A TAPESTRY OF BRONZE NOVEL

Titles in the Tapestry of Bronze series:

JOCASTA:
THE MOTHER-WIFE OF OEDIPUS

NIOBE AND PELOPS:
CHILDREN OF TANTALUS

NIOBE AND AMPHION:
THE ROAD TO THEBES

NIOBE AND CHLORIS:
ARROWS OF ARTEMIS

ANTIGONE AND CREON:
GUARDIANS OF THEBES

Learn more about the Tapestry of Bronze series at
www.tapestryofbronze.com

ANTIGONE AND CREON: GUARDIANS OF THEBES

VICTORIA GROSSACK
AND
ALICE UNDERWOOD

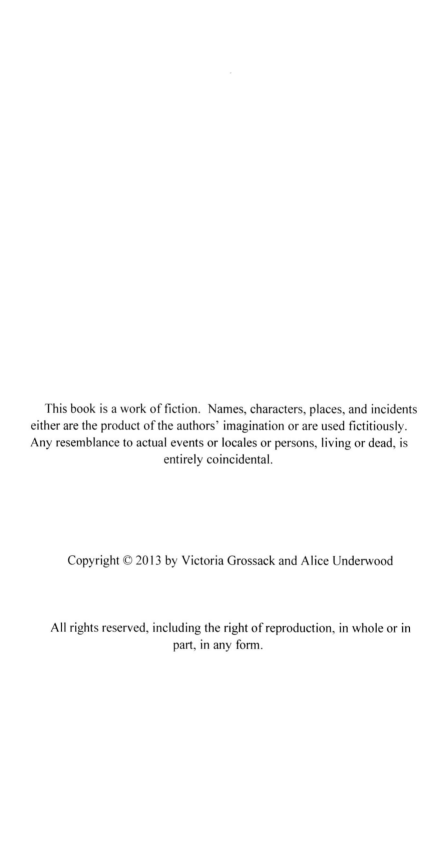

This book is a work of fiction. Names, characters, places, and incidents either are the product of the authors' imagination or are used fictitiously. Any resemblance to actual events or locales or persons, living or dead, is entirely coincidental.

ANTIGONE AND CREON: GUARDIANS OF THEBES

MAPS

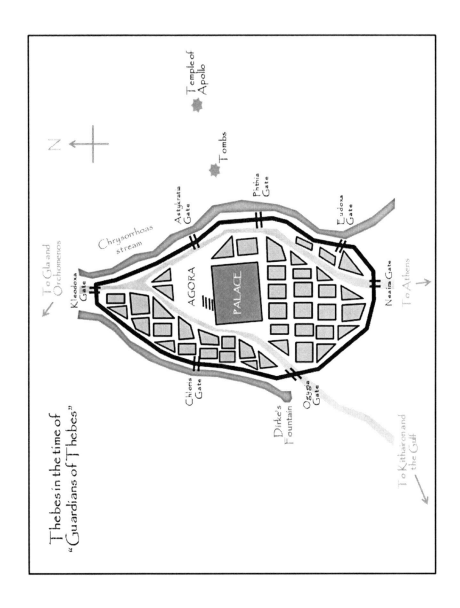

Thebes in the time of "Guardians of Thebes"

Temple of Apollo

Tombs

N

Astykratia Gate

Phthia Gate

Eudoxa Gate

Chrysorrhoas stream

To Gla and Orchomenos

Kleodoxa Gate

AGORA

PALACE

Neaira Gate

To Athens

Chloris Gate

Ogyga Gate

Dirke's Fountain

To Kithairon and the Gulf

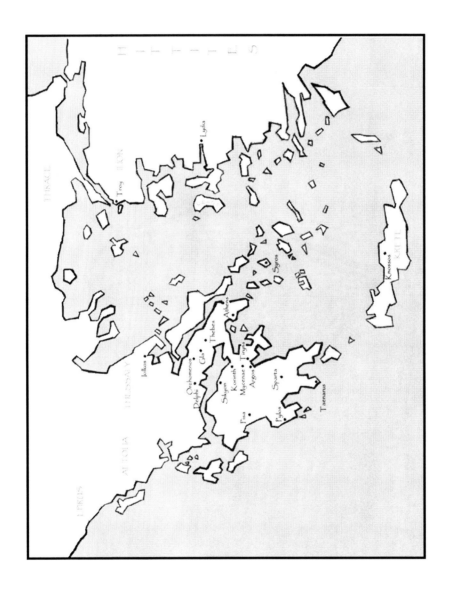

CHAPTER ONE
CREON

Creon leans on his staff as he walks across the shadowy room to stand at the window. Out beyond the city walls, an orange glow lights the horizon. The smoke of the corpse-fires wafts over the city, an odor of roasting flesh and a residue of charred bone all that is left of the common soldiers who attacked Thebes. Their leaders, criminals who started this battle remain – by Creon's order – unburied.

The war is over. Thebes has survived. There are scars, to be sure, but the crisis has ended. And yet he finds himself unable to sleep. There is too much to do, too many decisions to make and decrees to implement. He glances down – looking for signs of lamplight in windows, the glow of a torch lighting someone's path through the streets. How many Thebans share his sleeplessness this night?

The condition is widespread, no doubt. Wives mourning fallen husbands, aged fathers like himself who have lost sons. And, yes, sisters grieving over brothers slain in battle.

But grief cannot excuse the willful disobedience of his niece Antigone. Defiance like hers would lead to chaos! The burden Creon bears – the burden of maintaining order in a city wounded by betrayal, a city all too prone to the madness of the mob – that is his alone. Even his wife Eurydike does not understand. She made that clear when she asked that Antigone be spared. That is another reason Creon has sought the solitude of his study: avoiding the sorrow of his wife, her pleas that he listen to their son. Why Haemon should argue on behalf of Antigone, who deserted him so many years ago, is beyond Creon's comprehension.

But there are, he admits to himself, many things about this younger generation that he does not understand.

A knock at the door of his study interrupts his thoughts.

"Uncle?"

His nephews are dead; Antigone is shut away in a guarded room. Only his younger niece, Ismene, remains.

"Enter, if you must! I suppose you've come to beg for her too?"

The last of his sister's children slips through the door. "No, my lord king," she says softly.

Creon notes Ismene's resemblance to her sister – and, more strongly, the resemblance to her mother. For a moment grief clutches his heart so tightly that tears well up in his eyes, but then he masters his old-man's weakness and finds his voice.

"Then why are you here?" he asks gruffly.

She takes a seat on the chair nearest the hanging oil lamp: the shell-inlaid chair once preferred by her mother. With the dim light and his fading vision, he can almost imagine Jocasta sitting there.

"I couldn't sleep, Uncle. So many in our family have died – you're the closest relative I have left."

This is true: Ismene's parents are long deceased, her brothers freshly dead, her sister condemned.

"I felt so lonely – and then I thought that you must be lonely too."

He doubts her words; how can she have not come for her sister? Yet perhaps Antigone's fate troubles him more than it does Ismene. Antigone has been gone for so many years that the sisterly bond may have frayed. He realizes he does not know Ismene very well – this niece has always been so quiet.

Creon crosses over to the couch beside Ismene's chair; his aged joints complain as he lowers himself onto the cushions. "Loneliness is the curse of every king."

"And for many years you were king in all but name."

So many years of loneliness – these words Ismene does not say, but Creon hears them nonetheless. Jocasta once had this ability: a way of beguiling men into saying more than they ought, into making costly concessions and unwise promises.

"Ismene, I will not be lenient towards your sister."

She does not protest that she has not asked for Antigone's release; instead she pursues her original subject, while pouring them both cups of wine and water. "You were regent for my brothers, adviser to my mother and her – her husbands. You were always the one who knew what had to be done."

Creon knows flattery when he hears it; but, like all the best flattery, this is simply well-chosen truth. "What had to be done was not always pretty, Ismene. The full tale would shock you."

A sad smile curves her too-wide mouth, so like her mother's. "After everything that has happened – how could anything else shock me?"

Perhaps she is right. Ismene shed no blood in the war, but her spirit bears wounds as deep as his own. She may be the one person who *can* understand.

He knows that others have turned to Ismene when troubled. Jocasta confided in her before she died; his beloved son Menoeceus was close to her. Both dead now. But their secrets, their stories live on in this young woman. In his aching bones, the stoop of his shoulders, Creon feels the weight of his years – his own life thread will reach its end before many years pass; perhaps much sooner. If he too tells Ismene his story, will that ease the burden of the secrets that he carries?

Setting his fingertips together, he briefly marvels at how gnarled and spotted his hands have become. "Antigone is not the first, you know. I've sent other women to their deaths for the good of Thebes."

This does seem to surprise her; her dark eyebrows lift with curiosity. "Who, Uncle?"

He rests his lips against the edges of his forefingers. There is danger in giving voice to matters that have lain silent for so long. But it is difficult to imagine gentle Ismene using the knowledge to injure him, to damage Thebes.

Once, he had imagined confessing everything to Jocasta when the time was right. But that time never came – and Jocasta has been gone for years. All that remains is her daughter.

Yes, he will tell her. Where should he begin?

CREON

They say that wine poured into the earth wakes the ghosts of the dead so that they can speak to us. I've never known that to work. But wine poured into the throat of an old man like myself summons the spirit of youth.

Among my earliest memories are the construction of Thebes' walls and the beautiful music of King Amphion. Mountains of stone were moved to the sound of the king's lyre, until they encircled and protected our city. Amphion seemed like a god to me, as though Apollo himself had stepped out of the temple's wall painting. As a young boy I said something like this to my father, and his reply was harsh and stern: "Amphion's no god. The blood of Kadmos does not flow in his veins – but it flows in yours, my son."

As I grew older Father taught me the history of Thebes and of our family, and always I sensed his dissatisfaction that Amphion was our king. He did not seek the throne himself; the connection to Kadmos came through my mother, who had died when my sister Jocasta was born. I always believed that Father was resentful on my behalf, for he had named me Creon, which means, as you know, ruler – but given my situation today, and Father's later stint as the Tiresias, perhaps he was simply prescient. Who knows? Yet back then I discovered that not everyone was convinced of my mother's lineage and I developed doubts of my own. More importantly, I saw that Amphion was a good ruler. Why should Father question the king's legitimacy based on his grandfather's grandfather? One may choose a new chariot-horse for its sire, but the true test comes on the race course. No man keeps his swiftest horse in the stable because its bloodline is not pure.

Besides, I was not the only living male descendant of Kadmos. There was another, one whose ancestry was unclouded: Prince Laius, son of the man who had been king before Amphion. He lived in the court of King Pelops, far to the south, and before my birth had ceded his claim to the Theban throne.

One sunny afternoon when I was about twelve, our father chose to remind us of this. I was annoyed, because most of Thebes was celebrating the completion of a major portion of the walls – what would later be called the Chloris Gate – but Father decided that instead of staying to enjoy the songs and games being organized by King Amphion's sons, he would take my sister and me home. Father was never enthusiastic about Amphion's wall-building project; he pointed out many times that *Kadmos* had not thought walls necessary. Perhaps Father did not care for the sweat and the shouts and the endless moving of stone. Anyway that afternoon Father told us again how he had served as an envoy before Amphion took the throne, and had been sent to Pelops' court to determine young Laius' intentions.

"So he was only a little boy?" asked my sister, after Father described his encounter with Laius.

"Just the age you are now, Jocasta," Father answered.

"And King Pelops made him say he didn't want the throne, because Amphion is married to Pelops' sister? That's not fair."

Father spread his hands. "Perhaps not, Jocasta. But an oath made before Zeus is binding."

I scuffed my sandals in the pebbles in our courtyard. "Then so was your loyalty oath to Amphion," I muttered.

Father heard me and snapped: "And have I ever broken that oath?"

"No, but…"

"But what?" Father asked, yet the tone of his voice made it clear he did not want me to say anything. "The laws of the gods take precedence over the wishes of men."

This struck me as hypocritical. Father had never acted against Amphion, but he certainly made his disapproval clear. I lifted my chin and said, "If we do not behave rightly towards other men, whom we can see and hear, then how can we judge our behavior towards the gods? Besides, the king is the man the gods have chosen to rule our city. Isn't obedience to him the same as obeying the gods?"

Father's russet eyebrows drew together. "Creon, the gods do speak clearly at times – but you must listen to them. And right behavior towards other men should start with respect for your father!"

Other fathers might have cuffed or beaten their sons for my remark; mine did not. Instead he demanded that I apologize by kneeling before him and begging his mercy along with that of the gods.

When, several years later, King Amphion's children died suddenly and Amphion himself was torn limb from limb by an angry mob, my father declared this to be the will of the gods. I myself suffered briefly the same symptoms that killed the royal children, and Father warned me that my impiety would be the death of me if I did not make amends. I recovered, however, and took this as a sign that the gods wanted me alive – and they have kept me alive, when so many others have gone to their graves.

Of course you, Ismene, know very well what happened next: the long-absent Laius returned to Thebes and married my sister Jocasta. And it was because of Laius that I first brought about the death of a woman.

Threats come in all shapes and sizes. Only a fool would think that a woman, simply because she *is* a woman, is not dangerous. The lioness does the hunting for her cubs, and no beast is fiercer than a mother bear protecting her young. And though snake-haired Medusa turned men to stone with her ugliness, beauty is an even more potent weapon.

When Laius arrived in Thebes, he brought with him the mother of his two sons, a low-born beauty called Nerissa. Many men have bastard children by peasant women; kings often keep a mistress or two. But after marrying my sister and getting her with child, Laius treated Jocasta with loathing and contempt while showering Nerissa with gifts and fondling her in public.

The insult to my sister was bad enough; it appalled most Thebans and shocked visitors to our city, who could not understand how the king could so mistreat his charming, beautiful young wife. But more important was the fact that Nerissa had two sons, one of them a hearty seventeen-year-old with friends among Laius' soldiers.

Although it was difficult for her, Jocasta handled the situation well. She was always gracious – and Laius' mistreatment won her the sympathy of the city. It soon became clear to everyone in Thebes that Laius preferred swilling wine and tossing knucklebones to performing the duties of a leader. Jocasta's popularity soared while Laius' fell, but a certain faction remained loyal to the king, growing angrier and more defensive with each passing day. I heard rumors that Laius planned to put Jocasta aside before she was brought to childbed, and make Nerissa his queen – but the gossip always came third-hand; I never traced the original source. And I could not imagine that the citizens of Thebes would allow Jocasta to be sent away in disgrace.

Laius and his supporters must have recognized this. When she was eight months pregnant, Jocasta was ambushed on her way to visit a temple: brutally assaulted by armed men. Amazingly, she survived – a fact I attributed to the bravery of her bodyguard, who died protecting her; Father, of course, saw it as divine intervention. Perhaps it was both.

Laius denied having anything to do with the attack – but even if this were true, it must have been planned by someone seeking favor with him. My sister's life remained in danger.

We could not rid the city of Laius; he was surrounded by a cadre of loyal soldiers and had the support of the powerful King Pelops. More than this, I knew that Laius' death – so soon after Amphion had been torn apart by the mob – would bring utter chaos. Thebes needed Laius to remain king – but he needed to treat Jocasta as queen.

We needed Nerissa and her sons to go.

That would solve all our problems. It would remove a rival for Laius' affections and eliminate two possible pretenders to the throne. Whether the babe my sister bore turned out to be boy or girl, the child's life would be constantly threatened by the presence of two older half-brothers, no matter their bastard status. Eliminating Nerissa and her sons would also prove to Laius that he was not untouchable – and the fact that the people of Thebes would not mourn them would remind Laius that it was his wife, my sister, who was the city's darling.

But I did not see how to manage it. I was a lanky young man with little prowess at arms, while Nerissa's elder son was an athlete like his father. Perhaps I was a coward, but I dismissed any notion of carrying out the deed myself with the excuse that, for my sister's sake, there must be no way to trace it back to our family.

While I struggled with this problem, visitors arrived in Thebes: the King of Tiryns and his son Amphitryon. The King of Tiryns knew Laius from the Olympic Games, and had come to Thebes in order to negotiate for our beef and leather. Prince Amphitryon was several years younger than I, but he was already taller and more muscular than most full-grown men. I did not like him much, but while the kings drank and threw dice, I ended up spending a lot of time in his company.

One afternoon he and I were sitting in the palace courtyard, fletching arrows. Jocasta was spinning wool in the shade of the colonnade; across the way Amphitryon's father and Laius played senet, with Nerissa close by. Laius must have made a lucky throw with the knucklebones: he gave a triumphant laugh, and Nerissa clapped her hands.

Laius drew his blonde mistress onto his lap and kissed her. "You always bring me good luck, my dear," he said, the volume of his voice indicating how much wine he had downed already. "You're the most wonderful woman alive!"

"By Zeus," muttered Amphitryon, "how can he insult the queen so?"

I glanced at my sister and saw that the color had risen to her cheeks, but she looked pointedly away from her husband and his paramour. "I don't know."

"She's *so* beautiful," Amphitryon said, gazing at Jocasta.

This was true. Round-bellied with child, she was everything a young wife should be: fertile, gracious, healthy, kind, lovely. Her dark, curling hair shone like polished ebony and her full breasts were the color of sweet cream. Amphitryon was completely under her spell; he gazed at her constantly, but whenever she spoke to him he flushed bright red and stuttered helplessly in search of words.

Turning back to my work, I set the obsidian blade of my knife against a feather-quill and sliced carefully downward. "It's offensive for a peasant woman to put herself before the queen," I muttered.

"That low-born slut!" Amphitryon growled. "She needs a beating, that's what. If I knocked out a couple of her teeth I bet King Laius wouldn't find her so pretty anymore."

The violence of his anger astonished me; I set aside the two halves of my feather and studied the Tirynian prince. He was eager to do something for the object of his adolescent desire, and he was already a powerful young man. With only a little prodding he could be the solution to Thebes' problems.

"You would, wouldn't you?" I said.

"Beat a slave girl?" His brows drew together in puzzlement. "Of course! Why not?"

"Some men would be afraid to touch a slave that belonged to their host," I said cautiously.

Amphitryon wrapped a leather thong around the end of the arrow he had been fletching. "I'm not afraid of anything. I've already killed a man, you know." He knotted the thong and trimmed the ends with his knife.

I put as much disbelief as I could muster into my voice. "At *your* age?"

His freckled cheeks flushed. "Are you calling me a liar? I ran him through with my sword, I tell you! He vomited blood when I pulled out the blade."

"But you're not yet old enough for the soldiers' ranks," I said dubiously.

"So what? He was a bandit, who attacked me and my father when we were out hunting." He held up his right fist, big as a grinding-stone. "I slew him with this hand."

"Prove it," I said, lowering my voice. "Kill Nerissa."

My palms began to sweat as I uttered the words. I set my knife down on the bench beside me, fearing that it might slip from my damp fingers.

How would Amphitryon react to this suggestion? If he chose to betray me – or was simply careless with his words…

"All right," he said. "I'll do it."

Though my pulse raced, I managed to keep my voice even. For my sister's sake, I cautioned quietly, he must not be seen – and he must never tell anyone that we had spoken of it. I made him swear in the name of Zeus, and we sprinkled wine on the ground to seal the oath; his eyes were solemn as he took the vow, and I knew he thought himself manlier than I despite his youth. I was more than willing to confirm that opinion, if only he rid Thebes of Nerissa. I wondered if I dared suggest that he kill Nerissa's sons as well, but that seemed too much to ask. If events broke in my favor, perhaps he would find it necessary anyway.

Our pact made, we turned to discussing *how* it could be done – Nerissa's habits and daily routine, the streets of the city, the location of Thebes' springs, and the lay of the nearby countryside.

Engrossed in our plotting, we did not notice the two kings approach until they were standing over us. "What are you two talking about?" asked Amphitryon's father.

Amphitryon looked up. "Uh—"

Hastily I interrupted: "The best hunting-grounds near Thebes."

Laius laughed. "You shouldn't ask *that* boy about hunting."

I loathed being called a boy. True, my beard was still scant and my shoulders were narrow, but I had taken my manhood oath. I was older than my sister the queen; I shared with her most of the responsibility for ordering the city's affairs.

And I had just arranged a murder.

"Creon's arrows rarely hit his targets," Laius continued. "When did you last bring back something for the supper pot?"

"At least, my lord king, I know my way around Thebes." This barb reminded everyone that Laius had been away from the city for most of his life. Besides irritating my brother-in-law, these words achieved their real purpose: deflecting attention away from red-faced Amphitryon.

Since the failed attack on my sister and the death of her most loyal bodyguard, I had slept on a cot in her antechamber. But that night I could not sleep for thinking of all the things that could go wrong. Despite his bluster, Amphitryon might decide he lacked the stomach for killing a woman. But inaction would be better than a failed attempt that led to his discovery. If Amphitryon revealed my role, Laius would order his Peloponnesian soldiers to execute me.

Even if my plan succeeded, and Amphitryon said nothing – would the gods exact punishment? I might not fear the gods as much as Father thought I should, but never before had I planned a murder.

Yet Amphitryon's task proved simpler than I could have hoped. Because Nerissa was widely reviled – Thebans hurled insults at her whenever she appeared without Laius – she went about her errands at odd hours. At dusk, when the people of Thebes were sitting down to their evening meal, Amphitryon followed her to a quiet corner. There he throttled Nerissa and her youngest son.

He stopped me outside the palace kitchens at dawn the next morning and drew me aside, his eyes flashing in excitement as he told me of the killings. "Both of them," he said, as if daring me to question his manhood. "We didn't talk about the little boy, but he saw me."

"Then you did the right thing," I said, wishing only that he had dispatched Laius' older son as well. Well, this should make him fear for his life! Perhaps he would flee the city. I glanced around, making sure that none of the kitchen staff had wandered near. "Where did you leave the bodies?"

"In the alley, behind a pile of firewood."

I nodded. "You've done my sister and me a great service, Amphitryon. She must never know the truth – but I'll make sure she knows you're a man of great valor, a man to reckon with."

He pulled back his broad shoulders and grinned.

Amphitryon must not have hidden the corpses as well as he thought –

they were found quickly, and the news was delivered to King Laius that morning. I tried to seem as shocked as everyone else; I even asked Jocasta if she had been responsible for their deaths. No one could think *I* had done it – everyone knew I had not left the palace grounds since the attack on my sister. And since Amphitryon was only a boy, and a foreigner, no one seemed to think of him.

No one had seen the murders, or at least no one reported them. As each day passed, I breathed more easily. My main fear was that the boy himself would prove loose-tongued despite his oath. Always boastful, he needed to tell the tale: and so I listened to him describe how the cord had felt as he pulled it tight around the woman's throat, how she had struggled and then become suddenly a heavy weight in his arms. The little boy, whom Amphitryon had silenced with a kick to the head early on, was more easily dispatched. Hearing the Tirynian prince whisper of the dusky gloom of the alleyway, the stink of the dead woman's voided bowels, the slight weight of the child's body, I felt almost as though my own sweaty hands had done the deed. I dreamed of it, sometimes, and I praised the gods when the king of Tiryns, tiring of Laius' morose grieving, headed home with his son.

No further threats were made against Jocasta – and soon we learned it was her unborn child that Laius truly feared. He refused to explain, except to say he had been given a terrible prophecy. And so when the babe was born, Laius had him taken away and exposed on Mount Kithairon.

*

"Or so you thought," Ismene says softly.

Creon rubs his eyes. "Yes, so I thought. My sister had made other arrangements. One of many secrets she kept from me. I don't know if she even told our father. The prophet Tiresias died just at this time, and our father gave up his eyesight to assume the office. Yet later he must have realized who Oedipus was, for he killed himself to prevent the truth from coming out."

"So many secrets – so many sacrifices." Ismene sighs and looks up at the shadowed ceiling; to Creon it seems that she is blinking away tears. His niece is feeling ashamed of her origins, he guesses.

"It was always so with our family, I fear. But it is time to break that tradition. Now you know the truth of Nerissa's death. And I will tell you how Melanthe died, too."

His niece frowns and says: "Melanthe?"

Creon smiles and dips his cup in the krater of wine and water. "You know of her as the Sphinx."

CREON

After the events I have described to you, my sister and her husband Laius made a truce of sorts. They never shared a bed, but they lived together peaceably. These were good years for the city, and for me. Other than the tribute we paid to Pelops, our only real difficulty was the resurgence of the Maenad cult.

Their leader Melanthe was about my sister's age, the daughter of a Theban merchant by an Aegyptian woman. Whereas Jocasta seemed almost untouched by the passage of the years – perhaps, as people say, the necklace of Harmonia conveys eternal beauty on its wearer – Melanthe's life in the cult of the wine god had transformed her from a voluptuous golden-skinned girl to a sinewy woman with leathery feet and sun-baked shoulders. With her dark eyes and gold-capped braids, she was still striking, but as terrifying as Medusa. She wore the pelt of a lion as her cloak, and her followers said that she had killed the beast herself using only a knife. When seized by the wine-god's madness, Dionysus' followers are capable of extraordinary strength.

Other than occasional confrontations with Melanthe, whose Maenads stole livestock and trampled farmers' fields during their midnight orgies, I enjoyed my duties in service to Thebes; and when I was in my late thirties, I married your aunt Eurydike.

The following fall, King Laius made a pilgrimage to Delphi – only to be killed by men we assumed to be bandits before reaching the shrine.

Laius' sudden death provided both danger and opportunity for Thebes. Laius' sponsor and former mentor, King Pelops – who had demanded exorbitant tribute these many years – was still the most powerful man in Hellas, but less so, since quarrels with his two eldest sons had forced them to flee to Mycenae. Pelops would want to select Thebes' next king; but if we could make a better alliance for ourselves, we might finally be able to stop the drain on our resources.

Only the gods were stronger than Pelops in those days, and so we enlisted their help: to be precise, the help of the vine god Dionysus and his servant Melanthe. We arranged that Dionysus would choose Thebes' next king through a contest of wit. Melanthe would be the god's instrument – and ours.

When the day came, in late autumn, to proclaim the contest, we closed the seven gates of the city to prevent infiltration of King Pelops' agents. Melanthe wore not only her lion-skin cape but an outlandish set of false wings, evoking that creature of her mother's native land, the Sphinx – a blend of bird, lion, and woman. Her announcement seemed to cast a spell over the citizens; the mere memory of her voice sends a shiver down my spine. Even though I had plotted with her myself to bring all this about, I half believed her possessed by Dionysus – or by some strange Aegyptian beast-god.

All that winter the Maenads patrolled the city walls and kept guard at the gates alongside Thebes' soldiers. When spring came, Jocasta and I considered each suitor – and when she met Prince Oedipus of Korinth, the decision was sealed. Prince of a wealthy city without ties to Pelops or his sons, he was an excellent strategic choice; and besides all that, your mother fell in love with him.

Jocasta was terrified, though, when the contest of riddles turned deadly, and Melanthe's knife drew the blood of the first suitor. As the afternoon continued, and one man after another died, I realized how dangerous our Sphinx was. I, too, feared for Oedipus – would she kill him with the others?

Yet Oedipus solved her final riddle, and Melanthe kept her pact with us – or perhaps Dionysus stayed her bloodstained hand. Oedipus of Korinth was Thebes' new king.

Still, Melanthe remained a threat. She showed no intention of relinquishing the influence she and her Maenads had gained during the winter months. The day before your parents' wedding she came to me with more demands for her Maenads, a greater share of the harvest and other goods from the city stores. If I denied her, her followers might run riot and undermine the new king's reign; if I agreed, the next time they would expect even more. Who could say – she might declare herself queen!

For the good of Thebes, once more it was necessary to eliminate a woman.

This task I could not delegate. Melanthe's skill with the knife was too widely feared, her connection to Dionysus unquestioned. No one else would dare kill her.

Because Melanthe wanted a greater portion of grain for her cult, I agreed to meet her at the granary by the Astykratia Gate. Though I had grown in strength and experience since my youth, I was still no master of weapons. However, I now knew plenty about herbs and poisons.

I was fortunate that Melanthe arrived alone; she must not have wanted the Maenads to hear our negotiations. It saved me contriving an excuse to send her followers away.

"You are dismissed," I told the two soldiers standing guard at the door of the granary. "Wait for me at the gate."

The two men raised their hands to their foreheads in salute. "Yes, Lord Creon." Spears held stiffly upright, they strode away.

Melanthe watched them go, then scanned me with narrowed eyes. "Why did you send them away?"

I lowered my voice. "You're demanding an increase in the Maenads' rations. There's not enough in the city stores for me to increase the soldiers' portion too."

She set her hands on her hips, stringy muscles standing out along her sun-browned arms. "The stores cannot be so meager as that."

"See for yourself," I said, taking the torch from its sconce on the building's outer wall and pushing open the door. The yellow light of the torch revealed wheat-chaff dusting the floor and rows of tall earthenware storage-jars along the walls. Some of these pithoi had been wrestled out into the central space and emptied; many more stood sealed and waiting. A mouse scurried away from the torchlight, and a granary snake slithered after it. When the oaken door swung shut behind us, the great balance scale shifted as if it were some slow-moving beast roused by the thudding sound. Like a clutch of eggs, stone measuring-weights rested at its base.

Melanthe gestured at the sealed storage-jars, and then beyond them into the shadows. My eyes could just make out the oil-vessels and jars of olives, the containers of lentils, dried figs, and raisins, the stacks of amphorae cushioned with barley straw. "You see? Thebes has plenty."

"This has to feed *all* of Thebes until the harvest comes in," I argued. I slipped the torch into a fretted bronze stand and reached for the leather bag slung across my shoulder. Drawing out a wax-covered tablet, I read to her from the palace records: how much came in, the amounts that were distributed each day and month, the calculations showing how long the current stores would last.

I droned on in as boring a fashion as I could manage, worse than my father in his most pedantic lecture on religious ritual. I meant for this dull recitation to put her off her guard. Why should a creature as fierce as her fear someone like me, a glorified scribe?

"…under the best conditions, each of these pithoi holds enough to feed five families for a month. But the last harvest was smaller than it should have been, so they are not full. The Maenads keep trampling the crops – your orgies ruined the yield of three barley fields last season."

She glanced at the half-empty bins I indicated, suspicion in her dark eyes. "Why should I believe you?"

"If you'll just look here," I said, holding out the wax tablet, "I can show you…" I continued my analysis, pointing at various figures. As the daughter of a trader, she might have learned to read – at least she was not willing to admit it, if she could not. She came closer and peered down at the symbols scratched into the wax.

I noticed the lines in her forehead, the purplish circles beneath her eyes. Close to, she seemed weary and more human. Silver strands sparkled among her tight-woven braids. The woman smelled as though she had not bathed in a month; her lion's-pelt cloak was dirty and ragged. She was more than a head shorter than I, and appeared wholly unconcerned. My bronze stylus was long and sharp – should I act now? I gripped the instrument tightly, considering.

Shrugging, Melanthe waved the tablet away. "Then get more from our new allies. You've got the Korinthian prince now – and only because of me. Tell his city to send grain."

I allowed my shoulders to drop, as though I had hoped to convince her with logic. She expected weakness from me; let that be what she saw. In a low voice I said: "We need what Korinth will send to feed the soldiers."

"You owe me, Lord Creon," she said, threats glittering in her dark eyes.

I swallowed. "We – perhaps we could spare *half* of the Korinthian shipment for the Maenads."

She smiled, as if she believed she had won. But I knew that she had lost.

"That might do," she said. "If you provide two cartloads of oil and barley *now*."

"Melanthe…" I pleaded.

"My women are hungry, Lord Creon! Think what damage they will do if their bellies are not filled!"

I looked down, pretending to yield. "All right." I made notes in the wax and showed them to her, then snapped the folding tablet shut. "Two cartloads – but no more. The rest will have to wait until the Korinthian shipment arrives."

Melanthe shrugged.

"I need your word on this, Melanthe."

She pulled back her shoulders. "I've always kept my word, Creon."

"Still," I countered, "you must give me something in this bargain." I wanted her to believe that I expected the alliance between the Maenads and the palace to continue.

Melanthe folded her wiry arms as I spoke: her followers, I said, must not disrupt my sister's nuptials or the crowning of the new king. They must avoid trampling any more fields when they held their nighttime rites.

"…and you must not tell anyone of the bargain we have made," I concluded. "The people of Thebes cannot learn of this."

She lifted a sardonic eyebrow. "Very well. You have my word."

I nodded. "Then let us drink in the name of Dionysus to seal our bargain." Behind the scale, almost hidden in the shadows, an amphora rested upright in a bronze tripod; traders often concluded their transactions with a libation.

Melanthe agreed; wine was sacred to the Maenads.

I slipped the tablet back into my leather shoulder-bag and, my motions concealed in shadow, withdrew a small vial that contained a potent decoction of belladonna. I did not think it would kill Melanthe, but it would slow her down. I picked up one of the rough wooden cups the soldiers used and dipped it into the wine, then added a measure of belladonna with hands grown suddenly damp. I did not bother to add any water from the ewer on the floor nearby, but I wiped my sweat-damp hand on my kilt before dipping out a second cup of wine for myself.

My heart was thudding so loud I feared she could hear it as I handed her the cup. To cover my nervousness I said, "I've always admired you, Melanthe." I took a sip of wine, making sure I had kept the right cup for myself. Thick and heavy, without admixture of water, the wine calmed my nerves a little.

"Have you?" she asked skeptically, and set the other wooden cup to her lips.

"A worthy adversary," I said, inclining my head. "A valuable ally. And a beautiful woman." This overstated the case, but even those who mistrust flattery are usually willing to listen to it. "After that contest, your fame will last forever. The bards will sing of the deadly Sphinx and her riddles."

She drained her cup like one well used to unwatered wine – and, praise the gods, she detected nothing amiss in the taste. "Yes, I imagine they will."

I glanced at her cup. "More?"

"Yes," she said, handing it to me. "A good vintage. From the northern vineyards – about five years old, I'd say."

"The leader of the Maenads knows her wine," I said, moving back into the shadows to refill her cup. I set down my own cup and left it there, then slipped more belladonna into hers, wondering if her Maenad habits would make the drug work faster, slower, or not at all. Offering her the refilled cup, I prolonged the conversation. "And fierce as well as beautiful. They say you killed that lion yourself." I stroked the pelt as if I hoped to seduce her, knowing I was only postponing what must be done. Was I a coward not to strike?

"Yes," she said, smiling dreamily as if the memory pleased her. She explained that she and the beast had been tracking the same deer in the mountains some distance from Thebes. I did not know whether to believe her description of the encounter, but still I plied her with questions.

"I threw three knives at it," she said, her words beginning to slur. "They struck, but only angered the beast. After that I had just one blade left."

I felt like a prowling lion myself: my muscles tense, my shoulders taut, watching and waiting for the moment to spring. If I failed in this, I would be as dead as the beast whose skin Melanthe wore. "What happened then?"

"I drew my last blade," she said, pulling a gleaming knife from her girdle. "This one here. I knew I coul... couldn't throw it. Not the last one. Had to keep hold of it."

A chill seized my gut and I knew my moment had come. I stared at the knife, admiring the gleam of the curving bronze in the torchlight, and then reached toward it. Melanthe let me gently take it from her hand, as if proud for me to make a closer inspection.

Then I grabbed a fistful of her braided hair in my left hand, and with my right I plunged the knife into her belly.

Though I was never a warrior, I had offered many a blood-sacrifice to the gods. I knew that my knife-hand must be quick, must not hesitate. The victim must never sense hesitation. The blade must cut deep, and a strong sideways twist of the knife once it is in brings a quicker resolution.

Shouting curses, she struggled to wrest the knife from my hand, but the belladonna and the rush of blood from the wound had weakened her. I had the added advantage of height and leverage. Though the wash of hot blood made it harder to keep my grip on the knife's well-worn hilt, it also made it more difficult for her to pry my fingers away. I jerked her head back; instinctively her blood-smeared hands went up towards my face, and then – as if she had just remembered – she reached for her girdle, where no doubt she had another dagger concealed. I pulled her close, pinning her right arm against my ribs, and dragged the knife sideways through her flesh to widen the wound. She screamed, choking and coughing up blood. Her left hand moved weakly, slowly, and then fell limp as she sagged back in my arms.

I did not release my grip. Only days before, I had watched this woman kill four men. This could be a ploy – she could rush at me like a wild harpy the instant I let go. I counted my ragged, shaking breaths. Ten breaths, and the thunder of my heartbeat began to subside. Twenty, thirty, and still she had not moved.

Bending my head, I set my cheek before her upturned face and felt no movement of air from her nose or mouth. I pressed my ear to the curve of her throat and heard no heartbeat but my own. Finally, warily, I released my hold on her, remaining ready to pounce if she somehow returned to life.

But she was unquestionably dead.

I eased her to the floor and stared down at the corpse of the Sphinx.

To calm my nerves I swallowed the half-cup of wine I had left in the shadows and reviewed what I must do next. The body I hid behind a row of pithoi. Among the soldiers I had a few trusted men; I would arrange for them to remove it later. I kicked piles of wheat-chaff over the pool of blood that marked the spot of our struggle and the trail that I had left dragging the body across the floor. I used water from the ewer to rinse my red-stained hands and legs, then took off my kilt and turned it inside out to hide the stains. Finally I slipped the torch from its stand and left the granary, pulling the oaken door shut behind me. I shouted to the soldiers at the gate that they should resume their post outside the storeroom.

Slowly I climbed up the hill towards the center of the city, grateful that the evening's darkness hid me from those few who were out in the streets. With each step I re-lived some aspect of the struggle: Melanthe's wine-scented curses, the hot slippery feel of her blood flowing across my knuckles. At last I understood why soldiers tell so many tales of battle, and why young Amphitryon had been so anxious to whisper the details of Nerissa's death. Killing a human being is something far more awful and profound than sacrificing an animal upon the altar. As I struggled with Melanthe I had felt her life-thread fray and finally snap, as if I were an agent of the Fates.

By the time I reached the palace, I was calmer, though Jocasta looked at me quizzically. After dinner I ordered a hot bath and scrubbed away the traces of blood, but later I still could not sleep. My young wife also slept little – we had a newborn son – and I pretended that he was the cause of my wakeful night. But as Eurydike hummed lullabies to the child, I endlessly reviewed the rest of my plan. With my soldiers, I would hide the body and then spread a rumor that Melanthe had been spirited away in Dionysus' leopard-drawn chariot, in order to become the god's concubine. Her followers would believe this; her devotion to the wine-god was unsurpassed. We could even, I mused, build a shrine somewhere to celebrate the love between Melanthe and Dionysus.

And yet, in those moments when the baby stopped fussing and my wife slept, I imagined the voices of avenging Furies. I had killed the high priestess of the Maenads! My father – now the Tiresias – said that divine retribution always followed an act of sacrilege.

Who can say? Perhaps this latest disaster for Thebes is their retribution. Or maybe the Furies took their vengeance on some of my children. Whatever their reasons, they spared *me* for the time being and have now made me king.

The next day Jocasta married Oedipus; weary from lack of sleep, I relaxed, expecting that few eyes would turn in my direction during the ceremonies. But then – just as the festivities were concluding – Melanthe's body was discovered and I was forced to improvise.

I claimed that Melanthe, proclaiming her work in Thebes finished, had killed herself. My story sounded feeble, even to myself – until I reminded everyone of her skill in throwing knives at Jocasta's suitors only a few days before. It seemed unlikely that *I* could have killed her – or have prevented her from killing herself. Then your father, King Oedipus supported me, his well-chosen words transforming the occasion into one of triumph for Thebes and honor for Melanthe's memory.

*

Creon wipes his moist hands on his kilt. "Of course, Jocasta and Oedipus were both concealing dark secrets then, too – from me and from each other." Looking at his niece – so like her mother! – he continues: "About a year later I learned that Oedipus was the man who slew Laius just outside of Delphi. When I confronted him with this fact in my sister's presence, I learned that Jocasta knew the truth and had hidden it from Oedipus – exactly the opposite of what I had expected! But, then, Oedipus had never seen Laius before, and did not realize that the man he killed was the king of Thebes."

"Mother told me," Ismene whispers. "The night she died. She said that when Father described the fight outside Delphi, she knew at once that the old man was Laius – but she kept the truth from Father because she did not want him to think himself unlucky."

Creon shakes his head. "Unlucky! That is one word for it."

"He did not ask for his fate," his niece reproaches.

"No. But he could have acted more wisely." Creon's hips ache from sitting so long. Leaning on his staff, he pushes himself to his feet. "My dear, you must realize that your mother is the third woman I had to kill for the sake of the city."

His niece rotates her wine cup in her hands. Then she says: "You did not kill her, Uncle Creon."

He presses his lips together, feeling the old grief tighten the back of his throat. After a moment, he is able to speak again. "Not with my own hands, no. But I told her what had to be done." He remembers his sister's shining blue eyes – and his harsh words to her, the change in her lovely face when she too recognized the awful necessity. "Three women. One by persuasion; one by the blade; one by commission. But all my doing. And all for Thebes."

Ismene rises from her chair and touches his arm. "For Thebes, yes. But not all your doing. Mother took responsibility for herself in the end. And Amphitryon—"

Creon shakes her soft hand away, suddenly filled with self-loathing. "Amphitryon was a love-struck boy. I used him, Ismene, as surely as I used Melanthe's knife."

"He was old enough to take two lives," Ismene counters. "And you gave him sanctuary, later."

That is also true. Creon remembers how he spoke with his sister the queen and her husband the king, arguing on Amphitryon's behalf. "It took some doing. By Zeus, he had killed the king of Mycenae! But in public he swore it was an accident – and, privately, he reminded me that I owed him a debt. I convinced Oedipus and Jocasta to let him stay in Thebes, and after that Amphitryon and I never spoke of what he had done. So far as I know he never told anyone – not even his son Alkides. But I was relieved when he died fighting the bandits to the north."

"Still, you helped him, Uncle," Ismene says. "And you were always kind to his widow, and to Alkides."

"Far too kind, considering." Creon wonders, as he has often wondered, if later events were the gods' revenge. Then he puts his hand on his niece's shoulder. "Ismene, you're trying to make me seem more merciful than I was. I understand why, but I cannot help your sister. A king must uphold the laws he makes, or else those laws are worthless. A city without laws cannot stand." Looking out at the dark sky he repeats, resolutely, the same words he pronounced when he sentenced her: "Tomorrow Antigone will see the sun for the last time."

CHAPTER TWO
ANTIGONE

Antigone blinks as one of the soldiers shoves her through the doorway onto the terrace at the top of the palace steps. Overhead the sky is a brilliant blue and dotted with soft white clouds; the morning sun is warm on her face. She pauses, looking up, but the soldier pushes her with the flat of his sword.

"King Creon's orders," he says. "Move."

Down at the base of the stairs, another four guards wait, swords drawn; beyond them a dozen more, their spear-shafts held parallel to the ground, hold back a crowd of onlookers. Several soldiers have linen bandages wrapped around an arm or leg; all bear bruises of the war just past. That is part of why they hate her. But only part.

Lifting her chin, Antigone turns to face her escort. "Where are you taking me?"

"You'll see soon enough," says the man closest to her. He is younger than she, perhaps not even twenty; his dark brows meet in the center over his nose.

His partner gestures with his sword, its bronze blade flashing in the morning light. "Stop stalling, Princess." The last word is uttered with a sneer.

As she walks down the stairs, she searches the crowd for familiar faces, but they are hard to find. In the ten years she has been away, slender boys have become men with broad shoulders and bearded chins. Girls have become mothers, their figures altered by childbearing. Only a few middle-aged people look familiar: a woman who used to bring greens gathered from the forests to trade in the marketplace; a potter known for his vase-painting; a tanner. Where is her family, she wonders? Her sister, her cousins, her husband?

The crowd growls like a many-headed, many-armed beast preparing to strike. Old men jeer at her, calling her traitor. Women scream the names of men they lost in battle. Children laugh and pelt her with pebbles until six guardsmen form up around her, a wedge before and behind. The other men's spears hold back the mob until she has passed; then the horde closes ranks behind her and follows, shouting. Antigone notices gray-haired Rhodia the midwife in the crowd, and for a minute they hold one another's gaze; the old woman shakes her head, looking troubled.

Antigone focuses on the back of the soldier who walks before her, feeling her cheeks flush at each new taunt from the mob. *Porni!* Untrue – she is not and has never been a whore. *Traitor!* Unfair: she has sought only justice; she has not put Thebes in danger. *Abomination!* Perhaps they are referring to the circumstances of her birth, which she did not choose – but if so they should also revile her sister Ismene; they should not have let Eteokles rule as king, should not have given him a royal burial. *Disobedient wretch!* That one has an element of truth – and yet she has obeyed the highest law, the law of the gods.

She tells herself that such words do not matter. She must not feel shame because of ignorant insults, any more than she should be ashamed of her unkempt hair, or of her dust-streaked gown. She has done right in the eyes of the gods.

They pass through the Astykratia Gate; a dead body, one of the Argive warriors, the one called Amphiorax, hangs from above. As Antigone and her captors cross the Chrysorrhoas, the bulk of the shouting mob falls back – but another group has already gathered some distance ahead. Each step along the rocky path brings her closer to them; soon she recognizes many familiar faces. There is her sister, Ismene; close by, her cousins Pyrrha and Henioche and their young brothers – and small slim Daphne, elder daughter of the Tiresias. Antigone knows better than to look for Daphne's aged father, the greatest prophet in all Hellas; he is too ill to leave his bed. Still, she wonders what the Tiresias would say about this morning's events.

A white-robed man calls Antigone by name, extending a hand towards her. Her husband, Haemon: he is taller then she remembers, and thinner, but then Thebes has been under siege. Catching his dark and sorrowful gaze, she nearly speaks the words that have gone so long unsaid – but then decides it would be cruel. She does not want to involve him in her disgrace.

The soldiers urge her forward, past Thebes' leading noblemen and ladies. They halt a few paces before her uncle, King Creon.

Creon, the crown of Kadmos encircling his white head, occupies a gilded sedan chair, carried on the shoulders of four bearers. His wife Eurydike is seated in another, smaller chair which has been lowered to the ground. Her eyes are puffy; her face is pale; she appears to have been crying.

Creon's expression is as stern as a god's, but Antigone sees lines of age and worry carved into his face; blue veins stand out in the hands that grip the wooden armrests of his chair. He may be king, but he is mortal, and mortals are fallible.

"Antigone," says Creon. His voice is as cold as a winter night.

She inclines her head dutifully, respectfully. "My lord king," she says, then raises her head to look up at him. Will he admit that he was wrong?

She sees no mercy in the eyes of the man who is her uncle, king and father-in-law.

"You willfully defied my command. You knew the punishment. Now you must pay the price."

Antigone lifts her hands towards him, palms upturned. "My lord king, why did you try to deny my brother's ghost passage to the Underworld?"

Color rises to the old man's cheeks. "Polynikes was a criminal! A traitor! He besieged his own city—"

"He had been wronged," Antigone interrupts. "Eteokles was supposed to share the throne—"

"That does not justify what he did to Thebes: the criminal deserves to be left to crows!"

She raises her voice, hoping that even if she fails to convince her uncle, she can make others see the righteousness of her actions. "The gods demand *all* men be given burial, so that their shades may find rest—"

"Silence!" Creon bellows. "The gods demand that *you* obey *me*, your king! And for your defiance I will give you the burial you wished for your brother. My order stands: you will never see the light of day again."

He points, and Antigone's gaze follows the direction of his outstretched arm, indicating the space beneath a rocky overhang. "The twin caves were discovered after you and your father departed Thebes," Creon continues, "about a year before Eteokles and Polynikes reached manhood. They rarely agreed on anything at that point, but both recognized that the caves were suitable for royal tombs. Eteokles has been buried in his; you, Antigone, will occupy the other."

The entrance to each cave has been walled in, the white-washed stucco painted with two bands of swirling blue spirals, symbols of eternity. The bronze-bound wooden door of the right-hand tomb is closed, a young woman kneeling to place a wreath of flowers before it, but the door for the other – the tomb that should have been Polynikes' – has been removed, leaving a rectangle of darkness. Beside the gaping hole Antigone sees a small stack of square-cut stones, a large pile of mud bricks, a broom, and a wooden bucket filled with glistening wet mortar.

A cloud passes before the sun; Antigone shivers as the shadow sweeps over her shoulders. She looks back at the grim-faced soldiers, at the mob gathered behind. She has not convinced the people of Thebes, but she knows she has followed the law of heaven.

Creon nods to a priest standing near his chair. "Begin the ceremony."

Haemon shifts, looks up at the king. "Father—"

"Silence!" Creon thunders again.

The priest – Antigone cannot remember his name, but at least it is not her husband – steps closer to her. "Know now, daughter of Oedipus and Jocasta, that your fate rests with the immortal gods. You shall be given food and drink; you shall not die by Theban hand. If it is the gods' will that you be spared, then you shall be spared."

"You think to keep your hands clean, Uncle," Antigone says, "but the gods know which of us has obeyed their law!"

"They know which of us has been faithful to Thebes," he snaps. Then he looks down at his wife Eurydike. "Give her the basket."

"Antigone..." Eurydike rises from her chair and steps forward; a servant woman follows her, carrying a large basket. "Oh, Antigone."

In the decade since Antigone last saw her, Eurydike's face has become lined with wrinkles and her dark curls have turned gray. But her gentle manner has not changed; she reaches out to squeeze Antigone's hand. The older woman's fingers are warm and soft, and carry the fragrance of lavender that Antigone remembers from long ago.

"Aunt Eurydike..." Antigone's voice trembles, and for the first time she feels her resolve weaken.

"Please," Eurydike whispers, "take it."

It was Aunt Eurydike – not Antigone's remote, elegant mother the queen – who had tended the scrapes and bruises of childhood, who offered comfort and hugs, soothing songs and kindly advice. Though she had meant to refuse the food and water, Antigone cannot deny her aunt this last act of charity. She accepts the basket from the serving woman; its wicker handle is rough against her fingers.

Eurydike kisses Antigone's cheeks, leaving the cool trace of her tears to evaporate from Antigone's skin. The crowd murmurs at this. Some hiss, and a few shout that Antigone deserves no such kindness, but others seem uncomfortable.

"Enough!" Creon declares. "Astakus, put her inside."

The buzz of the crowd swells in volume. The young soldier Astakus grabs her upper arm with a calloused hand and yanks her away from Eurydike. Clutching the heavy basket, Antigone stumbles as the man drags her toward the tomb, but his powerful grip holds her upright. He pushes her into the shadows; she stubs her toe on the threshold but somehow keeps from falling.

She sets the basket on the cave's packed-earth floor and turns to look outside. The small patch of sky she can see is blue and cloudless. In order to see the glowing orb of the sun she would have to step outside – but the two armed men standing on either side of the door will not permit this. The crimson petals of a poppy, crushed beneath their heavy sandals, lie scattered in the dirt.

Her uncle's voice commands: "Brick her in."

The jeering crowd parts to make way for two workmen in leather aprons. The first uses the broom to sweep dust from the marble threshold; the second, a baldheaded fellow, kneels and begins to set a layer of cut stones into place. It does not take long to finish this row, a foundation to ensure that pooling moisture will not weaken the base of the wall; soon his partner is troweling on a layer of clay mortar and begins to lay the mud bricks. The smell of moist earth fills Antigone's nostrils.

Before long the wall is halfway to her knees.

She looks out, hardly able to believe what is happening – but the ugly shouts of the crowd, the tears on her aunt's cheeks, the distress on the face of her husband Haemon, the sight of her sister Ismene with one hand pressed to her mouth all assure her that this is real.

The men are sealing her in this tomb.

"This is wrong," she tells them.

The bald man sets the first brick of a new row into place; mud oozes out beneath it. Without looking up, he fits the second brick alongside, and then the third.

Perhaps they did not hear her over the noise of the mob. "I couldn't let my brother's ghost wander forever!"

At this the man glances up, his eyes pitiless. "Your brother Polynikes and his army killed my son."

The second mason spreads thick brown mud over the new row of bricks. "My wife was out visiting her shepherdess sister when those traitors first appeared." He rubs his arm, smearing a streak of mud over his freckled skin. "Haven't seen her since."

Antigone cannot meet his gaze. She glances back into the dim chamber; her eyes have adjusted to the gloom now and she can see the low, uneven ceiling.

"Why are you even talking to that traitorous *porni*?" growls the soldier Astakus.

"I'm *not* a traitor!" Antigone cries. "I tried to stop the battle – I tried to convince Eteokles to honor his oath! His oath-breaking and Creon's sacrilege will bring down the gods' anger on Thebes – don't you see that? What I did, I did for Thebes!"

"*I* know what it is to serve Thebes," snarls the soldier. "My father and I fought together – and I saw what the invaders did to my father's body, after they killed him."

Suddenly cold, Antigone hugs her arms tight across her chest. Such anger – such hatred. Are there no words that might reach them?

"Even Eteokles wouldn't want his twin to stay unburied!"

The freckled man snorts. "Tell it to him, Princess," he says, smoothing a new layer of mortar onto the growing wall, now waist-high. "Eteokles is right next door. Oh, but he's dead too."

It is no use. Even if she could win these men over – and she has never been good at persuading people – others would quickly take their place.

Antigone sinks down to the cave's cool floor; from there, she can still see a patch of blue sky. But the masons make quick progress, and the crowd's shouting begins to quiet – or is it only that the growing wall muffles the sound? With each new brick fitted into place the tomb grows dimmer. She watches, her eyes seeking every last bit of light. Soon there is only a glowing spot of brilliance against the gloom, and then the workmen's fingers settle the final brick into place.

Darkness envelops her.

She can hardly hear the crowd. Instead she detects the scraping sound of trowels moving across the outside of the wall, and she knows the workmen are plastering its outer surface. Before long even that bitter scrap of connection to humanity is gone.

Antigone cannot see her own hands held before her face. She hugs her arms around her knees, willing herself not to weep. She despises tears.

After measureless time she realizes she is shivering: from fear, from cold, from lack of food – or perhaps all three. She remembers glimpsing a blanket in the basket of provisions. Groping around on her hands and knees in the featureless dark, she finds the wicker container. Within it her fingers detect a loaf of bread and the pliant form of a water-skin: she pushes these aside, determined not to eat or drink. Why prolong her torment? The blanket, though, could make her final hours a little more comfortable.

Carefully she removes the woolen blanket from the basket and drapes it around her shoulders. It smells of lavender – Eurydike's perfume.

She can no longer hold back the tears; they slip down her face. The blanket enfolds her as Aunt Eurydike's arms did when Antigone was a child. Blessed Athena, how has it come to this? Her family, her uncle, has done this to her – while her very own husband looked on!

But her family has a long and terrible history.

So many years she longed to return to Thebes, simply wanted to come home, wanted things to be as they once seemed to be – as they never truly were.

Grateful for the concealing darkness, she drifts into exhausted, fitful slumber.

When she wakes, Antigone opens her eyes but sees nothing. She listens, but hears nothing except her own breathing, and even of that she is not certain. The darkness and silence are so complete, so inescapable – could she already be dead?

But her bladder is full. It seems unlikely that the dead pass water.

Letting the blanket fall, she creeps along the packed-earth floor until her hand encounters the cave wall's uneven stone. She starts to lift her skirt, and then a better idea occurs to her. Her hand brushing the side of the cave, she slowly rises to her feet and then edges along until her fingers encounter the mud-brick wall sealing her in.

After relieving herself against the wall – childish petulance, perhaps, but she must urinate somewhere – she starts back, and then realizes she is not sure where she left the blanket. Though it is surely futile – she does not have long to live in any case – she counts her steps, as her father learned to do when he was blind, pausing after each two to explore, her toes seeking the basket. As she moves further into the depths of the cave it grows cooler. Then she finds the blanket; she wraps it around herself and moves to the reassuring solidity of the wall. Remaining out in the center of the tomb seems too empty, as if she were floating in the void.

She closes her eyes, but images assail her: the army gathered outside the gates of Thebes; Eteokles' angry scowl; the bodies of her twin brothers, lying close by the sacred spring.

How long will it be until she joins them?

"Antigone?"

Antigone blinks, but of course her eyes reveal nothing. Has she imagined a woman's voice?

"Antigone!"

There it is again – a feminine voice echoing in the darkness. Is she dead after all? But then Hermes should conduct her to the Underworld, shouldn't he? Unless some other spirit has come for her... the voice seems achingly familiar.

"Mother?"

"What?"

Antigone hears a difference in the tone – *like* her mother, but definitely *not* her mother. "Ismene? Is that you? Where are you?"

"In Eteokles' tomb."

"Of course," says Antigone, feeling foolish – and then her heart races with unlooked-for hope. The gods have recognized the rightness of her cause: perhaps they have decided to spare her, and make Creon's error plain for all to see! "There must be a connection between the caves! Keep talking, Ismene."

Antigone moves as quickly along the wall as she dares, listening to her sister's voice.

"I'm at the back of Eteokles' tomb. Can you see the light of my lamp?"

"Not yet." She realizes that the wall of the cave is starting to curve away, taking her further from the source of sound. She retraces her steps, feeling carefully up and down the uneven stone.

"There are cracks," Ismene is saying. "That's all I can see."

Cracks. Cracks too small, narrow, and crooked to admit even the lamplight. Despondent once more, Antigone slumps down against the wall. "Of course. Why would the gods take pity on me now, when they did not before?"

"I'm sorry," Ismene says softly.

Sorry. Such a futile word. It fits Ismene well.

"Why did you come?" Antigone asks.

"You're my sister. I wanted to be with you now – to help you if I could."

"You can't help me," Antigone snaps. "Only the gods can do that." And apparently they will not.

Ismene does not reply, and after several breaths Antigone's impatience subsides. Has she driven away her only contact with the living?

"Ismene?" she asks, a little ashamed. "Ismene, are you still there?"

"Yes."

"Is it – is it night or day?"

"It's night – but the sun should be rising soon."

"Did you come alone?" Antigone asks, surprised. Ismene was always fearful of everything, including the dark.

"The guards are outside. I told them I wanted to be alone with my brother's body. But really I was hoping we could talk. I was planning to shout through the bricks from outside, if I had to, but this is better."

Antigone sighs. A conversation with the living will only make her death more wrenching – yet she is grateful. "I suppose." But what will she and Ismene talk about? They have never been close.

Ismene asks: "Have you eaten any of the food?"

"No."

"Ah! You're very brave."

"I'm not being brave. I just don't want to suffer longer than necessary."

"I helped Aunt Eurydike pack it," says Ismene. "There's wheat bread, olives, figs, and raisins – and that hard sheep's-milk cheese you like so much. But the bread will get stale if you don't eat it soon."

Despite herself, Antigone reaches for the basket and starts feeling the contents. "You should have put in a knife – or a flask of poison, so that I could end this sooner."

"What?" Ismene's voice is indignant. "I don't want you to die!"

"But the king wants me dead, little sister." Her hand encounters the loaf of bread. Suddenly her mouth fills with moisture; her stomach grumbles. "And the king's word is law."

Ismene does not answer.

As though they were small creatures not under her control, Antigone's hands rummage through the basket and grasp the water-skin.

No, she tells herself, *you will not eat or drink!*

Ismene's voice comes through the wall again. "You believe that what you did was right."

"Of course I do! The gods' laws are more important than a king's!"

"Then maybe the gods will still save you. Isn't it important to stay strong, and give them a chance to act?"

Antigone feels her resolve weakening. When did her sister learn to argue?

"Remember, they saved Father when he was a child."

Certainly that is true. Their father should have died as an infant on a hillside, condemned by the previous king, Laius. But the Fates intervened.

"Much good that did us," says Antigone.

"What!" exclaims Ismene. "Would you prefer not to have been born?"

It is Antigone's turn to be silent. Her sister, she thinks, asked the question rhetorically. But Antigone has pondered the question many times, without finding a satisfactory answer.

"Antigone?" Ismene's voice sounds anxious. "Antigone, are you there?"

"Where would I go?" She sighs. "I suppose the Fates wanted us and the twins to be born, or they wouldn't have worked so hard to keep Father alive. But you'll soon be the only one left, Ismene."

"Not yet. You're still here. And you're all I have left." After a pause, Ismene says: "Please, stay strong while you can. For me. Even if – even if the gods don't come."

This plea moves her more than Ismene's other arguments. Antigone has always striven to be strong when others faltered. To lead along the difficult but necessary path.

"Very well," she says.

Her hands reach once more for the bread. Suddenly ravenous – she has not eaten since the previous morning – she breaks off a morsel and stuffs it into her mouth, then feels for the water-skin with trembling fingers.

"Are you eating?"

Antigone swallows the food and drink. She considers a sharp answer to the sister whose request will prolong the process of her death, but reconsiders and says only: "Yes."

"I'm glad."

"Better than nectar and ambrosia." Antigone means these words ironically – but in truth, the nourishment sends a wave of warmth and strength through her. "Well, Sister, what shall we do while we wait to see if the gods will spare me?"

"Antigone, you've been gone so long..."

"I know." Ten years.

"What happened, after you left with Father? And why didn't you come back to Thebes when he died? I've missed you, Antigone."

The idea is surprising – but perhaps, Antigone thinks, only because she did not often think of Ismene during those years. Others had claimed her thoughts.

She takes another sip of water – it tastes sweet, as if Eurydike added honey to it – and wonders if she should tell why she stayed away so long. The reason is so painful that she can scarcely bear to remember it. But this is her sister, the last child of the parents they share; and the secrets have burdened Antigone too long.

"Very well," she says, "I'll tell you." She closes her eyes. With her eyes shut, the darkness seems to disappear; instead she sees Thebes ten years past.

ANTIGONE

My marriage was the turning point. Before I married, the world followed its proper order; everything was as it should be. After the wedding, nothing was.

Haemon and I married because everyone expected us to; even the Tiresias said we were well matched. We had always been close friends. All those warm summer nights when we left the adults to their wine in the megaron and went up to the roof garden to catch the breeze… as I recall, Ismene, you stayed in the torchlight with the other girls to talk about clothes and jewelry, while the twins played senet and swapped stories about weapons-training with their friends. Alkides and Megara usually slipped off to a dark corner where they could hold hands and exchange kisses. Haemon and I sought space to ourselves as well – but instead of kisses we shared his poetry and my musings about the gods.

Close as Haemon and I were, desire had not yet been a part of it; and when the time came – our vows exchanged, our nuptial bed made ready – we failed. I had been told what to expect, and when Haemon stroked me I felt the intimate tingling and the flood of warmth – but Haemon's flesh did not respond to my hesitant touch. This was supposed to be the start of our marital bliss; instead it was mortifying.

After a long while I drew back, biting my lip. "We're doing it wrong," I said.

Haemon moved away and swung his thin legs over the edge of the bed. His shoulders slumped; he did not look at me; instead he rubbed his brow as if his head ached. "We're not doing it at all."

I pulled the sheet up to hide my nakedness from the late afternoon light that filtered through the window-shutters. "It's because I'm not pretty enough," I muttered.

He twisted back to look at me, anguish on his face. "No – Antigone, *no*, don't think that!"

Tears threatened – and I struggled not to yield to them. "If I were pretty, you wouldn't have a problem."

"That's – that's not it," my husband stammered. "It's my fault, not yours. I've never–"

Before he could tell me what he had never done, there was a knock at the door. We stared at each other in horror.

"Who is it?" Haemon called out, although we both knew.

"Your mother," trilled Eurydike. "I must come get the sheet now, my dears."

I looked at the pristine white linen covering me. There was no bloodstain, as there should have been, to witness the consummation of our union. Everyone would think I had not been a virgin! How utterly humiliating – especially since I was *still* a virgin!

Aunt Eurydike eased open the door. She seemed embarrassed herself: as Haemon is her eldest son, this was the first time for her to perform this duty. "I'm sorry to interrupt you," she said, not meeting our eyes, "but the guests in the megaron are waiting! If I don't appear with the sheets soon, their dirty jokes are just going to get worse."

But when she examined the bed sheets and saw no sign of blood, her tone grew serious. She looked at Haemon, then at me. "Don't worry," she whispered. "Antigone, I know you haven't been with anyone else." She reached for a small pouch tied around her waist and began to undo the leather thong that held it shut. "You two have spent so much time together… I remember what it was like, to be so young and in love. Things happen. But we mustn't let people say that you two took liberties before your wedding day." She pulled a small ceramic vial from the pouch and unstoppered it, then splashed a few drops of crimson liquid onto one of the sheets.

I gasped, and Haemon stammered: "Wh-what–"

Eurydike smiled, showing dimples in her cheeks. "My dear children, do you think you two are the first to have this problem?" With her fingers she smeared the red droplets. "No one can tell the difference between goat's blood and the real thing."

Though this would hide my shame from the wedding guests, it only increased the depth of my embarrassment. The real reason for our problem never occurred to Aunt Eurydike. Then again, why should it? She had been, people say, a very pretty bride.

"Come, now," Eurydike said. "Get dressed; we must go out to greet the guests. Here, Antigone, I'll help you with your skirt-laces."

We managed to get back into our clothes while Eurydike stripped the sheet from the bed. Haemon took my hand. "I'm sorry, Antigone," he whispered almost silently.

Hand in hand we walked back to the megaron; we were greeted with whistles and cheers and one ribald joke after another. When Eurydike unfurled the bloodstained sheet, Alkides' shout could be heard above the applause: "Didn't think you had it in you, Haemon!"

Haemon's face went red as a sunburn. I swallowed, feeling ill: our marriage was a lie. We were deceiving the people of Thebes, and dishonoring the gods. Yet I could not have admitted the truth – not in front of my mother.

As regal as ever, she came over to embrace me. "Darling, you're a woman now!" Then she pulled back, holding my shoulders. "And you look so beautiful today!" But to me her tone sounded forced.

"Mother, don't," I muttered, further humiliated by her falsehood.

She shook her head, setting the tiny golden leaves and flowers of her crown aflutter. "Antigone, today of all days, let your mother say something nice to you! Give me a kiss."

After I kissed her, she stepped back to let Father take his turn. "I'm proud of you, Daughter," he said, wrapping me in his strong arms. Then, one hand on my shoulder, he turned to my new husband. "Haemon, you must always take care of my little girl."

"I'll – I'll do my best, my lord king," stammered Haemon.

Mother reached out for Father's free hand. "Remember *our* wedding day, Oedipus?"

Father's arm dropped from my shoulder, and he grinned down at Mother. "Of course," he said. "How could I possibly forget?"

For once I was relieved at the way Mother absorbed all Father's attention for herself. Haemon and I managed to accept congratulations from his parents and the various noble Thebans and honored guests. Eventually we took our places at the table and nibbled at our food. With the poor harvest that year, I had been anxious that there would not be enough for our wedding feast – but now I had no appetite. People joked about this, as they did about everything we did: every word we said and every movement we made prompted some off-color comment, as if we were supposed to be thinking of nothing but our marriage bed. After a while it became too embarrassing to bear – at least, if we went back to our room, we could escape the leers and jokes. When we excused ourselves the people cheered us, and their drunken shouts echoed down the hallway as we made our retreat.

After we banished the serving girl and the door swung shut behind her, Haemon sank down onto a wooden stool, resting his face in his hands. "I'm sorry, Antigone," he said softly. "I'm not man enough for you."

I went to sit on the floor beside him. "It's my fault. If I had my mother's beauty – if I were as pretty as your sister Megara–"

"It's not that!" he objected, his dark eyes shining in the lamplight. Then he looked away, sighing. "Maybe I should sacrifice to Priapos."

"That's a good idea," I said. Surely the fertility god, with his unfailing erection, could help. "Let's not try again tonight. We should wait until after you've made a sacrifice."

He looked so relieved at my words that the tears I had been fighting all evening broke free. I got to my feet and turned away so that Haemon could not see. My back to him, I untied my skirt-laces and shed my heavy clothes, then slipped into a linen night-shift. Haemon changed into a linen dressing-robe; I dried my tears as unobtrusively as I could and we lay down on the bed side by side, not touching each other, staring up at the ceiling.

Eventually his breathing deepened into soft snores, but I could not sleep. What if Haemon never made love to me? It was a woman's duty to bear children! But if I was so plain that my husband could not bear to touch me, what kind of woman was I?

Yet if our marriage was doomed, how could the Tiresias have said that we were well suited to one another? Was it only because neither of us was good enough for anyone else? I remembered how I had scorned Megara and Alkides and the fact that they spent their time together kissing, while Haemon and I had discussed the mysteries of the universe. But now I realized that Haemon had never caressed me because I was too repulsive.

Always before when something troubled me, it was Haemon who listened. But this problem involved Haemon. I sometimes went to Aunt Eurydike – but how could I speak to her of this? Wishing that the earth would swallow me up, that I could be anywhere but Thebes, morning birds were chirping before I fell asleep.

Then the lightning bolts came.

The skies were ominous all day; from time to time we heard the rumbling of Zeus' thunder, but no rain fell. Although the light was poor, we women worked in the weaving room, talking little as we spun new thread together. My head ached from lack of sleep and a heaviness in the air; I wished the storm, like Deukalion's flood, would come and drown us all. Then a servant burst into the room, shouting that the city was on fire. We rushed out onto the balcony to look and saw the thick black smoke rising from the storerooms by the Astykratia Gate. My first thought was that *I* had brought this upon the city. My failure as a wife – my deception of the people: these had offended the immortal gods. Staring, I spoke the thought aloud: "Are the gods cursing my marriage?"

"Of course not," Mother snapped. "Don't be ridiculous."

I shrank back from her and realized that I had been chewing at my fingernails, a habit she hated. I dropped my hand from my mouth. "How can you be sure?"

Her dark brows drew together. "If you don't believe me, go ask the Tiresias! He blessed your marriage!"

"We should pray," I said. "Pray for rain."

I remember that you, Ismene, helped Aunt Eurydike get her younger children to the nursery. I ran to the palace shrine to make an offering of incense and beg the Immortal Ones for mercy. But my words did not persuade Zeus to open the heavens to quench the flames. I knelt before the altar until my knees went numb, reciting every prayer said to be pleasing to the ears of Zeus, and still the rain did not come.

Zeus, of course, hates oath-breakers: did he hate me, and spurn my words, because my marriage vows were a lie?

I heard a commotion in the hallway; I rose to my feet and went to see what was happening. Was the palace itself on fire? Thank the gods, it was not; but the servants were taking food and drinking water to those fighting the flames.

I could not help the city with prayer, but with this I could help. I went to the palace kitchens and gathered up a basket of bread and cheese, then followed the servants rushing towards the eastern storerooms. The gusting winds drove bits of soot and ash through the air and the smell of burning wood and oil filled my lungs. When I got close enough to see the orange flames licking skyward, I found that the men of Thebes had formed up in dual lines to pass vessels of water up from the springs to the site of the fire and then end the empty ones back for more water. Noblemen and well-born youths worked side by side with peasants and slaves; it seemed that every pot in the city had been pressed into service – from fine vases that usually adorned the tables of the Spartoi to mean chamber pots from the peasants' huts.

Women moved along the lines with refreshment for the sweating men and boys; occasionally a woman stepped into the line to relieve a youth whose strength was failing. Handing out the bread and cheese from my basket, I found my husband Haemon working alongside Polynikes and Alkides. A servant boy no more than twelve was next in line, he was pale with exhaustion. Daphne touched the boy on the shoulder and motioned him aside, then took his place in line.

"Antigone!" Polynikes called out. "Have you got something to eat? Gods, I'm famished!" I gave him the last of my bread and then took his spot between Daphne and Haemon so that he could eat. If Daphne could do this work, so could I.

I glanced around to see how it was done, but there was little time to think: Daphne passed an ornate bronze urn to me. It was staggeringly heavy, and some of the water sloshed out as I swung it over to Haemon. Then there was another vessel, and another. Of course they were slippery, and to my horror as I tried to pass one to Haemon it slipped from my fingers and the terracotta shattered to pieces against the cobblestones.

I cried out in frustration, but Daphne said briskly: "Don't worry about it; just take the next one. Hold it like this, with one hand supporting the bottom."

I kicked the potsherds aside and kept working, ashamed that I – the daughter of Thebes' king and queen – should be so useless. But then, unlike most women in the city, I never fetched water from the spring: the palace servants did that.

Now we all worked to save our city, servants and well-born alike. The heat from the blaze was oppressive, and despite our efforts the fire was still spreading. The storehouse, filled with jars of olive oil, burned brighter than any lamp, and sparks had leapt across to adjacent buildings: like a glowing swarm of locusts the flames ate away at roof-beams, windowsills, and painted wooden columns.

Haemon's face was grimy with soot; he grimaced as he took the next jar from me and then gasped, "I have to rest." He tapped the peasant who stood back to back with him, handing empty vessels down towards the stream. "Let's switch places for a while." The man nodded and they exchanged places. For an instant it seemed strange for me to be jostling elbows with such a man, but I dismissed the thought – I was as filthy as any peasant.

I handed the next urn of water to the peasant, who passed it to Alkides. Though he was just a little older than the twins – thirteen or fourteen, I suppose – he was already as big and strong as the grown man working next to him. "Tired already, Haemon?" he teased.

"The gods didn't give all of us your strength, Alkides," Haemon answered wearily, rubbing his forehead.

"That's true," Alkides said. He was not being boastful; it was an acknowledgement of fact. Although *I* did not find him attractive – his bulk and his hairy arms and legs reminded me of a bear – most of Thebes' young women fawned over him and the young men envied him.

"Still, they gave us this fire to fight."

I glanced over my shoulder at Haemon. "Our marriage is cursed," I said quietly.

Haemon gave me a foul look. "You just want a reason not to be married to me."

I looked away, hoping Daphne and the peasant had not heard. I took the next vessel from Daphne's hands – a precious one, its painted surface depicting the wedding of Kadmos and Harmonia – and handed it to the man at my left. I was ashamed to admit it, but Haemon was right. And obviously *he* did not want to be married to *me*, either.

"Come," said Daphne, drawing me aside. "Let's let the men work for a while."

Polynikes, having finished his bread, came to fill the gap in the line. "What, ladies, giving up already?"

Daphne pushed a sweat-damp lock of hair back from her forehead; her shoulders drooped in exhaustion. "Maybe the gods don't want us to put out the flames," she said, lifting a hand to the dark clouds. "There's no sign of rain – and Zeus' own lightning struck the storeroom. Maybe we should let it burn as a sacrifice."

"What!" shouted Eteokles from where he worked in a parallel line several paces away. "Thebes must be protected!"

"Absolutely," agreed Polynikes. "No king would let his city burn!"

"Haemon!" called a female voice. "Alkides!" I looked up; Haemon's sister Megara was running towards us. Her cheeks and breasts were free of soot; the stray curls caused by her haste only made her look prettier. "The fire's under control to the south! Prince Eteokles, Prince Polynikes–"

Seeking the shortest route, she ducked beneath the eaves of a nearby building, one whose rafters were aflame at the far side. Just as she passed beneath, there was a terrible groaning sound – and the building began to collapse.

"Megara!" bellowed Alkides. He dropped the jar he had been holding and sprinted over to her. A shower of roof-tiles started falling from the doomed structure; Alkides held his massive arm over the girl's head and snatched her away. Women screamed as the building collapsed in a cloud of dust and glowing sparks; the flames caught one peasant woman's skirts and she slapped at them, shrieking. Alkides pushed Megara towards Eteokles and then snatched a water jar from the arms of the nearest worker, splashing it onto the terrified peasant woman and extinguishing the flames. It was all over in an instant, and then Alkides hurried to Megara's side. "Are you all right?"

"Alkides – you saved my life!" Megara gasped, clinging to him.

We all paused to admire Alkides. "I'll tell Father of your bravery," Eteokles said.

"I'll have the bards make a song about you!" added Polynikes.

"The fire may be under control in the south, but it's not out here yet!" I reminded everyone.

"Antigone, you're no fun," Alkides muttered.

What he said was true. I was always the one who reminded the others of their duties and responsibilities – the one who forced them to see realities they preferred to ignore. I myself had learned to do so long ago: every morning, I looked at my plain face in the mirror and knew that I could not change it.

"Wait, Alkides," said Megara, clutching his arm as he moved back to the line before me, "I have to tell you – tell everyone here – the reason the gods are angry. The king and queen have committed a terrible, terrible sin."

"What do you mean?" I asked, passing the full vase I held to Alkides.

Megara looked at me, then at my brothers. "Your father – he's your mother's son."

I did not understand her. "What are you talking about?" I snapped. "Father is the son of the king and queen of Korinth!"

Megara pushed a stray curl out of her face. "I'm sorry, Antigone," she said, "but he's not. He was adopted. King Oedipus is the son of Queen Jocasta."

"Impossible!" I said, full of horror and disbelief.

My brothers were just as appalled. "You're lying!" Eteokles pronounced, and Polynikes chorused, "Who would speak such filth?"

Haemon joined us, while his sister Megara persisted. "Your father was born to King Laius and Queen Jocasta. There was a bad omen, so Laius left the baby on the mountainside to die. But somehow he survived, and was adopted by the king and queen of Korinth…"

My mind reeled as she spoke. How could this be true? And yet – Megara seemed so certain. She had so many details. Who would invent such a story?

I noticed Haemon edging away from me, revulsion in his eyes.

"You believe her?" I cried. "You believe that my father is the son of my mother?"

He lifted soot-smudged palms. "Antigone, how would I know anything about it?"

Before I could say anything, a group of men appeared, led by a fellow called Melanippus. They were from the southeastern gate and had come to assist.

I set my jaw. "I'm going to the palace. I'll find out the truth."

"The fire's not out," Polynikes said, echoing my earlier point.

"Ah, let her go," said Eteokles. "With Melanippus and his team here now, we'll soon have this out. Come on, everyone, get back to work!"

I ran away, my heart pounding hard. It was a lie – it had to be!

But as reached the city's center, the mob of people surrounding the palace seemed to have heard the same lies – seemed to believe them. The smoke-filled sky grew darker and distant lightning flickered over the hills, as though Zeus himself was menacing me.

"Look," shrieked a woman, "there's the *porni's* daughter!"

"Sacrilege!" screamed an old man. "It's them what's cursed our city!"

A fat raindrop splashed my cheek; another hit my shoulder, and then the clouds burst open. Water pelted down, splashing in the streets. It should have been a sign of the gods' mercy – they were putting out the fires at last! – and yet it felt like an extension of their anger.

I hurried through the crowd, and although the insults continued, no one touched me. The marble treads of the broad palace stairway were slick, treacherous; I nearly fell but, driven by my need to learn the truth, I did not slow my pace. Ducking into the shelter of the palace at last, I sluiced rainwater mixed with soot from my face and arms and then turned towards the residence wing. Halfway down the corridor I nearly collided with Aunt Eurydike.

"Antigone! Is Haemon all right?"

"Haemon's fine," I said. "Megara's down there too. This rain will put out the fire."

"Oh, Antigone! The news – it's so awful…"

I knew she did not mean the fire or the weather. "Megara said my parents…" I stopped, unable to repeat the words, willing her to deny them.

But she nodded, squeezing my hands. "Creon is furious," she said. "He says they knew – that they must have known. That they've brought the wrath of the gods upon our city."

I drew back. "Where are they?"

"Your mother's in her room. Your – father —" she hesitated

awkwardly, because my father was also my brother now, then continued. "The king was livid. He and Creon shouted at each other, and then your father went to find your mother. He said – he said she must atone. That if she did not, he would …"

Pulling away from Eurydike, I ran down the hall. As I climbed the stairs I heard screams of anger and desperation, Father's and Mother's voices both – and then one piercing shriek.

There were guards outside my mother's room, but they did not stop me. I threw open the door. Mother was standing there dressed in a fine gown, the necklace of Harmonia around her slender neck. Tears streaked down her face, yet she was still beautiful as an ivory carving.

"Mother? Father?"

But Mother did not turn towards me; Father, slumped on her dressing stool, both hands covering his face, did not look up.

I stammered: "They're – they're saying the most terrible—"

With the pounding rain outside, the room was dimly lit; so it took me a moment to notice the blood seeping from between my father's fingers. "Father!" I gasped. "What's happened?" I ran over to him and pulled his hands from his face – and a horrifying wash of blood poured forth, down his cheeks, on to the furniture. One of Mother's dress-pins, as long as my hand and needle-sharp, clattered to the floor.

"Antigone?" Father said, his voice hoarse. "Antigone, is that you?"

I did not want to see the ruin where his eyes had been, and yet I could not look away.

"Father, what has she *done* to you?" I screamed.

"Nothing," said Mother, though the guilt was plain on her face. No blood marred her manicured hands, no gore stained her dress – but she was responsible all the same. She had known, I could see it: she had always known that he was her son. She had lied to him, to all of us, and now she meant to go on lying. "Nothing!" she repeated in a plaintive, nauseating tone.

"Nothing! You mean, everything!" Though Father's fingers held the pin, it was all her fault – *she* had done this. I glanced at their bed… though no child likes to think of their parents' lovemaking, now it was too much to bear: I swallowed back rising vomit.

I had to get Father away, out of the room where *she* had tricked him with her unnatural beauty into committing sacrilege.

Taking his bloody hand in mine, I pulled him to his feet. "Come, Father, come with me."

I settled his arm around my shoulders and led him to the door. He was unsteady on his feet, but I managed to get him down the hall – to the room that until my marriage I had shared with you, Ismene.

"Find a healer!" I yelled at the gaping servants, and made Father lie down on my bed. While we waited for a healer, I cleaned his hands and cheeks.

"I didn't know," he said, his voice cracking. "I didn't know."

"Hush, Father," I said, dipping the bloody sponge back into my washbasin.

It took time for a healer to arrive; most of them were tending burn victims. But finally the door creaked open.

"Who is it?" Father asked, lifting his head. A touch of hope animated his face.

"Rhodia, my lord king," she answered. Though Rhodia was officially a midwife, her healing skills were excellent.

"Oh." Father sank back against the pillows. "I hoped…"

He did not finish the sentence, but I knew what he was thinking. He had hoped that it was Mother.

Rhodia had the servants bring strong wine; she mixed several pinches of herbs into a half-filled goblet, then held the cup to my father's lips. "Drink, my lord king: it will ease your pain. Then I can treat your injuries."

He drank deeply, and then turned away. "Nothing can ease my pain."

The healer touched his shoulder. "Give it time, my lord king." Then she glanced at me, her eyes full of empathy and sadness. "The herbs need a little while to work." Young as I was, I knew that was not all that she meant.

While Rhodia positioned lamps near the bed and prepared her equipment, I waited, holding Father's hand. Eventually I felt his grip slacken. Rhodia must have seen the muscles of his arm relax; she came over to the bed and eased the pillow out from under his head, then brought over her polished bronze tools. They looked like table implements for some ghoulish meal.

She had a servant hold Father's head still as she worked. For the most part he bore it in silence, flinching only a little now and then. She scraped the bloody pulp from his eye sockets and washed them with sour wine. Then, using bronze tongs, she took up a glowing coal to cauterize the worst of the bleeding.

Dear gods, I'll never forget the smell!

He gasped, and his fingers tightened on mine till I thought the bones would break, but with a moan he relaxed. When it was time for the second eye we were both ready for the pain, and it was not quite so bad. Finally Rhodia settled small linen-wrapped poultices into each empty eye socket and tied a bandage around his head to hold them in place.

"Each day for a month," Rhodia said, "the wounds should be washed with sour wine. That will keep them from growing putrid." She slipped the pillow back beneath his head, then offered him an herb-infused goblet. "You should sleep now, my lord king."

He drank, as obedient as a child. Murmuring our mother's name, worn out from pain and emotion, he soon slept.

Rhodia and I watched his chest rise and fall, then she turned to me. "You should sleep too, Princess Antigone. There's nothing more you can do now."

"Sleep?" I whispered. "Merciful gods, how can I sleep? I just learned that my father and I both sprang from the same cursed womb!"

She grasped my arm and led me over to the second bed. "As dreadful as today has been, my lady princess, tomorrow may be worse. You should conserve your strength." I remembered, then, that this woman had assisted at my birth. Did she, too, feel betrayed by my mother's lies?

I did not fight her, but lay down on the bed and let her give me a sleeping draught. The herbs she gave me were bitter but I swallowed them gratefully, and soon I slept.

Dreams of fire and blood pursued me through the night. I woke with a start, hearing angry shouts in the distance and feeling rough hands upon me. "What—"

Polynikes was shaking my shoulder. "Wake up, Antigone. If we don't go out and face them, they'll storm the palace."

I blinked up at him stupidly.

"We could be killed like Pentheus," added Eteokles, standing beside him. "Like Labdakus and Amphion. The Theban mob does not like sacrilege." He glanced over at Father, who stirred as though he were just beginning to wake. "But I won't die for our parents' crimes."

I sat up. "But Father didn't know!" I protested.

"Will the gods forgive that?" Polynikes asked. "Will the people of Thebes? He *should* have known."

The rumble of shouting outside the palace was growing louder.

"He killed his own father!" Eteokles said, his tone harsh. "He *killed* his father and *married* his mother. What's worse than that?"

Still bleary with sleep, I rubbed my eyes. Mother's first husband, Laius – my father's true father – had been killed by a bandit outside Delphi. "What are you talking about?" Bewildered, I looked around the room. Uncle Creon stood just inside the door, his arms folded across his chest; Aunt Eurydike was nearby, a hand pressed to her mouth; my new husband Haemon stood a little behind her. And you, Ismene, I remember how weary you looked: beneath your eyes were dark shadows, as if you had not slept.

"It's true, Antigone," you said softly.

"Yes, it's true," Father confirmed, sitting up. "I must appear before the people. If someone would guide me..." He reached out his hand.

He was willing to sacrifice himself, if necessary, to save the rest of us. I darted to his side. "I'm here, Father. Antigone. I'll help you." Surely if the people of Thebes saw his contrition, the awful price he had already paid, they would not blame him! It was Mother's fault – *she* was the one who should face their wrath.

As I assisted Father to his feet, I looked over at Uncle Creon. "What about Mother?" I asked. "Is *she* coming?"

"The guards will bring her," Creon said.

How like her, I thought. Father was going of his own volition, ready to face the crowd's wrath – she had to be brought, by armed men. The Theban people would see the meaning of that well enough! In the throes of my anger, I almost welcomed the thought of her being torn apart by the mob. It would be a kind of justice.

"Chamber pot," Father muttered, and the disgust on the faces of the twins grew deeper.

"*I*'ll help you, Father," I offered, as everyone else streamed from the room.

We each used the chamber pot. I put on my sandals and helped Father with his. Then we made our slow way down the interior stairs and out to the terrace facing the agora. It was filled with restless people; several white-robed priests were conspicuous in their front ranks, and the Tiresias in his dark robe, his eyes bound by a blindfold and leaning on the arm of his daughter Daphne, stood near the top of the stairs. The crowd started jeering when they saw us, but Uncle Creon's shout hushed them. "Silence!" he shouted, "Hear me, Thebans! I have done everything in my power to protect you these forty years!"

Several of Creon's men stood on the marble stairway a few treads below us, their spears leveled at the crowd. If the mob swarmed the palace, how long would their loyalty last?

"You've been protecting them!" called one woman.

"Your sister did this to us! Your sister – and your nephew, Oedipus!"

"Yes," said Creon – and this single word brought silence once more. "And my sister Jocasta has paid the price." He turned back, beckoning to soldiers in the corridor behind us. I thought they would lead Mother forward to face the mob. What would she say? How would her beauty, her famous charm, help her now?

But Mother did not walk onto the terrace; instead four soldiers appeared, carrying a linen-draped bier. They walked forward and set their burden at Creon's feet; Uncle pulled back the fine-woven cloth.

In death, Mother's beauty deserted her at last. She was hideous: her face swollen beyond recognition, the color of an overripe fig. Still, I knew those fine hands, those dainty feet.

You, Ismene, let out a piercing wail. "Mother!" you cried, sobbing.

"Jocasta?" Father asked, a tremor in his voice. "Jocasta, are you here?"

"She's dead," Creon said coldly. "She hanged herself."

Father clutched my arm. "Dead?" he whispered.

Confronted with his grief, one part of my anger melted away – even as the remaining part grew more jealous and spiteful. "Yes, Father – she's dead."

"Let me touch her," he said.

I guided him to her body and helped him kneel beside it. For a moment, the crowd's fury ebbed away: they watched, breathless, as he took my mother's hand in his own. "My love," he whispered, so softly that I doubt anyone else could hear. His voice gained strength. "I should have killed you. I meant to kill you. You were braver than I.”

"Parricide!” hissed someone in the crowd.

Another shouted, “Look how he loves her still! Unnatural!”

Father dropped Mother's hand and stood. “Yes!” he cried. “Unnatural son that I am, my eyes looked upon her with love – and so I put them out!” He ripped the blindfold from his face, and the poultices fell away. The crowd gasped at the sight of his ravaged face and said no more.

In the sudden hush, Creon spoke. “Queen Jocasta is dead. Priests, if we banish Oedipus, will that cleanse the city?”

I turned to stare at the man who was my uncle, my great uncle, and my father-in-law. *“Banish* him?”

"Be silent," Creon snapped at me. “Let the priests answer.”

Bromius, Apollo's chief priest, glanced at the Tiresias. I wondered why the famous prophet had not spoken; even now he gave no sign. “That should be enough," Bromius said, sounding uncertain. “But we must make a sacrifice and read the omens to be sure of the gods' will.”

I stepped toward Creon. “How can you banish him?” I objected.

Creon looked down at me. “We must think of Thebes.”

"But he's blind!"

"I am blind," said the Tiresias, breaking his silence at last. “And yet I manage.”

"You are the greatest prophet in Hellas," I said, “honored and welcomed wherever you go! Who will welcome my father?”

Father patted my arm. “It's all right, Antigone," he said. “Tiresias, if I leave the city, will that lift the curse from Thebes?”

The old seer nodded. “Yes, Oedipus. Any curse occasioned by your offense against the gods will be lifted from the city.”

The people's fierce anger lessened. Though banishing Father seemed cruel, it was better than letting the crowd tear him apart.

"And my children?” persisted Father. “Will *they* be freed from the curse, if I go? No guilt remains upon them?”

How selfless he was! I gazed up at Father's face – how could anyone blame him for what had happened?

Bromius, Apollo's priest, stuttered: “I – I don't know, my lord king—”

"They're not to blame for your crimes, Oedipus," said the Tiresias, sounding tired. “Or for mine,” he added, so softly that I doubt I would have heard the last three words had I been any further away.

"Nor should they be," said Father. “It seems, then, my time in Thebes is done.”

I straightened my shoulders. “I'll go with you, Father.”

"But, Antigone," my mother-in-law objected, “you're newly married!”

I glanced at Haemon. A muscle twitched in his cheek, but he said nothing.

"My marriage—” I was on the verge of declaring my marriage a sham; but when I saw his face redden, I knew I could not shame him so. “My duty to my father is greater," I said.

"You have my permission to go," Haemon muttered without meeting my gaze. I believe he was relieved to be rid of me.

Then you stepped forward, Ismene. "I'll come too!"

"No!" The word came simultaneously from me, Creon, and Eurydike.

I did not want you with us: you had not helped tend Father's wounds – instead you had wept over Mother's body. *I* was the one who had earned the right to be by Father's side, not you.

"Not *both* of you," pleaded Aunt Eurydike.

"Ismene, you're still a maiden," said Creon.

You protested that you were only a year younger.

"Nevertheless, Ismene, I forbid you to leave. You are not as strong as your sister – for you it would be too hard."

Even though he said what I wanted to hear, my lips twisted sourly. You, the pretty child, Mother's favorite, must be protected. But I – the plain one, troublesome and outspoken, the one who might taint Creon's son – I was welcome to take up the wandering life of a mendicant.

"Eteokles and Polynikes must also stay," Creon said firmly. "The Tiresias has said this curse does not touch them; they are still royal princes, and must prepare to take their thrones."

Eteokles nodded. "Of course."

"That – that's our duty," Polynikes added.

"I see," said my blind father. "My daughters choose family; my sons choose power."

But I did not want the twins with us, not after how they had spoken about Father.

"Let's go, Father," I said. I led him down the steps and we made our way through the crowd. Demochares and his soldiers held them back, but despite the shouts of the mob I did not sense that the people still thirsted for our blood. They were content to have us gone.

"Which way are we going?" Father asked, as we descended a cobbled street.

"Towards the Ogygia Gate," I answered.

"Good," he said, nodding his blindfolded face. "From there let's head to the coast. We'll find a ship that can take us to Korinth."

Korinth – the city of his childhood, where the woman he had always thought to be his mother still lived. Yes, that was a logical destination. Perhaps the widowed queen would have mercy on us.

Before we reached the gate, a woman came running from behind us, calling my name. She was one of Eurydike's servants; she handed me a full waterskin and a leather traveling-pack. "From my lady," she said, helping me to settle the straps over my shoulders. "She'll pray to all the gods for your safety, Princess." The woman then whispered to me that at the bottom of the pack I would find a few jewels and beads of silver to help with emergencies. I told the servant to thank my aunt; the woman slipped back into the crowd.

Father's ankles had always pained him; our progress through the city was unhampered, but not swift. So I was not surprised to see that Haemon had reached the Ogygia Gate before us – however, I did not expect what came next: he approached us, and walked the last few blocks beside me.

"At least now we know," he said quietly. "This – this situation explains our trouble."

"Does it?" I countered. "The Tiresias said no blame attaches to my parents' children."

Haemon's face went red. "That must be it! What else could it be?"

I shrugged. "You know that as well as I." I had said it already, on our wedding night: I was too plain to rouse his desire. There was no need for me to repeat it now. "I suppose you're glad that I'm leaving."

"No, Antigone—" he began.

"Why not? You don't want me as your wife."

"Antigone—" He touched my arm, and I halted my steps to look at him.

Someone in the crowd shouted at us to keep moving, but I ignored them.

Haemon said, "You've always been my best friend. If you go, I'll have no one."

"I won't desert my father," I said, resuming the walk towards the boundary of Thebes.

"Antigone," Father murmured, "you shouldn't—"

"Don't, Father," I said. "This is what I need to do." I glanced back over my shoulder to see Haemon still standing there, looking stricken. "You could come with us," I said.

He hung his head. "Father would never allow it."

Well, I thought, so be it. Our marriage was a failure before it ever began; even if Haemon joined us, that would not change.

After Father and I passed through the city gates, the noise from the crowd abated. Old Bromius' voice rang out, invoking the blessings of Apollo now that the curse had been banished from the city.

So I left Thebes, with my banished father-brother, and then I remembered how, on my wedding night, I wanted more than anything to leave the city and had implored to the gods to give me a reason.

*

Antigone shifts against the hard stone wall. "So, you see, in that case the gods answered my prayer." She laughs, a bitter sound that echoes in the cave. "But, given how they did it, I wish that they hadn't."

CHAPTER THREE
ISMENE

Ismene stares down at the glow of her lamp, remembering the horror of those days — and considering the fact that they had been more horrible for her sister than she ever guessed. And for Haemon.

Realizing that the silence has grown long, she glances at the cave wall that separates them. "Antigone?"

"I'm not dead yet," her sister answers. "But why don't *you* talk for a while?"

An understandable request: what Antigone just shared was so personal, so painful that she must yearn to fall silent. But unlike her sister, Ismene has always been a listener, not a speaker. She is not sure what to say, but if she can comfort Antigone, she will do her best to talk. "What about?"

She hears a sound like a sigh — is that Antigone, or just the movement of air between the twinned caves? "Tell me about Eteokles' tomb."

Ismene holds up the terracotta lamp and looks around. "The side walls have been smoothed with stucco and painted. Across from me there's a fresco of a boar hunt. You can even recognize Eteokles' favorite dogs — Twig, the brown one, and Barley, the dun-colored one. They were both sacrificed on his tomb. They're buried at his feet now, in the direction of the door."

She stands, stretching her legs stiffly after sitting for so long on the tomb's packed-earth floor. Is this how the dead feel, when they arrive in the Underworld?

"The wall between the tombs," she continues, "shows Eteokles on the throne. There's a sphinx on either side, looking up at him." She carries the lamp toward the grave-mound at the center of the tomb. "He was buried with his sword, but his helmet and shield are on top of the grave mound. There are baskets of raisins and dried beef, and jars of honey and wine, lined up against the walls. His golden wine-goblet is here on a little table — oh, and there's his favorite camp-stool. I suppose I could bring that over to sit on while we talk, instead of sitting on the floor. Do you think Eteokles would mind?"

"I couldn't say," Antigone answers dryly. "You knew him better than I."

"I suppose that's true." Ismene feels her cheeks flush. So much safer not to be the one talking — it's always so easy to say the wrong thing! Why did she describe the food, when Antigone has so little food with her? She doesn't even have the comfort of a wooden stool! "Antigone, are you sure you want to hear all this? It's—"

A knock at the door makes Ismene jump; she falls silent, her heart pounding.

"Yes," Antigone says, "I do! Tell me about the rest."

"I – I have to go now."

"Why?"

"Someone's at the door."   Ismene's stomach lurches. Her uncle Creon would not approve of such contact with her sister. He did not expressly forbid it, but he could still take her presence here as an act of defiance.

"Ismene, wait," pleads her sister. "Don't leave me!"

Ismene hesitates. Is that panic in her sister's voice? She has never known Antigone to show fear or doubt.

"I'll come back as soon as I can," Ismene assures her. "I'll just go see what's happening." She sets down her lamp, walks past her brother's grave, and pulls open the heavy door. The sun has risen, and daylight dazzles her eyes. She makes out a group of people several paces away, silhouetted on a rise against the sky. What are they doing here – come to gloat over her sister's fate? To sympathize, perhaps? Maybe they're just curious – but all they can see is a wall of bricks.

"What is it?" she asks the guards, wondering if she is already in trouble with Creon.

The soldier nearest the door bows. "Pardon me, my lady princess – just wanted to make sure you were all right. You've been in King Eteokles' tomb a long time."

"I – I'm fine."

Her eyes adjusting to the light, she recognizes her aunt Eurydike and her cousin Haemon in the crowd. Haemon frowns and says something to his mother.

The guard bows again. "Yes, my lady princess," he says, stepping back to his post outside the other tomb.

Leaving the group, Eurydike and Haemon walk down the slope towards the tombs. Eurydike hurries over to take Ismene's hand; her aunt's plump fingers feel very warm. "Child, they say you've been here since before daybreak! I know you loved Eteokles, but he wouldn't want you to mourn all day in the dark."

Ismene looks down, feeling ashamed. While Antigone was speaking, she hardly thought of the brother whose body lay only a few feet away. "I – I couldn't sleep," she stammers. "I kept thinking how lonely he must be…"

"Are you really here because of Eteokles?" Haemon interrupts. He moves closer, his taller form blocking the light. His voice low but firm, he continues: "I think you're here for the same reason we are, Ismene.   For Antigone."

His bluntness startles her. Dropping her aunt's hand, she glances up to meet her cousin's dark eyes – and at once looks away. She knows more, now, about Haemon than he would want her to know. For a man there's no shame greater than being unable to make love to a woman – especially his own wife! Ismene wonders if that disastrous wedding night led Haemon to shun the pleasures of the bed altogether: in all the years since Antigone's departure, she has never heard of him taking a lover. And yet, despite all that, Haemon admits he is here because of Antigone.

Before their marriage, Antigone and Haemon were the best of friends – just one of the close bonds that surrounded Ismene without including her. Ismene's habit of remaining apart, watching and listening, has proved safer: her parents' passionate marriage ended in disaster; Haemon and Antigone have been estranged for years; and Ismene cannot bear to think of what happened between Haemon's sister Megara and her husband. And now the twins – once so close – have killed one another.

Yet if Ismene has learned anything during the war, it's that no one is always safe. She squares her shoulders and looks up again at Haemon. "What if I am?"

"Why were you inside Eteokles' tomb so long? What were you doing?"

Ismene glances nervously at the nearby guards, then up at the crowd on the ridge. She does not want the king to learn of this. But Haemon and Eurydike can discover the truth themselves simply by entering her brother's tomb.

"There's – there's a crack in the wall between the caves," Ismene whispers. "Antigone and I can talk to each other. It's not big enough to pass anything through – even the lamplight doesn't get through. But at least I can keep her company until the end comes. Please don't tell Uncle Creon!"

"We won't," Eurydike says quickly.

"Mother..."

"You're not disobeying him," Eurydike says, gently touching Ismene's arm. "The king has not forbidden you from visiting your brother's grave."

"No, he hasn't," Haemon says, studying her.

Ismene looks up at the group of people watching from a distance. A few more have arrived since she came out of the cave; soon everyone in Thebes will have heard where she is and what she is doing. Her aunt and cousin may assure her that she is not breaking the law, but Uncle Creon will not be pleased when he finds out.

It doesn't matter; she is bound by her promise. "I'm going back inside. Antigone needs me."

Eurydike nods. "I'm coming too. What about you, Haemon?"

Haemon shifts his weight, glancing uneasily from Eteokles' open tomb to the blank wall that seals the adjoining cave, the pair of soldiers standing guard there. Then he nods. "The guards won't interfere with the queen of Thebes and the chief priest of Apollo. But don't – don't tell Antigone I'm here."

"Tell her yourself, when you're ready," Ismene says, turning to re-enter the tomb. Her aunt and her cousin follow; Haemon pulls the door closed, and then only the small circle of light cast by Ismene's lamp remains.

Even after her eyes grow accustomed to the shadows, Ismene needs a moment to find the fissure. She points to it, traces the cleft with her finger; Eurydike and Haemon nod. Eurydike removes her cloak and folds it to make a cushion to sit on, while Haemon chooses a place further away. Ismene decides to leave her brother's camp stool where it is. "Antigone? I'm back."

"What was it?" comes the voice through the wall.

"The guard wanted to make sure I was all right." She resumes her seat on the floor and rests the lamp between herself and Eurydike. Haemon is a dark shadow, just at the edge of the lamplight. She waits a moment, offering her aunt and cousin a chance to speak, but they are silent. "Where were we?" she finally says.

"Ismene, tell me... tell me what happened after Father and I left Thebes. What did you do?"

Ismene glances at Eurydike, and over at her cousin Haemon. Eurydike gives Ismene's knee a soft, encouraging pat. Ismene cannot make out Haemon's face, but she sees him nod.

"What *I* did...?"

There is so little, really, that she has done. At least until recently. But the war has changed her, forcing her out of her quiet corner to act, and has made her question things and people that she never doubted before. Ismene seems to find only more questions, no answers. She no longer knows what offends the gods or pleases them. It is all shifting shadows and hollow echoes, like the people and voices in this tomb.

ISMENE

I have always been the least of our family.

I could never match Mother's beauty, Father's insight, or the political wiles of Uncle Creon. Even Mother's father was chosen by the gods to become the Tiresias, and served Apollo and Athena with distinction until his death. Our brothers displayed all the ambition and drive expected of royal princes, and were adored by the people of Thebes.

And you, Antigone: you've always been so clever, so quick – and brave! Going off with Father as you did... I offered to go with you, but when everyone insisted I wasn't strong enough I knew they were right.

You might think that with so few accomplishments, I'd hate hearing about the adventures of others. But I've always loved songs and stories. People say I have a pretty voice, but I'd rather listen to a new ballad than sing one I already know. I love examining well-made tapestries that show exciting tales, even when I know I couldn't weave anything so spectacular.

Spinning's all I've ever been really good at: I can spin long, strong thread. That, and listening. Sometimes I remind myself those things have value. Weavers need thread that doesn't break; bards need an audience that cares.

Did you wonder where I was, that night – the night of the fires? You were busy tending Father's wounds… maybe you didn't even think of me.

I was with Mother.

I stayed awake with her all through the night, and she told me everything. She admitted that she had done terrible things – but I couldn't help wondering: if the gods were so disgusted by our parents' marriage, then why didn't they stop it before it happened? Why did Aphrodite make them fall in love? Why did Dionysus let Father solve the Sphinx's riddle? The gods are powerful; they could have made their anger known before our parents brought four children into the world.

Uncle Creon told me that Mother had to die; if she did not kill herself, the mob would have ripped her to shreds. She *was* brave, Antigone, in her way. She sent me away, before the end, because she knew I wasn't strong enough to bear it. Even after it was done – when the guards brought out her body – I couldn't bear the sight of it. I closed my eyes and looked away.

You were strong, Antigone. You've always been strong. I turned into a puddle of tears that day, while you offered your shoulder to Father and led him out of Thebes.

The Tiresias and Priest Bromius said the curse was lifted, but we could not rest. Rain had washed away some of the ashes and the smell of soot; but there was much to do.

Uncle Creon took charge. He appointed men to muster teams of workers to clear away the charred rubble and salvage what they could. He ordered the palace scribes to review the records and inventory what had been lost. He told the city's leading men to come to the palace megaron at supper time, and then went to consult with the priests about Mother's funeral.

Aunt Eurydike worked with the palace steward to arrange a simple meal. There was roast mutton and fresh barley bread, cheese, olives, and small honeycakes. Nothing fancy – that would have been wrong, with so much of the city's supplies destroyed by fire.

I took a place at the dinner table. Uncle Creon and the twins had not yet arrived; the gathering was subdued. Adults' conversations trailed off awkwardly, and even the younger voices were quieter than usual. My cousins kept glancing at the empty thrones. I tried not to, for they made me want to weep. I could not believe that Mother was dead, that you and

Father were gone.

Our cousin Menoeceus nudged me. "You're not eating, Ismene," he said.

I stared down at my plate. "It doesn't seem right to," I said. "With the storehouses burned down... the city will be hungry this winter."

He dipped a piece of bread in olive oil and offered it to me. "Father's sending envoys to negotiate with Orchomenos and Gla," he said. "We still have plenty of leather to trade."

I accepted the morsel and put it into my mouth.

"That's better," he said.

Lasthenes, Master of the Herds, said: "We might have to cull the cattle."

"Then we'd have more leather to trade," observed the merchant Hyperbius.

"And more beef for our table!" said Alkides, who was wandering restlessly around the room. "Say, Haemon, are you going to eat that?"

Haemon glanced up. "Huh? Oh, here, go ahead." He passed his plate to Alkides, who grinned and took a large bite of mutton, chewing loudly.

"Alkides!" Megara teased him. "What manners! You eat like a starving dog!"

He swallowed his mouthful. "Like a conquering lion," he corrected her. Then his blue eyes went round, and he belched loudly.

"Hear the lion roar!" said Menoeceus. We all laughed – except for Alkides: his sense of humor soured when he was the butt of the joke.

Just then Uncle Creon and the twins entered the room. Alkides set the plate back down in front of Haemon and went to his seat beside Megara.

Uncle Creon was dressed in a dark blue tunic with gold-sewn borders that would have been suitable for receiving an embassy; his gray hair and beard were freshly oiled. Eteokles and Polynikes were also dressed in their best – but where Creon appeared solemn, their expressions were sullen. Eteokles kept glancing at Uncle Creon with narrowed eyes, and Polynikes was frowning.

Moving to stand beside the central hearth, Uncle Creon and the twins each took a cup of wine from a servant. The sun was just setting; all eyes were drawn to the light of the fire and the gleam of Creon's golden cup, held aloft. Or, rather, all eyes except the twins': they glanced at each other, then looked down at the floor.

"People of Thebes," Creon said, "the fire that burned our storerooms has been extinguished. The curse has been removed from our city." He dipped his fingers into his cup, then scattered a few drops of wine across the stuccoed floor as a libation. "The will of the gods has been satisfied."

Many in the megaron murmured words of thanks. The Tiresias was not present, but Apollo's chief priest Bromius nodded his large head approvingly.

Creon lifted his goblet once more. "There is much work to be done;

but tonight, let us drink to a new day in Thebes!"

Everyone raised their cups and drank. Then, leaving my brothers beside the hearth, Creon went to stand between the thrones. Resting his free hand on the king's marble chair, Creon said that he would arrange for trade with Gla and Orchomenos to keep hunger at bay, and that he had sent to Korinth as well. He informed us that Mother's funeral would take place in the morning. For the next seven days, traffic through the city gates would be restricted, as was the custom when Thebes lost its king. Then there would be a ceremony of purification for the city; we would re-sanctify each of our seven gates. "Bromius, you will coordinate the details of the ceremonies with the priesthood."

The priest bowed. "Yes, my lord."

"And let it be known," Creon concluded, squaring his shoulders, "that I will serve as regent until the princes come of age."

There was an awkward silence. Alkides gaped at the twins, but neither of them looked up. I could see Polynikes' jaw clench; Eteokles nudged a rough spot on the floor with one sandal.

They were the heirs to two thrones, Thebes' and Korinth's, though it had never been decided which brother would rule which city. But Uncle Creon had managed Thebes' affairs three times as long as the boys had been alive: as regent, he could help them prepare for the duties of kingship. Looking around the room, I could tell that the heads of the city's leading families – the Spartoi, men with streaks of gray in their beards and lines of experience etched into their faces – were thinking these same thoughts. Some, like old Demochares, had been Creon's friends since before I was born; but the leading men of the next generation, like Melanippus, also nodded agreement. Many lifted their cups to Creon.

Alkides leaned forward, his big fists clenched on the tabletop. "The twins should inherit *now!*" he hissed.

I don't know if he meant the comment just for Megara, but his voice carried. Eteokles and Polynikes looked his way, and an uneasy murmur arose from the graybeards.

I looked at him in surprise. The people of Thebes were so volatile – they needed a steady hand after the turmoil just past. And how would Korinth react? My brothers were only thirteen years old: they weren't ready to rule!

Haemon put down the wine cup he had been nursing. He stood, folding his arms across his narrow chest, and addressed Alkides. "My father's right," he said. "The princes are not yet men, any more than you are. There should be a regent until they come of age."

I remembered Haemon's own manhood ceremony, only a few months before: like the others just past their sixteenth birthday, he had placed his bronze sword at *my* father's feet and sworn his oath of loyalty. I think he spoke out because he meant to honor that oath: he was trying to protect Oedipus' sons.

But Alkides did not seem to hear it that way. He got to his feet and took a menacing step towards Haemon. Though he was two years younger, he was already a handspan taller and far more muscular. Haemon edged back, just slightly; Alkides' eyes flashed at this sign of weakness.

"Do you think you're more of a man than I am, Haemon, just because you've had the rites? You can't even keep your wife at your side!" Haemon flushed bright red; Alkides continued, "Both Prince Eteokles and Prince Polynikes did the work of men fighting the fire!"

Polynikes drew back his shoulders, standing tall at this praise; but Eteokles hesitated, rubbing his hairless chin. His gaze swept around the room, taking the measure of the Spartoi, of the soldiers who stood guard at the entrance to the megaron, even of the servants who stood in the shadows along the wall. "Alkides," he said evenly, "you should listen to Haemon."

Alkides stared, his jaw hanging open.

"Think about it," Eteokles continued. "Thebes has been dealt a terrible blow. If we take the throne now, every rival city will test us. We might even be invaded!" He paused, and many heads nodded in agreement.

At a nudge from his brother's elbow, Polynikes spoke. "It's true." He exhaled slowly and then, as though reciting a history lesson, added: "With Uncle Creon as regent for the next three years, there'll be time for transition. My brother and I will both learn from him. It's the best way for Thebes – and for Korinth."

Alkides let out a grunt of disgust. But the twins' words were accepted with relief and praise by the leading citizens. It was decided: until the twins reached manhood, the crown and scepter that had belonged to my father would remain in Creon's safekeeping.

"What about the treasures of Harmonia?" asked Megara.

I remembered Mother wearing these precious items: the golden necklace made by Hephaestus and the gown woven by Athena, shimmering with the color of a summer sky. Once I had wondered how Harmonia, for all that she was daughter of Ares and Aphrodite, could have been any lovelier. Of course, the necklace was supposed to give its wearer eternal beauty – and Mother remained beautiful long after the years should have left their mark.

Aunt Eurydike, holding little Pyrrha on her lap, suggested: "We could bury them with Jocasta."

"Mother!" protested Megara. "They were never buried with the queen before!"

"And never before has a queen of Thebes hung herself with the belt of Harmonia's gown," said Uncle Creon. "Who would want to wear it now? The dress will be buried with my sister."

Megara objected. "But she didn't hang herself with the necklace! Why bury that?"

Her father hesitated, considering, and then addressed his wife. "Eurydike, you should keep Harmonia's necklace until the city has a new queen."

"Me?" she asked. Her five-year-old daughter looked up with sleepy eyes, and began to fuss. Jiggling the child, Eurydike said: "Creon, I'm no descendant of Kadmos. It wouldn't be right for me—"

"I'll take it, Father!" Megara offered quickly.

But the voice of her brother Menoeceus drowned her out. "It should be given to Princess Ismene," he said loudly.

Everyone turned to stare at me; my face went hot.

Uncle Creon combed his fingers through his beard. "Ismene, you *are* descended from Kadmos and Harmonia. Are you willing to hold the necklace in trust for the city's next queen?"

"I – I suppose so." Keeping the necklace safe was something I could do to honor Mother's memory.

And so her cedarwood chest was delivered to my room. I thought I would spend that night remembering her – but, weak with exhaustion, I slept. The next day, Mother's body was laid to rest in a beehive tomb outside the city walls, alongside the bones of her first husband Laius – our grandfather, I reminded myself. It was the proper resting place for a queen of Thebes; but I wondered, would she want to be there? She had told me that she was infatuated with Laius at first… but then he rejected her. It was Father – her own son, may the gods forgive them both! – that she had truly loved.

The rest of the day was spent closing the city gates; we would reopen them on the seventh day, when Uncle Creon formally assumed the regency. The ceremony required walking to each gate in turn, where the priests would perform the ritual of closing. Just the thought of it wearied me – especially with all the hateful whispers I heard about our parents. Aunt Eurydike noticed and made excuses for me; I was permitted to return to the palace. Menoeceus accompanied me most of the way, seeing me safely into the servants' care; then he patted my back, and said he must return to his father.

The palace had never seemed so empty. Mother was dead; you and Father were gone; nearly everyone else was at the Closing of the Gates…the stillness weighed upon me, heavy and oppressive.

I returned to the room we once shared, you and I, and sat before the cedarwood chest that had belonged to Mother. I rested my cheek against its surface as though it were Mother's shoulder, and wondered if her spirit had already crossed over the River Styx into the Underworld. How long does the journey take, anyway? People die every day, so many of them – surely Hermes is fleet as he escorts each one.

I ran my fingers across the rosettes carved into the surface of the wood. Perhaps Hermes guided them down in groups, I thought, holding his caduceus high for all to follow.

How had Mother greeted the messenger god? He must have been captivated by her beauty and charm – visitors to Thebes always were. But would she receive a horrible punishment in the Underworld? That morning by the Eudoxa Gate, I heard one woman suggest that she hang for all eternity, choking forever as she swung from side to side. Poor Mother – she never meant to offend the gods! Her crimes were only beauty and love.

A knock at the door interrupted my musings. I thought a servant might be bringing me a meal – but, to my surprise, it was our cousin Megara.

"Mother and Menoeceus asked me to look in on you," she said. "They said you need cheering up."

"I suppose." Rising to my feet, I wiped my damp eyes. "It – it hurts to hear the people say such awful things about Mother. Megara, she had no idea! At least, not until the very end—"

"I know." Megara walked over and put her arm around my shoulder. "No matter what they say, your mother was a good queen. Thebes' wealth has increased hugely over the last forty years: everyone knows that!" She steered me over to the couch beneath the window; we both sat down. "And her beauty was legendary! Men risked their lives for the chance to marry her – some of them *gave* their lives for the chance!"

I blinked up at the afternoon sun. "That's true. Of course, they didn't just want her for her beauty – the man who married her would become king of Thebes."

"Yes." Megara bushed a lock of hair back from my face. "But do you think they would have risked their lives if she'd been homely?"

I considered. "No," I said. "I suppose not."

"She was the most beautiful woman of Thebes since Harmonia herself – everyone says so." Megara took my hand, and leaned close to whisper: "Cousin, may I see the necklace?"

I did not like to dig through Mother's things – that was just one more admission that she was gone. But I couldn't think of a reason to refuse. I let Megara pull me to my feet and over to the cedarwood chest.

Together we lifted the lid on its bronze hinges. At the top was Mother's best cloak, in the colors of Thebes that she had worn on state occasions in the winter. It had labyrinth-pattern borders almost a handspan thick, worked in shining golden thread. The crimson wool was thick and soft beneath my fingers. I pulled it out, wondering whether the scent of roses was from Mother's perfume or simply my own imagination.

"Gorgeous," Megara said, turning the edge of the garment so that the thread-of-gold caught the light.

Next was a round, painted ceramic box larger than any pyxis I had ever seen; I needed both hands to lift it. The scenes painted on its surface in swirls of red and black showed Hera, queen of the Gods, seated at her dressing table in the midst of a garden.

"That must contain the necklace," Megara whispered. But when we opened it we found a different treasure: the queen's crown. I realized the garden painted on the container echoed the crown's flower-wreath form. Tiny, shimmering flowers and leaves adorning the braided circlet of golden vines moved at my slightest breath.

"Not one of the treasures of Harmonia," said Megara. "But fine work nonetheless."

"No," I said, and solemnly I replaced the lid and set the container back inside the chest.

A rectangular ebony box, inlaid with mother-of-pearl, held Harmonia's magical necklace. The box was lined in calf's-leather, stained with the precious purple dye that comes from sea snails. The container alone was worthy of an Aegyptian queen – what it held was worthy of a goddess.

Megara reverently lifted out the sacred necklace. "Magnificent," she breathed, holding it up to catch the afternoon light. I had never looked at it so closely. As you know, the necklace is in the shape of two golden serpents. Each minute scale along the length of their slender bodies was depicted in painstaking detail with tiny, spherical grains of gold. "Look at those sapphire eyes," Megara said. "No one but Hephaestus could have made this."

"How did Hephaestus know that snakes would be right for his wife's daughter?" I asked. "Kadmos and Harmonia didn't turn into snakes until many years after their wedding."

"Maybe they became snakes *because* of this necklace," Megara speculated, caressing the gold with her fingertips. Then she unhooked the clasp. "Ismene, I *must* try this on!"

"Megara, I don't know if that's a good idea..." It seemed wrong – perhaps just because Mother had been buried that morning.

"What harm could it do?" she asked, fastening the ornament about her slender throat. She rose, walked over to the dressing-table, picked up my mirror and admired herself in its polished silver surface.

And she did look breathtaking. Her dark, glossy hair had been woven with strands of golden beads for Mother's funeral; her white teeth and dark, flashing eyes seemed to reflect the gleam of the golden serpents around her neck.

"Eternal beauty," she whispered, tracing the curving serpents with the fingers of one hand.

I cleared my throat. "Megara," I said, "we should put all this away. It belongs to the next queen of Thebes."

She sighed and set down the mirror. "I suppose." Reaching back to undo the clasp of the necklace, she said, "I think it really *is* magical. I can feel it."

"You don't need magic – you're already the most beautiful maiden in Thebes." I took the necklace from her and slipped it back into its padded box. "Besides, you don't really want to marry one of my brothers, do you? I thought you liked Alkides!"

Megara flopped down on my bed. "Father doesn't want me to marry Alkides."

"Why not?" I asked, refolding the red-and-gold cloak. That rose scent

– I was *not* imagining it. I held the cloth to my face for a moment, breathing in Mother's perfume.

"I don't think he likes Alkides much."

Reluctantly I put the cloak back in the cedarwood chest. "Because he challenged Uncle Creon about whether the princes were old enough to inherit?"

She propped herself up on one elbow. "Even before last night. Father says Alkides is too young for me."

"He's only one year younger than you," I said, shutting the lid of the chest.

"I know!" Megara pouted. "Father wants me to marry an old man, or something."

I sat down on my dressing stool. "Well, your father is many years older than Aunt Eurydike. It's traditional, I suppose."

"Mother says he wants the best for me. But what if Alkides is best? He's already the strongest man in Thebes. And so handsome…" She fell back against my pillows, and looked up dreamily at the painted ceiling beams.

For a moment I watched her, lost in hopes of romance, then wondered who would want to marry me. I was a child born of incest – a crime against the gods. Even though the Tiresias had declared us free of our parents' curse, no man would choose me as his bride. You, Antigone, were married already – even though you chose to go with Father rather than stay with Haemon. Our brothers were destined to be kings, one in Thebes and one in Korinth; they would have no difficulty finding wives. But I…

Megara sat up. "Anyway, Mother says you should join us in the weaving room tomorrow, Ismene. She says you need company."

Over the next few days I did go to the weaving room, though I occupied myself mostly with spinning. Uncle Creon gave me Mother's spindle; the feel of its age-mellowed ivory in my fingers comforted me. Occasionally the daughters of the Tiresias joined us. You must remember what a good weaver Daphne was; Manto showed promise of developing her older sister's skill. Both of them praised my tight, even thread.

Despite this domestic work, the days were strangely empty. With the city gates closed, there were no traders in the agora. Workers cleared away the rubble near the Astykratia Gate; in the potters' quarter, men shaped new roof tiles for rebuilding. We had no word yet from Korinth, but supplies and reassurance arrived from Orchomenos and Gla. People gained confidence that they would not starve over the winter, and the city's mood grew lighter. By the time of the gate-opening ceremony, Thebes was ready to celebrate and look to the future.

At dawn, Uncle Creon offered a ram on the altar in the agora. As we sang a hymn to Apollo, the priest Bromius supervised acolytes in collecting the beast's blood in silver bowls, and then we began the procession through the city.

We went first to the Chloris Gate. Uncle Creon gave the word, and soldiers slid aside the thick bar and swung open the tall oaken doors. Then Eteokles and Polynikes came forward and dipped bunches of laurel leaves into the bowls of ram's blood. Together the twins scattered crimson drops across the threshold, to sanctify the city boundary and signify that the curse had been banished. The Tiresias, leaning on his cornel-wood staff, stood by silently as his flower-garlanded daughters lit cones of incense at each gate post. Finally Bromius chanted a prayer to Apollo as god of absolution; once he had finished, the procession moved towards the Kleodoxa Gate.

Seven times we repeated this rite. Finally, at the Ogygia Gate, the smell of roasting meat overpowered the scent of incense. When Bromius completed his prayer a pair of flute girls emerged from the crowd, piping a lively melody, and everyone let out a huge cheer.

By this time my mouth was watering; I gladly accepted a skewer of spiced beef and a painted wine-cup from a servant. For the first time since Mother's death, I felt respite from grief. It was a lovely fall day; the sky was bright blue with wisps of high cloud. People laughed and danced, clapping their hands in time to the flute-girls' song. I saw Alkides with three skewers of meat in one hand and two in the other; from the way he was eating, all five would soon be empty. Giggling, Megara reached up to wipe a smear of grease from his cheek. Creon stood with Eteokles and Polynikes, one hand on the shoulder of each boy, saying something that elicited nods of agreement.

"It's good to see you smile, Ismene," said Menoeceus.

I looked up at his warm hazel eyes. "I guess I haven't forgotten how."

Haemon joined us. "I wonder how long that will last."

"Ismene's smile?" his brother asked, sounding offended. "Forever, I hope!"

"What?" Haemon shook his head. "No, I meant that," he said, gesturing to where Creon stood with my brothers. "The throne's not big enough for two."

"Maybe one of them should go to Korinth immediately," Menoeceus said. The king of Korinth had died less than a month ago; we assumed the queen, my father's adoptive mother, was acting as regent.

"Do you really think Korinth will accept either Polynikes or Eteokles as king once they learn King Oedipus was adopted – and that he married his *true* mother?" Haemon asked, crossing his arms. "I don't know the situation in Korinth, but every city has men full of ambition, who want power for themselves."

"Sweet Leto," I whispered.

"You may be right, Haemon," said Menoeceus.

I glanced at the Tiresias, standing between his daughters as he spoke with white-robed Bromius. The blind prophet said we were innocent of our parents' crimes – crimes they hadn't even meant to commit!

"Father's on his way to Korinth – maybe he can straighten out the

56

situation," I said hopefully.

"Maybe," Haemon continued, "but maybe not. And if not, what will the twins do?"

"I don't know." I looked over at my brothers, their russet hair shining like polished copper in the sunlight. They had been linked together since birth, but under too much tension even the strongest chain could snap.

"You're upsetting Ismene," Menoeceus reproached his older brother.

"I'm sorry," Haemon apologized, his expression still serious. "But we must face what is, and understand what may be. Better to see trouble coming while it's still some way down the road – while there's still time for precautions. And maybe I'm wrong. Maybe the Korinthians will welcome a son of Oedipus."

Menoeceus patted my shoulder. "Even if they don't, that doesn't have to mean trouble between Eteokles and Polynikes. Anything – anything could happen during the next three years."

"That's right," Haemon agreed, obviously trying to lighten the mood. "Anything could happen."

"My father once told me," interposed a female voice, "that when anything can happen, it usually does!" I turned my head and saw Manto approaching us.

"Well," offered Menoeceus, "if the Tiresias says it, then it must be true!"

Manto smiled and swept her long, straight hair over her shoulder with one hand. "Well, usually. But he *is* sometimes wrong about the weather."

"I suppose that's understandable," Haemon said, matching her lighthearted tone. "That's the domain of Zeus, while his patrons are Apollo and Athena."

"Just so," Manto agreed. "Actually, Father sent me to find Princess Ismene."

I blinked. "Me?"

"Yes, *you*, my lady princess! And don't worry, he's not planning any dire pronouncements – he's in a good mood today. Still, after so long on his feet he wants to go home. He asked whether you would visit us there this afternoon. Will you come with us now?"

"Of course," I said. "It would be an honor."

I had never heard of the Tiresias inviting someone to his home before. Of course, few of the men and women who hold that title keep a home at all. You remember how Grandfather never stayed long in one city after he became the Voice of Apollo. But this Tiresias, being not only blind but lame, had kept his house in Thebes.

Manto and I soon caught up with her father and her sister Daphne; the old man moved at a snail's pace, but fortunately the house was not far. A manservant opened the door with a respectful nod. I noticed that the Tiresias inclined his blindfolded head in return, though he could not have seen the servant's gesture.

We passed through the antechamber into a shadowy room. Daphne called for a servant to light the lamps, while Manto led me to a cushioned chair. In the dim light, my first impression was of a cramped space – but once the lamp-flames flared to life, I saw that the room itself was large. It was simply jammed from floor-tiles to rafters with objects.

One whole wall was lined with shelves in a slanting crisscross pattern that formed countless little nooks, and in each nook were five or six rolls of Aegyptian papyrus. Wooden masks with sharp, angular features hung on another wall, and beneath these two entire elephant tusks – carved all over in elaborate patterns – rested in bronze brackets. There were skins of striped and spotted beasts from the lands of Punt, and a large basket filled with brilliantly colored feathers. One long shelf held shoes and sandals, from tiny cloth baby booties to sandals large enough for a Titan: soft slippers from Sikyon and curl-toed Hittite boots, gilded toe-thongs from Lydia and some strange fur-lined construction that must have come from the land of the north wind. A table in a corner displayed a Kretan vase painted with an octopus; a pile of seashells in various curving shapes surrounded its base. An ivory carving of Hermes stood on a pedestal next to a massive anchor-stone.

Most terrifying of all was the skull of a monster with enormous jaws and teeth on a table far too close to me.

"A crocodile from Aegypt, from my father's days as a trader," Daphne explained, noticing my apprehensive gaze. "It lived in the Nile, their great river."

I nodded, and kept staring. I knew that this Tiresias had been a trader before becoming the Voice of Apollo, but this was my first time to see his exotic collection.

"Ah," sighed the Tiresias, easing his toes into a foot-basin his serving girl had brought. "That's better! Ismene, will you sit and take wine with me?"

"Yes – yes, thank you, Tiresias," I said, scooting my chair as far away as possible from the skull of the dead river monster.

Moving with grace, Manto brought me a cup, while her sister carried one over to their father. Even though they had played important roles in the day's ceremonies, neither bothered with cosmetics or jewels. Their only ornaments were the flower garlands that crowned their dark, straight hair and they wore their usual unadorned tunics – though clearly, from the wealth of objects that surrounded me, they could afford multi-tiered skirts trimmed in gold rondels had they wished. As they finally took their seats, they scarcely glanced at the precious items that filled the room. But why should they? This was their home.

"Don't you care for the wine, my dear?"

The hairs on the back of my neck prickled; how had the blind man known that I had not yet drunk anything? But, then, of course, he possessed the second sight.

Hurriedly I sipped the wine. "It's excellent, Tiresias, thank you."

"You're welcome, my dear." He lifted his feet from the basin and the servant girl toweled them dry; he dismissed her gently and then turned his face to me. "Princess Ismene, I wanted to tell you that I'm sorry for your loss. I first became acquainted with your mother when she was your age, before she became queen of Thebes. I remember her marriage to King Laius. She was a true queen from the very first, fulfilling her duties even when it was difficult. No matter her faults, Thebes is richer for her leadership. She will never be forgotten."

I remembered that Mother had described him as a kind man and a good friend. "Thank you," I said huskily, blinking back tears.

Daphne offered a plate of stuffed grape leaves. "Try one of these, Ismene," she said. "They're very good. The spices are from a land east of Babylon."

Glad for the change of subject, I accepted one and took a bite. The flavor of the barley and pine-nut filling was unusual: earthy, spicy, savory. It reminded me of cumin, perhaps with a hint of saffron, but the other spices left me puzzled.

"That's Daphne's favorite," said Manto. "But the flavor's not for everyone! It's all right if you don't care for it."

"It's unusual," I said, "but interesting. Like so many of the things you have here, Tiresias!"

He nodded. "Yes, curious things from curious places. You'd be surprised, the things a sea captain can pick up over the years." He turned his cup in his hands, running his fingers across the embossed silver surface. "But, my dear princess, I want to discuss some of *your* objects."

"What do you mean?" I asked, then pushed the rest of the stuffed grape leaf into my mouth.

"The necklace of Harmonia, given to you for safekeeping."

"Yes, Tiresias?" I asked, speaking awkwardly because my mouth was full.

"I must warn you about it."

I swallowed rapidly. "How so?"

"It is imbued with deep and ancient power and should only be worn by the rightful queen of Thebes. I must advise you, my lady princess: do not put it around your neck."

"It's not suitable for everyone," Daphne said.

I saw how solemn Daphne and Manto had become. "I—"

"Have you already worn it?" The voice that had seemed so kind a moment before suddenly turned ominous.

"No…" I said, not wanting to explain that Megara had tried on the necklace.

The Tiresias tugged at his blindfold, as if it chafed, and then turned his face directly at me. "I see," he said, and I was certain that he *did* see. Then he sighed, and smiled wryly. "Well, let us hope no ill fortune will come from it. Best keep it away from everyone else, my lady princess."

*

Ismene breaks off, realizing she has re-opened old wounds. Her aunt Eurydike has covered her face with her hands; Haemon has put his arm around his mother's back.

So easy to say the wrong thing! Why did she remind her aunt of Megara?

CHAPTER FOUR
ANTIGONE

When Ismene falls silent, the darkness of Antigone's tomb seems to intensify. She reaches up to touch her own face and confirms with cold fingertips that her eyes are indeed open. Without the distraction of her sister's words, fear swells anew.

"Ismene?"

"I'm here, Antigone." Her sister's voice sounds fainter than before. "My throat's just dry from speaking so long."

Antigone realizes she too is thirsty. She gropes for the basket of provisions, and her questing hands find the water-skin. It is not as full as she hoped; how long will it last? "Provisions for a day," was part of the sentence, and she was put in the cave yesterday. A little angry with herself for being weak enough to yield to her thirst, she takes a small sip, thinking that she will soon have no choice but to go thirsty.

She hears rustling on Ismene's side of the wall, then what sounds like quiet conversation. Carefully stoppering the water-skin and replacing it in the basket, Antigone asks: "Is someone with you?"

"I'm here too." The voice is achingly familiar.

"Aunt Eurydike?" Antigone asks, sitting up straighter.

"Yes, my dear, it's me. I had to come – it's not *right,* what Creon's done. We've all suffered too much already. Lost too many dear to us."

Feeling her eyes fill with tears, Antigone buries her face in a fold of the blanket, breathing in its faint scent of lavender. "It's good to hear your voice."

"I've missed you, Antigone."

Remembering how Aunt Eurydike comforted her against the scraped knees of childhood, Antigone wipes her eyes. "And I've missed you."

A male voice says: "What about me?"

Her heartbeat quickens in astonishment and alarm. "Who's that?"

"You've forgotten my voice, I suppose. It's Haemon – your husband."

Antigone's jaw goes slack in astonishment. Her husband – and even calling himself that!   "Haemon, I – the cave distorts sounds; I wasn't sure." Antigone hesitates, remembering the shameful truths she shared with her sister. "How long have you been listening?"

Ismene responds quickly: "Haemon and Aunt Eurydike came inside with me after I went to answer the door. They've only heard me tell what happened after you and Father left Thebes."

Antigone relaxes – and then wonders why she cares whether Haemon heard her speak of their failed wedding night. What does it matter, when she is about to die?

"Antigone…" Haemon's voice trails off, and there is a moment of silence. Then he continues: "I'm sorry we didn't get a chance to talk before you disobeyed Father."

She laces her fingers together. "Why – would you have stopped me? All I did was give Polynikes' soul a chance to find rest in the Underworld."

"Polynikes should never have attacked Thebes!"

"You're a priest of Apollo. You *can't* agree with your father's decree to leave bodies unburied. Besides, Eteokles wronged Polynikes."

"King Eteokles gave his life to defend Thebes."

Shaking her head slowly in the darkness, Antigone says, "There's no use trying to trace the Fates' thread back, wrong for wrong and blow for blow, to see which of my brothers was more deserving and which more at fault. Their lives are finished. It's not for us to judge them: that's with the gods now. But your father wanted Polynikes' spirit to wander forever. Is that fair – to exile him first from Thebes and then also from the Underworld?"

"A king can't ignore defiance," said Haemon. "Why didn't you try to persuade him some other way?"

"Haemon," chides Ismene, "We're not being good company."

Antigone smiles ruefully in the darkness. Though her sister dislikes anything resembling confrontation, she herself finds the argument invigorating. But she owes a debt to Ismene, the first to come to her.

"You're right, child," Eurydike agrees.

"Antigone, I'm sorry," Haemon adds. "I know your motive was devout."

She finds comfort in these words. Haemon's ability to consider all the various aspects of a question was something she admired in him when they were young. They did not always agree, but they always listened to each other.

"Let's change the subject," Ismene declares, with a determination Antigone finds slightly surprising. "Antigone, can you tell us what happened to you and Father after you left the city?"

"Yes, please," adds Haemon. "I'd – I'd like to know too." There is wistfulness in his voice. Does he, too, think about innocent summer nights spent in the roof garden, watching the constellations march across the sky as they talked until dawn? She remembers speculating whether they could fly up to the stars themselves, using wings like those crafted by Daedalus. If they flew at night, she argued, the hot sun could not melt the wax that held the feathers to the frame; but Haemon thought the stars were too far away to reach before sunrise.

She is reluctant to turn from those precious memories to the hard first days of her journey with her father. But even that is better than dwelling on the fate before her. Once more she closes her eyes to shut out the darkness, so that she can better see the past.

ANTIGONE

After we left through the Ogygia Gate, the jeers faded. We trudged along, step after step. The rains that had finally put out the fires made the roadway into muddy sludge, with ankle-deep puddles in the grass along the roadside and occasionally in the road itself. Father's footing was unsteady, and he often slipped; usually I was able to catch him – but once he went sprawling, smearing his kilt and traveling cloak with mud.

We stopped at a stream to wash and to ease our thirst; we ate some of the bread and cheese that Aunt Eurydike's servant had given me, and I topped off the waterskin. I looked worriedly at the wounds where Father's eyes had been: we did not have sour wine to rinse them as Rhodia recommended, but there was a cloth in the traveling-pack that I could use to replace the blindfold Father cast aside to show the people of Thebes the punishment he had inflicted on himself. I bathed his swollen ankles in the stream, then rinsed my own feet, noticing that my sandals had already rubbed blisters on my heels. But if we were to reach the harbor before nightfall we could not rest any longer. I shouldered the waterskin and the traveling pack once more and we headed on.

I realized I had never been so far from the city before – and I had never faced the prospect of finding some place to spend the night. Any excursion – to the festivals of Dionysus in the sacred grounds north of the city, to Artemis' temple east of town – ended at home, in the palace, and if I grew tired I could always ride on a cart or in a sedan chair.

"Father," I asked, "what if the sun sets before we reach the shore?"

"We make camp," he said, maintaining his slow pace, feeling ahead with his walking stick.

"But… I don't know how to make a fire."

"I suppose not." He took another step. "If we can't beg a coal from a passing traveler, we'll manage without."

His fortitude shamed me. He must be in terrible pain – the last thing he needed was a helpless daughter's complaints. I would manage, that was all. He needed me.

From behind I heard the sound of a donkey-cart. Even though we had just spoken of asking a fellow traveler for help, the sound filled me with fear. What if this was someone from Thebes, determined to snuff out the curse once and for all?

"Someone's coming," I whispered. "Should we hide?"

Father smiled crookedly. "What would be the use? Hiding from the Fates doesn't work." He stopped, and waited for the cart to arrive.

"Friend Oedipus!" called a man's voice. "Princess Antigone!"

It did not sound like someone planning to shed our blood.

"Who's there?" Father shouted. "Mnesikles, is that you?"

"None other!"

Sure enough, as the man came closer I recognized the Korinthian envoy's kindly, gray-bearded face beneath the straw brim of his hat. "Mnesikles!" I exclaimed with relief. Father had known the man since childhood; he was a friend of Father's parents – his adoptive parents. And he seemed glad to see us.

He pulled his team to a stop. "I thought your ankles might be getting tired by now, my lord," he said. "Care to ride?"

"Most gratefully, old friend. But you should not call me 'my lord' any longer."

I led Father over to the cart, and together Mnesikles and I helped him to climb into it. "I can't think of you any other way, my lord," Mnesikles objected.

Father stroked his stubbled chin with one hand. "You must, old friend. I'm just a beggar now. One thankful for your generosity."

Mnesikles' face grew grave. "I suppose it's better so, until we reach Korinth. If my sailors knew who you were, and all that has happened, they might refuse to take us."

"I won't lie," Father said, his voice sharp. "I've lived with lies too long."

I admired Father's honesty, but— "They might throw us overboard, Father! And Mnesikles too!"

He hung his head. "No more than I deserve. But I won't bring that on you, Daughter. Or on Mnesikles."

"You needn't lie," the Korinthian said. "The sailors have never seen King Oedipus up close, and they won't know the news from Thebes yet. They won't recognize you, so long as you don't say who you are. Once we reach Korinth, you may do as you think best."

Father sighed, and leaned back against the planks of the cart. "Very well."

I climbed into the cart and sat down beside Father, my blistered and aching feet grateful for the rest. Father wrapped his arm around me, and I laid my head against his broad chest. Mnesikles took his seat on the driver's bench and flicked the donkeys' rumps with a willow-wand; the cart lurched into motion. Before long I heard Father snoring softly, and I realized he must be more exhausted even than I. His ankles had never been sturdy – and the healer had given him strong herbs to lessen the pain of his ravaged eyes.

I wished I could sleep, but that comfort eluded me. Before long my arms were pink with sunburn, and my face was warm as well. "How foolish," I muttered in annoyance. I had not thought about it – always before when I went outside a servant walked beside me with a sun-shade. I asked Mnesikles if he had an extra hat; he laughed, and told me there were two, in fact, and pointed at a leather travel bag. I dug them out, settled one onto my head, then placed the other over Father's face. He did not need it to shade his eyes from the sun, but it would help hide his identity.

From beneath the brim of my hat I stared out at the landscape, wondering when – or if – I would again see Theban lands. The donkeys pulled us past a grove of olive trees; the small green orbs clustered thick among the branches. On the crest of a low hill stood a whitewashed hut with a roof of thatch; its door was open, and children laughed from inside. Father had brought prosperity to this land through careful stewardship, shrewd trading arrangements and peaceful relations with neighboring kingdoms. The olives, grain, beef and cheese of this countryside had fed me since my birth – but if they cast out my father, it was no longer my country.

The sun was low in the sky when Father stirred awake. "I smell the sea," he said, sitting up.

I caught his straw hat before it fell from the cart, then peered into the distance, squinting against the sun. "Are we near the port, Mnesikles?"

"Yes," the Korinthian answered as I settled the hat onto Father's head, tying the strings beneath his chin. "We'll be on board ship before dark."

We reached the harbor and made our way through its bustle of activity; Mnesikles reined his donkeys to a stop at the water's edge. A sun-browned man on the nearest ship waved and called out a greeting, ambling down the slanting wooden gangplank to meet us.

"What's this, my lord?" he asked, peering uncertainly at Father and me. "Passengers?"

"Old friends, Captain," Mnesikles said. "They'll sail with us to Korinth."

"But – a woman?" The captain shook his head. "Shipboard women are bad luck."

Mnesikles laughed and thumped the man on his hairy back. "It's hardly a day's journey," he said, steering the captain toward the boarding plank and motioning for me to follow with Father. "And you'll earn my gratitude."

Father stumbled as the plank shifted with the motion of the boat, but I kept him from falling; Mnesikles' strong hand gripped Father's elbow and guided him onto the deck. The captain, after scowling at me, sent a deckhand after the baggage in the donkey-cart.

"You can take my usual berth, old friend," Mnesikles told Father as he led us back toward the stern. There were two small cabins; their roofs formed a lookout platform where a lone sailor stood, winding rope into a coil. He paused to stare at us; Mnesikles looked up and waved, greeting the man by name. Then he ushered Father and me into a cabin and opened a window-shutter to let in the orange light of sunset. A rope hammock spanned the diagonal, and a narrow built-in chest formed a sort of bench beneath the window.

"Make yourselves comfortable," Mnesikles said kindly. "I'll have the baggage brought back, and a meal sent to you."

Father removed his hat; the gentle west wind ruffled his sweaty hair. He leaned against the window-sill, taking a long, deep breath. "Reminds me of my childhood," he murmured. "The rocking of the boat... the smell of the sea..."

"Excuse me?" The deckhand with our baggage stood just outside the open door.

"Put it over there," I said, pointing to the corner.

The young man nodded and dropped the bags. "Lord Mnesikles told me to say there's a package of healing herbs for your father in this gray one, Miss."

I blinked back tears at this sign of care from both Mnesikles and Rhodia. "Thank you." Looking away to hide my face, my glance fell on Father's muddy sandals. "Could you bring a foot-basin and some water, so I can wash my father's feet?"

"Sure, Miss. Seawater's good for that – very healthy. I'll be right back."

"Seawater?" I asked dubiously, but the fellow was already gone.

"He's right," Father said. "Seawater's the best thing for cuts and blisters. Stings a bit, but the brine keeps wounds from festering."

The deckhand returned with a wooden bowl and an urn painted with leaping dolphins; he set the water-filled urn on the floor and handed the bowl to me. "Uh, shall I bring back some supper for you both? There's fish stew, and the bread's from yesterday – not too hard yet."

I nodded and the young man left, closing the door behind him. I knelt beside the baggage and rummaged until I located the package from Rhodia. It contained fresh linen bandages, and two jars of ointment – one smelled of dittany and mallow, the other of myrrh. And there were dozens of small poultices of dried chamomile and clover, each wrapped in fine linen and tied neatly with strong thread – these, of course, were for Father's eye sockets.

I guided Father to a seat on the narrow chest beneath the window; I washed his feet with the briny water and smeared ointment on his blisters, then wrapped and tied clean bandages. My own feet throbbed; I decided to try this sailor's cure on my chafed toes. The seawater *did* burn when it first touched my blistered toes and heels, but the pain soon receded.

Just as I finished tending my feet, the deckhand tapped at the door. He had brought stew and bread, and a small jug of wine. I helped Father eat and drink; when Father had eaten his fill, I blotted his chin clean with the edge of his cloak and finished the last of the salty stew myself.

Father leaned against the wall of the cabin. "By Poseidon, I'm tired."

"Don't sleep yet, Father – I need to take care of your eyes before it's too dark." I untied the blindfold, wincing at the sight of my father's ravaged face. Seawater might be good enough for our feet, but not for washing Father's injured eye-sockets: I used wine, as Rhodia had showed me. Then I settled two fresh poultices into place and retied his blindfold. "There," I said, "that's done. Now you can rest." I glanced uneasily at the hammock – there was no way I could get him into that. I pulled a blanket out of our traveling bag and made him a pallet on the floor.

"Thank you, Daughter," he said, easing himself down onto the floor beneath the swaying hammock. Soon his breathing was even, regular; he slept.

I carried out the foot-basin and emptied it over the side of the ship. My life as a pampered princess already seemed to belong to another person. Sailors from our ship and the others were talking around a campfire on the shore. They were too far away for me to hear their conversation, but I heard their laughter; they seemed content. I looked up at the sky, where the stars were springing into view; a breeze refreshed me. Not wanting to return to the tiny cabin, I edged towards the deck, where I heard other voices.

"So, Mnesikles, who's this blind fellow?" one of the sailors was saying. "I asked the captain if it was a new Tiresias, but he says not."

"No," Mnesikles answered. "Just an old friend who's fallen on hard times. Suffered an unfortunate accident."

The sailor took a swig of wine, and I recognized him as the man who had been standing on the roof of the cabin when we arrived. "Still, he reminds me somehow of the old Tiresias – the one who killed himself last year to save Thebes from the plague."

The captain, sitting beside Mnesikles, nodded. "He does at that."

This was a dangerous line of thought, if the sailors should manage to put the pieces together. The old Tiresias had been the father of Queen Jocasta, who had married her son Oedipus, and hence our grandfather.

"Is there more stew?" I asked, coming into view and hoping to change the subject.

"Yes, my dear," said Mnesikles. He told the young deckhand to refill a bowl for me, and made room for me to sit on the deck beside him. "The new Tiresias is still alive," he offered. "At least he was when I saw him in Thebes this morning."

The oldest of the half-dozen sailors manning the ship for evening, a bald old fellow who seemed built of sticks and sinew, said: "He's a good seer, this one. But none of 'em have had the second sight the way the old woman did."

"Right you are," said the captain. "I met that Tiresias when I was a boy. Terrifying, she was."

"What was she like?" I said, glad the conversation had taken a safer turn – but curious, too.

Mnesikles and I relaxed as the subject shifted to ancient history, and the old fellow spoke of the woman who had been my grandfather's predecessor as the Tiresias. She died soon after Mother first became queen of Thebes – about forty years ago! – so memories were hazy, and the men could not agree on her size or shape, or the color of her hair before it went gray. But they were united in the opinion that she had been extremely gifted. If she turned her blindfolded eyes toward you, it was as if she saw not just you, but your past, your future and every impure impulse you'd ever had.

"It's because she never yielded to the sex impulse," said the wizened old sailor.

"How do *you* know that?" asked the captain. "Did you try her?"

The sailors laughed at this, but the old man only looked disgusted. "Try to seduce the Handmaiden of Apollo? That'd be a sure route to the god's curse!"

"Well," said the captain, grinning, "she *did* have a manservant who went with her everywhere…"

"Don't be ridiculous," countered the graybeard. "She never had children."

"Some women are barren," ventured the deckhand.

"But," I objected, "the current Tiresias had a wife; he's got two daughters. And the one before him had a family too. So *they* weren't virgins."

The captain looked at me and raised one eyebrow. "Men gain power when they make love to women," he said, "while women lose it."

"That's how we know Aphrodite is the most generous of goddesses," said one of the sailors. "The Maidens of Artemis keep their power all to themselves, while Aphrodite's girls give it away!"

"*Give* it away?" objected the deckhand. "When was the last time you went to the temple? They demanded three whole cones of Aegyptian incense!"

"Well," said the other, spreading his hands, "I'm *much* better looking…"

The man sitting nearest the deckhand elbowed him. "Your *own* cone must not have impressed them!"

I blushed and looked away; Mnesikles patted my shoulder. "Come, men, don't embarrass the girl."

"I told you, Lord Mnesikles," said the captain, "a ship's no place for a woman."

I excused myself; Mnesikles escorted me back to the tiny cabin, where Father slept soundly. Not daring to brave the hammock in the dark, I curled up on the wooden decking and – despite the hard floor and the rowdy sailors outside – soon fell asleep.

I woke at dawn to the shouts of the crew working outside. That was when I discovered that the cabin contained no chamber pot. Seeing no other solution to my dilemma – and grateful that Father still slept – I squatted and emptied my bladder into the wooden foot-basin. Then I got to my feet and carried my makeshift chamber-pot outside to empty it.

A team of men were hauling up the anchor stone, while others readied the broad square sail. The vessels on either side of ours had already departed. Soon we were floating away from the shore, the sailors pulling at the sail with ropes. I watched the shoreline recede until I could scarcely make out the people on the dockside; and as we left the shelter of the harbor the boat's gentle swaying grew more vigorous. The sparkling blue waves swelled into gray monsters that tossed the vessel; my stomach lurched, and I had to grab at the ship's rail to keep my balance.

"Let me get that for you, my dear," said Mnesikles, picking up the wooden basin I had dropped. I felt my face go hot, wondering if he realized why I was out here in the first place. Then the ship bucked beneath us, and I staggered. Smiling, he said, "Things must be kept secure aboard a ship under way! Here, I'll help you back to the cabin."

I looked out at the vastness of the sea. Alarmed, I asked, "Will we be safe? These waves—"

Mnesikles smiled. "A gentle day for sailing!" he said. "Nothing to worry about."

"Then you don't think the gods—"

He tucked the wooden bowl beneath one arm and caught my elbow with his free hand. "If Poseidon were angry, we'd know it. Look at that blue sky!" Lowering his voice, he added: "Don't worry, and keep quiet."

When I entered the cabin, I discovered that Father was up, his blindfolded face at the open window. "We're at sea!" he said, with a contentment I did not expect – until I remembered that in his boyhood he had sailed often.

We made the crossing without mishap; by mid-afternoon we reached the Korinthian shore on the northeast side of the isthmus. Unlike the gentle hills of Thebes, this landscape was dominated by the massive, jutting Akrokorinth. Its huge, steep-sided bulk loomed over the harbor and the lower town; from below, the palace and temples of the citadel on its plateau were only thin ribbons of red and white.

Though I had not exerted myself during the crossing, the thought of climbing the steep slope dismayed me. Fortunately that proved unnecessary; as I assisted Father off the ship, Mnesikles arranged for a donkey-cart.

Once we were seated, Father said: "Tell me what you see, Antigone."

I told him how the harbor we had just left was vast and crowded; dozens of ships bobbed at anchor, and others were pulled up to the shore for loading and unloading. There were traders of every description: slender, shaven-headed Aegyptians in white kilts, including a few ebony-skinned men from the land of Punt; Hittites with oiled beards and curling-toed boots; redheaded, sunburned Thracians and narrow-waisted Kretans wearing golden jewelry. Noblemen and a few richly dressed women, accompanied by servants holding sun-shades, walked among the merchants, examining the goods for trade. Father nodded, his expression wistful – it must have pained him to return to his boyhood home after so many years without being able to see it. As we made our way through the crowds he commented on the languages he heard, and on the scents of the different cargoes: spices from the East, loads of fish freshly caught – and leather.

He asked, "Are those skins from Thebes, Mnesikles?"

Our host shaded his eyes to look. "I believe so, old friend."

We made our way through the agora in the lower town, where merchants offered goods of every description beneath striped fabric awnings, and then passed the rows of neatly whitewashed houses where the artisans, ship-owners, and tradespeople lived. The crowds thinned as our cart climbed the slope; I told Father how the lower city spread out below us, with the blue of the gulf behind it and – off in the hazy distance – the far shore. The road was even and our driver knew it well; our pace was quick. When we reached the gates of the high city, the guards in their uniforms of Korinthian blue and tan recognized Mnesikles; they admitted us at once, and he had the driver continue to the palace.

The high city was beautiful; only the royal family and the most powerful of the nobility maintained residences here. The remaining buildings were temples. Mnesikles pointed out the famous Temple of Aphrodite, with its rose-tinted walls; it occupied the highest spot on the Akrokorinth, and I could see a young woman in a pale pink robe lighting the torches on the front columns. I heard a faint sound of music and laughter.

We continued to the palace and followed Mnesikles up the stone stairway, Father holding my arm. The soldiers on duty nodded respectfully to Mnesikles; he told them: "We wish to visit the queen."

"Of course, Lord Mnesikles." The man closer to us shifted his blue cloak, eyeing me and Father. "Who've you brought with you?"

Mnesikles glanced at us and then turned back to the soldier, squaring his shoulders. "This is Oedipus and his daughter Antigone. The queen's son, and her granddaughter."

Both guards gaped. "Oedipus of Thebes?" said the second man.

"Yes," Mnesikles answered simply.

"But – but he's blind!" the man blurted out.

Father's shoulders stiffened at this. "That's right," he snapped.

"Enough of this," Mnesikles interrupted. He was a man of power in Korinth, and clearly accustomed to being obeyed. "Take us to the queen."

"Yes," said the first soldier. "Yes, of course, Lord Mnesikles. But I must inform Regent Thoas of your arrival – and your guests."

"Regent Thoas?" asked Father. I heard apprehension in his voice, and I remembered that Thoas was the name of one of his Korinthian cousins.

"Very well," said Mnesikles. "Let the queen and Regent Thoas know we are here."

The guard sent a servant boy sprinting ahead to the queen's chambers with news of our arrival and then led us in that direction at a more measured pace. As we walked, Father muttered: "Thoas," and shook his head. I wanted to ask, but not while the guard was listening, so I turned my attention to our surroundings. The palace was high-ceilinged and airy; when we passed down an open colonnade I could see the blue waters on both sides of the isthmus. Most of the palace's frescoes featured scenes of ships or sea-creatures, and the bronze wall-sconces were in the shape of fish. How different the inland city of Thebes – with its wooded hills and grassy fields, its herds of cattle – must have seemed to Father, when he first arrived to contest with the Sphinx!

We were shown into a large sitting-room whose windows overlooked the lower city, and the sea in the distance. Long curtains of sun-bleached linen stirred in the breeze. I heard women's voices approaching; then the door swung open and a frail old woman entered. "Mnesikles – they told me you've brought—"

"Mother?"

"Oedipus! Oh, Oedipus, my son!"

She went to him, and Father wrapped her in his strong arms. I saw then that she was taller than she seemed, as tall as I in fact. "My son, my son—" she pulled back slightly, and touched Father's face with trembling fingers. "What's happened to you? Are you—"

"Blind. Yes, my lady queen, I'm blind."

Mnesikles cleared his throat. "My lady queen, let me not intrude on your reunion. With your permission, I will go speak with the regent."

The silver-haired woman nodded and waved him out without looking back; he left with a bow, closing the door behind him and leaving me alone with my father and the woman he had always believed to be his mother.

"What—" Queen Periboea began, staring up at Father's face. "How—"

"You should sit, my lady queen," he said. "Antigone, help me."

"Antigone! My granddaughter!" She reached out for my hand. "But – aren't you newly married, my dear? Your father sent word! Where's your husband – what's happened?"

"Please, my lady queen, take a seat," I said, helping her and Father to sit side by side on a padded couch, then pulling up a stool for myself.

Father groped for the old woman's hand. "You know, my lady queen, that I never returned to Korinth because of the oracle I received at Delphi—"

"Yes," she interrupted, "and you would never tell us what the oracle was, just that it was something terrible."

He nodded. "The Pythia said I was fated to kill my father and – and marry my mother."

"Oedipus, no!" gasped the old woman. "But..."

"You understand now why I refused to come home. I couldn't imagine how I could do such a thing, but it was always possible the gods would visit some madness upon me. I couldn't risk the danger to you, to your husband." He paused. "But the Fates have power over us all, no matter how we seek to evade it. I *did* kill my father, King Laius of Thebes. And I

71

did marry my mother, Queen Jocasta of Thebes."

"Oh…" Clasping his hand to her wrinkled cheek, she said: "My poor boy… I never dreamed…"

With an effort to steady his voice, Father related how he learned the truth amidst the chaos of the fires that nearly consumed Thebes after my wedding day. Enraged, he had confronted Mother, meaning to kill her – but he could not.

"I loved her," he groaned. "I still loved her. She was so beautiful." He clenched his free hand into a fist. "But for my eyes to look upon her with lust was a crime against the gods. So I destroyed them."

"Oedipus, your own eyes," whispered the aged queen. After a moment she asked: "And Jocasta?"

"Hung herself. Then Thebes cast me out. Only Antigone was loyal to me – Antigone, and Mnesikles."

"Oedipus, you're blameless in this! It's *my* fault, all my fault. I miscarried so many children… Polybus' family called me barren, and said that he should name one of his young cousins as heir, but he refused. When at last I brought a pregnancy to term it was as though the gods finally decided to smile upon us. But the infant lived only hours. I was desolate; I had failed my husband, my city." The old woman wiped tears from her brimming eyes. "Polybus, dear man, sent Mnesikles in secrecy to find a boy-child that we could raise as our own. When Polybus brought you to me – you made my life worth living. You were the son I always dreamed of. Your father and I could not have loved you more had you been our own flesh and blood. You *were* our son, in every way that mattered!"

"Except to the gods," Father said.

"Mnesikles stayed true to us, as did the midwife who buried the dead infant." She glanced over at me. "But, Antigone, there were troublemakers who said Oedipus did not look like the king."

"My cousin Thoas among them," Father said. "His taunting was the reason I went to Delphi."

The door swung open; a richly dressed man in his middle forties entered, followed by Mnesikles and a pair of soldiers. "So," said the man, folding his arms across his chest. "You've returned."

"Thoas—" began Queen Periboea.

"Cousin," Father said, turning his blindfolded head in the newcomer's direction.

"You're no cousin to me," Thoas answered. "And, given what Mnesikles has told me, I intend to convene the council of nobles and claim the kingship immediately."

Father's brow wrinkled. "Mnesikles?"

"I'm sorry, my lord king, but the truth will arrive soon enough – better that it comes from me." Mnesikles rubbed his bald head. "Creon of Thebes has asked Korinth for assistance."

Nodding, Father said, "I understand. But, Thoas, you are *regent* – not king. It's long been agreed that one of my sons would inherit the throne of Korinth. They are blameless in all this."

The regent snorted. "They've no right to the Korinthian throne. They're not of our royal family – they're the rotten fruit of your incest!"

The queen lifted a hand in entreaty. "Thoas—"

"Enough! You've lied to Korinth for forty years, my lady queen, you and Mnesikles both! I'll not hear another word from either of you!" He pointed at Father. "Guards, get this cursed man out of my palace at once – him and his foul daughter-sister!"

"How dare you speak to my father that way!" I cried, getting to my feet. But the next thing I knew one of the soldiers had hold of me, and I found myself struggling to escape his grasp.

Father stood. "There's no need for the guards, Regent. I'll leave the palace peaceably. But promise me one thing."

"You're in no position to make demands!"

Spreading his hands, Father said simply, "Allow Queen Periboea to remain here in comfort. Her acceptance of your reign will make you more secure."

"Perhaps," Thoas grunted. He hooked his thumbs into his bronze-studded belt. "In any event, I'm a man who obeys the laws of the gods, Oedipus – unlike you. I'm not one to cast an old woman onto the streets. As for Mnesikles, I'll send him back to Thebes at once with news of your disgrace."

"Very well," said Father. "Come, Antigone, we're not welcome here."

"Thoas, let me at least say goodbye to them!" Periboea cried, getting to her feet.

"Make it quick," Thoas said.

To my surprise – we had only just met – she came to me; the soldier released his grip so that Periboea could embrace me. In my ear she whispered: "Seek sanctuary at the Temple of Aphrodite." Then she turned to Father and clung to him affectionately, until Thoas cleared his throat and ordered the guards to take us out.

The regent's men led us out of the palace and down the stairs. "If you're smart, you'll get out of Korinth," one of them said.

I looked around nervously. It was dusk, and much cooler; how could I possibly get my blind father down that steep roadway in the dark? Holding his arm, I said softly: "The queen said we should seek sanctuary at the Temple of Aphrodite."

He nodded, unaware of the way people gaped at us. "That makes sense."

I knew the temple was on the highest spot – but which road would take us there? I was reluctant to ask for directions. At this hour, most of those on the streets seemed to be servants; and gossip moves among servants quicker than lightning flashes across the sky. One would think a blind man led by his daughter would receive looks of pity – but the stares of passers-by were scornful and hostile. Did they already know our story?

Well, if we kept moving uphill we would reach it eventually. "This way, I think." I led Father up a well-trodden roadway. He brushed against a passer-by; the man stopped to stare.

"Prince Oedipus?" he asked.

A gap-tooth fellow nearby laughed and pointed. "Aye, that's him – haven't you heard?"

"He's cursed!" shouted a man carrying an amphora over his shoulder. "Him and that girl both!"

"Mother-fucker!" called another.

I looked around in fear; more people were gathering. I urged Father to hurry, but he stumbled on a loose stone; I grabbed his arm and steadied him to keep him from falling.

"You're his daughter?" asked a man pushing a hand-cart filled with firewood.

"And his sister!" sneered the man with the amphora.

"You sleeping with him too?" someone shouted.

"Shut up!" I cried. Ahead I could see the torches illuminating Aphrodite's temple, and silently thanked the gods that I had chosen the right path. If we had gotten lost among that vicious crowd…

The sound of flute-song grew louder as I hurried my limping father onward; the crowd followed us, but kept their distance. As we approached the temple's entrance I smelled sweet incense. We were greeted by a young woman dressed in linen so sheer that it revealed more than it concealed. "Welcome to the Temple of Aphrodite. I am Myrrha. How may we serve you?" She spoke her words by rote, and she smiled at us the way she had surely smiled on a thousand men – but then her gaze fell on my father's blindfold, and on me, and the smile wavered.

"We ask sanctuary from the goddess," my father said.

"Sanctuary!" Myrrha exclaimed, with a glance at the jeering group of servants behind us. "How unusual!" With a graceful sweep of her arm, she said, "Aphrodite welcomes all into her temple. But the chief priestess must decide on your request for sanctuary. Come, I will take you to her."

We followed the young priestess into the temple; she led us down a torchlit corridor to a room that reminded me of Father's study – except for the erotic frescoes that covered the walls. A woman sat behind a desk stacked with wax tablets, working by the light of a three-wick lamp. She was of middle years, and a broad streak of white accented her dark hair, but she was still striking.

"A moment," she said without looking up, tapping her stylus against her chin; then she made a notation on the tablet she was reviewing.

"I'm sorry to disturb you, Kallia," said our guide, "but there's a request for sanctuary."

The woman raised her eyebrows and set the tablet aside. "Sanctuary?" She peered at Father, then at me. "For what reason?"

"I loved a woman I should never have loved," Father said.

Kallia smiled, revealing beautiful white teeth. "That crime the goddess should readily forgive. You must make a generous offering to her, and sleep with one of the acolytes tonight—"

"The woman was my mother," Father interrupted.

The chief priestess gaped at him for a long moment. Then, as if she needed to be sure that she had heard right she asked: "You made love to your own mother?"

"Yes," Father said. For the second time that day, he told the story. His voice stayed steadier this time, his relation of events matter-of-fact. I, too, found it less wrenching to hear; repetition was making me numb to the horror, just as a callus forms on one's heel where sandals previously chafed the skin raw.

But the tale was new to Kallia. Her face grew pale beneath its powder and rouge as Father spoke. When he had finished she shook her head slowly. "I… I must commune with the goddess to ask her guidance. Incest between a man and his mother – it's unheard of! And parricide is the crime the gods most abhor."

"But Father didn't know!" I objected. "He did everything he could to avoid the crimes that the oracle said he would commit. He had no idea that the king and queen of Korinth were not his parents!"

Kallia looked at me, tilting her head. "You're his daughter; of course you speak in his defense. But did he truly do everything he could? Was it not unwise of him to kill *any* older man, to marry *any* older woman?"

Father's face fell. "I was young and hot-blooded. And mad with love for Jocasta."

I was not willing to let Father accept the blame for this. "Doesn't such passion come from Aphrodite? She should help him!" A thought struck me. "We're her descendants, after all!"

The priestess picked up her stylus and turned it in her slender, well-manicured fingers. "A bold claim."

"Only the truth! We're of Thebes' royal line, descended from Kadmos and Harmonia – and Harmonia was the daughter of Aphrodite and her lover Ares."

I was glad to see my words hearten Father. He said, "Priestess, I don't deny my crimes. I put out my own eyes so that I could not look again with lust upon the woman who bore me. What more can I do to purify myself? I beg you – I beg your mistress Aphrodite – *help* me."

Kallia nodded solemnly. "I will confer with the senior priestesses and we will ask the goddess. Meanwhile, Myrrha, we must offer King Oedipus and his daughter food and drink, and prepare a chamber where they may sleep tonight."

"Yes, Kallia," said the younger woman, looking at us uneasily. "But, mistress, there's a crowd gathered outside. They may grow restless."

The senior priestess rose from her seat; she was tall and imposing. "I'll close the temple for the evening. No other men may enter now."

"*Close* the temple?" Myrrha's eyes went round.

"It's been done before, when necessary. And I'll remind the crowd that if they violate the peace of the temple the goddess will curse them – they'll never make love to a woman again."

She swept past us, striding purposefully as she left the room.

I considered this curse as Myrrha led us toward the center of the temple.

Haemon, I wondered then whether Aphrodite might have cursed *you* – whether that was the reason for our failed wedding night. But I couldn't imagine why the goddess would be angry with you. No, it had to be my fault – perhaps my incestuous origin was the problem. And that might mean Aphrodite would not forgive Father for his crime.

Such thoughts fled my mind when we entered the large central room of the temple. Perhaps a dozen men were there, though the tables and benches around the edges of the room could have accommodated five times that number. In one corner, an older woman played a double-flute; several young acolytes danced in a circle around the central hearth. The firelight shone through their sheer linen gowns, illuminating the ripe curves of breasts, buttocks, and thighs.   Their hair cascaded freely over their shoulders, swaying seductively with their movements; they smiled and winked at the men as the steps of their dance brought them close and then teasingly moved away. The men watched with eager eyes, scarcely noticing our entrance.

Myrrha led us to an empty table. Saying, "I'll have the girls bring you something to eat," she hurried away, as if glad to get away from us.

I looked around the room. The space was well lit, with the fire in the great central hearth and tall lamps of polished bronze at the sides of the room. A large painting on the far wall showed Aphrodite emerging from the sea-foam; her flaxen hair was damp, and droplets of water emphasized the fullness of her breasts and hips. Other walls showed couples – and groups – engaged in various sexual activities. I felt my face flush as I examined these, and was almost glad that Father could not see me looking at them. I wondered whether these paintings were an inventory of services available to the men who came to worship the goddess.

Before long two pink-clad girls appeared with foot basins, and proceeded to wash our feet in warm rose-scented water. They did not speak to us, other than what was necessary for their task, and regarded both me and Father with trepidation. When they had dried our feet and slipped our newly-cleaned sandals back into place they hurried away. Another girl brought cups of spiced wine and a stew of mutton, apples and onions. As we ate, the men at the other tables began to stare at us. I heard my father's name spoken.

Two men who were seated at the table nearest us got up and moved to the other side of the room. "He should never have come back to Korinth," one of them said loudly. "What if his curse contaminates the city?"

At this comment Father turned his head, but at least he could not see their hateful stares. I grew increasingly uncomfortable, and hoped that Myrrha would soon return to take us to a private room where we could be free of these men's revulsion.

The flute-player started a new song, and the acolytes' dance changed; but now fewer of the men followed their sinuous movements, and instead they watched Father and me. One of them, a tall man with hair of gold, rose from his seat and approached our table. I prepared myself for an onslaught of curses and abuse.

Instead he said, "Greetings!" and seated himself on the bench facing Father.

"What do you want?" I asked, suspicious.

"To speak with your father, King Oedipus."

Father shook his head. "No, you don't. Never has a man been so cursed by the gods as I."

The man laughed, and I realized the cup of wine he held was far from his first that night. "That's exactly why I want to speak to you! I thought *I* was the most cursed mortal alive. But you've bested me!" He lifted his cup to Father. "I hereby award you the olive wreath in the contest of catastrophe!"

I watched him take a swallow of wine. He was drunk, and in other circumstances I would not have welcomed his company; but his presence shielded us against the hostile stares of the other men. And perhaps his tale of woe, whatever it was, would distract Father from his heartache.

"What's your misfortune?" I asked.

The man peered at me. "Tell me your name, girl."

"Antigone – I was a princess of Thebes."

"Antigone… that can mean 'against birth.' I'll bet your mother had a difficult labor, eh? And now – now you might interpret that differently. The Fates have their laugh with all of us, don't they?" He emitted a sharp snort. "Well, Antigone-who-once-was-a-princess, I'm called Adrastos – and I've plenty in common with your father here. I'm also a man who should be a king. King of Argos, the land beloved by blessed Hera, queen of Heaven. And it was family that cost me my throne – though, thank all the gods, Oedipus, not the same sort of family problems that *you* have." He took another swallow of wine. "Three years ago my brother Pronax – my treacherous, scheming, thieving brother – stole my throne and forced me into exile."

"How?" I asked, I guiding Father's hand to his wine cup. "What happened?"

"It was during the sacrifice, just before I was to have been crowned. When Amphiorax slit open the beast's belly – gods, you never smelled such a stench. That cursed calf was rotten through and through. It's a wonder it was able to walk to the altar." He took another swallow of wine, then wiped his beard with the back of his hand. "Amphiorax – oh, sorry, I didn't explain, he's the chief priest of Zeus – he said he'd never seen a worse omen. I couldn't possibly take the throne. I'd bring ruin upon the city."

Father rubbed his unshaven chin. "A king should protect his people. If the Fates are against him, he must give up his throne, for the good of his city."

Adrastos nodded; then, realizing that Father could not see this, he patted Father's arm. "Of course! That's only right. But the calf that was sacrificed was not the one *I* offered!"

"What?" I asked. Other heads turned; I realized that men at nearby tables were listening to Adrastos' story.

Curiosity in his voice, Father asked: "Are you certain?"

"Dead certain," Adrastos answered, slapping the table so that the bowls and cups jumped. "*Mine* was unblemished. Pure white, perfectly healthy. I had inspected it just that morning – watched it eat a mash of calming herbs, so that it would go to the knife willingly, gratefully, without making a fuss. I placed a garland of roses on its head, to please Lady Hera. Then I went to prepare for my own role in the ceremony. I dressed and oiled my face; when the time came I approached the altar. One of the acolytes led calf forward. It was wearing the same garland – but it wasn't the same animal."

"Why didn't you object right then?" I asked.

"I didn't *realize* it right then," Adrastos groaned. "I was focused on the ceremony, reciting the names of all the previous kings of Argos. I didn't look at the animal carefully – I paid no attention to it until it started acting strangely. It tried to pull away as it was led to the altar – the herbs should have prevented that. Then it stumbled, a very bad sign. When Amphiorax started to cut its throat, it shook its head and lowed and tried to escape! Amphiorax had to make a second cut, and what with the calf shaking its head blood spattered everywhere. I could hear people saying I would stumble as king, that I would cover Argos in blood. And then when he read those foul entrails…"

Adrastos drained the last of the wine from his cup, and called for one of the serving girls to refill it. After she had poured for him she lingered nearby, listening. Everyone, it seemed, was listening; even the music had stopped.

"I just stood there, the scepter in my hand – totally dumbfounded. All I could think was: how could the gods turn on me like that?"

Father groped for the man's hand, and clasped it in both of his. "King Adrastos – my friend – I know all too well how you feel. When I was young, the gods gave me a warning; I took it. And I seemed to have earned their favor. Denied one kingdom, I won another. I won a wife of surpassing beauty, sired a healthy family. But the gods had tricked me—"

Adrastos freed his hand. "It wasn't the gods that tricked me. It was a man." He closed his eyes for a moment, his face twisting in fury. "I saw it. When the men who should have been taking oaths of loyalty to me started yelling that I had to be banished to save Argos, I stumbled over to the carcass of that cursed calf. I was dazed, like I'd taken a blow to the head. How could this be? And then I saw it. The garland of roses had slipped from its head – and behind the beast's ear was a brown splotch. The animal *I* chose was unblemished!" His whole body shook with anger.

"What did you do?" asked a wiry, sun-browned man who had been playing knucklebones.

"I protested, of course! I pointed out the mark on the beast's head. But the priests accused *me* of lying! Me! They said I had no proof that the animals had been switched. And so I was refused the crown and banished from Argos! My brother Pronax led the squadron that hustled me across the border – and I knew he was behind it. Now, of course, *he's* the king."

"Betrayed by your own brother," Father said quietly.

The onlookers – men and acolytes alike – murmured in sympathy.

"Treachery from my own flesh and blood." Adrastos looked as though he wanted to spit, but retained enough sense not to defile the floor of Aphrodite's temple. "Well, I hope the Argives are happy with Pronax as king! They're learning that he has no shame. Now that he's finished stealing from me, he's stealing from them. He'll ruin the city as sure as Apollo's chariot rises in the morning. Argos would have done better inviting a group of pirates to invade them."

"What are you going to do about it?" Father asked, resting his chin on his fist.

Adrastos blinked. "Do?"

"If you're concerned about your city's welfare, you should try to save it. I left Thebes to protect my city from the gods' wrath. But *you*—"

"Didn't you hear me?" interrupted Adrastos. "I'm *banished* from Argos. I'm not even allowed to see my children, or my sister! Pronax has the whole army at his command – how can I go back?"

"I don't know," Father sighed. "Maybe I have no business giving advice."

At that moment the chief priestess Kallia entered the room, followed by Myrrha and another woman. Their demeanor was particularly sober for servants of laughter-loving Aphrodite. I touched Father's arm and whispered; he straightened respectfully in his seat.

"Oedipus," Kallia said, "we have considered your situation, and consulted with the goddess. But we are unable to cleanse you of your crimes, and Lady Aphrodite will not permit you to take pleasure with any of her servants."

"I understand," said Father. "Can you suggest any other way that I might be purified?"

"My mistress Aphrodite says you must find that answer for yourself," she answered.

My shoulders fell. So Aphrodite would not help us after all.

After a moment, Myrrha said, "Lord Mnesikles' men have brought your traveling-bags; you'll find them in your room. I'll take you there now."

As I helped my father to his feet, the third priestess added: "Your presence is a blight upon this temple. You must leave at daybreak."

I shivered with fear. If our divine ancestress refused us shelter, who would take us in?

"Why not get rid of him now?" objected a plump fellow with thick eyebrows, who smelled of fish. "Him and this other one, they're distracting the ladies with their stories. I climbed that blasted hill and made an offering of three dozen good oysters. I came for one purpose, and it ain't listening to these god-forsaken fellows crying into their wine!"

Kallia spoke sternly. "It would violate the laws of our father Zeus to send even the worst criminal out into the night."

"Night or day, what does it matter?" argued the fisherman. "It's not as if he can see!"

"His daughter guides him and *she* needs light. Besides, they are descendants of our beloved goddess through her daughter Harmonia." Then Kallia smiled placatingly. "But of course, dear sir, you came to worship Aphrodite and we are here to accommodate you. Please, choose the woman who most pleases you." She turned to the flute-player in the corner. "And we must have more music!"

Myrrha came over to us. "Come, you must be tired," she said, ushering us away before we completely spoiled the mood.

Father and I followed her down the hall. I was relieved that we would not be turned out into the night – and grateful that, thanks to Mnesikles, we would not leave empty-handed. But where would we go in the morning?

*

Antigone pauses, remembering. The world seemed so hostile then, so unforgiving. But she and Father managed to find small joys in their mendicant wandering: warm sunshine and lilting bird song, cool spring water and the sweet scent of olive blossoms. Now even those things are denied her.

But at least now she has companionship. "Thank you for being with me," she says to those beyond the hard, thick wall.

CHAPTER FIVE
HAEMON

Antigone's voice fades and then stops. Haemon glances at his mother and Ismene: the women's faces are drawn and frightened in the lamplight. They also, he realizes, found Antigone's words too much like farewell. He whispers to them, "Could she have taken poison?"

"There was nothing harmful in the basket," his mother assures him.

Despite these words, Haemon is not sure. His father, expert in plants and toxins, could easily have arranged to smuggle a deadly flask to his niece. He might have even have considered it an act of mercy.

"Antigone?" Haemon calls, resting his hand on the wall that separates them. "Are you all right?"

"No worse than a moment ago," she answers. "Just remembering those first few days of traveling with Father…"

Haemon lets his fingers trail down the stone; his worst fear set aside, others surge up within him. In Antigone's tale so far there has been no mention of her missing him, no expression of regret for leaving their marriage. She has made her devotion to her father abundantly clear; she recalled tender thoughts of her aunt Eurydike, and even the healer Rhodia, but nothing of her feelings for him.

On the other hand, *he* is the man; he should be pursuing her.

"You should rest, Antigone," Haemon's mother says. "You sound exhausted."

"No!" cries Antigone, desperation in her voice. "Don't go, Aunt Eurydike – don't leave me!"

"We're not leaving," Haemon assures her. "But Mother's right. One of us should talk for a while."

Ismene nods her agreement. "What would you like to hear?"

There is another long silence – but then the sound of Antigone's voice comes again. "I'd like to know what happened after I left," she says. "With my brothers – and with *you*, Haemon."

"Then I'll speak," he says, taking heart at her saying his name. But how should he address her – as his wife? Does she even think of herself that way? They were friends, once, as children. Perhaps that is the best way to speak to her.

If ever Antigone needed a friend, she needs one now.

He glances briefly at Ismene and his mother. There are things he wants to share with Antigone that he would prefer not to reveal to them. But speaking the truth before others strikes him as bravery of a sort – a valor far better suited to him than bold deeds in battle. And after so much destruction, so many deaths, male vanity seems a foolish self-indulgence.

This is his last chance. He must seize the moment.

Besides, Antigone deserves the truth. All of it.

HAEMON

I remember the day that the friendship between Eteokles and Polynikes began to die.

It was less than half a month after we buried Queen Jocasta. Father had been declared regent until the princes came of age, and Thebes' gates were open once more. I was down by the Ogygia Gate, supervising the grain allotment. In return for the sheep, goats, and calves they brought to Thebes, the herdsmen rightly expected provisions for the winter. But we had lost so much in the fire that we couldn't give them full rations – not until fresh stores arrived.

"This?" protested a goatherd in a grimy brown kilt, holding up his half-filled sack of barley. "This is all I get? This won't keep my family even a month!"

I pushed back my hat and wiped sweat from my forehead. "It's just temporary—"

"I gave you my best cattle!" interrupted another man. His two front teeth were missing, and his breath stank worse than his unwashed body. "I guess you're new at this, youngster, but here's how it works: we bring in our animals, and you give us a winter's worth of grain!"

I held up my tablet and pointed at the wax-coated writing surface. "Yes, and I'm keeping track of what you've given. We're expecting more supplies to arrive shortly. This is just supposed to last until—"

"How can I trust *that*?" shouted the goatherd, waving his dirty hand at my note-tablet. "You know I can't read those marks! Besides, wax can be pressed down and changed!"

"Here," I said, handing him the pottery shard that I had marked for him. "Here's the same figure, and no one can change it." This gave him a moment's pause, so I quickly continued: "Keep it safe. It's your token to claim more barley – and your measure of olives, oil, and wine – next month. See? Look, that's the symbol for barley. And this is for olives."

He squinted at it. "That don't look like no olive."

"No," I countered, frustrated by his lack of imagination. "It looks like an olive *tree*." I took a deep breath of manure-tainted air, fighting light-headedness, and reminded myself to have patience. Peasants could not be expected to grasp the subtleties of writing.

"This says I'll get what I'm due next month?"

"Yes," I sighed. I had endured the same conversation a dozen times already that day.

Frowning, he said, "How do you know there'll be any then?"

"We're only short because of the fire," I began. "My father the regent has asked our allies—"

The gap-toothed cowherd held up the token I had given him earlier, shaking it at me. "And what if you Spartoi let it all burn up again?"

I resisted the urge to flinch away. "The city's atoned for the crimes of Jocasta and Oedipus. Thebes has been purified. There's no reason for the gods to strike us with lightning again."

This man had received his token; why didn't he leave, instead of staying to make trouble? But he wasn't the only one lingering, staring angrily at the jars of grain behind me. Alkides and the princes were with the Master of the Herds, out by the livestock pens; the soldiers were stationed at the gate. I had only an ancient scribe and a few palace servants with me, and the crowd of herdsmen was growing restless as the day's heat increased.

"We should just take what's left," said another fellow. I recognized him as a man who often brought cartloads of firewood to the palace. His muscled shoulders were enormous, and he was expert with an axe. Several peasants shouted their agreement, while others nodded encouragingly.

"If you do that, there won't be anything for people who come tomorrow," I said, raising my voice over the uproar. "Do you want your fellow Thebans, your neighbors, to be hungry this month?"

"We want our barley!" yelled the goatherd.

Involuntarily I took a step back. "You'll get the rest next month, I tell you!"

The woodcutter growled, "I want it *now!*" He put a large hand against my shoulder and shoved, hard.

I stumbled backwards. "How dare you!"

"Thebans!" interrupted a new and powerful voice. I turned to see Alkides pushing his way through the crowd of peasants, sweeping them aside as effortlessly as a man walking through a barley field. "You! Leave the regent's son alone!"

I'd never been so relieved to see Alkides, or the two princes trailing behind him. The crowd's mood quickly shifted, and the peasants shrank back from me.

"I – forgive me, my lord Alkides," said the woodcutter, looking at his feet. "Me and my friends, we just want our grain."

"We have wives and children," said the goatherd in the brown kilt. "We need to feed them during the rainy months."

"And you will!" Eteokles declared. "A runner's just arrived from the harbor – there's a shipment in from Korinth. Trust us, Thebans: my brother and I will take care of you."

"We always have," Polynikes added, pulling back his shoulders.

This was an exaggeration – my father had done far more for the city than the twins, who were still three years from their manhood ceremony – but their words calmed the mob. And when someone at the back of the crowd shouted that old Mnesikles had been sighted on the harbor road, leading a dozen or more wagons towards the city, the peasants began chanting the princes' names.

"Thanks," I muttered to Alkides.

"Any time, Haemon!" When he clapped me on the back, I realized he could have taken on the woodcutter and won. Two years younger than I, he stood a handspan taller and his shoulders were broad as a full-grown man's. He routinely won wrestling bouts against men in their twenties, and his beard was already better than mine – and he was still growing.

"Look," Alkides said, pointing. "There he is!"

"Mnesikles!" shouted Polynikes, lifting a hand in greeting.

Cheering, the crowd made way for the old Korinthian; at his side walked a younger man I didn't recognize. Behind them was the first of many donkey-carts, laden with large bags and storage jars. I scanned the traveling-party as best I could, hoping to see you, Antigone; but as far as I could tell, no women were among them. My rational mind told me there was no reason to expect you – you'd be with your father, of course, and he would not return to Thebes – yet I kept looking.

Eteokles strode forward. "Greetings, Mnesikles!"

"Welcome back to Thebes!" Polynikes added, clasping the Korinthian's hand.

I followed Alkides toward the visitors. "Did you bring any oysters?" he asked.

Mnesikles nodded, grinning. "There's an urn full of them right here." He pointed to the cart just behind him. It held several pottery storage jars, in addition to amphorae resting on their sides and cushioned with straw, with covered baskets stacked on top. "These provisions are meant for the palace; the rest are bulk foodstuffs." He gestured to the other wagons.

"We're glad for Korinth's friendship," said Polynikes.

"Absolutely," Eteokles agreed. "You must dine with us tonight."

"Thank you, my lords," answered the Korinthian, bowing. "Allow me to introduce Glaukos," he continued, indicating the younger man beside him. "He will take my place as Korinth's envoy." This surprised me, but Mnesikles did sound weary. He was an old man, older even than Father; it stood to reason that he'd want to retire.

"Prince Eteokles. Prince Polynikes." Glaukos made a tight bow to the princes. "I bring messages from Korinth for Regent Creon."

"We'll take you to him," Eteokles said courteously. "And you can tell us all about Korinth."

I caught Polynikes' eye. "I'll stay here to make sure everything is inventoried," I said.

"You're a good man, Haemon," said Alkides. "Me, I'm going to make sure I get some oysters!" Grinning, he joined the two princes; the three of them led the Korinthians and the cart of select provisions up the road towards the palace.

Someone had to take the inventory, of course. But I was glad for the excuse to avoid the others; I needed to collect my thoughts. There was no reason for you to return, Antigone – and yet the fact that you had not come left me feeling melancholy. Having work to do gave me something else to think about, helped me to master my emotions. By the time my brother Menoeceus arrived – he had heard that supplies were in from Korinth, and wanted to see for himself – I was ready to speak to someone other than the scribes.

Menoeceus helped me tally the barley and wheat, olive oil and wine. He moved among the wagons, shouting the numbers; I noted them in my tablet. It took us the rest of the afternoon – Korinth was generous. But of course they had been our closest ally for many years, ever since Oedipus became king.

I'd sent for additional soldiers; once the last of the barley-sacks had been counted, I addressed the ranking man. "Get this into the storerooms, and guard it well."

"Yes, my lord Haemon," he answered, saluting.

"And you—" I said, turning to the peasants who remained, staring greedily at the contents of the wagons, "go home. The sun's setting already. There'll be no more disbursements until tomorrow."

Reassured that their bellies would be filled, they did not complain, but obediently dispersed. A few hailed me by name, and offered words of thanks. Nothing like their excited shouting for the princes, of course, but then I was only the regent's son.

By the time Menoeceus and I reached the palace, the last glow of sunset was shading from orange to crimson; a man was lighting the torches in the wall-sconces. In the megaron, an eager group of young people surrounded the large urn Mnesikles had brought, looking on as servants scooped out the oysters. Each was tapped on the shell to check that it was still alive; those that responded by closing tighter were placed on the coals of the central hearth, and the dead ones were tossed into a refuse basket. Our Korinthian guests, Mnesikles and Glaukos, were seated in places of honor, sipping goblets of wine. My father was not yet in the megaron; he had other business that day.

Taking my usual seat, I called for a woman to bring over a washbasin. I rinsed my hands and splashed water on my face, dried my scanty beard and then allowed the servant to untie my sandals. It was a relief to soak my feet in the warm, rosemary-scented water.

As the servant scrubbed the grime from my toes, others entered the megaron. I remember you, Ismene, arriving with several other girls – and then the commotion when you, Mother, shepherded in my younger brothers and sisters, who wanted to check the oysters themselves. The dinner crowd, eager for news and oysters from Korinth, grew quickly. The Tiresias appeared too – he was always fond of a good meal – accompanied by his daughters, who always made me think of tree nymphs. Just as the servant woman was drying my feet and slipping them into soft house-shoes, Father entered the room; Bromius, the chief priest of Apollo, followed a few steps behind.

"Regent Creon!" announced the herald.

Those who were seated got to their feet; the din of conversation subsided as Father went directly to Mnesikles and clasped his hand. "Greetings, my friend!"

"My lord regent," said Mnesikles, bowing.

Glaukos cleared his throat loudly. "Regent Creon, *I* am in charge of this delegation."

Father released Mnesikles' hand and turned to face the other man. "And you are…?"

"Glaukos of Korinth," the man answered, adding a curt bow. "I must inform you, Regent, that Mnesikles has incurred grave disfavor in Korinth. Henceforth I will serve as my city's envoy. Mnesikles was sent only to facilitate the transition."

"I see," Father said coolly. "Welcome to Thebes, Glaukos. I thank you and your city for the goods you have brought in this time of need. If I may ask… is there a precise inventory?"

"Here, Father," I said, approaching with my tablet.

He opened it and squinted down, turning towards the hearth to get the best light as he perused the amounts. I saw his shoulders relax. Finally he looked back to Glaukos. "Korinth is generous," he said, closing the tablet and handing it to a scribe, who would copy the figures into clay. "Thebes will not forget this."

"My – ah, yes, Regent Creon." Glaukos shifted his weight uneasily. "Thebes has been an important ally for many years. We set great store by your friendship – and we value the trade of beef and leather in exchange for our fish and salt. But, Regent Creon, my city has an important message for you and the sons of Oedipus."

Eteokles and Polynikes moved closer. I wondered how they appeared to Glaukos: it must have been impossible for a stranger to tell one handsome, copper-haired youth from the other. Broad-shouldered Alkides stood behind them.

"We value the Korinthian alliance," said Eteokles.

Polynikes added, "Let us hear your message."

Glaukos bowed, a little more politely this time. He glanced briefly at old Mnesikles, as if seeking support, and then realized he would receive none. Squaring his shoulders, he said: "My lord regent, my lord princes, I bring serious news. My lord Thoas has assumed the throne and is now king of Korinth."

The color drained from Polynikes' face. "What!" he exclaimed. There was a swell of astonished reaction throughout the megaron.

Raising his voice to be heard, Glaukos continued: "The council of nobles has decreed that no son of Oedipus can claim the throne of Korinth.

You are not eligible now, and will never be eligible in the future—"

"What?" asked Polynikes.

"You have no right!" exclaimed Eteokles.

Polynikes lunged forward, raising clenched fists. "How dare you!" Glaukos did not move, but Father reached out to stop the prince. "Polynikes, this man's our guest!"

Polynikes halted his advance, but the rage did not leave his face.

"I will have order here!" Father shouted to the megaron at large. As the clamor abated, he turned back to the Korinthian envoy. "Glaukos, why has Korinth taken such a step?"

His eyes fixed on Polynikes, the man said: "Oedipus was born to King Laius and Queen Jocasta of Thebes. He is not, and has never been, Korinthian."

"That's not right," Eteokles objected. "Our father was the adopted son of the king and queen of Korinth."

"You can't deny us," spat Polynikes. "We'll take Korinth by force if we have to!"

Alkides came to his side. "I'll support you. And so will the rest of Thebes!"

"That would be unwise," Glaukos said apprehensively, taking a step backwards.

"Boys, be silent!" Father commanded. He looked each of his nephews in the eye, then fixed his gaze on Alkides – and I realized that, tall though my father was, Alkides was already taller. "You don't know what you're saying. None of you has ever seen Korinth – but *I* have. Korinth sits atop a crag far higher than the acropolis of Mycenae. Never mind that Korinth is our trusted ally – an attack would be utter folly. You'd need chariots drawn by winged horses to scale its walls. As regent of Thebes I forbid any such engagement."

Polynikes' face colored at this rebuke. "Uncle Creon—"

"Glaukos is right," Father interrupted. "What claim do you have to the Korinthian throne?"

Eteokles' jaw dropped. "But our father—"

"Oedipus has forfeited any claim," Glaukos broke in. "He admits his true parentage, and his incestuous crimes."

Mnesikles looked down at the floor. "That he has," he murmured.

"But *we* aren't cursed," said Polynikes, bristling.

Glaukos folded his arms. "How do you know?"

"Ask old Bromius," Polynikes answered, pointing at the priest. "Or the Tiresias!"

"The Tiresias is here?" Curiosity tinged Glaukos' voice, and he scanned the room's occupants.

"Yes." The old man spoke from where he was seated; people moved aside as if to give him a view of the Korinthian envoy, which of course made no difference to the blind prophet.

Glaukos bowed. "Tiresias, though your words are always true, they are not always to be trusted. What the gods give you to say is often not understood by mortal men until it has come to pass." He clasped his hands behind his back. "And you will understand that Korinth does not seek your advice in this matter."

"I understand," said the Tiresias, inclining his blindfolded head. His voice was tinged with regret, and I wondered what his advice would have been.

"Tiresias," Polynikes pleaded, "*tell* him—"

Father interrupted. "You and your brother will have to content yourselves with the throne of Thebes. *That* should be enough for anyone!"

These patriotic words silenced my cousins, at least for the moment, but both glared sullenly at Father and at the Korinthian envoy.

Father apologized to Glaukos for the outburst, continuing smoothly: "I hope this won't interfere with the good relationship Thebes has always had with Korinth. We greatly appreciate your city's generosity, especially at this difficult time. Would you care for some wine?" He beckoned to a servant holding a tray of painted wine-cups.

But Glaukos held up his hand. "It's been a long day, lord Creon," he said. "If I might retire…"

"Of course." Father snapped his fingers, and another servant stepped forward to escort the envoy to a guestroom; at Father's urging, people began to take their seats. Old Mnesikles remained; I heard him ask a servant to bring his favorite Theban cheese.

"One grows accustomed to certain tastes," he told Mother, who had come to sit at the head table. "Cow's-milk cheese is not as common in Korinth, and we make nothing quite like that one."

Eteokles and Polynikes remained standing; they had folded their arms and were staring at each other. "How can we *share* a throne?" Eteokles asked.

"There's precedent in such matters," Father said, looking over at them. "Amphion and Zethos were twins who shared the throne while I was a boy."

Of course, Father was shading the truth. Amphion and Zethos had not shared the Theban throne equally. Amphion ruled as king of Thebes, only yielding the throne to his brother when he traveled away from the city.

Alkides set one hand on each of their shoulders. "You'll work it out," he assured them cheerfully. "Right now, let's see about those oysters!"

The princes still looked dubious, but Alkides' friendly confidence seemed to comfort them. The excitement past for the moment, everyone else turned their attention to the oysters cooking on the coals. Servants refilled our goblets, set out bowls of salt and flasks of vinegar, and passed around baskets of fresh bread. Soon plates of steaming oysters were reaching the tables. People laughed as they tried to open the hot shells without burning their fingers. Mother had the servants handle this task for the younger children; my sister Megara spared her delicate hands by ordering Alkides to open hers.

The treat occupied everyone for some time, but eventually the last of the oysters were eaten, and people toyed with their wine cups or tossed bread crusts to the dogs. Conversation slowed, as it does when people are full and growing sleepy, when old Mnesikles remarked: "No one here has asked about Oedipus."

That did not mean no one cared, of course: I had not asked about you, Antigone, though I had been thinking of you all the while.

Silence descended on the megaron. It was broken only when my youngest sister knocked over a pile of oyster shells. They clattered across the floor tiles; two dogs barked excitedly and hurried over, and Mother called for the servants to sweep up the mess.

Father exchanged looks with the princes and then spoke. "Mnesikles, my friend – you know that Oedipus brought great calamity upon Thebes."

"If Father had managed the situation better, Thoas wouldn't be king of Korinth," said Polynikes.

Mnesikles set down his wine cup. "He was given a terrible fate, my lord prince." His voice was quiet and sorrowful. "An unbearable burden – one he sought to avoid."

"How is he?" asked Ismene softly. "Is he in much pain?"

"His flesh is healing," Mnesikles said. "But his spirit suffers."

Ismene's courage emboldened me to speak. I wet my lips, then said: "And Antigone – how is she?"

Mnesikles explained that Oedipus and Antigone had traveled with him to Korinth, but Thoas expelled them from the palace and ordered them to leave Korinth. He did not know where they had gone.

Mother clutched Father's arm. "A young woman and a blind, lame man, traveling alone…"

Guilt gripped my heart. My wife, and my father-in-law – I should have gone with them. Antigone, I'd told you Father wouldn't let me leave Thebes. But that's not the *real* reason I didn't go. I couldn't be the husband you deserved. I was doubly a failure. No one knew the depth of my shame, or seemed to notice my negligence – and somehow that made it worse.

"Let's hope the gods will protect them," said Father. "Tiresias, what can you tell us?"

The Tiresias shrugged. "Traveling has its dangers. One may be attacked on the road even when whole and sighted."

I closed my eyes, trying to push away my anxiety. Surely the gods would protect Antigone – she had done nothing wrong!

"True," Father remarked. "And we shouldn't forget that Oedipus caused *your* injuries, Tiresias."

"But I wasn't the Tiresias then," said the seer. "I was a different man: Pelorus, friend of King Laius – and neither of us guessed that our assailant was the son Laius long thought dead. Still, Pelorus' life continued, even once he was blind and lame – and the gods gave him many blessings." He patted the hand of his younger daughter, conceived after he lost his sight. Manto smiled, and touched her father's cheek.

"So," Menoeceus asked, "are Oedipus and Antigone all right? Or not?"

"Bandits usually prefer richer targets," opined the Tiresias.

That gave me hope: surely that was true! But Menoeceus muttered, "That's no answer." The Tiresias turned his blindfolded head Menoeceus' way.

"Perhaps the Tiresias cannot tell us at this time," Father said hastily.

"The gods have not commanded me to be silent," the Tiresias offered, his tone mild. He turned to face south, as if peering towards Korinth. "I believe they're alive. But their lives won't be easy."

"Will they die?" Ismene asked.

"Dear Ismene!" The Tiresias' voice was gentle. "Of *course* they'll die, as will you and I – we are mortals, after all."

Ismene blushed and looked down.

"She means, will they die *soon?*" Menoeceus persisted.

The seer paused for a moment. Then he said, "I don't believe so. They may even yet influence our lives here in Thebes."

Father frowned. "But Oedipus is banished from this city!"

"That's true," said the Tiresias equably. He plucked a grape from a bunch resting on a nearby platter and popped it into his mouth.

"But you're saying that he's planning to return to Thebes and resume control!"

Old Bromius interjected: "I don't believe that's what the Tiresias said, Regent Creon. Oedipus and his children still *influence* the future of Thebes. Certainly Prince Polynikes and Prince Eteokles do."

Everyone looked confused. Polynikes and Eteokles bent their coppery heads together and spoke in low tones, glancing up at Father or at the Tiresias from time to time.

After a moment Lasthenes, the Master of the Herds, cleared his throat and asked: "Tiresias, are you making prophecy now – or is this simple conversation?"

"It's so hard to tell the difference, isn't it?" The blind seer wiped his mouth with the back of his hand. "But let me remind you that though Oedipus and Antigone have left Thebes, both of them care about the city's welfare, and that of their family. That is, in fact, why they left: an effort to remove the curse from Thebes."

The old prophet's words stung my heart: Antigone was my family twice over, both my cousin *and* my wife. And we had been close friends as long as I could remember. She had acted selflessly to protect me and all of Thebes – and I had repaid her by feeling sorry for myself. I looked down into my wine-cup, pondering this.

Mother reached for Ismene's hand, murmuring soft words of comfort. Then she asked, "Tiresias, do you know where they are?"

"No – that I cannot tell you."

Father frowned. "And Mnesikles, you said you don't know either."

"No, my lord Creon," said the bald Korinthian. "Last I heard they were on their way out of Korinth. But that was several days ago."

"They could be anywhere by now," Father observed.

"If they boarded a ship, they could be halfway to the Hesperides!" said Alkides.

"Not quite that far," said the Tiresias, his lips curving in a smile. "But they could have reached Krete if Poseidon is feeling generous." He wiped his fingers on a napkin. "Regent Creon, by your leave – I'm an old man, and after enjoying your excellent table I fear my bed calls to me."

"Of course, Tiresias," Father said. I was certain I heard relief in his voice. I think that while Father enjoyed the prestige of having the Tiresias in Thebes, he did not like the fact that in some ways the seer outranked the regent.

With his elder daughter's help, the blind man got to his feet; his younger daughter handed him his wooden staff. Before leaving, the prophet turned to Mnesikles. "Old friend, we may never meet again," he said. "The years weigh upon us both; journeys are for younger men. May Hermes watch over your return to Korinth."

Mnesikles thanked him for this blessing, and with his daughters' assistance the Tiresias hobbled out of the megaron; the priest Bromius followed.

This departure gave others an opportunity to put down their goblets and leave. Old Mnesikles bade my father good night and headed for his guestroom; Mother left with Ismene and my younger brothers and sisters.

Father glanced over at Megara, who was whispering to Alkides. "Megara, help your mother and cousin get the little ones to bed."

Forced to leave Alkides' side, my sister pouted but obeyed. Father recommended that the princes also retire. "Tomorrow will be busy," he said. "You'll have a lot to do, overseeing the rations."

"And I should go home to my mother," said Alkides. "She's still not feeling well." He stood and bowed to Father. "As ever, many thanks for your hospitality, my lord regent." He grabbed a fistful of cheese-stuffed olives on his way out.

The lamps were burning low, the room nearly empty; I moved closer to the hearth. I was a man; Father could not send *me* to bed. I summoned a servant to bring me more wine.

As I stared down into the glowing coals, Father approached. "How many cups of wine have you drunk tonight, Son?" he asked, pulling up a stool to sit beside me.

I shrugged. "They've been well watered."

"I counted at least five," Father said, pulling a stool closer and taking a seat. "I've noted as much on other evenings. What's troubling you, Haemon?"

"Don't you know?" I asked bitterly. "You know everything that happens in Thebes – even how many cups of wine I drink."

"Not everything, of course, but I try. I want what's best for the city." He leaned closer. "And for my son."

I contemplated this. Did he really want what was best for me? Or was it just that he saw advancing my interests as a way to help his own? I did not especially want to discuss my feelings with him.

"It's about Antigone, isn't it?" he said.

My emotions churned, fueled by the wine. Fear for your safety, Antigone – longing to see you again – regret that I was not the man I should have been…

"Isn't it?" Father prodded.

"Of course I'm worried about her," I said defensively. "She's my wife."

"Is she?"

I looked up, feeling my face go hot. "What are you saying?" By all that was holy, did he know *that,* too?

"Well…" Father rubbed his beard. "She abandoned you."

Silently I gave thanks that Father did *not* know of my failure as a man – or at least he was not going to speak of it.

He continued, "It's helpful for the Tiresias to say she left for the greater good of Thebes; that protects your honor. You needn't let this wound your pride. Son, Antigone's no longer a useful alliance for you. Her very existence is a disgrace. She's the daughter of her own brother!"

My throat tightened with anger: that wasn't your fault! "The priest said no guilt attaches to Oedipus' children," I ground out.

"He did say that." Father peered at me closely. "Do you *want* to stay married to her?"

I stared at the painted decoration on the hearth's stuccoed rim: curving, stylized flames of red and yellow. I was drinking, as Father had noted, my fifth cup of wine – or was it the sixth? I felt it loosening my tongue; and there, in the shadows of the empty megaron, it was easy to let the words spill out. "I always assumed Antigone and I would marry. Always. Ever since we were children."

"I know," Father said. "And since she was the eldest daughter of the king and queen, I wasn't about to object. But I never understood the attraction. She's no beauty – and she was always a difficult girl."

That made me laugh a little – and made me miss you even more. "Yes," I agreed, turning the painted cup in my hands. "Yes, she was." Finally I looked up into Father's dark eyes. "Have you ever thought, Father, how the goddesses of Mount Olympus show us the different examples of womanhood?"

Father picked up a charred stick lying just inside the rim of the circular hearth and used it to poke at the coals further in. "Not really."

"There's Hera, of course – the queen of heaven, the goddess of marriage. But a woman like that wouldn't be right for me. A queenly woman needs a king, and I'll never be that."

Father shrugged. "That's up to the Fates, Son, but go on."

"Then there's Aphrodite…"

"Aphrodite!" Father laughed. "Antigone's *nothing* like Aphrodite."

I shook my head. "No – Megara, perhaps. She enjoys the attention her beauty brings her. Antigone isn't one for clothes and jewels and makeup, or flirting like Megara."

"I know," Father said darkly. "I'm keeping an eye on Alkides."

I nodded, smiling wryly. "Well, I didn't want a wife like Aphrodite." I hesitated, then said: "I suppose most men look for a measure of Demeter in their wives."

"Antigone's not much like Demeter, either."

"True." I picked a fragment of bread from my kilt and threw it into the hearth. Would Father laugh at me? "She's – she's always reminded me of Athena."

He didn't laugh; instead his dark eyes narrowed. "Athena? Well, Antigone *is* a clever girl."

"And a skilled weaver."

"Yes, another point of resemblance." He set his hands on his knees. "But, Haemon, the goddess Athena is a virgin."

"I should have thought of that," I said ruefully.

At this point Father chuckled, but to my surprise his laughter did not make me feel worse about myself. "Few marriages turn out well," he said, drawing patterns in the ash with his stick. "Even the gods can't manage it. Look at how Zeus and Hera bicker, and how Aphrodite cuckolds her husband Hephaestus. If the gods themselves fail, why should mortals expect to succeed?"

I paused with my wine-cup halfway to my lips. "Aren't you happy with Mother?"

"She's a good wife and a wonderful mother, but I chose her when I was far older than you are now." He touched my shoulder. "Son, you're still young – there's no reason for Antigone to ruin your life. We didn't know the truth about my sister and Oedipus before your wedding – I can have Bromius declare the marriage invalid. Take your time in choosing another girl; there's no hurry. And in the meanwhile… come, we're both men. Sleep with whoever you like."

But I didn't *want* our marriage to be revoked; I wanted everything *fixed*, somehow, impossible though that was. I downed the last swallow of wine. I didn't want any other woman. And – I wasn't going to admit this to Father, but I didn't think I could bed a woman at all. As long as you remained my wife, no one needed to learn about that.

"She's been gone less than a month," I said. "I don't think it would be fair to her to set the marriage aside."

"*Fair*?" Father exclaimed. He threw the stick into the center of the hearth; sparks flew up into the darkness. "Son, *fair* is beside the point.

You're not resolving a dispute between quarrelling merchants, or deciding which of two peasants has better claim to a calf. This is your future we're talking about."

I turned the empty goblet in my hands, studying its painted pattern of interlocked spirals. I felt that our lives, Antigone – yours and mine – were intertwined in the same way. Turning the cup did not change the pattern; even if I dropped the cup and let it shatter, the shards would still show the linkages.

"And hers," I said quietly. "I care about her, Father. If I set her aside, she'll have nothing. *Really* nothing. I can't do it."

Father sighed. "Well, she's chosen a dangerous path – the Fates may make you a widower anyway." He stood, stretching. "Now, what do you plan to do? I'll tell you right now I'm not going to watch you drown yourself in an amphora. If you have no particular plans, I've got some suggestions."

"What?" I asked dully.

"The high priest of Apollo is growing old. I want you to serve in the temple. I've already spoken to Bromius, and he's agreed."

Become a priest of Apollo? My wits thickened by wine, I considered the possibility sluggishly. I knew little about medicine, but I supposed I could learn. And while I didn't have a good singing voice or great skill at the lyre, I enjoyed music. I felt fairly sure I could manage to lead prayers and sacrifices. Serving in Apollo's temple might not be so bad. At least Father wasn't asking me to take over as Master of the Herds, or to become a captain in the army.

Father was walking a slow circle around the hearth, still speaking. "I'd expect you to eventually become the chief priest, Haemon. It will be a prestigious and powerful position. Especially once we have a new Tiresias."

I nodded. When the mantle of the Tiresias passed to a younger and healthier seer, that person would no doubt resume the Tiresias' traditional wandering across Hellas. Then the chief priest of Apollo would once more be the city's senior religious official.

"There are disadvantages, of course," he continued. "Apollo's priests can never take part in the orgies of Dionysus."

"That's all right," I said, too quickly.

Father peered at me with narrowed eyes, then briskly changed the subject. "That's not all. I need you to be my eyes and ears."

"At the Temple of Apollo?" I asked.

"Oh, you may learn some useful things from the petitioners. But that's not what I meant." He came to sit again on the stool beside me. "I have my sources throughout the city, but now *your* generation is reaching manhood, and I can't cultivate them as someone their own age can. Your cousins the princes, your brothers, Alkides, the sons of the Spartoi – you see them in different circumstances than I. They'll reveal to you strengths and weaknesses I might not perceive; they'll speak with you more candidly about their hopes, their plans. Observe them, all of them, and tell me what you think. I value your judgment, Haemon."

I blinked, surprised by his confidence in me. "Thank you, Father."

"This will be a difficult time, Son." He sighed. "Many times, I told Oedipus and Jocasta they should name one of the twins heir to Thebes, and the other to Korinth – but they never did it. The gods alone know why. Now we'll bear the burden of that failing, too. With the throne of Korinth occupied, we have one prince too many."

I had already thought this, of course, but when Father put the observation into words a chill ran down my back. Suddenly sober, I placed my wine cup on a table and promised him my obedience and loyalty.

The next morning I told Menoeceus that he and Alkides should take charge of that day's disbursements to the peasants, then tied on my sandals and left the palace. It was early; merchants were just putting up their awnings and setting out their wares in the agora. My route took me through the city's eastern quarter, the area ravaged by fire less than a month before. Still the smell of smoke lingered. Workmen were arriving to continue clearing away the charred rubble of homes, workshops, and storerooms; another month would pass before the quarter was ready for building again. Some areas were leveled to the ground; in other places charred stones and the remnants of wooden columns jutted upwards like the ribs of a corpse only half-consumed by its funeral pyre.

So much had been lost. But thanks to the Korinthian alliance – and the desire of that city's new king to maintain trade ties with Thebes, after taking the throne we'd expected a son of Oedipus to inherit – at least we could feed our citizens this winter.

I passed through the Astykratia Gate, greeting the guards on duty, and headed down the slope and across the stream of Chrysorrhoas. I could see the white walls of Apollo's temple on the top of the next hill, gleaming in the bright morning sunlight. As I worked my way up the slope, my stomach growled; I wished I had stopped for breakfast. Perhaps the priests and acolytes would share their morning meal with me, since I was to become one of their number.

A young boy was sweeping the broad marble-tiled forecourt; he watched me wordlessly as I passed the outer altar where burnt offerings were made. I ascended the stairs and passed into the temple, lit by the rays of the morning sun. There I found old Bromius, tending the flame that burned on the small inner hearth before the wooden image of the god. He lifted his head slowly, as though its weight was a burden to him. His face always reminded me of a pomegranate – round, red, and lumpy. I tried not to smile.

"The regent said you'd come," said the old man. He placed a few neatly trimmed twigs onto the flames, then dusted his gnarled hands against each other. I detected a pungent smell and guessed that the twigs might be some special type of wood – not a terribly fragrant one. Bromius continued, "Even the Tiresias seems to think this is a good idea. Well, I suppose I could use the help. Talk to Udaeus here about robes."

I was surprised to learn that the Tiresias had taken an interest in my serving Apollo – but before I could ask about this the old priest turned his back and shuffled away.

"Welcome, Haemon." A man about five years older than I with a remarkably large nose, Udaeus emerged from the shadows. I knew him slightly, as did all the members of the Spartoi, but given the difference in our ages that was the extent of our relationship. He eyed me with some suspicion; as the regent's son I outranked him, and could thwart his plans to rise in the temple. But as he showed me around his manner warmed, and I could see that he was a good-humored fellow. He showed me where the robes and incense and temple treasures were kept, then took me around to the areas that were outside the temple proper but were still considered part of the sanctuary. One was a section for guests and travelers, and another area was for those who were sick or injured. We spent more time in the latter, where Udaeus spoke of his training in the healing arts.

When the tour was over I asked him about food. He grinned and led me around back to the temple storeroom. I took an apple from a bowl sitting on a shelf, and Udaeus helped himself to a handful of dried figs from a storage-jar.

"First lesson you'll learn," he said, chewing, "is to eat when Bromius isn't around."

I bit into the tart apple. "Why? Does the high priest have to eat alone?"

Udaeus laughed. "It's not a ritual, if that's what you mean. It's just that he stinks so bad."

"I *did* notice an odd odor earlier."

"Oh, you'll notice it alright." Udaeus popped another fig into his mouth. "I swear he never bathes. And he won't have more than two sets of robes; says it's a waste of temple resources."

I considered as I wiped juice from my chin. "I could ask my father to make a special donation to the temple. It makes sense, if I'm to serve here. And if the regent offers several sets of robes, Bromius can't turn them down, can he?"

"I like the way you think, Haemon!" He gave me a nudge with his elbow. "The trick'll be getting the old fart to wear them. But anyway, I'm glad you're here. Be nice to have someone to talk to!"

I soon learned that in addition to his unpleasant smell, the high priest was growing hard of hearing, especially in his left ear. Sometimes I repeated myself more than once before realizing I was standing on his bad side. But that also had advantages; he didn't notice muttered conversation between Udaeus and me, and he was less likely to detect a slip of the tongue during a ritual and make me start again from the beginning.

The greatest frustration was that Bromius was a poor healer; he insisted on doing things the way his grandfather had done, and refused any innovation. The midwife Rhodia was extremely skilled with herbs, but Bromius insisted that "women's lore" had no place in the Temple of Apollo – even though the Shrine of Artemis was not far off and Artemis is Apollo's twin sister. Udaeus, who was very interested in medicine, confided to me that he often asked Rhodia's advice on challenging cases.

Udaeus taught me how to welcome petitioners, and how to assist those who came to sleep in the temple seeking the god's advice in a dream; I led animals to the sacrifice, held the entrails in a silver bowl for Bromius to examine, and helped Udaeus butcher the carcasses and offer the thigh-bones and fat on the god's altar. I studied salves and poultices to treat various maladies, and paid close attention when Udaeus showed me the secret store of healing herbs he'd obtained from the midwife.

Most difficult for me was remembering each detail of the longer rituals. If I mumbled along with Udaeus in approximately the right rhythm, Bromius didn't notice; but sometimes he made me say the prayers by myself, and he *did* notice when I found myself at a complete loss for words.

"Listen here, Haemon," the old man snapped one afternoon, "your forgetfulness dishonors the god!"

"I'm sorry," I said, taking a step back away from him, for his stink made me light-headed. I rubbed my nose, drawing a deeper breath under the slight protection my hand offered – we'd had no luck getting him to wear the new robes Father sent; Bromius insisted those be saved for special ceremonies. I looked up at the painted face of the god. *Apollo,* I thought, *doesn't his reek offend you? Can't you send a dream to tell him this?* But the god didn't answer me.

After a moment I said to Bromius: "To be sure we get the words right, why not write them down? At the palace, we always record how many calves the herdsmen bring in, how much produce the farmers—"

"Write them down!" Bromius sputtered. "Turn the holy words of Apollo into marks in wax? Or *clay?*"

"The god accepts terracotta offerings," I said, gesturing at the little votive statues brought by various petitioners. "Why would he object?"

"Prayers are holy!" hissed the high priest, slapping the side of the altar with his hand. "Sacred! Mysterious! They are the secret language we priests use to command the attention of the gods! If we wrote them down, they could be uttered by any common scribe!"

And then priests would lose their power, I realized, bowing my head to hide my expression. Bromius' hearing might be failing, but his eyes remained keen. "Forgive me."

"What? Speak up, young man! How many times do I have to tell you to stop mumbling?"

"Forgive me, Bromius," I repeated loudly. "I still have much to learn."

"You surely do," he snapped. "Now come back over here – no, stand right here, next to me! Repeat from the beginning: Apollo Phoebus, bringer of light…"

So close to him, the odor of his body made my eyes water, but I had to go through the entire prayer three times before he was satisfied. Only then could I escape to the woods behind the temple. Grateful for the fresh air, I snapped off a pine twig and stripped it bare, crushing the foliage between my fingers and breathing in the fresh green scent.

"He's especially ripe today," said Udaeus, walking over with a waterskin. "The women take his laundry tomorrow; it'll be a little better for a few days."

I rubbed my forehead and took a swallow of water. "How do you manage?"

"I burn a lot of incense," Udaeus said with a laugh. "Bromius doesn't like it; since he gets a share of the offerings he wants people to bring other gifts. But when he's not listening I always tell people the god favors incense above all. Especially strong-smelling resins like myrrh."

I remembered this the next day, when a worshipper brought sandalwood. After the man had left Bromius grumbled, "Why do they bring so much incense? You'd think Apollo was the god of smoke, instead of light!" He squinted at me. "We need better offerings. Tell your father the regent we don't need incense and robes – what we need is to refurbish the temple." The old priest gripped my upper arm with one hand, pointing with the other. "See? Look how faded the god's face has become. It's all that incense smoke, I tell you! His image needs repainting. And look up there, see that spot of light between the tiles? The roof needs replacing. With any hard rain we get water dripping down this wall – look how the fresco's being ruined. It's a scandal!"

I carried Bromius' requests back to my father; he agreed to repair the roof, but not to replace it, and he refused to commission an artist. He said that with the losses we'd suffered in the fire, Thebes had more pressing needs.

This did not satisfy Bromius. The priest insisted that keeping Apollo happy was the only way to ensure the city's prosperity. Shortly before the winter solstice, just after I was initiated into the priesthood, I thought I might have better luck with Father. He seemed pleased that his plans for me were advancing; so I thought I might sway him.

We were in his study; wax tablets were stacked in neat piles on his work table. After I posed my questions he closed the tablet he'd been looking at with a snap, and dismissed the scribe and servants. "Haemon, I'm proud of you. And I'm glad to see you taking your new duties so seriously. But you're missing the point."

"The fresco really *is* in poor condition, Father. And the god's image—"

"I'll have both repainted *after* you become Apollo's chief priest. At which time we will also replace the roof, and touch up the gilding on the columns. Perhaps some other improvements as well."

"When I'm chief priest? But – but who knows when that will happen, Father? Or even *if* it will happen?"

"Of course it will, Son. And the sooner Apollo wants his temple beautified, the sooner he'll make you chief priest."

I frowned at him. "Is that wise, Father, to bargain with the god?"

Father rose and dipped a cup in a krater of well watered wine. "Haemon, we bargain with the gods all the time! Every sacrifice at every temple is a business transaction. We give the gods what *they* want, and we ask for what *we* want."

Mulling this over, I sat on the couch by the window. Yes, nearly everyone who came to the temple with an offering requested something from Apollo: healing an illness or an injury, advice in a dream, increased musical skill – but still Father's attitude seemed impious. Finally I ventured: "Isn't it rude to make the god wait?"

"Apollo can wait a little while," he said, going back to his seat. "After all, he's immortal. It's *Bromius* who doesn't like it."

I doubted that Apollo would be pleased by my father's attitude, yet he had a point.

"The old man will need to retire soon. And by then you'll know exactly what should be done to improve the temple." He glanced up at me from beneath his shaggy brows. "Haemon, I'm glad to see how you've taken to your role. It's given you purpose."

"I suppose," I said. There had been no news of you or Uncle Oedipus for months, but my days at the temple gave me the chance to pray for you often, to ask Apollo to protect you and to guide you.

"Good," he said, nodding. "Now, on another subject – a large boar has been spotted southwest of the city. The princes are taking a hunting party after it tomorrow morning – they want to eat boar at the Kronion festival – and I want you to join them."

"*Me*?" Boars make dangerous quarry, and I was a wretched hunter.

Father grinned. "I'm not expecting that *you* take it down, Haemon. Just go along with the boys. Keep your eyes and ears open." He picked up his wax tablet. "I've already sent a messenger to Apollo's temple with word that you've other business tomorrow."

It was a small and inexperienced group that met outside the palace stables the next morning: the twins, Alkides, Menoeceus and me. Besides the half-dozen servants who were setting out sturdy boar-spears and preparing the dogs, the only seasoned hunter to join us was Father's friend Demochares.

Alkides and Polynikes were sharing a laugh, their breath making little white clouds in the chill morning air. Eteokles was tossing a stick for the liveliest of the boar-hounds, Blackfoot, while my brother Menoeceus – already a skilled archer – inspected his arrows.

I approached Demochares. "Who else is coming?"

"No one," he said. "It's not the party I'd have picked, but my lord princes insisted." Turning from me, he shouted to everyone to gather their weapons and supplies and make ready to go. We all had water-skins and pouches of food for the trek; each of us wore a short sword and carried a stout ash-wood spear. Menoeceus had a bow and quiver at his belt, and Alkides carried a heavy olivewood club. The servants had bundles of extra boar-spears strapped to their backs as well as additional food, water, and wine.

We headed down towards the Ogygia Gate. The dogs trotted ahead, then circled back, yipping to hurry us along. We passed the fountain of Dirke, where women were filling their water-jars, and continued southwest towards Mount Kithairon. It was a long walk; the north wind on the back of my neck made me shiver, and clouds blocked the sun. My hands and legs were soon thoroughly chilled – along with every other part of me that wasn't covered and several parts that were. Menoeceus, aware that I suffered dizzy spells, walked beside me most of the time but the one good thing about cold is that it keeps my lightheadedness at bay. We all kept a few paces away from Alkides, who was swinging his club around dangerously.

"Just wait till we bring the boar's carcass back to Thebes," said Eteokles. "I don't care whether we've had our manhood ceremony yet – no one will be able to doubt we're men, after that."

"Ready for the throne of Kadmos," his brother agreed, rubbing his hands together.

I looked ahead at the pair of servants leading the way; they were men in their thirties, but their presence would not diminish the twins' accomplishments. And Demochares, as our old instructor, was no rival.

Polynikes asked, "So, what's it like serving in the Temple of Apollo?"

I described Bromius' stink, which made everyone laugh. Then I told about working with Udaeus, and what I was learning about the arts of healing.

"Do you feel closer to the god?" Eteokles asked.

I pondered this for a moment, not sure how to answer. To cover my silence I kicked a large pebble on the roadway and promptly regretted it: pain jolted through my cold toes. Blackfoot barked and went chasing after the pebble, looking disappointed when it rolled to a stop.

Finally I said, "I'm no better with the lyre than I ever was - and Menoeceus is a far better archer. And though I'm learning about medicine, I don't have the knack for it like Udaeus."

"Maybe Apollo will give you the gift of prophecy," suggested Menoeceus.

I shook my head. "No sign of that! But I've become comfortable there. I suppose, serving Apollo so much, I *do* feel closer to him."

Close by my right side, Eteokles said: "You'll make an excellent chief priest."

"Much better than smelly old Bromius," added Polynikes.

Ahead of us the servants stopped by the side of the road; they were the ones who had sighted the boar yesterday; we had reached the turn-off. The dogs all bounded ahead; one of the men snapped a command, and the dogs stilled themselves, their noses twitching expectantly.

"All right," declared Demochares, his voice booming across the empty roadway. "Have a drink and a bite to eat, piss now if you need to. Once we turn off, we're in the boar's territory."

"All Thebes is *our* territory," grumbled Eteokles, but he followed the old hunter's advice.

As we fortified ourselves with mouthfuls of dried beef and swigs of watered wine, the trackers described what they'd seen. "It's up over there," said the shorter of the two, a curly-haired fellow. He waved his arm southward. "We spotted it in an oak grove, stuffing itself on acorns."

"A big one, my lords," his sunburned companion emphasized.

"Good!" declared Polynikes. "The bigger the better!"

After we emptied our bladders, the curly-headed tracker led us into the woods. "I'll go first," said Polynikes, pushing in front of his brother and Alkides. "Haemon, you come after me."

I was flattered by this; as a rule, neither prince sought my company. But I simply nodded and fell in behind him; now that we were tracking the beast in earnest, it was no time for conversation. The dog Blackfoot, all playfulness gone, came to Polynikes' heel; as we hunters walked in single file, the dogs wove their way in among us, moving as silently as shadows.

Polynikes was considerate, holding branches so that they did not whip back to slap me in the face. Scrambling upward through the brush was difficult; if there was a path, I never noticed.

"Balls!" cursed Alkides behind me. I glanced back to see him wiping a bloody cheek against his right shoulder; a thorn had raked across his face.

"Quiet," Demochares hissed from the back of our column.

The lead man halted, holding up a hand. Blackfoot and one of his companions, a sand-colored beast with powerful haunches, grew still and their ears pricked up. Both emitted low growls, but remembered their training and did not rush forward. All of us – men, boys, and dogs – gathered and waited silently until Demochares reached us. He motioned the lead tracker ahead.

The curly-haired man moved almost noiselessly into the brush and returned moments later. "My lords," he whispered, "it's in a clearing just beyond these oak trees."

All of us – even Alkides and the princes – looked to Demochares for instruction.

"We'll break up into three teams," Demochares said. I was, as always, amazed that a man whose voice was famous for its loudness could speak so softly when he chose. "You, lord Haemon, go with Alkides to the left – and you, my lord princes, go to the right. I'll come from below with Menoeceus. When I give the signal, the dogs will rush in to harry the beast." Then, as if unable to stop advising us, he added: "There's no beast more dangerous than a wounded boar – the lion is no fiercer. That creature is stronger than any of us – even you, Alkides. Brace your spears well, or it will wrench them from your hands."

"We'll do as you say," one of the princes reassured him. He and his twin nodded solemnly, their blue eyes hard and serious.

"Best you do, my lords," said Demochares. He signaled to the servants; the two trackers slipped off to opposite sides, each accompanied by another man. Two heavily laden servants lowered their packs quietly, then unbundled the extra spears so that they could be retrieved if needed. This done, they grasped their own weapons, edging slowly forward.

"Come along, Haemon," Alkides whispered. I followed him to the left, two of the dogs slinking beside us.

We came to a large, sloping boulder. It was awkward to climb; I used the butt of my spear like a walking stick, but Alkides – the powerful muscles of his thighs and calves bulging – simply crouched low and crept forward with a weapon in each hand.

"There he is," Alkides breathed.

The beast was grayish brown, the color of the dead leaves below its feet. Its head was huge; sharp white tusks, each longer than my hand, curved dangerously on either side of its ugly face. It seemed aware of us – or of something: it stopped snuffling for the acorns and lifted its snout. Its nostrils quivered as it looked suspiciously from side to side. Then it started moving towards the edge of the clearing.

"Ouranos' balls, Demochares, hurry!" whispered Alkides. "We'll never catch him in the brush!"

I realized that Demochares and Menoeceus were approaching from that direction. Would the animal charge them?

Demochares whistled, and the dogs bounded forward, barking madly. They closed on the beast, coming from several directions at once. An arrow flew up the slope to strike the beast in the shoulder. The boar bellowed with pain, much louder than I expected. Furious, it charged after one dog and then another, but the well-trained hounds darted easily out of the way. One of the dogs leapt at it, fastening sharp teeth in the boar's tender muzzle; it roared and shook the hound off, droplets of blood flying through the chill air. The dog landed with a thump, whimpering; its fellows charged, leading the beast away from their injured companion and thwarting the boar from escaping into the forest underbrush. They were wearing it down, making things easier for the next attack – *our* attack.

Then I heard Demochares' full-throated yell: "Hunters, go!"

My heart pounding, fighting faintness, I rushed after Alkides, gripping my spear in both hands and trying not to think of stories I had heard: men whose spears were wrenched away and then splintered against a stone, men who were gored and then trampled—

Alkides threw his spear; it missed.

I gripped the ash-wood shaft of my own weapon, determined not to throw and leave myself disarmed, though fearing that if I managed to get my spear-point into the beast it would toss me aside as easily as it had the hound. Just then the boar swung around and charged the twins. One prince had his spear ready for the throw – but then he stumbled and fell. The other prince launched his spear and, like Alkides, missed the mark.

The boar barreled forward, tusks down, whipping its head from side to side. The prince on the ground yelled hoarsely and rolled away, desperately trying to pull his sword. I saw white around the blue irises of his eyes, saw the death that he himself saw in the boar's bloodied tusks.

"Get up!" Demochares shouted. "Get up and run!"

I did not know which prince was on the ground, but I saw the bright crimson blood sheeting over his arm and covering one of the boar's ivory tusks. If I did nothing he would die. I had to help.

Yelling, I ran forward; the angry beast turned, and I felt dizzy as it fixed its black and beady gaze upon me.

Then a pair of dogs rushed in, teeth bared, and Menoeceus darted around to the right. The boar stopped, looking from the dogs to Menoeceus, then back to me.

"Come at me, you stinking turd!" roared Alkides, waving his club two-handed overhead. "Try it! Just try it!"

The boar turned to face him; Alkides swung his club this way and that. Demochares cast his spear; it caught the beast in the hindquarters. The boar looked back at him, bellowing in rage; and in this moment – amazingly – Alkides rushed in and dealt the beast a mighty two-handed clout to the head with his club.

The animal staggered; its forelegs crumpling.

I ran forward, holding my spear low as I had been taught; my point caught the boar in the ribs just as Menoeceus' arrow pierced its haunch, and one of the princes buried his spear in the animal's hairy neck, releasing a stream of blood that steamed in the chill air. Beside me Alkides shouted – we all moved back to give him room – and he brought down his heavy club once more. I heard the boar's skull crack and splinter; it trembled and was still.

Relieved but gasping for breath I dropped dizzily to the ground. Apollo did not want me to hunt, I decided; the next time Father suggested anything like this I would explain I could not. Above me I saw Menoeceus undamaged and whole. He held his bow skyward, laughing. "By the gods!" he cried. "By all the gods, we did it!"

"We did it!" Alkides agreed with a grin, leaning on his club with a self-satisfied air.

"I knew we would," said the uninjured prince. With my head clearing, I could see that this was Polynikes. "Tonight we eat roast boar!"

Prince Eteokles scrambled up from the mud, blood still dripping from his injured arm as he came to face his brother. "You tripped me!" he hissed, fury contorting his handsome features. "You wanted that thing to kill me!"

Polynikes' eyes went wide. "What? I – that's ridiculous! You must have tripped over your own clumsy feet!"

"Not a chance! You deliberately tripped me!"

"Don't be stupid," snapped Polynikes. "Of course I didn't!"

His kilt and cloak muddied, his arm bleeding, Eteokles looked at each of us in turn. "You're all witnesses! What did you see? I demand the truth!"

Gray-haired Demochares took a step forward. "My lords," he interposed, "in the hunt, accidents happen. The important thing is we have taken down our quarry." He motioned to me. "Here, my lord Haemon, help me tend Prince Eteokles' wound."

A servant came forward with a wineskin and a strip of linen; I washed the dirt from the prince's torn flesh and bound a bandage over the wound. Gritting his teeth, Eteokles bore the pain, and when I was done he said: "As your future king, I demand the truth. Each man here must tell me what he saw – and you, Haemon, will administer a holy oath."

Alkides walked over. "Is this really necessary?" he asked, his voice cajoling. "You two bumped into each other, and you fell; that's all!"

"Go ahead, Eteokles," said Polynikes angrily, "*I* know I didn't trip you."

Eteokles waved his uninjured arm at the dead beast. "Haemon, use the boar's blood to solemnize the oath."

Demochares beckoned the servants forward to deal with the carcass. They drew their knives and slit open its belly; scooping out the entrails, they cut them to pieces and threw them to the dogs. I dug into my pack of provisions; there was a little leather bag of raisins. I dumped out the raisins and collected blood from the slain boar in the bag. It was clumsy and inelegant, but I had enough for my purpose.

I'd only been a junior priest of Apollo for a short while, and had never administered an oath of truth before; but I had witnessed the ceremony often enough. "Zeus son of Kronos, lord of Heaven and Earth, master of oaths: hear me, Haemon, son of Creon." I dipped my fingertips into the small bag of blood and sprinkled a few red drops on the ground. "May this blood burn any who breaks his oath." Then I reached up and smeared a streak of red on Polynikes' forehead. "Prince Polynikes, do you swear in the name of Zeus to tell the truth?"

Polynikes' face was white and angry in the cold winter sunlight. "I swear in the name of mighty Zeus, Lord of Heaven and Earth: I did not deliberately cause my brother to fall."

Eteokles' jaw tightened, and his blue eyes flashed. He also swore in the name of Zeus. "I felt my brother trip me and send me into the boar's path. I'm not a fool; I know what's an accident and what's not."

"Obviously you don't," countered Polynikes.

"What do the rest of you say?" demanded Eteokles, turning first to

Alkides.

"There's no point in my swearing," Alkides said. "I was watching the boar, not you."

"Swear anyway!" insisted the injured prince.

"Very well," said Alkides. I stepped over and reached up to touch his forehead with my blood-smeared thumb; he swore in the name of Zeus. "I was looking at the boar," he repeated. "If Polynikes tripped his brother, I didn't see it."

Eteokles frowned. Cradling his bandaged arm, he turned to Demochares and Menoeceus.

Demochares took the oath and then said: "The princes were rushing in too close together. They should have been more careful. That's all that I saw."

After I daubed Menoeceus' forehead, he looked from one prince to the other and then shook his head. "By Zeus, I'm not sure. It's possible, but I can't say for sure."

Eteokles' expression became grim. "You see? It *is* possible."

"Possible doesn't make it true!" countered Polynikes, reddening. He flashed a look of fury at my younger brother.

"Haemon, it's your turn," Eteokles said. "*You* swear, and give a statement."

I hesitated. I felt the gaze of both princes; to confirm one was to deny the other. Each person here would bear witness to whatever I said: my brother, Alkides, Demochares, and the servants who would carry this story back into Thebes just as they carried the carcass of the boar.

I dipped my thumb into the blood and anointed my own forehead. I vowed in the name of Zeus to tell the truth. And then I said: "My lord princes, I saw you running near one another. I saw Prince Eteokles fall, but I did not see the cause. All I can say is that I am relieved there are no grave injuries and that our hunt was successful."

At these words, Polynikes looked smug, Eteokles furious; everyone else seemed relieved.

"There, my lords," said Demochares, "it's done. Now let's head back into Thebes. "We'll lose the light before long, and my old bones want to rest by a warm hearth."

The servants busied themselves with the boar's carcass; normally two spears would be enough to take the quarry's weight but because this one was so big they lashed together two sets of three spears each to form the carrying-poles, and bound the animal's hooves together over these. The servants must have been even more relieved than I that the way back to the road was downhill. Eteokles, disgusted with all of us, struck out ahead of the two trackers and I soon lost sight of him in the brush.

"I didn't trip him," Polynikes repeated. "How could he even think such a thing? Unless it was something he'd do himself, given the chance."

Demochares frowned. "My lord prince, your brother's frustrated that he lost his shot and fell in the mud. And with the wound to his arm, he's in pain. There's no need to seek darker motives."

Flushing at this rebuke, Polynikes nodded tightly. "Of course, Demochares."

Changing the subject, Menoeceus turned to Alkides. "I still can't believe how you took that beast down!"

"Yes," I agreed, eager to shift the mood. "You're as powerful as a demigod with that club!" As we headed back down the steep hill, conversation centered on Alkides' strength and hunting prowess. When we reached the road, where Eteokles waited, we started back towards the city. Eteokles' temper had cooled and he joined in praising Alkides.

"You saved my life," he told Alkides.

"An amazing blow," Polynikes agreed. "Knocked it right to its knees!"

"It *was* impressive, wasn't it?" Alkides said, wiping the blood from his club on the boar's shaggy pelt.

Eteokles said, "You should take the boar's tusks." I was relieved that Polynikes did not object.

"Thank you, my lord prince," Alkides said, then began talking of other beasts he wanted to hunt. "A lion skin – now *that* would be a trophy."

"There's an old one in the treasury room," ventured my brother Menoeceus.

"Yes," said Demochares, "it belonged to the Sphinx."

Alkides tossed his club with one hand and caught it with the other. "I want to slay one myself."

"I admire that about you," said Eteokles. "You want to earn your own glory, instead of stealing it from others."

Polynikes bristled at this, but said nothing.

A gust of wind blew a few cold drops on our faces. "Let's hurry," Demochares said, "my feet are turning to ice."

As we continued, Alkides still talking about fabulous beasts he wanted to slay, I pulled my cloak closer – and studied both princes surreptitiously. *Had* Eteokles' fall been an accident? Given the confusion of the hunt, the rest of us couldn't tell what happened – but one of the twins had to be lying. And if so, why wasn't someone's skin burning beneath the smear of boar's blood? Had I performed the ritual incorrectly? I might be as incompetent a priest as I was a hunter. Yet the Tiresias himself had said that my serving in the Temple of Apollo was appropriate.

"A huge python guarded the Oracle at Delphi," said Menoeceus, "until Apollo killed it. Maybe you could find a monster like that, Alkides."

"There must be others," Alkides agreed. "Like the serpent that used to live here, watching over Dirke's fountain." He pointed ahead to the spring, where a few peasant girls were filling up plain terracotta jugs.

The bearers put down their burden in order to get a drink of water; while everyone was gathered around the stream, I saw Polynikes dip the edge of his cloak in the flowing water and then scrub his forehead with the wet, cold cloth.

Eteokles noticed this as well. "Is it burning you, Brother?" he asked, his eyes narrowing.

"Not at all," his twin answered. "And, had I lied – which I did *not* – surely Zeus would have burned me up by now." He glanced at the girls with their water jars, who were listening with puzzled expressions. "But the matter's settled. We should all wash our faces. Why give people a reason to ask questions? The whole point of our hunt was to demonstrate our abilities to the people of Thebes; we don't want to distract from that."

Alkides agreed and splashed his face with water from the spring; Demochares, explaining to Eteokles that the incident was best forgotten, wiped his forehead as well. I did likewise; Menoeceus hesitated a moment but then washed his face too. That left only Eteokles with a smear of dried blood between his coppery eyebrows.

"Are you going to clean up, or not?" asked Polynikes. "Make your decision; the rest of us are cold."

Eteokles finally wiped his forehead. He said little as we went through the gate and climbed the hill in the fading light of late afternoon. The others were laughing and boasting, which made his anger less obvious. Making our way through the cobbled streets with the boar's immense carcass, we soon drew a crowd; people shouted praise to the princes, and Alkides held up his club with one thick-muscled arm.

Word of our return reached the palace before we did; Father was waiting for us at the top of the grand staircase. He smiled and welcomed back the princes, adding his congratulations to those of the cheering crowd. The boar was sent to the kitchens for butchering, and we hunters headed for the megaron, where a fire blazed in the central hearth. The room was decorated for the winter solstice festival to be held the next day: evergreen boughs framed the doorways and garlands of pine and bright red berries graced the tables. All the lamps and torches were lit, and we were accompanied into the room by a boisterous crowd of well-born youths and maidens. It was as though the Kronion festival had started early.

Glad to be out of the wind, I accepted a cup of hot mulled wine from a servant and eased myself into my usual chair. A servant woman brought over a foot-basin and removed my muddy sandals; I eased my feet into the warm water. Alkides took a seat nearby, and my sister Megara came to sit beside him, encouraging him to tell and retell how he killed the boar. Other maidens clustered round, exclaiming over his strength and squealing as they pointed to the blood-stains on his olivewood club; but Megara was by far the prettiest, and she commanded his attention.

Each member of the hunting party was given a skewer of roast boar-meat, but Father announced that everyone else had to wait: the rest would be saved for the Kronion feast. Instead the servants dished out a hearty lentil stew, and hot barley-cakes that we dipped in olive oil. To my surprise, Alkides excused himself early: asking the princes their leave, he explained that he had to go home to his sick mother and clean up for the celebration the next day.

Shortly after that Megara attempted to depart, but Mother caught her wrist. "Where do you think you're going, young lady?"

"Mother!" Megara wrenched her hand free. "I'm tired, that's all!"

Mother frowned. "You look lively enough to me."

"I want to rest before tomorrow's festival."

"No, you want to meet Alkides in secret."

"Mother!" gasped Megara, reddening.

"You're staying right here."

She continued to protest, but Mother wouldn't let her leave. Megara kept glancing toward the door, shifting restlessly in her seat. When Mother took our younger brothers and sisters off to bed, she told me to keep an eye on Megara.

As soon as Mother had gone, Megara turned her large dark eyes on me. "Haemon, I'm tired," she said, and gave a wide yawn. "Please, let me turn in for the night."

"Are you planning to meet Alkides?"

"No, of course not!"

It seemed to be a day of lies. "Then why's it so urgent? If Mother wants you to stay, stay. Go say something nice to Eteokles and Polynikes. I don't think you congratulated them at all, and this was *their* hunt."

Her arching brows drew together. "But—"

"You *are* planning to meet him," I said flatly.

"What if I am?" She flopped back in her chair, sighing. "Father has something against him. Mother just does whatever he wants – she always has."

I looked over at Father, who was inspecting Eteokles' injured arm. "Maybe because he thinks Alkides will take liberties with his daughter," I said.

"He's the best young man in Thebes! Father's just jealous because *he* was never much of a hunter."

I sipped my wine and pondered Megara's theory. Could that be the reason? No, Father's closest friend was Demochares, the best hunter of their generation.

"Haemon, let me go," she urged. "Alkides will wonder where I am!"

"You just pointed out that he enjoys the hunt. If Alkides catches you too easily, he'll lose interest."

Her mouth dropped open, as if she was appalled that I could suggest any male's losing interest in her; but she made no further attempt to leave. Perhaps my argument reached her after all. When Mother returned, Megara was still sitting beside me – and still did not look especially tired.

Father concluded his conversation with Eteokles, and approached me. Setting a hand on my shoulder, he said, "Let's go to my study, Haemon."

A servant carried a lamp to light our way down the corridor, but Father dismissed the man once he had kindled the brazier in the study. Taking a seat, Father said: "Tell me about today's hunting trip."

I sat beside him. "Alkides—"

"I don't want to hear about Alkides," he interrupted sharply. "There's been enough talk of him tonight! No, tell me about the princes. Demochares said they had an argument." I explained what had happened; Father listened intently. Finally, he asked: "And? *Did* Polynikes trip his brother?"

I looked down into the glowing coals, wishing I had the gift of sight and could read the truth in the patterns of red and orange. "I don't know," I said. "Maybe. But I don't know." I glanced up, seeing the deep shadows beneath Father's eyes, the horizontal furrows in his brow. "What do you think?"

"One of them is lying."

"Probably. But neither of them acted as if their forehead burned."

Father smiled briefly. "Immortal Zeus may take his time punishing the oath-breaker." He asked me more questions, and I found myself relating how both princes had shown me more attention than usual, even showing interest in my duties at the Temple of Apollo.

"Sensible," said Father, nodding slowly. "They both realize that they need to build alliances for the future."

This prompted thoughts of other possible alliances. It seemed to me that arranging a betrothal between Megara and Alkides – which Megara would certainly welcome – could be advantageous. After today's hunt, he was more popular than ever with the people of Thebes.

"May I ask something, Father?"

"Of course!"

"Why do you dislike Alkides?"

He did not answer right away, but tapped his fingers for a while on the table beside him. I sensed he was pleased with me for having the insight to ask, but displeased with the topic. Finally he said, "I knew his father very well. Amphitryon was handsome and popular – but also hotheaded and impulsive. He drank too much, and when he was drunk he had a raging temper. Alkides is much like him."

"But Alkides killed the boar today – he may have saved Eteokles' life!"

"Oh, he's capable, I grant you. People still talk about how he saved that woman during the fire." His dark eyes reflected the glow from the brazier. "He's more popular than the princes!"

That hadn't occurred to me; it was a little alarming. "Do you think he'll try for the throne?"

Father took even longer to reply this time. "I don't know. He's popular, but he's not descended from Kadmos – he's not even from Thebes – so I don't know if the people would accept him. It's true he has royal blood in him, but if he wants to rule a city – and I don't sense that he does – then he should go to Tiryns. On the other hand…"

"On the other hand, what, Father?"

"Everything is possible, my dear boy. But we already know which two will be vying hardest for the throne of Kadmos."

"Polynikes and Eteokles," I said, and a shiver ran down my spine, as I remembered the looks they had given each other during the day. "What will you do, Father?"

"I will try to help them reach an amicable settlement. But I am only Regent, my son. When they reach manhood, it will be up to them. May the gods protect Thebes! Now, Haemon, I thank you for your information. Now go back out and check on Megara – do what you can to keep her away from Alkides."

So I left Father's study and returned to the megaron, to discover that my sister and others were being entertained by a juggler. I sat down beside her, but my gaze soon went to the twins. I wished you were still in Thebes, Antigone, and could mediate between your brothers. And then I missed you on my own account, on that long night. For so many years, you were the one I shared my thoughts with, the one who helped me wrestle with difficult matters. But you were gone.

*

There is more, much more, that Haemon could say; but at least he has made a start.

CHAPTER SIX
ANTIGONE

The sound of Haemon's voice transports Antigone back to her youth. Back then, even though she had not appreciated it, life had been so easy, so innocent!

And yet the seeds of the future were already planted. The truth about her father's parentage; the fact that her twin brothers were destined to compete for a single throne. And her doomed marriage to Haemon. Even if events hadn't compelled her to leave Thebes, she was too plain to summon his desire.

At least he cannot see her now.

"Antigone?" It is Eurydike's voice. "Are you all right?"

She blinks, rubbing her face with chilly fingers. "Yes, I'm still here."

"I thought I put you to sleep," Haemon says.

Antigone smiles slightly. "No, not at all." Sleep would be a temporary escape from her lightless tomb – but if only a few hours remain to her, she would rather spend them talking with these people who care about her than wandering the land of dreams. "I didn't know about the boar hunt."

"Do you still have food and water?" asks her aunt.

Antigone reaches out for the basket of supplies, checking its contents. "There's some left." This is not a lie: *some* can refer to any quantity, large or small. In point of fact, her last crusts of bread will soon be too hard to chew, and the water-skin is more than half empty. But, as she intends, her words reassure her listeners, and Haemon resumes his recollections of Polynikes and Eteokles.

"Until that boar hunt, they were always friends and allies," Haemon says. "But I suppose it was inevitable, with two heirs to a single throne."

"Yes." Antigone sighs. "Fate is fate. An acorn sprouts an oak; you can't make it grow into a pine tree."

"You can't change its nature, perhaps, but you can pluck out the shoot before it grows tall," says Haemon, "the way a farmer pulls weeds from his field."

"That sounds like something your father would say," Antigone retorts. "I suppose he thinks Mother and Father should have weeded out one of the twins when they were born."

"Antigone!" exclaims her aunt. "You mustn't say such a thing." And yet Eurydike's tone of voice confirms Antigone's suspicion that her uncle *did* make such a suggestion, long ago.

"Father does what he thinks he must," Haemon says defensively. "For the good of Thebes."

"Uncle Creon thinks, as my father once did, that it's possible to escape the plans of the gods. Father did everything he could to escape his fate – and that's exactly what brought it to pass!" She challenges: "Haemon, as high priest of Apollo, you should know we mortals can't change the gods' plans!"

"If the gods never listen to us, why do we sacrifice to them?" he retorts.

They are arguing the way they did as children, and Antigone finds her intellect rising to the task. She is weighing possible responses when Ismene's voice interrupts: "Antigone, where did you and Father go after you left Korinth?"

"You're trying to change the subject," Antigone snaps. "You don't want Haemon and me to quarrel."

"And if I don't – what's wrong with that?"

Nothing, Antigone admits silently, ashamed of herself. Ismene's reluctance to face uncomfortable truths has always irritated her, and her relationship with Haemon is both confusing and painful. But they are here, and she is grateful for that. So close to the end she should not be impatient or petty. Even if *she* is disposed to be argumentative, isn't that wrong of her? Their final memories of her could distress them the rest of their lives.

"Besides," continues Ismene, "I want to know."

Eurydike adds her voice. "Yes, Antigone, tell us what you and your father did when you left Korinth."

Why does she never feel frustration towards her aunt? The sound of Eurydike's gentle voice dissolves her annoyance. "Very well," Antigone says. "Just a moment."

She picks up the water-skin and drinks about half of what remains. It refreshes her, just as the ghosts of the dead are revived by libations.

Antigone smiles in the dark. That *is* her situation, precisely. And so she owes those who have given her this offering to speak.

ANTIGONE

We left Korinth in the early morning, before the sun was fully risen. It was cool and foggy, and the mist helped hide our identity from inquisitive eyes.

Uncle Creon was right to forbid attacking Korinth: the path leading to the citadel was steep, narrow, and long. If Thebes had sent an army, it would have been quickly and thoroughly defeated. But as Father and I descended that morning, I was not thinking about military strategy; my concern was to keep him from slipping on the damp rocks. I held his arm tightly, and he used his walking-stick; still I was afraid that he would stumble and hurt himself.

"Where should we go now, Father?"

It frightened me to have no clear direction. I was used to having a goal, a plan. When I was a girl, my plan had been to marry you, Haemon – to be a good wife to you. Though I failed at that, my next task seemed clear: get Father safely to Korinth. But now we were banished – I had failed again. The future was shrouded in fog, like the path before us. What steep and treacherous drop was in store for me – for us both – if I took the wrong turn?

Father tapped ahead on the path with his stick, taking small, cautious steps. "To the harbor. But not the one we were at yesterday – the other one."

I shifted the traveling-bag on my shoulder, wondering if the bag slung across Father's back was throwing him off balance. If so, there was no help for it – I could not carry everything myself. Scanning the path for loose stones, I asked: "But *then* where?"

"I must be cleansed of my crimes before I die," he said, "or else the gods will punish me for all eternity."

His words chilled me – how lightly he spoke of his own death! But then I saw a shadow in the mists ahead, and focused on my immediate task. "A cart's coming," I said, pulling Father towards the inside edge of the road.

"Yes, I hear it," Father said. "And smell it. Full of fish, I think."

Only then did I detect the briny odor. The path was narrow here, close up against the shoulder of the mountain; Father and I pressed back against the rock face to allow the heavy cart as much room as possible to rumble past.

"I wonder what judgment the gods might render," Father said. "They have Sisyphus forever pushing a boulder uphill – that makes sense, for a king of Korinth. Every time he starts again, he must remember this road."

"But Sisyphus mocked the gods," I objected, leading him down through the fog once more. "He even chained up Hades himself! You've always been a pious man. You never meant to do anything wrong."

"Didn't I?" Father's voice was bitter. "I was given a prophecy in Delphi, but I thought I could avoid it by never returning to Korinth. I thought I could outwit Apollo! That was *my* hubris."

"What else could you do? It isn't fair!" The mist was starting to dissipate; above us the sky showed hints of blue, and I could see further down the road than before. But I felt no more clarity about our future.

"We've no right to call what the gods do fair or unfair. Can an ant judge the actions of a king? The gods are further above us even than that." He shook his blindfolded head. "All I can do now is beg for mercy. Perhaps one of the gods will show compassion. And your – our – mother … she could be suffering as we speak…"

I was resentful that he wanted to help Mother; wasn't she the source of all our problems? But I knew better than to bring that up. "Lady Aphrodite was no help," I said. It seemed to me that since love caused my parents' crime, she – of all the Deathless Ones – should have been most merciful. But, as he said, we mortals have no business judging the divine. "Which god shall we try next?"

Father had already considered the matter. As we continued downhill, he shared his thoughts with me. He held little hope of absolution from Apollo without the influence of some other deity; Apollo had given him the terrible prophecy in the first place.

Traffic was increasing; we encountered more travelers making their way up to the summit. I worried that someone might overhear our conversation, but Father lowered his voice even before I asked him. Leaning on my shoulder, he explained quietly that he wanted to petition Zeus, Lord of Heaven and Earth. As king of the gods, Zeus could command his son Apollo to relent.

"You were a good king to Thebes," I said softly. "Under your reign the city was peaceful and prosperous. Zeus is god of kings, as well as king of the gods; maybe that will help."

"Perhaps," Father agreed. "At any rate, I must go to Zeus first. Otherwise he might take offense – and then no other god would dare help me."

We reached the bottom of the slope, and now the morning fog was entirely gone. Seeing people gathered at a spring, I guided Father in that direction. We waited our turn behind servant women and peasants who were filling their water-jars and the sailors and merchants who came to quench their thirst. Thank all the gods, no one hurled insults or pointed accusing fingers at us; we remained anonymous, just a blind man and his daughter.

A bronze dipper was chained to the stone; I filled it with cold water from the spring and helped Father to drink. I swallowed a few mouthfuls myself, silently offering a prayer to the spring-nymph, and then moved Father away so that others might take their turn.

"Zeus has many temples," I said, taking Father's arm and moving towards the harbor. "Which one should we go to?"

"One of his favorites. Where we're more likely to get his attention."

The crowds were thicker now, but people made way for the blind man, and still no one recognized Father as Korinth's disgraced prince. I had no confidence that this reprieve would last; once the palace servants made their way down to the marketplace, the gossip would catch up with us. I wanted to be gone as soon as possible.

"Where do you suggest?" I asked.

Father fidgeted with his blindfold for a moment, as if he hoped that moving it would allow him to see. Then he sighed and resumed tapping ahead of his steps with his stick. "I think we should try Olympia."

He meant the place where the Olympic Games had been held, every four years, during the reign of King Pelops of Pisa. Though the games stopped after Pelops' sons quarreled with each other, Father said the temples Pelops built in Olympia remained, and were still attended by priests and priestesses. King Pelops was said to have been Zeus' grandson; given his extraordinarily long and successful life, he must have been a favorite of the king of the gods. Father believed that if Zeus listened to petitions anywhere, he would surely hear prayers from Olympia.

As we neared the busy harbor – the one on the other side of the isthmus – I saw ships of all descriptions anchored in the shallows; I stopped a few of the friendlier-looking sailors and asked if they knew of any vessels headed southwest. Eventually I found myself talking to the grizzled captain of a boat much smaller than the one on which Mnesikles brought us to Korinth.

"That's right, young lady," the captain said, squinting at me. "I'm headed out this morning, bound Pylos way."

"Will you continue to Pisa?" I asked.

"I'll stop wherever there's fish to be caught and trades to be made." He scratched his close-cropped beard. "You and your papa here both going?"

"That's right."

He grunted. "Don't usually like to have women aboard – and wouldn't want a blind man bumping into things, either. But I *could* stand to earn a bit extra this trip." He folded his hairy arms across his chest. "I might could give you space to sleep in the hold. What've you got to pay your way?"

Father broke in: "Before we discuss that, Captain, we need to know a bit more about your ship and crew. My daughter may be my eyes, but I know something of the sea."

With my help, Father assessed the vessel. He told me in a whisper meant to be overheard that it seemed seaworthy, if not particularly impressive. With his help I was able to negotiate passage for us with only a ring of amber and silver.

The normal travel time between Korinth and the port nearest Olympia, Father told me, was five or six days; but our captain seemed a lazy sort, and rarely sailed more than half a day at a stretch – often much less. When the fishing was good, we stayed at anchor all day; trading stops at various towns and villages also extended the journey. More than once the sailors bartered their fish for a large amphora of wine; then they drank and sang late into the night, and spent the next day at anchor recovering from their hangovers.

As the coastline slid slowly past, I described the scenes to Father – the steep, rocky cliffs against the bright blue of the water and the skies above; people beating trees with long sticks to harvest the last of the year's olives in hillside groves; the ship's crew casting nets into the sea and hauling up the catch; seagulls circling overhead and dolphins leaping alongside our boat when we were under way. Certainly the sea breeze had a healing effect on Father. I had been using sour wine and Rhodia's herbs to tend the wounds where his eyes had been, and saw no signs of evil humors – and, gradually, he grew better able to manage the small tasks of everyday life.

He could eat and dress and wash himself with little help now, and could tie on his blindfold and hat unassisted. Sometimes when we were at anchor he made the circuit of the ship without me, holding onto the side rail for support.

All in all it was more than half a month until we made port near Olympia, about noon on a cool autumn day. The harbor was a sleepy place, little bigger than that of the villages we had visited. The few carts traveling from the shore towards the city were all full to overflowing, with no room for passengers, so we walked the whole way.

At Father's slow pace, the trip took us the rest of the day. The shadows were growing long when we stopped at the Temple of Hermes so that Father could rest; I placed a stone at the base of the tall pillar in front of the temple – the traditional way of asking a blessing from the god of travelers – and then we continued. By the time we crossed the wooden bridge over the river Alpheios, which separated the twin cities of Pisa and Olympia, Father's ankles were terribly swollen and he leaned heavily on both me and his staff. The sun was setting behind us; it was too late to seek Zeus' advice. We needed a place for the night.

I found us lodging at the Temple of Hestia, where athletes used to stay when they were training. Fittingly for a place dedicated to the hearth-goddess, a large and welcoming fire blazed in its central courtyard. The evening meal was simple: a soup of barley, lentils, onions and salt; some bread and goat's cheese; apples and a very sour wine. Our small room was comfortable enough, with two sturdy cots and woolen blankets that were old but clean. Though we had been on dry land for hours, once I lay down I seemed to feel the swaying of the ocean. Somehow this was restful rather than dizzying, especially with no drunken sailor's songs to disturb me. I slept soundly and without dreams.

The next morning we went to the Temple of Zeus.

"What does it look like, Antigone?" Father asked.

It was the largest of the temples in the sacred district – but, as with many others, the painted colors of its façade were faded and cracked. Behind the temple I made out the long, flattened oval that had once been the chariot track; a set of rotting wooden seats sagged on its southern side. As the story went, King Pelops had won his bride Hippodamia by defeating her father in a chariot race. Now weeds invaded the sandy track; if another generation passed without resuming the games, the marble turning-post in the distance would be all that remained.

Still, Zeus' temple was an imposing structure. Its red marble forecourt – littered with fallen leaves that stirred in the chill morning breeze – was larger than that of Apollo's temple in Thebes. A waist-high marble altar stood at the center of the space. Thunderbolts of polished bronze adorned the closed temple doors, which were flanked on either side by marble columns whose capitals bore traces of gilt.

We approached the altar, its upper surface blackened by the fires of many sacrifices. Father paused, resting a hand on the cold stone, and I guessed he was offering a silent prayer.

Just then the temple doors creaked open; Father's head jerked up. "Who's there?" he whispered to me.

"An acolyte," I said, looking at the stocky young man. He wore an oft-mended robe that might once have been white; now its cloth was the color of dust – except the bottom hem, which bore the kind of ingrained dirt-stains that no amount of rinsing will remove. Yawning as if he had just risen, he began sweeping – and then jumped rather comically when he noticed us at last.

"Can I help you?" he said, making his way down the steps.

Father drew himself to his full height. With dignity he said, "I am here to ask the mercy of Zeus."

The young man nodded. "You'll need to make a sacrifice."

"What offering does the god prefer here?" asked Father.

"A healthy male animal. The bigger the better." He glanced at me; his eyes were large and round, and bulged outward, giving him a perpetually surprised look. "You can get something in the Pisatan agora."

I patted Father's arm. "I'll see to it," I said. I would move quicker without him, and he could spend more time praying to the god.

Leaving him at the temple with our traveling-bags, I took with me only the pouch of jewelry I carried for barter. Thanks to our journey the day before, I knew where to go: back over the wooden bridge into the city of Pisa, then up the slight slope towards the palace where King Augeas now ruled. The agora was a wide, flattened space with room for about twice as many merchants' stalls as were actually there. Of course, with the harvest behind us and the sailing season drawing to a close, this was not the busiest season; but I sensed that it was a long time since the marketplace was filled to capacity. A small boy and his sister ran through it, pelting each other with pinecones.

In Thebes we always offered bulls to Zeus, but none were available in the agora. I traded a silver dress-pin for a powerful-looking black ram, and arranged for the shepherd's boy to help me lead the animal to the temple. While the old shepherd fed the beast a mash of barley and calming herbs, so that it would submit placidly to the knife, I found a stall where a woman was selling garlands of dried flowers twined with colorful ribbons. The shepherd's boy tied the garland to the ram's curving horns for me, and we headed back to the temple.

When we arrived I described the animal to Father, and let him examine it with his hands. "It will have to do," he said after patting the beast's wooly flank. I felt sure that he was remembering the lavish sacrifices he had led as king of Thebes; in comparison a single ram seemed paltry. But those civic offerings – sometimes as many as a dozen bulls – had fed hundreds after the fat and thigh-bones were offered to the god; here in Olympia we had only ourselves and the temple staff, and a handful of locals who had gathered to watch the ceremony and claim a skewer of roast mutton.

The priest, a middle-aged man built like a storage jar, had the same protruding eyes as the acolyte; no doubt they were related. His robe was dark blue, and its borders displayed a gray-and-white zigzag pattern. He licked his fleshy lips as the shepherd's boy led the ram towards the altar. A matronly woman – probably the priest's wife – emerged from behind the temple; she looked at the ram and grinned, then winked at me.

"My uncle likes mutton," whispered the acolyte I had spoken to earlier. A second temple servant, a boy about twelve years old, came forward to help with the animal. I saw that kindling and firewood had been readied on the altar.

Looking cheerful, the priest stepped closer to Father. "Now that your daughter has returned, let us know your concern so I may offer your petition to the god."

Father nodded. He took a deep breath, and began to tell the tale. As the truth emerged, the once friendly acolyte edged away from me, disgust and loathing in his bulging eyes; the priest's face paled and then flushed an angry red. The locals who had come to watch, and the two boys holding the ram's lead rope, stared open-mouthed from Father to me. Standing beside the temple steps, the priest's wife pressed both hands to her mouth.

When the story concluded there was utter silence, broken only by the birds in the nearby bushes.

Finally the priest sputtered: "You – you killed your father... and married your *mother?*"

Father inclined his blindfolded head. "Yes."

"You are Oedipus, and you killed Laius of Thebes?"

"Yes," Father repeated.

"I do *not* believe Zeus will forgive this crime," the priest said, exchanging a nervous glance with the acolyte. "It's – it's abomination! To kill your own father – a good man, a king! – and then compound the crime by bedding the woman who gave you birth—"

"Forgiveness is for the god to decide, is it not?" Father interrupted mildly.

The priest fell silent, frowning.

Father continued, "Will you make the offering and ask him?"

The priest looked at the ram, and all the hungry people; finally he said, "Very well." After a brief consultation with the elder acolyte, they began the preparations. From within the temple the acolyte fetched a knife and a bronze bowl to catch the blood. As the woman tied a bloodstained leather apron over the priest's robe, the senior acolyte went back into the temple. He emerged with a flaming torch and a small silver box; his junior colleague led the ram toward the altar.

The priest chanted a prayer, then took a pinch of meal from the silver container and sprinkled it over the docile animal's head. With a practiced hand he grasped the nearest curving horn and slit the ram's throat.

As far as *I* could tell, the sacrifice was satisfactory. The priest extracted the ram's liver and entrails, which looked healthy; when he threw the fat and bones onto the altar fire, savory-smelling smoke floated straight up towards the sky. The senior acolyte handed the silver box of meal to the younger boy; then he took up the basin containing the ram's blood and organs and carried it into the temple while the priest intoned more prayers. As the ritual progressed without incident, the man grew calmer; his stammering outrage seemed to have been forgotten. He lifted his arms skyward, asking All-Powerful Zeus to make known his will.

Hope grew inside me. Watching the offering-smoke rise toward the blue autumn sky, hearing the priest's voice shape the ritual words, I dared to think that Zeus had heard us – that he would grant Father mercy.

Then a loud boom shook the air, followed by an ominous echoing rumble; Father jumped, and I grabbed his arm to reassure him. The rumble continued for a moment, then died away.

"Thunder!" announced the priest, lowering his bloody hands. "Zeus has heard you, Oedipus –but despite your sacrifice, he will not cleanse you."

Father's face fell; his shoulders drooped. But I was suspicious. "That was like no thunder I've ever heard," I objected, "and there are no clouds in the sky."

The priest stared at me. "Ah – what are you saying?"

His confused reaction fed my suspicions. "I think the sound came from the temple."

"Who are *you,* girl, to question Almighty Zeus?" The priest shook a bloody forefinger at me. "He can summon thunder as he likes! And if he chooses to speak from the temple—"

The rumbling noise sounded again – and this time I was *certain* something was amiss. Letting go of Father's arm, I ran up the temple stairs. Too stunned and too fat to hinder me, the priest shouted, "Stop! What do you think you're you doing?" For good measure, he added: "Blasphemy!"

I glanced around inside, scarcely noticing the image of the god painted on the rear wall; I was not looking for Zeus. Soon I spotted my quarry – there, crouching behind a charred stump of wood that looked as if it had been struck by lightning, was the acolyte. Beside him was a huge wooden bowl, resting on its side. A piece of oiled leather was bound tightly over the mouth of the bowl.

"What are you doing here?" the young man cried, his voice breaking into a squeak. "You're violating the house of Zeus!"

"Am I?" Anger and indignation gave me strength; I shoved him aside, and the wooden bowl rolled forward a handspan, making a now-familiar rumbling sound. This stoked my anger, and I gave the thing a good push; I felt something heavy – rocks, most likely – tumbling inside, striking the taut leather cover to generate the thunder-like rumble. Furious, I struck the leather with my fist, producing the same loud boom we had first heard. "*You* are the blasphemer!"

The acolyte glanced uneasily at the painting of Zeus: muscular and sun-browned, the god held two thunderbolts in each hand. I wanted Zeus to transform the gilt paint into real lightning and strike down these impudent charlatans who called themselves his servants – but nothing happened.

Aiming a last kick at the thunder-bowl, I went back to the threshold. "These men have made the false thunder themselves," I shouted, "as you just heard me do!"

The shepherd's boy and the assembled Pisatans stared wide-eyed; though the junior acolyte flushed bright red, the wife of the priest looked dumbstruck.

"Blasphemers!" cried Father. "It's your duty to appeal Zeus on my behalf – but instead you invent his answer yourselves!"

"Who are you to speak of blasphemy, Oedipus?" sputtered the priest. "You killed your own father! Sired that girl there from your own mother's womb!"

Father hesitated. "Without realizing it," he said humbly. "And I came here without guile, seeking penance."

I hurried to his side, glaring at the priest. "Zeus punishes oath-breakers," I hissed. "What oath did you swear when you became his priest?"

A vein throbbed in the man's forehead. "There's nothing I can do for you. Zeus will forgive you, or he will not; I cannot give absolution. Now take your curse from Olympia's soil."

Father was not inclined to obey the charlatan priest; he wanted to visit Olympia's other temples. But word of who we were traveled much more quickly than Father's limping pace. The priests and priestesses all refused to speak with us.

The sun was setting as we were turned away from the Temple of Rhea, and the chill wind was growing stronger. I pulled my cloak tighter around my shoulders and then adjusted Father's. "We should return to the Temple of Hestia."

Father sighed. "I hope they don't refuse us too."

That was my fear as well, but fortunately we were permitted to enter. The priestess who had welcomed us warmly the night before kept her distance from us as though we were lepers, saying only, "My mistress Hestia suffers you to stay another night." Her tone made it clear that we could not expect more. The other guests also knew our story, and stayed on the far side of the courtyard.

Only one ancient priestess, her thin white curls cut short, consented to have anything to do with us. Her eyes were milky with age, and her hands gnarled and spotted – but she brought us bread and oil, some pickled fish, and a flask of wine. Then she dragged over a stool to sit beside us. I glanced at her surreptitiously as I ate, wondering if she had lost her wits:

why did she seek us out, when others shunned us?

She asked about our visit to Zeus' temple; Father related much of the story as I watched her by the light of the hearth-fire. "Your voice is like his, you know," she said.

Father paused, wiping his fingers clean with the last of his bread. "Like whose?"

The old woman grinned, showing her gums. "Laius."

"You knew him?" I asked.

"Oh, yes... *many* girls did." She nodded, smiling. "I was one of his early favorites, before his beard came in. But later he decided I was too old for him." Laughing a little, she added: "I think I was twenty-two. Too old!"

I had never thought much about King Laius – my mother's first husband, the man who had sired Father. He had been such an unpopular king in Thebes that little good was ever said about him; certainly Mother never mourned him.

"He organized the games here for years," the old woman continued. "He even helped build this temple, including your guest-room. The Fates have their little jokes with us, don't they?" Her tone growing nostalgic, she said, "He helped me get a place here as a priestess. He was kind to us girls, you know, even after his eye wandered on. And he loved spending his evenings here, drinking with the athletes."

Suddenly, as if the gods granted me a vision, I imagined this toothless old crone as a young and pretty maid – and the grandfather who had died before my birth as a lusty young man. It was peculiar, yet somehow reassuring, to hear something pleasant about him. I was glad to learn that he had not been miserable all his life.

"Laius was always popular; the young men all admired him, and he was very close to King Pelops." After a moment's pause, she added: "There's a saying here, of a young man who's particularly randy – they say, 'He's had more girls than Laius of Thebes!' Even the young folk who never knew Laius, they still say that."

"If he was so popular here," Father said slowly, "I suppose there was never much chance for the man who killed him to receive absolution at Olympia."

This observation renewed my puzzlement over the old woman's demeanor. "Priestess, why do you seek our company, when everyone else shuns us?"

She reached over to pat my arm. "Child, I've seen evil in my day. Old King Oinomaios – he passed on the seed of malice to his daughter Hippodamia, and she to the sons she had with Pelops. I've lived through all of that. I know the difference between an evil man, and one the Fates have given a terrible burden."

With that she fell silent, and for a while we listened to the crackling of the flames. The other guests had gone to their rooms; the crescent moon was slipping lower in the sky. A few dead leaves danced across the courtyard, propelled by the evening breeze. The old woman reached down and grasped one of them, then cast it into the fire. It flared briefly bright and then curled away into ash.

Staring down at the embers, the crone said quietly: "The gods' mercy is not something you can be granted here in Olympia. The games haven't been held here since the quarrel between King Pelops and his sons Atreus and Thyestes, and Atreus took much of the holy treasure with him to Mycenae. The gods no longer favor this place."

I thought of the temple of Zeus, the priest with his false thunder – and how the priests and priestesses of the other temples refused even to speak with us. Yet here at the temple of Hestia, piety remained. I made some comment on this to the ancient priestess, and she nodded.

"Remember, child, Lady Hestia renounced her throne on Mount Olympus in order to tend the hearth fire. She's not proud or ambitious like the other gods and goddesses; she doesn't need a temple adorned with gold. All she asks is firewood, and the forests provide plenty of that." She tossed a small branch in the fire. "We keep her flame burning; that's our duty. The other gods will return to this part of the world someday."

Father nodded and stroked his beard. "Where should we go to seek them, priestess?"

"Oedipus son of Laius, I cannot tell you which god might aid you. My mistress Hestia remains apart from the intrigue that occupies her divine brothers and sisters." She gazed at Father with her milky eyes; in her expression there was compassion and kindness. "I think you should go to Pylos. Ask the advice of King Neleus and Queen Chloris. They're celebrated for their wisdom."

So the next morning we headed back to the port. At first, none of the merchants or farmers would give us space to ride in their carts, even though I offered to pay with a necklace of agate beads. Only the addition of an ivory bracelet convinced a man hauling amphorae of wine to give us room in the back of his oxcart. When we reached the port, all the sea captains had heard who we were, and decided we were bad luck – even though Pylos was not far away. Finally, after I offered jewels worth three times what we had bartered for the trip from Korinth, the greediest and most disreputable-looking of the captains relented. Fearing that he planned to steal our baggage and pitch us overboard, I insisted that he seal the bargain with an oath on Poseidon's altar there in the harbor. Even if the captain had few scruples, I hoped that fear of the Lord of the Seas would constrain his men.

During this short and wind-tossed journey I kept my jewelry-pouch tucked tight against my side, worrying: what would we do, once our meager wealth ran out? Never mind bargaining for berths aboard ships; how would we even *eat?* And shelter – the days were growing colder. We could not sleep outside in the winter.

Thank all the gods, the sailors did not threaten us – and though the passage proved rougher than previous days' sailing, we arrived safely on Pylos' sandy shore. As Hestia's priestess had advised us, we sought an audience with the elderly king and queen – and, to my complete surprise, they welcomed us warmly even though they knew our story.

"Thebes is hard on her rulers," said Queen Chloris solemnly. She herself was a refugee from Thebes; her father, King Amphion, had been torn limb from limb by the mob – which was how King Laius and my mother came to the throne.

"Yes," King Neleus said, patting his wife's hand. "That tradition goes back many generations." He had seen much history himself, almost as much as the ancient priestess of Hestia; I guessed he was in his late seventies. He was bald as a cabbage, except for his ears – these stuck out like jug handles, and had tufts of white hair sprouting from them.

Queen Chloris nodded, her expression filled with compassion. In her youth she had been celebrated as a great beauty; perhaps ten years younger than her husband, she was still slim and handsome, with thick white hair and large gray eyes. "I grieved to learn of Jocasta's death. She saved my life, you know. Your mother had a brave and loving heart."

Your mother. The term applied to both Father and me, of course. I flushed at the reminder, and Father's grip on his walking-stick tightened until his knuckles turned white. He pressed his lips tight together; after a moment's silence he said: "Do you know how I can cleanse myself of my crimes? And Jocasta – can I somehow atone for her?"

"That is a difficult question," said King Neleus. "We must consult the leading priests and priestesses of Pylos, and seek the guidance of the gods." He nodded his bald head. "This will take time."

Queen Chloris smiled. "The season for traveling is nearly over. Stay here in Pylos as our guests; we can offer you a room in the palace."

This generosity, after our recent experiences, brought tears to my eyes; Father and I expressed our gratitude as best we could. It was an unanticipated luxury to live in a palace again; even though we had only a small pair of adjoining rooms and no servants of our own, we ate as well as the royal family and the palace staff treated us with respect. The crown prince – King Neleus' son by his long-dead first wife – proved as gracious a host as his father and stepmother; the many children of Neleus and Chloris also made us welcome.

On winter's milder days, I took Father to walk along the sandy shore; as always, the scent of the sea cheered him. When the ocean breeze was too cold for such excursions, I spent the days with Queen Chloris. She was an expert weaver; she taught me how to work with linen, a thread far finer than wool, and explained the making of various dyes: brilliant reds that reminded me of poppies and pomegranates, blues deep as lapis or pale as the winter sky, glowing shades of yellow and gold. She offered me the use of a loom in her weaving-chamber, and I found a quiet satisfaction in choosing the right colors, tying the warp-weights into place, and passing the shuttles back and forth. We chatted as we worked; I enjoyed the stories of her youth, her days with the Maidens of Artemis. She showed me many beautiful tapestries she had made – one depicted the fearsome wolf-men that once raided the flocks of Arkadia; another showed the huntress band in their short tunics, loosing their arrows to bring down a stag; a third portrayed Artemis herself, riding her silver moon-chariot across a starry sky. Under Chloris' supervision I began a tapestry depicting Kadmos' marriage with Harmonia.

King Neleus, we discovered, had never been a hasty man, and in his old age he made decisions at the pace of a reluctant tortoise. Over the winter months he spoke with Father again and again about his situation, and called in one after another of the priests and priestesses to offer their insights – but no one seemed to indicate any particular course of action. Everyone took this in stride, explaining that King Neleus' careful nature had made Pylos very prosperous. Only Father, concerned that Mother was suffering torments, fretted out of concern for her.

One day, just as winter was yielding to spring, the consultations involved Prince Nestor, a son of King Neleus and Queen Chloris. A man of middle years, Prince Nestor was high priest of Poseidon; he had curling dark hair that mostly concealed the protruding ears he had inherited from his father. After months of reviewing various rituals of purification – and the histories of Thebes, Korinth, and Pylos – the men concluded that we should ask the sea god to intercede with Apollo.

I rubbed my nose doubtfully, looking out the window of King Neleus' study towards the sea in the distance. "I know that Poseidon is the patron of Pylos – but does he have much influence with Apollo?"

Nestor leaned forward. "We believe so. Remember, Poseidon protected Leto when she was seeking a place to give birth to Apollo and Artemis. Jealous Hera declared her husband's mistress would find no rest anywhere under the sun. Then Poseidon sheltered Leto on the island of Delos, striking the waters with his trident to make waves so high that the sun's rays could not reach the little island."

"Perhaps we should go to Delos," Father mused. "That might be the best place to seek Apollo's mercy."

"Before you decide anything, consult Poseidon," Queen Chloris said. "We should be sure that he will grant you passage."

"Just so, my dear," said King Neleus, tugging on the hair growing out of his right ear. "Mustn't be hasty."

Prince Nestor turned to practical matters. "Poseidon's preferred animal is the horse," he said.

"Then we will offer the very best horse from our herds to win his favor," Queen Chloris said, patting my hand. "I owe your mother that much."

The morning of the ceremony dawned clear and crisp. As I led Father through the palace courtyard, I noticed the hyacinth coming into bloom; I hoped the flowers were a good omen. We met King Nestor and Queen Chloris in the foyer of the palace, and followed the royal couple down the staircase and through the streets of Pylos. A crowd gathered behind us as we made our procession towards the harbor; it seemed like a festival day. The mood was one of curiosity; Pylos' citizens were not cheering us on, precisely, but neither were they hostile – it was as though Father and I were some unusual spectacle. Not a monstrosity like a two-headed calf, which would be a sign of the gods' anger, but also not a wondrous apparition like a ram with golden fleece – rather like some strange beast from the land of Punt with a neck longer than its legs.

More people awaited us at Poseidon's temple. Prince Nestor was there in his priestly garb, robes of blue with a garland of dried seaweed crowning his dark curls. He held the reins of a young stallion taller and larger than any I had ever seen. His skin was as white as seafoam; he had a dark gray mane and tail, and he seemed as strong as the ocean itself.

"He's magnificent," I gasped.

"He's the best of a herd that started from Poseidon's own stock," said Queen Chloris proudly. "The stable-hands call him Arion."

The stallion was so tall that I could not see over his back, even if I stood on tiptoe. Father, if he still had his eyes, could just have managed it. As though he sensed my interest, the horse Arion glanced at me with one huge dark eye; he snorted and tossed his head proudly, but made no attempt to pull away from Prince Nestor. He shifted his weight, and his well-groomed hooves clacked sharply against the cobblestones of the temple forecourt.

I was sorry to think that this handsome, vibrant creature would die – but it could not be avoided. We needed to give Poseidon the best; obviously the ram offered to Zeus in Olympia had been insufficient. As the people took their places, I described the horse to Father; he thanked King Neleus and Queen Chloris for their generosity, and squeezed my hand tight. I felt hope radiating from his grip like the heat of a newly kindled flame.

An acolyte called for silence; the crowd fell silent and then King Neleus spoke the ritual words, asking his son Prince Nestor to call upon the sea god. Nestor nodded solemnly, then chanted as two acolytes sprinkled meal mixed with salt over the horse's forelock. When the prayer was done, the senior acolyte handed Prince Nestor a huge double-headed axe with bronze blades polished to a flawless sheen.

Though the other acolyte was murmuring reassuring words to the horse, the flash of bronze caught the beast's eye; before I could blink the magnificent horse reared sharply, ripping the reins from the acolyte's hand and letting loose a sound like a battle-cry. Nestor swung up the axe, but the horse was too quick and too powerful; it brought its hooves down upon the broad flat blade, knocking the weapon from Nestor's grasp. With a mighty kick Arion then felled the acolyte who had given Nestor the weapon. Neighing furiously as if to say, "I am a king among horses! How dare you threaten me?" the enormous horse barreled off, plowing through the horrified and shrieking crowd like a warship cutting through the waves.

"What's happening?" yelled Father. "What's going on?"

Shouting over the noise of the crowd, I did my best to explain; Father dropped his walking-stick and fell to his knees. "Cruel Fates!" he shouted, beating against the cobblestones with his fists. "Cruel, vicious Fates!"

King Neleus and Prince Nestor worked to restore order. The acolyte, who took a kick to the head, died instantly; but healers were summoned to help those who were injured in the white horse's escape. A few started shouting that we had brought a curse to Pylos, and called for our blood. The king's soldiers protected us and took us back to the palace while Queen Chloris sternly reminded her people that we were royal guests.

But we could not remain in Pylos. Later, the king, queen and Prince Nestor summoned us to a small audience room in the palace. "Oedipus, the god has made his will plain," said Nestor, his arms crossed. "Poseidon does not forgive you."

For once, old King Neleus did not hesitate. "You cannot remain in Pylos. I have never witnessed such a clear omen – the horse has fled from us; all I hope is that Poseidon does not reject Pylos, too."

Father nodded. "I understand, and I thank you for your hospitality this winter. No ship would take us now. We must leave on foot."

"But Father, your ankles!" I exclaimed, unable to completely hide my terror at what we were being forced to do. "Besides, where should we go?"

Queen Chloris counseled us to seek the Maidens of Artemis. She pointed out that Artemis was closer to her twin brother than any of the other gods; with the help of the Huntress we might soften Apollo's heart. We were given a cart full of provisions and a sturdy little donkey to pull it; after what happened with Arion, the king would not give us a horse. I doubt I could have managed one anyway.

Even though she had served among the Maidens before her marriage, that was decades ago; Queen Chloris could make only vague suggestions as to how to find them. The path taken by the itinerant band of huntress-priestesses through the forests of Hellas varied each year. Occasionally they made camp on the outskirts of one city or another, inviting the local girls to participate in Artemis' moonlight rituals, but they followed no fixed schedule. I had been initiated myself into the Mysteries of Artemis a few years before, joining the Bear Dance under the stars – but my memories yielded no hint as to how to succeed in the task we now faced.

Since leaving Thebes, Father and I had traveled mostly by sea. We relied on the ships' captains to set our course, lay in provisions, and deal with the dangers of the journey. I had guided Father to and from the ports, but that meant following well-established roads. Now we would pursue an elusive quarry through unfamiliar, mountainous country. Bandits and brigands could be lying in wait – not to mention lions and wolves. As we left Pylos, I tried to conceal my anxiety from Father, but I feared our wanderings would finally kill us.

We journeyed inland, north and east into the wilds of Arkadia. The first night we made camp I lay wide-eyed by the fire all night, shivering each time I heard wolves howling in the distance. Eventually I managed to sleep some each night, but our pace remained slow – while our stores of cheese, raisins, and dried fish shrank like snow in sunshine. I did not mention this to Father; I pared back my own meals to stretch out our provisions. At first my stomach ached with hunger, but in time I grew used to smaller portions. I envied our little donkey, who ate whenever he liked, munching grass and leaves along the roadside.

The mountain villages all looked the same to me. Whenever we approached a cluster of thatch-roofed huts, herd-dogs greeted us with a chorus of barks, and a grimy, gap-toothed boy would come running out to see what was the matter. Once it became clear we were no threat to the flock, the young shepherd would shush the dogs and shout to his mother or grandfather that strangers had come to town.

These rural folk were kind to us, usually offering a meal to the blind, lame beggar and his skinny daughter, sometimes giving us a roof to sleep under. We were grateful even for space in a lean-to stable, and I learned to make myself comfortable on a pile of straw beside the goats' pen. One by one, I sometimes traded our few remaining jewels for hard cheese or dried figs to augment our dwindling supplies.

Always we asked where to find the Maidens. Whenever we heard they had been sighted, we turned our donkey-cart and followed in our slow, trudging pace – but each time we reached the indicated destination, Artemis' followers were already gone. I began to despair of ever catching up with them.

One rainy afternoon in late spring, the right front wheel of our cart mired itself in mud. Even with two of us pushing the cart from behind our little donkey lacked the strength to pull it free. Father suggested prying out the wheel with a tree-branch, so I poked through the underbrush along the side of the road while rain dripped from the hood of my cloak into my face. I wedged the branch under the stuck wheel, and hauled against it with all my strength as I shouted at the donkey. Father shoved at the back of the cart, to no avail; finally, verging on tears in my frustration, I leaned my full weight against the branch and kicked the donkey's flank. The beast jumped forwards, and the wheel popped loose. I landed on my side in the muck and Father fell too, but at least the cart was moving – until the opposite wheel slipped off the far edge of the path and the whole cart flipped on its side, dumping out all of our possessions. Yanked to a stop, the donkey brayed in alarm.

Pushing himself up from the roadway, Father asked: "What? What's happened?"

I slapped the muddy ground, despair and frustration tightening my throat as I told him.

Eventually we righted the cart and collected most of our scattered belongings. I salvaged a pouch of dried apples and another of mutton jerky, but our last loaf of bread was ruined and the jar of olives had shattered against a rock. Worst of all, our fire pot had tumbled into a puddle, extinguishing the precious embers.

That night we huddled beneath a sodden dirty blanket in the bed of the cart, too cold to sleep.

Father put his arm around me. "Antigone, I'm sorry."

"Why?" I asked, still angry with myself. "*I* let the cart overturn."

"That's not important." He drew me closer, resting his chin on the top of my head. "I'm the one who brought this wretched existence upon you. My crimes cursed you from birth – and now the blindness I inflicted upon myself forces you to do the work of a slave."

"You're my *father,*" I said, trying to keep my teeth from chattering. "It's my duty to help you."

"Your brothers felt no such duty."

"They were very young." I felt I should defend them – even though they were surely sleeping in warm, comfortable beds that night, with their bellies full. "They weren't yet men."

"They're older now," Father observed.

"Not that much. It's been only half a year or so since we left Thebes."

"Is that all?" There was surprise in Father's voice. "It seems longer."

I nodded against his shoulder. When we first left home, I kept hoping that all the awful things that had happened would turn out to be a dream – that all of this was just a terrible nightmare, and I would wake beside Haemon and everything would be fine. But now it seemed that my childhood in Thebes was the illusion: that this life wandering with a donkey cart was my true state, and I had only dreamed of being a princess.

"Anyway," Father continued, "sons have a duty to their father."

I rubbed my chapped lips with fingers that tasted like mud and felt like ice, then stuck my hand beneath my arm in an effort to warm it. If the twins had been with Father, *they* would have never let the cart overturn. Or if they had, they would have made a fire even without embers to start it. They would be able to hunt, so that Father would have fresh meat to eat, I thought, my stomach growling. Rich, savory venison, charred in a proper campfire…

I woke with the scent of roasting meat in my nostrils – but no, that was only what I had been thinking of as I finally fell asleep. There was no campfire; Father and I were cramped up together in the bed of the donkey-cart. I threw back the damp blanket, blinking against morning sunlight – and gasped with surprise.

"What is it?" Father grunted, sitting up.

Two young women stood over us. They wore short tunics; one had arms and legs tanned brown as a boy's, and the other was covered with freckles. The freckled girl grasped the ears of a freshly killed hare; the other, taller and thinner, carried a basket filled with greens.

I rubbed my eyes. "Are you Maidens of Artemis?"

The freckled girl grinned. "Of course!"

"We heard you're looking for us," her taller companion added. They helped us down from the cart and the freckled girl took charge of the donkey; we followed the pair unquestioningly, and with each step the smell of roasting meat grew stronger. My mouth watered as we entered the Maidens' camp, a circle of tents surrounding a campfire with perhaps a dozen women going about various morning tasks.

A tall sinewy woman stepped into our path, her hand resting on a dagger at her waist.

"Greetings," I said. "I am Antigone, and this is my father—"

"We know who you are," she interrupted. Her cautious gaze swept slowly over me and Father; then she took her hand from the dagger's hilt and folded tanned arms across her chest. "You're hungry," she said, and jerked her chin towards the fire. "Eat, and then we'll talk."

I helped Father sit by the fire; a girl handed each of us a skewer of meat taken from some small animal – squirrel, we were told. It was tough and stringy but I quickly devoured it. Then there were boiled vegetables: the freckled girl explained that they were cardoons – the same purple thistles that our little donkey often ate along the side of the road. I had not realized that thistles could make a tasty dish, but these – flavored with a touch of salt – were surprisingly good. We finished with cakes made of pounded hazelnuts and served alongside tiny strawberries, tart and delicious. By the time the senior priestess came to sit beside us, my hands no longer shook with hunger and the fire and sunshine had dried our clothes.

"You're most hospitable, Priestess," Father said, wiping his beard with the edge of his cloak. "Please accept our gratitude."

"You may call me Hyale," she said. She paused a moment, running her fingers through her gray-streaked hair. "What do you want from us, Oedipus?"

Father explained his desire for absolution for himself and our mother, his hope that Artemis might intercede with her brother Apollo to grant it.

Hyale frowned, pulling at her lower lip. "The sacred pool of Artemis is reserved for maidens. No man or married woman can be cleansed there. Only virgins may enter the waters."

Perhaps I should have said something to this, but I was embarrassed— and perhaps the priestess would not believe me if I explained I was still a virgin. Anyway, the mere fact that I was married would likely be reason enough for Artemis to reject me.

Father continued: "If Lady Artemis cannot cleanse me, could she intercede with her twin brother on my behalf?"

"Or at least offer us advice?" I added.

"I'll bathe in the sacred pool myself. Perhaps my mistress will give me a vision to share with you." Hyale rose and tossed a few pieces of wood on the campfire, then continued: "But you must make a gift to the goddess."

I glanced over at our cart. We had so little – our bag of jewels was down to unmatched beads and spangles, and I did not think the goddess would want a mud-smeared bag of dried apples. What could we offer?

Father held out his fist in Hyale's direction. "Will you accept this ring?"

"What ring is that?" asked the priestess.

Father pulled off the ring and held it for her to take. "When I gave up the throne of Thebes, of course I gave up my royal signet ring, but I kept this one – one given to me by my wife on the tenth anniversary of our marriage. It shows me challenging the Sphinx, with Jocasta in the background."

"Father, are you sure?" I asked.

A sad smile touched his lips. "What letters will I write now, Antigone? Besides, if it helps your Mother…" The scene on the ring showed Father rescuing Mother the first time; I knew he was trying to rescue her again.

Priestess Hyale took the jewel from Father and examined it. "I believe Lady Artemis will value this," she said. "Sometimes, before the gods can give our lives a new direction we must show that we are willing to give up our old treasures."

I remembered how, when I married, I brought Lady Artemis a brightly painted lamp in the shape of an owl – the one that had lit our room all throughout our childhood, Ismene. Perhaps my offering had not been enough.

"How long does the bathing ritual take?" Father asked.

The priestess shrugged. "It takes as long as it takes. I won't start until the moon rises, late this afternoon. Until then, I invite you to rest."

Sated, Father dozed off. I washed my face and hands, and changed into my spare sandals and a fresh gown. I washed my mud-spattered sandals and gown and hung them from a tree branch to dry, and set out fresh things for Father when he woke. Then I watched the Maidens as they worked. They set up a tripod over the fire and hung a soup-pot from it, adding spring nettles and forest mushrooms to the broth. I approached the freckled girl, who was skinning the hare, and asked how they lived off the land.

The young woman explained that they gained their skills over years of training and practice, but she and her companions could teach me a few things that day. Hazelnuts, I learned, could be eaten at once – but acorns needed to be leached and chestnuts roasted to make them edible. Once cooked, nettles lost their sting and were nourishing – and the purple thistles called cardoons were plentiful throughout Hellas. I knew dandelions could be eaten, from the roots to the blossoms. The Maidens counseled me against gathering mushrooms; it was too easy for the inexperienced to confuse safe varieties with those that were deadly. But wild figs and rose hips were safe and easily identified, as were myrtle berries, pine nuts, and walnuts. They explained that making fire was an arduous task, so they always carried two fire pots; one of the Maidens gave me a spare.

A Maiden near my age invited me to join them for archery practice while the soup simmered over the fire; I quickly learned I could not have hit the side of a palace had one been in the clearing. I thanked the huntresses for their patience and returned the bow to its owner.

Father woke and I helped him change into clean garments, then rinsed his cloak and tunic and hung them beside my gown to dry. As the sun approached its zenith, a woman whose belly was swollen with child arrived with baskets of freshly baked bread and soft cheese. The mother-to-be consulted with Hyale and asked Artemis' protection for the remaining months of her pregnancy. Afterwards, the Maidens shared around the bread and cheese and ladled out the mushroom soup. A while later a pair of huntsmen arrived, bringing a haunch of venison as a thanks-offering to Artemis. The Maidens spitted this to roast over the fire.

Late that afternoon the ghostly white moon made its appearance against the pale blue sky. Without saying anything to Father or me, Hyale picked up a leather bag and disappeared into the forest. The Maidens built up the fire for the night and we shared an evening meal of venison and wild onions. After sunset the Maidens sang songs around their fire; their voices were sweet but I kept looking for Hyale. The sky was inky and full of glittering stars by the time the chief priestess, her damp hair smoothly tied back, returned to the camp.

"What did Lady Artemis reveal to you, Priestess?" Father asked after I helped him to stand. His voice did not tremble, but I heard his desperate yearning for absolution.

Hyale guided us to a log and helped us to sit down next to her. "I entered the sacred pool, Oedipus, and asked the goddess to share her wisdom with me. But for a long time, the reflection of the moon on the water's surface told me nothing. My mistress was letting me know that this matter is no concern of hers."

My shoulders slumped; after chasing them for so long, were we to learn nothing from the Maidens? Father's hand tightened on my arm. "But—"

"I persisted on your behalf," she interrupted. "I reminded my mistress that you'd journeyed long to seek her advice and help, that you'd offered up a precious gift from your mother-wife. I asked Lady Artemis to speak with her brother."

Beside me Father nodded.

"The sun slipped behind the hills, but still Artemis brought me no message from Apollo," the priestess said. "Finally, as the sky shaded from blue to black, I heard the voice of the Huntress whispering in the trees. She reminded me that while her twin brother is god of prophecy, one must also consider the *subject* of the prophecy."

"But *I* was the subject," Father said, looking troubled. "Do you mean I cannot—"

"The prophecy dealt with marriage," the priestess said firmly. "That is

Hera's realm. Unfortunately, Lady Hera is famous for her temper."

"Hera?" Father wondered aloud. "But how—?"

"The queen of the Gods does not wander in the wilderness, but if you go to Argos she may consent to hear your plea," said Hyale. "Argos is Lady Hera's favorite city."

So Father and I set off for Argos the next day. We had clean clothes and full bellies, and most importantly we had good directions and a definite destination – one I was sure we could reach before running out of provisions, for the Maidens had supplied us with onions, nuts, and dried meat; and now I knew how to supplement our meals with fresh greens. Warm sunlight filtered through the trees, and blackbirds trilled overhead. But as I led the donkey along the rocky path, I wondered what would happen when we petitioned the queen of Heaven.

"Why should Hera be angry with you?"

Father sighed. "Anything that offends the sanctity of marriage offends Hera. And *my* marriage—"

"But you didn't *know*," I protested, as I had done so often before. "Besides, we're Hera's descendants. Shouldn't that matter to her? Kadmos' wife Harmonia was the daughter of Aphrodite and Ares; and Ares is the son of Hera and Zeus!"

"But we're descended through Laius, and I killed him," said Father. "Besides, Kadmos' sister Europa was one of Zeus' lovers – as was one of Kadmos' daughters. Hera has no reason to be fond of Thebes."

Contemplating this, I scratched the donkey behind his ear. It seemed unfair to punish us for the deeds of our ancestors – but then perhaps it was also unfair to expect our lineage to earn us any favor. And as Father would point out, fairness only applied to doings between mortals, not between mortals and gods.

Father nodded his blindfolded head agreeably. "If Hera's anger is the source of our difficulties, perhaps I can make peace with her. And if not – well, I'll do my best to persuade her to help. Zeus may listen to her. A husband listens to his wife."

I hoped so, for so far it seemed that the gods were united in turning their faces from us.

The weather continued fair, growing warmer as we descended from Arkadia's hills towards the sea. I added variety to our diet with cardoons and dandelion greens. When a spoke on one of the cart's wheels started to crack, I bound leather thongs around it as tightly as I could manage, while asking Hermes to protect us. We approached Argos with the cart still rolling.

The guards on duty at the gate yawned as they looked us over. "What's your business in the city?" one asked.

"We've come to petition Hera," my father answered.

The guards squinted at us in the noonday sun. "Not likely to have much to offer the goddess," muttered one of them.

His companion shrugged. "Let Lady Hera be the judge of that," he said, and waved us through.

Argos is wealthy; it has strong ties to both Pisa and Mycenae, and its vassal city Tiryns on the eastern coast is a busy port. Although I felt fit and strong, we made a poor showing, as we made our way through the crowded streets.

The Heraion was lovely, its forecourt tiled in green marble and its wooden columns painted vivid blue and topped with polished bronze. To enter such a place, we should have been freshly bathed and richly attired. Instead Father and I were sweaty and bedraggled, our clothing and our little donkey cart streaked with dust. I found a street-urchin to hold the donkey outside the grounds, offering him dried venison for his effort. Then I took Father's arm and led him towards the temple.

As we approached, temple servants nudged each other, shaking their heads and frowning. I tried to remember I was born a princess of Thebes as I led Father slowly up the treads. Shading my eyes, I glimpsed a magnificent statue of Hera within: the goddess' face and arms were sheathed in polished ivory, her hair gleaming gold. An expectant young woman dressed in flowing scarlet robes moved past the goddess' form and stepped out onto the terrace.

I paused, taken aback by her beauty. Her hair was honey-gold, her lips and cheeks rosy pink, and her large eyes a shade between blue and green. Some women grow haggard when carrying a child, but pregnancy lent this mother-to-be a vital glow. As lovely as a goddess, I thought, more conscious than ever of how dreadful we looked. Then I saw the acolytes following her and noticed the deference in their movements.

"This must be the chief priestess," I whispered to Father. Guided by the sound of her footsteps on the marble, he turned his blindfolded head in her direction.

"Away!" She said, sweeping her hand, glittering with emeralds, in a gesture of dismissal. "Peasants may only approach the queen of Heaven and Earth on festival days!"

Drawing himself to his full height, Father spoke in his most regal manner. "We are not peasants, Priestess, but of royal blood – descended, in fact, from divine Hera. We have come to seek her mercy."

"You?" she scoffed.

"I am Oedipus, once king of Thebes." He touched my shoulder. "This is my daughter, Antigone."

Her blue-green eyes narrowing, she inspected us more carefully and seemed to reach some conclusion.

"My name is Eriphyle; I am Hera's senior priestess." She descended the stairway towards us, stopping a short distance away, as if coming too close could pollute her. "My brother speaks of you often. He will want to see you."

Father nodded politely. "Who is your brother, Priestess?"

She blinked – then frowned at me, and back at Father, as if appalled by our ignorance as well as our filth. "My brother is Adrastos, king of Argos."

I remembered the name, but the man called Adrastos had been no king.

Father voiced my thought. "Adrastos? We met him last year, in Korinth, but—"

"Much has changed in the last few months," interrupted the priestess. "Lord Oedipus and Lady Antigone, you will be welcome at the palace. There you can prepare yourself to approach Queen Hera in proper state."

She ordered an acolyte to guide us, and a slave ran ahead to announce our impending arrival. I retrieved our donkey-cart from the boy who had watched it for us; he accepted his payment and followed behind us in evident curiosity. By the time we reached the palace, we had accumulated a crowd of onlookers; I heard our names spoken, and caught snatches of conversation. Our family's story seemed known here, and yet the palace guards did not turn us away, but led our little donkey-cart away to the stables as though it were the stately conveyance of a visiting dignitary. A palace steward showed us to a suite of rooms with an adjoining bath.

The bath attendants assured me that they could take care of Father without me, so I left him in their care and surrendered myself to luxury. While Father was being bathed and barbered, one servant pumiced my calloused feet and another brought me honeyed barley water and dates stuffed with almonds. Then I was led into the bath chamber, where I sank blissfully into a deep, steaming terracotta tub. A bath-girl sponged the grime of travel from my skin with practiced hands.

Afterwards, a maidservant dressed me in the brightly dyed skirts proper for a Hellene princess, and an open-fronted jacket edged with golden spangles that would have brought Father and me a year's worth of provisions in Arkadia. My hair was twisted up away from my face, and bound with blue and yellow ribbons that matched the skirt; then a servant girl brushed my upper eyelashes with kohl and dabbed alkanet rouge on my lips and cheeks.

The woman looking back at me from the polished bronze mirror was like a long-lost acquaintance, someone I felt I should remember better than I actually did. The bronze-studded sandals they gave me rubbed uncomfortably against my newly soft feet, and I had almost forgotten how to move in wide, flounced skirts.

Father wore his new clothing more easily; the long gold-bordered tunic fitted smoothly across his broad shoulders. With his russet beard neatly trimmed and his hair combed, he radiated a tragic dignity. A soft blue cloth was tied around his head to hide his ravaged eyes, and even his walking stick had been cleaned and polished. No one would mistake him for a peasant now: he was clearly a man of royal blood, ready for an audience with a king. A servant arrived to guide us to the throne.

The Argive megaron was crowded with richly dressed people, abuzz with conversation. But as the herald announced us – Oedipus of Thebes and his daughter Antigone – the great room fell silent. I led Father towards the throne, where our onetime drinking companion from Korinth was seated. Sober and clad in kingly robes, he looked more handsome than I remembered. A crown rested on his waving golden hair, and a broad smile lit his face.

"Oedipus, my friend – welcome to Argos!" He turned to the people standing near his throne. "Daughters, this man is my benefactor!" Two dark-haired girls smiled and nodded. "Amphiorax, your wife – my sister – has delivered him to me!" A swarthy fellow, not too tall but very muscular, peered at us – Amphiorax, I presumed.

Father smiled wryly – he could not see the people that the king was introducing. Adrastos seemed to realize his error. Jumping down from his throne, he took Father's hand and guided his fingers to the royal scepter, which was topped with a golden pomegranate: the fruit sacred to Argos' patron goddess, Hera. "Feel this, Oedipus! This is the birthright that you helped return to me!"

Inclining his blindfolded head in respect, Father said: "I congratulate you, my lord king."

The Argive king laid his hand on Father's shoulder. "You, Oedipus, showed me that I was *not* the man most cursed by the Fates. Because of you, I dared reverse my fortunes." He went on to explain how he regained the throne, winning the support of Amphiorax – chief priest of Zeus and a well-respected soldier – by arranging for him to marry his young sister, Eriphyle. As Adrastos spoke, I studied the king's relatives, especially Eriphyle. There was a likeness between brother and sister: not just the fair hair but also the straight, proud line of the nose and the full, curving lips. It was easier to see the resemblance between brother and sister than between the king and his daughters, who must have taken after their mother.

Adrastos concluded: "Oedipus, my friend, you and your daughter must stay here in Argos! I'll give you a house and servants – all that you need." He turned toward Eriphyle. "Sister, will Queen Hera smile upon this decision?"

Father lifted his chin slightly, as blind people often do when they don't know where an answer might come from.

The golden-haired priestess approached us. "Friend Oedipus, I have asked the goddess this question. Your crimes are known to her; but so is the fact that you were a loving and devoted husband."

Father's lips parted slightly, as if he were surprised by her words.

"My mistress Hera values fidelity in a husband: too few demonstrate it. Men often come to the temple seeking her forgiveness for the terrible way they treat their wives. But you, Oedipus – your transgression was one of love."

"Yes," Father said, his voice rough. "I loved Jocasta. I – I miss her more than I can say. And I am worried about her."

Eriphyle's voice softened. "Certainly it's unusual – and wrong – for a

135

man to wed his mother. But Queen Hera values an appreciative son." I heard murmurs all around me – people were taken aback by her reasoning – but King Adrastos and the priest Amphiorax nodded, and I realized that Eriphyle had already discussed our situation with them. Serenely she continued: "We all know that the queen of Heaven and Earth can be pitiless with her enemies – but she is kind to those who earn her favor. And with you, Oedipus, she is inclined to be generous. I foresee no danger to Argos if you and Antigone remain with us for now."

Father squeezed my hand. "Will I – will I be purified of my crimes?"

The priestess exchanged a glance with her brother and her husband; apparently they had yet not resolved this point among themselves. "We shall see."

"Certainly you can attempt cleansing rituals," suggested her husband Amphiorax.

King Adrastos smiled. "Oedipus, Antigone – welcome!"

After so many months of wandering, Father and I had a place to live.

*

Antigone shifts, stretching her arms above her in the darkness. Just remembering their journey tires her. "After the purification ritual, Father was more at peace than he had been since we left Thebes, even though the priestess told us that Hera could not offer complete absolution."

"King Adrastos was kind to you," concludes Ismene. "Were you and Father happy in Argos?"

What a question! But Antigone nods, and then shakes her head as she realizes her gestures convey no more to her unseen listeners than they had with her blind father. "I suppose so. King Adrastos put us in a little house near the palace, and assigned servants to see to our needs. It was as comfortable a life as we'd known since Thebes – more even than in Pylos, because the people of Argos welcomed us." She rubs her eyes. "But I didn't trust the Fates. I had our traveling cart mended, and kept our little donkey nearby."

CHAPTER SEVEN
EURYDIKE

Listening, Eurydike clutches her arms tight to her chest. She wishes she could hold Antigone now as she had when her niece was little. Queen Jocasta never knew how to handle her eldest daughter; the two seemed to grate on each other from the moment Antigone was born. Jocasta had been less awkward around quiet, yielding Ismene, but she showered the bulk of her attention on the twin boys. And, of course, on Oedipus.

Jocasta's beauty attracted men and made women jealous: Eurydike recalls moments of envy herself, but she does not blame Jocasta for everything. Antigone was always a willful child, not easy for a queen with so many demands on her time.

Antigone is talking of how the king of Argos offered a new home for her and Oedipus. But her voice is hoarse; her words falter. Poor girl, her throat must be getting sore: some hot wine mixed with honey and willow-bark, that's what she needs.

If only she could rewind the Fates' skein! And go back to those days when Antigone and her own children were small, when the twin princes were alike as a pair of barleycorns. However tall they grew, Eurydike still thought of them as children. So many brave, beautiful children lost: Eteokles, buried just a few steps away; her own Menoeceus – and beautiful, vivacious Megara. Now Antigone would soon join them in the Underworld.

Antigone pauses, and Ismene says, "King Adrastos was kind to you."

Anger flashes through Eurydike: she bears great ill-will towards the Argive king. He may have helped her niece and brother-in-law, but Adrastos is responsible for many Theban funerals.

Now Antigone has stopped speaking. It is quiet in Eteokles' tomb, with just the sound of the three of them breathing – but not as quiet as it must be in Antigone's. Eurydike inspects the lamp: throughout Hellas, it is the task of women to keep the fires burning. The lamp's two wicks are in good shape, but more oil is needed. Well, olive oil is here among Eteokles' grave offerings – even a striped stirrup-jar which she can reach without rising. Eurydike grasps it, pulls the stopper and carefully refills the lamp.

Of course, Antigone's cave must be completely dark.

Haemon rises to his feet, stretching as much as the tomb allows, and then edges closer toward the fissure in the wall. His movements cast huge shadows on the wall-paintings. "You're tired, Antigone," he says, voicing Eurydike's own thought. "You should rest now, and let one of us speak. Do you want me to tell you what happened with your brothers, here in Thebes?"

"Yes," Antigone answers. Eurydike imagines the girl who was once like one of her own daughters leaning forward, thirsting for knowledge, craving to understand everything that had led to the battle between the twins. "Tell me about—"

"No," Eurydike says, interrupting.

"Mother!" Haemon looks down at her, his eyebrows raised, as if he had not expected an objection from *her*. "Why not?"

"She should hear what happened, Aunt Eurydike," Ismene says.

"Yes," Eurydike agrees, her decision firming. She pushes herself to her feet, her joints stiff from sitting so long in one position. "She needs to know everything. And so do you, Ismene. And you, Haemon. It is time I told *all* of you the truth."

"What do you mean?" Haemon asks, taking her elbow. "What could you know that I don't?"

"More than you realize," says Eurydike. She picks up her folded cloak, and places it closer to the crack in the stone wall. "People tell me things."

Haemon frowns; then his expression clears. "Of course. Father—"

"Not your father," she interrupts with some asperity. "Or rather, not *just* your father."

Eurydike arranges her skirts as she takes her seat on the makeshift cushion by the wall. She glances in the direction of the door; she wonders what is happening outside. From the amount of lamp-oil that has burned, most of the morning must be gone. But that does not matter just now.

"Antigone," she asks, "can you hear me?"

"Yes, Aunt," says the voice on the other side.

"What did people tell you?" presses Ismene. She is turning out to be as inquisitive as her sister.

"Secrets," says Eurydike, staring at the twin flames of the lamp. "Shameful secrets."

EURYDIKE

After the boar hunt Haemon told you about, Antigone, your brothers were never friends again. It tore my heart – the twins had always been so close! And things soon grew worse. The city of Thebes was like a tightly-woven cloth: though battered and twisted, even burned around the edges, it was still strong and sound at its core. But all it takes is one small nick to sever the weave, and then the strongest cloth can be ripped in two.

Eteokles started letting people know his version of the boar hunt. My son Menoeceus told me about an afternoon archery practice, when a man's shot went far wide of the target – so bad that the assembled men burst into laughter. The man threw down his bow and grabbed one of his fellows by the shoulder. "You pushed me, you stinking dog! Couldn't stand to see me win – you're as bad as Prince Polynikes!" Polynikes was on the far side of the range, but the man's voice carried. Menoeceus said he saw his cousin's face go red with fury; the prince stalked away from the archery field without a word.

But that night, after dinner, Menoeceus came across Polynikes talking with a group of soldiers. "I've heard Eteokles is saying that I pushed him," Polynikes said, spreading his hands. "But he *tripped,* by the gods! He tripped over his own feet, and then tried to blame his failing on me! That's no leader of men." The listeners offered words of support, scorning Eteokles' clumsiness. "Don't forget," Polynikes added, "he's a liar, too."

You know how folks are, when the days are cold and the nights long. There's not much to do, so people talk; and they love to have something to argue about after dinner. Seems like each winter, a handful of arguments crop up over and over again. Well, that winter there was just one: who was telling the truth, Eteokles or Polynikes?

Since no one could prove what really happened – even the other members of the hunting party weren't sure! – these arguments weren't about facts. Instead, people took sides with one twin because their friends did – or because someone they didn't like backed the other twin. You see, with the scar on Eteokles' arm, everyone could finally tell them apart, and they were no longer "the twins" but two competing princes. Some called Eteokles the virtuous brother, wronged by conniving, treacherous, jealous Polynikes; others said Polynikes was the one who had been wronged, by a liar who couldn't even manage a weapon and would rather smear his brother's good name than admit his clumsiness. Each side grew more firmly committed to one version of events, refusing to consider another possibility. A few arguments turned into brawls.

The twins scarcely spoke to each other; they sat on opposite sides of the megaron whenever possible. But one issue still united them: they both wanted to be declared men.

Polynikes was the first to come to Creon with the request, just as winter was releasing its grip. Creon told me about it that night as we prepared for bed. "What did you say?" I asked.

"That if he was trying to take the manhood ceremony without his brother, he was wasting his time."

And so both boys came to our rooms a few mornings later. Creon was eating breakfast, and my maid was arranging my hair. "Show them in," Creon said to the servant.

The twins entered awkwardly; neither, I guessed, wanted the other to walk in first – and yet the door wasn't really wide enough for two abreast. As soon as they had crossed the threshold they stepped apart, glancing from my husband to one another and back again.

Creon dipped a piece of bread in a bowl of wine. "What is it?"

"You said you would consider our doing the manhood ceremony together," said Polynikes. "Here we are, making the request. Together."

"I have already considered it," said Creon, putting the morsel in his mouth. "You're fourteen years old. That's too young."

"Why should that matter?" Eteokles objected. "It's a man's *deeds* that count."

"Ah, like your glorious boar hunt? Tell me, how did that turn out?" Creon wiped the bowl with the last of his bread.

Polynikes stood taller, throwing his shoulders back, while Eteokles scratched his scar and frowned. Neither of them had an answer for Creon.

My husband put down his bowl. "Now, I want all this nonsense about what happened during that hunt to stop. As though I needed any reason to prove that fourteen is too young – which I do *not* – you've given it to me. Your quarrel is causing dissension in Thebes. If you were ready to be leaders – ready to be *men* – you'd understand that Thebes' princes must bring the city together, not shatter it into pieces." He pointed at the door. "You may go."

I hoped that the fact they'd come to us together was a good sign – I hoped they'd take Creon's words to heart. They did stop talking about the boar hunt; but as far as I could tell, during the year that followed, that was the only improvement. Every night at dinner, each time there was a ceremony in Apollo's temple or any other public event, the twins positioned themselves as far apart as possible. They scarcely spoke – and when they did exchange words, it was usually to contradict one another. If Polynikes praised the venison, Eteokles found it too dry; when Eteokles said the day was sunny, Polynikes scanned the sky for clouds. And the competitions! Footraces, javelin throws, archery, wrestling – when one worked to excel at something, the other matched him. In every race they crossed the finish line neck and neck. Neither could consistently out-distance the other with the javelin, or out-score his twin at archery. One wrestling match went on so long, that Creon called off the bout and said that while he was regent they could not wrestle each other.

We had a good harvest that autumn, and the winter was mild. The following spring Thebes' herds did well in the calving, and the peasants began bringing in the winter crops to refill the granaries. On the afternoon before the ceremony in which Menoeceus and Alkides were to come to manhood, the twins arrived at their uncle's study. Megara and I were there; we had been reviewing the plans for the next day's events with Creon – I remember we were talking about garlands; the palace servants hadn't completed as many as we needed.

Since Jocasta's death, because I was the regent's wife I had taken on many of the duties of a queen. That taught me just how much my sister-in-law had done for the city. I wasn't afraid of hard work – raising a large family is no garden stroll! – but I just wasn't as clever as Jocasta. Back when she and Creon discussed their ideas and strategies, they often leapt ahead so quickly that they left me behind. Now, with Jocasta dead, I just did the best I could. I gave constant thanks to Hera for your assistance,

Ismene, and for my daughter Megara.

Megara had her father's sharp mind and much of her Aunt Jocasta's beauty. I felt sure *she* would make a wonderful queen – actually, she'd received offers of marriage from several kings and princes; even the new young king of Athens expressed interest. But her heart was set on Alkides, so she found one reason after another to reject the various marriage proposals. Creon doted on her, and did not – as so many fathers would have done – simply tell her to marry the man he thought most advantageous.

But I was speaking of the twins, now fifteen years old. When they came to see Creon, he was already in a bad mood. The Tiresias had sent word that he intended to attend the manhood ceremony, and Creon was uneasy about what the seer might say. I wasn't worried about it – this Tiresias was a friendly, even jolly old man, much less intimidating than my father-in-law when he served as the Voice of Apollo – but Creon never liked surprises, even pleasant ones.

My husband looked up from his work-table, assessing his two nephews. His gray brows drew together in irritation. "Before you ask," he said, "you may *not* take part in the ceremony tomorrow. You're not yet men."

The twins scowled. "We're as tall as Menoeceus," Eteokles snapped.

"And faster than Alkides," boasted Polynikes, folding muscular arms across his chest.

"Menoeceus and Alkides are in their sixteenth year," said Creon. "You are not."

"In other cities, that's not the rule," Polynikes argued.

"Thebes is not some other city," Creon answered, tapping his stylus against the table. "If you want to be initiated this spring, try one of those other cities."

Eteokles scratched his jaw; he was, truthfully, as tall as Menoeceus, but his red-gold beard was just beginning to come in. "Aunt Eurydike, can't *you* convince him?" He smiled in entreaty. "What harm could it do?"

I could not see the harm, myself; the boys were so close with Menoeceus and their friend Alkides – why shouldn't they join the ceremony, even if it *was* a year early? I opened my mouth to speak – but when I saw the dark frown on Creon's face, I changed what I was going to say.

"Why be in such a hurry to grow up?" I asked. "Have one last year to enjoy yourselves, and let your uncle take care of things."

Polynikes sputtered, "You're just saying what your husband wants to hear!"

Megara drew in a sharp breath at this disrespect; but Eteokles went further, leveling an accusing glare at Creon. "Right! And what he wants to hear is that *he* can stay in charge of Thebes!"

Creon slapped his stylus down on the table with a sharp crack, but his voice remained level. "What idiocy – if I wanted the throne, don't you think it would be mine? I've had every opportunity during the last forty years."

The twins' eyes widened.

"Despite all I've taught you, you still think kingship is about hunting and racing and feasting and setting that gods-cursed crown on your empty heads! I hope between this year and next you'll manage to understand that being a king means more than planting your buttocks in a fancy chair!"

Eteokles pulled his shoulders back; I remember thinking how red the scar on his left arm still looked. "It was worth a try," he said. "And next year, *we'll* be the ones to say what being king means."

"You can't delay us again," Polynikes added.

Creon leaned back in his chair, folding his arms across his chest. "Tell me, what happens next year? How will you share the throne?"

The twins were silent. They glanced at each other briefly and then looked away, in different directions.

"You could divide up the duties," I offered. "One of you could supervise plantings and harvests, while the other manages trade."

But the twins remained silent, both frowning. My suggestion did not please them.

"You see?" Creon smiled, but not in affection; it was that sharp-edged expression he gets when he's pleased to have proved himself right. "Until I know how you'll share Thebes' throne, how can I yield the regency? You two must come to an agreement on this before next year's manhood ceremony."

Polynikes hooked his thumbs into his belt; Eteokles rubbed his scarred bicep. Neither spoke.

Megara leaned forward in her chair. "Why not take alternate years? Then there's just one king at a time – one of you next year, and the other the year after that. You could trade each spring."

This idea caught everyone's attention; my husband and nephews stared at my daughter with respect.

"It might work," ventured Eteokles.

"Better than trying to sit on half a throne," agreed Polynikes.

"Then all that's left is to decide who goes first!" I realized I'd said the wrong thing when both twins frowned.

Before a new argument could start, Creon raised his hand and said: "Enough! You have a year to solve that question. I have issues to deal with for tomorrow. Away, both of you."

Polynikes shook his head, then turned on his heel and left. Eteokles paused to bow slightly before following his brother. Their footsteps echoed down the corridor.

Megara rose. "I'll go check on those rosemary garlands, Papa."

Creon reached for her hand. "Your suggestion was excellent, Daughter. Very clever." This time his smile contained real warmth.

"Thank you, Papa." She leaned over to kiss his cheek, then glided gracefully out of the room, leaving the fragrance of rose petals behind her.

"We do have a clever daughter," Creon repeated as the door closed again. Then he cleared his throat. "Our *nephews* are a different matter."

I shifted my chair closer to his work-table. "Don't be too angry with them. They're young."

"Yes," he said wearily. "And that's why they're not ready for the manhood ceremony. If I remain regent another year, I give Thebes another year of peace – and protect my nephews from themselves."

He sighed; the afternoon sunlight filtering through the window-curtains showed deep lines in his forehead. It struck me, then, that my husband was beginning to look like an old man… and that frightened me a little.

"A year seems like a long time to them."

"But you and I know how quickly it will pass, Eurydike." He shook his head, looking down. "Jocasta should have exposed one of them."

Appalled, I drew back. "Creon!"

He shrugged. "It was suggested, you know, when they were born. It would have been the sensible thing to do."

"She could have *never* done that," I objected. "Abandon a healthy child on the mountainside to die? Especially after her first-born was taken away from her!"

"You're right; Jocasta was too softhearted to make that choice." He rubbed his eyes again. "And even if she *had* exposed one, he might have returned to Thebes anyway. Oedipus did."

"Let's not worry about that," I said, anxious – for both our sakes – to change the subject. "Megara's clever, isn't she?"

"Yes," he said.

We finished the day's business, and had a quiet evening; the morning of the ceremony was, as always, very busy. My primary task was to ensure that all my children were appropriately dressed and that they went to their designated places at the appointed times. Henioche and little Pyrrha had new gowns for the occasion, dyed with saffron; my younger sons had new tunics. Megara was radiant; she wore a flame-colored jacket and skirts that echoed the same shade, alternating with tiers of rich russet. I noticed that she borrowed your carnelian necklace and earrings, Ismene – they looked so stunning with her dark hair, and went well with her golden bracelets. You looked very pretty too, Ismene.

At midmorning Creon and I made our appearance on the terrace atop the palace staircase. I was so proud to see you standing there, Haemon, tall and dignified in your robes – your first major ceremony as high priest of Apollo since old Bromius died. And, to my great relief, Eteokles and Polynikes stood back as Creon greeted the crowds gathered in the agora. Watching them take their places on either side of his chair, no one would have guessed they'd accused him of wrongful ambition the day before.

The Tiresias was at the foot of the grand stairway, supported by his daughters. As always, Daphne and Manto wore simple woolen shifts and no makeup; but, with garlands of hawthorn flowers adorning their hair, they were like a pair of forest dryads. A few men cast hopeless glances their way; for ten years Daphne had refused all offers of marriage, saying her place was by her father, and Manto seemed likely to do the same.

Antigone, your sister's sweet voice carried over the crowd as she and Megara led the procession of maidens from the Kleodoxa Gate, scattering rose petals as they sang. Next came the youths about to be proclaimed men. They walked proudly, shoulders back and chins held high; all wearing new tunics and cloaks. I thought of the many hours the mothers of Thebes had spent at their looms to make sure their sons would look magnificent. My eyes sought Menoeceus; as the highest-ranking youth, he led the procession – but even though I looked at him with a mother's love, I realized that most of the cheers were for Alkides.

At that point I had nothing against Alkides – but selfishly I was sorry that the order of the procession put him so close to Menoeceus. Menoeceus was a handsome young man, but Alkides stood more than a head above the rest, with shoulders like a young bull. He had shining curls of dark gold, and a square chin with a dimple at its center as he did not yet have a beard. Ribbons of red and blue were tied around his forehead, emblems of his victories in competitions. Alkides outshone his peers in the javelin cast and the axe throw; though he was not the fastest, he was by far the most powerful, and could wrestle a calf to the ground in the blink of an eye. The princes were better off waiting a year, instead of sharing their manhood ceremony with Alkides.

Hearing the applause Alkides grinned; he waved to the crowd and especially to his mother Alkmene. She had managed a place in the front ranks, and her height made her easy to spot. Alkides had been an enormous baby; she labored three full days to birth him, surviving despite all expectations. Afterwards, though, she was never healthy, and rarely appeared in public – but the widow would never have missed the initiation of her only son into manhood.

The maidens finished their hymn; dividing into two groups, the flower-crowned girls moved to either side of the youths who stood at the base of the stairs. Megara waved at Alkides – not as discreetly as she probably thought – and he acknowledged her with a wink.

Creon gave the signal; Haemon stepped forward, his chalk-whitened robes brilliant in the sun. He held up a jeweled goblet.

"Come forward, my son," Creon told Menoeceus.

Menoeceus ascended the stairs, halting to kneel on the final tread. He drew his sword and laid it at Creon's feet, then accepted the golden cup from his older brother. He poured out a few drops of dark wine; then, looking up at his father, he spoke the words of the oath: "As I, Menoeceus, son of Creon, offer this wine to the gods, so too I offer my sword and my life's blood in service of Thebes."

Tears spilled from my eyes as my husband answered: "And I, Creon, Regent of Thebes, accept your oath of loyalty."

Receiving the cup from Menoeceus' hands, Haemon declared: "You are a man of Thebes."

The people cheered as Menoeceus re-sheathed his sword and rose to his feet. He turned to descend the stairs, and Alkides moved as if he expected to come forward; but when Menoeceus was still a few steps above the level of the agora, the Tiresias lifted his staff.

"I would speak," he declared.

The people of Thebes fell silent. And, though I had not been concerned the day before, suddenly my heart clenched with fear. What had made me think I knew better than Creon? Yes, this Tiresias was a kindly old man – but the gods who spoke through him were *not* always kind. Creon had told me the words of others who had worn the blindfold and carried the staff of the Tiresias. Words that ruined lives.

But the Tiresias was the most powerful seer in all Hellas. We could not order him to remain silent.

A vein pulsed in Creon's forehead. "Thebes is listening, Tiresias."

The blind prophet beckoned Menoeceus closer; his daughters gestured that Menoeceus should kneel. Then the old man reached out to touch my son's face. I saw his fingers tremble slightly.

Hail, Thebans, hail;
Yes, hail one and all
His stalwart heart and noble blood.
When the waves crash
Against Theban walls,
His sacrifice holds back the flood.

The people cheered, shouting that my son would be a great hero; but I did not understand the seer's words. Thebes was inland; how could waves threaten our walls? Even in the wettest autumn, both Dirke's stream and the Chrysorrhoas combined could never flood the city. The word *sacrifice* made me especially uneasy; Menoeceus was named for Creon's father, who had offered his own life to cleanse the city of plague. But then, I thought, maybe the prophecy meant the gods wanted Menoeceus to become a priest like his older brother. That could be it.

I looked to my husband, hoping he could make sense of the prophecy; but Creon's brow was creased as if he was likewise puzzled.

Menoeceus, though, did not seem either confused or concerned. In fact, when he stood to face the people of Thebes, it was as if the prophet's touch had filled him with Apollo's golden light. He shone from within, handsomer than I had ever seen him.

"I thank you, Tiresias," he said in a strong and earnest voice. "I am proud to serve my city." At this the crowd's shouts grew louder. Menoeceus acknowledged the citizens graciously as he moved aside to let the next young man take the oath.

I wished I could discuss the prophecy with Creon, but Alkides was already climbing the steps. The muscular youth knelt and placed his gleaming bronze sword at my husband's feet; Haemon passed over the libation goblet and Alkides poured out the gods' portion, then spoke the words of the oath.

Creon paused for a moment; I was not sure why, but I knew Creon disliked Alkides. But my husband's hesitation did not last long. He nodded and said: "I, Creon, Regent of Thebes, accept your oath of loyalty."

Haemon lifted the goblet from Alkides' big hands and declared, "You are a man of Thebes."

I could not tell which group offered louder acclaim: the soldiers, or the female population. Alkides was tremendously popular with the soldiers, but if rumor was to be believed, Alkides had bedded at least half the women and girls. I had lived in the palace long enough to know that rumors swell faster than a loaf of rising bread – but also long enough to know they are often based on truth.

Megara was as smitten with Alkides as any; she clapped enthusiastically and an eager smile lit her face. Then the Tiresias held up his staff once more, and the city fell silent while Alkides walked down the stairs and knelt before the prophet.

Releasing his daughter's supportive arm, the Tiresias put his aged hand on the young man's face. The prophet said nothing; he lowered his head as if he could stare through his blindfold at Alkides' sunlit curls. Anticipation grew: was the Tiresias listening for some divine whisper? Or did the gods send him visions? However it was done, it took a long time, much longer than it had for Menoeceus. Finally, almost reluctantly, the Tiresias let his hand fall.

Golden Alkides, it is the Fates' plan
That you shall exceed every other man.
Greatest hero Hellas has ever known,
Even Lord Zeus will claim you for his own.

Unlike the prophecy for Menoeceus, this one's meaning was plain enough! The assembled people of Thebes erupted into wild and massive cheering. Flower petals, garlands, and ribbons were tossed in the air; soldiers stamped their feet and bellowed their approval, while Megara cried out in delight, and all across the agora even respectable matrons shrieked like giddy girls. Alkides climbed to his feet and swept his mother into his muscular embrace; there were tears of joy on her cheeks. The soldiers clustered around them, shouting, "Alkides! Alkides!" Even Menoeceus went over, grinning widely, and clapped a hand to his friend's thick shoulder.

I tried to be glad for Alkides and his proud mother; it was petty to resent his eclipse of Menoeceus when my son himself did not mind. But if

Alkides was to be Hellas' greatest hero – exceeding every other man – what did that say for the princes who were heir to Thebes' throne? Both twins looked pensive; Polynikes scratched his chin, and Eteokles' eyes narrowed.

Trouble was coming.

While the jubilation continued, the Tiresias left the agora with his daughters; then Creon and Haemon brought enough order to the agora so that the remaining youths could take their oaths of loyalty. I pitied them; after Alkides' prophecy, I suspected that even their own mothers had lost interest in them. But at last the ceremony was complete and we could return to the palace and prepare for the evening's banquet. As Creon and I walked through the corridors, I worried that things might get out of hand. Thebans are excitable people, and what the Tiresias had said about Alkides was so remarkable – what if he quarreled with the princes? Whose side would the people take?

For once in my life, I was thinking of Theban politics when my thoughts should have been on my own family. Creon and I had just reached our rooms – my maidservant was still slipping off my sandals, and Creon was shedding his cloak – when Megara burst in, her cheeks flushed with excitement. "Papa! Papa! Did you hear what the Tiresias said?"

Creon laughed, and handed his cloak to a manservant. "How could I not, my dear? People are still shouting it in the streets!"

She ran to him and took his hands. "So then you'll say yes, won't you? You'll let me marry Alkides!"

My husband's mouth drew into a hard, tight line. "No, Megara," he said at last. "I won't."

Megara dropped his hands. "What? Why not? How can you say no?"

"You are descended from Kadmos and Harmonia," said her father. "You should be a queen."

"But I don't *care* about being a queen!" Megara wailed. "I love Alkides!"

I rose from my dressing-stool and tried to comfort her. "Megara, you're young—"

"I've always loved him!" she said, ignoring me, even turning away from me. "I've been *waiting* for him!"

"He's not good enough for you." Creon's voice was stern.

"Not *good* enough!" she shrieked. "After that prophecy? Not good enough?"

Even I could not understand my husband's logic.

Grasping her upper arm, Creon walked Megara over to the stool I had just vacated. "Daughter, sit down."

"But—"

"Sit down, and listen to me." He folded his arms across his chest. "Megara, I know this is not what you want to hear – but Alkides is a reckless, drunken womanizer."

"No!" Megara shook her head vigorously. "He'll be the greatest hero

147

ever!"

"Prophecies always turn out differently than people expect."

"There's nothing *to* turn out different," she objected. "That's exactly what the Tiresias said. He'll exceed all other men!"

Creon sighed; he paused a moment, and I could tell that he was choosing another line of argument. "Let's set aside the prophecy for now. And instead of the future, let's talk about the present. Alkides may be stronger than any bull, but that's not what makes a good husband. This boy—"

"He's a man now!" she objected.

"This *man* has no throne to give you, no family fortune. His father was an outcast. He drinks too much and he beds every woman who'll lift her skirts. What is there about him that would make him a good husband for my precious daughter?"

I knelt beside her. "Your father loves you, Megara. He only wants what's best for you."

She sniffled and wiped her eyes, smearing her makeup. Although she let me put my arm around her, I could almost hear her thoughts racing as she considered what Creon had said. Alkides' drunken carousing was well known; it was one of the reasons he was so popular with the soldiers. And Megara *had* to be aware of his amorous exploits.

She bit her tear-swollen lips. "He's with other women because he can't be with me." Looking up at Creon, she ventured, "Papa, before you married Mama, weren't *you* ever with other women?"

His face colored above his gray beard. "That's different. And you should show more respect, young lady." Thrusting a finger towards his daughter's face, he declared: "I don't care what the Tiresias said. I won't allow you to marry Alkides, and that's final."

"Papa, you can't!"

"Megara, I can." He turned to me. "Eurydike, our daughter is overwrought. Take her to her room. I don't think she's in any condition to attend the banquet tonight."

"No! I want to see Alkides!"

"Not in this state," said her father.

"Come on, my dear," I said. "The world won't end tonight. What you need right now is a nice warm bath. Maybe the herb-woman can bring you something to calm your nerves – and then, perhaps—" I looked at Creon "—perhaps you can go later if you've calmed down."

"Perhaps," said Creon coldly. "But she'll stay away from Alkides."

Megara was furious. It wasn't easy for me to usher her out and down the hallway to her room; but by the time we reached it, she was a little calmer. Once she was freed from her festival gown and wrapped in a soft robe, I sent her servants out to fetch the herb-woman and arrange for the bath. I set aside the carnelian necklace and earrings to return to Ismene, and helped Megara wash the smeared makeup from her face myself.

"Megara," I said gently, "you must deal with the world as it is. Your father will never consent to a marriage with Alkides."

Her heartbreak had passed from anger and disbelief to quiet despair; I felt her pain as if it were my own. "Why not? *Why* does Papa hate him so?"

I wiped a last trace of rouge from her cheek, and set aside the cloth. "I don't think hate is the right word, dear. But Alkides' father was a violent man. He had to seek sanctuary in Thebes after killing someone."

"But if Papa didn't approve of Amphitryon, why did he allow him sanctuary?"

"I don't know, but I believe that was the decision of your aunt and uncle."

"They must have had good reasons—"

"The point, Megara, is that Amphitryon was a murderer. He died just a couple of years after his son was born, so you don't remember him – but your father fears Alkides inherited his temperament as well as his blood-guilt."

"Maybe." She picked up a hand mirror and glanced at her reflection, then – looking dissatisfied at what she saw – set the mirror down. Lowering her voice, she confessed: "I can't help it, Mama. I love him. He's – he's like a god!"

"Alkides is handsome and strong," I admitted. "But so are other men. You haven't ever met the king of Athens, but people say he's very good looking. And so wealthy! Just think, dear, you could be queen of Athens!"

"I don't want to go to Athens," she mumbled, toying with an alabaster perfume bottle.

"All right – then why not marry one of your cousins? You could be queen of Thebes." I suspected that this was what Creon wanted, anyway; and that was why he had not pressed her into another marriage. In Megara he saw his sister Jocasta again.

Megara turned the polished stone bottle on her dressing-table, pursing her lips. After a moment, she said, "But I'd only be the queen every other year." A puff of laughter escaped her. "Unless you want me to marry both of them?"

The return of Megara's usual wit heartened me. I clucked my tongue and said, "I don't know about *that*."

She shrugged, twisting her full lips. "Unusual circumstances call for unusual methods. And they're hard to tell apart anyway."

At that point Megara's personal maid stepped in to announce that the bath was ready; I watched her climb into the steaming tub, and saw to it that she drank a calming draught prepared by the herb-woman. Feeling drained by the day's events, I had the herbalist prepare a soothing tea for me as well.

Megara and I attended the banquet, but only briefly. She kept making cow's-eyes at Alkides, so her father sent her back to her room. But as you know, servants talk. At some point that night, after the young men were well into their cups, Alkides learned that Creon had forbidden any consideration of marriage between him and Megara. Thank Dionysus, by that time the carousing had moved out of the palace into the streets of the town – which meant that instead of threatening my husband in person, Alkides vented his anger in other ways. A soldier who was even drunker than Alkides laughed and wondered aloud how Alkides thought he'd have a chance with the regent's daughter in the first place. Alkides smashed the fellow with a mighty fist, causing him to lose two teeth. Then he went on a rampage through the lower town. In the potters' quarter he threw to the ground dozens of earthenware pots waiting to be painted; he kicked over some of the piss-pots standing outside the tanners' shops so that the area stank even worse than usual. My son Menoeceus and the princes tried to calm him; Alkides responded by plowing his fist into the nearest door. This splintered the door, but also injured his hand, and the pain shocked him out of his rage enough to let him listen to reason. At any rate Eteokles took him aside after that, and finally managed to quiet him.

My scandalized maidservant reported all this to me early the next morning; I relayed everything to Megara myself. She listened to me solemnly, and did not try to defend his actions; I believed she was learning to accept the fact that marriage to Alkides would be a catastrophe. Around noon, while most of Thebes' citizens and especially its new men were still sleeping off their hangovers, I spoke with Creon in his study.

"I should banish him," he said grimly.

"Creon, he was just proclaimed the greatest hero Hellas will ever know. By the Tiresias himself. You can't banish him."

"That boy is dangerous."

"He's a man of Thebes. You accepted his oath yourself. And how many soldiers would we have left if we banished all the ones that drink and break things?"

"I suppose you're right, my dear."

"One good thing may come of it," I said. "I think Megara was horrified to hear about his rampage."

"I hope so." Some of the tension left his shoulders; he drummed his fingers on the tabletop. "As you say, he's popular with the soldiers – except for the one who lost his teeth. With spring here and the travel season started, we've been having trouble with bandits in the mountains north of the city. Dealing with that should keep him out of trouble – and away from Megara."

"That's a wonderful idea!" I leaned over to kiss Creon on the cheek. "You know, last night I suggested to Megara that she marry one of the twins."

My husband raised an eyebrow. "Really? What did she say?"

I did not repeat her joke. "I think she's considering it. I think she would make an excellent queen of Thebes."

"Yes," he said slowly. "I've always thought so, too…"

I was right; that was why Creon had not tried to arrange another marriage for Megara. "The Tiresias himself said no taint remains on the twins," I reminded him of what the old prophet had proclaimed when Oedipus accepted exile.

"I remember," said Creon. "Megara was very shrewd, wasn't she, suggesting that they alternate years on the throne? She'd be an asset to any king. And in the end she would be far happier with one of the twins than if she married Alkides. I'll speak to the princes about this."

Alkides and some of the soldiers were soon hunting bandits in the north, and Megara gave me every reason to believe she had dismissed him from her thoughts. She never spoke of him, never asked for news. Instead, she began receiving courtship visits from the princes – separately. As her mother, it was my duty to chaperone such visits, but I wanted to give the young people a chance to talk without imposing my presence too heavily. The palace courtyard worked well as a setting. I brought my distaff and spindle, and sat some distance away; close enough to ensure nothing untoward took place, but far enough to be removed from the conversation.

Not to say I didn't eavesdrop. Of course I did! I did my best to hear every word – any mother would.

Polynikes was the first to call upon her – and, as the spring ripened into summer, he visited more often than Eteokles. Megara seemed to look forward to their conversations; she took care in deciding what to wear when she knew they would share an afternoon, and applied her violet-scented perfume. He always brought her some charming gift: once a huge bouquet of narcissi, another time a nightingale in a wicker cage. He praised her beauty and her wit, professed himself intoxicated by her presence; he kissed her hand and sat close beside her in the shade of the laurel tree. He seemed to charm her – he certainly charmed *me*, and I wished that I was young again and as lovely as Megara. In my youth I was pretty enough, but never a beauty on a par with Megara or Jocasta – and giving birth to so many children ages a woman.

Eteokles came as well, but less frequently and far less ardently. "You're very pretty, Megara," he observed one afternoon, with the same matter-of-fact tone that someone might say: "The cow on that hill is brown."

"Thank you, cousin," was Megara's crisp reply.

"You don't really want to marry me," he continued, "and I don't really want to marry you."

My daughter's eyebrows went up at this observation, and I confess I stopped my spinning to listen more closely.

"Nevertheless," said the prince, "an alliance between us might be mutually beneficial." He then lowered his voice, and I couldn't make out his next words – not for lack of trying! But I could tell from my daughter's expression that she found them very interesting.

At any rate, the twins' individual efforts to woo Megara continued through the summer. Meanwhile Alkides succeeded in routing out the gangs of bandits in the north, enriching himself and Thebes with their coffers of stolen gold and gems. Creon, still preferring to have him away from the city, sent him to work with the herds. He did well there too: not even Lasthenes the Herd-Master was better with the animals. Alkides attended a few banquets at the palace that year – Creon could not find excuses to keep the young man away all the time – and he was handsomer than ever, with his skin tanned nut-brown and gleaming sun-bleached streaks in his dark blond curls. But I only caught him and Megara staring at each other once. Most of the time Alkides was at Eteokles' side, and surrounded by a cluster of adoring young maids that excluded my daughter. And all through that autumn and winter I never heard the least gossip that Alkides minded the twins' wooing Megara.

Polynikes' manner reminded me of his father as a young man: the twins looked very much like Oedipus when he first arrived in Thebes. Oedipus had truly been in love with Jocasta, I thought sentimentally – even if it turned out to be terrible incest. But Polynikes was not as quick as Oedipus in pressing his suit. I supposed he was waiting for his own manhood ceremony to be closer. It wasn't until spring that he broached the key subject. One afternoon, with the crocus just coming into bloom, he took Megara's hand in both of his. "Marry me," he finally said. "I'll be a good husband to you, Megara."

Sitting several strides away in the northeastern corner of the courtyard, I did my best to keep my spindle moving at a steady pace. I lowered my lashes, trying to seem as if I wasn't watching them at all.

Megara smiled, a dimple gracing her cheek. "In what way, cousin?" she asked playfully.

"In every way. I swear it." He shifted on the bench they shared; dappled sunlight filtering through the young leaves played across his shoulders. "I will cherish you as the treasure you are – as the queen that you must be. I will shower you with jewels from every corner of the world: lapis lazuli from Lydia, pearls from the depths of the southern seas, golden amber from the far north…"

I saw a spark of delight in my daughter's eyes; she adored jewelry. She opened her mouth to speak, but Polynikes reached up and set a finger to her lips.

"Not yet – don't say anything yet. Not until I've given you this." He withdrew a box of polished ebony from a leather pouch at his belt.

Megara took the box and opened it. Inside was something that shone with the rich luster of gold; my daughter held it up in the sunlight. I could tell that the gift was a bracelet, but that was all I could see.

Breathlessly, Megara said: "Two interlaced serpents… Polynikes, it's like the necklace of Harmonia!"

The youth came to stand beside her. "Yes. It's yours, Megara – as the necklace of Harmonia should be. Marry me. Be my queen."

She slipped the bracelet onto her slender wrist and held out her arm to admire it. Then she looked up at her handsome cousin, arching an eyebrow. "Your brother could say the same. The necklace belongs to the queen of Thebes. If I marry either one of you, I'd be able to wear the necklace only half the time."

"He *could* say the same. But *has* he?" He took her hand. "Megara, be my wife. I'll give you perfume so enticing that Hera herself will wish to borrow it. I'll have your skirts sewn from fabric delicate enough to make Athena jealous. You'll bathe in milk and rosewater every day, until your soft skin is the envy of Aphrodite."

"Your words are sweet as honey, Polynikes," she said, sounding impressed despite herself.

"Only because you inspire me." He lifted her hand to his lips and kissed it.

I saw her hesitate a moment, and then draw back her arm rather abruptly. She turned away, rubbing the back of her hand where he had kissed it.

Polynikes frowned. "Megara – Megara, you *don't* want to marry Eteokles. He's not to be trusted." His voice grew strained. "You *know* he lied about what happened at the boar hunt, don't you? He tripped – and then he tried to blame me! If that's how he treats his own brother, how do you think he'd treat his wife?"

She nodded, not looking back at him. "You have a point," she said in a quiet voice.

The prince brushed at the folds of his kilt and straightened his shoulders; his polished manner returned as he reached out to touch her shoulder. "Think about it, Megara. Please."

My daughter sighed. "I will, Polynikes. I promise. But I won't decide until after the manhood ceremony."

After he left, Megara walked back and forth along the pebbled path that circled the courtyard. "What is it, darling?" I called to her. "You look troubled."

I thought she was wondering which prince was telling the truth about the boar hunt, and which prince was lying. That was certainly the direction my own thoughts had taken. Polynikes was so clever with words – was his desperate tone when he spoke of Eteokles that of a brother wronged, or one trying to cover up his guilt?

But Megara said nothing of such thoughts. "Not at all, Mama!" She held out her arm to show me the golden bracelet. "Look – see how pretty it is? Eteokles never gave me anything like this."

Eteokles came to see her the next day; he brought a cloth bag with him. "There's something inside for you," he said.

Megara loosened the drawstring and took a small round-bellied jar of honey out of the bag. Looking down at it, she pursed her lips.

"It's the very best," he said. "That's what the merchants say. The best honey comes from Hymettos, outside Athens – not from my brother's lips."

"But your brother's offered more than honey," she said, setting the jar on the bench between them.

"Sometimes the package is more important than what's inside," said Eteokles. "Even if what's inside is sweet – or if it shines."

I didn't completely understand him then; I thought he was trying to be clever and poetic, and not doing it very well.

Megara sat primly upright, folding on her lap the bag that had contained the jar of honey.

Eteokles leaned forward, speaking too quietly for me to hear. Megara nodded a few times but said nothing; finally Eteokles shrugged and got to his feet. "If you want to marry my brother I won't stop you," he said in a louder voice. "Enjoy the honey, anyway." He glanced my way, gave me a brisk nod, and departed.

"I will," Megara called after him.

I set down my distaff and spindle and walked over to her. "What were the two of you discussing?"

"Nothing," Megara said, her cheeks flushing.

"It didn't *look* like nothing. He practically insulted you, leaving you to his brother. That's not like him. And it's not like *you,* either, not to be angry with him about it."

"Oh, Mother." She shook her head. "Eteokles and I have been friends since we were little. I'd never given any thought to marrying either him *or* Polynikes until you brought it up. If he has other plans, why should I hold that against him? We're still friends."

I frowned. "He has his eye on another girl?"

She shrugged. "I suppose so. I think he only paid court to me to see if his feelings might change."

And, I thought, because he had to compete against his twin for everything – whether it was something he really wanted or not. Perhaps Eteokles was giving up pursuit of Megara because he knew he couldn't outdo his brother in romance… and withdrawing from the contest would appear more honorable than losing it.

"He told me he wants us to remain friends, though," Megara continued. "And that's only right, isn't it? Since we're cousins and all."

I happily reported to my husband that Megara was leaning toward accepting Polynikes' hand; Creon was pleased to hear it. But I was wrong: Megara had fooled us all. I'll come to that in a moment.

The remarkable thing about the manhood ceremony that spring was how *unremarkable* it was, compared with the prior year. The twin princes, heirs to the throne of Thebes, were assuming the mantle of manhood – and yet the Tiresias stayed silent. Unlike the year before, the rites went entirely according to schedule; we had no dramatic outbursts. The people's mood was festive, of course, and they cheered the handsome princes; the banquet was delicious, and everyone had a marvelous time. I think Alkides left early to take care of his ailing mother, who had not attended – at any rate, I don't remember him being unusually drunk. I do remember Polynikes trying to steal a kiss from Megara, but she only let him caress her cheek – then she made her excuses and retired. For once there was no squabbling between the twins, and even Creon seemed relaxed.

"Tomorrow I can retire," he told me, his eyes twinkling. "Imagine – after tomorrow, I can sleep late! No more inventories scribbled in wax to strain my eyes. I can laze beneath the trellis in the courtyard, or enjoy a game of senet with my sons."

"You'll never retire," I teased him.

"Tomorrow I step down as regent," he said seriously, "and one of the princes will take first turn as king. Which one, I wonder?"

"I hope Polynikes," I whispered. "Then Megara can be queen sooner." I watched the princes – officially men at last – make their way around the megaron, speaking with one and another of the leading citizens. After a moment I added: "I suppose it doesn't really matter, though."

"It might," Creon said. There was a note of caution in his voice. "It might matter a great deal." I realized that for all his words about wanting to relax, he was leery of relinquishing his beloved Thebes to either of his young, untried nephews.

Because the twins could never agree which one of them would first sit on the throne, they had decided months ago to leave the choice up to the gods by drawing lots. But the exact procedure for this took more negotiation. Eteokles didn't want to draw straws: with only two straws, he argued, it would be too easy to guess which one was the shorter – and how would they decide who should draw first? He suggested that instead each of them should place a tile marked with a chosen symbol into a bag. Polynikes agreed to the concept, but insisted that a third party must draw out the tile to determine who would rule first. Creon proposed that Haemon, as chief priest of Apollo, should do this.

I recall Eteokles saying, a few months before the manhood ceremony: "But then who will hold the bag? It can't be you, Uncle – you must preside over the event."

Creon nodded. "True."

"What about Alkides?" ventured Eteokles.

"Absolutely not!" my husband snapped. "He has no place in this matter – he's not of the line of Kadmos." After a moment's consideration, he said: "How about your sister?"

"She'd be too nervous," said Eteokles. "Besides, Ismene would hate to play any part in choosing between us."

"Megara could do it," Polynikes suggested.

"Megara?" asked Eteokles, and then objected: "We all know she favors you—"

"Perhaps, but she wouldn't touch the tiles," Creon said. "She'd only hold the bag for Haemon to draw from."

Eteokles frowned. "I suppose," he agreed reluctantly.

With this process agreed, each prince needed to choose an emblem for his tile. The sphinx, commemorating Oedipus' victory in the riddle contest, was the royal symbol of Thebes. But for just that reason, Creon said they were only entitled to use the sphinx when they sat on the throne.

Polynikes quickly chose the lion as his personal symbol. When the two ivory tiles had been carved – and verified identical in size and weight – Polynikes had the palace artisans paint a lion on his. He also had a small statuette of a lion cast in bronze, which he gave to Megara. And he had his ox-hide battle shield painted deep crimson, with a roaring lion in gleaming gilt. Eteokles selected a serpent, celebrating Kadmos' victory over the serpent which had led to the founding of Thebes; he had the palace artisans depict a coiling red serpent on his shield, against a rich yellow-gold ground.

And so on the day after the manhood ceremony, Thebes gathered once more in the agora; we of the royal retinue took our place in the square. Antigone, my dear, your brothers were so handsome in their kilts and cloaks of red bordered with thread-of-gold; both wore a slender red-and-gold diadem tied around their heads, and with their coppery curls and polished bronze-studded belts and sandals they shone like twin gods. Creon, with his flowing silver beard, looked handsome and distinguished – and you, Haemon, you were magnificent in your white robes.

At the very center stood Megara. She was glorious – and that's not only the fond claim of a mother. People in the crowd talked about it. Some said she was even more beautiful than Jocasta! She wore flounced skirts of red and gold, and a red jacket sewn with polished gold spangles; her lips and cheeks were rouged red, and her nipples gilded. Strands of golden beads and red ribbons wove through her dark curls – Hyperbius the merchant said she was like the city of Thebes, transformed into a woman.

Dried flower-petals were thrown, and music played. Finally Creon lifted his hands to the crowd's swelling cheers; then he lowered his arms slowly, the crowd quieted, and the serious part of the ceremony began. Each of the twins poured a libation of wine, and Haemon led them in swearing a holy oath to Zeus. Together they vowed that they would always protect Thebes, lead well during their time as king and serve faithfully when their brother held the throne, and abide by the order established in the drawing of the lots.

The oath done, Creon inclined his head and said: "Then I am ready to relinquish Thebes' rule." With dignity, he beckoned Megara forward.

She held a bag dyed deep red, like the color of drying blood; its mouth was bordered with golden braid. Holding it open, Megara showed the bag to both princes, to her father and brother, and then to the public, to demonstrate that it was empty.

Polynikes withdrew his ivory tile from his belt and held it up to show the gilded lion on its surface. Then he dropped it into the bag, saying: "May the gods choose the Lion of Thebes!" A cheer went up among his friends and he waved at them, smiling. Finally he stepped aside.

Then his brother Eteokles stepped forwards. I remember thinking how alike they looked – identical in height, in their trim physique, in their blue-eyed good looks, with only the scar on Eteokles' arm showing a difference. Even their voices sounded the same. Eteokles held up his own tile, saying: "A serpent guarded Thebes before Kadmos arrived; Kadmos and Harmonia took that form when they left Thebes. May the gods choose this symbol to protect Thebes now!"

Eteokles' faction shouted approval from the other side of the agora as he dropped his tile into the gold-trimmed bag.

Then the crowd fell silent: the moment of decision had come. Maybe it shouldn't have seemed so momentous: after all, the brothers had just sworn to rule in alternate years – it should make no difference which of them took the throne this first year. And yet we all held our breath in suspense. I had more reason than most to care about the outcome: as I'd told my husband, I wanted Polynikes to be chosen so that Megara would marry him and become queen at once. My heart pounded as Creon asked our son to make the determination on behalf of our city's patron god, Apollo.

Haemon lifted both hands to the blue sky overhead; fingers spread wide, he chanted a prayer imploring the gods to guide his hand. Though I should have been listening closely, repeating the words of his prayer in my heart, I found my attention drawn back to Megara. I expected to find her gazing at Polynikes – but instead I saw her glance briefly at Eteokles. This puzzled me, but there was no time to ponder it further. Haemon finished his prayer and stepped over to Megara, who held open the bag. He put his hand into the bag and drew out a tile.

He glanced at it, then held it up for all to see. "The serpent!"

Eteokles grinned in triumph; his friends shouted, whistled, and stamped their feet.

"What?" Polynikes cried against the noise. "Let me see that!" he said, grabbing Haemon's wrist.

Creon moved closer and inspected the tile along with Polynikes. "It is the serpent, Nephew."

Polynikes turned to Megara. "The bag, let me see the bag – is my tile even in there?"

Megara upended the bag, and a tile dropped into Polynikes' palm. With Haemon and Creon beside him, Polynikes inspected the ivory token. It bore a lion, his own lion.

Gripping the tile in his fist, Polynikes turned on you, Haemon. "You cheated! You purposely picked the serpent!"

I'd never seen you look so angry, Haemon. Your face darkened, and you said: "By Apollo, Zeus, and all the gods, I did nothing of the sort!"

Alkides pushed his way to the front of the crowd. "Be calm, my lord prince! Eteokles was lucky, that's all. It'll be your turn next year."

As Polynikes' fury subsided into disappointment, I wondered why he

157

had been angry in the first place. One of the twins had to win the draw, and one had to lose. The gods had selected Eteokles for first turn on the throne, that was all. I was disappointed too, because this meant I'd have to wait a year to see Megara become queen. But that was as the gods willed.

Except that it wasn't.

I didn't learn the truth until much later, when Megara finally told me what she had done. She'd altered the lining of the bag so that there was an extra division hidden within it. Polynikes dropped his tile into one side of the bag – the side that was slightly deeper. Then Megara adjusted the way she held the bag so that when Eteokles dropped his tile, it fell into the other division – where another tile was already waiting, a tile marked with an identical serpent, supplied to her earlier by Eteokles.

So when you reached into the bag, Haemon – into the shallower portion Megara made available to you – your fingers found two tiles, just as you expected. You couldn't know that *both* of these bore the sign of Eteokles.

Megara told me that Eteokles had given her a similar bag before, when he delivered the honey, and then they practiced this trick until she was confident she could do it correctly, leaving none the wiser. Her only moment of fear was when Polynikes demanded to see the bag. Fortunately for Megara, shaking the lion tile into his hand proved sufficient – if he had still insisted on searching the bag itself, he might have discovered the extra compartment holding the extra serpent tile. But he did not.

Later, Megara crushed the extra tile and threw the bag in the fire.

But at the time we knew none of this. Alkides calmed Polynikes, and Creon hushed the crowd. The palace herald brought forward the crown of Oedipus, resting on a purple-dyed cushion, and Eteokles placed it on his head, covering the princely diadem. He spoke words of blessing to the assembled crowd, and then said: "I will hear oaths of loyalty from my subjects."

These were to be done in order of rank – and the highest ranking was Polynikes, of course.

Tension gripped the crowd. Eteokles' supporters looked on with narrowed eyes, waiting to hear what the rival prince would say; Polynikes' faction leaned forward, hands near sword-hilts. I thought worriedly of the violence the Theban agora had known in the past, and whispered a prayer to Apollo to protect his city now.

Haemon handed the sacred wine-cup to Polynikes. "Repeat after me," he said. "I, Prince Polynikes, son of Oedipus, swear loyalty to King Eteokles of Thebes."

Resentment was plain on Polynikes' face. He took the goblet, sprinkled a few drops of wine on the ground, and said: "I, Prince Polynikes, swear loyalty to King Eteokles of Thebes – *for the next year.*"

Ranking next after Prince Polynikes, my husband took the oath; each nobleman of Thebes came in turn to swear his loyalty, and then King Eteokles called for music, food, and wine. He led the well-born up the palace stairs and into the megaron; with a flourish he pulled away the cloth that concealed his father's throne, and seated himself to applause.

People took their places, and the servants brought out the meal that had been in preparation all day; there were toasts and laughter and music, and although Polynikes and his friends still looked sour, most joined in the toasts to the new king. I heard Alkides' voice at one point, reminding Polynikes that it would be his turn next year, and hoping that the celebration would be every bit as good. After the meal, King Eteokles and Alkides started a drinking game that involved tossing a pebble at a cup of wine; those whose aim was good could choose to drink it themselves, or choose another player to down the cup. This quickly grew riotous with laughter; my son Menoeceus, the soldier Melanippus, and even old Demochares joined in. Before long Megara excused herself, saying that she had a headache.

I was standing with Creon near the central heath when the Tiresias and his two daughters entered the megaron. "Gods," Creon muttered as the revelers made way for the prophet. "I'd hoped the old man had gone to bed."

Briefly the Tiresias turned his blindfolded head our way, and I remembered that he had keen hearing. I touched Creon's elbow to remind him to behave.

King Eteokles paused in his game, pebble in hand, and called out: "Welcome, Tiresias! Would you care for a cup of wine? The vintage is excellent, I assure you. I won't even make you toss for it!"

"No, my lord king, I thank you," said the Tiresias, leaning against his wooden staff. "The gods have asked me to deliver a message to you."

At these words all conversation stopped; someone shushed a tipsy flute-girl, and her song trailed off with an awkward squeak.

Eteokles set down the pebble and straightened his stance. "Very well, Tiresias. What is this message from the gods?"

"King Eteokles, if you and your brother are to reign peaceably in Thebes, you must obtain your father's blessing. Without his blessing Thebes will suffer."

The new king frowned. "Even though he had to be banished to cleanse the city?"

Shrugging, the seer said, "That is the gods' message."

King Eteokles folded his arms across his chest. "Does anyone even know where he is?"

After a short silence, Ismene ventured: "He and Antigone were in Argos a while back. But I don't know if they're still there."

Everyone looked at the merchant Hyperbius, who as the one who traveled most for his business, was the one who generally brought news of the exiled king and princess. Hyperbius' mouth was full – the man loved a good meal – he had to chew and swallow before he answered. "I haven't been to Argos for months, my lord prince – I mean, my lord king."

159

"Very well," said Eteokles. "At first light, we'll send a messenger to Argos. Father has suffered enough for his crimes. It's time to bring him and Antigone home."

Speculation about the meaning of this prophecy, and the whereabouts of Oedipus and Antigone, took over the crowd. My curiosity piqued, I joined in the conversation – and failed to realize that Alkides had left the room.

It was not the first time that he and Megara managed to meet.

My clever daughter – she and Eteokles outsmarted all of us, even Creon. When she came to us not long after this to say she was pregnant by Alkides – and that King Eteokles had already sanctioned their marriage – I was completely flabbergasted. Creon was furious, but there was nothing he could do. With his daughter carrying Alkides' child, he would never get another man to marry her – and he could not defy Eteokles' will without challenging the royal succession he had worked so hard to stabilize.

And so Eteokles was on the throne of Thebes and Megara was in Alkides' bed. Everything was exactly as they had planned, starting that day in the courtyard so many months before.

*

Eurydike shakes her head, remembering. "Megara was clever. But in the end it did not help." Remembering where her daughter's cleverness led is so painful that Eurydike must push those memories away. That happened later, anyway; it is not part of the story she's telling now. "Eventually," she continues, "the messenger returned from Argos. But he said Oedipus and Antigone were gone."

CHAPTER EIGHT
ANTIGONE

Eurydike's voice stops. Antigone shifts, and realizes that she has not moved her right arm for a long time; it tingles as though a thousand tiny bronze needles are pricking her skin.

"By then we'd left Argos," she says, rubbing her arm vigorously with her left hand. The discomfort, though annoying, reassures her: here in the lightless tomb, she is still alive.

"Why?" asks her sister.

"I'll come to that," Antigone says. Feeling is returning to the fingers of her right hand; she shakes it, and accidentally strikes the rocky wall of the tomb. Stifling a curse, she pushes herself up to stand, feeling stiffness in her legs. "But this trick Eteokles and Megara used – Haemon, you didn't know?"

"No!" His disembodied voice is full of anger. "I had no idea."

"Eteokles stole the throne from the very start," Antigone muses. Carefully she walks a few steps, her fingers trailing against the stone wall for guidance; then she turns and walks back, brushing the rough wall with her other hand.

"Why should I have suspected anything?" Haemon says, sounding defensive. "As Alkides pointed out, *one* of the twins had to be first. And like everyone else, I thought Megara preferred Polynikes."

"Does Uncle Creon know?" Antigone asks. "Did you tell him, Aunt?"

"I – I've never told this to anyone until now," Eurydike answers. "But he may have guessed, especially after Eteokles approved our daughter's marriage to Alkides. Creon's always been shrewd."

"What Megara did—" Haemon begins, and then stops. Hearing the tightness in his voice, Antigone imagines him clenching his fists. "She helped bring this war upon Thebes."

"But she loved Alkides so much!" interjects Ismene. "Eteokles just took advantage of that!"

"She paid the price for what she did," say their aunt. "So did Eteokles."

Antigone pictures the three of them looking at Eteokles' burial mound. "At least Eteokles had a proper burial," she snaps. "If Uncle Creon guessed the truth, he should have allowed Polynikes the same dignity!"

Eurydike reminds her: "You performed the rites, Antigone. His soul is at rest."

"Perhaps." Antigone recalls how she knelt beside Polynikes' corpse, sprinkling a handful of earth on his face and chest, chanting the prayer to summon Hermes. Her uncle's soldiers pulled her away before she could do anything further. "But his body is still out there, being eaten by crows. What I did doesn't feel like enough."

"That doesn't mean it wasn't," says Ismene. "You're always so angry, Antigone – don't be angry at yourself now!"

"Maybe I had to be angry for both of us," Antigone snaps. "You've always been too forgiving: Mother, Uncle Creon, Eteokles, me – well, once I'm gone, to even the scales you'll have to start showing some spine!"

"Antigone!" her aunt exclaims.

"You don't know what your sister has done the last ten years," says Haemon.

Anything? Antigone wonders, but this time manages to hold her tongue. "I – I suppose not."

"She was brave during the siege," continues her aunt. "And she's here with you now."

Antigone's anger drains away. Suddenly she is very tired. "You're right. I should not have spoken so."

"You're upset," says Ismene, her soft voice full of understanding – making Antigone ashamed of her outburst. "Of course you're upset. You have every reason to be. Anyway, you said you'd tell us why you and Father left Argos."

A wry smile twists Antigone's lips. There is, after all, one thing Ismene can always be counted on to do: listen.

"So I did," Antigone agrees.

And she will keep her word, although talking will dry out her throat. Settling back down on the packed-earth floor, pulling the blanket close to breathe in the scent of lavender, she resumes her story.

ANTIGONE

As I said, King Adrastos gave us a little one-story house, with a tiny courtyard garden and a pair of servants to take care of us. It was not luxurious, but after so many days of wandering without assurance of a roof over our heads, both Father and I were grateful. In fact, the small size of our new home proved helpful: Father soon learned his way around, and could walk through our few rooms without bruising his shins on the furniture.

We spent much of our time at the palace: King Adrastos liked introducing us to his visitors. A gregarious man, he obviously enjoyed the scandalized reaction we evoked. Father was his good-luck charm, the man who had reminded him he was a king. Throughout Argos we were treated the way huntsmen treat an old, flea-bitten, three-legged dog who nonetheless manages to scent the prize stag: we were welcomed, rewarded with treats, but not embraced too closely.

The king had two young daughters and an even younger son; their mother had died during Adrastos' banishment and he had not remarried. Having seen him in Aphrodite's temple in Korinth, I guessed that he preferred to keep a variety of mistresses – but it was probably also to his advantage to leave his options open, for he had only recently gained the throne and Argive politics were complicated. Amphiorax, husband of the king's lovely sister Eriphyle, was high priest of Zeus and seemed to lead another faction, while other noblemen dressed almost as richly as the king himself, and bowed to him less deeply than they should.

The summer solstice occurred shortly after our arrival. Because it was the first time for this festival to be held under Adrastos' rule, he arranged an especially extravagant event: four full days of games, musical contests, and feasts, culminating in a chariot race – in which King Adrastos himself would compete.

Peasants streamed in from the countryside, pitching tents around the athletic grounds. There were guests from Athens, Tiryns, Sparta, and wealthy Mycenae – but Argives made up the bulk of the chattering, excited crowds. The peasants wore wreaths of bright flowers on their heads; the noblemen and their ladies were splendid to behold. The ladies rode in cushioned sedan chairs, with strands of gold and silver woven through their hair; their husbands, sons, and brothers wore brilliantly dyed kilts, and carnelians and agates adorned both sword-sheaths and sandals.

I described all this to Father as we made our way toward the festival grounds. "Argos must be very rich," I said. I glanced down at my own skirts, a gift from the king; they were almost as good as what I had owned as a princess of Thebes – and they were merely the king's gift to a suppliant.

"Or at least King Adrastos wants everyone to think that," Father replied, a little too loudly.

"Father," I whispered, "People can hear you." He sometimes forgot that even though he could see no one, others heard and saw what he did.

We passed through the city's western gate and made our way towards the gathering. Guards ushered us to the area reserved for the nobility; as we approached the tiers of wooden benches shaded by a broad striped awning, a servant indicated that we were to take places near the king.

Seeing us, Adrastos grinned and called out: "Friends, visitors – this is Oedipus, formerly king of Thebes, and the unluckiest man alive!" The noble Argives were used to us, but the foreign visitors stared.

While we waited to climb to our seats – several people before us moved slowly – I scanned the nobles and told Father who was in attendance. I started with the king's sister, golden-haired Eriphyle and her husband the priest Amphiorax. It was already warm and the priest was fanning his wife with a small fan. The king's stocky, curly-haired nephew Kapaneus – son of an elder sister long deceased – was also there, with his wife and small son. I mentioned Iphis, an older man, the father of King Adrastos' dead wife; he sat between Princess Argia and Princess Deipyle – the daughters of the king and Iphis' granddaughters. I described Hippomedon passing a wineskin to his companion Parthenopeus. Small and dark, with crooked teeth, Hippomedon was a favorite of the king and seldom far from the lanky, freckled Parthenopeus, a member of the minor nobility. The two of them were hard drinkers and loud braggarts; I wondered how they would fare in the athletic contests.

"*Oedipus* of *Thebes*?" asked an Athenian trader. "King Adrastos, you harbor a monster whose presence will bring pestilence!"

Adrastos beckoned us forward, grinning, and I led father towards him. "Not at all! My dear sister welcomed them to Argos in Hera's name."

Another visitor, decked in Mycenaean gold, rubbed his nose and objected: "Hera may be your city's patron goddess, King Adrastos, but her husband Zeus is king of the Gods—"

The king of Argos shook his head and turned to his brother-in-law. "Amphiorax, share your wisdom as Zeus' high priest. Do we offend the gods by giving sanctuary to Oedipus and his sister-daughter Antigone?"

Handing the small fan to his wife, Amphiorax rose. A heavy, broad-shouldered man, he had never seemed particularly pleased by our presence – but perhaps his thick black eyebrows and narrow eyes made him look perpetually suspicious. He stared at me and Father for a moment, then up at the sky, then finally peered in the direction of an oak tree; the nobles all around us fell absolutely silent.

The priest observed the movements of the clouds and the oak leaves, then announced: "Whoever keeps Oedipus safe in his kingdom will fare well. The city that garners his tomb will prosper throughout the ages. This is the will of Zeus."

The crowd around us murmured in astonishment; beside me, Father sighed with relief. King Adrastos rubbed his hands together triumphantly. "You see! You see! What have I been saying? It's the law of Zeus himself: hospitality! The gods favor those who take pity on the unfortunate!"

Amphiorax scowled as he sat back down. His expression suggested that he did not quite agree with King Adrastos – and yet he did not dispute the king's words.

We were finally able to press through to our places, and I helped Father take his seat while the king's remaining guests arrived. Then the Argive herald shouted for silence; by the third time this command rang out across the crowd, conversation ceased and the people gave their host respectful attention.

King Adrastos stepped out from under the awning; his golden crown flashed in the sun. Holding his arms wide, he declared: "Welcome! Welcome, Argives and neighbors, countrymen and friends. Today and the three days that follow you will witness contests of strength, speed, and talent to rival even the Olympic Games of King Pelops' day!"

People whistled and stamped their feet; even the Mycenaean envoys appeared to accept this in good spirits, as homage to the heritage of their ruling family rather than a challenge.

"We begin today," Adrastos continued, "with the contests for heralds, musicians, and bards; tomorrow we shall see feats of strength; the third day will test our men's skill at arms; and on the fourth day we will see who is most fleet of foot over distances short and long, and which man is master of the chariot."

When the applause subsided, King Adrastos called for his sister and brother-in-law to invoke the gods' blessing. A tawny bull-calf was sacrificed to Zeus, and a sleek brown heifer to Hera; the beasts' organs were pronounced well-formed, and the offering-smoke rose towards the heavens in the straight, unbroken columns that indicate the gods' favor.

Father enjoyed the first day of the competition. Even a sightless man could choose his favorite among the loud voices of the competing heralds, and Father had firm opinions about the various flautists, lyre-players, and praise singers. King Adrastos often asked Father's opinion, pointing out to the young king of Tiryns that a blind man might be the most honest judge in such contests, since he could not be swayed by a singer's good looks or a lyre-player's charming smile.

But as the day wore on, Father grew pensive, and during the feast at the palace Father said he wished to speak with the priest Amphiorax. I helped him up, set his staff in his hand, and led him over to the priest, who was conversing with a nobleman from Mycenae. Noticing our approach, the priest touched his companion on the arm and said something I could not hear. The man glanced our way and nodded to Amphiorax, then left.

"Yes, Lord Oedipus?" said Amphiorax.

"I want to thank you for your favorable pronouncement this morning, but I still have questions." Father hesitated, shifting his weight. "Forgive me; I've been deceived by oracles in the past – or deceived myself, hearing only what I wished to hear. That's why I must know, Amphiorax: is there any hidden meaning in your words?"

Amphiorax folded muscular arms across his chest. "I'm a plain-spoken man, Oedipus. I know silver-tongued Apollo prefers riddles and poetry, but I was called by Zeus himself. The city where you are laid to rest *will* prosper. And no harm will come to the city where you reside."

I saw the tension leave Father; he inclined his blindfolded head, as if making a silent grateful prayer. Then he raised his face and said, "Thank you. It's a relief to know we can stay here without bringing evil upon Argos. I owe my daughter a better life than that of a wandering beggar."

"Father," I murmured, "don't worry about me."

He patted my hand, but continued: "Amphiorax, has Zeus forgiven me? Or is there still a curse upon my soul? And – on my – Jocasta?"

The priest scratched his dark-bearded jaw. "I don't know. These are weighty problems, which we cannot resolve now – especially with the festival just beginning. We'll speak later."

Father slumped a little, but then he nodded understanding and thanked

165

the priest for his time. "I'm tired, Antigone," he said. "Let's go back to the house."

In the morning Father was fatigued and irritable; I guessed that worries about Mother and his own soul kept him from sleeping well. As that day's contests progressed, I tried to tell him what was taking place on the sand, but I was no expert on wrestling or boxing. Only when one fellow knocked his opponent unconscious did I know the result before the judges made their announcement. When the contests changed in the afternoon I had an easier time; I could report which man flung his discus the furthest, and which made a longer jump than the rest. Father and I retired early that night, and though the noise of the drinking-parties throughout the city could be heard in our little house he managed to rest. By the third day of the festival, his spirits were better, and he cheered with Kapaneus' wife and little son when the barrel-chested man won the javelin contest and congratulated Hippomedon after that fellow took the prize for archery. The afternoon brought mock battles with sword and javelin – and, to my surprise, the priest Amphiorax won both contests. The Argives seemed to expect this – apparently Amphiorax was celebrated for such skills – but it had not occurred to me that a high priest of Zeus could also be a city's leading warrior. When I voiced this thought Father chuckled, and said that perhaps in Thebes our priests were too soft.

I was less surprised to see lanky Parthenopeus win the next day's distance-race, although he lost to a man from Sparta in the morning sprint. But even as King Adrastos set the victor's garland on Parthenopeus' head, all talk turned to the festival's final event: the chariot race.

The crowd erupted into applause as the four chariots approached at a walk, each driven by the racer's horse-trainer. King Adrastos and the other contestants stood and made their way down towards the chariot-track. Since the king was to compete, Amphiorax assumed the presiding role for the event. The two young princesses, Argia and Deipyle, clapped and called out encouragement to their father the king.

Each man brought his two-horse team into position at the near end of the sand-covered oval racetrack. The herald announced them, starting with King Adrastos. His wicker chariot-car was painted with a large red pomegranate on each side; purple-dyed ribbons were twisted around his chariot rails, and woven through the neatly braided manes and tails of his dun-colored horses.

Next came the king's nephew Kapaneus: his bronze helmet bore a horsehair crest dyed in hues of red, orange, and yellow that matched the bright ribbons streaming from his horses' manes. I observed to Father that, although Kapaneus' ebony steeds were both beautiful and graceful, the thick-set man would surely be a heavy burden.

Hippomedon and Parthenopeus were the last two charioteers. Hippomedon's vehicle was simple and unadorned, and his horses – one brown, one dappled – appeared healthy and strong, with manes and tails streaming free in the warm breeze. Parthenopeus, on the other hand, had used enough decoration for several vehicles: his entire chariot was painted blue, and he wore a matching blue kilt and a bronze helmet with two whole boar's tusks affixed at the front. After I described the tusks, Father chuckled and whispered: "Like a young buck just getting his first antlers!"

Finally the charioteers were in position. The herald held his arms wide and then clapped sharply; the sudden noise set the horses' hooves in motion. I had to shout at the top of my voice so that Father could hear me over the thunder of pounding hooves and the shrieks of the crowd.

The race interested me more than I expected – my days driving our little donkey-cart had given me an appreciation for the charioteer's art. King Adrastos, positioned at the inside of the track, quickly pulled into the lead. Kapaneus lagged behind: he was too heavy for his team. Early on, Parthenopeus overtook the king's nephew; but as the four chariots completed a circuit of the oval track, I realized that Parthenopeus was turning too wide. In Hippomedon, who had the worst starting position, I recognized real skill. He edged past Kapaneus and then, just after the circuit was completed, pulled ahead of his lanky friend Parthenopeus and moved tighter inside. He was gaining on the king.

King Adrastos glanced back over his shoulder; seeing Hippomedon closing in, he grimaced and slashed his willow goad at his horses. The crowd's roar grew louder and louder: by the completion of the second loop, it looked as if Hippomedon might overtake the king.

But then, in the third and final circuit, I saw Hippomedon pull back on the reins. Before my journey through Arkadia, I would not have noticed it: but now I knew enough of draft animals to tell that the horses were not slowing out of fatigue. It was a slight thing, but just enough to ensure that King Adrastos' chariot crossed the finish line first.

While King Adrastos took his victory lap, I said: "The king has won."

"What is it, Antigone?" Father's eyebrows drew together above his blindfold. "Is something wrong?"

Even with all the noise of the crowd, Father could detect the dry note in my voice. "It's nothing," I said, not wanting to shout about what I had seen. "I'll explain later." Watching the sandy-haired, handsome king smile and wave at his subjects, I wondered if he realized that Hippomedon had not done his best.

He *had* to know, I decided – the man was not stupid. And surely he knew more about chariot-racing than I did. But when he knelt so that his daughter Argia could tie the victor's ribbon around his forehead, the king's broad grin gave no indication that his joy in his victory was diminished by that knowledge.

That perplexed me. Adrastos was not a bad fellow – he had been very generous to Father and me. But how could he be so content with undeserved glory? To be sure, a man may want to be king whether or not the throne rightly belongs to him: the position brings wealth and privilege, so that part I understood. But I was starting to realize that many men – our host apparently among them – crave praise for its own sake, whether genuinely earned or not. Some thirst for it like a drunkard thirsts for wine; they lie and cheat to make themselves appear greater than they are – and yet *they* must know the truth about their deeds – as do the gods.

I glanced at those around me, curious whether any realized what had happened. The priest Amphiorax was studying Hippomedon, one dark eyebrow raised. Apparently he had *noticed* what had happened, but was he *disturbed* by it? I shrugged. I was new to Argos and did not know its ways; perhaps letting the king win was the custom here.

The chariot race was the festival's last contest. The spectators poured out of the stands, and many offered their congratulations to the king. He clasped hands with his competitors, praising their performance in the earlier events, and then invited us to feast with him beneath a canopy located just beyond the athletic field. As I led Father down the wooden stairway and in the direction of the delicious smells, a Mycenaean said: "There's nothing like a good chariot-race! King Adrastos, your horses are as beautiful as any I've ever seen."

A nobleman from Tiryns added, "Such a joy to watch. And you handle them with skill, my lord king."

The king smiled at this praise.

Hippomedon scratched his nose. "A good chariot-team is wonderful," he said. "But chariots themselves are limited."

King Adrastos frowned at this drop of negativity. "What do you mean?"

Waving back in the direction of the racetrack, Hippomedon replied: "Chariots need level ground. And even on the best terrain, you can only turn so quickly. Too sharp a turn and you find yourself kissing Mother Earth."

His words reminded me of how our donkey-cart had tipped and how miserable Father and I were afterwards, shivering in the cold wet mud without any means of warming ourselves. What a relief it was to leave our wandering behind! I guided Father to a group of tables and benches beneath a broad canopy where the well-born would be served. The peasants would also have meat today, but they would roast their own skewers over the bonfires that ringed the fields.

At our table, long-limbed Parthenopeus nudged Hippomedon. "You'd become a centaur if you could!"

"Only if I could change back into a man when I liked!" Hippomedon laughed. "But seriously, the thing is to find a horse tall enough to carry a man on its back. Centaur by day, man by night – that's the thing." He winked at a serving-girl sauntering by; she giggled and hurried her steps. "Just think – then you could go anywhere a horse could go. Up a steep slope, through a forest – even across a river!"

"Few horses are large enough to carry a man," said King Adrastos.

"One's been seen running wild in Arkadia," said Hippomedon, his voice wistful. "A stallion white as snow, with a smoke-gray mane and tail. They say he's as tall at the shoulders as a man, and fleet as the wind. No one's been able to catch him."

"Antigone, could that be Arion?" Unfortunately, Father's question came at a moment when the rest of the table was silent.

The men turned towards us. "Arion?" Hippomedon asked.

I glanced uneasily from him to Father. "That was the name of a horse we saw in Pylos," I said. "The one you're describing sounds similar, my lord."

Kapaneus objected: "But this horse is in Arkadia, not Pylos. Could it have run so far?"

"Of course it's possible," said Hippomedon. "Oedipus and Antigone have walked as far, and horses outrun men."

"I suppose so," said Father slowly. We had never explained the precise circumstances under which we left Pylos.

"I gather there's a story here," said King Adrastos. "Tell us about this Arion – even if it's not the same horse."

Father must have felt the tension in my grip; he patted my hand reassuringly, and in a calm voice explained how we had sought Poseidon's favor in Argos. I watched the faces of the Argives and their noble guests as Father related the tale. When he told of Arion's escape, a few men edged away from us, muttering at the bad omen. Eriphyle grimaced, and set a hand on her pregnant belly; her husband moved closer to her, concern on his face.

"King Adrastos, are you *sure* this man isn't cursed?" asked a seafaring merchant. He needed Poseidon's good will.

Adrastos shrugged. "The high priest of Zeus told us that Oedipus has not brought his curse to Argos. Right, Amphiorax?"

The priest glanced up from his wife. "Yes, my lord king."

Rubbing her belly – perhaps the babe inside was kicking – Eriphyle commented: "Poseidon created the horse. Horses are special to him – perhaps he wanted this one to live."

"If the horse I've seen is your escaped Arion, it would be a crime to sacrifice him," Hippomedon concurred. "What an animal!"

"My dear," Amphiorax said, beckoning to the servants that carried Eriphyle's sedan chair, "let's get you home."

The blonde woman, obviously fatigued, nodded. "Yes, I think – I think that would be best."

The king's sister and her husband departed, while Hippomedon quizzed Father and me about Arion. Some of his questions, such as the horse's ancestry, neither of us could answer; and of course only I could describe his looks and behavior.

"I'd wager it's the same animal," Hippomedon concluded, despite my faltering responses.

King Adrastos had a gleam in his eye. "What if Poseidon spared him so that he could be ridden by men?"

"We'd have to catch him first," said Kapaneus, scratching an insect bite on his thick neck.

"And once we did, we'd have to find a way to get a rider on his back," said Hippomedon.

"But how hard can that be?" asked Adrastos. "Think about it: bull-dances have been a Kretan tradition since ancient times. I think most of you have seen them at one time or another. If youths and maidens can stand on the back of a full-grown bull – and flip themselves over its horns – then why can't a man sit astride a horse?"

"I think they do, in the north," opined a Spartan, reaching for a handful of olives.

"But that's where the centaurs live," said the king of Tiryns, who was about my own age. He was a fellow of average looks, which had not been improved by the sunburn he had acquired these past few days. The skin on his nose was starting to peel; he rubbed at it absently. "I expect someone saw a centaur and thought it was a man sitting on a horse."

This turned the conversation to centaurs and other creatures. "I think we should go home," Father said. We slipped away from the revelry before the roast nuts and honeycakes were served.

The next day, the peasants returned to their duties in the fields and the visiting nobles straggled away from Argos. Then Father sought an audience with the priest Amphiorax to pursue the question of how he might receive absolution. But Amphiorax replied that this matter should be brought jointly to Zeus and Hera, and his wife was not feeling well and might not be able to help us until after she gave birth.

"A delay of many months," Father said glumly, as we returned to our little garden.

The lavender was in bloom. Normally this cheered me – the scent always reminded me of you, Aunt Eurydike – but Father's sour mood affected me as well. Instead of enjoying the perfume I frowned at the bees attracted to the purple flower-sprays.

"The gods are avoiding me," Father sighed.

"Maybe not," I said, waving a bee away from his face. "They might just be waiting for the right moment."

He tugged on his beard, a habit he had lately acquired. "Time means nothing to the deathless ones. But I'm mortal – I must find absolution before I die."

"Maybe that's not necessary." I put my arm around him. "Amphiorax said the gods would bless the city where you're laid to rest. Why would they do that if they hadn't forgiven you?"

"I don't know," he said, running his fingers through the curls of his beard and then twisting the silver-and-copper hairs around his knuckle. "But I don't *feel* their forgiveness." He lowered his voice. "What if she's suffering, Antigone? What if she's being punished?"

I could not help myself from snapping. "Why do you want to help *her*?" She was the source of all our troubles, after all!

"I *loved* her, Antigone – I love her still."

"I know, Father. I just don't understand why," I said, trying to quell my frustration. "Get some rest. I'm sure Amphiorax and Eriphyle will see us soon – long before the Fates clip your thread." I decided I needed fresh air; I told the serving woman to watch over Father and headed towards the agora, hoping a walk would help me shed my irritability. The sun was sinking low in the west, and merchants were bundling up their wares, but the packed earth of the agora still felt hot as a bronze-smith's forge beneath my sandals.

Was that it – was it just the heat and the crowds that had put me on edge, these last several days? My monthly blood was not due for some time, so I did not think that was the cause of my ill temper. Silently I scolded myself, telling myself that Father deserved better. He needed me. He needed me to—

I stopped short, and someone collided with me from behind. Muttering with annoyance, a peasant woman carrying a basket of undyed wool stepped around me.

Perhaps, I realized, the problem was that Father did *not* need me so much lately. Not the way he had needed me when we were trudging up and down the hillsides of Arkadia. Now we had a roof over our heads, and a home in which he could find his way around without me guiding his every step. We even had servants again. What Father needed now was something I could not help with – and after having been challenged for so long, I had little to do. In Pylos, I had occupied myself with weaving alongside Queen Chloris. Well, I told myself, our house had no loom, but I could certainly spin wool into thread. Spinning was less interesting than weaving, but at least it would be productive.

Nearly two months after the festival, Father and I received a summons to meet with Amphiorax and Eriphyle. They received us in the roof garden of Amphiorax' house. By then the worst of summer's heat had receded from Argos; though our meeting took place at mid-afternoon, the shade of a vine-covered trellis offered a pleasant refuge. In the dappled light, Eriphyle's skirts – cascading in alternate pale and dark shades of blue – made me think of water rippling over her heavily pregnant body. Her breasts were full and round; she reminded me of a polished ivory figurine.

Amphiorax offered us seats in the shade; his wife arranged her skirts gracefully as she settled onto a gilded chair. Her toenails elegantly colored with henna, but her ankles were swollen from her pregnancy. Father inquired after her health.

"This is my first child so I don't know what to expect," said Eriphyle, "but the midwife assures me that I am well, even if I don't feel so. Now that the worst heat of the summer has passed, it is a little easier."

"You look fine," I told her.

The priestess raised an eyebrow, as if she begged to differ, but then seemed to decide there was no point in discussing beauty or the inconveniences of pregnancy with me. "Thank you, Antigone," she said politely and changed the subject. "Oedipus, we are sorry my condition forced me to delay seeing you. I know you have spoken to my husband, but tell us again what it is you want."

Father explained how he wished to make sure that his soul was pure, and that our mother was not being punished in the Underworld.

Amphiorax squinted at him. "Describe the cleansing rituals you have performed, or attempted to perform, since leaving Thebes."

Father spoke of what happened in Korinth and Olympia and Pylos, and of our time with the Maidens of Artemis. "What must I do?" he finished plaintively, "for myself – and for Jocasta?"

Eriphyle rested her hands on her swelling belly. "You loved her very much."

"I did," Father whispered.

"They say she was the most beautiful woman in Hellas," Eriphyle said.

Father smiled wistfully. "I always thought so." Then gallantly he added: "I've heard that you are beautiful too, my lady."

"I have posed your petition in the sacred oak grove," Amphiorax said, "But Zeus has told me nothing so far. My dear, has Lady Hera revealed anything to you?"

"Only that Oedipus was a devoted husband, and she bears him no grudge. But she has not shown me what he must do to find peace."

Folding muscular arms across his chest, Amphiorax said: "Oedipus has tried sacrifices, and rituals of bathing. Being blind and lame, he cannot win the gods' favor with athletic events or heroic deeds. What if he seeks the deathless ones in a dream?"

Eriphyle pursed her red lips and nodded. "In the realm of dreams, Oedipus and Jocasta can petition the gods together – even though she's no longer among the living. That could be the solution."

They discussed the matter further, and concluded that three nights after the next full moon Father should make an offering of incense and sleep through the night in Hera's temple; then he should repeat this ritual the following month in the Temple of Zeus. "You may have to be patient," Amphiorax warned. "I believe the gods will take their time about answering you."

I wondered why Father should bother with the ritual before the gods were ready, but Eriphyle answered my question before I could voice it. "But you should come anyway. The gods are honored by consistent devotion."

"Thank you," Father said. I could tell that the promise of a new tactic encouraged him.

I was likewise heartened by the conversation – it looked as if we would not be traveling soon – and ventured to ask a favor of Eriphyle. "My lady, would it be possible to set up a loom in our house? The rooms are too small for a large loom, but there's enough space for a little one."

"You enjoy weaving?"

"Very much."

"Then you must go to the weaving room in the palace! I'm a poor weaver myself – I was my mother's last child – a surprise, actually; she thought she was finished bearing children. When I was old enough to learn her fingers were too stiff to teach me. But my nieces should learn. You could teach them, Antigone."

Thus I became acquainted with the young princesses, Argia and Deipyle, and helped them with simple designs. My own first project was a tapestry of the horse Arion, hoping that this would please Poseidon if he were offended – and hoping that the result would satisfy the unending curiosity of King Adrastos and his friend Hippomedon. I never saw Eriphyle weave, but she occasionally joined us in the workroom, often bringing a lyre-player, especially during the last couple of months of her pregnancy when the weather had turned wet and cold. She gave birth to a boy shortly before the winter solstice.

That first year, Father received no helpful dreams, but Amphiorax and Eriphyle urged him to be patient. Zeus and Hera were not always in perfect harmony with each other, and so it might take several cycles between their temples to achieve anything.

During this time Hyperbius the Trader brought us news from home – and a kind message from you, Ismene. Hyperbius said that Creon was serving as regent until the twins came of age, and assured us that everyone was well. Father never said this, but I sensed that he hoped his other children might come to visit. Sometimes we cannot speak our deepest desires. I did not ask the merchant about you, Haemon – Father did that. I felt my face redden when the man replied you had sent no message.

As one year turned into the next, King Adrastos continued hosting lavish banquets and games; I noticed that he often gave rich presents to his friends. And the city teemed with his friends: men who enjoyed drinking games and pretty flute-girls after a day's chariot-racing, and who gladly accepted golden arm-rings and new cloaks as gifts from the Argive king.

As always, I described to Father what he could not see. "I wonder where his wealth comes from, that he can be so generous," Father remarked one night after we had returned to our little house.

"Tiryns," I said. We both knew that the young king of the nearby port city, famed for its thick walls, gave Adrastos support.

"I'm still not sure that's enough. If Adrastos continues like this, he'll empty his storerooms." Then he smiled and shook his head. "Ah, Daughter, who am I to complain? I'm not a king any longer. I don't need to tell Adrastos how to run his kingdom."

As the seasons changed, Eriphyle became pregnant with her second

son. Adrastos' daughters Argia and Deipyle grew faster than their tapestries
– like their aunt, they lacked talent at the loom – and the king's young son
turned from a toddler to a little boy. I began to worry about Father's health;
in the cooler months of autumn, Father complained of new aches and pains.
When he slept at the Heraion during the autumn rains, he caught a chill and
coughed violently afterwards. The king sent his own healer; the man
frowned more than I liked as he made his examination, but his syrup of
poppy seemed to help.

About a month after our second winter solstice in Argos, and a very
cold night at the Temple of Zeus, Father finally had a dream to report. In
the morning's gray drizzle I came to escort him back to our house, and
before we left the temple he described his dream to Amphiorax and to me.

"I was standing outside Delphi, at the place where three roads meet –
the place where I encountered my father Laius, though I did not know it was
him. A chariot rushed towards me."

He hesitated, uneasy, and Amphiorax prodded: "Describe the horses."

Father twisted his fingers through his beard. "The horses – there were
three; I know that is strange – the one in the middle was creamy white, with
a dark mane and tail. It was Arion – the horse from Pylos."

The priest nodded and pursed his lips. "And the others?"

"Both solid black."

"And was your father Laius – the man you killed – driving the
chariot?" Amphiorax asked.

"No…" He sounded troubled; I reached for his hand, and he squeezed
my fingers. "Jocasta was driving. She was so beautiful… as lovely as
when we first met. Her dress was black but she wore a garland of red and
yellow flowers. She asked me to join her in the chariot, but I hesitated, and
she drove away without me."

"Interesting," commented the priest, his eyes narrowing. "What do you
think it means?"

"I don't know," said Father. "I was hoping you would tell me."

"You didn't join her," I ventured. "You knew it would be wrong."

"Perhaps, Antigone." Father shook his head. "All I know is that my
heart leapt with joy when I saw her – and fell with despair when she drove
away."

He still loves her, I thought, despairing in my own way.

"Amphiorax, what do *you* think it means?" Father asked.

The priest looked up into the shadows of the temple rafters. "I'm not
sure," he admitted. "You had the dream here, so it should be a message
from the king of the gods. But the meaning is not yet clear. Three horses
pulling the chariot – as you say, that is strange." He turned back to Father.
"In the dream, did either of the horses neigh, or make any other sound?"

Father's graying brows drew together. "I – I don't think so."

The priest shrugged. "The gods will make their meaning clear in time,
Oedipus. I will discuss your dream with my wife – but I think you will

have to seek another vision at Hera's temple next month."

The next day I visited Eriphyle, who had recently given birth to her second child, another boy. She invited me back to her rooms and took a seat at her dressing-table. She had the finest mirror I had ever seen: held upright in a bronze stand, it was square in shape, and its silver surface was formed and polished so perfectly that there was hardly any distortion in the reflection. Eriphyle glanced at herself and tucked a stray lock of golden hair behind one ear. She frowned slightly and said, "I'm not sure about this new hairstyle."

I had not noticed the difference, but when she mentioned it I realized that her servants had piled the curls higher than usual, and twisted several tiny braids around the back of her head. "You look as lovely as you always do, my lady."

She turned away from the mirror and smiled. "Ah, Antigone – how I envy you!"

"Me?"

"Yes, *you*, Antigone! You have such confidence. And you never seem to worry about your hair, or whether your sandals match your dress."

I glanced down at my sandals, slightly alarmed. Did this pair look wrong with my skirts? Not that I had much choice; despite King Adrastos' generosity, my wardrobe was far more limited than when I lived as a princess of Thebes.

But Eriphyle was not looking at my sandals; in fact, she had turned back to her mirror and was brushing a finger over one gracefully arching brow. "You're so skilled at the loom – and you've journeyed halfway across the world! Whereas my day is spoiled if my hair isn't just right. I wish I were more like you, and didn't care how I look!"

The remark stung, though she did not mean to insult me. Pretending to have the nonchalance that she perceived in me, I shrugged. "Worrying about it wouldn't help me, my lady. I've never been beautiful." I hoped the words did not sound as bitter as they tasted.

"I'm with child again," she said. "This will be the third pregnancy since my marriage started. Women's beauty attracts men, which gets us with child, which ruins our beauty."

"But you've no reason for concern – you're the most beautiful woman in Argos!"

She turned away from her mirror, her expression wry. "Not all of Hellas?"

I couldn't tell whether she was mocking my praise, or mocking herself. Perhaps both. To my surprise, I found myself trying to reassure her. "I've not traveled to *all* of Hellas," I said, "but I can truthfully say you outshine the women who serve Aphrodite in Korinth."

"You're as word-careful as a prophet!" she said. "But you didn't ask to meet so that you soothe my vanity. Come, why are you here, Antigone? Your Father's dream?"

As he said he would, Eriphyle's husband had already told her the key points. She asked if Father had described the flowers in Jocasta's hair. "Amphiorax said they were red and yellow. Do you know what kind they were? Could the yellow flowers be narcissi?" she asked.

"Yes, I think so," I said. "I think Father may have mentioned that."

"What about the red flowers? Roses or poppies?"

"I don't know."

"Could they be pomegranate flowers?" asked Eriphyle.

"Perhaps," I said. "Father did not say. Is it important?"

"My husband thinks so," she said.

I thanked her and went home, wondering. Pomegranate flowers were never used in garlands because plucking them destroyed the fruit, but they were bright red. Pomegranates were favored in Argos as Hera's preferred fruit and a symbol of fertility – but pomegranates could also represent death. Swallowed pomegranate seeds had compelled Persephone to remain in the Underworld with Hades.

I brought these ideas back to Father. He listened and said that he had not mentioned the flowers in our mother's hair, but that Eriphyle was right, the yellow flowers were narcissi and the red were pomegranate. "And you said Eriphyle said that her husband asked about the flowers?" Father asked.

"Yes," I said.

The next day, despite the fact that he wasn't feeling well, Father insisted on going to Zeus' temple. There to my desperate embarrassment, he loudly challenged Amphiorax: "What kind of seer are you, that visions remain hidden for so long?" Irritation plain in his voice, he continued: "Or is it that you know and won't tell me?"

At first I thought Father's question rude – but when I saw Amphiorax's parted lips, I realized that Father had somehow guessed the truth. Amphiorax did know more than he was telling.

The large priest raised his hand in a calming gesture, then seemed to realize that Father could not see him. Instead he approached us, speaking slowly. "Oedipus, Lord Zeus has finally given me his answer," said Amphiorax. I stared at him apprehensively, fearing he was about to foretell Father's death, but he said something I had not in the least expected. "Oedipus, you must go to Athens."

I blinked; in unison, Father and I asked: "To Athens?"

"Yes. For some time I have suspected you would have to go there eventually, but I was not sure when – and obviously King Adrastos likes having you here. But this very morning, just after dawn, I saw an eagle headed in the direction of Athens. You must go to the district of Colonus, outside the city of Athens, and seek absolution from the Kindly Ones."

*

There is a long silence from the other side of the wall. Finally Haemon says: "So that's what made you go to the Kindly Ones."

Exhausted, trying not to think of her thirst, Antigone nods in the darkness and rests her head against the stone wall. "Yes. The ancient goddesses of vengeance and retribution – called the Kindly Ones only because it is too dangerous to call them anything else."

CHAPTER NINE
ISMENE

Ismene shivers, remembering her terror at Colonus.

Her aunt Eurydike rises slowly. "Antigone, you sound exhausted. You should sleep."

Antigone's disembodied voice answers: "You're right, I *am* tired. But..." The words grow fainter, becoming incomprehensible. Ismene listens intently, unable to tell if her sister has stopped speaking or if she herself simply failed to hear.

"Antigone?" Haemon presses, frowning. "But what?"

"I – I don't want you to go."

Ismene is sure that if *she* were walled up in a dark cave to die, that she would be babbling with terror; nevertheless it is unsettling to be reminded that her bold sister Antigone is afraid to be alone. "We can't leave her like this," she whispers to her aunt and cousin.

"I want to speak to Antigone," Haemon says quietly. Then he clears his throat. "I'll stay with you, Antigone. Mother and Ismene will step out for a little while, but I'll keep you company while you sleep."

"I can stay too," Ismene offers.

Antigone's voice comes through the wall. "No, Ismene – please go with Aunt Eurydike."

"Come, Ismene," Eurydike says. "You've been here longest - you need fresh air."

Ismene allows herself to be pulled to her feet. Once again she is yielding. Always yielding. Her sister complains that she yields too easily, and yet compels her to do it again.

She follows her aunt to the door of the tomb. After sitting for so many hours, her arms and legs are stiff and uncooperative, but the two of them manage to pull open the door. The outside air is warm and sweet, the sunlight painfully brilliant. The guards touch the backs of their hands to their foreheads in respect when they see their queen.

"Wait," Eurydike says beside her. "My eyes..."

Blinking against the blinding daylight, Ismene waits as she is told. What is it, she wonders, that stops her from resisting the orders of others – from insisting on her own desires? Her siblings never yielded so easily. Eteokles, Polynikes, Antigone: all three spirited, all unafraid – while she, Ismene, does nothing. Is nothing.

Of course, her brothers are dead – and Antigone will soon join them in the Underworld. But they made their short, vibrant lives their own.

As her eyes adjust, Ismene discovers that the crowd on the rise beyond the tombs has grown. Have the same people been watching all day, she wonders, or is this a new and different group? A few gesture towards her and her aunt, making Ismene feel shy and exposed – do they realize that while she has been sitting in Eteokles' tomb, she has been speaking with her renegade sister? Guiltily she turns away, as though turning not from the onlookers but from the bright sun. Toward the wall of mud bricks imprisoning her sister.

On the ground lie several wreaths of flowers and pine, offerings of mourning. Have they been left to honor the dead king – or to show respect for her sister? In truth they seem a little nearer to the bricked-in entrance, but the cave openings are so close to each other that it is hard to tell.

Curious, Ismene approaches a guard. "Soldier, did you move the flowers?"

He shakes his head. "No, my lady princess; they are where the people put them."

"Look," says Eurydike, bending down to examine them. "Roses, and sprigs of lavender."

"They're for Antigone!" Ismene feels a glimmer of relief. There must be others who do not hate her sister.

"You may be right," her aunt says. "Guard, who left these flowers here?"

The man's face turns stony, impassive. "My lady queen, I did not see."

How can that be? Before Ismene can ask the question, the answer arrives in her mind – in Antigone's voice: *Of* course *he knows who put the flowers before the wall! He just doesn't want to tell Queen Eurydike. Her husband's the one who condemned me.*

This guard sympathizes with Antigone! Ismene's spark of hope swells into a warm and comforting flame. A man who shed blood for Thebes – the wound on his arm still ugly and scabbed – he feels for Antigone!

What if I were you, Antigone? What would I do now? Ismene has never before asked herself that question. But an answer comes to her immediately: *I'd break down that wall!*

The thought is so bold, so unlike her, that she catches her breath and sways.

"Are you all right?" asks her aunt.

The strange, daring notion sputters out like a torch in a downpour. "I don't know."

Even the two soldiers look concerned. "You were in your brother's tomb a long time, my lady princess," says the soldier with the injured arm.

Eurydike takes her hand. "Oh, my dear – of course you're not all right. None of us are. And you must be hungry and thirsty: you arrived here long before Haemon and I did. Let's return to the palace and get you something to eat."

Ismene looks back at the mud-brick wall. How could she imagine tearing it down – even if it were not guarded by armed men? She couldn't possibly succeed. Why even try? There is no point.

In this thought she hears an echo of Antigone's words just now, dismissing her – and an echo of a thousand other thoughts and words over the years, a thousand other reasons to say nothing, do nothing, be nothing.

Perhaps, she thinks, *I could get food and water to Antigone.* That would not be a complete victory – but during the siege of Thebes she has learned that the first goal is always one more day of life.

As she and Eurydike make their way through the somber crowd, one woman says: "May the gods bless you, my lady princess. You *and* your sister." Ismene recognizes her, a peasant woman who sells goat cheese in the agora.

"Thank you," Ismene answers.

Before they can go more than a few steps, a dark-haired man approaches. Judging by his tunic and sandals – plain, but clean and well-made – he serves a noble household. He bows formally and asks, "My lady, are you Princess Ismene?" At her nod, he continues: "My mistress invites you to take some refreshment in her pavilion." He gestures northeast where a broad tent of striped fabric has been erected a little distance from the road. Two of the tent's four sides are rolled up and secured with ropes, leaving a shaded space beneath the peaked roof. Carpets cover the ground; there are three-legged tables and richly patterned cushions. A veiled woman occupies one of several folding chairs.

"May my aunt accompany me?" Ismene asks.

"Queen Eurydike?" asks the servant. He bows even more deeply. "My mistress would be honored to receive her."

Ismene and Eurydike exchange a glance, and then Ismene nods. It is only a few paces away. There is a crowd of Thebans nearby, and Theban soldiers stand guard outside the tombs. Whoever this woman is, surely no harm can come to them.

As they approach, the woman rises gracefully from her chair. Fine white fabric covers her hair and face, and swathes her shoulders and breasts; only her large eyes are visible.

The servant announces Ismene and Eurydike by name; then his mistress says: "I am called Phyle. I am a priestess whose duty has called me to this place." With a wave of her hand, she invites Ismene and Eurydike to be seated. "Will you honor me by accepting food and drink? There is water with mint and honey, and I have fresh bread and figs and cheese."

"Thank you," Ismene says, her mouth watering. She sits; after the hard stone floor of her brother's tomb, the cushioned chair is soft and comfortable. She sees four soldiers near the tent, dressed in blue kilts and carrying shields each decorated with a gray-colored owl: the emblem of Athens.

"You are very welcome," says the woman. Turning to her manservant, she says: "See to it."

"Yes, my lady," he says, bowing low before he departs. A serving woman wearing a long, dark blue tunic offers Ismene and Eurydike goblets of water; a second, a few months pregnant, awkwardly hands them terracotta plates. The manservant returns with a small bronze table laden with bread and other delicacies, which he places between their chairs. The cheese is delicious, the bread soft, the minted water refreshing. If only she could get some of this to her sister!

"It's excellent," says Eurydike, after draining her goblet.

Ismene wipes her fingers clean with the last morsel of bread, swallows it and then asks: "What duty do you have here, priestess?"

"I wish—" The veiled woman hesitates, clasping her long-fingered hands in her lap, and then begins again. "I wish to understand what has happened here."

Ismene frowns. "Do you mean the sentence King Creon has imposed on my sister?"

The foreign woman inclines her head. "In part. My training as a priestess bids me understand the larger pattern of events here at Thebes. I was told that there was a prophecy —one given by your father Oedipus. Some claim he foretold Thebes would fall if attacked – and yet Thebes has prevailed."

"At great cost," Eurydike says bitterly.

"Yes," acknowledges the priestess. "That, too, is part of what I must understand." She turns back to Ismene; above the veil, her brows draw together. "Do you know, Princess Ismene, your father's exact words?"

Ismene clasps her hands together. Strange that the priestess should pose *this* question: her father's last words came so soon after the events her sister just described. It seems that the Fates mean for her to re-visit the past: first in the darkness of Eteokles' tomb, separated from her sister by an unyielding wall of stone – and now here, caressed by a warm breeze, with an Athenian priestess and a crowd of curious Thebans for her audience. They stand at a respectful distance, but she can tell that they are listening intently.

"I remember his words," says Ismene. The memories are not pleasant.

"Will you tell me?" asks the priestess.

Ismene's inner voice asks why she is so ready to yield once again – especially since she would normally be too shy to speak before so many people. But, oddly, she does not feel shy. Perhaps war and loss and everything else have finally worn away her timidity. Perhaps the Fates want this story told, so they have given her strength.

Ismene lifts her chin. "Yes," she says. "Yes, I will."

ISMENE

When my brothers reached manhood, they drew lots to determine who would first rule Thebes as king, and Eteokles won. Just after this, the prophet Tiresias received a vision; he told Eteokles that Eteokles and Polynikes needed my father's blessing. Without it, he warned, the city would suffer.

My father and sister had been gone from the city for three years; we heard that they had settled in Argos. So Eteokles sent an envoy to Argos, charged with bringing Father back to Thebes.

The day that this messenger left, Eteokles came to my room and demanded that I give him the queen's crown and the necklace of Harmonia.

Weakly I objected: "Those should only be worn by the queen of Thebes – and you're not married!"

"Married or not, I'm the king," he said. "And the treasures belong to the throne." He crossed the room to the chest containing the precious relics and lifted its lid. I remember how the late spring sunlight caught the delicate gold-work of the necklace, casting scattered sparks of light across my brother's face. "You have protected them faithfully, Ismene – but they're no longer your responsibility." He settled the necklace back into its case, snapped shut the lid of the chest and carried it away.

My servants witnessed this, and servants talk; soon people wanted to know why the king had taken possession of Harmonia's treasure. Even Polynikes drew me aside. "Is he planning to marry?"

I spread my hands. "Not that I know of. I don't think he spends time with any girl in particular, other than Megara." Both my brothers had been courting her, and Polynikes' expression changed at the mention of her name. Softly I said: "Polynikes, you should know – she's still in love with Alkides."

Since you're not from Thebes, Priestess, I suppose I ought to explain: Alkides was another young nobleman, very handsome and popular and strong. My cousin Megara had been in love with him for years, but her father – my uncle Creon, who's now king here – opposed the match.

When I mentioned Megara's feelings for Alkides, Polynikes' eyes narrowed. "Perhaps," he replied. "But love's not the only reason to choose a husband." He stalked off, shaking his red-gold head.

He may have been right, but love was reason enough for Megara. With Eteokles on the throne, at last there was a power in Thebes greater than her father's – and Megara convinced the new king to sanction her marriage to Alkides. At the time, I thought Eteokles agreed mostly so that his twin would not win her. Uncle Creon was angry, but he would not undermine his nephew's new rule with a show of defiance – especially as Megara claimed to be carrying Alkides' child. Even so, the ceremony was hurriedly planned and performed, as if Megara wanted to make sure that no one stopped her.

A few days after the wedding, I was sitting on the palace's southern balcony. With the summer heat, the breeze up there was welcome. More importantly, this balcony offered a good view over the city, out to the hills and mountains in the distance – and I hoped to catch the first glimpse of my father and sister returning to Thebes. I whiled away the hours by making thread and watching the people in the streets below. That afternoon my cousin Menoeceus joined me, sitting beside me on a bench. I praised the poem he had recited at his sister's wedding, and asked how his newest work was progressing.

"Slowly," he said, tapping his bronze stylus against the small folding tablet he always carried. He was the only poet I ever knew to make notes about his work; others said that interfered with the inspiration from the muses, but Menoeceus claimed that his note-taking helped him to piece together the words in the manner that would most please Apollo. "I envy your spinning, Ismene: your fingers never struggle with what to do next!"

I caught up my spindle and wrapped the length of new thread into the skein. "I suppose not. But my thread's not nearly as interesting as your poems."

Menoeceus turned the stylus in his fingers; the line of spirals incised along one side caught the light. "Why is that, I wonder? Why *don't* people find simple, everyday things interesting?"

I smiled as I affixed a tuft of wool to my distaff. "I don't know. Have the muses ever suggested that you should create a poem about spinning?"

My cousin grinned. "No! It seems that even they prefer more excitement – secrets, scandals and squabbles. Speaking of squabbles," said Menoeceus, giving me a sidelong look as he guided our conversation in a different direction, "do you know that yesterday Eteokles accused Polynikes of sitting on the throne during the morning and countermanding his orders about how to allot the grain?"

"And Polynikes denies doing any such thing," I said, setting my spindle into motion again. "*He* says that Eteokles changed the orders himself, just to make Polynikes appear disloyal."

Menoeceus rose from the bench and walked over to the balustrade. "I wish they didn't look so much alike. It makes everything confusing."

"Even Mother had trouble telling them apart."

"Eteokles warned the noblemen not to accept orders unless they can see the scar on his arm, or take an imprint from his seal-ring. But the twin on the throne yesterday was wearing long sleeves."

"Which is strange in this hot weather," I said "So perhaps it was Polynikes."

"Or Eteokles, pretending to be Polynikes pretending to be Eteokles."

I shook my head; my cousin had too much imagination. "Perhaps when Father returns, they'll be friends again."

"Perhaps," Menoeceus said, shading his eyes as he peered into the distance. "But the messenger from Argos should have returned by now."

This was true, but I did not want to admit it. Before I could form any sensible response, the thread I was making broke; my spindle went rolling across the stuccoed floor. Menoeceus bent down to catch it, and returned it to me. He sat beside me again but I looked away, using the excuse of mending the thread to avoid meeting his eyes.

"I'm sorry," he said gently. "There are a hundred different reasons your father and sister could be delayed and still be perfectly well. The king of Argos may want them to participate in a ceremony. Or they might have broken a cart wheel – that happens often enough."

"I know," I said, twisting the wool fibers between my fingers. "But it could be something much worse."

He patted my shoulder. "Sometimes I think the worries of travel are worse for those who stay home, waiting. Travelers face all sorts of inconveniences, but at least their thoughts are occupied by their adventures. Those of us who remain home let our fantasy run wild. We imagine monsters and shipwrecks, instead of bedbugs and broken cart wheels."

"I suppose you're right," I said.

"I'll pour a libation to Hermes, and ask him to protect them," offered Menoeceus.

Apparently the god of travelers heard my cousin's prayer, for Eteokles' envoy, a trader called Hyperbius, came back to Thebes soon afterward. Despite my many hours of vigil on the balcony, I missed his return into the city, and learned from a servant that he was with the king in the megaron. I hurried there, and glanced around the group of gathered nobles – but saw no sign of Father or Antigone. Eteokles was frowning; Polynikes, Uncle Creon and Aunt Eurydike, standing together near the throne, also looked troubled.

Eteokles leaned forward on his raised marble seat. "What do you mean, they *won't* return?" he demanded of the portly trader.

Not wanting to disturb anyone, but hungry for information, I edged closer to where the Tiresias stood with his two daughters. "They're still in Argos?" I whispered to Daphne, who was closest.

She shook her head. "They're at Colonus, a village near Athens," she replied softly.

Puzzled, I turned my attention to Hyperbius. "...I explained your wishes, my lord king. But they refused. And, given the – ah – sacred nature of their hosts, I could hardly force them."

Eteokles' jaw tightened. "Why would they refuse?"

The trader tugged his tunic. "My lord king, they would not say – perhaps your father's health is not up to the journey. His lameness seems worse, and the years have not been kind to him."

Poor Father! He was so much younger than Uncle Creon – but for the curse that had struck him, he should have been in the prime of his life!

"However," the man continued, "your father did make one request. He asks Princess Ismene to visit as soon as possible."

At his words, all eyes turned to me, and although I took a step backwards, there was no escape from the attention. "Why – why *me*?" I stammered.

Hyperbius spread his plump hands. "I asked repeatedly, my lady princess, but they would not tell me – all I can say is that your father and sister were most insistent." He turned back to Eteokles. "I sought an audience with the Athenian king as well, my lord king, in hopes that *he* might persuade your father and sister to return with me to Thebes. But King Theseus refused to send Oedipus away – and he *also* called for Princess Ismene to visit her father."

Eteokles' eyes narrowed as he looked at me; unaccountably I felt my cheeks flush. "If Father's so eager to see you, Sister, surely you can convince him to give Thebes his blessing. We'll leave tomorrow."

"I'm coming too," Polynikes interjected. I could tell he did not want Eteokles speaking to Father without being there himself.

Eteokles glanced briefly at his twin, but did not object. "Of course. Uncle Creon, I want you to accompany us as well." He appointed three men – old Demochares, Megara's new husband Alkides, and the captain of the palace guard Melanippus – to manage things in his absence; then he turned to the seer. "Tiresias, will you travel with us to Athens?"

The prophet shuffled forward, leaning on his daughter. "My lord king, I doubt this journey will be any easier for me than for your father. I'm just as lame and blind as he, and far older—"

"Tiresias," Eteokles broke in, a note of entreaty in his voice, "if we are to seek my father in the lair of the Kindly Ones, we need your wisdom."

My brother's words filled me with horror. *The Kindly Ones?* Father and Antigone were being held captive by the dark goddesses of vengeance and retribution – and now they wanted *me?*

The Tiresias turned his head and seemed to stare with his blindfolded eyes through the walls; later I realized that Athens lay in the direction of his unseeing gaze. "Very well then, my daughters and I *will* join you – I have long felt that I should spend some time with Athena, and obviously this is the moment."

Daphne saw my dismay. "Don't be afraid, Princess," she murmured.

A straightforward imperative – banish my fear – but I could not comply. Like every child I grew up hearing stories of these ancient goddesses with snakes for hair and huge bat's wings on their backs. They chased their victims relentlessly, whipping them with brass-studded scourges. How could their cult be anything other than horrifying? Yet the Kindly Ones hold special grudges against those who violate sacred duties: of host to guest, of ruler to suppliant – and of child to parent. Ignoring Father's summons would surely bring their fury upon me.

"But why do they want *me*?" I asked her, panic creeping into my voice.

"I don't know," she admitted. "But they save their worst for oath-breakers. You haven't broken any oaths, have you, my lady princess?"

"I don't think so," I said, casting my mind over my short life's deeds and acts – but Daphne was right: I could not have broken any oaths because I had never, to my recollection, made one.

"My father serves Athena as well as Apollo, and Athena has a special bond with the Kindly Ones," she added. "I'm sure Athena will temper their wrath with her mercy."

This comforted me a little, and I was extremely relieved that the Tiresias and his daughters were joining us, but at dinner I was still too anxious to eat the stew of veal and figs. While I stirred the contents of my bowl with my spoon, a servant informed me that the king wished to speak with me privately. Eteokles had already left the megaron – he had to prepare for our departure on the morrow – so I went to meet with him in his chambers. Our cousin Megara was with him, even though she no longer lived in the palace; she had moved into Alkides' house when they married. So far marriage agreed with her, for she was more beautiful than ever.

Eteokles had the servants pour watered wine for us, and then dismissed them. "Ismene, I've been thinking," he said. "We should forge closer ties with Athens. King Theseus once expressed interest in making Megara his wife. That's no longer possible. But *you*, Sister…"

I stared. "Me?"

He grinned, his eyes sparkling in the lamplight. "Why not? The fellow may not have killed a Minotaur like the famous ancestor he's named for, but he'll make you a good husband."

"But—"

"An alliance between Thebes and Athens would benefit both cities," he continued. "That's why Theseus was interested in Megara, but you're the *sister* of the king of Thebes – not just his cousin. What better way to make a strong alliance? I'll wager that's what he's thinking."

"But Hyperbius said it's *Father* who wants me to come."

"Father wants the alliance, too, of course! Why else would you be needed in Athens?"

I had no answer.

"Certainly it must be better than being summoned by the Kindly Ones," said Megara.

Yes, on the face of it, marriage to the king of Athens seemed far better than meeting with the goddesses of vengeance. And yet my heart was galloping like a frightened horse.

"Look at her!" laughed Eteokles. "I don't think she agrees with you. I think she'd rather go to her doom."

"N-no, of course not," I stammered. "It's just that – I can't believe it. If he wants to marry me, then why doesn't he say so?"

"Perhaps he thinks the females in our family are too choosy. After

Megara turned him down, he may want to be sure of you before he proposes an alliance."

"Or maybe he just wants to meet you before deciding to marry you," suggested Megara.

I twisted my hands in my lap, guessing that my beautiful cousin doubted that any man who had once wooed her – as lovely as a swan – could be content with a dull thrush like myself.

"Anyway, make sure you bring the girl who does your hair and makeup, and pack your finest clothes. Megara here will help you; she's an expert in such matters."

So that evening I let my cousin Megara choose which skirts and jewelry I should take. She made various suggestions about how best to attract King Theseus, but I was too nervous to pay close attention. She said something about admiring everything he did, but the rest of her advice I quickly forgot.

"Make him fall in love with you and you'll be queen of Athens," Megara concluded. "You'll be married to a great man!"

Putting aside my own concerns, I wondered how happy my recently married, newly pregnant cousin was. Did she like living in a house rather than the palace – and not just with Alkides, but with Alkides' ailing mother? Did she ever doubt her choice? "The Tiresias said that *your* husband is going to be the greatest man in all Hellas," I reminded her.

"*Going* to be," said Megara, as if she needed to remind herself as well. But she recovered herself and added: "Don't worry, Ismene; there's no other man for me! Now, get plenty of sleep – sleep's a better beauty tonic than almond milk and fenugreek seeds."

Good advice, but I couldn't follow it. That night I tossed and turned, worrying about my father and my sister, King Theseus, and the Kindly Ones. When I closed my eyes, it seemed my maid was waking me only moments later.

The sun had not yet risen, but she was saying: "You must get up, my lady princess. We're leaving from the Neaira Gate at dawn."

She gave me my breakfast, bread soaked in wine, and after I dressed we hurried down to the gate which led to Athens. Despite the short time for preparation, everything was ready. The first pink light was just glimmering in the east as we gathered. There were no clouds, and the morning air was cool – but before long I would be glad of the sun-shade my maidservant carried.

"It will be a long day," my brother the king announced, "but if the horses make good time we'll reach Eleusis before nightfall."

As the Tiresias' daughters settled the old seer into one cushioned horse-cart, my cousin Menoeceus helped me into the other. "Is Haemon coming?" I asked. He was dressed in his white priestly robes – appropriate for asking a blessing on us, but not fit for the dust of travel. "Doesn't he want to see Antigone?"

Menoeceus shook his head. "He believes his wife should come back to *him*."

"What a shame. Before they married, they were such good friends."

"Maybe you can talk to her about it," he suggested.

I looked down, smoothing the folds of my skirt. "I don't know. Maybe it's wrong to expect happiness in marriage. My parents were the happiest couple I've ever known – and look how that turned out."

"They *were* happy, weren't they?" In the dim light I could not see his expression, but his voice sounded melancholy. "Goodbye, Ismene. I hope – despite everything – you'll be happy in Athens."

My brothers were busy preparing their chariots; sure they would not overhear, I blurted out the truth. "I don't know that King Theseus wants to marry me – and I don't know if I want to marry him. *Thebes* is my home." I had never gone any real distance from the city; my stomach clenched at the prospect of leaving forever.

He touched my hand. "Then why are you going?"

I blinked back tears, hoping he could not see them. "It's my duty as a princess of Thebes."

He opened his mouth as if to speak, but his father Creon interrupted, patting his son's shoulder. "Ismene's right, Menoeceus. Thebes comes before any of us."

Creon continued to his own chariot; my cousin dropped his hand from mine and gazed up at the city wall. Perhaps – perhaps he was thinking of our grandfather, for whom he was named. No doubt you know the story, Priestess – but you might not remember that the last Tiresias, the one who sacrificed himself for Thebes by throwing himself from the highest point of the walls, had been my grandfather Menoeceus before he gave up his name and his identity to serve the gods.

I'm sorry... where was I? Oh, yes, we were departing for Athens. Eteokles shouted orders to the guards; the men hauled aside the stout bar that held shut the city gate at night and pushed back the tall bronze-bound doors.

Menoeceus looked as if he wanted to say something more, but there was no time; my driver had already shaken the reins to start the horses walking. "Wait," said my cousin, fumbling at his belt. "Here, take this." He held up his stylus, the one he used to note down the words of his poems.

"What?" I said, startled. "No, cousin, you need that for your poetry."

Moving to keep up with the cart, he said, "I want you to have something to remember me by."

"There's no need for that," I said. I would not forget him in any case, and the cart was already pulling away. "Be well, Menoeceus," I called out, but I saw disappointment on his face before he turned away.

My brothers led the column in their chariots, followed by Uncle Creon and two chariots of guardsmen. The cart carrying the Tiresias and his daughters came next, then my own cart; two more chariots brought up the rear. Eighteen horses churn up a great lot of dust, and as the sun climbed higher in the sky I felt like a loaf of flour-covered barley-bread baking in an oven. My maid did her best to keep the sun's blaze off my face, and dabbed my neck with water whenever I took a drink.

The landscape moved past, and soon we were further from Thebes than I had ever been before. The hills grew more rugged, and I saw far more sheep and goats as opposed to cattle. Once in a while I caught a scrap of melody from some shepherd-boy playing his pipes in the distance. With the heat and the cart's swaying motion – and my lack of sleep the night before – my eyelids grew heavy, and I was yawning by the time we stopped to water the horses and take our midday meal.

Sitting by the roadside, under the shade of some of trees, my brothers and uncle said little; but the Tiresias spoke more than enough to make up for them. He had been a merchant in his youth, and being again on the road lifted his spirits. He told us tales of distant places: Olympia when the games were at the peak of their glory; the faraway eastern court of Lydia, where old King Tantalus ruled before going mad; the port city of Tyre, where the best purple dye was made. "From hideous sea snails, covered with thorns. And the smell! I'd be amazed if the breath of Hades' three-headed dog Kerberos smells worse!"

Perhaps because she had heard these stories a hundred times, Daphne suggested that we trade places for the next leg of the journey. I agreed, and what with the afternoon heat and the soothing sound of the old man's voice I nodded off to tales of Aegyptian tombs huge as mountains, guarded by statues of dog-headed gods twice as tall as a man. When I woke, I realized from the position of the sun that I had slept for some time – but the old prophet had dozed off as well, and was snoring unevenly. His younger daughter Manto smiled when she saw me stir, and whispered that her father's stories often had the same effect on her.

For all that my brothers pushed the pace, night had fallen by the time we reached Eleusis. We took shelter in the portico of Demeter's shrine, welcomed by the priestesses. Eteokles asked me whether I was ready to meet King Theseus the next day.

"I suppose so," I said, settling down onto the cushions my maid had arranged. "But I don't know what to say to him."

"Tell him you're fascinated by sailing," Uncle Creon suggested. "Athens has a large fleet, and he's certain to be proud of it."

"But, Uncle, I've never even *been* to the sea!"

"Then, say that you've always *wanted* to sail," advised Polynikes.

I glanced over at the Tiresias, whose daughters were helping him out of his sandals in a corner of the shrine. "That's not exactly true—"

"*Pretend*, Ismene!" my brothers chorused.

I nodded and fell silent, wondering how well I could feign interest in something I had never given any thought to. My sister Antigone would never do it, out of principle; my cousin Megara, I was sure, could convince a sailor – or any male, for that matter – that he was the most fascinating man alive. I certainly didn't have Megara's charm. But for once the twins were agreed on something: that my marriage to King Theseus of Athens, with his great fleet and his rich silver mines, would be good for Thebes. I resolved to ask the Tiresias about sailing in the morning, and stay awake to hear his answer.

Shortly after dawn Eteokles sent a pair of soldiers ahead in a chariot, to let King Theseus know of our impending arrival. My maid dressed me in my most flattering skirts, with a tight open-fronted jacket trimmed in blue braid; she rouged my lips, cheeks, and nipples and arranged my hair, adding some fresh flowers that Daphne and Manto had picked behind the shrine. Then we shared a simple breakfast of bread and cheese, and offered incense to the goddess in thanks for her hospitality. As we journeyed on, the Tiresias complained that his bones ached, but he did so with a rueful grin and a good-natured tone, so I took Daphne's place once more and asked him about traveling by sea.

I tried to pay more attention to the prophet's stories than to the olive groves we passed through and the great beige rock of the Acropolis towering before us – but his words about ships and harbors fled my mind when we sighted the Athenians. A long column of foot soldiers in blue-trimmed white cloaks carried tall spears; their shields had the newer, rounded shape with the crescent indentation at the bottom that allows a spearman to thrust at his foe from underneath. At the front of this procession was a tall, dark man, his white-painted chariot drawn by two gray horses. He was flamboyantly dressed, his kilt and cloak dyed entirely in purple – I thought fleetingly of the stinking sea snails of Tyre – and trimmed with shimmering gold rondels that echoed the richness of his heavy gold bracelets and jeweled crown.

Manto whispered to her father: "The king of Athens – and *many* of his soldiers."

My stomach knotted itself up like one of the sailor's ropes the Tiresias had mentioned. Would this man be my husband?

Eteokles moved his chariot slowly forward. "King Theseus," he called loudly, "we come in peace to meet our father. You've no need for your whole army."

The dark-bearded man grinned. "But, King Eteokles, these are only a few of my troops!"

I could not see Eteokles' face, but his horses shifted restlessly, as if sensing his uneasiness. "I've not come to count your men. I've come to see my father."

"Of course!" The Athenian king handed the reins to his charioteer and jumped down from the vehicle. Gesturing back to his soldiers, he said, "We're near the sacred grove; we should leave our horses here. Allow me to provide an escort. The walk will do my men good."

"Certainly," Eteokles said, sounding anything but certain. He gave his charioteer the reins and descended, indicating that Polynikes and Creon should do the same. His eyes narrowed as he appraised his twin suspiciously for a moment; then he turned back to the Athenian. "Allow me to introduce my family. This is my brother, Prince Polynikes – perhaps you know one another already?"

"No," King Theseus answered, "but I'm pleased to make his acquaintance."

I hated to see that Eteokles thought Polynikes might be conspiring with Athens – and yet I, too, watched closely. Polynikes offered our host a shallow bow; I detected no hint of recognition.

"My uncle Creon," Eteokles continued, "and my sister, Princess Ismene, sitting beside the Tiresias." He pronounced the seer's title rather too loudly – as if to emphasize any protection that his holy presence might afford, in case the Athenian king was contemplating violence. "Sister, come join us."

The cool of morning had long baked away; sweat dampened my brow and thighs. Wishing I had been forgotten, I let Daphne help me down from the horse-cart. I smoothed my skirts as best I could and approached King Theseus.

"Welcome to Athens, my dear princess," he said. "I hope your journey has been pleasant."

"Pleasant enough, my lord king. But I suppose an overland journey is never as pleasant as sailing."

"A Theban princess who enjoys sea travel?" he asked, lifting his eyebrows.

"Well, ah, yes—"

Polynikes interrupted: "We understand, my lord king, that you specifically asked for Ismene to accompany us."

"Closer alliance between Thebes and Athens would be most welcome," Eteokles added. "While our cousin Megara is wed, our sister Ismene would establish an even stronger tie."

My cheeks flushed; I felt like a haunch of meat being hawked in the agora, and not necessarily the choicest cut.

"Ah!" King Theseus looked me up and down, and I felt my face go hotter still when I realized there was more pity than interest in his eyes. "Your sister is a lovely maid, sons of Oedipus. But I recently concluded negotiations for a different bride – that betrothal is sealed." He turned from me to Eteokles. "Nonetheless, King Eteokles, I too would welcome tighter bonds between our cities."

"There are many grounds for alliance," my uncle Creon interjected. "Perhaps Athens could use more leather? Athenian silver is always welcome..." As the men fell into conversation, King Theseus led them back along the column of his soldiers, and then turned from the main road onto a side path.

Burning with shame – if King Theseus had found me sufficiently beautiful, I was sure he would have forgotten the other betrothal – I stopped listening and focused on my efforts not to burst into tears.

Coming to my side and handing me a linen handkerchief, Manto whispered: "Why are you upset, my lady princess? I thought you didn't want to marry him."

"I didn't," I said. And if the Athenian king was already betrothed, he wasn't rejecting me personally. I wouldn't have to marry a stranger; I could return to my home in Thebes. Feeling better, I blew my nose – not very elegant, perhaps, but that was no longer a concern.

Leading her father slowly toward us, Daphne said, "You were ready to do your duty for Thebes, Princess Ismene. That's what matters."

"Yes," I said, straightening my back. "But I didn't have to."

"There are other ways to serve," said the Tiresias, tapping the path before his feet with his wooden staff. And then, despite the heat of the day, I shivered – remembering that we had been summoned by the Kindly Ones.

We followed the path taken by the king of Athens with my brothers and uncle. Two Theban soldiers fell into step behind us, and at least a dozen Athenians. Soon the rocky trail led us towards the forest; tree branches formed a roof of greenery above, shielding us from the hot summer sun. I was as terrified as if I were approaching the Underworld, guarded by three-headed Kerberos. A rustle in the underbrush made me jump, even though it was probably only a hare. Large spider webs linked branches and leaves on both sides of our way; in one a moth struggled. As we walked the shadowed path, even the birds sounded mournful to me.

Why had my father and sister come *here,* of all places? And why did they – or the Kindly Ones – want *me?*

We reached a glade with more space and light. As a place of worship, it seemed strangely empty; there was no altar, no temple, just the trees and foliage that surrounded us. In the middle was a large wooden post; beside it sat a woman in a gray robe. When she saw King Theseus she rose from her rock, came forward and bowed.

"Welcome, King Theseus – have you brought us some criminals today?"

I realized then the reason for the wooden post. Wrong-doers were bound to it and whipped.

King Theseus did not answer her question directly. Instead introduced her to us as a priestess of Athena, explaining that some of Athena's priestesses served here, helping to moderate the fury of the Kindly Ones. Then he introduced my brother King Eteokles, and the Tiresias, to the priestess. He ignored the rest of us.

The gray-robed woman turned to my brother. "Of course – the son of Oedipus. Make your request at the shrine, and perhaps the Kindly Ones will answer you."

This puzzled me – I saw no shrine. But Manto touched my arm and pointed. My brother, standing closer, had perceived it already: he stepped towards what seemed like a curtain of foliage, but was actually a structure. Not very large, it seemed more like a thing that had *grown* there than a building made by human hands. Its wooden walls were covered by vines, its roof scabbed with moss. There was no bright color, no ornamentation that you see in the temples dedicated to the gods who sit with Lord Zeus on Olympia. But the Kindly Ones are ancient goddesses; no wonder that their temple seemed ancient as well.

The priestess said: "Knock on the door and make your request."

He pounded on the wooden door and declared loudly: "I am King Eteokles of Thebes. I wish to see my father Oedipus. Is he here?"

For the space of several breaths there was no answer. Then the door creaked open, revealing at first nothing but darkness. Finally three women emerged: one was young, about my age, the second matronly in years, the third a crone. All three were garbed in robes black as night, wrapped round the waist with braided leather belts that ended in long tassels tipped in bronze; their matted, dirty hair hung in twisted, snakelike ropes. They narrowed their eyes as they walked into the sunlight; the eldest shaded her brow with a gnarled, blue-veined hand as she peered first at Eteokles, then at Polynikes, Creon, and King Theseus. Her searching stopped when her gaze fell upon me. The hand left her face, and she pointed a palsied forefinger at me.

The other two women came to stand on either side of me. "Princess Ismene?" asked the youngest.

I flinched – I could not help myself – but answered: "Yes."

"You are still unmarried?" asked the one of middle years, who had a sprinkling of gray in her ropes of knotted hair. "A virgin?"

"Y-yes." In the cool of the glade my cheeks flushed once again.

"Very good," said the white-haired crone, shuffling toward me. "Lady Ismene, as you know, your father has committed grave crimes: to kill one's father, take carnal pleasure in one's mother – for this a man must suffer eternal torment in the Underworld! Unless, that is, his soul is cleansed before he dies."

We were all silent. After a moment, Creon spoke: "How can that be done?"

The old woman rubbed her hands together as if in anticipation. "Only the blood of a virgin can purify him – and relieve your mother."

"What?" exclaimed Eteokles, taking a step toward me.

I was faint with fear. "My blood, you mean?" I glanced at the bronze-tipped belt that circled the old woman's waist: would these women whip me to death, at the behest of their terrible mistresses?

"Yes, my lady princess," said the middle-aged priestess, and I wondered if this answer applied to my unspoken question. "Your sister is a married woman; her sacrifice would be useless."

"No!" said Polynikes. "It's not right! Ismene's innocent – why should she sacrifice herself for Father, who is guilty?"

193

Eteokles frowned. "But since she *is* innocent, she will not be punished in the Underworld. Father will, unless—"

"Silence!" ordered the eldest priestess, holding up her hand. When everyone was quiet, she spoke to me directly. "Your sacrifice must be voluntary, my lady princess."

How can something be voluntary when every face turns towards you, waiting for you to act? Afterwards, people called me brave, but in truth it was cowardice that drove me. I was afraid to refuse.

I looked at my brothers, at my uncle – and then I turned towards the Tiresias. His sightless gaze seemed to be directed at me from behind his blindfold, and I remembered his words from a short while ago: *There are other ways to serve.*

My parents' souls could be cleansed: their sins washed away by my blood. This was why Father and Antigone wanted me here. And the Tiresias himself – the Voice of Apollo – had said as much. I dared not deny the wish of my own father – certainly not in the holy grove of the Kindly Ones themselves, the goddesses who punished ungrateful sons and daughters!

"I – I am willing," I whispered.

"Good." The middle-aged priestess grasped my upper arm, her fingers strong as bronze. "We must hurry – come with me." She ushered me into the darkness of the shrine. I trembled as I walked, dazedly thinking that at least I was being led away from the whipping post – but terrified by the idea that the worst tortures might be saved for the darkness.

At first I could see nothing at all; but there was a damp, earthy smell, and the floor yielded with a softness like rotting leaves. I heard the two other women close the door behind us. Even in this dank space, black as a cistern, the priestess led me unhesitatingly forward as though her eyes could see in the dark like an owl's.

This must be how the heifer feels when she is led to the altar, I thought numbly. Sacrificial animals, I knew, were given calming herbs: would they be merciful, and do that for me? Animals wore garlands on their way to the knife, and fittingly I was dressed in my finest; I hoped my finery would please the gods, although I wondered if they could see me in this place where no sunlight reached.

I moaned softly in terror.

Our steps led downwards; the structure tunneled into the earth and was far larger than it seemed from the outside. We turned a corner, and a glimmer of light appeared; I wondered if it came from the lantern of the ferryman waiting to take me across the River Styx to the Underworld.

But instead of the ferryman, I saw the familiar face of my sister Antigone, sitting on a low three-legged stool beside a wooden cot. The light came from a lamp on the bedside table, and on the bed lay a blindfolded, gray-haired man.

"Father..." I whispered.

"They may not speak to you," cautioned the priestess. "It is forbidden."

"But—"

I wanted to protest that I should be allowed to speak to my nearest kin, parted from me for so long, before meeting my end. Yet my words caught in my throat and I only nodded, meeting my sister's mute gaze. Did she feel sorry that she had called me here to die? No, I reproached myself. If she could save Father from an eternity of torture, she would have given her own life already. But a married woman was barred from the sacrifice.

The two other women emerged from the darkness behind me. The youngest held a goblet carved from rough, pockmarked stone; the aged crone carried a knife with a ripple-edged flint blade. This gave me hope that my death would be quicker than the torture I had feared, but still my blood rushed loudly in my ears. I loved my father, but I did not want to die.

You have no choice, I told myself. *This is your fate – the Tiresias said so. Besides, Father and Mother need your help. And the Kindly Ones will hound you forever if you refuse.*

"Kneel," said the woman who gripped my arm, pressing me down.

Apparently there would be no calming herbs. I knelt, feeling the dampness of the floor beneath my knees seeping into my skirts.

The young priestess came to stand before me, holding the stone goblet just in front of my breasts. Water, or some other liquid, shimmered within it. "Raise your palms upward," she ordered.

Weakly, I complied; my hands shook like leaves in a gale.

The middle-aged priestess released my arm and grasped my hair, yanking my head back. I had heard it said that slitting the throat was the quickest, kindest way to dispatch a sacrifice; I closed my eyes tight and prayed that was so—

I cried out, feeling the stone blade slice into my flesh – the flesh of my left hand, not my throat! I opened my eyes as my head was released, and the white-haired priestess with the knife grasped my wrist and held my bleeding hand over the ancient stone cup. Confused by what had happened, I watched crimson drip down. Then the crone nodded, and the other priestess wrapped my hand in a linen bandage smelling of thyme.

"Rise, Lady Ismene," said the ancient priestess. She used the flint knife to stir my blood into the other liquid.

Shakily, assisted by priestess who had bandaged my hand, I stood. "That's all?"

The white-haired priestess held out the goblet, saying: "You must give your father the sacrificial drink yourself. He may not speak to you until he has finished it."

I took the rough vessel from her, willing myself with all my might not to drop it, though my knees felt ready to give way. Antigone rose from the stool and silently offered it to me; grateful, I sat, and held the cup to Father's lips. He drank, pausing once, and I helped him to sit up so that he could more easily finish the goblet's contents. When he was done, I handed the pockmarked vessel back to the wizened priestess.

"It's done, Father," I said.

"Ismene..." he rasped, lifting an uncertain hand as if hoping to touch my face. My heart ached when I saw this demonstration of his blindness – I had done my best to forget the terrible memory of his last days in Thebes, to remember him instead as the vigorous king he was before.

I reached out and grasped his hand in both of mine, pressing his fingers to my lips. "Father."

"Lord Oedipus," said the eldest priestess, "my mistresses the Kindly Ones have given you and your mother-wife the gift of their mercy. Your soul has been purified. You shall join Jocasta in the Underworld without stains upon you."

Father sank back against the cot. "Blessed be the Kindly Ones," he whispered. "And bless you, Ismene, for your sacrifice."

"It was nothing." The pain in my hand was already subsiding.

"You didn't know that. But you offered yourself anyway."

Embarrassed by this undeserved praise, I changed the subject. "How are you, Father – and you, Antigone?"

Father smiled slightly. "I'm ready for eternity."

Antigone's only answer was a slight shake of her head; I could tell she was worried about Father. The priestesses had hurried me back here so quickly – did they think he might die any moment?

"I'm not alone," I said, words gushing forth. "Many have come with me. The twins, Creon – even the Tiresias."

"My sons? Creon?" His mouth twisted. "Where have they been all these years? My devoted daughters are all I need before I die."

"Father, don't speak of death!"

Antigone broke her silence. "Don't be foolish, Ismene – everyone dies." She was as impatient with me as she had been when we were children. When she turned back to Father her voice softened. "How's your pain, Father?"

His lips curved slightly. "The potion helped."

Confused, I said: "Father, please – won't you speak with your sons? And Creon?" I squeezed his hand.

He settled his other hand over mine, and his fingers lingered on the fresh bandage. "Very well, Ismene. Because *you* ask it, I will speak to them."

Antigone's expression was grim, but to my surprise I noticed tears at the corners of her eyes. "Can you walk, Father?"

He struggled to push himself up, but only for a moment before sinking back against the cot. "No, my dear."

My sister pressed her lips together. "Then we'll carry you." She beckoned the acolyte. I offered to help, but Antigone waved me away and told me to carry the lamp instead. I discovered that the cot on which Father lay was a stretcher resting on a frame; together Antigone and another woman lifted it from its resting place. It gave them no trouble: Father, once such a strong, muscular man, now weighed little more than a child.

At Antigone's direction I walked alongside or before her, while she and the other woman carried the stretcher around a corner and up the stairs with practiced skill. As we passed back out into the forest, I squinted at the brightness just as the others had done earlier, while Antigone and the young priestess placed the stretcher on the ground. My uncle and brothers stared in dismay at Father's wasted form, but King Theseus was unsurprised by Father's condition.

"Father?" ventured Eteokles. "Is that really you?"

Father turned his blindfolded head. "Who is that?"

"Eteokles," he answered, moving closer. "Your son, the king of Thebes."

"I'm here too – Polynikes." He went to the other side of the stretcher, dropping to one knee.

"And I, Creon," said my uncle, though he remained standing.

"I asked only Ismene to come," Father objected, his voice fretful. "Why are the rest of you here?"

Eteokles knelt down too. "We've come to take you home, Father."

"Thebes needs you," added Polynikes.

"Thebes *needs* me?" Father's voice was faint but his anger was clear. "The city banished me – turned Antigone and me both into homeless beggars, dependent on the charity of others. I owe Thebes nothing!"

Eteokles glanced up at the Tiresias, who leaned on his staff a few paces away – but the Tiresias offered no guidance. Finally Eteokles continued, "The Tiresias has told us that we need your blessing, Father."

Polynikes added, "Your return will protect us, Father. And Ismene and Antigone."

Father gave a bitter laugh. "You were quick enough to blame me for Thebes' misfortunes."

"*We* didn't banish you, Father," Eteokles objected. "We weren't men yet. Creon was in charge."

"And even Creon has come to ask you to return," Polynikes said.

Creon clasped his hands behind his back. "Perhaps I was too hasty, Oedipus. But we were all shocked to learn the truth."

Father turned his head away. "So was I."

"I know." Creon's voice wavered. "But we must put Thebes before our own feelings. Do you think I wanted Jocasta to die?"

"You could not have loved her more than I," Father whispered.

Creon stiffened. "She may have been your wife for nearly twenty years, Oedipus, but she was my sister more than twice that long!" He paused, and when he continued his tone was more controlled. "But I gave up even her to safeguard Thebes."

"Father, the past is done," Polynikes broke in. "We must think of the future."

Father smiled slightly. "Is that so?"

Eteokles straightened, saying, "I brought a cart full of soft cushions; the journey will be easy for you."

Father shook his head. "Tell me, Sons: why did you never come to visit your sister and me in Argos?"

Polynikes, still kneeling at Father's side, said: "We've only just reached manhood, Father. We were not permitted to come – before."

Father adjusted his blindfold with one hand; his fingers trembled in a way they had not been a few moments ago. "Antigone did not wait for permission to come with me."

Although this reproach was aimed at my brothers, I felt it too. "I should have come too, Father."

"Ismene, at least you offered, child."

Eteokles began: "Father, we can't change the past. But you can come—"

"Enough," Father interrupted. "Don't ask me again. I will die here at Colonus."

Polynikes objected, "Father—"

"Here at Colonus," Father went on, "and within the hour."

"What?" asked Eteokles and Polynikes simultaneously, while Creon spoke sharply: "Oedipus, what are you talking about?"

"The mercy of the Kindly Ones," Antigone said, her voice matter-of-fact. "His soul is cleansed, his pain will end – even Mother is redeemed." She wiped her eyes brusquely. "It is done."

I realized that poison had been in the stone vessel – the vessel into which my blood was mixed, the vessel from which I helped Father to drink. *I* had poisoned him. I pressed both hands to my mouth to keep from wailing aloud.

"My sons – my sons and my brothers – you did not fulfill your duty to me before. Now it's too late – you will suffer for it." He licked his lips, and when he spoke again his voice was fainter. "But listen to me: beware of what you most desire. Whatever you treasure more than your duty to the gods, will be used by them to destroy you."

"But, Father," Polynikes objected, "I—"

Father held up his hand to stop the words. "Enough. Antigone, my spirit is ready."

"Yes, Father," my sister answered.

Antigone went to the head of the stretcher while the young acolyte moved towards the foot; they lifted Father once more.

Eteokles rushed forward to block their path. "Stop! You're not taking my father anywhere!"

In an echoing voice the gray-garbed priestess of Athena cried: "Eteokles of Thebes! Would you thwart your father's will – *here*, in the sacred grove of the Kindly Ones? Would you interfere with the servants of the dark goddesses? Think carefully, Eteokles of Thebes!"

My brother's face went white. "He's *my* father—"

"Father will die in the sanctuary," Antigone said, "as he has elected to do." She and the other young woman simply moved past Eteokles and carried the stretcher back into the gloom. I was too stunned, at first, to take up the lamp and accompany them. They disappeared into the darkness before I realized I should have followed.

A hand touched my shoulder. "Princess Ismene," said the Tiresias, "your father's soul will find peace."

Eteokles cast a wary glance at the gray-robed priestess of Athena. Then he folded his arms and looked at his twin. "Our business here is finished."

"You are welcome as my guests in the palace," offered King Theseus. "Surely you wish to rest and refresh yourselves, after your journey. I believe we had a treaty to discuss."

The Tiresias turned to face them. "My daughters and I will remain here, at the sanctuary of the Kindly Ones."

Uncle Creon addressed Eteokles and the Athenian king. "It's time for my daughter-in-law Antigone to return to her husband."

"I'll go and get her," said Polynikes. "And take charge of Father's body."

The priestess of Athena shook her head. "You may not enter the shrine of the Kindly Ones, lord Polynikes. No man may see what lies within."

Polynikes protested: "But Ismene and Antigone—"

"Are not men."

"What about my father?" asked Eteokles, sounding confused.

"He is blind. As is the Tiresias."

My brothers looked so dumbfounded that King Theseus actually chuckled. "Sons of Oedipus, come with me," he told them. "It's better than risking the wrath of the Kindly Ones. We'll send word to your sister Antigone later."

*

Ismene stops speaking, her awareness returning from the past back to the present. A fly lands on her skirt; she shoos it away.

"Your brothers did not take the body, did they?" Phyle says.

"No – the body was buried in a place known only to King Theseus. My father's grave was supposed to ensure greatness to the city where it was buried, so he wanted to keep it for himself." Ismene frowns; a priestess from Athens should know this.

Eurydike, quiet until now, interjects: "Theseus took what wasn't his! If he hadn't, perhaps Thebes wouldn't have suffered so much!"

"Perhaps not," says the priestess Phyle.

From the corner of her eye, Ismene detects movement among the crowd of listeners. Turning, she sees why. A white-haired man in a sedan chair is being carried towards them.

"My uncle," she says to the other women: "King Creon is coming!"

CHAPTER TEN
CREON

King Creon touches the outer surface of the Eudoxa Gate's thick wood, open again at last. Its bronze-bound strength has protected Thebes for decades – but now the oak planks are charred and splintered. "May you find no rest," he mutters to the corpse dangling above the gate. Kapaneus the Argive: his fiery attack cost many Theban lives.

"This gate is in the worst condition," Creon says. "Have it fixed first."

"Yes, my lord king," replies the scribe beside him, making a note on his wax tablet.

Creon ponders the cost of the repairs that must be made. Fortunately, the assailants' own wealth will cover most of the expense. Immediately after the final battle, Creon and a trustworthy few tallied the goods stripped from enemy corpses. Some of the weapons and armor were now displayed in the agora as trophies; the gold and jewels had been brought to the palace, to be used for the common good. A rich cache – but lacking the treasure Creon most hoped to recover, stolen years ago by Polynikes. Perhaps Polynikes had deemed the item too precious to take with him on a battlefield – although Creon had hoped Polynikes might consider it a talisman, and had brought it with him for good luck. Who knew? Polynikes might have even lost it years ago, or could have bartered it away for a bowl of stew.

Curse his traitorous soul, Creon thinks, wiping black soot from his fingers.

"All right," he says, walking back towards the royal sedan chair. "On to the final gate." He takes his seat and gestures to the bearers. They are well-muscled men and skilled in their task, but nonetheless he grips the arms of the chair to keep himself steady as they hoist the wooden poles onto their shoulders.

Moving ahead through the crowd, Creon's escort of soldiers clears a path for his bearers. The city's mood remains subdued; but along the way to the Phthia Gate, Creon notes signs of recovery. A crew works on the wall of one of the granaries. Women are returning from outside the walls, some carrying baskets full of newly washed laundry, while others bring in fresh greens: mint and nettles and dandelions. During the siege, fresh food was impossible; Thebans had lived on stored grains and dried beans and very little towards the end. But now grain and livestock have arrived from Gla and Orchomenos; even the tanners are again treating fresh skins in urine-filled vats. Most importantly, Thebes' children no longer wail with hunger; some small boys play a game with pebbles in a side street, laughing and clapping as one makes a throw.

As the royal procession leaves the tanners' quarter, Creon looks down from his seat and sees one of the daughters of the Tiresias. "Daphne!" he calls, but the young woman does not respond. "Daphne!" he barks out, annoyed. Her father's status is no excuse to ignore the king!

Finally she glances up. "My lord king – I am Manto, not Daphne."

Irritated by his mistake, Creon snaps: "You two look too much alike." It is true that the seer's daughters share the same small, slender shape and long straight hair. But, now that she is looking up at him, Creon recognizes Manto's younger face.

"Indeed, my lord king," Manto acknowledges, shifting the basket of greens she carries and making a slight bow. "Is there a message I may take to my sister Daphne?"

"I wish to know how your father is."

Her thin shoulders slump. "He's very weak, my lord king."

"I assume that is why he did not attend my coronation."

"Father says he will only leave his bed once more – and for this he must guard his strength."

Creon frowns. So – the Tiresias did not consider *his* coronation sufficiently important! But then, the prophet's pronouncements were not always favorable; perhaps his staying at home was just as well.

"I hope he's not in too much pain," Creon says gruffly, aware that Manto is grieving – and likewise aware that, despite his frailty, the prophet still wields great power in Thebes.

"He sleeps most of the time, my lord king."

Creon nods and makes a gesture of dismissal; the young woman bows and departs. Creon orders his bearers to continue towards the Phthia Gate. Rubbing his eyes, he wonders – as he did so often during the siege – why Thebes must have so many gates. Yes, seven was a lucky number, and King Amphion had named the gates for his seven daughters. But Amphion, who was a clever man, should have realized that seven gates meant seven weak points.

Still, Amphion's walls *did* keep out the enemy. Wishing the idea had occurred to him earlier, Creon decides that he will pour a thanksgiving libation at Amphion's tomb. He and the Tiresias are among the last living Thebans who helped build those walls; perhaps that occasion will coax the seer from his bed, and make his last public appearance a fortunate one.

Acknowledging the salutes of the guards at the Phthia Gate, Creon descends to make his inspection. This gate is less damaged than the last; but, just outside, piles of rubble and broken ladders remain from the enemy's efforts to scale the wall – and scattered all around lie the shards of pots that citizens threw down upon the heads of would-be invaders.

"I want this cleaned up," Creon orders.

His scribe writes on the wax tablet.

Creon notes one of his guardsmen – Astakus – glaring up at the corpse hanging over the gate. He has forgotten which Argive this is, but does not ask; he rather likes that the criminal is nameless in death.

Creon walks back through the gate; his guards follow. With Astakus' assistance, he climbs the stairs to stand on the top of the wall. He notes repairs for the stone workers to make; then, gazing to the east, he perceives a crowd gathered in the distance.

"What's going on there?" he asks, pointing.

The young soldier tells him that people are visiting King Eteokles' tomb.

"Are they?" This bears investigation – especially as Antigone is walled up in the adjacent cave. Creon makes his way down the stairs and orders his bearers to take him there

As they approach, Creon sees a sizeable gathering of people, old and young. Some have even brought food and drink, as if intending to spend the entire day here. Saying little, seeming more wary than surprised at Creon's arrival, they make room for his escort. They bow to their king, but Creon finds it difficult to read their mood. Are they in mourning? Or have they come to witness Antigone's death? A public execution always draws a crowd, but watching a blank wall does not offer the excitement of a beheading.

From the height of his sedan chair, Creon studies the twin tombs. They are guarded by two armed men, per his orders. The door to Eteokles' tomb is shut; the wall built to seal in Antigone remains intact. But at its base Creon sees pine branches and sprays of flowers, their colors – red, lavender, and sunny yellow – brilliant against the drab mud brick. He frowns.

Then he notices a tent erected further to the east, just a little north of the path. His eyes narrow: what is this? He does not recognize the structure, but it is surrounded by another small crowd.

"Take me there," he tells his bearers, pointing; the crowd parts to let him through.

Someone calls out, "Long live King Creon!" – and then, unexpectedly, a different shout: "Free your niece!"

Creon's jaw tightens, but he does not seek out the speaker. Better not to call attention to the dissent. His bearers reach the striped canopy. Three women are seated in its shade; they rise to their feet. He recognizes two of them. "Eurydike – Ismene!"

The third woman is veiled, but the richness of her garb indicates high status. "King Creon," she says, bowing.

"I am King Creon." After all these years of standing beside the throne, the title still feels strange to him.

"Would you honor me by accepting refreshment?" the veiled woman asks, gesturing to a table laden with dates, cheese, and bread.

Creon surveys the woman's attendants. There are three servants, a man and two young women, and half a dozen armed guards dressed in the livery of Athens. His own escort is large enough to provide security, and his wife and niece seem at ease.

"Very well," he agrees, and signals to his bearers. They lower the chair, and a servant hands him his staff. Creon walks over and takes a seat on a folding chair. After the long morning he is hungry and thirsty; the thought of sweet dates – a delicacy he has not tasted since before the siege – brings moisture to his mouth. He picks up one of the dark, sticky fruits – but pauses to ask his hostess: "Who are you? It may be rude of me to demand your name, but Thebes has been beset by enemies and we have learned the value of caution."

"I am called Phyle, my lord king," says the woman. "I am a priestess."

Creon bites into the date. In the shade of the canopy the air is pleasantly cool; two of Phyle's servants wield broad wicker fans, making a breeze that dries the sweat in Creon's beard. He accepts a cup of wine; the vintage is excellent, mixed with fresh spring-water.

Creon turns to his wife. "Eurydike, why are you here?"

His wife glances at Ismene, then says: "We came out to visit Eteokles' tomb, and remained inside for a while. We were headed back to the palace when Phyle offered us refreshment."

"We have been speaking of Eteokles and Polynikes," Ismene adds. "What my brothers were like before they became enemies."

"Before Polynikes became *Thebes'* enemy," Creon corrects harshly.

Phyle breaks in: "My lord king, I have been called here to learn what happened in Thebes. Wasn't there an agreement between Eteokles and Polynikes to share the Theban throne?"

"There was."

"And yet they did not share."

Creon lifts an eyebrow. "No. They did not."

"May I ask why, my lord king?"

Creon studies the strange woman and her retinue and ponders her request. "The king of Thebes need not answer questions posed by a stranger."

"Of course not," affirms the woman, whose eyes – wide, blue-green, undeniably beautiful – stare back into his. "But this priestess seeks the benefit of your knowledge. Your experience. Your wisdom."

He taps his staff on the ground, considering. It is a lovely afternoon;

after so many months stuck behind Thebes' walls, it is refreshing to be outside. All Hellas knows of the siege; and, now that Eteokles and Polynikes are both dead, the best way to ensure stability and safety for Thebes is for everyone to understand what happened between them.

Besides, he is an old man, and old men love nothing better than the attention of attractive women. Eurydike, who has listened to him faithfully throughout the years; Ismene, his own sister's child; and now Phyle, a mysterious priestess with eyes that remind him of the sea. He recognizes his weakness for what it is, but decides that in this case there is no harm in indulging – and perhaps real benefit for Thebes to be gained.

"Very well," he says. "I will tell you, Priestess, the truth of what transpired."

CREON

The twins agreed to rule in alternate years; the first year's reign, determined by drawing of lots, went to Eteokles. Not long after Eteokles took the throne, Oedipus died and his body was buried in the sacred grove of the Kindly Ones, near Athens. His daughter Antigone, who had accompanied him into exile, elected to stay in Athens as an acolyte of Athena.

I urged my son Haemon to renounce his marriage to Antigone and to take another wife. When he demurred, I contrived for him to cross paths with the city's prettiest, most eligible maidens – all to no avail; instead he devoted himself more intently to the service of Apollo. Meanwhile my daughter Megara and her new husband Alkides were devoting themselves to the service of King Eteokles.

Megara was the beauty of her generation – and as her belly swelled with Alkides' child she grew even lovelier. Some whispered that this was the effect of Harmonia's necklace; Eteokles, unmarried, allowed her to guard this treasure. Megara never wore the necklace in public, but as I still commanded the loyalty of many servants she had brought from my household, I learned that she often wore it in the privacy of her rooms. As Polynikes criticized his brother for allowing Harmonia's treasures to leave the palace, Megara realized that she would keep the necklace only so long as Eteokles kept the throne.

Megara's husband Alkides was immensely popular; many of Thebes' prominent men came to his house to dine. Because Alkides' mother was an invalid, Megara assumed the role of hostess. My sources described how she served them roasted meats; laughed at their jokes, poured cup after cup of wine, mixing in very little water but substantial amounts of flattery. Subtly, adroitly, she turned the leading citizens against her cousin Polynikes.

One evening Lasthenes, the Master of the Herds, told how he and Alkides had wrestled down one of Thebes' prize bulls after it bolted from its pen. Megara praised their strength and bravery, then asked Lasthenes what it was like to defend the herds from lions and wolves. She gazed at him from beneath long eyelashes as he detailed his exploits, and listened with apparent interest as he then explained why Theban cattle were the best in all Hellas. And then Megara said that she heard – perhaps she didn't understand perfectly, being a sheltered noblewoman and all – she had heard that Polynikes, when he ascended the throne, was planning to trade many of the best animals away to Thrace.

"Why would Polynikes do that?" spluttered Lasthenes.

Megara dipped his cup in the krater of wine. "Because he prefers Thracian gold to Theban bulls, I suppose." She smiled as she passed him the wine. "But perhaps I misunderstood – I know so little of such matters!"

Another time, Melanippus – the commander of Thebes' foot-soldiers – came to dine. Megara asked about the successful campaign he had recently led against a group of bandits, and thanked him for keeping Thebes safe. After the meal, Melanippus and Alkides played a game of senet; Megara remained nearby, encouraging the soldier to tell her more.

"I know the king values your experience," she said after Melanippus concluded one of many tales. "The current king, that is. But Polynikes…"

His eyes narrowing, Melanippus scratched his gray-streaked beard. "What about Polynikes?" he asked, and picked up the knucklebones.

"I think he plans to bring in a general from Athens to take charge of the troops," she said.

Melanippus cast the knucklebones with such force that one skidded off the game-table. "An *Athenian*? In charge of Theban soldiers?"

Shrugging, Megara said: "He admires the Athenians so."

"That's true," Alkides added.

"Treason!" fumed the grizzled soldier.

Megara retrieved the escaped knucklebone and pressed it into Melanippus' calloused hand. "I could be wrong, of course," she said in a soothing voice. "But King *Eteokles* would never do such a thing. He knows Thebes belongs to Thebans!"

Another of my sources overheard Megara speaking with Hyperbius the trader one afternoon in the agora. She suggested that once Polynikes took power, he would increase taxes on imported goods. "The royal share has always been ten percent, but I heard that he's going to take half."

Hyperbius gaped. "Half? That's mad! That would completely ruin trade in Thebes!"

"Well, I might be mistaken." Megara shrugged, rubbing her pregnant belly. "But Polynikes has so many ambitious projects in mind – if he wants to complete them in his year as king, I guess he'll need resources."

Not long after this Megara went to see Aktor, the best of the bronze workers, to have a new set of sandal-buckles made. Leaning close over his shoulder as he showed her samples of his work, she exclaimed: "It's so hard to choose! All your work is so beautiful. And to think – such delicate detail shaped by your strong hands!"

The bronze-smith stammered some embarrassed reply, wiping his brow with a burn-scarred forearm. Once Megara had made her choice, she said, "I *knew* you were just the craftsman for this job, Aktor. My cousin Polynikes doesn't know what he's talking about."

Aktor shifted the left strap of his leather apron. "What do you mean, my lady?"

"Complaining that the greaves you made him aren't the right size – he must be fastening them incorrectly!" She touched Aktor's muscled shoulder. "I'm sure anything you make would fit perfectly. If he's so determined to go to another armorer next time – well, it'll be his loss!"

As the months passed, Megara skillfully bent the loyalties of Thebes' most influential men in Eteokles' favor. Old Demochares might have seen through her, but he was ailing and died one night in his sleep. I must say that Polynikes, for his part, did little to help himself. The more adherents Eteokles gained, the more loudly and publicly Polynikes disagreed with his twin. He made a point of saying things would change when *he* ruled Thebes – which played right into Megara's dainty hands.

In late winter, nine months into Eteokles' first year as king, Megara was delivered of a healthy boy. Alkides gave his son the name Creontiades. Of course I knew this was intended to flatter me – and yet I was moved nonetheless. That afternoon I visited my daughter and my new grandson; beaming with pride, Megara placed the infant into the crook of my arm.

"Isn't he handsome, Father?"

I had to agree. "And so heavy for a newborn!"

Megara dimpled. "Aren't you glad that you let me marry Alkides, after all?"

Alkides was out, and his invalid mother was resting in her room. Except for the servants, my eldest daughter and I were alone. "You're not queen," I reminded her, shifting the baby's weight to rest against my side. "If you had married one of your cousins you would sit on the Theban throne."

"But instead I've married the man the Tiresias says will be the greatest hero Hellas has ever known! And King Eteokles values us."

My grandson squeezed his eyes tightly shut and let loose an impressively loud wail. Laughing, Megara retrieved the baby and put him to her breast.

"I'm sure he does," I said, lifting an eyebrow. "Given what you're doing."

Her cheeks colored. Still looking down at the child, she said, "I don't know what you mean."

"Of course you do, Daughter. You're providing Eteokles very useful assistance. Drumming up support for him while spreading lies about his brother."

Megara did not insult me by attempting to deny it; her large brown eyes met my gaze directly. "Do you intend to do anything about it?"

I folded my arms across my chest. "I'm not the king. I'm no longer even the regent."

"But you're still influential, Father. People listen to you."

"My concern is what's best for Thebes – and for my family."

The corners of her mouth curved upwards just slightly, and she stroked the baby's head.

I looked around the room. The marble floor-tiles were well swept, but the wall-paintings were drab and faded, as though they had not been touched up since Alkides was a child. This modest home seemed too small to contain a man as big as Alkides – a man who fancied himself the greatest hero in the land. "Tell me, Daughter – does Alkides take good care of you?"

Megara blinked. "Of course he does!"

"He's young to be a father. The child's crying doesn't make him – impatient?"

"That will soon pass." She shifted the child to her other breast.

"I hope so." Leaning back in my chair, I asked: "Where is this someday-very-famous husband of yours this afternoon?"

"Lasthenes is hosting a drinking party," she said. "To congratulate Alkides on our son's name-day."

"I see." I combed my fingers through my beard. "Lasthenes has a pair of pretty daughters, doesn't he?"

Megara's full lips tightened. "Alkides can't help it if other maids throw themselves at him – they always have. But he's *my* husband."

"That doesn't stop—"

"Father!" she hissed. "Why must you bring this up?" She glanced down at the child in her arms, as though my words might disturb him.

I waited until I saw the muscles of her jaw relax. Then I said softly: "Even if you choose not to *speak* the truth, my dear, it's important to *know* it."

She did not answer, but I hoped she would take my words to heart. Though her infatuation with Alkides blinded her to his faults, Megara usually had a keen sense for men's motivations. She and Eteokles had won over most of Thebes' leading citizens, and as the winter barley fields began pushing forth green shoots their arguments for staying with Eteokles grew more direct. It was foolish for Thebes to change kings every year; the city had prospered under Eteokles, but Polynikes said he would take Thebes in a new direction. The city would be like a witless traveler, marching east one day and west the next – resources would be squandered, and nothing of consequence could be achieved. One by one, Thebes' key men agreed that Polynikes should be stopped from assuming the throne – but most were reluctant to take part in a conspiracy.

"All you need do," Eteokles assured them privately, "is support me when the time comes."

As Eteokles' year drew to a close, he reached out to his twin in a conciliatory manner. They must not argue any longer, he said; for the good of Thebes, the two of them should work together to ensure a smooth transition. He did not deny the friction between them, but said that civic duty must override any disagreements. Those who had been uneasy about the brothers' strife were relieved by Eteokles' overtures – even Polynikes seemed reassured. The day before Polynikes was to be crowned, he accepted an invitation to join his twin at a party hosted by Alkides. I was not one of the guests – this event was for younger men – but my sources in that household later told me that the evening began in good spirits. Wine was poured generously, and there was roast lamb and herbed cheese.

"I'm looking forward to a respite," Eteokles declared. "Now *you* can sit and listen to the reports on the barley fields, brother! *You'll* be the one who gets to decide which peasant to believe at court." He stood, raising his goblet. "To the next king of Thebes!"

As the evening continued, Megara lessened the proportion of water in the mixing krater, and the guests grew more raucous and then drowsy; by midnight she was sending her guests staggering home. But Eteokles remained – as did Polynikes, collapsed over the table and snoring loudly.

Alkides barred the main door and returned to the dining room. Swaying slightly, he folded his thick-muscled arms across his chest and frowned down at Polynikes. "You're sure that dose won't kill him?"

Megara snapped her fingers to dismiss the servants – but one loyal to me remained in the shadows just outside, and heard her say: "Your mother often takes poppy juice, Husband, and it doesn't kill her even as frail as she is. I was very careful with the dose."

"I should hope so," Eteokles said sharply. "We agreed, there's been too much killing in my family already. I don't want to risk the gods' anger."

As the Fates would have it, my source could not relate all this to me until the following evening. But I remember he said that Eteokles had seemed as drunk as Dionysus while the other guests were present; now he was sober as Apollo.

"Of course not," was Megara's response. "Any more than we want to risk losing the support of key noblemen. He'll wake up tomorrow." She reached out to pull the empty goblet out of Polynikes' slack fingers. "*Late* tomorrow."

Alkides lifted Polynikes' unresisting form and carried him back to the couple's private rooms. Exactly what happened there is not difficult to reconstruct. Alkides removed Polynikes' clothing and signet ring, while Megara used her cosmetics to conceal the scar that Eteokles had received during the boar hunt – hiding the one obvious difference in the twins' appearance.

The next day, in the dim light just before sunrise, I watched a prince in a rust-red cloak bordered with a pattern of tawny lions stride into the agora. A large crowd was already assembled for the rites that would mark the passage of power; though a few men looked the rougher for a night's heavy drinking, all Thebes brimmed with anticipation.

"Greetings, Prince Polynikes!" Udaeus, the junior priest of Apollo, bowed respectfully. Straightening, he scanned the crowd for a moment and then asked: "Ah, where is your brother, King Eteokles?"

I was wondering this myself, so much so that I looked at the arm where the scar should have been – but it looked fine to me. I wondered, too, if Eteokles were off planning some other mischief.

"Alkides, are you here?" he called out.

"Yes, my lord," Alkides said, stepping forward from the front ranks of noblemen.

The prince lowered his voice. "Is Eteokles awake yet?"

"He's still heaving his guts into a chamber pot," Alkides answered, his voice uncharacteristically low; I doubted that more than a handful of us could hear his words.

The prince rolled his eyes. "He *was* drinking pretty deep last night." He glanced at the eastern horizon, then turned back to Udaeus. "But we can't keep Apollo waiting, can we?"

I cast a glance at my wife, whose lips pursed in disapproval; then I looked back to the priest. Udaeus shifted uneasily under my nephew's gaze. "No, my lord. I'll – uh, I'll tell the chief priest we should begin without him."

The ceremony proceeded without further incident. Though it seemed odd to mark the transfer of power in Eteokles' absence, the sacrificial bull – one chosen by Polynikes, in fact – yielded willingly to the axe, and Haemon pronounced its organs without blemish. When the first rays of the rising sun touched the altar, the fat-wrapped thigh bones were laid upon the flames, and fragrant smoke rose in a straight, unbroken column towards a cloudless sky.

Haemon nodded solemnly. "Apollo accepts you, son of Oedipus, as the new king of Thebes." He rinsed his hands and then beckoned forward the palace herald, who carried the golden crown of Thebes on a crimson-dyed cushion.

"Before Apollo," my nephew answered, "I swear to protect my city and the people of Thebes." He took the crown in both hands and placed it on his head. Then Haemon handed him the sacred wine-goblet; he sprinkled a few drops onto the ground as a libation to seal his oath and then, still holding the goblet, walked towards the palace stairs. The people of Thebes, bowing respectfully, made way for their new king. He ascended the first three steps, so he could be seen all across the agora, and then said loudly: "I will hear the oath of loyalty. Alkides son of Amphitryon, come forward!"

Alkides strode to the base of the broad marble staircase, and accepted the golden cup. As always, his appearance stirred forth a cascade of feminine sighs; my daughter Megara scowled. Alkides dipped his fingers into the liquid and said loudly: "I, Alkides son of Amphitryon, swear loyalty to the new king of Thebes!"

The young king smiled and accepted the cup once more. "And I am pleased to receive your oath, Alkides." He turned to me. "Creon son of Menoeceus, let us hear your oath next."

The sun was now fully risen. As I walked towards the palace stairs, I appraised the young man who stood above me. He had Polynikes' ruddy hair and piercing blue eyes; he wore Polynikes' favorite cloak, and when I drew near I recognized Polynikes' lion engraved upon the face of his signet ring. His left arm appeared to have no scar.

And yet when I met his gaze I knew this young man was Eteokles.

He handed the goblet down to me. "Do you, Creon son of Menoeceus, swear loyalty to me as king of Thebes?"

I hesitated only a moment. Then I shook a few drops of wine onto the earth before my feet and said: "I, Creon son of Menoeceus, swear loyalty to you as king of Thebes."

After returning the goblet to his hands, I went to stand beside Alkides, at the side of the palace staircase. I was certain that Eteokles had just been re-crowned as king, and I wondered when and how the deception would end. Was Polynikes alive or dead?

As each man came forward to give his oath to the newly crowned king, I studied their faces. Which of them knew the truth, and which were deceived? By their demeanor, certain men revealed that they were party to the secret: Melanippus gave the young king a sly smile, and the trader Hyperbius subtly winked when he accepted the chalice from Eteokles' hands. Others I judged to truly believe they were speaking with Polynikes, whereas in some cases I could not be sure. My grown sons, for instance – as far as I knew they were not especially close to either twin, and neither revealed anything through their expression or gestures.

Admiration grew within me as the morning wore on – though it seemed strange to watch such a scheme unfold without having been its creator. This was a clever plan, and Eteokles proved meticulous in each detail of its execution: he stated the oath in such a way that no man actually said Polynikes' name in repeating it, and yet he managed not to call attention to this fact.

How long could this misdirection last? Eteokles was too canny to think he could assume his brother's identity for the full year if Polynikes still lived. And yet – if Eteokles was willing to kill his brother, what need was there to assume his identity? I could not then guess all the details; but I knew that, like plans I myself had conceived over the years, this scheme could go violently wrong. I made sure my wife and my younger children were near me as I waited for it to play out.

But the ceremony proceeded without incident. Before long the last oath was sworn, and the butchered carcass of the sacrificial bull was roasting over the cook-fire. Its savory aroma made my mouth water, and I dared to hope that the day would pass peaceably for Thebes, whatever Polynikes' fate. Palace servants came out into the agora offering baskets of freshly baked bread, platters of cheese and olives, and cups of wine; I tore off a hunk of bread and took a cup of wine, when—

"Thief!"

I turned to look, as did all those near me – and saw a furious Polynikes barreling through the crowd.

"Treason!" he shouted! "Oath-breakers! The Kindly Ones will flay you alive!"

Dressed in a tunic far too large for him – bunched up where it was belted and hanging sloppily from one shoulder – Polynikes struck out against surprised citizens who found themselves in the way of his rush toward the palace. The confrontation I was expecting had come; how would Eteokles handle it?

"So, Brother," said my red-haired nephew from his elevated position on the stairs, "you decided to attend the ceremony after all?"

"Gods curse you, Eteokles!" The poorly attired Polynikes looked around, his blue eyes wild. "That's Eteokles! Don't you see it? My thieving brother has stolen the throne! It's *my* turn – *I* am the rightful king of Thebes!"

As gasps and confusion rippled through the agora, the men Megara had been cultivating all through the last year edged forward. Broad-shouldered Aktor and another bronze-smith exchanged a glance; they nodded, and moved toward Polynikes to block his way, preventing him from climbing the palace steps. Lasthenes drew his dagger, and at a gesture from the trader Hyperbius several of his stevedores pushed closer, while Captain Melanippus and his troops fell into place around the king on the steps.

"I don't think so," said Eteokles.

"Thebans!" screamed his twin, turning towards the people, "*I* am Polynikes – that throne is mine!"

"Seize him," Eteokles ordered. Melanippus and another soldier darted forward and grabbed Polynikes by the arms.

"Let go of me!" Polynikes bellowed, red-faced. "How dare you lay hands on your king!"

Shaking his head, Eteokles smiled. "Brother, *I* am the rightful king of Thebes. I arrived here for the ceremony – you did not."

"Because you gave me a sleeping potion and locked me away!" Polynikes yelled.

Eteokles spread his hands. "The priests sacrificed a bull on my behalf and the entrails were good," he countered. "The sacrifice was accepted by the gods. I have heard oaths of loyalty from all Thebes' leading men; I wear the crown. It is done." Turning away from his twin as though from a disgruntled peasant, he told the palace steward: "Bring out the meats!"

The meat of the sacrificial bull was still roasting, and would feed many; yet more meat had been prepared in the palace kitchens. Servants emerged bearing broad wooden platters heaped high with slices of beef, veal, mutton and lamb. Some of the Thebans of lesser birth, who tasted meat only on special occasions, moved away to claim their share. A clever distraction, I thought.

"Curse you, oath-breaker!" cried Polynikes, struggling against his captors. "Give me my crown!"

Surrounded by armed supporters, his brother shrugged. "It's mine. The citizens have sworn loyalty to me."

"They didn't know what they were doing!"

"Are you sure?" Eteokles smiled with the confidence of a man who knows he has already won. "Only one last oath remains to be made. Will you swear loyalty to me, Brother?"

"Of course not! *I* am king now. *I* am Polynikes!"

"Yes, you are Polynikes." Eteokles twisted off the lion signet ring and threw it at his brother. "But *I* am king. If you won't swear loyalty to me, you will leave Thebes. Now." He snapped his fingers, and four palace guards bearing spears moved to assist the two men holding Polynikes. One of the guards bent down to pick up Polynikes' fallen ring.

Eteokles' admission caught the attention of some of the peasants, who wiped mutton-grease from their chins and gaped. A discordant tumult – some shouting in favor of Eteokles, some against – gathered volume. Pressing my wife and younger children back, I drew my dagger, readying myself for what might come. I remembered the mob that clamored for my sister's blood after the facts of her marriage to Oedipus were discovered; in my youth, the people had ripped King Amphion to bloody pieces in this very agora, and in prior generations other kings had met similar fates. I did not doubt for an eye-blink what these people could do.

Polynikes twisted in his captors' grasp. "Thebans! Do you want to be ruled by this traitor?" he yelled. "Support me!" Some of the herdsmen and farmers shouted their agreement – but most of the Spartoi and all of Melanippus' foot-soldiers drew their swords. Those shouting Polynikes' name soon fell silent.

"It's your choice," Eteokles said calmly. "Swear loyalty to me as king of Thebes, or leave this city forever. What will it be, Brother?"

Polynikes' face was crimson with rage. "I'll never swear loyalty to you, oath-breaker! That's *my* crown!"

Eteokles nodded. "We thought it might come to this." He lifted a hand. "People of Thebes: see now that your king respects the ties of blood, and shows mercy." He fixed his gaze on his twin. "Your chariot and horses have been made ready, Polynikes. They await you at the Astykratia Gate. Give him his ring, Melanippus, and see him out of the city."

Before Polynikes could say more, Melanippus jerked his arm roughly and pulled him away. Fewer than a dozen onlookers followed as the soldiers forced Polynikes, struggling and cursing, out of the agora. Eteokles' men clustered round to congratulate their new king; other Thebans

213

turned back to their feast. Even among the lower classes – those who had not heard Megara's blandishments or enjoyed Eteokles' bribes – most seemed content: perhaps they were glad to have greater stability for the city, or truly thought Eteokles would make the better king.

Eteokles had succeeded.

Realizing that the flash point had passed – the citizens of Thebes would not whip themselves into a bloodthirsty mob this day – I sheathed my dagger. Bending down, I told my wife Eurydike: "Remain here at the feast; stay close to Eteokles. I'll return soon." I slipped through the crowds towards the Astykratia Gate. I could always hear Eteokles' version of events, but this could be my only opportunity to learn from Polynikes anything I might need to know.

Polynikes' angry struggles slowed Melanippus and the other soldiers, so I had no trouble catching up. I found my nephew and his guards not far beyond the stout wooden doors of the Astykratia Gate; a handful of gawkers hung back by the gate, or stood atop the city wall to watch.

True to his word, Eteokles *had* prepared Polynikes' chariot; it stood just the other side of the stream Chrysorrhoas. Contained by the soldiers' leveled spears, Polynikes was inspecting the vehicle and the provisions with which his twin had stocked it. "Water-skin, food, cloak, tunic, sandals, shield – where's my sword?"

"King Eteokles had the servants put your dagger in the leather pouch there, my lord prince, along with your arm-rings and your cloak pins." Melanippus shook his grizzled head. "Be grateful for that much." Grumbling, Polynikes fastened the dagger-sheath to his belt.

He turned to face me when one of the guards acknowledged my approach. "Creon!" he snarled. "Were *you* behind this, Uncle?"

"No," I answered simply.

Polynikes folded his arms across his chest, the extra fabric of the too-large tunic bunching awkwardly. "Come, Uncle. *You,* of all people – you must have known Eteokles was stealing the throne."

For a moment I considered lying, but decided there was no advantage to be had in it. "It's been clear for months that he was up to something, but I wasn't sure what – until this morning. And even then I didn't know exactly what was happening. The two of you look so alike, and Eteokles obviously did something to hide the scar on his arm."

"Why did you let him do it, Uncle?" Moisture sparkled in his eyes. "That's *my* crown – I've waited a whole year for it!"

"I had no power to allow this, Polynikes – or to prevent it." I stepped closer. "This is between your brother and you. It always has been. And since you cannot agree to share the throne, only one of you can rule Thebes."

"We *had* an agreement!" Polynikes snapped. "And he's betrayed it!"

"Perhaps," I said. "But over the years I've learned that the gods reward those who simply take what they wish. Any throne, in the end, goes to the strongest – and that's as it should be. The strongest ruler can best protect his city."

He looked down, scuffing the dirt with one sandal. "The strongest," he said through gritted teeth. Then he fixed me with his bright gaze once more. "You'll let me be banished, then?"

"Polynikes, *I* am not the king," I said, spreading my hands wide. "King Eteokles has banished you – and his word is the law of Thebes."

He muttered something under his breath; I did not hear the words clearly, but they might have been, "For now." Then he went to his horse-team and stroked the neck of the nearer beast, murmuring the sort of endearments a man gives to his favorite steed; this seemed to calm him as much as it did the animal. Finally he climbed into the car and took up the goad that rested across its front rail.

"Tell my brother, Uncle Creon, that I thank him for the provisions. The food and water should last me several days, and I've enough gold to buy more when that runs out." He gave me a crooked smile. "I have always been fond of jewelry." With that he snapped the goad at his horses, and soon they vanished beyond a curve in the roadway; the dust of his passage quickly settled. But the whirlwind Polynikes would stir up was only beginning.

*

Creon pauses, wiping his sweaty palms on his cloak. "Polynikes was cleverer than I realized," he says. "More so than my daughter and her husband realized. They were horrified when they discovered what he had done. For months they sought to remedy the situation themselves, and then sought Eteokles' help. Only after the three of them had exhausted all their ideas did they come to me for advice." He looks up at the veiled face of the priestess. "You see, Polynikes knew that the necklace of Harmonia was in Megara's safekeeping. While shut in her private rooms, he found it. And, when he left Thebes, he took our most sacred heirloom with him – hidden inside that tunic he took from Alkides."

CHAPTER ELEVEN
ERIPHYLE

Phyle's mouth twitches; she is grateful for the veil that hides her expression. With an effort she keeps her hands folded in her lap.

King Creon taps hard on the ground with his staff. "But you know all about that, don't you? You may have an Athenian escort, but you are Eriphyle, the sister of King Adrastos of Argos."

At Creon's pronouncement, horrified astonishment washes through the Thebans: Princess Ismene gasps and Eurydike stares, while the other spectators draw closer. Though the canopy no longer blocks the sun's slanting late-afternoon rays, and they are warm on Phyle's arm, a chill races down her back. Her mercenaries step forward, drawing their swords, but they are outnumbered by the Theban soldiers.

Phyle reaches up and pulls loose her linen veil, then draws down the fabric around her neck. Sitting erect, raising her voice, she says: "Yes, my lord king, I am Eriphyle, sister of King Adrastos of Argos, and widow of Amphiorax, priest and soldier. Knowing this, will you order your men to kill me?"

"Creon—" Eurydike begins, her voice soft, pleading.

"Quiet!" he snaps, and his wife closes her mouth.

Phyle has only one option: to brazen it out. With a wave of her arm, Phyle signals her bodyguards to step back, then turns again to Creon. "Well? Have you made your decision, my lord king?"

The old man's age-spotted forehead folds itself into deep furrows. "You have served me wine and bread. Attacking one's host is forbidden by sacred law."

"Yes," Phyle agrees, her voice sounding much calmer than she feels. The time has come for what she must say, what she has come here to say: "But you're already violating the laws of the gods, my lord king. You are not allowing the dead to be buried."

A corner of the old man's mouth quirks upward, but his smile is not kind. "Are you *trying* to persuade me to kill you, Eriphyle?"

Princess Ismene breaks in: "Uncle, no!"

Creon frowns at his niece, and then glances at the Thebans gathered round. Phyle wonders whether he will consider their wishes – but she does not know what these people actually want. During Creon's story, more locals approached; they seemed curious, mostly, but now that they know her identity, they may demand her blood.

"Husband…" pleads the queen.

Phyle struggles to keep her expression serene, though her fingers clutch the arms of her wooden chair tightly. All her life, her greatest influence has been on men – but today women may be her best allies.

Creon points at her with his staff. "Lady Eriphyle, you show more courage than your brother. But I suppose a man who flees from battle *would* send his sister into danger, to negotiate in his stead."

Keeping her gaze fixed on Creon, Phyle says: "If my brother Adrastos came to negotiate, would you kill him, my lord king?"

The old man laughs without humor. "Of course!"

"And me – will you kill me?" she repeats, making her voice both melodic and strong, even though her heart is galloping like Adrastos' magnificent steed.

Creon's dark eyes narrow. "No," he says at last. "Not now – not yet."

There are many sighs in the surrounding crowd; Phyle hopes they are of relief and not disappointment. She presses her advantage. "So, then, will you let me take the bodies for burial – or will you wall me up with your niece for trying to do what is right?"

The Thebans fall silent in anticipation. Of course, Antigone's imprisonment – not the tomb of their recently fallen king, not the unexpected appearance of Eriphyle of Argos – is what has brought most of them here. But Phyle does not know how these people feel. Are they angry at Antigone's punishment? Do they approve of it? Or have they simply come here to revel in another's misfortune, hoping to hear moans and pleas from behind the wall?

More immediate to her own situation: will King Creon go against his own word not to kill her simply because she has asked a question? He presses his long fingers together. "No, you may not take the bodies," he says, "and I advise you not to make suggestions you may regret."

In the front row of spectators a babe wails; the mother puts the child to her breast, and the high-pitched cries stop. Phyle sees a small white butterfly, indifferent to human tension, flutter haphazardly between her and Creon.

Phyle returns her gaze to the king, wondering what she should say next. She does not want to accept the refusal, but she is unsure how to proceed. If only she could consult with those who have accompanied her! But she dares not call attention to them.

"My lord king," she begins, her voice low, "please..."

"I have already answered you," Creon says. He seems about to summon the men who carry his sedan chair – and if he leaves, Phyle's best chance at retrieving the bodies will have failed.

Then Princess Ismene speaks. "Priestess, you shared Polynikes' years in Argos. You can tell us what happened there."

"I can," Phyle concedes, realizing that Ismene also does not want this meeting to end. But she does not look at the princess; she concentrates on Creon. "My lord king, would you like to learn what happened when Polynikes arrived at the Argive palace?"

Those nearest in the crowd edge closer. Every Theban citizen, Phyle realizes, must ache with curiosity about their exiled prince's life in Argos. This time Creon does not glance toward his subjects, but Phyle is certain he is aware of them – just as a man, without having to look, knows what his hands and feet are doing.

"Very well," he says at last.

Phyle feels the muscles in her neck and back relax. While words flow freely, no blood will spill. A story, well-told, can keep violence at bay – and though a lie has its uses, truth is more powerful.

ERIPHYLE

I did not lie to you when I said I was called Phyle; it is the name my family and close friends use. And as you know, Polynikes joined our family. But before I can tell you about him, I must tell you what Argos was like before he arrived.

One autumn morning not long after Oedipus and Antigone left the kingdom, I went to the palace and to the room my nieces shared. I had noticed blemishes marring Argia's skin; I was bringing her a tincture of basil made by a local herb-woman. When I reached the girls' room Argia wasn't there – but her younger sister Deipyle was curled up on a couch, one hand pressed to her side.

I went over to her. "What's wrong, dear?"

"Nothing," she mumbled, turning her head away from me – but I saw tears on her face.

I was only a few years older than Deipyle myself, and I recognized the symptoms. "Your monthly blood has started, hasn't it?"

She shook her head in mute denial.

"Deipyle, don't be embarrassed." I set down the vial I'd brought, and carefully lowered my pregnant body on the end of the couch. "It's nothing to be ashamed of – it's something to celebrate! You're a woman now!"

Rubbing her nose, she mumbled: "I don't want to be a woman."

"Nonsense – you can't be a child forever," I said, stroking her hair. I glanced around the girls' room; the cloth dolls they once carried everywhere now collected dust on a high shelf. "Strange that your time should come before Argia's, though."

This statement released Deipyle's tears in earnest; I drew her head on my shoulder, trying to soothe her. And then my own words struck me. "Yes, *very* strange for your month's blood to start before your sister's. She's more than a year older."

My niece made no response to this.

Sternly I continued: "Deipyle, I am the chief priestess of Hera and you must tell me the truth. Is Argia already a woman?"

She glanced at me with swollen eyes and nodded.

Calling for servants, I ordered one to find Argia and bring her back, and another to fetch a valerian tonic from the herb-woman for Deipyle's cramps. But when Argia arrived, she remained defiant. "That's wrong – my cycle hasn't started." She stood just inside the door, her arms crossed. "Don't you think I would have told you, Aunt Phyle?"

"I expected you to," I said. "But your sister says you've kept it from me."

Argia shot Deipyle an angry look.

"Niece, don't lie." I peered at her more closely. "You've stopped growing taller – and your breasts and hips have filled out."

"No," Argia said stubbornly. She pressed her folded arms tighter against her chest.

"I'm Hera's priestess," I reminded her.

"And *I* do not bleed!"

My temper rising, I lifted my swollen body and stepped toward her. "If my acolytes strip you bare and check each day for the next month, will we still find no blood? I'll have them do it, Argia, unless you tell me the truth."

The sisters exchanged a glance; I clasped my hands behind my back and awaited their answer.

Deipyle said: "We can't hide it."

"We *have* to hide it," answered Argia.

"Girls, this is an offense against Lady Hera!" I scolded. "You can't deny the goddess!"

"Aunt Phyle's right," Deipyle told her sister.

"I know it's been hard for you girls, growing up without your mother. But I thought you trusted me to help with such things." I reached out to stroke Argia's cheek. "How long ago did you start?"

"Last winter," she conceded sullenly. "Almost a year."

"And you, Deipyle?"

Kneading her side with one hand, she said: "This is only my second time."

"All right." I took Argia's hand and drew her over to sit beside me on the couch. "Here's what we must do. You both must make offerings to the goddess, and ask her forgiveness for neglecting the rites. That can be arranged. But, girls, *why* have you kept this hidden?"

They didn't want to tell me; I had to probe for their motives. Did they wish to remain virgins and join the Maidens of Artemis? No – both hated the idea of sweaty days chasing game through the forests, and shivering nights spent under the stars. Were they frightened of dying in childbirth, as their own mother had? A little, Deipyle admitted, but the girls recognized that death came to everyone, and the Fates controlled each life-thread. They both enjoyed playing with my babies, so they did not dread the responsibilities of motherhood.

"Then what is it?" I asked. "Are you afraid of men?"

"Not all men," Deipyle said, her face reddening. "Just – just *those* men."

"Hippomedon and Parthenopeus." Argia spat the names as one might spit out a stone encountered in a piece of bread.

"Ah!"

Hippomedon and his friend Parthenopeus were two Argives who had supported my brother when he needed it. But they were unlikely to catch a young woman's fancy.

"We overheard Father talking to them after he came back home to Argos," Argia said. "They were all drunk, and didn't realize Deipyle and I were listening. But we heard."

Deipyle shuddered. "We can't marry them."

"I'd kill myself first," her sister declared.

"Argia! Don't talk like that!"

"Me too," Deipyle agreed quietly. "Enough poppy juice would do it. Or eating belladonna. I know what it looks like!"

"Girls, listen to me – even if the man you must marry is not one you'd choose, it's not worth *killing* yourself!" I lowered my voice and spoke earnestly. "No marriage is perfect."

Though my husband Amphiorax was considerate, I did not love him. When he came to my bed, I closed my eyes and tried to think of pleasant things: which gown I would wear the following day, how I would arrange the flowers at the temple for the next ceremony, what bath-oils I would use to rid my skin of his scent.

"Aunt—" Deipyle reached out and squeezed my hand. "At least Uncle Amphiorax is a good man. He's kind to you, we can tell. But do you really think Hippomedon and Parthenopeus would make good husbands?"

I considered: neither had even a fraction of Amphiorax' wisdom, nor his worldly goods, nor his illustrious ancestry. So, releasing my niece's hand, I said: "What if—what if I talk to your father about finding different husbands for you two?"

"That would be wonderful, Aunt Phyle!" Deipyle smiled for the first time that day.

Argia was more cautious than her sister. "Only if they're *better* husbands."

"But Aunt Phyle's right. We can't keep our womanhood secret forever."

"Thanks to you, it's no secret at *all!*"

"I'll talk to him at once," I told them, quashing the tiff before it mushroomed into an all-out quarrel.

I asked the servants regarding the king's whereabouts and learned that my brother was in his private study. Walking through the corridors, I tried to think of arguments that might sway him. If only someone had argued against my marriage, I thought – but what was done was done.

When I arrived at the king's study I was compelled to wait; Adrastos was yelling at Hippomedon. I could not help overhearing: Hippomedon had informed my brother that an important cargo ship had sunk, and my brother was venting his fury and frustration at the top of his voice. I won't repeat my brother's curses, or Hippomedon's apologies and excuses, but they continued for a while.

My brother finally calmed down. "No, no, I don't blame you, Hippomedon, but find out what happened! Was there a problem with the vessel? Was the sacrifice to Poseidon inadequate? Don't come back until you have answers!"

Hippomedon departed, his head down; my brother beckoned that I should enter.

"Ah, Phyle, my dear sister," said Adrastos. "Come in and sit down. Your visit is a welcome respite from the burden of ruling a kingdom!"

I lowered my awkward body on to a couch. I couldn't help thinking that his complaint was unreasonable: hadn't he wanted to be king of Argos? I, on the other hand, was with child for the third time in three years not by my own wish but because of his desire to be on the throne. But many people yearn for a shiny red apple high up on a tree, only to discover it sour when they bite into it.

"To what do I owe this pleasure?" he asked, pouring us both cups of watered wine.

I told him what I had learned about his daughters: how they were both now women and how they had hid that development, not wanting to be married off to Hippomedon or Parthenopeus.

"I see," he said, drumming his fingers on the table.

"What will you do?" I asked.

"They should obey me," Adrastos said. "I am their father and their king."

I doubted that maidenly reluctance would sway my brother, so I tried policy. "What sort of alliance would those men bring you?"

"They have served me well."

"In the past, yes. What about the future?"

Adrastos lowered his brows, as if my point was worth considering, but before I could press, a panting runner arrived with a message. The bridge that my brother was building over the Inachus River had collapsed!

My brother slumped back on his chair. "This day is cursed," said my brother. "Why have the gods turned against me?"

"I don't know, Brother," I said.

"Could it be because my daughters are disobedient?"

A chill crept down my back at his suggestion. "I don't know," I repeated. "Their offenses seem rather mild – could that really cause such a reaction on the part of the gods?"

"Who knows what pleases the gods?" asked Adrastos, rising and putting on his cloak in preparation to depart. "That's a serious question, Phyle, one I want you as the chief priestess of Hera to consider – and tell your husband about it too. Now I must go to the river and see what happened."

I left the palace as well. The streets were muddy from a storm that had swept through the day before. Holding my skirts above the muck, I went to Hera's temple and arranged for ceremonies on my nieces' behalf. I also lit incense and posed my brother's question to the goddess but received no inspiration that might lead to an answer. Then, rather tired, I headed back to my husband's large house.

As the sun had come out, the nursemaid had taken my boys into the courtyard; I paused to watch them from the colonnade. Baby Amphilochus lay on a blanket beneath the laurel tree; little Alkmaeon had found a feather and was using it to tickle his brother's plump stomach. The nursemaid laughed and clapped her hands; Amphilochus shrieked happily, flailing chubby arms and legs. As soon as things quieted, the toddler twitched the gray feather to begin the hilarity anew.

"They're lively this afternoon."

I started at the sound of my husband's voice. "Yes," I answered, "they should sleep soundly tonight."

"Then perhaps I could join you in your chambers this evening, Phyle." Amphiorax reached out to stroke my shoulder. "You're so beautiful…"

I kept walking, wishing that my pregnancy could be used as a reason to refuse him – but the midwife assured me it should not, as long as my husband was gentle. "I've been thinking about the womanhood ceremonies for Argia and Deipyle."

"I heard you ordered offerings for them," he said, letting his hand fall to his side. "Strange, isn't it, that they both reached womanhood on the same day?" My perceptive husband guessed more quickly than I that the sisters had concealed their womanly status.

"It is unusual." I looked up as I passed the next red-painted column, frowning as I noticed a cobweb linking it to the ceiling; I would complain to the housekeeper. "My brother will want them wed soon, but I think he should seek other suitors for his daughters. Hippomedon and Parthenopeus bring no useful alliances."

"No *foreign* alliance," Amphiorax corrected me, "but they'll seal the loyalty of factions here in Argos."

I stopped and turned to face him. "But – *Hippomedon?* And *Parthenopeus?* Those poor girls!"

My husband spoke in a low voice. "I know it's hard for you."

"For me?" Resuming my path along the colonnade, looking upwards as if I were seeking more cobwebs, I said: "I don't know what you mean."

"Of course you do, my dear. Much as I wish otherwise, I know you didn't want our marriage."

I avoided his gaze. Amphiorax was one of Argos' greatest warriors, but he had killed my father. He swore it had been an accident; nevertheless his hand had done the deed. Yet my brother Adrastos had needed Amphiorax' support to claim the Argive throne, and still needed his support to hold it. Which meant my brother needed me to do my part.

So, like the goddess I served, I honored my marriage and my husband even though I found no joy in his company. Of course, I mused, Zeus often forsook Hera's bed to seek pleasure in other women's arms. Sometimes I wished my husband would do the same!

I changed the subject to the ill-fated sinking of the ship and the collapse of the bridge and told Amphiorax that Adrastos wanted to consult with him about making sure we had the favor of the gods. "Of course," said Amphiorax and left to find my brother.

Their consultation was inconclusive but my husband promised to petition Zeus just as I had petitioned Hera. But my brother's ill-luck was not finished. Two days after the collapse of the bridge, he was thrown from his chariot and broke his leg between the knee and the ankle. The healers gave him a heavy dose of poppy-juice against the agony of setting the bones, and would not allow us to see him until the next morning.

The room stank; some noxious herb had been used for the poultice on Adrastos' swollen, splinted leg, and though the servants assured me all the chamber-pots had been emptied a sour smell of vomit and urine lingered. I ordered the staff to open the curtains; it was a brisk fall day, and as the cool breeze poured through the room Adrastos' eyelids fluttered open. "Phyle?" he said muzzily.

I sat down on the stool at his bedside. "Yes, Brother, I'm here."

He tried to push himself up a bit in the bed, and grimaced. "Gods, it hurts!"

I looked at his wounded leg, propped up on a cushion. The splints ran from ankle to knee, and though the bandage covered most of that I could see that his foot had puffed up to twice its normal size. The healers assured us that he would live, though, and that an amputation was not needed.

"Do you want some poppy juice?"

"Not now – it puts me to sleep," he said, rubbing his eyes. He moved his head slightly so that he could stare at my husband, who stood between the bed and the window. "Oedipus was my talisman of good fortune. I should never have let him go."

"It was the gods' will, my lord king," Amphiorax reminded him. "Besides, he's dead now."

"So what should I do? The next stroke of misfortune will kill me! You say you're a seer – what has Zeus told you?"

"I believe he has told me something," Amphiorax spoke slowly. "It concerns your daughters, and who they should marry."

Despite the breeze, my brother's forehead was beaded with sweat. A bowl of water and a sponge stood on the bedside table; I moistened the sponge and blotted his brow. Adrastos gave me a weak smile of gratitude.

"And?"

"It is not the gods' will," my husband continued, "that you marry your daughters to Hippomedon and Parthenopeus, my lord king."

I squeezed water from the sponge and listened.

"Oh?" asked my brother, glancing at me suspiciously, then returning his gaze to my husband.

"That is the reason for your chariot accident, my lord king," he said, gesturing to my brother's injured leg. "To warn you that the gods have other plans for the princesses. Parthenopeus' bridge across the Inachus River collapsed; that's a straightforward omen that he should not be allowed such clear access to Argos – that is to say, marriage to either of your daughters."

The argument was a good one. As I resumed sponging my brother's forehead, relief filled my heart. One of my nieces was spared.

"Huh," Adrastos grunted. "And Hippomedon?"

Amphiorax folded powerful arms across his chest. "He oversaw the lading of the ship that sank – a sign that you cannot trust him with something so precious as a daughter."

I listened intently, my nausea forgotten. Was Amphiorax doing this for *me*? Or was he moved by pity for our nieces? Perhaps Zeus *had* revealed something to him – whatever the cause, I could have wept with gratitude for the girls' sake.

My brother Adrastos, to my surprise, did not object; perhaps he agreed that Hippomedon and Parthenopeus would add little to our house, or perhaps the pain from his broken leg simply sapped his appetite for argument. "Then who should they marry?" Adrastos asked. "They're women now."

"I'm not sure, my lord king. Perhaps we should not be too hasty, but let the gods lead us."

My brother and I exchanged quick smiles. If there was one thing we agreed on, it was that Amphiorax was *never* hasty.

"Phyle, why don't you let the girls know that they can remain maidens a little longer," said Adrastos. "I have a few more things to discuss with Amphiorax."

I put down the sponge, rose and went in search of my nieces. They were elated at the news, at least at first. Both of them hugged me and thanked me for my efforts for them.

"But you'll both have to marry someone," I warned them, "and who knows – your father may choose men worse than Hippomedon and Parthenopeus."

Neither could imagine worse, but they were young and inexperienced and I decided it was better not to fan their fears. A few days later my husband and I were again in my brother's chamber – from the reduced swelling, it was clear his leg was improving – and my husband informed my brother that he had received advice from Zeus concerning my nieces' marriages.

"Let's hear it," said my brother, as a servant oiled his skin and scraped it with a strigil.

Sitting on a chair with cushions, but finding little comfort, I too turned to watch my husband, wondering what he would say. Amphiorax faced away from us, his broad-shouldered form silhouetted against the luminous blue sky. "Zeus has given me the interpretation to a dream. Let us discuss the dream first, and then the interpretation. My lord king, you and your daughters walked through the woods; they came to a clearing where a boar and a lion were fighting. The girls shrieked, and the beasts stopped their battle."

"A boar and a lion?" I asked.

"Yes. The girls walked ahead – and one of them climbed onto the lion's back."

I folded my hands on my swollen belly. "What did the other girl do?"

"King Adrastos picked her up and set her onto the back of the boar. It snorted, but did not throw her off. Then there was a chariot. No horses, just the chariot. The king harnessed the beasts to it."

The baby inside me kicked. "A lion and a boar – harnessed together?" I asked.

Amphiorax nodded. "Yes. The king stepped into the chariot – and suddenly the chariot was decorated with gold. He shook the reins and the beasts headed off, your nieces riding on their backs."

"And how do you interpret this dream?" asked my brother the king.

"You must marry your daughters to a lion and a boar."

"I see," said my brother, holding out his left arm so the servant could scrape it.

"What do you mean, you see?" I asked. "A lion – a boar? One girl would be eaten and the other gored!"

Amphiorax shrugged. "That is Zeus' interpretation of the dream, Eriphyle."

"But it doesn't make any sense!" I objected.

"It will in time," said my husband. "We must trust the gods."

"Amphiorax, I thank you," said my brother. He then indicated that we should leave, as his healer had arrived and was about to help him stand and move around the room. I understood that he did not want anyone to witness his struggles with pain and weakness, and so we left.

The girls were visiting their grandfather Iphis at his house, so I could not tell them about the prophecy that day, but when they learned about it they came to see me. I sat in a chair while they sat on a sheepskin rug and played with my boys. Naturally they were appalled at the prospect of being married to beasts. Having had time to think about it, I tried to console them by reminding them of Europa, who ran off with Zeus disguised as a beautiful white bull.

"But Zeus is already married to Hera," Argia objected, tossing a ball to my elder son. "He can't marry again."

Deipyle pulled my younger son on to her lap. "What about that queen of Krete, who fell in love with a bull? She gave birth to a monster!"

"The Minotaur," Argia said. "Half man, half bull. It *ate* children."

"Well…" I struggled to find something optimistic to say. "At least you don't have to marry Hippomedon or Parthenopeus."

"But – *wild animals?*" exclaimed Deipyle.

"I won't do it," declared Argia. "If Father tries to make me, there's always belladonna."

"Don't say that, Argia," I said, shifting uncomfortably. "Perhaps the dream meant something else."

Over the next month my brother's leg started to mend. As soon as he could return to his throne he made another announcement: just as he had given sanctuary to Oedipus, he would give sanctuary to others who needed it. I was occupied by the birth of my third child – my first daughter – so I did not see the first group of unsavory characters who made their way toward Argos, but even in confinement it was impossible not to hear about them.

My brother believed that the worst ruffians would bring the best blessings. After all, Oedipus had killed his own father and sired children on his own mother – and *he* had brought Adrastos good fortune! Some other man, despised everywhere else, might be my brother's new harbinger of luck. Since there were few merchants in the cold months, Adrastos let the newcomers pitch their tents in the agora, and naturally quarrels broke out among them; black eyes, broken teeth, and bloody noses were common. Sometimes the brawls spilled over into the streets of Argos. My brother listened frequently to citizens' complaints of broken crockery, ripped awnings, and figs and raisins trampled underfoot; he had Amphiorax investigate each incident, and compelled the culprits to make restitution with goods or labor. But like a winter-sown crop, the visitors' tempers quickened with the warmth of spring.

I hoped he would turn away some of the men, but my brother found another solution: athletic contests to drain off their energy. By this time Adrastos could manage short distances with a walking stick, although to reach the athletic fields he needed to be carried on a litter. Nonetheless he enjoyed the competitions greatly, as did most of Argos. Occasionally my brother asked me if I thought any of the contestants resembled a boar or a lion. The victor of a wrestling match had crooked tooth that was a bit like a boar's tusk; another time a sprinter had long tawny hair – but I did not want my nieces wed to such criminals, so I did not comment on the likenesses to my brother.

But one rainy night in late spring, as we were all gathered in the palace, listening to a bard sing of Narcissus and Echo, loud shouting interrupted the song. "They're at it again," I sighed, and signaled the musician to stop plucking his lyre. "Despite the rain!"

"Probably that pair from Korinth," Adrastos said, more amused than annoyed. "They're always fighting. Do you think the bald one will win again?"

"Maybe," said Argia. She and her sister monitored new arrivals warily. "He's strong."

Deipyle wrinkled her nose. "But the one-eyed fellow is tricky."

"Brother," I said, "I can understand your giving *one* of them sanctuary – but why both?"

My husband Amphiorax patted my hand. "Which should he choose? He might reject the one meant to bring him good fortune." He raised an eyebrow at my brother. "Besides, the king enjoys the excitement of a good fight."

Adrastos only grinned. "You know me well!" Pulling himself up with the help of his walking stick, he said: "Let's go see!"

I seemed to be the only one who preferred music to fighting, so I let Amphiorax assist me to my feet. The girls fell into step behind us. As we passed through the torch-lit hallways, the shouting grew louder – and then we heard the clang of bronze on bronze.

"My lord king," cautioned Amphiorax, "they're using deadly weapons."

But my brother only shrugged. "Well, that could settle their argument for good." At his gesture the guards opened the heavy palace doors, and – flanked by armed soldiers – we walked out onto the landing of the palace stairway. A half-circle of onlookers cheered the two combatants. Given the rain and the dark, it was hard to see, but I could tell that the men facing each other with raised shields and bared swords were not the two Korinthians. The two men before us moved with strength and grace, and both had two good eyes and full heads of hair: one dark, the other russet.

"They're new," Deipyle whispered behind me.

"And *handsome*," observed her sister.

"You knew that was my place!" spat the dark one, who was shorter and broader across the chest. "How dare you!"

"By all the gods," the copper-haired youth shouted, "no criminal like you will tell *me* what to do!"

The other laughed. "Who are you to call upon the gods? You're cursed – your whole family is cursed!"

"I'll have your blood!" The taller youth lunged, his sword flashing, but his opponent parried the blow with his shield.

"My lord king," Amphiorax said quietly, "we should stop this. A fistfight is one thing, but killing will ruin Argos' reputation for sanctuary."

"You're right." My brother lifted his hand. "Stand down!" he shouted. "As king of Argos I command you to stop!"

The crowd fell silent; the two combatants glanced up to see us standing above them.

"Lower your weapons!" Adrastos ordered, while Amphiorax went down and inserted himself between them.

Breathing hard, the two men slowly complied, but each kept his shield facing the other.

"Good," my brother continued. "Now, identify yourselves and state your grievance."

"Tydeus of Kalydon, my lord king," said the dark-haired one.

"*Formerly* of Kalydon," interrupted the second foreigner. "He was banished for murder."

The Kalydonian twitched his sword-point. "I'm kin to King Adrastos, you wretch! How dare you insult me before him!"

The russet-haired man did not answer; instead, he gazed up at my brother. "I speak only the truth, my lord king. The man has been exiled for murder."

"And who are you?" Adrastos asked.

"Polynikes, son of Oedipus," he answered, inclining his head. "The rightful king of Thebes. A man denied his throne – as you once were, my lord king."

"How bold," Argia breathed and I silently agreed with her. Few men would dare to remind a king of his prior disgrace.

"Hush," I hissed at her.

"Polynikes, son of Oedipus, you are welcome in Argos," my brother declared. "And, Tydeus, I recognize you as a kinsman and I will hear your case. Now sheathe your swords, both of you, and set aside your shields; then you may enter my palace, and we'll discuss your grievance."

Polynikes slipped his sword into its sheath; only when Tydeus had done likewise did he lower his shield – and then as the men ascended the stairs, so that the torchlight showed them better, my heart skipped a beat.

"Look!" whispered Deipyle, grabbing Argia's elbow and pointing.

Tydeus' shield was embossed with a boar; Polynikes' bore the image of a lion.

"*That's* what Uncle meant!" cried Argia.

I was stunned by the sight – but on a dark, wet night, before a crowd of ruffians, this was no time to discuss my husband's prophecy. "Hush," I said again, "do *not* mention it – not yet."

I managed to silence my nieces, while my brother had the two wet, muddy young men – surrounded by watchful guards – brought after us to the megaron. Adrastos seated them on opposite sides of the hall, and called for servants to bring towels and foot-basins and to clean them up. Eventually, despite frequent interruptions, we learned that they had been arguing over a camping spot.

Tydeus – formerly a prince of Kalydon – was in fact a relative, although distant. He had killed a cousin – in self-defense, he asserted: he claimed the cousin had planned to murder the Kalydonian king and seize the throne.

Drying his hands on a cloth, Polynikes interrupted: "If the killing was justified, why did your father banish you?"

Tydeus glared at him. "My cousin's family is powerful. They told my father that they would throw him off the throne unless he punished me."

"And because of how he killed his cousin," interjected Polynikes. "He was vicious – not just in killing the man, but to the body afterwards. He stabbed it over and over again."

"So, I was filled with the anger of Ares – what does it matter, what I did to a dead man?"

"Let me ask our chief priest of Zeus," said Adrastos. "What do you say, Amphiorax?"

My husband spoke gravely. "Defiling the dead is serious, but men can be purified of this crime. Was the body treated properly afterwards?"

Tydeus assumed a more respectful mien. "Yes, Priest Amphiorax. The body was burned while I left Kalydon."

"If you agree to atone, kinsman, you are welcome in Argos." Adrastos gestured for the dark-haired youth to take his seat once more. "And I bid you both – Polynikes and Tydeus – make peace with one another. I believe the gods have brought you to Argos for good reason."

We dismissed the young men without informing them of the prophecy, but – once my nieces were sent off to their room – my brother, my husband, and I discussed the matter well into the night. Amphiorax advised letting the gods' will run its course, rather than attempting to influence matters, but my brother was pleased at the idea of his daughters marrying men with claims to other thrones. "My grandsons could rule in Thebes and Kalydon!"

The young noblemen had caught the girls' and the king's attention; and, whether out of lust or ambition or both, the newcomers soon set about wooing the king's daughters. By some attraction of opposites, rough Tydeus sought the hand of gentle Deipyle while Polynikes pursued the stronger-willed Argia. By midsummer both girls were wed. Their unions were happy enough; both brides were soon with child.

At Tydeus' request, Adrastos sent word to the king of Kalydon. The messenger was publicly rebuffed, yet later the Kalydonian king sought him out under cover of night. He provided a rich gift of gold for the young couple, but sent the envoy back to Argos with a father's message of love and firm instructions that for his own safety Tydeus could not return to Kalydon. The message did not pacify the young man: he swore to spill the blood of those cousins who had turned his city – "and my own father!" – against him. He pressed Adrastos to support him in a raid, but Adrastos demurred. "Bide your time," he advised. "If your father falls ill, we will reassess the situation."

As fall passed into winter, and we spent more time within doors, I sometimes studied Argia's new husband – not with lust, but with appreciation for his beauty, as one contemplates a perfectly executed wall-painting. Oedipus had obviously been a handsome man before his blinding, while Jocasta, Polynikes' mother – *and* grandmother – had been celebrated throughout Hellas for her beauty.

Polynikes, unlike Tydeus, did not demand that Adrastos send an official envoy to Thebes. Instead he made friends among the Argive noblemen, and when travel became possible again the following spring, some of these friends found reasons to journey to Thebes. Kapaneus reported that King Eteokles insulted my brother, asking why he chose to fill his city with garbage and marry his daughters to dogs. This enraged Adrastos, but once he calmed down Kapaneus added that a few of the Theban nobility had welcomed him; when out of Eteokles' earshot these men asked after Polynikes' health. Parthenopeus also made a trip to Thebes that summer and found many were curious about Polynikes' newborn son Thersander – especially since King Eteokles remained unwed.

My nieces adored their baby sons, born within two months of each other; the girls spent their days together while their husbands trained at arms, helping Adrastos integrate the stream of newcomers into the Argive army. I often joined them, pleased to see the young brides settling into the responsibilities of motherhood.

I have observed, as a priestess of Hera, that some women are greatly changed by marriage and motherhood; others, like my nieces, become more fully themselves. Sweet Deipyle retained much of the plumpness of her pregnancy, but the lush curves of her breasts and hips suited her, and the dimples in her cheeks accented the prettiness of her smile. She could always calm either babe, no matter how fussy, and she was happiest with a child in her arms. Argia proved fiercely protective of little Thersander, scarcely letting her son out of her sight. She had great plans for him, and it was she, one sunny afternoon in late autumn, who first mentioned the idea of war against Thebes.

Our babies – for I had brought along my youngest, a girl – lay in the center of the broad bed that Deipyle shared with Tydeus; Deipyle reclined near them, shaking a silver rattle to coax forth their smiles. I was sitting near a window, while a maidservant pumiced my feet. Argia paced restlessly along the far wall.

"Hippomedon just returned from Thebes, you know," she was saying.

"Did the trading go well?" her sister asked, not looking up.

"Your father says the shipment of leather is good quality," I offered.

"Good," Argia agreed, "but not the *best*. That they send to Athens."

I bent down to check the girl's progress on my heel; the skin still felt rough. "Continue," I told her, then spoke to Argia. "King Eteokles will never give us his best."

Argia nodded briskly. "No, he'll never give Polynikes his due. But the common people of Thebes know that he stole my husband's rightful place. That's what Hippomedon says."

I looked down again so that she would not see my smile. It amused me that Argia put stock in Hippomedon's word, given how much she had reviled him earlier. But many people seek out what they wish to hear.

Shaking the rattle again, Deipyle said, "That's as it is, Argia – there's nothing you can do about it."

"You're wrong, Sister. What's not given when owed must be taken by force."

Deipyle's eyes widened. "You mean, attack Thebes?"

"Yes!" Argia took two quick steps to my side. "Remember, Aunt Phyle, the prophetic dream? The chariot drawn by the lion and the boar was covered with gold. Our husbands will bring wealth to Argos – and clearly that wealth isn't coming through trade. It must come through conquest."

Argia was the first to mention attacking Thebes to me, but soon I heard it discussed in the megaron and even in the streets. Men have always been excited at the prospect of war – and, given the violent types my brother's policies attracted, Argos was a heap of dry tinder ready to burn.

Polynikes was slower to advocate war, at least in large groups; he let others speak for him. One winter evening, as the servants cleared away the plates and refilled men's cups with mulled wine, my nephew Kapaneus held forth.

"Thebes has seven gates. Seven!" He emphasized his point by holding up seven fingers and wagging them. "We can surely get through *one* of them."

Before that night, my brother had never publicly joined the speculation; but that evening he was nursing his fourth or fifth cup. "The best way to conquer a walled city is from inside." The king fixed his gaze on Polynikes. "Is that possible?"

I remember leaning forward: what would the handsome Theban say?

Polynikes hesitated, then spoke in a low voice. "My brother Eteokles spread lies about me. Because we look alike, he sometimes tricked people into thinking he was me, and did things to blacken my name."

Argia set a hand on Polynikes' forearm. "But not everyone was fooled, Husband. Some know the truth."

"*Some* do. At least now that I'm in Argos, he can't blame me for his misdeeds."

"Once a cheat, always a cheat," Tydeus said harshly. "Eteokles betrayed his own brother – he'll turn against others too." Deipyle nodded agreement with her husband, as she always did.

"And then the people of Thebes will remember how badly he treated Polynikes!" Argia added.

"They may, Daughter," said Adrastos, sounding thoughtful. He turned to Hippomedon. "You're the last one here to visit Thebes. What do you think?"

Hippomedon rubbed his nose. "My lord king, the city walls are impressive: they're high and sturdy. Each gate is manned by a squadron of guards – and the Theban forces are well trained." He glanced at Polynikes. "They're led by two men: Melanippus, an older fellow with a lot of experience, and a younger man called Alkides."

"Alkides is strong as an ox," Parthenopeus added. "All the men love him."

"More than they love Eteokles, that's for sure," Kapaneus said, and then belched.

My brother turned back to Polynikes. "This Alkides could be the key. Can you win him to your side?"

"I don't know." Polynikes scratched his coppery head. "We three were the best of friends as boys: Alkides, Eteokles and I – once I thought nothing could destroy our bond. But Alkides helped my brother betray me."

"Maybe he's realized that was a mistake," Argia said. "Maybe he's come to see Eteokles for who he really is."

"Hmm," said Adrastos. He looked up at my husband, who was just returning from a trip to the chamber-pot. "What say you, Amphiorax? Should we attack Thebes? You told me the lion and the boar would add to Argos' wealth. They've given me grandsons, but my treasury's no larger."

"They will in time, my lord king," my husband answered as he walked past the central hearth.

"When?" demanded Tydeus.

Amphiorax stopped and looked down into the fire. His eyes narrowed as the golden light washed over his face. "I cannot say. Things must first change."

My brother frowned. "*What* must change?"

For a long moment my husband studied the dancing flames. Then he turned to face Adrastos, his thick-fingered hands spreading in a gesture of helplessness. "My lord king, the gods don't tell me everything. When the time is right, they'll reveal their will, just as they showed us that you would have a lion and a boar for your sons-in-law."

Adrastos slumped back on his throne and drummed his fingers on the arm.

"I don't like waiting," Tydeus grumbled.

"Especially when you don't know what you're waiting for," Kapaneus agreed.

My husband shrugged. "The gods value patience. Train hard; keep building the Argive forces, my lord king. The time will come. Someday Argos will prevail over Thebes."

"*Someday?*" Parthenopeus asked in a caustic voice. A chorus of grumbling swelled in the megaron; none of the men liked this prophecy – and my nieces looked as displeased as their husbands.

But the king raised his hand for silence, and the disgruntled comments subsided. "I've had to be patient before," he said. "But time means little to the deathless ones. Priest, can you tell me if I'll live to see this day?"

Amphiorax hesitated. He looked around the hall, his gaze sweeping across each of the men present. "Yes, my lord king," he said at last. "If you wait for the right time, yes – although it may be years. And one of your grandsons *will* be king of Thebes."

"Years?" the men muttered, clearly disappointed.

But my brother, studying my husband closely, was not unhappy. "Let's not object: we want the gods on our side!" He smiled and lifted his cup. "Besides, a late victory's far better than an early defeat. Let's drink to Argos – and to victory!"

So for the time being, the matter was tabled. Winter yielded to spring, and my brother's leg healed enough that he no longer needed a walking stick. Some talk of war with Thebes continued, but sightings of the horse Arion dominated discussions; a number of my brother's men tried – and failed – to capture the animal. Hippomedon got close enough to throw a rope over its neck, but the horse flung him off, leaving him with nothing but a bruised arm and a frayed piece of rope.

I bore another daughter that summer, but Deipyle miscarried and Argia was slow to conceive a second time. Hoping to secure Hera's aid for their fertility, I trained them in the rites of the goddess. Tydeus rarely came to the temple, but Polynikes frequently escorted his wife to the Heraion. Perhaps that is why Argia conceived while her sister's womb remained empty. At any rate, Argia's pregnancy progressed well through the cooler months, and late the following spring she delivered another boy.

The day before the babe was to be named, Argia and Polynikes came to Hera's temple to make a thanks-offering. I was arranging the most recent offerings in the wall niches that framed the central fresco when they arrived; Polynikes had an armful of fresh lilacs. "Beautiful flowers for Hera and her beautiful priestess!"

I could not help smiling at the compliment. "The goddess will enjoy their fragrance. Argia, my dear, are you strong enough to find a vase for them?"

"Of course," she replied, looking a bit irritated that I would question her strength – though most mortal women need time to recover from childbirth.

"Shall I come with you?" Polynikes offered.

"No – I can do it." She took the flowers from her husband and went to fetch the vase; Polynikes and I found ourselves alone with an awkward silence. I could not help but think what a good husband he was to my niece, despite her stubborn independence. And I was struck by how very blue his eyes were…as blue as the spring sky, and warm and penetrating as Apollo's rays.

Realizing that I was staring, I cleared my throat. "Would you hand me that gold cup, Polynikes?" I asked, pointing at the basket near his feet.

He retrieved the object from the basket, turning it to catch the morning light. "Who gave this, and what crime did he commit?"

"Eurystheus, the king of Tiryns – and he committed no crime; he just wants the favor of Lady Hera."

My brother's policy of welcoming outcasts had increased our treasury.

Whether or not banished from their cities, many wrongdoers reasoned that Argos could offer atonement; others, like King Eurystheus, made large donations to win blessings from the goddess even though they had no particular guilt to purge. Offerings of gold, silver, jewels, and incense enriched our temples; blood sacrifices provided meat to feed our growing army.

"This much gold could buy King Adrastos a Thracian steed."

"Perhaps," I said, moving aside an ivory statuette to make room for the goblet. "But now we must display it for Hera's enjoyment."

The most recent gifts were placed in prominent locations, but there were so many that the Heraion overflowed with treasures – golden goblets, bronze tripods, daggers and swords, vessels of marble and alabaster. Storing them all in the temple would have been impossible. So, after being exhibited to honor Hera, a valuable gift – especially if the donor was unlikely to visit Argos again – would be quietly transported to the palace. After all, argued my brother, Argos was Hera's city, so Argos – and Argos' king – deserved the goddess' support. Hera's bounty meant fine horses for the king's stables, yes; but also well-maintained roads, new armor and weapons for the soldiers, and festivals for the Argive people.

The Theban prince held out the goblet to me, but he did not let go of it immediately, so that for a moment we both grasped it. "Is this the most valuable treasure ever given to the Heraion?" he asked, looking down at me with his brilliant blue eyes.

"I'd have to think about it," I said, a little breathlessly. "This goblet is certainly precious, but others have made generous offerings."

"And did those gifts win the goddess' favor?" he pressed, finally releasing the cup.

I considered, but before I could answer, we heard shouts and screams in the forecourt. Hurriedly I put the object in its niche and started that way, calling out to the other priestesses: "What's happening?"

Polynikes came with me – and in the portico we encountered Argia, her face ashen. She clutched her husband's arm. "Polynikes," she cried, "there's a monster out there!"

"What?" I gasped.

Polynikes' eyes widened, then his jaw tightened as he resolved to act. He detached his wife, then strode to a nearby table. From among the objects dedicated to the goddess he grabbed a gilded scepter, topped with a pomegranate carved in red marble. He swung it to test its weight, then asked: "Where's this monster?"

Argia pointed towards the forecourt; Polynikes ran that way.

I turned to appeal to the painted image of the goddess. "Lady Hera, protect us," I prayed. Telling Argia to stay behind, I hurried after Polynikes, my heart pounding hard.

The forecourt was a scene of utter confusion. At its center was a huge, growling, shaggy creature – but it moved on two muscular legs, and swung a club in its human-looking hands. Acolytes and temple slaves darted out of the monster's reach, screaming in terror. Black-and-white painted pottery were shards scattered across the cobblestones, and the lilacs lay trampled underfoot. Polynikes was moving towards the beast, holding the scepter dedicated to Hera as though it were a sword.

The beast bellowed incoherently at Polynikes' cautious approach – and then, to my surprise, intelligible speech emerged from its mouth.

"Sanctuary!" it cried. "I ask sanctuary!"

My heart pounding hard, I shouted: "Stop!"

The creature paused and looked at me.

"Stop!" I repeated. "I am Eriphyle, sister of King Adrastos and chief priestess of Hera. I can offer sanctuary – but you must put down your weapon."

At first I wasn't sure it understood me.

"Put down the club," I tried again, slowly and distinctly.

The creature took a step towards me, which sent a thrill of terror through me – but then, praise be to Lady Hera, queen of Heaven and Earth – it dropped its heavy club. The weapon landed with a thud on the cobblestones.

"Kneel," I said, cautiously descending the short staircase.

The beast hesitated and then fell to its knees, reaching towards me in a gesture of entreaty. Its arms looked human enough, but they were corded with muscle and thick as an ordinary man's thighs. Even without a weapon this creature could kill me easily.

I stopped on the final stair tread and looked down into its face. It was a man, not a monster. But he was enormous – even kneeling, he was nearly as tall as I, though I stood on the step above him. Beneath the rancid pelt he wore as a cloak, his hairy chest was thick as a storage-jar; his legs were like tree trunks. Black dirt crusted his fingernails and the calloused palms of his hands; he stank of sweat, and his light brown hair and beard were matted with twigs and grass. A wound on one thigh oozed a yellowish fluid; now that he was still, a pair of flies landed on the lesion. He did not seem to notice.

"Forgive me," he moaned. "Beautiful priestess, have mercy!"

Polynikes edged closer and picked up the club with his free hand. "Be careful, Phyle," he said softly.

The wild man looked back to see who had spoken, and his eyes widened. "King Eteokles!"

Polynikes frowned and took a step closer, peering at the filthy madman. Then he said, "Alkides? What are you doing here?"

"Forgive me, Eteokles!"

Polynikes shook his head. "It's me – Polynikes."

"Polynikes?" repeated the man. Then the giant crumpled; it was like a mountain falling in on itself. Great wracking sobs shook his chest. Now and again a word came through the moans: *banished*, he said, and *dead*, and *madness.*

When the man's sobs finally stopped, I said: "Whatever you have done, you may seek sanctuary from Lady Hera. But you're in no state to petition the goddess."

Polynikes handed me the scepter and then reached out to touch the man's bulging shoulder. "Come with me, Alkides. I'll find you bread and meat – and a bath."

Alkides looked up; pale streaks showed on his face where his tears had run through the grime. He took Polynikes' hand in his great fist and allowed himself to be led away like a child.

*

Phyle, her throat dry, pauses in order to drink from her goblet. Only now does she see the tears spilling down Queen Eurydike's cheeks, and the dark cold anger in the eyes of King Creon.

CHAPTER TWELVE
EURYDIKE

"Alkides," Eurydike says. Memory, sorrowful memory, descends upon her like heavy fog. For a moment she can see nothing, hear nothing, feel nothing, and she wonders whether this is what it is like to perish of grief.

But her husband's furious words pierce the mist. "Alkides! *Alkides?* You welcomed that gods-cursed animal too? Woman, you and your brother made Argos into a dung-heap – you're no better than the flies buzzing about it! I should crush you as my men crushed your soldiers! Guards, come forward!"

"Uncle, please," Ismene breaks in, "I'm sure they made Alkides atone for his crimes—"

"Y-yes, my lord king, we did," Phyle stammers.

For the first time Eurydike hears fear in the voice of the foreign priestess. The Argive servants step back while Thebes' soldiers draw their weapons. The Athenian soldiers stand their ground, but they glance around nervously, as if seeking a way to escape.

"No atonement could be enough," Creon declares.

"Do you want me to kill her, my lord king?" asks young Astakus, raising his sword.

Violence, thinks Eurydike. *Men always answer violence with more violence.* For Creon to be so angry, so ready to strike, is unlike him; even with Antigone his decision was deliberate. Of course, the last few months and days have provoked him sorely – to say nothing of the burden of Kadmos' crown dropping suddenly on his head. Hoping to keep bloodshed at bay, she reaches over to touch his arm. "Creon, calm yourself, I beg you—"

He pushes her fingers away. "I will *not* be calm! Why should I be calm? This woman has fed and clothed countless criminals – men who killed our children! And the children of many other Thebans!" Anger swells in the crowd, and Eurydike fears that there will be more slaughter. So do Eriphyle's women, cowering behind the dark-haired manservant.

"Uncle Creon!" Ismene's voice rings out again, high and clear as a nightingale's. "Perhaps Argos should not have given Alkides sanctuary – but remember that *Thebes* granted sanctuary to Alkides' father, before that!"

Creon stops his rant, and turns to study his niece; the crowd, watching him, falls silent. "We had to," he mutters. "I – we – owed him."

His statement puzzles Eurydike, but now is not the time to pursue this matter. She says only: "You see, Husband? We're not blameless in this either. You sheltered Alkides' father; and we didn't insist enough that Megara—"

"I know! I know! But to help that monster Alkides—" Creon turns towards Phyle. "After what he did! Do you know all of Alkides' crimes? Do you understand what he did?"

Phyle begins: "He told us—"

But Creon cuts her off. "Never mind what that beast told you! I will tell you! *I* will tell you, you Argive insect, what sort of garbage you welcomed to your city!"

"No, Creon," Eurydike says.

"What?" her husband sputters. "What do you mean, no?"

"Let *me* tell what happened," Eurydike says.

"*You*?" His tone is sharp with disbelief.

Since she was a girl, Eurydike has admired Creon for his intelligence and insight. She has been a dutiful wife, guided by her husband in nearly everything, except those matters belonging solely to women. But on this day other women have inspired her: her niece Antigone, condemned to die for her piety; Eriphyle, daring to plead for her city's dead; even Ismene, usually so quiet, has spoken up. She, Eurydike, is risking little compared with them – though her responsibilities, as Thebes' queen, are greater. She cannot remain silent.

"You're my husband, and my lord king," she says, trying to sound as reasonable and soothing as possible. "But Megara was my daughter. A daughter tells her mother things she does not tell her father. *I* must explain what Alkides did."

Creon frowns; his eyes narrow. But he folds his arms and leans back in his chair. "Very well," he says, "we're listening."

EURYDIKE

Eriphyle, as a priestess you must have heard of the golden necklace given to Aphrodite's daughter Harmonia when she wed Thebes' first king, Kadmos. Hephaestus himself made the necklace, which is said to give the woman who wears it lasting beauty. It has been the prized possession of Thebes' queens since those ancient days – and its powers kept my sister-in-law Jocasta beautiful to the day of her death. But after Jocasta died, Thebes had no queen; so my husband, then regent, asked Princess Ismene to keep the necklace safe.

When Eteokles assumed the throne, he took Harmonia's necklace from his sister, saying that as king, the sacred heirloom belonged to him. But that was not his true reason. He knew that my daughter Megara coveted the treasure; he gave it to her in secret, so that she could benefit from its magic. Not long after this, Megara married Alkides – against my husband's wishes and mine, but with the king's blessing – and in nine months' time gave birth to our first grandchild: a darling little boy, Creontiades.

As all Hellas knows, at the end of Eteokles' first year of rule he tricked the people of Thebes into keeping Polynikes off the throne. What's not well known – what I learned later from my daughter – is that Megara and Alkides helped him. Because Alkides' ailing mother took poppy juice for her pain, they always had plenty of it in their house. They held a drinking-party the night before the ceremony that should have transferred the throne to Polynikes – and they dosed Polynikes' wine so that he slept through what should have been his own coronation. By the time he woke in Alkides' house, the sun had been up for hours; he guessed what had happened. He went to confront his twin; but Eteokles refused to yield the throne, and ordered Polynikes to swear loyalty instead. Polynikes refused, and was banished from the city.

We didn't realize until later that he had taken Harmonia's necklace with him.

I don't know how he found it. Maybe he was looking for a weapon – or just for jewels to steal; perhaps he guessed that Eteokles would force him into exile. But anyway he had the necklace hidden in his tunic when he left.

Of course Megara was the first to discover it was missing, but she didn't notice until that night. She only wore it in secret, you see. By then Polynikes had nearly a full day's head start. And naturally Megara waited till daylight to search through her whole house to make absolutely sure it was gone. She told me she interrogated each of the servants and even her mother-in-law, lying on her sickbed – hoping desperately that one of them might have hidden the treasure away somewhere. But none of them knew anything. Alkides came home late that night and found her beating the servants, and that's when he learned she had been wearing the necklace, every now and then, as a charm to increase her beauty. Shaken and angry to learn that his desire for her had been influenced by magic, he bellowed that even a fool could see Polynikes must have taken it – and this disaster was *her* fault, for having the sacred necklace in the first place. *She* needed to tell the king what had happened. Tearfully Megara pleaded with her husband not to make her go alone, and in the end he agreed to accompany her. So the next morning, the two of them went to the king's private study and explained what had happened.

Eteokles was livid. "What!" he shouted, red-faced. "How could you be so careless?"

"I don't know – I – I didn't think," Megara answered, cringing.

The king grasped her arm. "People will say my reign is cursed – that this shows Polynikes should be on the throne. That Kadmos and Harmonia would have it no other way!"

"I know, I know!" Tears coursed down her face. "I'm sorry!"

"You're a vain, careless fool, Megara!"

"That's my wife you're insulting, my lord king," Alkides growled, even though he had used the same language to her the night before.

Eteokles dropped his hand from Megara's arm and glared up at her tall, broad-shouldered husband. "You'll have to go after him to get it back. Only you, Alkides. No one else can know that the treasure is gone."

Alkides folded his massive arms across his chest. "No."

The king's eyes narrowed. "What do you mean, no?"

"I mean I'm not going after Polynikes."

"I'm your king!" Eteokles said grimly.

"You're the king because *I* helped you," he retorted.

"Alkides, I *order* you—"

"Polynikes was my friend once," Alkides interrupted. "I don't like what we had to do; I only did it because the two of you couldn't share a throne. But if he outsmarted you this time…" He shrugged his broad shoulders. "I guess it was his turn after all."

"Please, Husband," said Megara, softly stroking his arm. "Do it for me."

Anger flashed in his eyes. "I said no!" he snapped, and stalked out.

Megara was horrified. She had always been able to get Alkides to do what she wanted before. Had her persuasive powers vanished because the necklace was gone?

She promised Eteokles she'd do her best to change Alkides' mind and hurried after her husband. By the time she caught sight of him in the agora he was talking with his friends Aktor and Hyperbius; she couldn't press the matter in front of them. When Alkides returned home after midnight, sodden with wine, she tried to broach the topic once more – but he only collapsed into bed and was soon snoring.

Knowing her husband would have a fierce headache and fiercer temper the next morning, Megara waited for evening to try again. She had her servants prepare his favorite meal, lamb with a relish of onion and mint, and made sure the wine was mixed with plenty of water. As Alkides polished off the honey-drizzled hazelnut cakes, she dismissed the servants and stood behind his couch to rub his neck and shoulders.

"You're the most magnificent man who ever walked the streets of Thebes," she murmured into his ear. "The Tiresias himself said you'll be the city's greatest hero."

"Mm," he agreed, smiling. "More to the left – ah, yes, there."

"This is your chance, Husband. You can save the city – by retrieving its greatest treasure."

He chuckled. "A necklace won't save the city. That's what walls and soldiers are for."

"But—"

"Be quiet, Megara. Or do you want me to have the bath-girl rub my back instead?"

Thinking she might have made some headway – he hadn't denied her outright, after all – Megara let the matter drop for the evening. But she was persistent: at least once each day she pressed him, coming up with a different argument. The gods might curse Thebes, she argued, for letting the divine treasure be stolen: Alkides must think of his son's future! And what better way to ensure King Eteokles' favor? Besides, if Megara should bear her husband a daughter, that girl might be queen of Thebes someday; she would deserve to wear the necklace of Harmonia.

Alkides shrugged off these suggestions with growing irritation. After several days, he forbade her to mention the matter again. To Megara, this was yet more proof that her beauty had lost its hold on him, which only fueled her desperation. She persisted despite her husband's order; each time she spoke of it he grew angrier, and reminded her that a wife should obey her husband.

Finally, late one night, she asked once too often – and Alkides jumped up from his couch with a ferocious growl. He threw his terracotta wine-cup against the wall; it shattered, splashing dark lees across Megara's arms like streaks of blood.

"Alkides!" she gasped.

He kicked over the low table; the wine-krater spilled a great dark pool across the painted floor but did not break. Alkides grasped the huge vessel like a discus and hurled it with all his might at the far wall. With a sound like thunder it burst into fragments.

Megara shrieked in alarm.

"If you don't stop harping on this, woman, I'll throw *you* against the wall next!"

She collapsed sobbing to the floor, covering her head with her arms as though to ward off a blow – and this display of fear brought Alkides back to his senses, as did some fretful words called out by his mother from her bedroom. Alkides told his mother nothing was wrong, then knelt beside Megara. He apologized and carried her gently back to their bed where they made love.

In dawn's rosy light she dared to whisper of the necklace. Alkides set his thick forefinger to her lips. He did not shout, but he told her very firmly: "Do *not* ask me again."

Realizing that Alkides would never go after Polynikes and the necklace, Megara confessed her failure to Eteokles. By this time my nephew's anger had cooled; he pointed out that as long as he did not marry the theft need not be made known, and he was in no hurry to wed. This eased some of pressure she felt – but of course the king's anger was not the only reason Megara wanted the necklace returned.

As my daughter's second pregnancy progressed, I could tell that something was upsetting her. She tired more easily than she had done when carrying Creontiades, and she rarely smiled. One afternoon, as we sat together on a bench in her courtyard, I asked what was wrong.

She looked down at her sandaled feet; when her gaze met mine again I noticed how dark the shadows beneath her eyes had become. "Mother, how

– how old was Father, when you married?"

"Thirty-eight, dear. Why do you ask?"

"And you were about the age I am now, weren't you?"

Creontiades, on my knee, began to fuss; I bounced him to distract him. "No, my love, I was a few years younger."

"I suppose Father didn't stay out late all the time." She drew an arc in the dust with her toe. "Alkides was out late again last night. At Lasthenes' house. And tonight he's playing senet with Melanippus – and you know Melanippus has that dancing flute girl."

"If you feel left out, why not have his friends here? That's what you did last year."

"I can't – because of the baby, and anyway I'm so tired in the evenings." Her lower lip trembled. "So he's out every night having fun, drinking and flirting. Lasthenes' daughters – I've caught them looking at him before. And that sister of Aktor's. Alkides just laps it up, I know he does!"

"That's natural, Megara. He's still a very young man."

"I'm losing him, Mother!" Her voice cracked, and the tears spilled forth. "How can he love me, when I look like this?"

"What?" I asked, bewildered. Yes, she looked tired, but Megara was still lovely. "How can you say that?"

"Because it's true!" she wailed. "Look at me! My face is puffy, and my ankles are as thick as logs!" She grimaced down at her belly. "My waist will never be what it was before, even after this baby's born—"

"It feels that way, I know – but you just need a good tonic," I suggested. "And more servants, to help with Creontiades and your mother-in-law."

She shook her head. "That's not what I need."

"Megara," I said, "this will pass. Alkides loves you. How could he not, when you've given him such a healthy son?"

She sniffled.

"The first few months were always tiring for me too, dear. But you'll soon regain your sparkle. Remember how radiant you were while you carried Creontiades? Every maiden in Thebes was jealous!"

Instead of the smile I'd hoped for, she broke into sobs. I caught the words, "You don't know, Mother – you don't know!"

At this I grew concerned. I gave Creontiades to the nursemaid and dismissed all the servants from the courtyard. "What's wrong, Megara? Is there anything I can do to help?"

For a while she wept against my shoulder; eventually her tears lessened. When she was able to speak, she swore me to secrecy – and then she confessed how she had helped Eteokles gain the throne and had assisted him in tricking Polynikes – who had stolen the necklace of Harmonia from her keeping.

I loved my daughter; but my stomach churned at her confession. Such treachery! Perhaps it was the gods' own punishment that our city's treasure was gone.

This matter was beyond my meager abilities; I told Megara that I needed to consult her father.

Nodding, she wiped her reddened nose. "Yes. Tell Father – *only* Father. If anyone can get the necklace back, he can."

That evening in the privacy of our chambers, while we prepared for sleep, I related Megara's tale of deceit to my husband. But he was not as shocked as I expected. Instead he nodded, saying: "So *that's* how it was done! Very clever of Eteokles."

"Creon, he betrayed his brother!"

My husband dipped a cup into a krater of wine mixed with water and then set it on a table. "He thought Polynikes tried to kill him during that boar hunt."

"Polynikes wouldn't have—"

"Are you sure?" Reflected lamplight glittered in his dark eyes, as he opened a small box of dried thyme and another of dried rosemary. "It was obvious the twins could not share the throne. And Eteokles has proved himself the abler of the two."

"With trickery," I allowed, shifting uneasily against the bed-pillows.

Creon crumbled pinches of the herbs – he said they made his thinking stronger – into the wine. "Yes. The bloodless weapon of Hermes. Deceit has its uses, my dear."

"I suppose." Sighing, I added, "But it's such a shame. They were such good friends when they were little. Do you remember, when all the boys raced tortoises one summer? The twins decided to train only a single animal, so they would win or lose together." I realized that Creon, sipping his wine, wasn't listening. "Of course, that's not important now. The necklace of Harmonia—"

"An unfortunate loss," he agreed. "I'll be interested to see what Eteokles does to get it back. The theft could give him the excuse he needs to rid Thebes of the remaining threat."

"Threat?"

He smiled thinly. "Polynikes, of course."

"But Polynikes is gone," I said – and then, suddenly guessing his meaning, I stared open-mouthed at my husband. "You – do you mean Eteokles should *kill* his brother?"

"It might be wise," he said, joining me in our bed.

The linen window-curtains billowed inwards with a sudden gust; I shivered, and pulled the blanket up to cover my shoulders. "This is our *nephew* you're talking about," I whispered. "Jocasta's son…"

"This is Thebes I'm talking about, Eurydike." He set his cup on the side table and folded his arms behind his head as he lay back on the pillow. "Imagine you're a shepherd. A pack of wolves has been raiding your flock. You band together with other shepherds, and with great difficulty and risk to yourself, you kill the wolves."

"I don't see what this has to do with—"

"Let me continue," he interrupted. "You've averted the immediate threat. And then, you come across the wolves' den. It's full of half-grown pups – not so young as to need a mother's constant care, but not old enough to endanger you and your sheep – *yet*. What do you do?"

I clutched the blanket tighter. "What do you mean?"

"Do you kill the half-grown pups, or do you let them live?"

"Men aren't wolves," I said uneasily. But I knew Creon had dealt with such matters since before I was born, and he was usually right.

He enfolded me in his arms. "You're right, my dear; men are not wolves. And I'm not king – I'm not even regent. This is Eteokles' problem to solve."

I nodded against his shoulder. "But what about the necklace? Megara wants it back. Desperately."

"Harmonia's treasure belongs to Thebes – Polynikes should never have taken it. But Eteokles is king, and he must deal with this. Of course, he can't admit that it was ever gone – not until it's back in his possession."

"Why not?"

"People would question his right to the throne," he answered. "And Thebes has had enough unrest."

"Megara swore me to secrecy," I told him. "She told me I could tell you, but no one else."

He stroked my back. "I'm glad you're not like other wives, always gossiping."

I nestled closer against my husband and listened to the sound of his heartbeat, the slight roughness of his breath and the whisper of the breeze against the curtains. Eventually I surrendered myself to uneasy dreams of shepherds and wolves.

That summer was the ninth since Thebes last celebrated the Laurel-Bearer festival in honor of Apollo, and so it was time for this event once more. Lasthenes' young son was chosen as the Laurel-Bearer; I pitied the boy since everyone kept comparing him to Alkides who had been it last. You would think that Thebans would show enough respect for the god to be quiet during the ceremony – and yet even as the laurel-crowned boy led forward the chorus of maidens singing the hymn, I heard one person whispering about how much taller Alkides had been at that age. Another recalled that Alkides had carried the olivewood staff unassisted, whereas Lasthenes helped his son with the heavy ritual object as the Laurel-Bearer's father usually did.

Megara was proud to have so much attention paid her husband, and yet it also made her uneasy. She clutched his muscled arm tightly, and her jaw tightened when the prettiest girl in the maidens' choir cast a sidelong glance at Alkides – who responded with a broad grin.

Despite such distractions, my son Haemon preserved the solemnity of the ritual. I was so proud to see him presiding as Apollo's chief priest! When Lasthenes helped his son to place the olivewood staff – with its bronze spheres representing the sun, moon, and stars and its ribbons of purple and saffron for the days of the year – into its socket, Haemon received the offering with grace. His voice was confident as he spoke the final words of the prayer. For a moment, just a moment, the people of Thebes were united in reverence.

And then the ceremony was done. King Eteokles stepped from his place near the altar out onto the temple's sunlit terrace; lifting his voice, he called out towards the back of the crowd: "Hyperbius, was that you slinking in just as the procession started?"

Laughing, the crowd moved aside to let the plump trader approach the temple. He bowed to Eteokles with a flourish of his short crimson cloak, saying, "Most profound apologies, my lord king. I meant to be here two days ago, but Poseidon and the winds had other ideas!"

Eteokles started down the marble stairs and beckoned Hyperbius forward, so that the two met halfway down the flight of steps. From where I stood with my family at the front of the crowd, we could hear what was said.

"Your cargo?" Eteokles asked, a note of worry in his quiet voice.

The trader smiled. "All safe, my lord king. Our leather and dried beef were welcome; and my men will have the trade goods in your storehouses by the end of the day."

Eteokles nodded, his stance relaxing. "Good," he said, his voice pitched louder, so that all the assembled citizens would hear. "As always, Hyperbius, my trust in you is rewarded. Besides the success of your trading mission, what news from our friends in the south?"

"Last year's flax harvest in Pylos was excellent, my lord king, and the linen's even better quality than usual. We've brought four yearling horses from Taenarus that show real promise. The Athenian honey is plentiful – and the Tiresias and his daughters are doing well, as is your sister Antigone. They plan to stay in Athens for now."

At this mention of my daughter-in-law I glanced over at Haemon; fortunately, he was out of earshot, congratulating Lasthenes and his son.

"Anything else?"

Hyperbius shifted his weight, setting one foot on the next lower stair. "Yes, my lord king. We stopped in Argos."

"And?"

"My lord king, your brother Polynikes is there now."

Eteokles reached up with one hand to touch his golden crown, as if reassuring himself it was still secure on his head. "Argos! Why *there*?"

My husband Creon stepped forward. "Argos welcomes men that others shun, King Eteokles. And your father Oedipus stayed there."

The trader nodded. "You're right about that, my lord. King Adrastos makes no secret of it – he says the cursed bring Argos luck."

"A strange attitude," remarked my son Menoeceus.

"Yes," Hyperbius agreed. "But King Adrastos really believes it. He's even married his two daughters to exiles who've sought refuge with him: a fellow called Tydeus who was once a prince of Kalydon – and Polynikes."

Menoeceus gave a low whistle; Alkides chuckled. Eteokles' face went red. "The king's daughter," he repeated in tightly-clipped syllables. "My brother's done well."

"Not a pup anymore," muttered my husband. "A full-grown wolf, so quickly…"

Megara interrupted: "Hyperbius, tell me – is Polynikes' wife a great beauty?"

The trader shrugged. "Princess Argia's rather ordinary looking, my lady. But the newlyweds seem happy with their match."

"I see," Megara answered vaguely.

Alkides frowned down at her. "Why do you care?"

I realized that Megara hoped to learn whether Polynikes had given his wife the necklace – apparently he had not – but Alkides' jealous tone reminded me that Polynikes had once courted Megara.

Eteokles cut the conversation short, and declared that the gathering should proceed back into the city for the midday banquet. At the palace, Megara cornered the king for a private conversation – a conversation she recounted to me later.

"You could send soldiers," said my daughter.

Closing his eyes, Eteokles rubbed his temples. "We've discussed that already. And now he's the son-in-law of the Argive king."

"Well… what about sending someone to negotiate? My father's clever, and he can keep a secret."

He grimaced. "Here's how that conversation would go: Uncle Creon says the necklace belongs to Thebes – so my brother retorts that *he* is the rightful king of Thebes."

"But—"

"A successful negotiation requires concessions and gains on both sides. What could your father offer Polynikes in exchange? We have nothing of equivalent value except the throne itself – and I won't give that up."

"We could tell him he'll be cursed if he doesn't send it back," she suggested. "Or say the necklace itself is cursed."

Eteokles spread his hands. "Who do you expect to do the cursing? We have no control over Delphi. The Tiresias is still in Athens – and persuading the Tiresias to say what you want him to say is impossible anyway." For a moment he looked away, gazing out the window of his study. Then, in a speculative tone, he continued: "We might have better luck with your brother Haemon – but I don't think his words would influence Polynikes."

Megara bit her lip. "What about your sister?"

"Antigone? She's more unpredictable than the Tiresias!"

"I meant Ismene."

He laughed. "She'd never curse Polynikes!"

"But we could send her to persuade him."

"Not a chance! *No* one listens to Ismene." Eteokles patted his cousin's shoulder. "I want the treasure back in Thebes, too, Megara. But we'll have to wait for the right opportunity. And just now, we'd better get to the megaron – they can't start the feast without me."

A few days later I went to see my daughter. Alkides was in a good mood that morning; he dropped a kiss on my cheek and spent time playing with little Creontiades. As the sun reached its zenith, he departed for his shift guarding the Ogygia Gate – but not before sweeping Megara into his powerful embrace and exchanging a few tender words with her.

Megara left me in her rooms with the baby while she checked on her bedridden mother-in-law. When she returned, she dismissed the servants and brought up the subject of the necklace, telling me about her conversation with the king and asking if I could think of a way to recover the precious heirloom.

"My dear, you and Eteokles are cleverer than I've ever been," I said, rocking the baby in my arms. "I can't think of anything else."

"Then what will I do?"

"You'll have to manage your husband as other wives do – without charmed necklaces." My grandson had drifted off to sleep; I placed him gently in his cradle. "Alkides spoke very sweetly just now."

She clenched her fists. "Words are one thing; actions are another. Did you see how he looked at Aktor's sister during the Laurel-Bearer's ceremony?"

I sighed. "My dear, she's the daughter of a bronze worker – you're descended from Kadmos himself!" Though I tried to reassure her, Megara refused to be consoled. She needed the necklace to give her confidence.

My second grandson, Deicoon, was born early the next year. Though old Rhodia the midwife assured me that my daughter's life was never in danger, for months afterward Megara was nearly as feeble as Alkides' mother. She spent listless days in bed, not bothering to have her maidservants dress her or arrange her hair. Rhodia gave her herbs to make strengthening teas, but they were bitter-tasting and Megara did not drink them. At my urging, Haemon had his colleague Udaeus visit her; he suggested that she spend a night in Apollo's temple to seek a healing dream from the god. But the god sent her no dream messages.

What finally roused her was Thebes' spring festival of new wine. Not the festival itself – though I did persuade Megara to dress in her best jacket and skirts, and have her servants do her hair and face. I hoped that looking pretty would raise her spirits; but while the other women cheered on the procession of carts carrying the great terracotta jars of wine, Megara was glum and silent. Alkides made a great show of lifting the heaviest jars, ones usually carried by two men. Of course the people laughed and shouted praise; young women sighed and called his name – and each time some girl squealed "Alkides!" the corners of my daughter's red-painted lips drew further downward, making an unattractive scowl.

Menoeceus, Ismene and I urged her to stay, but Megara left the festival just after sundown, before the drinking-contest even began; she insisted that she needed to check on Creontiades and the baby Deicoon. Alkides, of course, remained and won the drinking contest.

The next morning, while most of Thebes was still sleeping off the wine, Megara came to see Creon and me. She had just thrown a cloak over her night-shift; her hair was pulled back in an unkempt braid that looked as though she had slept in it.

"Alkides made love to other women last night!" she wailed.

Creon pushed his breakfast-plate aside. "Men do that, Megara," he said. "Especially during festivals."

"They say he had three different women last night! *Three!*"

I went to her; taking her hand, I led her over to sit on the couch. "I told you not to go home so early, dear. If you'd stayed—"

"Mother! You think this is *my* fault?"

In a way, I suppose, I *did* think that. If only she would forget about the necklace, and just be the way she was before…

"Megara!" Creon snapped. "You will not speak to your mother that way!"

"But—"

"Daughter," he continued, his voice cold, "I forbade you to marry that man, and you disobeyed me. If you want him to give up other women, speak to him – not to us!"

Megara wrenched her hand from my grasp and fled. I rose to follow her, but Creon stopped me. "She's a grown woman, Eurydike. A wife and a mother. It's time she behaved like one. We've coddled her too long."

I pressed my lips together, distraught, but I thought Creon was right. We couldn't solve this problem for our daughter; it was between her and Alkides.

Megara did speak to her husband – over and over. They quarreled, and as the days passed their arguments grew louder and angrier. The neighbors began to complain about the shouting and the broken pottery, and finally the boldest of them approached the king and begged him to rule between the husband and the wife. This put Eteokles in an awkward position; Alkides was always very popular, and a favorite with the soldiers. But Megara was his cousin, and had helped him gain his throne.

King Eteokles found a temporary solution: he stationed Alkides in the mountains north of Thebes with a dozen soldiers, with instructions to rid the area of bandits and make the pass safe for travelers. I hoped – as, I imagine, did Eteokles – that separating the young couple would allow their anger to cool, and that their love would flicker back to life. But things were no better when Alkides returned at the end of the summer. He'd grown used to late nights by the fire with his fellow soldiers; rumor said that they took the comeliest bandits' women for themselves. I suppose most men stationed with warriors, away from civilization, develop rough manners; Alkides now shouted orders at his wife as if she were a slave rather than a noblewoman. A few nights after his return he invited his friends over for a drinking party. They played kottabos, tossing wine-lees at a target, and were so loud they could be heard throughout the neighborhood. Megara tried to retire to her rooms, but Alkides insisted she stay – insisted, in fact, that she serve the wine herself. She called him a drunkard and refused. He bellowed that no wife of his would defy him, and demanded she bring over the wine-pitcher. When she poured – whether her hand was unsteady with the pitcher, or his with the cup – the dark liquid splashed across his saffron-colored tunic.

"You bitch!" he roared, throwing his cup aside. "You did that on purpose!" His huge fist lashed out, knocking her to the floor.

That changed matters. Under Melanippus' protection, Megara fled sobbing with her small boys. They came to the wing of the palace where Creon and I lived, and word spread like fire that Alkides had struck his wife. She remained inside, ashamed of the huge purple bruise that ringed her left eye, but the servants had seen, and servants talk.

Thebes was more sharply divided than when Eteokles and Polynikes contended for the throne. Most of the soldiers remained loyal to Alkides, and said it was a man's right to discipline his wife. But most noble and influential men remarked quietly that a man as big and strong as Alkides should be able to control his wife – a woman half his size! – without resorting to violence. Thebes' matrons clucked their tongues in sympathy, remembering what it was like to be a young wife with small children. But some of the maidens – and a few of the younger wives – saw an opportunity.

At first Alkides reveled in his quasi-bachelor status, bedding one woman after another, and boasting that no man could match him for wine or for Eros. Drinking parties stretched across two or three days, with torch-lit dances through the streets of Thebes and even out in the fields. The Maenads of Orchomenos came to join the debauchery; Creon, and others among the elder generation, scowled, recalling the bad old days when Maenads destroyed Theban crops and attacked our livestock.

But even Alkides had limits. Drunken nights led to hung-over mornings; as time went on, the parties featured less dancing and more sodden conversation over the wine-cups. The Maenads tired of this, and returned to Orchomenos for the harvest festival. The banquets dwindled, as Alkides' friends tended the chores of autumn. Rumor had it his ailing mother scolded him, saying that his father Amphitryon would have been ashamed. "He was a good man – a loyal husband to me, and a father to his son! You spit on his memory!"

On a gray day when winter's chill was first making itself felt, Alkides came to the palace and asked to speak with his wife. Eteokles and Creon were out inspecting the new storerooms by the Chloris Gate, and I was with Megara and Ismene in the weaving room. Megara agreed to receive her husband on condition that several from the king's bodyguard also be there.

Megara seated herself in a chair like a queen preparing to receive a petition; I went to stand at her shoulder. Baby Deicoon was asleep in a cradle, tended by a nursemaid; the toddler Creontiades stood by one of the looms, staring at the soldiers with large, solemn eyes. Ismene remained on a bench by the wall, rhythmically casting her spindle and drawing out new thread.

When Alkides arrived, I was shocked at his appearance. His eyes were bloodshot, his beard and hair unkempt, his tunic grimy and stained.

"What do you want?" Megara asked sharply.

"I'm here…" He knotted his huge hands together; the cords twisted in his forearms. "I'm here to ask you to come home, Megara."

"Why should I?"

"Please, Megara. I love you."

My daughter lifted her chin. "That's why you treated me like a slave?"

He moved closer to her chair; I saw the soldiers' hands go to their sword-hilts, but Alkides dropped to one knee so that his troubled eyes were level with his wife's gaze. "I – I was drinking too much. You said so, and you were right. The wine-god made me mad; he does that to people. But I'll never drink again – I swear it!"

Megara tilted her head to one side, but said nothing.

"I miss you… I miss you so much, Megara. And the boys." He glanced over at his eldest son, and I saw unshed tears sparkling in his eyes. "Mother misses all of you too. We need you to come home."

Bitterly she replied, "Really? What about all those other women?"

"They meant nothing. Nothing! Megara, I'll never so much as *look* at another woman again."

"I don't know," she whispered.

"You're the only woman for me, Megara. Without you I'm worthless. Look at me!" He lay his head on her knee; his tears dampened her skirts. "I'm a wreck. I can't sleep; I can't take care of myself. I need you. You know what's right for me better than I do myself – you always have. I was just too stupid to realize it until you were gone."

My throat tightened with unexpected emotion; a glance at Ismene told me that she, too, was moved. Alkides really *did* love Megara; it was remarkable to see such a powerful man rendered so helpless. But Megara had seen something like this contrition before; she was not so ready to yield. They spoke for a long time, and finally she told him she would think about it. When Alkides and the guards had gone, she said that she needed to be *sure* that he would keep his word.

"Let's ask Haemon's advice," I said. "Alkides seems unwell – perhaps Apollo can help heal him."

"I think you should consult the Maenads," Ismene suggested in her soft voice. "They know the ways of Dionysus better than anyone."

Most of the Maenads were away in Orchomenos, but a few from that cult, too old to travel, remained in Thebes. Their leader recommended that Alkides wear an amethyst on a chain about his neck; since these stones are formed when Dionysus spills wine from his sacred goblet, they protect against drunkenness. Alkides traded some of the booty from his bandit raids for the largest amethyst to be had in the agora, and had a skilled goldsmith set it in a sturdy chain; then, under Haemon's supervision, he offered a pair of doves to Apollo and swore an oath to remain faithful and sober.

Megara and her sons returned to her husband's house, but my daughter remained cautious. She reconstituted the household staff so that the only female servants were aged, ugly, or both. Alkides, still sorry for his misdeeds, did not object. The new cook was fat and cross-eyed; the woman who now nursed Alkides' mother had been badly scarred in the great fire at the end of Oedipus' reign; and the young woman brought in to help with the boys had a harelip – she was called Rabbit, because of the way her two front teeth were exposed. I was surprised that she was not exposed as an infant, but some mothers don't think how deformities will cause their children to suffer. Megara did not let Rabbit wear a veil, and it was always shocking to see her ugliness.

In the fourth year of Eteokles' reign, at the end of the harvest, Alkides' mother finally died. I hoped the end of her suffering might bring greater peace to my daughter's household; and when Megara's third child was born – another boy, Ophites – it seemed a chance for a new beginning.

But not all beginnings are good ones. About this time, Alkides began drinking again.

At first it was just a cup or two at a friend's dinner party, when Megara was home with the baby; but Megara smelled the wine on his breath. He tried to hide it by chewing mint leaves; this increased Megara's anger, because he compounded oath-breaking with deception. The late-night arguments escalated once more; Creon and I heard disturbing reports from the neighbors.

I went to Megara one morning when I knew Alkides was away helping Lasthenes with the calving. The spring rains were pouring down; my cloak was drenched. Rabbit took it to dry beside the fire in the main room, and I went back to Megara's chamber.

She sat slumped at her dressing table.

"Daughter," I urged her, "come back to the palace."

Megara glanced up at me; her eyes were swollen. "Father will say 'I told you so.' He'll say I should never have married Alkides."

"Yes, he will. But wouldn't that be better than this?"

"I don't know," she whispered.

I reached out for her hand, held her arm up to catch the rainy morning's gray light. Ugly bruises, purple and green, ringed her wrist like a bracelet of snakes. "Alkides did this, didn't he?"

"He doesn't know his own strength," she said, her tone defensive.

I dropped her hand. "It's not safe for you to be here!"

Ophites whimpered in his cradle; Megara pushed herself up from her dressing-stool to go to him. It seemed to me that she was limping, and when she picked up the baby I saw her wince. "I don't understand," she said softly, looking down at the child in her arms. "The Tiresias said your father would be Thebes' greatest hero." She glanced at the two older boys, who were rolling their toy chariots across the bench beneath the window, and then met my gaze. Tears slipped down her face.

Little Deicoon looked up at her with dark round eyes. "Mama, don't cry!"

"I'm sorry, dear." Megara sniffled; shifting the baby in her arms, she wiped her nose against her shoulder. "I'll try to stop."

Four-year-old Creontiades stood, folding his small arms across his chest. "It's Papa's fault, isn't it?"

"Don't worry about it, darling," she told him, then called out, "Rabbit! Rabbit, come here!"

The hare-lipped girl came quickly; Megara told her to take the toddlers to the kitchen and get them milk and honeycakes. When they had gone, she sat down on the edge of the bed, looking down at the infant. "Your father *could* be a great man – I can still see it in him."

I went to sit beside her. "Don't worry about prophecies, Megara," I urged her. "They don't always mean what you think. What's important is that you're unhappy – and Alkides is dangerous. Please, come with me."

She bit her lip. "He apologized, this morning. Before he left, he told me how sorry he was – that the wine brings madness. He had the servants pour out all the wine in the house. He said he'd go by Apollo's temple before he comes home, and renew his vow."

I glanced out the window; the sky remained dark and gray, but the rain had stopped. "Come with me now. We'll just get the boys from the kitchen and go."

"I love him, Mother. I have to give him another chance."

"Megara…"

"I'll think about it, Mother," she promised. "I promise I will."

There was nothing more I could say. I kissed her and the baby, and returned to the palace.

Rain soaked the city again the next day; the following day the clouds began to clear – but that day Alkides did not arrive to help the cowherds, as had been agreed. Finally, around noon, Lasthenes sent a runner to fetch him.

The man found the door of Alkides' house standing open; he called out, but got no answer, so he ventured inside. I'll never forget the terror on the man's face, the quaver in his voice, when he came to the palace to report what he had found.

No living thing remained in the house. The servants had fled; Megara lay dead in the main room, her neck broken. The baby and the two small boys – sweet Leto, it tears my heart to say it – their skulls had been crushed and their small bodies thrown into the fire, partly burned. Alkides was nowhere to be found.

Alkides' friends did not want to believe he could be responsible. But who could have overpowered his titanic strength? Besides, his most precious things were gone: his amethyst necklace, his dagger, his club.

King Eteokles ordered his soldiers to search all of Thebes: every room of every structure was checked, from the rudest shelters to the finest apartments in the palace, from the granaries to the back rooms of the potters' workshops. They found nothing. None of the guards stationed at the city gates reported seeing Alkides leave the city, but one man posted at the Ogygia Gate said he heard something just before dawn.

"A sort of crashing sound in the bushes, my lord king," he said, hands clasped behind his back.

"Did you see anything?" Eteokles demanded.

"The light was poor, my lord king – it was hard to tell what it was…"

Creon interrupted harshly: "A man?"

"Looked too big to be a man, my lord," the soldier said uneasily. "It didn't run on all fours, exactly, but it didn't run upright either."

"It could have been Alkides," growled Creon.

Eteokles held up a hand. "Uncle, I respect your grief. But we must have facts, not supposition." He turned back to the soldier. "*Could* it have been Alkides?"

The man shrugged helplessly. "It's possible, my lord king. The sun wasn't up yet, and you know how thick the clouds have been. Whatever it was, it was moving away from the city, so I stayed at my post."

A monster, said Alkides' friends. A monster must have killed Alkides and his family.

Creon refused to believe any monster other than our monstrous son-in-law was at fault. He sought out the servants for questioning. The scarred nurse who once cared for Alkides' mother had left the household after the invalid died; she was of no use. The cook lived with her own family, walking early every morning from her home near the Kleodoxa Gate to Alkides' house; along the way she stopped to fetch bread from the bakers and to barter in the agora.

At Creon's urging, Eteokles summoned her and a few others to be questioned. The stout woman leaned on a walking stick as she limped into the megaron; I saw that one foot was bandaged.

"My lord king, I did not go to Alkides' house that morning," she claimed.

From her tone, I thought she was lying – but with her crossed eyes, it was hard to judge her expression.

"Why not?" asked the king.

She gestured at her foot. "Because I'd sprained my ankle, my lord king."

Eteokles' eyes narrowed. "Bring forth the baker," he ordered.

A short, bowlegged fellow came forward; I knew his bread to be of good quality. He wiped his palms nervously on a flour-dusted tunic, and swore that Alkides' cook did indeed stop at his shop to pick up bread the morning that Megara and her sons were found dead.

Eteokles turned back to the cook. "Why are you lying?" he asked coldly.

"I – he must be mistaken, my lord king! He must have meant someone else!"

"*Your* eyes are crossed, woman, not his!"

The woman gripped her staff, looking anxiously both ways at once, while spectators snickered at the king's wit. But I found no humor in it. I clutched my husband's hand, anxious to hear what would be said. My daughter and my grandsons were dead – I needed to know the truth.

"You went to Alkides' house, didn't you?" Creon prodded. "You saw the bodies."

She fell to her knees; her walking-stick fell to the floor with a sound that made people jump. "Yes, my lord, I did – forgive me for not telling the truth! But I had nothing to do with it, I swear – I would *never* have hurt the mistress, or the little ones! Never!"

"Is that when you really twisted your ankle?" Eteokles asked.

"Yes, my lord king," she sobbed. "It was so terrible to see – I ran away fast as I could, like the Kindly Ones were chasing me – and about halfway down the street I stumbled..." Eteokles and Creon questioned her further, but we learned nothing new. Megara and the boys were already dead; the cook had fled after only discovering the carnage.

Finally Creon said, "I think she's telling the truth, my lord king – *now*. But she lied to you initially. And if she had raised the alarm at once, we might have caught Alkides before he made his escape."

"Or whoever the murderer was," said Eteokles gravely.

"Of course, my lord king," my husband agreed. But under his breath he muttered, "It was Alkides."

The king sentenced the cook to a public flogging for her lies and her failure in her duty as a citizen. But there was still another servant to be questioned.

Rabbit was found the following day, trying to escape towards the north through the Kleodoxa Gate. She had veiled her face, which made the sentry suspicious – and of course once the veil was removed there was no question as to her identity. They brought her before the king that evening.

The deformed girl shook with fear, but – perhaps because she knew the flogging a false witness would receive – she told the truth from the beginning.

"It was raining that night," she reminded us, "but the master went out anyway. He went to dine at the house of Aktor the bronze-worker. He promised the mistress he'd only stay a little while, and promised he wouldn't drink any wine." Nervously, she licked her lips; I looked away from her misshapen mouth. "The mistress and the boys took their supper in the main room, and then Cook went home; I asked the mistress if she wanted me to take the boys to bed but she said no, the master would be home soon."

"Was he?" asked Eteokles.

"No, my lord king." She explained that the boys had fallen asleep; Megara was pacing back and forth, back and forth. Rabbit drifted off to sleep, waking when Alkides returned – and slammed the door so hard that the whole house shook.

"You're late," Megara accused, going to take his wet cloak. "You said you wouldn't be late."

"Well, I'm here now." He set a new log on the fire in the central hearth, and prodded the coals with a stick to rouse the flames. "Quit scolding me! What man wants to come home to scolding?" His voice was slurred.

Rabbit edged her stool back into the shadows, knowing she needed to be close by to watch the sleeping children, but not wanting to call attention to herself.

"I wouldn't scold if you came home when you said you would!" retorted Megara, spreading the cloak over a chair to dry. "I've been up all night, waiting for you."

"Waiting for it, eh?" A grin spread across Alkides' face. "I won't disappoint you." In two broad strides he crossed the room; his hand closed over Megara's arm, and he brought his face close to hers. "Tell me you want me."

She grimaced and pushed him away. "You've been drinking!"

"No, I haven't!"

"Don't lie to me! I can smell it!"

"All right, so I drank a cup of wine at Aktor's! How could I refuse my host?" Gripping her shoulders with both hands, he bellowed, "What kind of man can't have a cup of wine now and then? You've made me a laughingstock! No one respects me any more – and it's all because of you!"

The baby awoke and began to cry, but Rabbit didn't go to him. She had seen Alkides in this mood before – he'd struck her before, too. She stayed out of sight.

Wrenching herself from her husband's grasp, Megara walked across the room. "You swore to keep sober, before Apollo and Dionysus and Zeus! Do your oaths mean nothing to you?"

"You stupid woman!" yelled Alkides, clenching his huge fists. "Do you think the king of gods would ever give up wine?"

She slapped a couch cushion in frustration; little Deicoon looked over at her, rubbing his eyes with a chubby fist. "You're not Zeus Almighty, you know! An oath is an oath!"

He took a step closer. "I kept an oath tonight, Megara. Aktor's sister wanted me to bed her – but I refused, because of you. So come here and do your wifely duty."

"Shut up, Alkides. You're drunk!"

Knocking a chair out of his way, he closed on her. "How dare you deny me!"

"Don't you touch me!" cried Megara.

He grabbed her long hair with his left hand, and began to fumble at her clothing with his right. "You're my wife," he said. "And a wife has to spread her legs for her husband—"

"I will *not!* What kind of husband are you? I'll go back to my father!"

"Be quiet," he growled, covering her mouth with his hand. "It's not your words I want, woman—"

Megara bit his fingers; he roared in indignation and pain, and slapped her hard across the face. Megara fell back, her cheek bleeding where Alkides' ring had slashed open the skin. From her stool in the shadows Rabbit watched, horrified, wondering if she should try to help but terrified of her master's strength.

Another came to Megara's rescue. Young Creontiades ran forward and began to pummel his father's thick leg with small fists. "Stop it, Papa!" he yelled. "Don't you touch her again!"

"Get off of me, whelp!" replied Alkides, furious at the interference. With one hand he grabbed the child and flung him away.

Creontiades sailed through the air and hit the wall head first. The impact made a sickening thud; then the small body slid down the wall and lay still.

Their argument momentarily forgotten, Alkides and Megara stared at their son.

Megara was the first to react. "Creontiades? Baby?" she said hoarsely, crawling towards him on her hands and knees. "Talk to me, darling. Talk to me!" But when Megara lifted the child, his head fell back at a strange angle. Rabbit realized that his neck was broken. There in the shadows she stuffed her fist into her mouth to keep from sobbing aloud.

"You monster!" screamed Megara, her tears streaking down her cheeks in black kohl-stained lines. "You killed your own son!"

"No!" Alkides said, stumbling towards her. "He's not dead!" He tried to take Creontiades from her, but she enfolded the small corpse in her arms.

"Yes, he is! You murdered him! I'll see you dead for this, you beast – my cousin the king will chop off your head! When they learn what you've done, the people of Thebes will cheer your death – they'll spit on your corpse, and the ravens will feast on your eyes!"

"Shut up!" he yelled. "Shut up!"

The neighbors, Rabbit knew, had heard many arguments as loud as this; but with the rain pounding outside, the words would be drowned out. They would not know that little Creontiades was dead, killed by his own father; they would know only that Alkides and Megara were raging at each other once again. They would simply pull the blankets over their heads and stick their fingers in their ears. No one in their right mind would interfere when Alkides was angry.

Megara continued her furious ranting, describing in bloody detail how Thebes' citizens would dismember and trample the corpse of Alkides the murderer.

Rabbit was sure her own life was in danger: if Alkides realized she had witnessed Creontiades' death, he would kill her. She glanced around in terror, knowing there was no way she could escape the room without being seen. Her only chance was to hide, and hope that Alkides had not seen her. Nearby in the shadows, in the corner of the room, was a wickerwork chest for linens and tableware; Rabbit, a small woman, climbed into the chest and pulled shut the lid. Her heart pounding hard, Rabbit peered warily through the spaces in the wicker, waiting for a chance to escape.

Finally Megara set down her eldest son's corpse and got to her feet. "Everyone will know what you've done!" She went over to the couch where the baby Ophites lay wailing and picked him up. "Deicoon, come with me!"

"Where are you going?" asked Alkides, moving to block her path.

"To my father, you murderer!"

"No, no—" stammered Alkides, sounding truly frightened. "Megara, please, don't leave me! We'll say Creontiades was an accident."

"An accident?" raged Megara. "An accident!"

She tried to push her way past him – but he snatched the screaming baby from her arms.

"Give him back to me! Now!"

He held the baby above his head so that Megara could not reach him. "Promise me you'll stay!"

"Please," she sobbed, "give him to me!"

Alkides staggered back a step. "You've told me my life's worth nothing if you leave. Swear to me that you'll stay, or this one meets the same fate as Creontiades!"

"You can't! You wouldn't!"

Megara jumped up, trying to reach the baby; Rabbit could not see clearly what happened next. Did Megara push Alkides off balance, or did he deliberately slam the baby's head against the wall? She wasn't sure. But, however it happened, Ophites' short life was ended.

"No!" Megara shrieked wildly. "No! No! No!"

"Quiet!" Alkides bellowed. "Shut up!"

But Megara would not – or could not – stop screaming. Alkides grabbed her hair once more and covered her mouth with his huge hand. She struggled, but couldn't twist free of his grasp; she kicked him, and in his fury he shifted both his hands to circle her slender neck. Her eyes bulged;

her mouth gaped wide, but no sound emerged as her face went red, then dark purple, and her struggles grew feebler. Finally Alkides dropped his wife's body, and she was silent as he had ordered. He looked down at her, swaying slightly, and Rabbit saw that he knew what he had done.

After a moment he straightened his shoulders and turned to his last living child. Deicoon was crouched under a table; moving decisively, like a warrior confronting a cowering enemy, Alkides hauled him out by one ankle. The boy whimpered and then shrieked in that high, piercing way that only young children can manage. The sound stopped abruptly when his head slammed into the wall near the bloodstained spot left by his infant brother.

For the space of a few breaths, the only sound was the crackling of logs on the fire and the rain pounding against the roof. Inside the wicker chest Rabbit kept her hands pressed to her mouth, praying that Alkides would not hear her shuddering breath.

But Alkides was not looking her way. He knelt beside the body of his wife and stroked her face. "I'm sorry, Megara," he said. "I didn't mean to…"

He looked around the room – the house looked as though an army had invaded it. Furniture was overturned; blood stained the walls, and four corpses lay motionless on the painted stucco floor.

"I didn't mean to," Alkides repeated. "It was an accident!"

But even addled with wine as he was, Alkides knew he was at fault. He buried his head in his hands; his huge shoulders shook with sobs. "Oh, gods – what have I done?" he wept. "What have I done?"

Eventually his tears subsided; he rubbed his eyes with the heels of his hands and stood. "Done is done," he muttered to himself. "Can't be undone. Have to go."

He wrapped his cloak around his shoulders, and then glanced back. "The bodies," he mumbled. "Must get rid of the bodies." He tossed the small corpses of his three sons into the fire; then he grabbed his club and hurried out.

Rabbit waited, sickened by the smell of burning cloth and hair, until she was sure that Alkides would not return; then she emerged from her hiding place and fled.

I listened in horror as Rabbit finished her tale. My beautiful Megara, her three sweet little boys – it was all so pointless!

Creon was the first to speak. "Alkides is guilty."

"Yes," King Eteokles agreed grimly. "And he should be brought to justice. But he has left Thebes – that's clear."

I reached for my husband's hand, thinking of how I had asked my daughter to come with me just a few days earlier. If I had only convinced her, she would still be alive! I should have insisted – I should have *made* her come!

"What do you want to do about her?" the king asked Creon.

My husband looked vaguely towards the throne. "What?"

"The nursemaid," said King Eteokles.

Rabbit threw herself to the floor before the throne. "Please, my lord king – please have mercy!"

"Her duty was to care for the boys," Creon said. "She failed."

"Creon, she could never have stopped Alkides," I interjected.

He dropped my hand. "And because she ran away, we didn't catch him." He turned back to Eteokles. "But this is a matter for the king to decide."

After consideration, Eteokles sentenced Rabbit to flogging and banishment, and he sent his soldiers in search of Alkides. But, as you know, he was gone – to Argos, where you gave him sanctuary.

*

Dabbing at her eyes with a corner of her cloak, Eurydike glances at Creon. His eyes are tightly shut; his face is a mask of mingled anger and sorrow. She guesses that he, too, would shed tears of grief for Megara and her boys, but is resolved to show no weakness before the Argive priestess.

She turns back to the priestess Eriphyle. "Now you know what sort of criminal you welcomed to your city."

CHAPTER THIRTEEN
ERIPHYLE

As matronly, gray-haired Eurydike of Thebes concludes her story, Phyle realizes that the crowd's mood has grown even more hostile. King Creon's eyes are clamped shut, his fists clenched in anger. Beside him, Princess Ismene looks troubled; fidgeting, she glances anxiously over at the tombs.

Seeking to regain some measure of control over the situation, Phyle says: "These were terrible crimes." She knew that Alkides killed his wife and children, but this is the first time for her to hear the awful details; she hopes the king and his wife can hear the sincerity in her voice. "I grieve for your loss."

King Creon's eyes open, two dark slits. "But you did not execute the criminal."

Phyle spreads her hands. "He came to Argos seeking sanctuary."

"Sanctuary!" he snorts.

Phyle ventures: "Argos did not harm your daughter Megara or her sons." But even to her own ears these words seem feeble.

"True," snaps King Creon. "But you cannot say the same of how Argos treated *my* son. Guards – seize this woman!"

Two Theban soldiers grab her, pulling her out of her chair, while others level their bronze blades to prevent Phyle's servants from coming to her aid. Behind her a young woman whimpers fearfully; Phyle resists the urge to glance back. Those with her knew the risks in coming; she can do nothing for them now.

"Uncle," Ismene objects, "please—"

"Enough, Ismene!"

Now it ends, thinks Phyle. She closes her eyes, realizing the best she can hope for is a quick death. The body of a priestess – especially a priestess from an enemy city – will certainly not be sacrosanct. Perhaps she will soon join her husband, decaying at the end of a rope, hung over the highest gate. The breath of one of the men holding her is so foul that she wonders if she is already smelling her own rotting corpse. *Give me strength,* Hera, she prays silently. *Let me not shame you in death.*

A male voice pierces Phyle's terror. "What's happening here?"

The moment lengthens, and the cruel blade Phyle is expecting does not arrive. Cautiously she opens her eyes to see a man in the long white robes of Apollo's priesthood pushing his way through the throng. He is slender and youthful, not yet past thirty; his curling brown hair and beard are clipped short.

Princess Ismene starts to rise from her chair – but the priest holds out his hand, and Ismene sinks back into her seat, as if she has questions which she wants to ask but which she knows must wait.

This is not about me, Phyle realizes, her glance darting between Ismene and the white-robed young man.

"In the name of Apollo I ask again, Father: what is happening here?" says the priest.

Ah! So this is Haemon! Eldest son of Creon and Eurydike, and long-estranged husband of Antigone – Phyle sifts through what she knows of this man in search of some insight that she can use.

The aged king answers his son reluctantly. "We are speaking to this woman – this woman from Argos."

"*Speaking* to her, with bared blades?" Haemon gestures to the folding tables, to the wine-cups and the remnants of bread and cheese. "After accepting her food and drink?"

"She sheltered Alkides," growls King Creon, his face darkening.

Queen Eurydike wipes away her tears with an angry gesture. "And Argos did not punish him."

"Excuse me, my lady queen," Phyle breaks in, "but we *did* punish him."

"How?" demands the mother of Alkides' murdered wife.

On firm ground at last, Phyle says: "If you let go of me, I will tell you." King Creon nods to the men, who release their grip on her and step away. Phyle, shaking, sits back down. Her heart is thumping hard; she wishes that she could take time to recover from her fear, but that is not possible. Is this what soldiers experience when, having slain one enemy, they are beset immediately by another?

Taking a sip of wine, Phyle appraises her audience: the stern priest, the aged king and queen, the princess who may not be as timid as she appears, the volatile crowd of Thebans, and the guards with their weapons. She sorts through her memories, aware that her words may save her life – and the lives of the Argives behind her.

ERIPHYLE

My brother and my husband soon heard about the disturbance at Hera's temple; they came to learn more about what had happened, arriving as the temple servants swept the last bits of shattered pottery from the forecourt. My niece Argia and I described the wild man's appearance and actions to them.

"I thought he was a monster," Argia said, still trembling. "Everyone did – until Polynikes recognized him."

I nodded. "Polynikes called him by name: Alkides."

"That's Thebes' mightiest warrior," observed my brother.

"Alkides son of Amphitryon," added my husband Amphiorax, who prided himself on his knowledge of the royal houses of Hellas. "An interesting symmetry: Amphitryon was banished from Tiryns as a criminal. Now his son Alkides seeks sanctuary."

My brother pushed his cloak back over his shoulders and reached up to adjust his golden circlet-crown. "I want to interview this man."

Polynikes, we were told, had taken Alkides to the soldiers' training-ground. This made sense – it had a bath house and a kitchen, so the man could be washed and fed without making him the guest of anyone in particular. Argia went home to tend her newborn, but the rest of us headed towards the training grounds. As we walked, I noticed my husband glancing up at the sky. "Can you read the omens?"

Amphiorax shook his head. "They are mixed. Clearly the man has done something terrible."

"So have others we've given sanctuary," my brother said.

"That's true," I agreed. Still, remembering how flies had settled on Alkides' wounded leg, I felt uneasy. The Kindly Ones send vengeful spirits in the form of flies to pursue those guilty of heinous crimes.

"We'll know more soon," panted my brother, as we walked uphill.

When we reached the crest, the training-grounds came into view. Usually pairs of men practiced with wooden swords or engaged in wrestling bouts; but today they clustered near the bath-house. Some wore armor and held their helmets by the chin straps; others still had the sand of the wrestling-pit on their shoulders. All had halted their exercise to look over the newest fellow seeking sanctuary in Argos.

Fright can magnify the object of fear, but Alkides was as astonishing as I remembered. Even though he was seated on a bench, his head was almost level with Polynikes' – and Polynikes was a tall man. Alkides had bathed, and his leg had been bandaged, but he wore only a loincloth – no doubt they had trouble finding a garment large enough for him. He was eating a leg of roast lamb.

"Impressive," commented my brother, starting down the slope. "Looks as powerful as a Titan."

I wasn't sure this was a good thing. "Argos is overflowing with strong men. Do we really need another?"

Adrastos shrugged. "What do you think, Amphiorax?"

My husband stopped in the center of the path, squinting up at the sky once more; there were few clouds to be seen. A few white wisps trailed off to the east, in the direction of the harbor; another trace of cloud hovered over the western hills. There was no wind, and no birds flew overhead, though one chirped in the distance.

"The gods are not in agreement," he finally said.

My brother asked: "What does *that* mean?"

"Some gods favor this man, my lord king; but others are against him," Amphiorax clarified. "You should not harm Alkides – that would incur the wrath of his divine supporters. But it would be almost as dangerous to give him sanctuary."

My brother grunted with frustration. "Perhaps we can still find a use for him," he muttered to himself. "A strong man needs a challenge."

As we approached, I noticed that – once his filthy hair and beard had been washed and trimmed – Alkides was good-looking in his way. But his eyes remained swollen and bloodshot, with dark shadows beneath them. Noticing my brother's crown, he set aside the bone he was gnawing, wiped his mouth with the back of his hand, and got to his feet. Dark-haired Tydeus, usually the most powerful man in any crowd, studied him warily.

But Polynikes was at ease in the giant's shadow. "My lord king Adrastos, I present to you Alkides son of Amphitryon. He comes to Argos seeking sanctuary." His coppery brows drew together as he added: "He has not yet said why."

My brother drew back his shoulders as if trying to appear taller. "What is your crime, Alkides?"

The big man muttered something unintelligible.

"Speak up!" Adrastos commanded.

"There... I..." Alkides glanced at my brother, then at Polynikes. "It was an accident. But people will say I killed them."

"Killed who?" asked my brother.

"Who will say?" Polynikes broke in. "Eteokles? Or did you kill *him*?"

Alkides shook his head. "Your brother's alive."

"Then who is dead?" Adrastos repeated.

The fugitive covered his face with his hands; his massive shoulders trembled. To my astonishment I realized he was weeping. "It was an accident," he moaned.

His voice harsh, my brother said: "You ask my help, but won't say who you killed?"

"Forgive me, my lord king," the man mumbled, his broad shoulders slumping. "I can't."

For a moment Adrastos scowled at this refusal; then his face cleared. I sensed he was actually suppressing a smile. "No matter – the truth of your deed will reach Argos soon enough. But, Alkides, those who seek sanctuary in Argos both confess their crimes and bring an offering to our patron goddess Hera. You have not confessed, and you arrived empty-handed."

"And feeding him would cost Argos a fortune," Kapaneus said, in a loud whisper clearly meant to carry; Hippomedon and Tydeus snickered.

Wiping his face, Alkides said, "I'm sorry, my lord king. I'll serve you in whatever way you wish. I'm good with cattle—"

"Thebes is famous for its cattle," interrupted my brother, "but your strength would be wasted on our sheep and goats. Nevertheless, Alkides son of Amphitryon, I have a task for you."

He paused, catching the attention of all who were present – I could see the curiosity on the men's faces, wondering what challenge the king would give to this giant.

After a moment's silence, Adrastos continued: "There is a horse – a magnificent wild stallion called Arion, swifter and stronger than any other in Hellas. Bring him to me, and I'll consider your request for sanctuary."

So *that* was the reason for my brother's change of mood. It was clever: this task would either keep Alkides busy and away from Argos, without offending any gods – or else bring my brother what he most desired.

Many of the assembled men had tried to capture the fabulous horse for the king, all without success; they also reacted to my brother's challenge. Some muttered; others chuckled. A few shook their heads, casting pitying looks at Alkides, while others surveyed the giant as if they wondered if he might be the one who finally succeeded. I noticed Hippomedon rubbing the arm he'd injured in his attempt the year before.

When the murmuring died down, Alkides clasped his hands behind his back. "My lord king, do you want this horse Arion dead or alive?"

The men burst out laughing; over the tumult Adrastos roared, "Alive, of course! I want to ride him!"

As the men's laughter continued, the towering fellow said: "*Alive…* that will make it more difficult."

The next afternoon was the naming ceremony for Argia's newborn son. Wisely, my brother wanted Alkides out of the city to avoid any possible disruption of the rites; so the man was sent away that morning with a description of the stallion and its last known whereabouts. Polynikes saw him off, then joined us in the palace courtyard where family and friends had gathered for a light meal in advance of the ceremony – with the exception of Iphis, my brother's father-in-law, who was great-grandfather to the newborn. Iphis' wife was ailing so they would only join us for the ceremony.

"So, did you find a tunic for Alkides?" Tydeus asked, as Polynikes crossed the space towards us.

"A bed-sheet might be big enough," said Parthenopeus.

Hippomedon shook his head. "Have to sew together two of them." He winked at his young wife, whose belly was round with child; she giggled.

"Actually, we used one that belonged to that fat old potter." Polynikes sat beside Argia, who held their newborn son. "It's too short on Alkides, though. I told him he'd better wrap his loincloth mighty tight."

Everyone laughed at this – even my two young sons, happy to be included in a board game with other, older boys – the sons of my brother Adrastos and my nephew Kapaneus. My three-year-old sat with one of her cousins on a bench beneath a laurel tree, playing with cloth dolls. My youngest was with her wet-nurse, in a shady corner along with the women watching my nieces' two-year-old boys.

As the laughter died down, Adrastos posed a question to the group: "Do you think he'll succeed?"

"Not a chance," said Tydeus, who had failed to capture the stallion earlier in the spring. He offered a bowl of olives and radishes to his wife;

Deipyle took an olive and popped it into her mouth.

Kapaneus, who had also chased the animal in vain, folded his arms across his thick chest. "Alkides may be strong, but that horse is fast. He'll never catch it." Standing beside him, his wife nodded supportively.

"He said he knows cattle," Hippomedon offered. "But there's a big difference between a bull and a stallion. You can't treat them the same way. Even if he catches Arion, how can he bring it back alive?"

Adrastos looked to my husband for his opinion – but Amphiorax turned to Polynikes. "You know him best, Polynikes. What do *you* think?"

"I'm no seer, Amphiorax," replied Polynikes, his tone clipped – as if emphasizing that my husband should not be asking others about the future.

My husband frowned, but said nothing; in the meantime, my brother spoke up. "We'll know soon enough," Adrastos said smoothly, as if he were indifferent. But I knew he had told his groomsmen to make room in the stables for another horse.

Parthenopeus washed down a morsel of bread with a swig of watered wine. "We still don't know why he left Thebes."

"Yes, we do," said Kapaneus' wife. "He killed someone."

"But we don't know *who*," Kapaneus countered.

"Someone important," said Argia, smiling at her baby, "or he wouldn't be banished."

"You're right, dear," Polynikes agreed. "Alkides was very popular. The soldiers loved him."

Deipyle reached for a radish. "Well, he said it wasn't King Eteokles. So who could it have been? Who would be that important?"

"My uncle Creon, maybe," Polynikes speculated. "*That* would mean exile – he's been a pillar in Thebes forever. Or perhaps it was the Tiresias."

"The blind prophet?" asked Amphiorax.

Polynikes nodded. "Alkides did say it was an accident – and the Tiresias is a frail old man. Alkides might have knocked him down unintentionally."

Tydeus grunted. "Wouldn't be much of a seer if he let himself be killed."

"Seeing the future does not mean being able to prevent it," my husband pointed out.

There was a pause in conversation; knucklebones clattered against a wooden tabletop, and my nephew counted spaces as he moved his pebble around the board.

We had overlooked something, I realized. "He said *them*."

"What's that, Phyle?" asked my brother.

"Them," I repeated. "His words were: 'people will say I killed *them.*' More than one death."

"The Tiresias always had one or both of his daughters with him," Polynikes mused.

"We don't know that the Tiresias was involved at all," said Amphiorax.

Adrastos turned irritably to my husband. "Enough about what you *don't* know. What *do* you know, seer?"

Frowning, Amphiorax got to his feet. "The gods do not choose to reveal everything to me, my lord king." He glanced down at me, then made a curt bow to my brother. "If you will excuse me, my lord king, I will go to the temple and ensure all is in order for your grandson's naming ceremony."

My brother waved his hand in dismissal; an awkward silence lingered over the group after his departure. Finally Polynikes changed the topic of conversation. Leaning forward, he said: "My lord king, we have a great opportunity – things have changed in Thebes. Eteokles no longer has Alkides – Thebes' most powerful warrior – at his side. With Alkides' strength added to ours, Argos can easily conquer Thebes! Your daughter and I can take our rightful places as Thebes' king and queen!"

Argia glanced up at her husband, her eyes shining. "Yes."

My brother leaned back, considering this. "Well..."

"Don't count on Alkides," Tydeus said, shaking his head. "If he doesn't catch that horse, he won't come back."

"He'll never catch that horse," Kapaneus declared.

"Even if he doesn't," said Argia, cradling her newborn, "you don't need Alkides to win."

"That's right!" agreed Parthenopeus. "The Argive army is the strongest in all Hellas!"

"True," my brother said, "but Thebes has strong walls."

"It does," acknowledged Polynikes. "But there are seven gates. Only *one* has to open for us."

"Open, or be broken down," said Kapaneus.

The boys, hearing this talk of war, abandoned the knucklebones and pebbles of their game to join us. "Why are there so many gates?" asked Alkmaeon.

Polynikes smiled at my five-year-old son. "The king who built the walls named the gates for his daughters. And he had seven daughters."

"Taking a walled city – that's difficult," said Hippomedon. "I don't care how many gates there are."

"Someone in Thebes will help Polynikes," said my nephew Aegialeus. "Won't they, Father?"

Adrastos glanced at Polynikes. "Will they?"

The Theban hesitated only a moment; then he nodded. "By now, my brother must have enemies. I can't be the only one he's double-crossed. And Alkides has a lot of friends."

"Ah, to see you and Argia on the thrones of Thebes!" exclaimed my brother. "And my grandson Thersander and his new little brother as your heirs!"

"Thebes *is* wealthy," said Parthenopeus.

The men grinned at this; Kapaneus' eyes lit up. "Think of the spoils!"

"Spoils?" Polynikes exclaimed. "Thebes is my city – we won't plunder it!"

Adrastos interrupted the sounds of disappointment that ensued. "Come, now, Polynikes, you can't expect these men to risk their lives for nothing!"

Polynikes opened his mouth as if to object; then he glanced at his wife and baby son, and clamped his lips together.

"It's not as if the people of Thebes treated you well," Tydeus pointed out. "They deserve punishment."

Polynikes drummed his fingers on the table. "Perhaps…"

"Pick the richest men who betrayed you and execute them," Hippomedon suggested. "Then give their property to us. We'll be compensated for our efforts, and you'll be rid of your enemies."

Polynikes' ruddy eyebrows drew together. "They have treated me poorly."

"I'm glad you realize that," said my brother. "Now, Polynikes, what about your brother?"

At this question the courtyard fell silent once more, but for the sound of swallows chirping in the eaves. One of the toddlers shrieked; little Diomedes had tripped and bloodied his knee. Deipyle picked him up and held him in her lap, and he shushed.

Perhaps this distraction gave Polynikes time to collect his thoughts. He flushed, as redheads often do, but his voice was calm. "I'll treat Eteokles as he did me. He can choose between exile and death." Clasping his hands, he leaned forward and added: "I intend to make sure he chooses death – but if he chooses exile, I'll have him hunted down and killed. He can't be trusted."

My brother nodded. "I'm glad you're not squeamish. Only Eteokles' death will ensure the safety of my daughter and grandsons. Still, going to war is serious – before we go I need to make sure the gods are on our side."

"And if Alkides returns with the horse and agrees to fight with us?" asked Polynikes, watching my brother keenly.

"Even *Amphiorax* would have to admit that those would be two very good omens," said my brother. "Don't you think so, Phyle?"

As my husband had already gone to his temple, everyone turned to me. "I cannot speak for my husband," I said cautiously. "But this Alkides has not yet come back with the horse, nor has he atoned for his crimes – or agreed to fight for you, Polynikes."

"True," said my brother, nodding. "It's premature."

Still, talk of war continued until it was time for the naming ceremony; it resumed during the banquet to honor the king's newest grandson, called Adrastos like his grandfather. I wondered if Polynikes had planned to do this all along, or if he chose the name to encourage my brother's support for the war. The idea of attacking Thebes seemed to catch the imagination of every young man in Argos while Argia, who wanted a throne for herself as well as her husband and son, fanned the flames among the Argive noblewomen.

After my husband and I returned home that night, I asked his opinion of the matter. "Without Arion, your brother will never agree," he said. "And he'll have to learn to ride it, too."

"*Ride* it!" I exclaimed. "Is such a thing possible?"

My husband only grunted.

"I understand," I continued, "given that he can't walk far, he needs another way to move around. He could hardly lead men into battle on a sedan chair. Do you think Alkides will capture that horse?"

Again, my husband did not answer, and I dropped the subject and went to check on my children.

My brother quelled the war talk, telling Polynikes and Tydeus – the most eager – that we were not quite ready to attack another city, but he encouraged them to train hard. And so the talk died down – a little – but I know my brother often consulted with Hippomedon about where Alkides might be, and how to train a horse should he capture Arion.

About a month later, my husband and I were visiting my brother in the palace, discussing the offerings at the temples of Zeus and Hera and how much could be spared from each for the business of Argos, when we heard a loud commotion outside: people shouting, women shrieking, the thunder-like sound of many running feet.

"What is *that*?" asked my brother.

"Is Argos under attack?" I asked, for I had not forgotten the talk of war.

My husband simply went to the window, peered out of it and frowned. "My lord king, you will want to see this," he said.

My brother and I joined Amphiorax at the window – there was no invading army. Instead, a crowd of Argives surrounded a tall blond man who was leading the largest and most magnificent horse I had ever seen.

"He did it," I whispered.

That was what the people down in the agora were shouting: "He did it!" and "He's back!" and "Alkides!" and "Arion!"

"By Zeus," whispered my husband, leaning against the wall, as if he needed support.

My brother whooped with exultation, clapping his hands together. "By *all* the gods! Come, both of you – we'll discuss temple offerings later." He rushed out, moving as fast as his bad leg would take him; Amphiorax and I hurried after.

The palace doors were wide open; seeing my brother approach, the gaggle of staring servants parted, bowing, to make way for us. Adrastos had enough sense of the moment to pause just inside the threshold and collect himself, so that he strode out into the sunlight in a kingly manner rather than dashing out like a boy hearing that a relative has arrived with a gift.

"Alkides," he declared in a loud voice. "You've been successful!"

As the crowd's cheers subsided in respect for the king, my husband and

I followed Adrastos out onto the marble-tiled terrace. Alkides had brought the captive beast to the foot of the palace steps – and truthfully I had never seen its like. Its legs, flank, neck, and face were white as snow; the mane and tail were a deep gray, the color of a storm cloud about to burst. Its large, dark eyes flashed with intelligence – and though the beast shifted restlessly, clearly unnerved by the presence of so many excited people, Alkides' hand on its shoulder kept it calm enough not to strain against the rope circling its graceful neck.

Alkides grinned up at my brother, shouldering his stout club. "Yes, my lord king! I first arrived in Argos empty-handed, but now I bring a worthy offering."

Wonder on his face, Adrastos slowly descended the steps. As Amphiorax and I followed, I noticed Hippomedon and Parthenopeus pushing their way through the crowd's furthest edge, while Kapaneus and Tydeus approached from the side. Polynikes already stood near the fabulous horse.

"How did you manage this, Alkides?" my brother asked.

"He's strong as a Titan!" someone shouted.

Another added, "And swift as the north wind!"

Alkides laughed. "I'm both fast and strong, King Adrastos. But that's not how I captured him."

My brother stopped on the third step; there he could still gaze down at Alkides and the horse rather than looking up. "How, then?"

The big man gently patted the horse's shoulder. "Just as I learned from the Master of the Herds back in Thebes. A prize stallion's proud as a champion bull, but more delicate. A kingly beast like this can't be wrestled down. You have to gain his trust – to look him in the eyes and tell him your intention."

Adrastos stepped down to stand beside Alkides and the stallion.

Alkides stroked the beast's neck slowly. "Arion," he said, his voice gentle but firm, "this is your new master. He'll treat you well."

Tilting its head, the horse stared at my brother with one great dark eye, as if sizing him up. I was only a few steps away; I could hear the animal's breath, smell its earthy scent.

My brother lifted a hand. "Argos will be your home now, Arion," he said. "You'll have the sweetest hay and clover, and the best of the season's apples. Your stable will be the largest and most comfortable, and you'll have your choice of mares. And you will earn glory greater than any horse who has ever lived."

Arion blinked his long-lashed eyes.

My brother moved closer, and at Alkides' encouraging nod he reached out to touch the horse's shoulder. Arion whinnied and jerked his large head up and down, but did not pull away.

"He gives his consent!" someone said. "Look, the horse chooses King Adrastos' service!" The crowd shouted and cheered once more, and the horse looked nervously from side to side.

"We should take him to the stables, my lord king," Alkides said.

My brother nodded briskly. "Of course." He turned to the crowd and declared loudly: "Argives, make way – I will take Arion to his new home."

Gripping the horse's lead-rope in his massive fist, Alkides followed my brother around the side of the palace. My husband and I, and my brother's advisors, followed a few steps behind, careful not to crowd the horse.

"Amazing," Parthenopeus said. "I can hardly believe it!"

"If Alkides can do this, think what else he can do," Kapaneus was telling Hippomedon. "Think what a fighting force he'll be for us!"

Hippomedon shook his head in amazement. "Him, and that horse!"

"It's only one horse," my husband muttered. "And only one man."

We were approaching the stables. The stable-hands looked almost as excited as my brother – as though it was all they could do to restrain themselves from jumping up and down. The master of horse, a bowlegged little fellow, hurried forward and took the rope from Alkides.

"So this is the magnificent Arion!" he exclaimed. "My lord king, I can see why you don't want him for your chariot – we'd never find one worthy of teaming with him."

"Too true!" Adrastos was still smiling like a boy with his first bronze sword. "Can we train him to accept me on his back?"

The master of horse nodded, looking up at Arion with an expression little short of love. "It'll take some time, my lord king – a few months, maybe, especially since he's full grown and used to the wild. First we'll get him used to a harness; and then accustom him to carrying a bit of weight. Like training a donkey – but a spirited beast like this, he'll take a bit longer…"

Adrastos clapped the man on the back. "Only fitting—but we'll manage it." He turned back to the Theban. "Alkides, I'm in your debt."

Clearing his throat loudly, Amphiorax moved closer. "I beg your pardon, my lord king, but this man has only done the service you required of him in order to seek sanctuary. We still do not know the nature of his crime."

"Eh?" My brother looked back over his shoulder, his smile slipping slightly. "Ah, yes, Amphiorax, that's true. Well, anyway, Alkides – now you may petition Hera."

I picked up the hem of my skirts and stepped carefully around a pile of horse-dung. "We'll have to make preparations at the temple," I told my brother. "And the petitioner – ah, the petitioner needs a bath."

Alkides looked at me, then down at his grimy, too-short tunic – and burst out laughing. "You're right, Priestess! I surely do!"

My brother ordered the servants to make ready the best guest room in the palace, and have a hot bath prepared for Alkides. But even once the huge fellow had left, my brother and the rest of the men clustered around the horse like a group of maidens sighing over a handsome bard. They talked of training techniques, and what the beast's diet should be, and how he should be groomed... I was pregnant and quickly tired of it all, so I excused myself. Looking pensive, Amphiorax said that he also had obligations to attend, and came with me.

"Something troubles you about that horse," I observed as we walked back into the agora.

Amphiorax shook his head. "Not the horse. The man. Alkides. I—"

"My lord priest! My lady priestess!" Our conversation was interrupted by the approach of a portly man in a red tunic. As he came closer I recognized the close-cropped hair and beard of Hyperbius, the Theban trader.

"Greetings, Hyperbius," I said. "My brother will be glad to meet with you later, I'm sure, but just now he's occupied with other matters."

"Yes, my lady," he said. "Everyone in the city's talking about the horse. I know my shipment of leather – good quality though it is – can't compete with the likes of Arion. But – if I may, my lady, my lord – I'd have a word with the two of you before speaking with the king."

Amphiorax and I exchanged a glance. "Yes?"

Hyperbius looked around as if concerned we would be overheard – which seemed unnecessary, actually. We were in the midst of the crowded agora, with people milling all about. Judging by the snatches of conversation I overheard, everyone was still talking about the horse Arion; people would be likely to assume that was our topic of conversation as well.

In a low voice, Hyperbius asked: "Is Alkides really the one who brought the horse here? Alkides of Thebes?"

"Yes," my husband confirmed.

Hyperbius bit his lip, looking increasingly anxious. "You're sure it's him? Not just someone using the same name?"

"Polynikes recognized him," I said. "And given his size, he'd be hard to impersonate."

"Alkides," Hyperbius whispered. "By the gods."

"He has not yet petitioned the goddess for sanctuary," my husband continued, "but we understand he's guilty of murder."

The merchant looked at me, his eyes filled with horror and mourning. "Murder hardly describes it, my lady priestess."

Amphiorax folded his arms across his chest. "Describe it, then."

"He – he killed his whole family, my lord priest." The knot in his throat bobbed up and down as he swallowed. "His beautiful wife, Megara, and all three of their little boys. Strangled Megara; smashed the children's brains out and threw their bodies into the hearth-fire."

I stared at him, open-mouthed in disbelief. Around us the excited crowd was still talking about Alkides and the fabulous horse he had brought for the king; people were happy, laughing, yet I seemed to see dead children and hear a woman begging for her life. "Dear Hera!" I whispered.

Amphiorax said, "The king must hear of this. And he must hear it from

271

you, Hyperbius."

When we told Adrastos that Hyperbius had arrived in Argos, and could shed light on Alkides' crimes, my brother insisted that Alkides be present in the megaron as well. My brother was still giddy with delight over his new horse – and ready to believe that anyone who spoke ill of Alkides was lying. I was apprehensive – what if Alkides grew violent? – and asked for three extra pairs of my brother's guards, armed with spears, to be there. Adrastos patted my cheek and said I was growing like my husband and worrying too much, but agreed.

The late-afternoon sun cast slanting blocks of light through the megaron; dust motes floated through the air. The large room buzzed with curiosity; people glanced at Hyperbius, who stood near my brother's throne, who shook his head silently when anyone tried to ask him questions. Many were still talking about Arion; Tydeus was telling Deipyle and Argia, who had not yet seen the horse, of the animal's strength and beauty.

All fell silent when Alkides' bulk shadowed the door.

His hair and beard were still damp from the bath; the tunic he wore was too short for his height and displayed the full length of his thighs, bulging with muscle. I was glad to see he did not carry his club. As Alkides passed through the doorway he was speaking with Polynikes, who accompanied him – but then both men, seeing Hyperbius, fell silent.

"Alkides," my brother called from his throne, "this man, Hyperbius, brings news of your deeds in Thebes."

The enormous fellow blanched beneath his tan. "No," he said, his eyes going wide.

Polynikes stared up at his fellow Theban – and then began to move away, as you might edge away from a wild bear surprised in the forest.

I glanced at the guards and was glad to see them wary, grasping their spears in both hands.

"You *will* hear him out, Alkides," my brother commanded. "Hyperbius, say your piece."

"No!" bellowed Alkides, loud as a trapped bull. He raised his great fists, and the guards leveled their spear-points at his abdomen. "No!"

The stout trader looked Alkides in the face and declared: "This man murdered his wife and his three young sons!"

"No," moaned Alkides, sinking to his knees. The megaron fell silent as a tomb.

Finally Polynikes, remaining out of the giant's reach, said: "You killed *Megara*?"

Alkides made no answer; he lowered his head to the floor, sobbing. But Hyperbius spoke again. "He did, my lord Polynikes. Megara and their three sons. All of them."

Polynikes stared at the Theban. "But he loved her!"

"I did," moaned Alkides. "I loved her so much…"

Amphiorax glanced up at my brother. "He does not deny the murders, my lord king."

His face wet with tears, Alkides looked up. "It was an accident. An accident!"

"An accident!" Hyperbius cried, indignant. "An *accident*, that you threw the bodies of your three little boys into the fire, trying to destroy the evidence of what you'd done?"

Many in the megaron gasped with horror. Deipyle leaned against her husband Tydeus; standing beside them, Argia moaned and covered her mouth with her hand.

"This is the gravest of crimes," Amphiorax declared.

Kneeling on the floor, Alkides reached both hands toward the throne. "Please – please, my lord king, forgive me. I was mad with anger, and I made a terrible mistake. I put myself in your hands."

My brother's expression remained stern; his gaze flicked from one face to another: Polynikes, my husband, Hyperbius, me. Finally he said: "This is a troubling matter. We must seek the guidance of the gods." He gestured to the captain of the guard. "Remove all weapons from his guest-room, and then confine Alkides there. Maintain four spearmen inside the room and six outside at all times."

The soldiers managed to get Alkides to his feet; half stumbling, half carried by two brawny men, he departed.

My brother thanked Hyperbius for his testimony, and sent him to a different guest room with a pair of guards for protection. Then my brother told his family and closest advisors to accompany him to his study. As we crowded in, he seated himself behind his work table, pressed his fingertips together and looked up at us. "Do you think it's true?"

Tydeus cracked his knuckles and said, "He didn't deny it."

"He acted like a guilty man," Kapaneus agreed, taking a seat on the couch.

My brother nodded. "He did say it was an accident, though."

"An accident!" I exclaimed. "An *accident* that he killed four people – his whole family?"

"Megara was my cousin – I knew her my entire life. She supported my brother – she helped him betray me – but she was beautiful," Polynikes said hollowly. His wife Argia looked at him in dismay, but he didn't seem to notice. "And the children... so young! The eldest was born only the year before I left Thebes."

"Hera will not forgive this," I said firmly.

Deipyle set her hands on her hips. "No – how could she?"

"But he brought me that horse," Adrastos objected.

Hippomedon pointed out: "You could refuse the gift, my lord king."

My brother hesitated, glancing at my husband who was standing by the window, scanning the sky. My brother then said: "I would rather not do that, if it's at all possible."

Tydeus shrugged. "So keep the horse, and kill the man."

Adrastos said, looking at my husband, "How can I do that? It would break the laws of hospitality and offend Zeus. Isn't that true, Amphiorax?"

My husband turned away from the window. "Yes, my lord king. Despite his crimes, I believe Alkides is still favored by some of the gods – at least by Zeus."

"Surely Zeus does not approve of a man killing his wife and children!" I exclaimed.

"No, Eriphyle, he does not," said my husband. "Zeus is willing for us – for Hera – to punish Alkides, but we may not execute him."

"If Hera wants him dead," Kapaneus suggested, "he might die in battle when we attack Thebes."

"Adrastos," I said, "he can't be part of our army – Lady Hera would be furious!"

My husband concurred. "Besides, if he would kill his wife and children, then how could you rely on him for anything?"

"Furthermore, he can't stay in Argos," I said. "You can't even give him sanctuary. It would offend the goddess." I said this with great certainty because I knew Alkides' presence would offend me.

My brother drummed his fingers on the table. "Very well, what about Tiryns? Alkides' father came from Tiryns."

"And they pay us tribute," said Amphiorax.

"He still needs to be punished," I said. "Severely."

My brother nodded, then said, "I have an idea," which he presented to us. We discussed it at length, and my husband and I both made suggestions, to which Adrastos agreed. Then my brother stood, stretching his arms behind his back. "Parthenopeus, you're a swift runner. At first light tomorrow you'll take my message to King Eurystheus of Tiryns."

Tiryns is only about a summer hour's walk from Argos; Parthenopeus must have reached it before King Eurystheus finished his breakfast. He returned about noon, saying that the vassal king had agreed to our plan, and by early afternoon our patrols reported a group of chariots approaching from the northeast. My brother ordered Alkides brought to the temple of Hera.

Adrastos' heralds went through the streets, shouting that Alkides' petition would soon be heard. Excited at the prospect of this new spectacle, people streamed towards the temple from every direction – by the time Eurystheus and his men arrived, a large crowd filled the temple forecourt.

Four Argive soldiers surrounded Alkides. He stood slump-shouldered, barely looking up to see King Eurystheus – his cousin – stride through the crowd toward the temple stairs where I stood with my brother.

Eurystheus was not physically impressive: he was not tall, and despite his youth tended to flab. But for the similar shape of his nose, no one would believe that he and Alkides were first cousins. However, Eurystheus made up for his lack of good looks with ostentatious clothing. On that day, aware that all Argos would be watching, he wore a cloak dyed a rich brown, worked around the edges with thread-of-gold in a crenellated pattern that brought to mind his city's stout walls. His circlet crown was brightly polished, and jewels flashed on his fingers as he lifted a hand to welcome my brother. "Greetings, King Adrastos!"

My brother inclined his head. "I greet you, King Eurystheus."

"And I greet you as well," I said, "in the holy name of my mistress Hera, queen of Heaven and Earth."

Eurystheus glanced back at the hulking figure of Alkides. "I understand there is a service I and my city may perform for Argos – and for lady Hera, queen of Heaven and Earth."

Movement rustled through the crowd, like leaves in a breeze. No doubt people wondered whether we would have Eurystheus execute his cousin. I saw the Theban trader Hyperbius, near the front of the throng, watching attentively.

I drew myself to my full height and fixed my gaze on Alkides. "You have come to ask sanctuary," I said. "To seek atonement."

He looked up at me. "Yes, my lady. I acknowledge my guilt." He was clearer-eyed than I had ever seen him – I sensed that he truly did repent of his deeds. "I will do whatever the goddess demands of me."

"Atonement will not come easily," I said. "You must—"

"What?" interrupted a shout from the crowd. People gasped at this show of disrespect, but Hyperbius pushed his way forward, his expression incredulous. "You're not going to execute this – this abomination?"

Surrounded by armed soldiers, Alkides looked back at his accuser; the huge man's posture suggested that he might have accepted a death sentence as due justice.

"Hyperbius," my brother cautioned sternly, "you did a valuable service bringing this man's crimes to light. But I will not tolerate disrespect for Hera or her priestess."

"Disrespect!" The man's plump face flushed red beneath his close-cropped beard. "If you truly respected the goddess of marriage, you'd slit this monster's throat! I knew Megara – a lovely woman – and I knew their children. He *killed* them!"

I bit my lip, conflicted; though Hyperbius had interrupted me and challenged my brother's authority, his motives were righteous. Was Hera speaking through him?

But my brother's patience was at its limit. "You are a guest in our city—"

"No longer!" shouted the Theban. "I'd spit on the ground between us, Adrastos, but I've got more reverence for the goddess than to defile her temple as you're doing. And for a *horse!* I'd not have thought your honor could be bought so cheap!" He turned his back on my brother and stomped away; the shocked citizens made way for him.

My brother's face colored; I think the trader's barb touched him. "Let him go," Adrastos told the guards.

But Hyperbius was not finished. Before he reached the far edge of the crowd, he turned to point an accusing finger at Polynikes. "And you!" he shouted. "I wasn't sure I believed what your brother said about you before. But if you'd help shelter that creature...." He ended with a snort of disgust, and walked away.

The crowd erupted into scandalized discussion; my brother had his heralds call for order, and eventually silence reigned. "Argives," Adrastos told them, "you came here to witness the judgment of Hera. Let us now complete that sacred task." He gestured to me.

Regaining my composure, I faced the criminal Alkides once more. "You say you will do whatever penance the goddess demands."

The huge man nodded. "Yes, my lady."

"To atone for your crimes, you must complete ten difficult tasks. And because your crimes are hateful to the goddess, you must not show your face in her favorite city until your penance is complete. Instead, King Eurystheus of Tiryns will supervise your labors."

"Yes, my lady," Alkides agreed.

Eurystheus stepped forward and faced his cousin. "A lion has been menacing the flocks in the hills near the city of Nemea," he said. "Your first task is to kill this animal."

Alkides nodded. "And after that?"

There were whispers and a few titters in the crowd at Alkides' calm acceptance of this task; Eurystheus snapped, "I'll tell you your next task if you survive the first, criminal."

Alkides' huge fists clenched; obviously he did not relish such scorn from his small, soft cousin, but he kept silent.

"The goddess has one more demand," I said.

There was still irritation in Alkides' face when he met my eyes – and I was glad of it. If physical labors did not trouble him, debasement at the hands of his cousin Eurystheus seemed to. Which meant that the next part of his penance might make him suffer – and if any man deserved to suffer, it was this one.

"All glory must reflect on the goddess – not on the wrongdoer who seeks her mercy. From now on you will have a new name: one that honors the goddess, and not you. If you triumph in these labors, she will be praised, and not the wife and child-killer called Alkides."

He opened his mouth as if to protest, then shut it again, and nodded. "What is my new name, Lady?"

"From this day forward," I said, "you are Herakles."

*

Phyle's mouth is dry. She holds her goblet out for her manservant to refill, and indicates that he should offer more minted barley water to her listeners.

As she drinks, her manservant catches her eye; she nods slightly. She has not yet achieved what she came here to do. She must try again, as soon as her opponent provides an opportunity.

"Did the lion kill him?" King Creon asks.

"No," Phyle concedes. "But his labors are far from over." And at least her hearers know, now, that she and Argos did what they could – in this matter, anyway. "The king of Tiryns has sent Herakles on another dangerous mission."

The priest Haemon speaks up. "Remember, Father: the Tiresias foretold that Alkides would be the greatest of heroes."

The crowd murmurs in the fading light; some clutch amulets to ward off evil spirits, while others speculate about the man once known as Alkides. For so many years he had been one of them, working alongside them, eating with them, drinking with them, bedding the women and out-swaggering the men. The Thebans cannot help themselves; they are curious about him.

But King Creon's thick white eyebrows draw together; his eyes are like two hard chips of obsidian. "Enough stories! I'm an old man, Eriphyle; I have no time to waste. The sun is setting – it's time for me to return to the palace." Leaning on his staff, he rises to his feet and gestures to the crowd as he turns to leave. "It's time for the rest of you to go home, too."

Phyle glances at her manservant, at her anxious serving women, at the few soldiers she persuaded to accompany her from Athens. The thing has not gone as she had hoped; her first petition already failed. Yet, like the commander of an inferior force who finds himself and his men surrounded, Phyle has no choice but to press on. Cowardice will avail her nothing.

"I may be from Argos, King Creon, but I am still a priestess," she says. "I have come to perform the rites demanded by the gods. Allow us to bury the corpses of our husbands, fathers, sons, and brothers."

The Thebans gasp as if one creature instead a disparate group of men, women and children; collectively they turn their heads towards their aged ruler.

King Creon's face darkens but he stops moving towards his sedan chair. "No! I have already told you, no!"

Although her hands shake with fear, Phyle continues, raising her voice to be heard. "The body of my husband Amphiorax – the father of my children – hangs from one of your gates. You defile a high priest of Zeus, Lord of Heaven and Earth!"

A ripple of discomfiture spreads in the crowd around her. It is one thing to abuse the body of a soldier; quite another to defile the body of Zeus' earthly representative.

Creon shrugs. "The Astykratia is our highest gate. So your husband is as close to Zeus as is possible in Thebes."

Phyle feels her hackles rise. "How can you speak so? The gods will punish such disrespect—"

"The gods have made clear what they think of Argos!"

"Yes, but the gods may still choose to punish Thebes!" Phyle feels the heat of her anger flaring; she wrings her hands together, struggling to speak calmly. "My lord king, it is the custom to allow the defeated to bury their dead."

"I forbade my own niece to sprinkle earth on their corpses! Why should I allow Argive women to do more?"

"Antigone was right, King Creon!" Phyle says, rising to her feet. "You must let the spirits of the dead enter the Underworld. If the gods decide those spirits still deserve punishment, they will be punished. It is not up to you!"

Behind her, a woman whimpers. Phyle realizes her words may get them all killed. She had not meant to speak so boldly, but she feels the rightness of what she has said: perhaps the spirit of Hera possessed her. Creon himself appears amazed at such defiance in one so vulnerable, while Eurydike, Haemon, and Ismene glance at one another as if exchanging some silent word of agreement.

A woman in the crowd calls out: "Creon, free your niece!" A few others echo this sentiment, and then more voices join the calls of "Yes!" and "She's right!"

Stunned, Phyle realizes that some of the Thebans – who, not long ago, would have torn her limb from limb – agree with her! The flowers she saw before the mud-brick wall: they are not just for Eteokles – some, at least, have been left for *Antigone*!

But not everyone agrees. One soldier's face turns red as the setting sun; he waves his spear at the crowd. "Who dares shout for that *porni*!"

Haemon – son to Creon, chief priest of Apollo, and husband to the condemned woman – adds to the clamor by yelling at the soldier. "This is a priestess of Hera!" Then he turns to the king. "Father, I think—"

"Silence!" thunders the king. He turns back to her; sweeping his staff in a low arc he knocks over the table, scattering goblets and bread-crusts on the ground. "I will hear no more of this. Be glad that I am tired of death, woman. Get yourself and your borrowed Athenians gone from my city." He walks over to his sedan chair, sits down and signals to his bearers; they raise him on their shoulders.

The king addresses the crowd. "The rest of you will go to your homes. Tomorrow you will not come here. We have work to do." He orders his soldiers to disperse the people, and his bearers to take him back to the palace. Phyle watches in frustration as he departs, his crown glowing like a ring of fire in the setting sun's rays.

Behind her, the dark-haired Argive servant orders the others to pack; they hastily take down the canopy, pick up the folding chairs and the upended table and put the leftover food in a basket, while the Athenian soldiers stand guard. The dark-haired man comes to her. "We must leave, now," he says, then adds, "my lady priestess."

"But, the bodies…" Phyle says.

"Go, now, or I'll kill you here!" snarls one of the Theban soldiers, an angry-looking youth whose brows meet over his nose.

Feeling the despair that comes with defeat – is this how her husband felt before the end? – Phyle leads her group away from Thebes.

GROSSACK & UNDERWOOD

CHAPTER FOURTEEN
ISMENE

Ismene watches her uncle depart, his sedan chair borne high on the shoulders of four strong men, his wife a little behind, but on foot.

After a moment she rises from her seat. She considers going to speak with the priestess Eriphyle; but Theban soldiers surround the foreigners as they prepare to leave. Other soldiers are urging the crowd away, telling people to go home, obeying King Creon's orders.

Two steps bring Ismene to the side of her cousin Haemon. "How is she?" Ismene asks. She does not have to say her sister's name.

"Asleep," Haemon reports, looking troubled. Then he squares his shoulders. "I must go speak with Father." He turns away and with long, lanky strides makes his way through the crowd.

Ismene glances down towards the tombs. She cannot be certain at this distance, but it seems that the heap of flowers and offerings has grown. She thinks of going that way, but the surge of people – hurried along by her uncle's armed men – pushes her toward the city instead.

I'm a coward, she thinks, as her steps lead her away from the tombs, away from her sister. *A coward. A coward.*

No other member of her family lacked courage. Her mother, who ruled Thebes for generations – her father, who braved the deadly Sphinx – her brothers, who led men into battle – and Antigone, bravest of them all. Their deeds are worthy of song.

Hers are not.

She pauses, letting the people stream past her, and turns to look back. Eriphyle's servants have taken down the canopy and are packing away the folding chairs. The Argive woman with golden hair stands straight and tall, her garments stirring in the evening breeze. Her posture radiates dignity and courage.

Ismene's shoulders slump in shame. Even the enemy has more valor than she, challenging her angry uncle in front of a dangerous crowd. Whereas all she does is make softly worded suggestions and creep around in the dark. Yet what else can she do? She does not have the agility to cut down the bodies hanging over the gates, nor the strength to break down the wall of Antigone's tomb. And if, as Haemon says, her sister is sleeping then her rest should not be disturbed. Turning away, Ismene resumes the plodding walk back to the city. The crowd is so thick, she breaks away and turns north in the direction of another gate – her new route is a little longer but her pace is much quicker.

Thebes' walls are dark in shadow, silhouetted against the fading orange light of sunset. Here, at the Astykratia Gate, the walls reach their highest point; here, far too many men lost their lives. Ismene can just make out the form of the Argive corpse dangling from its rope – Amphiorax, the husband of the priestess Eriphyle. The people of Thebes cheered when the body was hoisted up above the gate – but Eriphyle has reminded Ismene that this man was not just an enemy soldier, but a husband, a father, and a priest of Zeus. Is his spirit angry, sending curses down on Thebes?

Eurydike has also chosen the longer route – both Ismene and Eurydike have an attachment to the Astykratia Gate – and waits for her near the makeshift bridge across the Chrysorrhoas stream. "He's very upset, you know."

Ismene's heart leaps wildly, and she wonders whether her aunt can see the shade of the slain Argive. "Who is?"

"Your uncle, of course." Eurydike takes Ismene's arm as they step onto the rickety planks, rudely lashed together. The old bridge, destroyed in the war, had been much more substantial.

"Oh." Ismene looks down at her feet, careful not to trip. She believes that others have far more reason to be upset than her uncle Creon; but naturally Eurydike is concerned about her husband. "Because people are challenging his authority?"

They step off the creaking bridge onto solid ground, then walk up the steep slope. "No king likes that. But that's not what I meant." Eurydike squeezes Ismene's arm and casts a glance at the soldiers manning the gate, their faces stern in the torchlight. Once the two women enter the city proper, Eurydike bends close and whispers: "He's not sure he made the right decision about your sister."

Ismene frowns. "Really? He was loud enough about it."

"That's what I mean," says Eurydike. "Your uncle and I have been married nearly thirty years; I know his ways. When he's confident he speaks quietly – he doesn't need to shout."

Ismene ponders this as they head up the hill towards the palace. After a time she asks, "Do you think he might change his mind?"

Puffing with exertion – the grade is steep – Eurydike says: "Not without a reason. A good reason."

Isn't being wrong reason enough? But Ismene knows her uncle well enough to understand Eurydike's meaning. Creon is a proud man – and he has only just become king. He will not change his policy on such a controversial matter without a justification that reinforces his position and salvages his pride.

"Maybe we can think of something," Ismene says, though she feels stupid with sleep and hunger and has no idea what a solution might be.

"Meanwhile – can you talk to him, Aunt Eurydike?"

"Not tonight," Eurydike says. "He's upset, and his bones will be aching. In the morning, maybe, once he's had a bit of breakfast."

Antigone will receive no breakfast, Ismene worries, and no dinner this evening. But she does not know how to get food and drink to her sister.

By the time they reach the agora, the crowds have thinned. Most people have headed home, seeking the comforts of a hot meal and a night's sleep. But one small woman, standing under the torches that line the palace stairs, calls out to them. "Princess Ismene? Queen Eurydike?"

The speaker is Daphne, the elder of the Tiresias' two daughters. The siege has left her thinner and more ethereal than ever, but a closer look reveals signs that are all too mortal. Daphne's eyes are puffy; her face lined with exhaustion and grief.

"How is your father?" Eurydike asks. The Tiresias has not been seen in public since shortly before the end of the war.

"Troubled, my lady queen. He wants to know what is happening. Could one of you come to him?"

Eurydike releases Ismene's arm. "Ismene, can you go? I must see to my husband."

"Of course, Aunt Eurydike," Ismene says. Even though she is tired, she is relieved to have a reason to avoid her uncle. She and Daphne walk south past the palace, towards the Ogygia Gate. "How is the Tiresias?"

Daphne brushes a strand of long, straight hair out of her face. "He's dying – and he's in great pain. Each breath is torture."

Ismene bites her lip. "A man so devoted to the gods can't fear death," she says at last. "Surely he could petition the gods to release his spirit from his body."

"Yes. But he says he has something still to do – he's refusing to let Hermes take him. Hermes listens to him, I think. Perhaps because Father was such a traveler before he became the Tiresias." She shakes her head. "But I don't see how he can *do* anything! He can barely speak."

Daphne hurries through Thebes' narrow streets as if fearing they might arrive too late – that Hermes might claim the old man against his will. But when they reach the house and open the door, the sound of the invalid's labored breathing is unmistakable. Her thin shoulders relaxing, Daphne leads Ismene through the main room, past the shadows of treasures accumulated in many long-ago foreign journeys, towards the yellow glow of lamplight in a chamber at the back of the house.

A window is open, admitting the night breeze, but a sour odor of illness lingers. Daphne's sister Manto rises from a stool beside the old man's bed and offers it to Ismene. As Ismene sits down, Daphne announces loudly: "Father, Princess Ismene has come to talk with you."

The Tiresias is past eighty, possibly the oldest man alive in Thebes. Scattered wisps of hair frame his brown-spotted scalp; a small bubble of spittle at one corner of his mouth moves with each wheezing breath. But there is something troubling about his appearance beyond the signs of age and illness – Ismene needs a moment to determine just what. Then she realizes: he is not wearing his blindfold.

Unlike others who have served as the voice of Apollo and Athena, this Tiresias did not have his eyes put out during the ceremony; an accident took his sight years before he became Hellas' most powerful prophet. His eyes move slowly, sightlessly, tracking nothing in particular.

It's rude to stare, Ismene tells herself. "Good evening, Tiresias," she says, speaking loudly and clearly, like Daphne.

The old man wheezes, struggles to speak, but manages no words.

"You said things have happened outside the city walls, my lady princess," Daphne prompts her.

"Father wants to hear about them," adds Manto, mixing a goblet of water and wine and pressing it into Ismene's hands.

The Tiresias' head moves almost imperceptibly, his nod so slight that Ismene is not sure if she has imagined it; but she trusts the daughters to know their father's wants. She tells her three listeners everything: from her pre-dawn visit to Eteokles' tomb and the conversations with Antigone and the others to the sunset petition of the Argive priestess Eriphyle. The tale takes a long time – how many words she has uttered today! The lamp-oil burns lower as she talks; the old man's labored breaths grow slower, and he closes his sightless eyes.

Finally Ismene reaches the end. The Tiresias says nothing, but his rasping breaths reassure her that Hermes has not yet taken his soul. Mustering her courage, Ismene says: "I need your advice, Tiresias."

He does not answer; the rhythm of his wheezes does not change.

"He's asleep, Princess Ismene," Manto whispers.

Perhaps sensing Ismene's disappointment, Daphne offers: "He may have advice for you when he wakes, Princess. Apollo could send him a dream."

Ismene sets her hands on her knees and rises from the low stool, a little dizzy. She stretches slightly, rubs an ache in her lower back. "I should go."

"You need sleep too, Ismene," Daphne says. "Thank you for coming."

Manto walks her through the darkened house. Opening the door, she says softly: "I never thought that once the war was over, things would still be so hard."

Ismene searches for comforting words, but finds none. She touches her friend's arm and departs, but the sisters' words echo in her ears with each slap of her sandals as she makes her way through Thebes' dark streets. She, too, once believed that winning the war would solve Thebes' problems – and yet the problems seem only to have multiplied. Fatigue and hopelessness weigh upon her, burdens she feels in her shoulders and thighs as she climbs the palace stairs.

A guard opens the bronze-bound door for her, inclining his head. Ismene nods to him, though this small gesture saps her further. She looks dully at the wall-paintings as she walks through the corridors. The palace was not harmed in the war – in that the Argives never breached the walls, never stormed through these halls. Just as Ismene was not harmed in the war, in that no blade pierced her skin. But the palace feels empty. Her brother Eteokles will never again light the megaron with his charming grin – and so many other precious lives are lost.

No servant waits for her in her chamber. Ismene's personal maid died during the hostilities, and the replacement now has other duties. Ismene has not yet chosen another. But someone has dusted the room, emptied the chamber pot, and lit the lamp on the bedside table. The water-ewer is full, a lidded bowl next to it.

Ismene does not mind being alone. She pours herself a cup of water and drinks thirstily, then lifts the bowl's painted lid to see what is inside. A mixture of dried figs, dates, walnut meats and roasted almonds. A few handfuls stop her stomach from growling. These basic needs attended, she sits down on the bed; she unfastens her sandals and kicks them off. After loosening the laces of her corset she sinks back onto the bed to rest, just for a moment.

When she wakes later, she realizes guiltily that she left the lamp burning – but that is not the extravagance it was during the siege, when even the lowest-quality olive oil was conserved. How much of the night has passed? Rising stiffly, rubbing her side – foolish, to sleep in one's day clothes – she goes to the window. The sky is still inky black and scattered with stars, but the scent of fresh bread baking wafts up from the palace kitchens. Dawn is not far away.

But not for Antigone! Her sister remains trapped in utter darkness, her supply of food and water dwindling, if not gone.

Ismene decides she must do something. Perhaps it would be possible to pour water through the crack in the stone wall that separates the tombs? At least she can try.

Hastily she readies herself. Before leaving she downs another cup of water and fills a pouch with dried fruit and nuts. She takes the ewer – still mostly full – and hurries out, hoping her movements will remain undetected, at least until she exits the palace. Only a few servants will be up so early, and most will be women, fetching water from the springs.

As she passes through the slumbering city, an idea occurs to her. Aunt Eurydike said that Creon would need a reason to release Antigone – would he, perhaps, be willing to free her on the condition she leave Thebes forever? Argos welcomed Antigone once; that city might accept her again. She could live, perhaps, with Polynikes' widow – or find a place in the local temple. After the way Eriphyle challenged the king, Ismene feels sure the Argive priestess would work to ensure Antigone's safety.

The moon lights her steps as she heads downhill. Before the siege, dogs would have been roped to some of the door-posts, dogs that might have barked at her as she passed – but no longer. Thebes' dogs were sacrificed to stew-pots to fill hungry bellies.

So much destruction and loss. Uncle Creon might not be willing to release his niece to live with the Argive enemy.

And even if Ismene can convince him, Antigone may refuse to go. From the time they were children, Ismene has never understood her sister's reasoning; Antigone has so often done the surprising, the unexpected. Why would anyone choose death over life, as Antigone has by performing the burial rites for Polynikes? Then again, last night Ismene was wondering why the Tiresias chose life instead of death.

The most challenging path, in both cases, Ismene thinks. Whereas *she* always chooses the least challenging path.

Or does she? After all, she's out before sunrise – again – to see if she can help her sister. Even though it most likely won't work, at least she's *trying.*

The thought encourages her, and she smiles boldly at the guards as she passes through the sally port near the Phthia Gate. Once through the gate, Ismene hastens her pace and reviews her plans. After speaking with Antigone – and, with luck, getting her some water – she must find Eriphyle. But, after Creon's hostility yesterday evening, what if the priestess and her retinue decided to chance traveling at night? They could already be far from Thebes!

Well, then, you must go after them, some part of her responds.

Startled by this bold thought, Ismene narrowly avoids stepping in a pile of ox droppings. Herself, traveling alone, chasing down a group of foreigners? Absurd!

Or is it? Here she is, outside the city walls before sunrise – not as dangerous a place to be as it was during the war, but it still is not safe. Creon could order her walled up. Brigands could assault her. There could be hungry wolves on the prowl. She is already taking risks. She shivers, but hurries on.

From the top of the rise she looks down at the twin tombs. Two watchmen squat near a small fire; their faces look weary in its orange light.

Her footfalls make little sound; the guards, laughing over some joke, do not notice her approach. When she clears her throat to get their attention, they jump guiltily to their feet.

"My lady princess!" says one, straightening his kilt and scratching his bandaged arm.

"Lady Ismene," acknowledges the other, who badly needs a shave. Both men smell of wine; an empty jar lies on its side by the fire.

"I'm not here to check on you." Ismene feels a little amused that she, weak and useless, could cause these thickset soldiers any anxiety. "I'm here to visit my brother's tomb."

"I'm sorry, my lady princess," reports the nearer of the two, stifling a yawn. "We can't allow that. King Creon's orders."

"But my lord Haemon is inside Eteokles' tomb," admits the unshaven man.

"Why will you allow him, and not me?" Ismene asks, feeling infused with her sister's courage.

"He, uh, he had an offering to make."

"He's the priest of Apollo," says the man with the bandaged arm. "Besides, he said he wouldn't stay long."

Ismene sets the ewer of water on the ground. Her arms ache from carrying it so far, even though she learned to carry water like common-born women during the siege.

She cannot claim Haemon's religious status – and of course Haemon is the king's son. Or maybe it is another connection that swayed the guards: a man asking to speak with his wife. If Haemon wants privacy, it might be better not to intrude even if she could convince the guards to admit her.

As Ismene hesitates, the door to Eteokles' tomb swings open. Haemon emerges, his face pale in the moonlight. "Ismene!" he says. "You're here early!"

"As are you, cousin." Has he been in there the whole night, while she slept on a comfortable wool-stuffed mattress? "I'll go in now."

But the guards bar her way, and Haemon shakes his head. "There's no point."

Ismene's stomach lurches. "No – already?"

Her tall cousin grasps her elbow, leading her away from the tombs and the guards. "No, she's not dead," he whispers. "But she's asleep. She's exhausted, and it would be better if we let her rest just now."

Ismene closes her eyes and silently thanks the gods that her sister still lives.

"I'm going to the Temple of Apollo for the dawn ceremony," Haemon continues. "I plan to pray for her. Will you join me?"

"Yes – wait just a moment." There is no point in carrying the heavy ewer to Apollo's temple; she offers it to the guards. They accept, looking a little surprised at this gift from a princess; she smiles shyly and goes back to her cousin. The eastern stars are fading, the first early glow appearing on the horizon. If they wish to reach the temple by daybreak, they need to hurry.

Ismene crosses her arms and falls into step beside her cousin. "I—I suppose you and Antigone have a lot to talk about," she ventures.

"Yes." Haemon's brisk pace does not falter. "She explained that she told you what happened between us. Or what *didn't* happen."

Warmth floods Ismene's face. "Well…"

"Each of us blamed ourselves for that, Antigone and I," he says, not looking at her. "And we avoided each other instead of confronting the situation. We were cowards."

"Cowards?" The word surprises her.

"Yes. Cowards and fools. We've wasted so much time – perhaps our entire lives. And now I think – I think we could find a way to be the friends we once were." Bitterness creeps into his voice. "Except that my father has walled her into a tomb to die."

"Is there any way to get her out?"

"I gave the guards a gold arm-ring each to let me smuggle in an axe, and I tried to break through the wall." He holds out his hands, which are bloodied and blistered. "I thought there might be a weak spot by the fissure. But all I managed to do was damage the fresco and give Antigone a headache. If we're going to break down a wall, it'll have to be the one made of bricks."

"Which means people could see." They are walking uphill; Ismene struggles to keep up with her cousin's quick pace. "But, Haemon, what if we could convince your father to release her? Maybe banishment would be enough. She could go to Argos."

He stops to let her catch up, then takes her arm. "Even if we could convince Father, I don't know that Antigone would agree. You know how stubborn she is. She wants her death to show that obedience to the gods' laws is paramount."

Ismene considers this. "I don't see how her death would help the gods and their laws."

"That's what I told her."

"What did she say?"

Haemon sighs. "Just that she was tired, and needed to sleep. Which could mean she knows her reasoning is poor but she doesn't want to admit it. Or it could mean she really *is* too weak to argue. For Antigone, that would be a bad sign."

They are approaching the temple; the pale marble of the forecourt glows in the growing pre-dawn light. Before Haemon can start up the stairs, Ismene catches his hand in both of hers. "You want her released, don't you?" she asks.

"More than anything," he says, his voice rough. He pats her hand, then gently detaches himself from her grip. "I must prepare for the dawn offering. May Apollo show us the way!"

Haemon ascends the steps. The ceremony is simple; he lights incense in a lovely bronze tripod donated decades before by Alkides' father Amphitryon, celebrating victory in a battle against the bandits to the north. Kneeling before the tripod, Haemon faces the rising sun with upstretched arms, imploring Apollo to make this day the day that Antigone is released.

Ismene watches from the forecourt. Her own prayer is silent: *Apollo, patron of Thebes: help me to help my sister. You too have a sister you love—*

A hand touches her elbow. Ismene jumps, imagining for a fleeting instant that the god himself has come to her – but the man beside her is too ordinary to embody any god.

"Your pardon, Princess Ismene," he says. "May I assist you?"

"Thank you," she says, recognizing the healer Udaeus, one of Apollo's senior priests. "I – I was just offering a prayer." The sun has risen, now; its rays illuminate a wall painting of Apollo leading his cattle up a mountain that looks like Kithairon. "At least the Argives didn't damage the temple."

"They took all the food, the wine, the healing herbs and the bandages, but they didn't hurt the building itself. I suppose Polynikes prevented it; he hoped to be king here, so why offend Apollo?" Udaeus gestures towards the temple with a bowl-shaped basket he is carrying, full of freshly picked mint leaves. "Now that the siege is over, our routine is back to normal. Travelers pitch their tents on the grounds; we priests treat the wounded and the sick."

"Travelers?" Ismene asks, hope blossoming in her chest. "Is one of them a priestess of Hera?"

"The *Argive* priestess?" Udaeus' mouth twists wryly, showing that he has heard, at least in part, the events of the day before. "She and her servants made camp behind the temple. Shall I take you to them?"

"No, thank you," Ismene says hastily. She does not want anyone else to overhear her discussion about Antigone. "I know my way – and I'm sure your patients need you."

Udaeus bows. "As you wish, my lady princess."

Crossing the tiles of the forecourt, Ismene passes into the laurel arbor beyond. The Argive encampment is easy to spot in the clearing behind the temple: a tent of striped linen; a scattering of wooden stools and folding chairs; a campfire encircled by fist-sized stones. Several Athenian shields lean against a nearby tree; bedrolls are neatly tied and stacked alongside. One of the young serving women, a blue-and-yellow striped blanket clutched around her shoulders, pokes awkwardly at the coals with a long stick.

A slim hand pushes aside the flap of the tent and the priestess Eriphyle emerges, staggering a little, as if shaking off the bonds of slumber. Her golden hair strays from an unkempt braid; she rubs her eyes with the knuckles of both hands and yawns. Her beauty is still undeniable, but she is not the elegant, poised creature of the day before.

Ismene pauses in the fragrant shadow of the laurels. Now that she is here, she is not sure what to say or do.

The servant woman does not hurry to her mistress' side. Instead, Eriphyle herself pulls a camp-stool closer to the fire and takes a seat. "Dear Hera, I need more sleep. But that bed is as comfortable as a pile of stones."

"And Father snores," says the maidservant, grimacing.

The tent-flap stirs again; the other maidservant – the pregnant one – steps out, clad in a brown nightshift and carrying a wooden bowl. She hands the bowl to Eriphyle; the priestess thanks her, takes a dried fig from the bowl and begins to eat. Then – to Ismene's astonishment – both servants take seats beside their mistress.

Ismene frowns. Eriphyle is priestess to Hera and sister to a king; her servants should treat her with more respect! Even Ismene's own maid was never so familiar, and Eriphyle has so much – so much *presence.* Are customs different in Argos? Antigone mentioned nothing of the sort.

"Are you going to try again?" asks the maidservant in the brown nightshift.

Eriphyle sighs. "I don't see what good it will do."

"You *have* to try again," says the one wrapped in the blanket. "Tydeus – you know what they've done to his body!"

Ismene blinks. *Tydeus?* The most barbaric of the assailants – and a son-in-law of King Adrastos.

"Of course I know," Eriphyle snaps. "They've done the same to my husband. But you heard King Creon; he was too angry to parley." She takes another fig from the bowl, then passes it to the pregnant maidservant.

The pregnant woman helps herself from the bowl, then stares at Eriphyle with narrowed eyes. "Could we offer them something?"

Letting the blanket fall from her shoulders, the other servant says, "A trade?"

Eriphyle rises from her stool and turns away, lifting her hand to her throat. "I don't know."

Yes, Ismene thinks, *a trade!* In exchange for the bodies, the Argive women will take Antigone off Theban hands. She is about to step forward and suggest this – but then a dark-haired man comes out of the woods that mark the glade's northern edge; Ismene recognizes him as Eriphyle's manservant from the day before. He strides toward the three women without hesitation or humility.

"Good morning, ladies!" he calls. "Glad to see you're finally up!"

"The sun's just risen," Eriphyle says, sounding defensive.

"And I rose with the moon." He takes the bowl of figs and pops one into his mouth. Still chewing, he says: "So are we leaving? Our Athenian soldiers are ready to go – they don't want a fight. They *say* it's because it will make their king unhappy, but I think they're afraid. They're an escort, not an army."

"We still don't have the bodies of our husbands, Father!" objects the maidservant with the striped blanket.

Father? Husbands? Ismene looks at the maidservants more closely.

The man strokes the young woman's hair. "I know, Deipyle. But they're dead. And our lives are in danger."

"Ismene?" After years of officiating at the Temple of Apollo, Haemon's voice carries. "Ismene, where are you?"

"Here, Haemon," Ismene says, finding her voice at last.

The four people before the tent freeze, like hares trying to escape the attention of a circling hawk.

"I'm here, Haemon," Ismene repeats, as her cousin comes closer. Then she points at the dark-haired man: "And that man is King Adrastos of Argos."

CHAPTER FIFTEEN
ADRASTOS

Adrastos stares helplessly, as unable to move as if he has grown roots into the ground like one of the laurel trees between the encampment and the temple. If only Arion were here! But the horse, more recognizable than its owner, is necessarily kept at a distance. Adrastos has no means of escape.

A tall, slender man in the white robes of a priest emerges from the grove of trees. It is Haemon, King Creon's eldest son. Behind him is a young woman Adrastos also recognizes: Princess Ismene of Thebes.

"Well?" insists the priest. "*Are* you Adrastos?"

Adrastos swallows hard. He hears the echo of his brother-in-law's bitter voice: *You will survive the war.* But prophecy is slippery and the Fates are fickle – with the fighting over, he could be in mortal danger. Surviving the war need not mean living to see Argos again.

The priest steps closer. Lanky and narrow-shouldered, he does not have a soldier's build. His only weapon is a dagger at his belt.

Don't be a coward, Adrastos tells himself.

Facing the Thebans squarely, he draws himself to his full height. "Yes." With one hand he removes the dark wig that has hidden his sandy hair.

Haemon spits on the earth. "I should have you killed!" His dark eyes hold the same flash of rage King Creon displayed the day before.

"Won't that defile the sanctuary?" Adrastos asks. "I've spent the night here, shared your food, offered incense at Apollo's altar. I'm your guest."

The Theban priest frowns, but says nothing.

"We are bound by blood and marriage," Adrastos continues, appealing to the young woman. "Princess Ismene, my grandsons are your nephews. My daughter Argia is your sister-in-law." He rests his hand on Argia's round shoulder.

"Blood!" cries Haemon. "And what of the Theban blood you've shed? You led an army against us!"

"Cousin," Princess Ismene interrupts softly, "too many have died. On both sides." She moves past Haemon, stepping closer to Argia. "You're Polynikes' wife?"

"His widow," Argia corrects sharply.

Ismene gestures to Deipyle. "And you must be—?"

"My niece Deipyle," Phyle answers the question. "Both make poor maidservants, I'm afraid. My brother is better at feigning servility."

Adrastos' hackles rise at his sister's drily spoken words. "I'm a man of many talents," he retorts. "As was Polynikes. And – having once lost my throne to a treacherous brother – I had sympathy for his cause."

"Eteokles *did* steal the throne from his twin," Haemon says grudgingly. Adrastos sees the priest's clenched fists loosen, the cords of his thin forearms relax. "I only learned the depth of his duplicity yesterday. But that does not justify your attack on our city."

Adrastos glances at the daughter who should have become queen of Thebes. Argia's face is clouded with emotion, a mixture of rage and loss. Still, he is in no position to argue. "Perhaps not," he concedes. "The gods granted the victory to you."

Ismene returns to her cousin's side; she whispers something Adrastos cannot hear. The young priest strokes his beard, his dark eyes narrowing, before murmuring a response. Ismene nods, and walks closer to the campfire. She regards each of the Argives in turn, then says: "You want my uncle to release the bodies, so that you can perform the funeral rites."

"Please," begs Deipyle, her voice breaking, "let their shades find rest!"

"It's not our decision," Ismene says slowly. "But Haemon and I may be willing to speak with the king."

Adrastos raises his eyebrows. "If...?"

"Tell us how you came to attack Thebes," Haemon says, challenge in his voice. "Polynikes was in Argos for years. What changed? Why did you attack when you did?"

Adrastos hesitates; the circumstances leading up to the failed war are not events he wants to remember.

"Is that all you want? Then you'll negotiate with Creon for us?"

"We make no promises," Haemon says belligerently.

"But," Ismene adds gently, "we still want to know."

Adrastos studies the two royal Thebans. Something else is going on here, he thinks, and wonders shrewdly if it concerns Antigone. Ismene is Antigone's sister; Haemon her long-estranged husband.

In the meantime they have asked a question; he is sure that he will be judged on his answer. And who knows? He may somehow win back the bodies, and by doing so soothe his daughters' hearts and prevent angry ghosts from wandering through Hellas. At any rate, a story, an hour's breath, is easy enough to give – he only hopes it calms these two rather than inflaming them, the way that Phyle's story about Alkides did.

"That will take some time," Adrastos says smoothly. "Please, share our breakfast. Deipyle, fetch chairs for our guests. And some more food."

His younger daughter looks at him crossly, as if the revelation of her identity should spare her from further servitude, but she complies. Ismene sinks down onto the offered chair with an air of relief, but Haemon lowers himself suspiciously, as if he fears the light folding chair could transform into a monster and swallow him. Deipyle passes around bowls of dried fruit and parched chickpeas while Argia sullenly offers cups of watered wine. Phyle resumes her seat, her expression impassive, hands folded in her lap.

Before sitting down himself, Adrastos drops more wood onto the campfire. "Very well, you asked how the decision was made to go to war," he begins at last. "When—"

"Wait," Haemon interrupts. "Before you speak, Argive, pour a libation and swear to tell the truth. All of it, with no lies mixed in."

"I—"

"You fled the final battle on your horse, leaving your men to die without you. You've been slinking around in disguise. Why should we trust you without an oath?"

"It's a fair point, Brother," Phyle says.

Adrastos clenches his teeth. His sister has aggravated him greatly the last few days. That last barb, about feigning servility, was especially annoying. Now this: agreeing with the Theban priest that he is both craven *and* untrustworthy!

But he knows they are, all of them, still reeling from defeat. It is easier to make, and take offense at, tart remarks than to directly face the enormity of the situation. Yet that is what this young priest – what the gods themselves – now demand.

Adrastos dips the fingers of his right hand into his cup and scatters droplets onto the ground. "I will tell the truth of what led to the war, as best I can." He touches the surface of the liquid a second time, casting another small shower of watered wine near his feet. "May Zeus, Lord of Heaven and Earth, punish me for any falsehood." He submerges his fingers a third time, rains down a third spate of blood-red drops. He glances at Apollo's priest; Haemon nods in grudging approval, indicating satisfaction with his oath.

Adrastos sips from the cup while he gathers his thoughts. "Very well," he begins again.

ADRASTOS

Like Polynikes, I had a crown stolen from me by a treacherous brother. My younger brother Pronax duped the people of Argos into thinking me cursed, and had me banished from the city. My daughters and my pregnant wife were forced to stay behind; Pronax wanted them as hostages, even though the gold I was allowed to take with me in my chariot was not enough to hire an army to threaten him. A few months later, my wife birthed a boy; though the child lived, the mother died. I suppose knowing I had a son at last should have cheered me – but it only reminded me that I could not see him, could not go home.

I felt thoroughly defeated, completely and utterly abandoned by the gods. Days stretched into meaningless months, and though I settled in pleasure-loving Korinth I found no joy in anything. Driving my chariot, gambling games – I won this black wig from an Aegyptian trader – even the beauty of Aphrodite's girls in the temple on the Akrokorinth – all the things a man should relish were as juiceless as a dried gourd. I was *supposed* to be king of Argos, ruling the proudest city of southern Hellas. Instead I was a wastrel, lacking both purpose and city, with a son who might never even see my face. Scorn filled people's voices when they spoke of me. I felt like the unluckiest man alive.

But then, Princess Ismene, I met your father Oedipus. He challenged me, made me see things differently: after all, I was *not* the man the gods most despised! And, unlike Oedipus, I could *do* something about my situation.

I remembered I still had a few friends at home, and I set about doing what I could to win more. I invited anyone journeying from Argos to join me for a drink, filling their goblets with the best vintages while keeping mine well watered. And so I learned what was happening.

Time out of mind, Argos has been ruled by three powerful families: mine, that of my father-in-law Iphis, and a third headed by Amphiorax. Iphis, I learned, had quarreled with my brother. So when a lucky toss of the knucklebones won me a silver chain from an Athenian merchant, I traded it for several amphorae of my father-in-law's favorite Chian wine. I sent them to him with words of regard, wishing continued good health to him and his wife, and expressing hope for the health of my children. I received a promising message in return – nothing so explicit as inviting me to return home, but an acknowledgement that my children were his grandchildren, and that he and I had shared interests.

Making alliance with Amphiorax was more challenging: he had killed my father, King Talaus. Oh, not in a way as to cause blood-feud! You see, Father liked sparring with younger fighters. He said it kept him fit. And since they used only wooden training-swords, Father insisted that no blows be pulled. In one of these bouts, Amphiorax landed a blow that shattered Father's helmet; the old man collapsed, and died two days later. Amphiorax swore it was an accident, and he was a senior priest of Zeus, so my family accepted his oath – but, as you might imagine, it made things awkward.

Even before that, Amphiorax and I had never been friends. We had little in common. He was a swordsman and a wrestler, valuing personal strength and hand-to-hand combat; I preferred chariot racing and archery, sports he despised. I enjoyed parties and pretty flute-girls; he claimed such pursuits sapped a warrior's discipline.

But if *I* had little in common with Amphiorax, my brother Pronax had less. I learned this near the end of the sailing season, when my young friends, Parthenopeus and Hippomedon, came to Korinth to visit the temple of Aphrodite. Over a game of senet in a corner of the temple, they related that my brother Pronax had developed a passion for an Aegyptian dancer.

"He wants to marry her and make her his queen," said Hippomedon. He was small, dark and quick – like a ferret with bad teeth.

"A *slave!* Queen!" This exclamation from Parthenopeus amused me; most of his own ancestors were peasants, but he brimmed with ambition. I've noticed men are often quick to see their own worst faults in others, while remaining blind to the exact same failings in themselves.

"And I'm sure she was sleeping with that Lydian lyre-player before." Hippomedon cast the knucklebones and began to move his pebbles. "Though now she *says* he's her cousin."

I grinned at the thought of my brother being played for a fool – until I remembered that *I* had been played for a fool by *him*. What did that make me? "What does Amphiorax say to all this?" I asked.

Hippomedon jerked his chin. "He's scandalized. Says it's beneath the dignity of a king of Argos." He imitated Amphiorax' voice and pompous manner so well that I broke out laughing.

"Well," I said, "he's never had an eye for the ladies." I gestured around the crowded room, admiring one and another of Aphrodite's lovely acolytes. "All this would be wasted on him, eh?"

I had thought this would get another laugh – but the two men fell silent, exchanging a wary glance.

"What is it?" I prompted.

Hippomedon cracked his knuckles before saying: "Actually, it seems Eros' arrow has struck him at last."

"Really?" I asked, picking up my wine cup. "Who's the maid – or is it a boy?"

"It's Eriphyle."

The musicians began playing again just as he spoke; I wasn't sure I'd heard right. "My little sister Phyle?" Eriphyle was the youngest of my family, conceived after my mother thought her childbearing days were finished. My parents treasured their baby daughter. Some years later – Phyle was about seven or eight – my mother suffered sudden chest pains and died; after that my father doted on his little girl all the more.

"That's right," Hippomedon said. "Your sister."

When I'd been banished from Argos three years before, Phyle still seemed like a child; but a little reckoning made me realize she was nearly fifteen. "How is Phyle?"

"Glorious," sighed Parthenopeus. "Graceful as a water-nymph."

"She's become a very beautiful young woman," Hippomedon agreed. Then he frowned and nudged Parthenopeus' arm. "You rolled a four, not a five."

Mumbling an apology, Parthenopeus moved his pebble back a space.

I rubbed my chin. "Anyway – will Pronax permit the marriage?"

Hippomedon shook his head. "Amphiorax won't give the blessing of Zeus for Pronax to marry the Aegyptian. So Pronax won't let him marry your sister."

Here, as unexpected as Phyle's conception in the first place – here was my opportunity! "Tell Amphiorax that *I* think he would make an excellent husband for Phyle. If I were king, I'd sanction it."

Parthenopeus grinned. "Will do."

An inquisitive spark lit Hippomedon's dark eyes. "But how would you become king?"

"That's a good question," I said slowly.

A girl came by with wine; Hippomedon waved her away. "What you need is an accident," he said quietly.

Parthenopeus' eyebrows went up. "Right – an accident! You know, King Pronax, he's very careless."

"A chariot accident, maybe," mused Hippomedon. "Wheels can break."

Parthenopeus rubbed his bulbous nose. "Pronax don't race much, though. And a fall like that might not kill him."

His small, dark friend picked up the knucklebones. "Perhaps the gods will manage something else." He cast, and made the high throw.

As Hippomedon moved his pebbles, I said: "If something *does* happen, and I regain my kingdom... I'd elevate you both to positions of responsibility in Argos. You're among the few to visit me in my exile. So I know you're true friends – men I can rely on."

Little more was said as they finished their game. I could almost hear their thoughts: they were ambitious fellows, and if I became king their prospects would multiply tenfold. Before leaving to choose their favorites among the temple girls, each of them clasped my hand warmly and wished me the gods' favor.

Through the cold days that followed I prayed frequently to Zeus, king of the gods and god of kings. I reminded him that my brother stole the sacrifice I'd intended for him, and replaced it with a diseased animal – a grievous insult. I promised Almighty Zeus that if he restored me to Argos I'd honor him without fail: I'd offer unblemished beasts and the finest incense on his altar, punish oath-breakers, and set an example to all Hellas in following his laws of hospitality. As king of Argos, I promised, I would welcome even the humblest. My time of exile, you understand, taught me to value a good host above all men.

You asked for the absolute truth, and I've sworn by Zeus to give it. But I can only tell you what I know. A few months after my conversation with Parthenopeus and Hippomedon – spring was just starting – Pronax fell from the rooftop garden and broke his neck. He died instantly. The only person known to be with him that night, the Aegyptian dancing girl, followed my brother from the rooftop to the rocky ground below. The palace guards said she screamed "No!" as she plummeted to her death. Some thought this proved her love for my brother: unwilling to live without him, she wanted to accompany him to the Underworld. Others thought she'd pushed him over the balustrade in a fit of anger, then killed herself to escape whipping and beheading. And a few suspected the Lydian lyre-player, though there was no evidence he'd been to the palace that night.

I don't know what actually happened. One of those theories could be right. But it's also possible that Parthenopeus or Hippomedon – or both of them together – heaved my brother over the balustrade, then, to be rid of a troublesome witness, tossed the Aegyptian dancing-girl after him. Later, I questioned each of them; both denied any involvement with Pronax' death. Maybe they were lying. Maybe the Fates just decided to snip my brother's life thread. At least his death was quick.

As soon as I heard the news, I set sail towards home – but I did not want to pass the herm pillars marking the borders of Argive lands without assurance that I was welcome. So I remained in the port city of Tiryns and sent messages to Amphiorax, to my father-in-law Iphis and to my sister Phyle.

Unsure about the loyalties of Tiryns' king, I did not announce myself to him; instead I remained in the lower city by the harbor. I offered Iphis and Amphiorax a meeting where the road from Argos neared the northern edge of Tiryns' stout-walled citadel, well away from the main eastern gate. My servant returned with the news that I could expect a group from Argos in two days' time. Hopeful but wary, I positioned myself on the rise east of town to watch for their approach. About midmorning a pair of chariots and a mule-cart approached from the northwest. I made my way down the rocky slope towards the group.

As my servant and I drew closer, I recognized the two charioteers: Amphiorax and my nephew Kapaneus, orphaned son of my eldest sister. Old Iphis, my sister Phyle, and my children rode in the cart with a pair of servants, and a few more servants walked alongside.

Iphis descended from the mule-cart to greet me, and then reintroduced me to my daughters. Argia ran forward to kiss me, but Deipyle hung back shyly. When Iphis urged his grandson – the son I had never met – to say hello, the boy only clung to his nursemaid's skirts and stared at me with mistrustful eyes.

"Give him time," said Phyle, walking gracefully forward. As my friends had told me, she had blossomed into a lovely young woman; her golden hair, arranged with rose-colored ribbons that matched her skirts, shone in the morning sun. "Brother," she continued, taking my hand, "I'm sorry we didn't support you against Pronax. Welcome home."

"I'm not home yet," I pointed out, taking this opening to discuss the main subject. I turned to Amphiorax. "So – may I cross the boundary into Argos and assume my father's throne? Or am I still cursed?" I rested my arm on Phyle's shoulders, intending this gesture of affection to remind Amphiorax that since my brother and father were dead, he needed *my* permission to marry her.

He handed his chariot-reins to a servant and took a step towards me –

but stopped several paces away. "You must purify yourself first."

"That calf with the bad entrails – that wasn't mine," I protested. "Pronax substituted it for the one I'd selected."

He made no response; I wasn't sure if he believed me. But then I detected something in his expression, the way his eyes moved beneath those heavy black brows. I realized he kept his distance not because he thought me impure, but because he was uncomfortable approaching Phyle too closely.

"You say I must be purified," I prompted. "What sort of ceremony is needed?"

"An – an offering," he said, as though each word cost him an effort to speak. "We'll read the gods' will from the omens."

That seemed reasonable enough. "All right. This time, I'll keep a closer watch on my offering!" I laughed, and saw Kapaneus smile; but Amphiorax' expression scarcely changed. His gaze remained fixed on my sister; the knot in his throat bobbed as he swallowed. Deciding that he was too bashful to say what needed to be said, I dropped my arm from her shoulders. "Come, Amphiorax, let's talk in private."

I steered him into the shadow of Tiryns' limestone fortifications. We walked far enough away that the others could not hear us, stopping beside a stretch of wall where the stones were particularly enormous. I looked at one, thinking it was so large that the strongest pair of oxen could not possibly have budged it. The people of Tiryns say their walls were built by the giant one-eyed Kyklopes; certainly no man – not even a dozen men – could lift a single one of the boulders that make up that wall.

But construction techniques were irrelevant to the matter at hand. "So," I said, quietly but directly: "will you support me or not?"

"Yes, if…"

"If what?"

He glanced back at my sister, but still said nothing.

Not wanting to wait all day, I broached the topic myself. "I hear you want to marry Eriphyle?"

"Yes." Earnest desperation saturated the single syllable.

Trying to keep from smiling, I said: "I'll approve the marriage, as long as the omens are good and I become king of Argos."

He nodded, gazing back towards where Phyle stood with the others, her golden curls spilling past her shoulders.

"Do you want to speak to her now?" I asked.

He stared at me in alarm. "No! I – I mean, yes, I do, but…."

I almost pitied the man. "You lead one of Argos' great families," I said. "With my brother dead and me banished, you could take the throne for yourself and marry my sister anyway."

"Take – *take* Eriphyle?" he stammered. "No, I… she… I mean, I can't even…"

I rested a hand on his thick-muscled shoulder. "Shall I speak to her for you?"

He nodded with relief. "Would you?"

"All right." It required great effort not to laugh – but try as I might, I couldn't keep the grin from my face as I walked away. Amphiorax, the soldier's soldier, head of a great house and Argos' high priest of Zeus – so in awe of a fifteen-year-old girl that he couldn't even speak to her! Oh, Eros' arrows wound us all, but usually only downy-cheeked youths are laid so low – not thick-chested men with full beards.

I nodded to Iphis and Kapaneus, signaling that the conversation had gone well; then I approached my sister. Phyle and the children had been watching the chariot horses graze on spring grass along the roadside; she looked up at my approach. I beckoned to her, and we walked a few paces away from my daughters.

"I want to come home, Phyle."

She nodded. "You *should* be home. You should be king."

"And I will be. Under one condition." I explained that Amphiorax loved her – that their marriage would ensure my place on the throne.

"Really?" Phyle glanced over at the dark soldier-priest. He was watching us, but abruptly turned away when we looked in his direction. "But how can that be? He never speaks to me. I don't think I've ever even seen him smile!"

"The anguish of passion," I said. "Trust me, he loves you."

She moved away from me, folding her slender white arms. "But he killed Father."

"That was an accident." Still, Phyle had been our father's favorite; she was close to him, especially after our mother died. "Phyle, don't forget – Father was the one who wanted those training bouts. He loved sparring with young soldiers. He *liked* Amphiorax." That last might have been pushing the truth, but certainly Father had respected Amphiorax' fighting skills.

She looked up at the men patrolling Tiryns' walls. Our gathering had been noticed; two men with feather-plumes on their helmets stood at the tightest curve of the walkway far above, looking down at us. "I suppose," Phyle said softly.

I tried another angle. "If you marry him, you can stay in Argos. You wouldn't have to go away to some foreign city. And I'll be there in Argos, with you."

Her hands fell to her sides; she nodded, but still she did not meet my gaze.

"Phyle, I don't want to force this on you. Amphiorax doesn't want to force this on you. He's a good man." Looking at her slender form, her shining curls and graceful hands, I realized that this was not the baby sister I remembered. I lowered my voice. "Is there any reason you *shouldn't* marry him?"

She turned back to me, arching an eyebrow. "Such as?"

"Such as you're already with child by another man. Or you want to join the Maidens of Artemis. Or because – I don't know! Maybe you're really a mermaid with a fish's tail beneath those skirts!"

This coaxed a smile from her at last; it was like glimpsing a rainbow in the spray of a waterfall, making what was already beautiful even more so. "No, there's nothing like that."

I took her hand. "So you agree to marry Amphiorax?"

She nodded.

"Excellent!" I bent down and kissed her soft cheek. "You won't regret it." I called out to Amphiorax, and beckoned him over.

"My sister has agreed to the marriage," I said.

He did not smile; in fact, he looked away from her when he nodded. I understood why Phyle had never perceived his interest.

I glanced over to where Iphis and Kapaneus stood with the children, alongside the mule-cart and the chariots. They were watching with interest, but too far away to hear our words. "So," I continued, "if you agree to certain terms, I'll sanction the wedding."

Amphiorax squinted at me. "What terms?"

"You'll back my decisions as king. Without question." I had Iphis' loyalty; I needed Amphiorax' as well. And I had to ensure that the citizens of Argos *knew* he was with me.

His thick dark brows knit together. "Don't you want honest advice?"

This was a good point – I've never had the hubris to think I have all the answers. "How about this: if we ever disagree, Phyle will arbitrate between us. Being your wife as well as my sister, she'll judge fairly."

My sister's lips parted in surprise. I had shown her great consideration in asking her acquiescence to the marriage; now I was assuring her power in the future as well.

"Besides," I added lightly, "this will guarantee that you treat her well."

"Of course I'll treat her well!" Amphiorax said hoarsely, indignant at the suggestion of anything else. This was not a man to tease, I realized.

"Then you should have the advantage. What's loyalty to a brother compared to the marital bond?" I stepped toward him, extending my hand. "Do we have an agreement?"

He clasped my hand, and together we swore an oath. We were just finishing this when a party of Tirynian soldiers arrived with an official from the palace. Young King Eurystheus and his regent offered hospitality, which we accepted: performing the purification rites in Tiryns would allow me to be cleansed before setting foot on Argive soil. The next day I sacrificed a ewe and a ram, and underwent a ritual bath; after that I was able to return to Argos and assume the throne. Amphiorax and Phyle married, and my sister – as the wife of Zeus' high priest – became chief priestess of Hera, our patron goddess.

I set about consolidating power in Argos. I banished the Lydian lyre-player, and – as promised – I gave Parthenopeus and Hippomedon positions of responsibility. Parthenopeus I put in charge of public works; citizens feel confident when they see new buildings, bridges, and roads constructed. Hippomedon had a gift with horses, so I had him supervise the royal stables and organize chariot races. I worked to ensure that the peasants were properly fed and productive, and to re-establish my friendships among the Argive nobility.

Shortly after Phyle gave birth to Amphiorax' first son, Amphiorax told me that Zeus had blessed him with the gift of prophecy.

The two of us were walking around the newly upgraded chariot-racing grounds, inspecting work just finished by Hippomedon and Parthenopeus. I stopped by the marble turning-post and studied my brother-in-law. "I thought prophecy was the province of Apollo."

"It is," Amphiorax agreed. "Zeus had his son grant me this ability."

I ran a hand over the cold, smooth-polished white marble as I considered this. My brother-in-law was widely acknowledged to be Argos' greatest warrior, and famed for his devotion to the gods; this would swell his reputation even further. And if he was known to be a prophet, how could I ignore anything he said? Yet I could think of nothing to do but to offer congratulations. So I offered them, then pulled my cloak tighter against the wintry wind.

"I thank you, my lord king," he said, as we started down the far side of the sandy racetrack. Then, always one to judge the wineskin half-empty rather than half-full, he added: "But foresight is a burden as well. Sometimes I see the future but cannot do anything about it."

"That must be frustrating." My friend Oedipus, who by then had taken sanctuary in Argos, was the ultimate example of attempting and failing to circumvent the Fates. "But let's see if we can turn your gift to the city's advantage."

I had been pondering ways to expand Argos' wealth and influence; military adventures seemed a natural strategy. Amphiorax expressed concerns about this, saying it would be wrong to start a war without provocation. I explained I had no intention of attacking without cause, but wanted Argos to be ready – and able to take full advantage – in case we *were* provoked.

Amphiorax sought the will of Zeus in the sacred oak-grove behind the temple. This was the message he brought back for me:

You'll survive no battle that you lead,
Unless you have the swiftest steed.

Disturbing words, but I wasn't sure what to make of them. Amphiorax hadn't claimed to have second sight until just recently, so his ability was untested. Yet with Oedipus living in Argos – Oedipus, who tried to escape prophecy as his father before him had tried, both without success – it was impossible not to take *all* prophecy very seriously.

So I pondered the words carefully. On the surface, they suggested I should not start a war. But what if Argos were attacked? My only protection would be having a fast horse – the *fastest* horse. The two I had taken into exile, now returned with me to Argos, were dear to me but past their prime. Others in the palace stables were good – but how could I be sure an enemy would have nothing better? I told Hippomedon I wanted the best horse in Hellas. I had him search out the top trainers and breeders; and, to the enthusiastic approval of my subjects, I instituted regular chariot races to test the steeds.

Meanwhile I needed to find ways to refill the palace coffers – and to secure my position on the throne. I realized the vow I made to Zeus, that desperate winter in Korinth, gave me a way to do both. Strangers and suppliants, I let it be known, were welcome in Argos. After all, the much-cursed Oedipus had given me heart when I was at my lowest; he brought me luck. Spending time with the unfortunate reminded me of my own good fortune; and wealthy travelers often made a generous gift at an Argive temple in return for purification. Other suppliants brought a different kind of good fortune: many strong young men, exiled from their home cities for one reason or another, came to live in Argos, and they gave their allegiance to me rather than to Iphis or Amphiorax.

We had good harvests; the temple treasuries filled with petitioners' gifts; rootless young men swelled our forces. I strengthened ties with Tiryns and cultivated relationships with Athens, Mycenae, and Kalydon. I was sure I had the gods' favor. Then Oedipus, my luck-charm, left the city – and misfortune struck. A bridge under construction collapsed; a shipload of cargo was lost; I broke my leg in a chariot accident.

That was when my sister told me how my two daughters had hidden their womanhood because they did not want to marry Hippomedon and Parthenopeus. It is true that I had *considered* making them my sons-in-law, but had never agreed to formal betrothals. I had reasons for reluctance. They were useful, but their blood was not good – they had no great ancestors or tales of glory themselves. Perhaps they had thrown my brother off the roof and had enabled my return to Argos and the throne. Yet even if I owed them, how could I marry my daughters to men who had murdered their uncle? And if they had not killed Pronax, well, then, I did not owe them!

Besides, they were ugly men. What if one of my grandsons inherited Hippomedon's weak and crooked teeth? He would have trouble chewing. Or even worse, what if a granddaughter were cursed with Parthenopeus' large red nose? She'd never find a husband!

What could I do? I lay there, recovering from my injury, swilling poppy juice in such quantities that the healer cautioned me that I might start imagining things. The warning gave me an idea, and in private I told Amphiorax that I had had a troubling vision. You've asked for the entire truth – and so I confess that the dream that Amphiorax interpreted – the one about the chariot being pulled by a boar and a lion – was something I invented and then asked him to explain. I was thinking of Mycenae when I spoke of a lion; an alliance with that wealthy city would have been convenient.

Amphiorax listened to me with gravitas; he behaved it as if my vision were real. After meditating in the oak grove behind Zeus' temple, he gave me his interpretation. He told me that my misfortune was caused by the husbands I was planning for my daughters. Rather than the men I was considering, the gods wished me to wed Argia and Deipyle to a lion and a boar. I let my brother-in-law take credit for the prophecy; and if my daughters were a little fearful, well, that seemed a reasonable punishment for deceiving me. Of course I had no intention of sacrificing them to wild beasts, but the prophecy provided a good reason to find other, less fastidious maidens to wed Hippomedon and Parthenopeus.

Then Polynikes and Tydeus arrived, bearing a lion and a boar on their shields.

After seeing their shields, I spent several nights wondering about the nature of prophecy. True, Polynikes was from Thebes and not Mycenae, but I had never told anyone of that part of my fantasy. Was it so surprising that what I imagined came true? A potter knows the shape of the urn he wants to make before he grabs a lump of clay and turns his wheel. A weaver chooses threads in accordance with the design she plans for her tapestry. A bronze-smith does not guess whether he is forging a dagger or an axe: he selects the proper mold. We all imagine that the future holds *something*. If we imagine a particular thing, and do our best to make it happen, isn't it more likely to come true?

Yet the episode was extremely unsettling. I did not consider myself a prophet; I had been the unwitting agent the gods used to bring about Amphiorax' prophecy. I realized why the gift of second sight troubled Amphiorax, and thought with compassion of those who go mad in service of the gods, like the Pythias who mutter incoherently at Delphi. No wonder your Tiresias must be blind – it would be too much for a mortal to bear, to see the future clearly while simultaneously watching the events of the day.

But I'm straying from the story. Argia married Polynikes and Deipyle married Tydeus. And though my new sons-in-law were loyal to me, they were – like so many others among the newcomers – restless and ambitious. A king needs to keep such men busy.

So I organized journeys to Korinth to visit the Temple of Aphrodite. I held games, contests, and hunts. Upon rumors of monsters or powerful beasts, I sent the men on quests. And of course there was always the horse Arion – surely the steed of Amphiorax' prophecy: I challenged the men to capture him, though none succeeded.

We staged mock battles, dividing the soldiers into groups led by various noblemen to encourage competition. Polynikes chose the lion as badge of his troops, and Tydeus the boar; Hippomedon opted for a winged horse. I decided on the pomegranate, the fruit favored by Argos' patron goddess Hera, for my own battalion – besides, a red oval on a white background is easy for men to see. But Amphiorax refused to select anything.

"I need no such trappings," he said. "It's enough that my men are capable soldiers."

"But the men enjoy it!" I pointed out. We were standing on a hill above the training-grounds, where Tydeus' men were about to charge those commanded by Polynikes. The Boars were shouting the rousing battle-cry Tydeus had composed for them, while Polynikes' troops roared like lions.

Amphiorax folded his arms across his chest. "They should take their duties more seriously."

"You could choose the eagle as your symbol," I suggested. "The noble bird of Zeus."

"Why? Can my soldiers fly like eagles? They're men, not birds."

Parthenopeus, overseeing the mock battle, stuck two fingers in his mouth and let out a piercing whistle; the opposing forces sprang to action. Amphiorax and I watched the play of wooden training-swords and blunted spears; from time to time a referee judged a man a casualty and ordered him onto the sidelines. Gradually the din subsided, and conversation was possible once more.

I pointed to one corner of the battle, where a group of Boars – the highest-ranking wore a hammered bronze helmet with two whole boar's tusks jutting out from the brow – was gathering to defend a comrade from a pair of opponents with lions painted on their shields. "It's not just a matter of choosing something to inspire them. It keeps things organized."

"Vanity," Amphiorax grunted. "I've trained my men properly. They know to follow me."

Though he never admitted I was right, not long after this Amphiorax had the shields of his troops painted blue. When I asked him the reason for this choice, he would not answer, but later I realized the color was the hue of Eriphyle's eyes. Perversely, his soldiers seemed proud of having no emblem at all; and the Blues, as they called themselves, won more than their share of training battles.

I knew that I had the finest fighting force in Hellas. The men knew it too. They thirsted for a real battle.

Warriors need to shed blood; if they go too long without real combat they fight among themselves. Arguments sprang up over women, boys, wine, chariot-horses. Drunken insults led to brawls that left men injured or dead. My sons-in-law were always urging war: Tydeus wanted to take Kalydon, while Polynikes argued for invading Thebes.

Having created this force, I needed to lead it. Yet I still lacked the horse I needed to survive a battle. I did not have Arion.

By then, my best men had been chasing the horse for years, without success. And yet, when he arrived, Alkides – I suppose I should call him

Herakles – managed it so quickly! The gods were at work, shifting the currents of fate. Through the remainder of the summer and into the fall I made the magnificent horse my friend – that's a story in itself, one for another time – and with the assistance of a Thracian trainer I mastered the skill of riding. My leg was weak ever since my accident; I could not walk long distances, and driving a chariot was agony. But riding a horse… that, I could do.

Riding a horse is different from sitting on a donkey. You're lifted high. You see much more – like standing at the top of the Akrokorinth. There's freedom: horses can turn quickly, and race across rocky ground and through trees where chariots would fail. I don't know if I can explain. Arion and I, we became like a single creature. We understood one another; he responded to my movements and voice, and I listened to what he told me in return. The toss of his head, his snorting breath, the flash of his dark eyes: I knew his thoughts as well as I knew my own.

The swiftest steed was mine. The time for war had come.

I spoke of this to Amphiorax at the celebration for the winter solstice – but he did not give me his approval. "My lord king, I'm not sure."

"What do you mean?" I cried, the heat of my anger driving away winter's chill. "Arion *has* to be the horse of your prophecy! And without Alkides, Thebes is ripe for the picking."

"It seems that way," he said, and walked away from me.

I glanced up at Zeus' altar, where a pair of junior priests were butchering the sacrificial bull. Then I limped after my brother-in-law. "The men won't be contained another year," I said quietly. "They're restless already, and winter's just starting."

He gazed at an oak tree with brown leaves still clinging to its branches. A gust of wind stirred them, so that they fluttered and a few fell to the ground.

"Thebes is the logical target," I urged.

Amphiorax shrugged, still not meeting my eyes. "I can't argue with that."

"Then don't!" I grasped his shoulder. "Support me, Amphiorax!"

He let out a long breath. "Let me seek Zeus' will."

"The signs are plain enough to me," I snapped. Turning away, I limped back to where I had tethered Arion and, with my groomsman's assistance, climbed onto the horse.

Amphiorax stopped coming to the palace; he did not appear at the soldiers' training bouts, and even missed my morning audiences. When I told Phyle I needed to speak with her husband, she said she had seen little of him herself lately; he was spending most of his time in Zeus' temple. He was avoiding me when I most needed his support – and when Polynikes and Tydeus and other men kept urging me to make a decision.

After several days of this, I summoned both Amphiorax and Phyle to my private study. I remember a cold rain pouring down outside. When the servants had gone, closing the door behind them, I glared at my brother-in-law. "You said you'd come to me with a decision about making war on Thebes," I said. "What's taking so long?"

He glanced at Phyle, who was gazing indifferently at the wall paintings, and then faced me. "It's difficult, my lord king."

"Has Zeus given you an answer or not?"

"Well…"

"And? Will you support this endeavor?"

"My lord king, I would – I would rather not."

I slapped my hand on the table. "What's wrong, Amphiorax? My grandson is supposed to rule Thebes! How can he take the throne unless we go to war?"

For a long moment there was nothing but the sound of the rain outside. Finally my brother-in-law said: "He cannot."

"Then we have to attack!" I stepped around the table. "Amphiorax, why are you so reluctant? You're said to be brave – but your attitude stinks of cowardice!"

Though Phyle said nothing, her eyes widened; she *was* paying attention.

Amphiorax flushed darkly. "I cannot guarantee victory, my lord king."

"Did I ask you to?" I asked. "Let me and Arion see to that!"

"Adrastos, even *you* cannot command the Fates!"

"What are you talking about? Arion must be the horse from your prophecy – you yourself said he'd bring victory!"

"No, my lord king, I said he would save your life. That is not the same thing!"

I needed a few moments to comprehend. "You mean, we'll *lose*?"

"Not exactly… but…"

"But what?" I fumed.

"I – I cannot see the end of the battle. All grows dark."

Suddenly I understood why Amphiorax was avoiding me, avoiding this discussion. He believed this battle would mean *his* death. Could I blame him for not giving me his blessing? He wanted to live. That was natural enough.

But I also wanted to live. And if I did not take my men to war, I would face riots and rebellion.

Folding my arms across my chest, I said evenly: "I'm king of Argos, Amphiorax. I've decided to make war on Thebes. And *you* will lead your Blues into battle with the rest of the Argive army."

Amphiorax' jaw tightened. "I told you I would be a faithful counselor… and that I would tell you if I thought you were making a mistake. That's what I believe. Defeating a walled city is nearly impossible."

"If no one inside helps. But Polynikes is *from* Thebes. Surely someone will come to our side."

"Perhaps," he said. "But I believe our losses will be severe."

"Do you know this?" I pressed him. "Did the gods send you a vision?"

"No," he admitted. "But I still oppose this war."

I considered challenging his fear of death, but decided that would solidify his opposition. "We made an agreement, once – that, should we differ, Phyle would decide." I took a seat on the couch. "Sister, it's up to you. Shall we attack Thebes?"

For the first time she spoke. "You ask *me?*"

I nodded solemnly. "You know what's at stake, Phyle. You know the mood of the soldiers – and you know that Thebes has lost its greatest warrior, Alkides. If Argos is ever going to war, now is the time."

"You're trying to influence her," Amphiorax objected.

I laughed, getting to my feet once more. "And you won't? You're her husband; you have five children together. You have the clear advantage."

"I should," he muttered. His tone suggested doubt, but Amphiorax was always grim.

Phyle rose and walked to the far side of my study. The murals depicted various stories involving Argos' patron goddess; Phyle stopped near the image of Io in the form of a cow, guarded by a many-eyed watchman. "I must ask Hera for guidance," she said. She pulled her cloak tight and departed for the Heraion.

Amphiorax and I agreed to let Phyle pray over her decision in peace. But throughout the day – despite the rain – others made their way to Hera's temple. Kapaneus, Polynikes, and Tydeus all made offerings to the goddess; no doubt they sought to convince my sister that war was not only the best course for Argos but the will of the gods. Around dusk Amphiorax sent their eldest son, Alkmaeon, to the temple with a warm cloak and an offer to walk Phyle home. She refused, saying that she needed a night to commune with the goddess.

By morning the rain had stopped, and a large crowd gathered in the temple forecourt, hoping for word. Eriphyle emerged looking more radiant than ever. Because of the cold weather, her robes covered her from neck to toe, but a garland of evergreen twined with red, white, and rose-colored ribbons crowned her golden hair. Lifting slender arms, she announced that she would sacrifice to Hera in order to ascertain her will.

As Hera's acolytes, Argia and Deipyle brought forward a tawny heifer. I knew both my daughters wanted war: Argia, because victory would make her husband the king of Thebes; Deipyle, because her husband Tydeus could prove his valor and then argue for a second war against Kalydon. But I don't think the girls knew what Phyle would say. Both looked nervous, their gaze darting from their husbands to their aunt and back again.

Anxiety swelled within me. What if Phyle spoke against me? I would lose all authority!

The leaders of my battalions stood with me, watching as the beast was readied for sacrifice. Argia sprinkled meal on the animal's forehead, and brushed her hand down its nose to encourage its nod of consent. As the heifer's head dipped, my men stood straighter. Polynikes grinned; Hippomedon elbowed his friend Parthenopeus in the ribs and arched an eyebrow. Tydeus tugged nervously at his dark beard.

Amphiorax stood apart with his children. He had one hand on the shoulder of his eldest, Alkmaeon, while the other rested on the shoulder of his second son Amphilochus. Their little daughters were a few paces back, supervised by a serving woman. The younger boy muttered something when Phyle's knife drew across the heifer's throat, bright crimson blood welling up – but Amphiorax shushed him, warning him not to interrupt a ceremony sacred to the gods.

The kill was clean; the heifer crumpled to the ground, and soon its fat-wrapped thigh bones sizzled on Hera's altar. The morning was clear and windless; smoke streamed upwards to the domain of Hera and Zeus. Phyle wiped her bloodied fingers on a cloth that Argia offered her, and then tossed the red-smeared cloth onto the altar flames. Afterwards she turned to face the citizens of Argos, her blue-green eyes brilliant as jewels.

"We go to war," she said.

*

Adrastos looks at his sister, at his daughters. He remembers the excitement and elation he felt at Phyle's announcement – he recalls how the Argives cheered, how his daughters clapped their hands with joy. Now the girls' faces are twisted with sorrow and regret; Phyle's expression is more difficult to interpret. The Athenian soldiers, who returned from Apollo's temple while he was speaking, look on impassively from the edge of the laurel grove.

Resting his hands on his knees, he turns back to the young priest Haemon. "*That* is how the decision was made."

CHAPTER SIXTEEN
HAEMON

Haemon turns from the king of Argos to stare at the man's sister. "So *you're* responsible for what happened to Thebes. I can hardly believe it of a woman."

Phyle holds out her slim, long-fingered hands, palms upwards, the gesture of a suppliant. "My husband was right; I didn't understand war. If I'd known the horrors of battle, I would have decided otherwise – but songs of glory were all I knew. And every man in Argos, except my husband, wanted war. Still… I could have refused. I bear responsibility. That's why I've risked my own life by coming here to ask for the bodies."

Haemon's cousin Ismene nods. "It *is* brave of you," she acknowledges.

Not wanting to concede any virtue in the Argive woman, Haemon folds his arms across his chest and says nothing.

"Please, help us bring rest to our husbands' shades," says Deipyle, a tremor in her voice. "Amphiorax and Tydeus are at the mercy of the crows – they deserve better than that!"

Haemon feels his lip curl. "After what *your* husband did to Melanippus, he deserves far worse."

"We must punish the living when they offend," Phyle says. "But the dead should be sentenced only by the judges in the Underworld."

"I agree," says Ismene. "As does Antigone."

A sad smile graces Phyle's face. "Princess Ismene, your sister is the most courageous woman I've ever met."

"She is," Haemon agrees quietly. Grudgingly, he remembers that Phyle and Antigone were friends for years.

Phyle clasps her hands together. "Prince Haemon, might your father accept a ransom in exchange for the bodies?"

Haemon considers. "Such as?"

The Argives glance at each other. "They must have already stripped the corpses of every gem, every bit of gold and silver," says King Adrastos.

Ismene is about to speak, but Haemon holds up his hand to stop her; he is still not ready to trust these people. "You have your horse," he suggests.

A spasm of anguish crosses Adrastos' face, as if he had been asked to give away his daughters. After a moment he says: "Prince Haemon, Arion is a willful beast. He will not permit most men to mount. King Creon – at his age, he should not risk it."

A fair point, Haemon admits silently. "Well, then… tribute?"

None of the Argives meets his gaze. Haemon senses that they are hiding something – but whether it is a cache of jewels or complete penury he cannot tell. Before he can pursue this further, Ismene breaks in: "Would you consider taking Antigone with you?"

Haemon flicks a reproachful glance at his cousin, but now that the topic has been raised it must be pursued. He turns back to the Argives, and sees the king's eyebrows lift as if this has not even occurred to him.

"Of course!" says Adrastos. "But why would this move King Creon? He wants her to die."

Hesitantly, Ismene says: "I believe – I believe he regrets his decision. He might welcome a reason to change it. But if he releases her she couldn't stay here."

"You think he would give us the bodies if we take Antigone?" asks Deipyle.

"Maybe," says Haemon. "But first we should make sure Antigone is willing to go with you."

King Adrastos stares at him. "You mean she might prefer to *die?*"

"She has her own priorities," Phyle says. "I remember how little she cared about clothes and jewels, about making herself beautiful. She chose exile to be with her father. She might choose death to be with her brothers."

Haemon studies the Argive priestess, considering. Finally he says, "She is very strong-willed. And my father would not offer her freedom unless he was sure she would accept it."

"Of course not," says Adrastos. "No king would."

"So," says Ismene, "let's go ask Antigone."

Haemon sees confusion on the Argives' faces. "We've been talking to her from the tomb of Eteokles," he explains. "There's a crack between the caves." Belatedly, he remembers the Athenian guards; he glances back at them, then shrugs. It makes little difference that they know.

"Very well," says Phyle, rising to her feet, briskly taking charge. "At the very worst, she or Creon will refuse – but who knows? They might agree."

"Wait," Adrastos says. "We're in danger if we stay; yesterday King Creon told us to leave Theban lands. Will you guarantee our safety, Prince Haemon?"

Haemon lifts his chin. "I will. As high priest of Apollo, I can do that. Leave your Athenian mercenaries here – it will be safer that way."

These words do not fully dispel the Argive king's frown; but when his sister and daughters make ready to go, Adrastos gets to his feet and puts the wig back on his head. Soon the five of them are walking together down the hill. Haemon steals a glance at the priestess of Hera – this woman who has been Antigone's friend. If he cannot convince his wife to accept the bargain, perhaps Phyle can.

And as a priestess of Hera, goddess of marriage, surely she will allow Haemon to accompany his wife to Argos.

What will it be like to live in the city of the enemy?

His father will never forgive him for going. But he allowed his father's will – and his own shame – to keep them apart before. He will not make that mistake again.

The sun is high and the air warm by the time they reach the caves. In accordance with the king's orders, no one loiters nearby; but people are passing along the path that leads from the city past the tombs to the Temple of Apollo. And some of those passers-by must have stopped along the way, because there are even more flowers at the base of Antigone's wall.

The night watchmen have been replaced by the morning guards; the new men look on Phyle with suspicion. One points at her, saying: "The king ordered you and your people to leave."

"They're here on my authority," Haemon says, his tone reminding the man that he is Apollo's high priest and the king's eldest son. "They are my guests."

The soldiers exchange a glance, and the one who has not spoken shrugs. Without further objection they step away from the door and let Haemon push it open.

Entering the tomb has become like returning to a familiar room. Ismene takes the lamp he left burning by the door and places it in a central position; she adds oil and another wick to increase the light. Haemon notices that Adrastos keeps his distance from Eteokles' grave-mound, as if his presence could offend the dead. *Eteokles, be at rest,* Haemon silently instructs his cousin's shade. *This man is here to help your sister. And after what I've learned of you lately, you have no right to claim wounded dignity.*

As the others take seats on the floor, Haemon walks over to the wall. Wryly he notes that although his efforts with the axe were futile, at least the fissure is easier to find. "Antigone!" he shouts. "Antigone!"

There is no answer.

"Antigone!" Ismene draws close and adds her voice to his. "Sister, we're here!"

Haemon calls out again; his voice echoes in the chamber, but still there is no response. Fear swells within him. Is Antigone already too weak to answer? Surely it is too soon for her to have died! "Antigone!"

"Hush," whispers Ismene, holding up one hand. She presses her ear to the wall. "I hear her!"

Haemon falls silent; his heartbeat pounds loud in his ears. Then he detects his wife's voice, faint and raspy: "Still alive… but, my throat… hurts to talk…"

"Then just listen for now," Ismene tells her. "Haemon and I have others with us – people from Argos. You know them: Eriphyle, Argia and Deipyle – and King Adrastos. They're willing to take you back to Argos with them. If you agree to go, we'll ask Uncle Creon."

There is a long silence; finally, Antigone says: "He'll refuse."

"Please, Antigone, let *us* worry about that," Haemon says. "Just tell us you agree. Father will have to be sure of that."

This time there is only a moment's hesitation. "The gods mean to punish your father for his lack of piety." Her words are suddenly strong and clear, as if she has been nourishing herself with this thought, gnawing on it after finishing the stale bread. "He knows he's in the wrong, and the guilt he will suffer for my death is the gods' punishment."

"Forget about Uncle Creon!" Ismene cries. "Antigone, we want to help *you!*"

"Please, Antigone, listen to your sister," Phyle adds, and the king's daughters add their voices: "There has been enough death!" "We want to help you!"

"Only the gods can help me now."

"The gods," Haemon mutters, too softly for her to hear. He has been praying to the gods these last few hours – these last few days – these last few months – these last few years. Their assistance seems so close at times – and at other times so impossibly distant.

"Are you so sure you know the gods' will?" challenges Argia.

Haemon shakes his head; this is exactly the wrong thing to say to Antigone. Predictably, she retorts: "Are *you* sure?"

Haemon slaps his hand against the wall in frustration. After so many years they are finally speaking to one another, connecting with one another; will she throw away the chance to be together? He cannot let that happen.

"Listen to me, Antigone. Listen, and for once don't argue. After I tell you what happened during the war, perhaps you'll have more sympathy for my father. And once I tell you why I want you to live – and how we can be husband and wife at last – perhaps you'll be willing to try."

He glances around at his listeners. Parts of this story will be difficult to tell with so many people listening. But Ismene already knows much of it. And the Argives – why should he care what they think? Beyond the gods and ghosts who may be listening, the only audience that matters is his wife, who has good reason to be disappointed in him. But perhaps the deity he serves will help him reach Antigone's heart.

He gazes at the flames burning in the lamp. "Bright Apollo, bless my words," he prays, then begins.

HAEMON

It was the middle of spring when the stranger arrived at Apollo's temple. Udaeus, although much more skilled with medicine than I, asked me to join him in the healers' area.

The window-shutters were open to admit the sunlight; a breeze freshened the air. Passing the bedside of a man who had broken his arm during the calving, I offered Apollo's blessing. I asked an acolyte how an ailing old woman was doing, and learned that Udaeus had decided to treat her with foxglove. I nodded. The medicine would either cure her or kill her, but either way should end her misery.

Then I came to where my colleague sat with the stranger. I was shocked by the color of the patient's skin. "He has the liver sickness?"

Udaeus looked up. "I thought so, but he tells me all his people look like that."

I pulled up a stool. "Where's he from?" The patient's eyes were long and narrow, more so even than an Aegyptian's, and his beard was only a scanty collection of black whiskers. Beads of fever-sweat dotted his brow and dampened his hair, which was as coarse and straight as a horse's tail.

"East," said the stranger. "Far, far east – five year travel, yes. Five year." His accent had an odd rhythm; he lengthened some words and clipped others short.

"Five *years*?" That seemed unlikely; surely you would reach the ends of the earth in less time than that. But I wasn't about to call the man a liar. "Why journey so long?"

"Ah," he said, his black eyes flashing as he held up a single finger. "Seek fruit of immortality. Eat one, live for thousand year."

"That's why I asked you here, Haemon," my colleague said. "Do you think he means the golden apples of the Hesperides?"

I considered. "Possibly."

The stranger struggled to sit up – then grimaced and hissed with pain, clutching his belly. Udaeus placed a gentle hand on the man's thin shoulder. "Don't tire yourself, Shan. You must rest."

"But – you know this fruit! Where? How far?"

Udaeus explained, "He begged me to ask you about it."

"No one really knows," I admitted. "At the western edge of the world, they say."

"How far?" the man called Shan persisted. "How many day travel?"

"Delphi is the center of the world," I told him. "And that's only a few days' journey from here. The western edge of the world must be at least as far as you've traveled already."

"So far..." he whispered. He closed his narrow eyes for a long moment; when he opened them again, they sparkled with moisture. "So far I can never go. I healer – know illness. I live two day, maybe three. Then die for sure."

"Maybe not," I said. "Udaeus is skilled."

But Udaeus touched my arm and shook his head slightly before saying: "We'll do what we can to make you comfortable." He called for an acolyte to bring a basin of water and a sponge, and asked me to stay with the traveler while he prepared a dose of poppy juice.

Shan sighed as the youth daubed his brow with mint-scented water. "Thank you," he said. He touched a pendant he wore on a glossy cord around his neck; it was carved from some milky stone with a greenish tinge – a more delicate shade than green marble, serpentine, or malachite. "You good people. At least not die alone."

"You've traveled such a long way," I said. "You must have seen so much."

"Yes, much." He shifted his tunic so that the boy could sponge his chest. A spasm of pain struck; Shan drew a sharp breath between clenched teeth. Udaeus hurried over with the poppy juice. The foreigner swallowed it with difficulty, and soon the lines of anguish in his tawny face began to soften.

"You good people, but I die," he said again. "You take my possession. Open bag."

I protested that he might yet live.

"You not understand," he said. "Open bag now to explain. If I dead, you ask – I cannot answer." His command of our language was imperfect, but his logic was sound.

I thought perhaps he carried gold and jewels to trade for the fruit of immortality; but instead the treasure was dozens of cloth pouches tied shut with cords of different colors. Udaeus sniffed and his eyes widened at the mélange of scents. "Healer's herbs?"

"I collect," Shan said. "From home, from my travel. Hold up and I say what they do."

Udaeus opened the first packet and poured into his palm a pile of things like tiny, fragrant brown nails. Shan called them cloves.

"I've heard of these," said Udaeus. "They help with toothache."

"Also digestion," said Shan. "First thing I try, when pain start in belly. But clove cannot cure *this*."

Udaeus replaced the cloves and tied shut the pouch, then opened another; it held small, dried berries of black, green and red. "Pepper," said Shan. "Grind, make you sneeze. Aegyptian put in nose of dead."

That substance was unfamiliar to us, but the next few Udaeus and I knew: wolfsbane and spikenard, belladonna and mint. Others followed – herbs and medicines from distant lands with unfamiliar names, some sweet-smelling and some pungent. The last item, from the very bottom of the bag, was a large pouch of brittle gray leaves. "From silver-fruit tree. Help men have sex."

I blinked. "What did you say?"

Shan smiled weakly. "Not help all men. Only men who faint."

Antigone, my wife – listen to me now. Listen carefully. If you've ever blamed yourself for my – my failure on our wedding night, you must stop. The fault was mine.

I was too ashamed to speak of it, then – and too young to understand. Already I hated myself for being unmanly: I was a poor hunter, a miserable athlete, easily tired and dizzy. And then, to make it worse, I proved a total failure as a husband. But over the years that I served in Apollo's temple I learned that other men sometimes had such symptoms. Finally I confessed my weakness to Udaeus. He offered various cures for my impotence – lentils, bitter bulbs, truffles and leeks – but nothing helped. I could not have taken another woman to my bed if I wanted to. Not that I wanted anyone else, Antigone! It was *you,* always you.

Now Shan, who had traveled so far, offered a completely new cure – and he came from the east, the land of Apollo. Perhaps these leaves from the distant silver-fruit tree were, at last, a gift from the god – the cure I had begged him for.

I asked the traveler several more questions, and then – with a pointed glance – Udaeus tied shut the packet and handed it to me. I tucked it into my tunic.

By then Shan was drowsy from the poppy syrup. Udaeus urged him to sleep; the man nodded, saying he thought he would not die just yet, and closed his eyes. Udaeus carried the precious bag of medicines across the room and placed it in a chest painted with Apollo's sun-chariot, where we stored our rarest herbs. The light of the afternoon sun streaming through the west-facing window lit the brightly colored chest, and – though I've never been especially gifted with the art of reading omens – it seemed like a sign of the god's blessing.

I was about to ask Udaeus what he thought of Shan's silver-fruit leaves when we were joined by a new arrival: a runner sent by King Eteokles.

"Lord Haemon," he panted, "you're needed at the palace. You as well, lord Udaeus."

"Why?" I asked. "What's happened?"

The messenger rubbed his side. "The Tiresias has returned from Athens."

As Apollo's high priest, my greeting him made sense. But since Udaeus was summoned too, I asked if the Tiresias was unwell.

"The king wants our best healer," said the runner.

"Of course," Udaeus said, and went to fetch his healer's bag.

I bent down to adjust my right sandal, which needed mending. Without looking up, I asked the messenger: "Who came with the Tiresias?"

Antigone, I wanted to know about *you.* I thought this too could be an omen, a sign of the Fates' mercy – the Tiresias arriving from Athens on the same day that the barbarian gave me what might finally be a cure. Perhaps you had come as well! But I was too ashamed to ask about you directly.

"His daughters," the messenger said, accepting a cup of water from an acolyte. "A few servants, and the driver of their mule-cart."

I tinkered with my sandal to hide my disappointment. If you had come, the fellow surely would have mentioned it. But at least, I reminded myself, the Tiresias and his daughters would bring news of you. And Shan had warned me that the treatment needed time to work.

Udaeus returned with his bag, and we left for the city. Our walk seemed unremarkable at the time, but now… now, thinking back, I'm struck by how *normal* everything was. The trees were in their first flush of green; violets and crocuses dotted the edge of the path. I saw peasants carting in wood for the city hearths; a pair of small boys threw sticks for their dogs to fetch, and down at the stream women were rinsing laundry. At the time I paid no attention to the beauty all around me; instead, I was annoyed as we crossed the bridge over the Chrysorrhoas because my sandal kept slipping at the heel.

When we reached the palace it was late afternoon; the king was on his throne and many of Thebes' nobility, including my father, had also gathered in the megaron. The Tiresias, it seemed, had just been carried into the room on a litter; his servants rested this on a pair of benches placed near the central hearth. Though the seer had once been plump, now he was wasted and frail. Hearing the herald announce me and Udaeus, he struggled to push himself up onto his elbows.

"Apollo," he said, his voice weak and unsteady. "Apollo tells me – danger!"

Around me, people gasped. Fear struck me like cold, wind-driven rain; dizzy, I reached out to steady myself against a column.

King Eteokles rose from the throne and descended towards the prophet. "What do you mean, Tiresias? What danger?"

The old man fell back against the litter. He reached beneath his black-dyed blindfold to rub one eye, as though that might help him see more clearly. "Danger to Thebes," he said, his voice growing fainter. His daughters bent over him, concern on their faces.

King Eteokles turned to me. "You're the high priest of Apollo. What is he talking about?"

I shook my head helplessly, and glanced at my father. I knew he mistrusted the Tiresias' prophecies – not because they failed to come true, but because they were so often fulfilled in unexpected and inconvenient ways. This vague warning, though, was different than the Tiresias' usual puzzling prophecies.

I asked Daphne, "Has he told you anything else?"

She shook her head. "I'm sorry."

Manto knelt beside the litter. "Can you say anything more, Father?"

"Thebes – danger comes." The old man shook his head feebly, then muttered a few slurred syllables that I couldn't make out.

"That's *it?*" King Eteokles' voice grew louder. "What *kind* of threat is it? How soon?"

Next to Eteokles in his red and gold tunic, little Manto in her plain brown dress was like a tiny sparrow confronting an eagle. "It must be serious, my lord king. Father insisted we come as quickly as possible."

The king sighed. "Perhaps he'll say more later. Udaeus, see what you can do for him."

My colleague nodded. "Yes, my lord king."

Eteokles then turned to me. "Haemon? What can you do?"

"I'll seek Apollo's guidance overnight." Noticing the king did not seem satisfied, I added: "And offer sacrifice tomorrow at noon, when the god's chariot is directly overhead."

"Noon tomorrow," said Eteokles, then turned to talk to Melanippus, the captain of the guard, while Udaeus and I followed the Tiresias' litter out of the room.

"He's been very agitated," Daphne offered as we walked toward the rear door of the palace, which was closer to the Tiresias' house. "He insisted we come to Thebes as quickly as possible."

Manto added, "He wanted us to keep moving through the night! But the driver said he and his mules didn't have the second sight."

"Still," Daphne said, "Father insisted we break camp at dawn."

"A hard journey, for an old man," Udaeus said. "Even one in the best of health." Which, of course, the Tiresias was not.

The sun was nearing the horizon by the time we reached the seer's home. A servant who tended the place in the family's absence opened the door for us, and lit several lamps. Udaeus and I followed the Tiresias' litter through a room filled with treasures from faraway lands: ancient, eyeless marble heads from the islands; a bronze statuette of a strange, many-armed goddess; unfamiliar weapons with odd, curving blades; the skulls of many animals, including a monstrous one that Daphne said was a crocodile from the Nile in Aegypt. I wondered if any came from Shan's distant home.

The servants settled the Tiresias into his bed, then Manto removed his blindfold. "It irritates his skin," she told Udaeus.

Udaeus felt the old man's pulse and listened to his heart.

"Sometimes he has trouble breathing," Daphne said.

My colleague nodded. "Does the breath come too quickly sometimes, and other times very slow?"

Daphne nodded. "Last night I worried he'd stopped breathing altogether. But then he woke with a gasp."

The prophet seemed unaware of what we were saying. His unseeing eyes were open; their slow motions seemed random, but the eyes themselves were not milky, as some old people's become. Of course, he had lost his sight from a wound to the head rather than any injury to his eyes.

Udaeus took his bag to a side table and began preparing a mixture of herbs. "He's dehydrated; make him drink more water. With more water in his system, he may be lucid. These herbs should help too." He explained the dosage to Manto and Daphne.

We needed to get back to the temple, to offer prayers to Apollo and prepare for the next day's sacrifice. But as Manto escorted us to the door, I finally asked the question pressing my heart. "What can you tell me about Antigone? Is she still in Colonus?"

"Yes." Manto stopped at a table near the front door, running her finger over a round-bellied vase painted with jagged dark lines. "Look at this dust! The servants have gotten lazy."

"Is she well?" I prodded.

"What? Oh, yes, Antigone! She's fine, Haemon. She's still serving as a priestess to Athena. Everyone admires her weaving – her last tapestry showed Apollo slaying the python at Delphi."

The servant ahead of us opened the door, and Udaeus stepped out into the dusk; we needed to go. Still, I paused to ask: "Does she ever mention me?"

Resting a small hand on the doorjamb, Manto tilted her head. "Not often. Once, though, a man asked to marry her... she explained she was already married."

My heart thudded hard. "Does – does she *often* receive such proposals?"

"I couldn't say. I happened to be visiting her when this particular man came to call. He was a cloth merchant from Tyre – a widower, and very impressed with her skills at the loom. But, given what she said, I don't think she would accept any man's offer of marriage." Manto smiled knowingly. "She hasn't forgotten you, Haemon."

These words gave me hope – but just then I could do nothing more. My duty was to Thebes, and helping the king make sense of the Tiresias' vague prophecy. Udaeus and I returned to the temple, hurrying as night fell. Udaeus checked on the patients in the healers' wing; he reported that the foxglove was helping the elderly woman and that the fellow with the broken arm needed his bandage changed. While Shan still lived, Udaeus agreed with the traveler's self-diagnosis: that type of abdominal spasm always killed within a few days.

After lighting incense and chanting prayers, Udaeus and I and the junior priests placed our pallets before the image of Apollo to seek his guidance in dreams. But I didn't sleep well – perhaps the effect of my first dose of silver-fruit leaves, but also my restless mind kept turning to thoughts of you, Antigone, mixed with worries over the Tiresias' warning. King Eteokles expected me, as chief priest of Apollo, to find the truth; but my best insights had always come from discussions with you.

Eventually I slept, but the god sent me no dreams, and none of the other priests reported any helpful visions. So we set about preparing for the mid-day ritual. By late morning the temple forecourt was jammed; everyone in Thebes had heard about the Tiresias' warning, and wanted to know what the future held – whether the danger could possibly be averted. I saw the Tiresias' daughter Daphne at the front of the crowd, standing with you,

Mother, as well as you, Ismene, and my brother Menoeceus and my other siblings; nearby, at the base of the temple steps, King Eteokles consulted his advisors. Captain Melanippus was reacting to some comment from Lasthenes the herd-master; King Eteokles shook his head, and turned to ask my father something. Though the king was elegantly dressed in a saffron-dyed cape and kilt with thick red-patterned borders, he looked as though he had slept even less than I. There were dark circles beneath his eyes; lines of fatigue creased his forehead.

I signaled to the junior priest holding the lyre, and he plucked the first notes of the sacred melody. The crowd fell silent, and I stepped out onto the highest tread of the temple stairs. The sky was full of patchy gray clouds, an uncertain omen; but the ritual went according to plan as I led the opening hymn. Just as the sun reached its zenith, an acolyte led forward the sacrifice: a fine-looking ram with perfectly curved horns. But as I sprinkled meal across the animal's head, I noticed the nervous movements of its eyes – and I feared that the calming herbs had not worked. I could not speak without interrupting the ritual, but I did catch Udaeus' eye; that was enough to warn him. When I lifted the knife and took the ram's forelock, it struggled, and the startled acolyte dropped the lead-rope. If Udaeus had not been quick and strong the animal would have darted out into the crowd – an unmistakable sign of the gods' disfavor.

But Udaeus managed to snatch the rope and keep the beast under control long enough for me to slit its throat. After that I was afraid to see what dire signs lurked in the animal's entrails – but of course, the ceremony had to be completed. To my relief, the organs were well-formed and healthy. I rose from the carcass slowly and carefully, lest a dizzy spell strike me; when we laid the god's portion on the altar-flames, the smoke rose straight up towards the cloudy sky.

What was I to say of the omens? The people of Thebes had accepted me as Apollo's chief priest – partly because of Father's reputation for wise leadership, I think, and partly because I have a good singing voice. But I've never thought myself blessed with the gift of prophecy. In my years as Apollo's priest, I've simply tried to draw some logical connection between the signs and the events of the day. Apollo is the god of reason, after all; perhaps that satisfies him.

I drew my shoulders back, and said loudly: "As the ram struggled against the knife, Thebes may face struggles as well. But the organs were sound, and Apollo has accepted our sacrifice – so whatever dangers we face, if we persist, we will prevail."

This brought a cheer from the gathered citizens; King Eteokles smiled at me and then turned to face his people. "We will prevail!" he repeated.

The people seemed greatly reassured, and soon were talking more about the smell of roasting mutton than about the as-yet-unspecified danger. But King Eteokles beckoned me. "The god told you nothing of what this danger is?"

I reached up to adjust my laurel garland. "No, my lord king. But the city has not lost his favor. The god will make things plain to us at the proper time."

We had less time to wait than I thought. Even as I spoke, there was a commotion on the crowd's southern edge. I heard the words *war* and *attack* – and then the people parted to make way for a sweaty fellow in traveling clothes, breathing hard. "My lord king," he gasped, "Argive soldiers are coming!"

It took only a heartbeat for this announcement to register. "Polynikes!" said King Eteokles, and his twin's name sounded like a curse. Then he demanded: "How long do we have?"

The traveler bowed and removed his broad-brimmed straw hat. I recognized him – a metals trader, one I'd met in the workshop of Aktor the bronze-smith. "I was in Athens, my lord king," he said. "The Argive ships arrived there the day before yesterday."

"Just after we left!" Daphne exclaimed.

Eteokles nodded his gold-crowned head. "Go on."

"When I heard they were going to march on Thebes, I came as fast as I could, my lord king. They can't move as quick as I did, not with that big army—"

"*How* big?" interrupted Melanippus.

The trader let out a low whistle. "Big. Forty, maybe fifty ships?"

"A day for them to unload and form up," Melanippus speculated. "Three days' march, if they push hard."

Lasthenes counted on his fingers. "That means they're here two days from now."

"Best plan for tomorrow," Father advised.

Eteokles nodded briskly. "Melanippus – send out scouting parties. At once." The man bowed, gathered a team, and loped off toward the city.

Clutching his hat, the trader added: "I warned all the peasants I saw along my way, my lord king. They'll be headed here."

Eteokles drew a deep breath and released it slowly, as though preparing himself. Then he turned to the Master of the Herds. "Lasthenes, do what you can with the cattle. Bring as many animals inside the walls as you can manage." Next he summoned the young nobleman Eurymedon, who had been supervising repairs at the Chloris Gate; after receiving a brief status report, Eteokles sent him off with orders to press every stonemason and carpenter in the city into service. He asked my father to take soldiers with him and to identify and expel all foreigners, as they could be spies; merchants' goods were to be confiscated. "Tell them we'll pay them later."

Father tapped his staff on the ground. "Most will want to leave Thebes in any event. I'll advise them to go north, and remind them they'll travel faster with no burdens."

Eteokles ordered the trader Hyperbius to empty the granaries south of the city, bringing all the grain and flour inside the walls: "Stack the bags in the street, if you have to. And anything else that might be stored in the countryside – wine, dried fruit – get that inside. Let's not feed the enemy." He charged Aktor the bronze-smith with arming all Thebes' fighting men, and told my brother Menoeceus to send runners to the allied cities Orchomenos and Gla, asking for support and assistance. Mother and Ismene were to supervise the women of Thebes in filling every available amphora, pot, urn, and vessel with water; if fire broke out, the wells inside the walls might not furnish the needed water quickly enough. My job was to transport the treasures of Apollo's temple, and the patients in the healers' wing, safely into the city. "I don't trust Polynikes to respect the sanctity of the temple," the king said.

I wondered whether Eteokles' ban on foreigners would extend to poor Shan – but that night he died anyway.

Before last spring, I knew nothing of war. My first lesson was that war is as much about waiting as it is about fighting. We were busy with preparations, we had a sense of purpose; yet the battle was not upon us. Each time I looked up at the watchmen patrolling the walls I wondered how long it would be until one of them cried out that the enemy had been sighted.

Meanwhile peasants and their flocks streamed into the city, until Thebes was like a grain-sack bursting at the seams. Some made camp in the agora or in the side streets; others were given a place to sleep on the floor in various houses around the city. Everywhere I went there were crying children; each time I turned a corner I startled a flock of geese, or stepped into a pile of goat-dung, or collided with some toothless grandmother carrying a basket of dried figs.

The day after the metal trader's warning, Melanippus' scouting parties announced that they'd located the advancing army; given the Argives' speed, we had another day to prepare. Aktor supervised the distribution of weaponry to those who did not have their own; throughout the city archers readied their arrows and bows while soldiers honed their spears, swords, and javelins. Because the alarm had not yet gone out, only the men stationed at the gates and along the walls carried shields and wore their helmet, cuirass, and greaves; but Eteokles sported his war-helmet because the red-dyed horsehair crest made him more visible as he gave commands.

He stopped to speak with me near the Neaira Gate; I was supervising a chain of men as they passed stones of various sizes – baskets of rocks small enough for slings, individual stones large enough to crush an invader's head if he ventured too close – up to the top of the wall. As we worked, peasants streamed through the open gate; they clutched runny-nosed children, ragged blankets, leather sacks and wicker baskets stuffed with whatever they considered valuable.

Looking at the refugees, Eteokles folded his arms across his chest. "Despite everything, right now I wish Alkides was with us."

I understood. He'd murdered my sister and my nephews – but in wartime he'd be an asset. "I just hope he's not helping the Argives."

Beneath his ivory-tiled helmet, the king's blue eyes narrowed. "He swore an oath of loyalty to Thebes."

A few paces away, my brother Menoeceus observed: "Not all men keep their promises." Just then a pair of lambs strayed from the flock of sheep that a peasant girl was herding; Menoeceus left to usher them towards a makeshift pen along the wall.

Eteokles stared after him, the line of his lips hardening. I wondered if he remembered his own promise to yield the throne every other year to Polynikes.

"Runner!" shouted a watchman atop the wall, pointing south. "Runner approaching!"

Menoeceus left the livestock and shoved his way through the crowd. "Make way! Make way!" Somehow he cleared a path, and the runner in his drab scouting-tunic sprinted through the gate. "Not long now," the man gasped. "They'll be here soon!"

I told the team conveying stones we were done for now. They put their last load into place, and then made room for the king on the stairs. Menoeceus and I followed.

Eteokles looked down at the crowd of peasants outside the walls. "Thebans!" he shouted. "Hear your king! Make haste! Pass word back – those further away should go to the Eudoxa Gate!"

There was shouting and consternation down below; those nearest surged towards the gate, and I feared some would be crushed, but the gate soldiers used the butt-ends of their spears to block what might otherwise have become a stampede. Most of those further away turned northeast; the Eudoxa was not far. The guards urged forward a man with a donkey-cart laden with firewood, and helped a pretty young woman with two small children inside.

"There, my lord king," said the watchman, pointing. He was a potter's son – a young fellow with keen eyesight and a fondness for pranks, but his beardless face was deadly serious. I followed the direction of his outstretched finger and saw the dust cloud rising in the distance.

"They'll be here soon," Menoeceus said.

"Archers!" Eteokles shouted. "Archers, to the walls!" The cry was echoed back through the crowd, and men with bows pushed towards the stone stairs on either side of the gate.

Grizzled Melanippus pushed his way through the crowd; he donned his war-helmet and hurried up the stairs towards the king. My brother and I stepped back to make room.

"My lord king." He bowed, the polished knob of brass that topped his helmet gleaming. "They won't attack from the march – we can keep the gate open until they come closer to weapons range."

Eteokles nodded. "I want all Thebans inside. But shut those gates when you have to."

I shaded my eyes with my hand, trying to see more, but could not make out details. Then I heard the sound of the enemy's keras horns. Feeling dizzy, I gripped the parapet. I realized this was the first time I'd felt dizzy since trying the silver-fruit leaves; maybe they *were* helping. I was a poor soldier – but perhaps the silver-fruit leaves would make it possible for me to fight. A man who cannot help defend his city is no man.

"How many are there?" the king asked Melanippus.

"Best guess, about two thousand. A hundred chariots, maybe, the rest foot soldiers. Advance force of two hundred or so, approaching with flanking forces. Don't know how they'll form up as they get closer."

The keras sounded again, and beneath their notes I heard a low rumble, like distant thunder. The sound of four thousand marching feet, two hundred horses pounding the earth, pack animals and servants… I detected movement, now, in the distance. A dark line, lit by the occasional flash of a spear-point catching the rays of the late afternoon sun. The line grew longer and thicker, as it approached – and gradually I made out individual forms.

"Close the gates! Bar all but Kleodoxa!" Melanippus bellowed. Along the walls to our left and right, men echoed his order, passing the word to their fellows nearer the next gate.

Praise Apollo, by then all the refugees who had been down below were inside or on their way to another gate; stragglers could still pass through the Kleodoxa until that was barred as well. I heard the creaking of the Neaira Gate's two bronze-bound doors, each twice as tall as a man, as they swung in their pivot-holes; I felt the thud as men slid the heavy oaken crossbar into place.

"I see two chariots," said the potter's son, squinting. "No, three. And – and – a *centaur!*"

"What?" exclaimed the king.

My brother Menoeceus shook his head. "That's no centaur – it's a man, riding a horse."

"That's the biggest horse *I've* ever seen, my lord," the youth responded.

With so few approaching, this had to be a parley rather than an attack. Straining my eyes to make out the details as the enemy drew closer, I recognized my cousin Polynikes in one of the chariots. A second carried a tall, handsome warrior with dark hair spilling out from beneath his helmet; a boar's head was painted on the front of his chariot. The third assailant was a stocky, muscular man with a blue-painted shield; his charioteer wore a blue-dyed kilt.

Then there was the man riding the horse. The steed was breathtaking in its size and beauty: creamy white, with red cords binding its dark gray mane into an elegant line of tufts. The rider's beard was sandy blond, sprinkled with silver; I guessed this was King Adrastos of Argos.

The main army remained behind, beating their swords and spears against their shields in a sinister rhythm to summon the war-god Ares and his sons Fear and Terror, as the three chariots and the warrior on the horse approached.

"No archers," Melanippus observed. "Just the men and their charioteers."

"They could have bows concealed in the chariots," said my brother.

"Our archers are ready," Eteokles said, sweeping his gaze along the line of the wall. Twenty of our best bowmen had lined up, bows ready, each ready to let fly through one of the gaps in the battlement.

The warriors drew to a stop about a spear's throw from the walls; behind them the army's keras blared, and the warriors stopped pounding their shields. In the sudden silence, the warrior in the chariot painted with a boar's head jumped down. With a quick glance back at his charioteer and the others, he strode forward, holding up something much shorter than a sword.

"What's in his hand?" I asked, puzzled. "A dagger?"

"An olive branch," said the potter's son. "Ha, maybe he's come to surrender!"

"Take aim, archers, but hold your fire," Eteokles commanded. "Shooting someone carrying an olive branch will anger the gods, unless they attack first."

Below, the warrior spread his tanned, muscular arms wide. Now he was close enough that I could see the olive branch for myself. "I am Tydeus of Kalydon!" he shouted in a booming voice. "Son-in-law to King Adrastos of Argos and brother-in-law to King Polynikes of Thebes! Hear us out, Thebans, and you may avoid bloodshed!"

Menoeceus and I exchanged glances.

"*King* Polynikes," Eteokles muttered. "The gall!"

"Open your gates, Thebans!" the man called Tydeus continued. "Open your gates to your true king, and no one need suffer!"

Eteokles rested both hands on the parapet. "*I* am king of Thebes! Not that pretender Polynikes!"

"Some king Polynikes is," commented the potter's son. "Sends another man to do his talking. Not like Eteokles." Melanippus silenced him with an angry hiss.

Then I heard Polynikes' voice – fainter than that of Tydeus, but discernible. "You're a liar, Eteokles! A liar, and a cheat!"

"People of Thebes," boomed Tydeus, his gesture with the olive branch taking in all the archers positioned along the wall. "You need not die for Eteokles!"

That drew jeering from the archers, the watchmen, and even the people in the streets down below. Among the cresting wave of shouts, hisses, and boos I heard: "Who are *you* to tell us who's king?" and "King Eteokles!" and "*You'll* die, not us!"

Eteokles grinned, surely heartened by the Thebans' mood. "You can't take this city! Our walls are strong – and our people are stronger! Be gone, or we'll send you for a swim in the Styx!"

"You choose war, Theban?" bellowed Tydeus.

"No, my brother chooses it!" Eteokles shouted. "If he wants to die a traitor, so be it!"

Tydeus relayed the information to the two other commanders standing in their war chariots, and all three charioteers turned their vehicles around – with obvious skill – as did the man on the horse. The first two chariots, carrying the war commanders Polynikes and Amphiorax, departed, then Tydeus climbed into the back of his. He tossed aside his olive branch, and yelled: "Then war it is!" Before his chariot headed to regroup with the Argive army, he took a javelin from his chariot and hurled it towards Eteokles.

It was an amazing cast, though largely symbolic: Eteokles had time to dodge. But as the Fates would have it, the potter's son, who had turned away to call down information, took the weapon in the throat. The bronze blade pierced the back of his neck and split all the way through, emerging below his chin awash in bright crimson. I'll never forget the look on his young face: utter astonishment. Then he choked, blood spilling from his mouth, and crumpled. Men behind him jumped away from the javelin-shaft as he fell.

"Archers!" cried Eteokles. "Let fly!"

But the enemy chariots were already speeding back towards their army; a chariot horse took an arrow in its rump, but that was the only damage we inflicted. Quickly the targets were beyond range of our arrows and the archers stopped their volley.

Eteokles watched them depart, then looked down at the fallen youth, surrounded by shocked and horrified friends. "He gave his blood for Thebes," he announced to us all, and then, to a senior officer, "See that he gets a proper funeral." This said, he turned and headed down the stairway, beckoning for me, Menoeceus, and Melanippus to follow; as we went down the narrow steps, I saw my father had arrived. When King Eteokles reached the base of the stairs people cheered, as though we'd won a battle – though the only person to die had been a Theban. To me it seemed wrong, but Eteokles smiled and let the cheering go on a while before he lifted his hand for silence. "Thebans: the time has come to defend our city! We all have work to do – from the warriors defending our walls and gates to the women tending the water supply. Together we will prevail!"

The cheers rose again; under cover of the noise, Eteokles addressed those of us standing closest. "Melanippus, go close the Kleodoxa. Menoeceus – check your gate; I'll check mine and send runners to the rest. Then get a good night's sleep. Our war council meets at the palace in the hour before dawn."

King Eteokles assigned one of the Spartoi to command the soldiers at each of Thebes' seven gates. He himself took the Ogygia Gate, closest to the sacred spring where our founder Kadmos slew the serpent. Hyperbius, more familiar with the terrain between Thebes and Athens than any of us, was given the Neaira; Lasthenes the Astykratia; my brother Menoeceus the Phthia. Though Eurymedon had been supervising repairs at the Chloris, the king placed him at the Eudoxa: the young man's family home was in the southeast quarter, while the bronze-smith Aktor, from the west side of town, received responsibility for the Chloris. Eteokles thought each man would fight most fiercely for his own neighborhood.

I, of course, had no gate to command.

Father must have sensed my mood as the warriors and messengers departed. "It takes more than muscle and bronze to win a war," he said. "We're needed too. Come on – let's get to the palace."

As we pushed through the crowded streets, I pondered this. In his youth Father had not been a warrior either, but now his age and his wise counsel shielded him from any criticism. All I had were my priestly robes, which I had brought with me from Apollo's temple. And my sandal still needed mending.

Perhaps I could learn to give good advice, like Father. I shared the evening meal with him, Mother, and my younger siblings at their table in the palace megaron. We spoke of the relative advantages and disadvantages of the city and the attackers; Father pointed out that so large a force would be difficult to feed, and the Argive warriors would grow restless without a battle to fight. Possibly, I ventured, they would lose interest in Polynikes' cause. Father nodded, but said that would depend on how skillfully he had convinced them that his cause was their own.

After dinner, I went to my old room; I took a dose of silver-fruit leaves, then extinguished the lamps. The complete darkness felt unfamiliar: in Apollo's temple, we always kept flames burning. But I was not in the temple, and a city under siege must conserve its oil.

We – Eteokles' war-leaders, Father, and I – gathered before dawn in the palace courtyard, the sky above us just shading from grey to pink. Servants brought bread, milk, wine and cheese to break our night's fast. I was surprised by Captain Melanippus' filthy appearance, until I learned that he and another man had gone on a scouting mission overnight. They ventured out through the sally port by the Kleodoxa Gate around midnight, first smudging their skin with soot for concealment.

"What can you tell us?" asked King Eteokles.

"As we saw from the walls before sunset, they've split their forces and set up camp outside each of the gates. Roughly equal numbers – maybe thirty squads of ten at each gate. We didn't venture too far from the Kleodoxa – tried to learn what we could there. Seems the force there is led by that loudmouth, Tydeus of Kalydon."

Lasthenes said: "They can't have brought many days' provisions. We've brought in the grain and oil; the herds not in the city are scattered in the hills. And the season's wrong for foraging, unless they've got a liking for dandelions."

"Orchomenos and Gla are loyal," said the merchant Hyperbius. "They won't trade with invaders."

"That's true," said my brother Menoeceus, "but they can bring supplies from Athens."

"And send men to the coast for fish," Eurymedon added.

Remembering the conversation I'd had with Father the night before, I asked: "How patient will the Argives be with a siege? Polynikes may have married King Adrastos' daughter, but this isn't really the Argives' fight."

"Don't be so sure," Melanippus broke in, lifting a soot-smudged hand. "My man and I crept close enough to a campfire to hear what they were saying. The traitor's promised Theban loot to every soldier. Polynikes' plan is to kill the men and make slaves of the women. Those that kill the most will get the best of the plunder – the houses of the Spartoi, the lands and the herds."

We fell silent, contemplating this; for a time the only sound was that of the swallows chirping in the eaves. Finally Father said: "I wondered why Polynikes doesn't seem concerned by making enemies in the city he wants to rule. But that won't matter if he intends to kill us all."

"You're right, Uncle Creon." Eteokles' blue eyes looked as hard as sapphires. "All Thebes must hear this – men, women, and children. This war's not about exchanging one son of Oedipus for another: it's about their very lives."

We finished our morning meal; before the men left for their gates I poured out the last of the wine and asked the blessing of Apollo, urging him to protect his city.

We rose, and Eteokles instructed the war-leaders: "Remind your men: this is going to be a long-distance race, not a sprint." The men bowed to their king, and headed out. Eteokles caught my arm, saying, "Haemon, go to the Tiresias. See what advice he can offer, then join me at the Ogygia Gate."

I headed for the rear door of the palace, closest to the Tiresias' home; in the corridor I encountered Ismene – she had been in the palace kitchens, ordering fresh bread and other provisions sent to the men at each gate. She stopped me to ask if I'd seen her personal maidservant. "She went to fetch her parents from their farm north of town – they should have been back before the gates closed yesterday."

"I'm sorry, Ismene, but I haven't seen her," I said. "But if they were bringing animals, they might have needed her help getting everything settled."

"I'll ask at the Kleodoxa." She bit her lip. "I still can't believe Polynikes is doing this."

I knew her affections were torn between her brothers, but just then I had trouble finding sympathy for Polynikes. "He's made his choice. Now we have to think of Thebes."

When I reached the Tiresias' home, his daughters welcomed me, but said their father was still sleeping. I asked whether he had said anything as the Voice of Apollo, or offered any advice for Thebes – but they told me he had not. So I continued towards the Ogygia Gate.

The morning sun was warm on my shoulders; the afternoon would be hot and sweaty. Women stood gossiping in the street, since they could not take their laundry out to the streams beyond the walls; old men gave advice as their young grandsons staged mock battles with wooden swords. I saw more peasants from the surrounding fields and hills than city-dwellers, but sensed no resentment from the citizens who had been asked to share their homes. We were all Thebans: together we would live or together we would die.

My father had reached the Ogygia Gate before me; looking up, I saw King Eteokles' red-crested helmet as he walked along the walls speaking with the archers, slingers, and javelin-men. An archer pointed down to me; Eteokles waved, and descended the limestone stairs.

I reported that there was no message from the Tiresias. Eteokles frowned briefly, but quickly reasserted his confident demeanor and asked me to offer prayers to bless the gate. I hoped the gods would hear me even in my workaday tunic and without a laurel wreath. I found a man with a wineskin, and scattered just a few drops at the base of the gate-post as a libation. Then I asked for the blessing of Apollo, patron deity of Thebes; of Athena, who led Kadmos the founder; and of the war-god Ares, whose serpent once guarded the spring just outside the gate. I reminded Ares that though Kadmos slew his serpent, the men who sprang from that serpent's teeth became the Spartoi, the leading men of the city – so we were Ares' people too. Seeing that the men – and the king – were comforted by my words, I lengthened my prayer. When I was finished, and the soldiers went back to their tasks, Father said quietly: "You see, Son? They need you too."

Eteokles went to speak with the spearmen by the gate; there was little for me and Father to do, but we waited with the others. The sun rose higher; when it was about halfway to its zenith, we heard the pounding rhythm of the enemy's weapons against their shields. "They're coming!" yelled an archer.

The king headed back up to see; perhaps more curious than sensible, I followed.

The enemy was approaching in a wedge formation: one chariot leading, two more chariots flanking this, and perhaps thirty foot-soldiers in two orderly ranks continuing the angle to either side. Each infantryman carried a shield painted deep crimson, with the emblem of a yellow lion – Polynikes' symbol.

The first chariot halted beyond the range of our bowmen; the next two took positions on either side, and the foot soldiers brought their two doubled lines together in front of the chariots, their shields held high: the men in the first rank holding shields forward, the next rank holding them slanted overhead. Polynikes, dressed in a red-dyed kilt bordered with shining thread-of-gold and holding a shield and spear of his own, jumped down from the lead vehicle and took a position at the front tip of the infantry wedge. They marched forward in formation, their shields held so close that our archers did not have a clear shot.

"Impossible," I heard one bowman mutter.

"Well done," said a second, with grudging admiration.

Only the spray of red-dyed feathers cresting Polynikes' helmet was visible. When they were close enough for his voice to reach us, he ordered his guard to halt, and then addressed us at the Ogygia Gate. "Eteokles!" he bellowed. "It's you I want! If you won't yield the throne, come out and fight me, Brother – spare Thebes from war!"

"You're a traitor, Polynikes!" Eteokles shouted back. "You've three dozen men down there. Why should I trust you to fight fair?"

"Do you fear me, Brother?" Polynikes addressed his next words to the men who guarded our walls. "Thebans, would you have a coward as your king?"

"Go back to Argos!" Eteokles yelled, red-faced. "Thebes will never support you – we know your plan to slaughter the men and enslave the women!"

Polynikes' shield dipped for an instant. "That's a lie!" He brought the shield back up, continuing: "Don't believe his lies, Thebans! He lied to me – he lied to us all when he said we'd share the throne!"

"Go back to your Argive wife, Polynikes," Eteokles shouted. "She'll open for you, but Thebes never will!"

Polynikes shook his spear. "I'll come again tomorrow, Eteokles! Maybe by then you'll find some courage!"

Their next maneuver impressed us even more: the Argives marched backwards, still in formation, their shields still held like the overlapping scales of a snake so that our arrows and rocks were useless. When they reached the chariots they broke apart; one Theban slinger sent a stone in Polynikes' direction, but it fell short and he was scolded by a senior officer for wasting ammunition.

Eteokles and I went back down to speak with my father. "You heard?" the king asked.

Father nodded. "They won't storm the gates today. Their men are still resting from the march."

"I agree," said Eteokles, running a finger under his helmet's leather chin-strap. "Uncle Creon, you hear all that's said in the city. The traitor's trying to foster treason here within the walls – if the people start to waver, I need to know."

"He hopes to make you look weak," Father said, leaning on his walking stick. His eyes narrowed. "You did well to remind Thebes of the fate we'd suffer at Argive hands."

Polynikes did come again the next day, but to the Chloris Gate; again he challenged Eteokles to a duel. This time Eteokles did not answer, and Polynikes, after shouting many insults, eventually withdrew. On the third day he approached the Kleodoxa Gate, where the enemy were led by Tydeus of Kalydon who had the boar as his emblem – and this time an Argive fighter failed to maintain position. One of our archers planted an arrow in his calf, and his comrades had to pull him back out of range, taking sling-stones and arrows on their shields. Though it was not a kill, Eteokles gave the archer a silver arm-ring for having drawn first blood for Thebes.

But Polynikes returned the next morning, continuing his circuit of the walls by issuing challenge at the Astykratia Gate, where the force with blue-painted shields maintained the siege. We had heard, by then, that this force of Blues was commanded by Amphiorax, the Argives' senior priest of Zeus and a fearsome warrior.

"He's making a circuit of the city," I said, joining my parents and siblings at their dinner table.

Father nodded. "He's showing us that we're surrounded."

"He can't keep this up," said my brother Menoeceus. "Having too obvious a routine exposes him."

"Going to different gates means everyone in Thebes will hear him," Mother observed. "Maybe he really is trying to win people over. Maybe what Melanippus heard about his plans was wrong – I just can't imagine Polynikes would really kill the Thebans who were his friends and neighbors."

Father disagreed. "He's brought an army here, my dear. Blood has already been shed."

I was surprised at how easily the city settled into life under siege. Polynikes' daily challenges continued, but Menoeceus was right; after completing one circuit, Polynikes varied the order of his challenges to the gates – but every day he came to one, and made sure he was seen and heard. I led prayers in the agora just after our pre-dawn war council and then would visit one or more of the gates. In the afternoons I went to the house of the Tiresias. Often he slept – his daughters said he slept as much as a hedgehog – but sometimes he was awake, and then I asked him for guidance from the god. But he only shook his head, and say that the way ahead was clouded. After a month had passed, I almost stopped wondering when the Argives would attack in earnest; once I said this to my brother, and he said that was exactly what our enemy was hoping for: that we would be lulled into torpor, and be unprepared when they brought in the battering-rams. "That, or they're waiting for us to grow hungry."

Hunger was, of course, a serious matter; despite rationing, we could not hold out forever. We needed the Argives to lose patience before we ran out of food.

At first our deprivations were light. The trader Hyperbius joked that he would use the war to rid himself of his paunch, and for a time Thebes' men did begin to look fitter and more muscular. I felt healthier myself, though I guessed it was due mostly to the silver-fruit leaves. I discussed the matter with Udaeus; about a month into the siege, I realized that my dizzy spells had stopped altogether. And there were… well, other hopeful signs: signs that told me I could be a real husband to you at last, Antigone. I felt as if my own personal curse had been lifted. My years of devotion to Apollo had finally borne fruit, silver-fruit! I desperately wanted the siege to end so that I could go to you in Athens. I prayed with all my heart to Apollo to protect his city, to bless us, to deliver us. Each morning when I led the city in prayers – each time I made sure that my movements were precise and graceful, my words sincere.

Apollo was the god of pestilence as well as the god of healing. He had struck down the sons and daughters of blasphemous Niobe. He could strike down the Argive invaders. But why did he wait? I convinced myself that the time of the summer solstice – the day when the sun god has his greatest power – would be the day for Apollo to save his city. I planned and executed a glorious ceremony for the solstice dawn; we offered the best of the remaining bulls in sacrifice. The people enjoyed a banquet, and a few hours of excitement; but the god did not end the siege, either that day or during the days that followed. And the indulgence of the feast only heightened our awareness of how meager our meals were afterwards. I admit I felt as if Apollo had abandoned us, but I said nothing and continued leading prayers and visiting the Tiresias.

Each morning, Ismene checked our water supplies and supervised women refilling urns and amphorae around the city. I learned to ignore the stench of so many unwashed bodies, but as supplies of firewood dwindled Father recommended rationing it and compelling the bakers to fuel their fires with dried animal dung instead. Father had helped administer Thebes' resources for decades – including another time, years ago, when Thebes' gates were closed. He knew which stores kept the longest, which needed to be eaten first, and what measures could be taken to stretch our provisions. The goats and pigs were spared the slaughter that befell the cattle, since they could survive on refuse: eggshells, apple cores, onion skins, and table scraps that people found inedible. But using their dung fouled the taste of our morning bread somewhat – when we *had* fresh bread, which was only every third day.

We knew, from Captain Melanippus' nighttime scouting missions and from what we could see and hear during the day, that the Argives had things easier. They could bathe in the streams, hunt in the hills, and gather from our lands. Sometimes they found a shepherd who had fled to the heights rather than come into the city; always they bragged of their kills, taunting us with the names of the men they had slain and the peasant women they had taken for their pleasure.

One morning, about two months into the siege, Tydeus approached the Kleodoxa Gate and boasted: "Thebans! Your little princess, Ismene – I killed her! But don't worry – she didn't die a virgin!"

Word spread quickly; I was with my brother Menoeceus at the Phthia Gate that day; his face turned gray as ash upon hearing it. "That can't be! I saw her in the palace this morning!"

I gripped his arm and steadied him. "I saw her too—"

"Could they have gotten inside?"

"They're lying," I assured him.

Still, we had a very bad hour until one of my younger brothers, serving as a runner, located Ismene. We met her and King Eteokles at the Kleodoxa Gate... Ismene, I remember the relief Menoeceus and I felt on seeing you. It sickened me to think that Polynikes would do nothing to stop his sister's rape and murder.

"He wants to kill *me*," Eteokles said dryly. "And I'm his twin."

Quickly we consulted on the course of action, and it was decided that I should go to the top of the walls. After so many years leading prayers, I could make my voice heard; and as Ismene's cousin and priest of Apollo my words might carry some weight. I climbed the stairs to stand beside Captain Melanippus; Eteokles, Ismene and Menoeceus climbed as well, but they remained on the stairs, invisible to the enemy. "Tydeus of Kalydon," I shouted, "I am Haemon son of Creon, priest of Apollo. In the god's name I ask: how do you know your innocent victim was my cousin, Princess Ismene?"

He did not challenge my wording – either he was pleased to be thought a killer of innocents, or my voice failed to carry. "I have her jacket," he bellowed, holding up a pale blue garment. "King Polynikes recognized it."

"My maidservant!" Ismene gasped. "I gave her some of my old clothes last year!" She pressed a hand to her mouth, looking ready to burst into tears. Menoeceus put his arm around her, while King Eteokles gave me another question for the enemy.

"And Polynikes," I shouted more loudly, not wanting this to be misunderstood: "Polynikes approves this crime against his own sister?"

Tydeus laughed. "She's fair game – she supported Eteokles!"

I turned to Eteokles and quietly asked: "Should I tell them Ismene's alive?"

Eteokles considered, then shook his head with a swish of his horsehair crest. "No. If Polynikes has any natural feelings left, he'll be angry with Tydeus for killing her. If not – it doesn't matter."

"Besides," said Menoeceus, "if the city falls, Ismene will be safer if they think she's already dead."

"What?" sputtered Eteokles. "Thebes will prevail! How dare you suggest anything else?"

"I'm sorry, my lord king," Menoeceus apologized. "I was only thinking of Ismene."

A javelin-man stationed to the west shouted: "Polynikes – Polynikes is coming!"

"How did he know I would be here – did someone tell him?" As always, Eteokles feared treachery from within. He looked with suspicion at Menoeceus.

My brother countered: "How could anyone tell him, when we didn't know you'd be here ourselves? Obviously the Argives lured you here by having Tydeus claim he killed Ismene."

Eteokles frowned at this; and, because I was watching the two of them, I did not see how Polynikes and Tydeus greeted one another. Later, some said Polynikes looked angry; Melanippus claimed it was just the expression of a man jumping down from his chariot onto rocky ground. But I heard Polynikes' voice: "Come out and fight me, Eteokles, before more Thebans die!"

Eteokles clenched his fists, then jumped up the last few steps – and for the first time since the beginning of the siege, he answered his challenger. "Never! My blade's too good for the flesh of a traitor!"

Polynikes lowered his shield a little and pulled off his helmet, so that those on the wall could see his face. "You're a coward, Eteokles! You shame our family! Thebes deserves a *true* leader, not a coward!"

Eteokles ordered archers to shoot, but before they could let their arrows fly, Polynikes' men had surrounded him with their shields. King Eteokles turned away, his face red and angry; the taunts were wearing him down. He hurried down the stairs – stopping halfway down to gesture impatiently to Melanippus and me, as though we should have known to join him.

"I've had enough," he said when we reached the ground.

We all have, I thought, but did not say it.

"What will you do, my lord king?" asked Melanippus.

"Take the battle to them," said Eteokles. "But on *my* terms, not his."

*

Haemon coughs, interrupting his narrative; Adrastos offers his wineskin.

"No," he says, pushing it away. "I don't want to drink anything while Antigone can't."

"I know you want to save your wife," says the Argive king. "But how will it help if *you* suffer? You need to remain strong."

Yielding to his logic, Haemon accepts the skin and takes a swallow of wine. Then he calls out: "Antigone, are you still listening?"

All those in Eteokles' tomb fall silent.

The answer is faint. "Yes."

"Will you agree?"

As the silence lengthens, Haemon's face begins to burn with embarrassment. Why doesn't she speak? He has bared everything for her.

"Haemon—I love you. And now I know you love me. But..."

"Antigone!" He slams his fist against the wall, unable to control his frustration.

King Adrastos reaches over to catch his wrist. "Haemon, your wife needs time to understand all this."

"There's no time left," Haemon protests.

"There's a little," says the king of Argos. "I think I should explain our side of the – the conflict."

Conflict, thinks Haemon. Such a mild word for months of death and desperation. He wants to make a harsh retort – but if all goes well, if he frees his wife, they will live in Argos. He cannot afford to offend this man. He glances at Ismene; she nods encouragingly. "Very well," Haemon says.

But before the king of Argos can begin, the door opens.

CHAPTER SEVENTEEN
ADRASTOS

The dazzling sunlight stuns Adrastos with the force of a physical blow; for a moment he is unable to breathe. When at last the air makes its way into his lungs, it comes with the recognition that he and his family are helpless as trapped rabbits if the Thebans come in with blades bared.

Thebans, he knows, have long been a murderous lot. They might welcome the chance to soak the burial mound of their dead king in Argive blood – offering Adrastos, his daughters, and his sister like sacrificial beasts.

He should never have let his women talk him into this: he should have left the dead to hang where they might. The defeat remains a humiliation, no matter what. A few days ago, he worried that allowing his women to appear more valorous than he would compound the shame – but now that argument is weak as water. What use is glory, if one cannot live to enjoy it?

"Prince Haemon," he urges, "you swore to protect us—"

"Calm yourself," Haemon interrupts, looking at the person silhouetted in the doorway. "It's only my mother."

His heartbeat slowing to a more normal pace, Adrastos sees that it is in fact only a single person, a woman – and as she steps inside and shuts the door behind her, he recognizes her. But Eurydike is not just Haemon's mother; she is Creon's wife and the queen of Thebes, and she bears a deep grudge against Argos.

It might be better, he thinks, to keep his identity concealed from her – to remain only the servant of the priestess Phyle. As Haemon explains to his mother that Antigone is not yet convinced that seeking asylum in Argos is better than allowing King Creon's death sentence to run its course, Adrastos edges further back into the shadows. Best not to call attention to himself.

Then Haemon turns to him and calls him by name.

Queen Eurydike's jaw drops. "King Adrastos? *Here*?"

So much for taking the safer path! Adrastos bows his head in respect. "My lady queen," he says.

"I've guaranteed his safety, Mother," Haemon says. "Safety for him and his daughters, and his sister Eriphyle."

The Theban queen looks up at her son as if struggling to believe what she has heard. Finally she says, "Haemon, the soldiers have changed their watch. Astakus is out there now."

"Who is Astakus?" Phyle asks.

"The man who wanted to kill you yesterday," answers Princess Ismene. "And after what Tydeus did to his father, he'd be glad to kill all of you—no matter *what* Haemon says."

Deipyle moans; Argia clutches her rounded belly.

From beyond the wall separating the tombs, Antigone says: "This is wrong."

The seven of them – three Thebans, four Argives – fall silent, awaiting more from their group's unseen eighth member. At last Haemon prompts: "What do you mean, Antigone?"

"All of you, risking your lives for me!"

The Thebans answer with a rush of words, speaking over one another: "Don't be ridiculous!" "Antigone, you're not the only one who can be brave!" "Creon's wrong, and he knows it!" Their desire to save the woman trapped in the next tomb – sister, wife, niece – blazes clear as the daylight that cut through the darkness a moment before, and Adrastos becomes even more aware of his danger. With a man like Astakus standing just outside – a soldier with a blood grudge – the Thebans could easily conclude that there might be a simpler way to save Antigone than by negotiating with Creon to allow her sanctuary in Argos. The life of a Theban princess for the death of an Argive king: that bargain would be easy to strike. Haemon might have given his word, but Adrastos knows how easily men break their promises.

Somehow, he must win the sympathy of these three Thebans.

"Prince Haemon," he breaks in, "if you will – allow me to explain how it was outside the walls."

The priest narrows his eyes. "Your oath from before still holds."

Adrastos nods. "I will speak the truth. And, my lady Antigone – you are brave, but there has been enough death. Choosing life also takes courage."

ADRASTOS

The bards sing of heroes and villains. That makes for a better tale – but in truth, most men have their moments both of courage and of cowardice. Afterwards we get painted in only one color or the other: the Fates either crown us with glory or tarnish us with infamy, and that's how later generations remember us. Think of Alkides – before he murdered his family he was a favorite in Thebes – a hero for his exploits against bandits and fierce beasts! Now he's called Herakles, and hated for his crime. Which is he, hero or villain?

My sister was the one who finally resolved the question of whether we went to war. But of course I'd urged it for months – as had every man in Argos save her husband Amphiorax. In fact, as we were loading our ships in the northeastern harbor of Epidauros, a large group of men mobbed us, begging to join the expedition. "On to Thebes!" they chanted. "On to

Thebes!" They were peasants: farm workers, herdsmen, carpenters, stonemasons, and plenty of belligerent drunks – but their energy and enthusiasm raised our soldiers' spirits further. These volunteers were poorly armed – more scythes and clubs than swords – but their hunger to fight was infectious.

Mounting my horse so that I could see and be seen, I shouted: "No man who wants to fight for Argos will be refused!" The newcomers, the soldiers, the stevedores loading the ships – everyone cheered this at the top of their lungs.

My brother-in-law Amphiorax, of course, was the worm in the apple. Although everyone else was laughing and confident, his mouth twisted with dismay. "My lord king, no!"

"No, what?" I asked.

"We can't accept all these extra men!"

Fortunately, it was too noisy for others to hear this challenge to my authority. I gave the crowd a last cheerful wave, then dismounted and handed the reins to my groom. "I just did."

"But they're not trained! They've got no proper weapons – no provisions!"

"Amphiorax, it's already done. And before you ask, I'm not calling my sister over to settle the dispute – there *is* no dispute."

Amphiorax had insisted that Phyle come along to see the result of her decision first-hand. My daughters also traveled with us – Argia because she expected to soon be queen of Thebes, and Deipyle because she could not bear to be separated from her husband Tydeus when her sister and aunt were joining the expedition. King Theseus of Athens had agreed to let the women stay in his city until Thebes fell; we believed it would take a few days for Polynikes' supporters to open the gates for us.

"My lord king—" Amphiorax began again, but I cut him off, setting a hand on his muscular shoulder.

"Supplies will be plentiful once we've taken Thebes," I said, walking him back to a ship his Blues were loading. "And anyway I'd rather have the troublemakers along with us than leave them behind in Argos to cause problems for Iphis and the other graybeards."

"Hmph," grunted Amphiorax. "No shields, no helmets – they don't even have decent sandals, most of them."

"Let them go barefoot, then," I said, taking my leave. "That's what they would do here."

I'll admit I did regret the extra men during the next day's sea journey to Athens. We were as crowded as barleycorns in a sack. Half the men on my ship were seasick; I learned later that my daughters and their maidservants, aboard their husbands' ships, spent the day vomiting over the side. At least none of the women fell overboard; one barefoot herdsman from Hippomedon's ship went over along with his breakfast when a wave tossed them. The man couldn't swim, so though Hippomedon threw a rope out to him it was useless.

We'd given the horses herbs to soothe their nerves, but they were still terrified; I spent much of that interminable-seeming day with Arion, stroking his neck and trying to reassure him. I told him that this day on the water would soon be over; that it was better to regroup in friendly territory than risk ambush along the isthmus. He made a sound that was as much a whimper as a whinny, but stopped tossing his head and stamping his hooves. After that the other horses were calmer. They recognized him as their king, I believe, and looked to him for leadership.

We'd asked the Athenian king to keep our plans secret as long as possible, to give Thebes the least amount of time to prepare. But of course King Theseus had to send word to his men at the harbor by that afternoon, so that they would know Athens was not under attack. Even though they expected us, Athenians gaped and pointed and shook their heads in wonder as we pulled in. When I stepped ashore, in the orange light of the setting sun, I heard shouts that we had the largest force ever assembled. This put heart into my seasick men; they quickly regained their enthusiasm, and grumbled happily about their sunburns and sore backs as they unloaded the gear and made camp.

A keras horn roused our army just before dawn; the sky promised good weather, and the breeze carried the sweet scent of olive blossoms. Riding on Arion to inspect the forces, I offered praise and encouragement to each of my war-leaders. Amphiorax' Blues were best organized, but Tydeus' Boars, answering his booming call to arms, were eager for the march. Polynikes led his men in a hearty lion-roar as they came into formation.

I called the war-council to meet at the head of the column, just as the sun was rising above Mount Hymettos to the southeast; King Theseus met us to take charge of our women. Polynikes scanned the Athenian king's entourage and asked: "My sister Antigone – she's not with you?"

King Theseus shook his head. "I sent a runner to Colonus when your arrival no longer had to be kept secret, but he was turned away from the shrine. He was told that a holy rite for Athena and the Kindly Ones was under way, and could not be interrupted."

Phyle said, "We'll speak with her, Polynikes, when she's available."

Polynikes nodded. "Tell her I hope she'll come home to Thebes once I take the throne."

"You're sure you won't join us, King Theseus?" asked my nephew Kapaneus. "Your own men are saying it: this is the biggest army the world has ever seen. Athens could be part of it!"

Theseus shook his head. "I've no love for Eteokles, but this isn't my fight. You're free to use my harbor, and I'm pleased to welcome your ladies as my guests. But I'm not ready to risk Athenian blood."

"Anyway, we couldn't feed the Athenian army in addition to our own," Amphiorax said. Though he directed his words to Phyle, he spoke loud enough for all of us to hear over the sounds of the army behind us preparing to march. I bit back a retort; there was no point in quarreling in front of everyone, especially on foreign soil.

"My husband must appear as the true *Theban* king," Argia said, taking Polynikes' hand. "There's too much history between Thebes and Athens. We can't have people saying that Athens put him on the throne."

"You're right, my dear," Polynikes said, smiling down at her. Then he turned to the Athenian king. "We thank you for your hospitality, King Theseus – and we look forward to better relations in the future."

My daughters took leave of their husbands more slowly than Phyle, who accepted Amphiorax' kiss on her cheek and then joined the Athenian contingent without a word. Argia and Polynikes exchanged a tender embrace, and Tydeus had to pry himself free of Deipyle's arms. But soon they went in one direction, while we took another.

Wanting to make good time, we marched the men hard, camping only when the gathering dusk forced us to stop. We thought we glimpsed Theban scouts once or twice; clearly the peasants were warned, for the farmsteads along the road were deserted. But we did not slack our pace to search the hills. We reached Thebes the second day, as planned.

Even Polynikes didn't think Thebes would surrender immediately. He hoped that people would begin to question, that first night, whether they really wanted to fight for Eteokles – and that his challenge the second day at the sacred Ogygia Gate, near the spring once guarded by Ares' serpent, would prompt Eteokles to come out and fight. When that didn't happen, we prepared to lay siege in earnest. Our men settled into permanent camps outside each of the seven gates, and we had the low-born volunteers cut brush and beat down weeds to convert the footpaths and game-tracks that circled the city into roads good enough for chariots. We established regular patrols, to ensure that our blockade held firm – that the Thebans could not escape over the walls between the gates, or bring up fresh provisions. Eteokles no longer even answered his brother's challenges, and Polynikes' scorn swelled.

"What a coward!" he said on the fifth night of the siege. He snapped the wooden skewer he held and threw it into the campfire. "How can the people of Thebes stand him?"

We were meeting for our evening war council, that night held in the camp of the Blues outside the Kleodoxa Gate. "Give it time," said Amphiorax, moving his camp-stool closer to the fire. "You're making your bravery clear to them. Wait till the storerooms start to empty. They'll tire of him then."

"There are a lot of peasants crammed in there," said Hippomedon, who had led scouting parties to assess the situation in the countryside. "They'll eat through their supplies quickly."

Parthenopeus nodded, and reached for another skewer of roast pork. "Let them starve. They'll be hungry. Easier to fight."

"What if we set fire to their supplies?" asked Kapaneus. "Burn up their oil and grain?"

"I don't want to burn down the city I plan to rule!" Polynikes folded his arms. "I want them to *welcome* me."

"How about storming one of the gates?" asked Tydeus.

"We'd take heavy losses," I said. "An assault like that would put our men in easy reach of their arrows and javelins."

"Our shields could block a lot of that," Tydeus objected.

"Give it time," Amphiorax repeated. "Walled cities are rarely taken by force."

I swallowed my last morsel of meat, then stood and stretched my bad leg. "Let's put our men to use. We've more than enough to besiege Thebes, and still send out hunting and fishing parties. Hippomedon, you said some peasants decided to stay on their lands. There must be a few pretty women left, and supplies of food. Tydeus, that'll keep your Boars busy."

My dark-haired son-in-law grinned. "I like that idea."

"At this point," I said, pacing back and forth, "we must assume that – for now – Eteokles has the loyalty of most of the soldiers. So any Theban who wants to help you, Polynikes, can't just open a gate. Too obvious. But we only need a small group of sympathizers to give us a sally port – or even just an unguarded stretch of wall. Timed properly, we could get enough fighters inside to open a gate for our main force."

Amphiorax scratched his jaw. "That will take coordination with allies inside."

"Has Zeus told you it will work?" Parthenopeus asked eagerly.

"No," said my brother-in-law, shortly, his tone reminding me that he had never wanted this war.

"But he hasn't told you it *won't* work, either," I prompted.

"No," he conceded, "it's a sensible strategy." He looked south, towards the high Theban wall, and I followed his gaze. A patrolling sentry passed a gap in the battlements, creating a brief shadow against the moonlight. "If you have friends, Polynikes, they will come to us in darkness, so as to hide their intentions from Eteokles. Our own guards need to allow for this. They need to determine the motives of any who approach, rather than just striking them down."

Polynikes nodded, and glanced back to where his charioteer was waiting with his vehicle and horses. "I'll tell my men as well when I return to camp."

I reached down to rub my aching calf. "Enough for tonight. Each of you: give orders that if anyone approaches asking for truce he must be disarmed and brought to you at once. Then send word to the rest of us."

But, night after night, no one came. Once Tydeus reported his men had heard something moving in the brush; they called out a challenge but got no answer, and concluded it was a stag. Another time Kapaneus' men outside the Eudoxa thought they saw something in the moonlight, but no Theban appeared with an offer.

As the spring wore on and summer approached, Amphiorax became more vociferous about our provisions. We sent some of the peasants who joined our cause at the last moment in search of Thebes' scattered herds and flocks, and they brought back goats, sheep and cattle from Mount Kithairon. I pointed out to my brother-in-law that the late volunteers had proved useful for more than road-building; he retorted that our supplies wouldn't be low if I'd turned them away.

The summer solstice arrived without measurable progress. That morning we heard music and laughter from within the walls: all the sounds – and the smells – of a happy feast. Not wanting the men to lose heart, we put on a feast of our own. I rode to each camp, reminding the men that the Theban revelers were just bringing the day of their defeat that much closer. That evening my war-leaders and I shared several amphorae of wine that my own forces, stationed outside the Phthia Gate, had discovered in an underground cache near the Temple of Apollo.

The celebration cheered Polynikes, and he supervised the mixing of wine like a host at a dinner party. "Theban wine is excellent, isn't it?" When the men shouted agreement, he reminded them: "That's because Dionysus, the god of the vine, was born here! Don't forget, he's a relative of mine. He'll want us to finish this war before the harvest festival – no city's harvest festival is like Thebes'."

"Look!" cried Parthenopeus, pointing at the eastern sky with one long, slender arm. "A falling star!"

"Falling as Thebes will soon fall!" Hippomedon declared, raising a fist in a gesture of triumph.

With the glow of the wine upon us, the warm evening breeze, and the humming of grasshoppers in the brush, it did feel like a good omen – as if the gods of Thebes were welcoming us, even though the people were not. Yet.

"Mortals follow the gods' wishes," Tydeus said, lifting his cup. "They have to. You'll see, men: our fortunes will soon change!"

Even Amphiorax did not argue. "You may be right."

As the days passed, our raiding parties ventured further north and east, finding more peasants. They killed the men and took the women as slaves – most of them, anyway. Some were not docile enough, and had to be slain. One of these seemed well-born; she fought Tydeus without fear, and spat in his face as he raped her. Even after, she attacked him with a dagger, and he was forced to kill her. "Too bad," he said over the campfire that evening. "She was good-looking."

"Did she give her name?" I asked. I'd ordered the soldiers to take names when they could. I reasoned that hearing the names of the men we'd killed and women we'd taken would sap the spirit of the Theban archers.

Tydeus refilled his wine cup. "No. But maybe you can tell who she was, Polynikes. We burned the body, but we've still got her jacket and bracelet." He called his charioteer to bring them over, who gave them to

Tydeus, who then passed them to me as I was seated between my sons-in-law.

The bracelet was just a simple copper bangle, but the jacket, though worn, was elegant. I could not determine its true color by firelight, but it was some soft hue – perhaps light blue or gray – and trimmed with dark ribbon.

Polynikes ripped it from my hand. "You murdering bastard!" he screamed at Tydeus. "This was Ismene's! My *sister!*"

Tydeus only shrugged. "How was I to know? What was she doing in a peasant's hut, anyway?"

Shaking the jacket in his fist, Polynikes said: "Maybe – maybe Eteokles thought she'd be safer!" His voice cracked on the last word.

"Then, more fool he," Tydeus said, taking a swig of wine.

I put my hand on Polynikes' shoulder. "Tydeus couldn't have known," I said quietly.

"People die in wartime, Polynikes," said my nephew Kapaneus. "You knew some Thebans would die." I think he meant to calm the situation, but the words were tactless; Polynikes' scowl deepened.

"She *would* have been more useful alive," commented Hippomedon.

"Too late now," Tydeus said. "If she'd told me who she was—"

"—you'd still have raped her," accused Polynikes.

Tydeus emitted an ugly grunt of a laugh. "Maybe."

I grabbed Polynikes' arm before he could strike; we could not afford to let this escalate into conflict between the Boars and the Lions. "You can't fight the Fates, Polynikes. They've cut her thread. But maybe we can still use this."

The news of Ismene's death – what we thought was Ismene's death – provoked Eteokles into responding to us. He was clearly enraged. But instead of finally coming out to face his brother, he claimed he'd *never* do so.

The next two days – or was it three? – Eteokles reverted to not answering Polynikes' challenges at all. Kapaneus speculated that he'd been assassinated, and the city would soon be ours. Amphiorax expressed his doubts at this, but his outlook was always contrary. On the night of the new moon, the war-leaders left for their own camps at sunset; no doubt some of them started drinking early. I know I did.

I'm not so young any more – older than most of my soldiers, to be sure. I craved the glory of victory, but I yearned almost as much to be back in my own palace, where I could have my servants draw a warm bath and then enjoy freshly laundered linen sheets on my wide soft bed. Oh, my tent was comfortable; I'd brought my three favorite servants, and pillows stuffed with lamb's wool for my camp-bed. I'd claimed a pretty shepherd girl with well-rounded hips and raven-black curls to liven my nights. But, lingering over my wine that evening, I remembered the sweetly perfumed girls of the Argive palace, with their soft feet and softer hands. I longed for fresh leavened bread dipped in cumin-spiced oil. The warm summer breeze stirring the flaps of my tent, the sounds of the men talking at their cook-fires and the sentries patrolling beyond – these had lost their allure. Wishing that it would be over soon, I called for extra wine and told the shepherdess I preferred to be alone. Perhaps, I thought as I dropped off to sleep, perhaps *this* would be the night that some Theban weary of siege finally approached us.

Perhaps Parthenopeus was thinking the same thing. It would have been a good ruse for the enemy to get close to his camp.

All I know is that my head was aching and my tongue thick when my manservant woke me the next morning. "My lord king – they're calling for you to go to the Chloris Gate."

"Great Hera," I grumbled; the Chloris was the gate furthest from my own camp. "Why?"

"There's been a raid, my lord king. Lord Parthenopeus is dead."

I was the last Argive war-leader to arrive. By then the sun was directly overhead, and triumphant Thebans had gathered on the battlements. They were too far away to hear, but their jubilation was obvious in their gestures – and galling as I looked at the corpses, and parts of corpses, strewn about the camp. We counted three dozen men slain. Amphiorax surveyed the carnage and concluded that the Thebans had first overpowered the sentries and then murdered the others – including Parthenopeus – while they slept. As dawn broke and the remaining Argives finally roused themselves to respond, the Thebans had thrown lit torches into the nearest tents and then retreated back to the gate under cover of their archers, slingers, and javelin-men.

"Curse that coward brother of mine!" Polynikes stabbed his spear-point into the ground and turned to shout back at the city: "He sends men to slit Argive throats in their sleep – but he won't face me! Is *that* a king?"

The people along the walls certainly could not hear his words, but they saw his impotent fury; they cheered and laughed all the more.

Sick to my stomach, I slid down from Arion's back and handed his reins to a soldier. The nearest corpse, I noticed, belonged to a youth who'd taken his manhood oath a few months before. His arm had been sliced open to the bone, and the force of the enemy blade had broken the bone between elbow and shoulder; the arm lay at an unnatural angle in a pool of blood covered with flies. With my foot, I nudged the arm closer to his body. His widowed mother had been so proud! What I would tell her when I returned to Argos?

Amphiorax walked over, looking as though he had something critical to say – but then, seeing my face, he clamped his jaw shut. It didn't matter: I knew his thoughts anyway. *It was folly to take these untrained boys to war, Adrastos.*

Kapaneus was talking to Hippomedon, but I don't think the short dark man heard anything my nephew said; he was staring at the bloody face of his closest friend. Parthenopeus' mouth hung open in death, as though his shade were still screaming; the gaping wound on his throat was like an echo of that soundless cry.

Tydeus was the only one not downcast. "We knew we'd take casualties," he reminded us. "We just need to make sure it doesn't happen again. And plan a revenge to make them regret they didn't open the gates the day we arrived."

"He came here for glory," Hippomedon said, half-choking on his words.

"I'll have the bards make a song about him," I promised. "His name won't be forgotten."

"Thank you, my lord king." Hippomedon rubbed his forehead with both hands as if he could wipe the grief away. "He needs a funeral. Him and his men. Their shades must find their way to the Underworld."

"We'll burn them," said Kapaneus.

I nodded agreement.

Amphiorax added: "From now on we must improve our night watches."

"And *I'll* remind the Thebans what kind of coward they call king," said Polynikes, wrenching his spear free of the ground. "Yesterday I challenged him here, today I'll go to the Kleodoxa – Tydeus, they may try attacking there tomorrow night. Make sure your men are ready."

Tydeus nodded. "I'll come with you. Let the others prepare the funeral pyre." Walking together almost as though they did not hate one another, my sons-in-law returned to their chariots.

As king it was my duty to supervise; I made the men add the half-burned tents to the pyre, and told the senior-most man remaining from Parthenopeus' troops to find an animal suitable for sacrifice. As the Chloris Gate did not have the strategic importance of the others, many of the troops were raw; these peasants' normal tasks were to fetch wood and water, but that morning they were terrified and begged for an armed escort. Eventually we brought the camp to order, gathered up the scattered human remains, and performed the funeral rites. I sent word to my forces that I would stay at the Chloris overnight; Amphiorax sent for three squads of his Blues, including a man to assume command in place of Parthenopeus.

Our council that afternoon, in the shadow of the pyre, was sober. Polynikes reported that once again Eteokles failed to appear and answer his challenge. When he questioned whether his brother still lived, the Theban who commanded at the Kleodoxa – a veteran called Melanippus – shouted down that of *course* Eteokles was alive, but he had better things to do with his time.

"Melanippus said he led the raid here," Polynikes added. "He promised more of the same if we don't withdraw."

"Some of my men deserted today, when they heard the news," Hippomedon said. "Mostly new recruits, but also two whole squads led by that fellow with the squint. I thought it was better to let them go than have a battle among my own troops – especially in sight of the Theban sentries."

"We need a raid of our own," Tydeus said. "That'll put heart in our men. We know their patrol schedule well enough. Let's take ladders to that quiet stretch southeast of the Kleodoxa. My soldiers are willing. All we need is two squads over the wall. Twenty men could take the gate."

"Possibly," Polynikes said.

"Come north with me tonight," Tydeus urged. "I've got the men picked out. Tomorrow you'll brief them on the terrain just inside, which buildings are where. We can do this."

In the last light of the setting sun we lit the pyre, and Amphiorax led the men in prayer; then all the war leaders departed for their various encampments. I stayed with Parthenopeus' men and the well-drilled Blues. The pyre glowed long into the night, smelling of burning oil and seared flesh. I listened to our patrols' call-and-response; the remaining men were more attentive now that they realized their lives truly depended on vigilance. Our guards would not fall asleep on night watch any time soon.

In the morning we stirred the pyre's ashes, and I had the peasants cover over the charred bones with soil. I prayed to Hermes, asking his protection for those Argive souls as he guided them to the Underworld. Then I headed north to help supervise the preparations for our raid.

It failed, of course. As you know. The Thebans were quickly on us; those Argives who managed to get over the parapet found themselves surrounded and massively outnumbered. They killed only a few defenders before being slain; and then the Thebans flung our ladders back from the walls. Argives near the top of the ladders died in the fall; others suffered broken arms and legs. A few were killed by arrows or javelins. And while the daring Boars that Tydeus picked for the mission were being slaughtered near the Kleodoxa, Melanippus tried another raid – this time at the Ogygia. But Polynikes' troops were alert even in his absence, and the Lions repulsed the effort with few losses.

The Thebans had more success later at the Neaira; Hippomedon lost eight men, and killed only two. We Argives now hated Melanippus as much as Polynikes hated Eteokles. Tydeus opined that the boldness was a sign of Theban desperation: "They must be getting hungry in there!" But our men showed signs of desperation too. Desertions increased – especially among the untrained peasants, but several experienced warriors who'd come to Argos for sanctuary decided likewise to seek their fortunes elsewhere.

We needed to inspire our forces. Kapaneus pressed for us to attack with a battering-ram. I listened to his idea: cutting down a large tree and using it to smash into a gate. I wasn't sure this was a good idea – Amphiorax warned we'd take heavy losses – but if the tactic worked, victory would be ours at last. Polynikes said he would think about it.

The following morning, I was slow to rise. My leg was aching; I decided to remain in camp and have my manservant massage it with oil.

We had no special plans; Polynikes was making his challenge elsewhere, and the Thebans stationed at the Phthia Gate, which my forces guarded, yawned in the day's baking heat. The Chrysorrhoas had dried to a trickle; we were fetching our water from the Ismenus. I had my servants roll up the flaps on either side of my tent, but still there was no breeze; the day was stifling and I dozed. When Hippomedon's runner arrived from the Neaira, I needed a moment to shake off my drowsy confusion.

"Polynikes' sister?" I repeated dumbly. "But she's dead. Tydeus killed her."

"My lord king, King Polynikes' *other* sister. The one who serves Athena and the Kindly Ones. And your daughters and sister have come with her."

My servants whispered nervously: they feared the Kindly Ones even more than Theban raids. But I thought Antigone's appearance might be the good sign that Argia had hoped for as we were leaving Athens, what seemed like an eternity ago. I went over to the wash-basin and splashed tepid water on my face, then shouted for my groom to make Arion ready to ride.

When I approached our camp near the Neaira Gate it was buzzing with activity. A group of Athenian soldiers were putting up four new tents, while servants unloaded supplies from a pair of donkey-carts. I handed Arion's reins to a soldier, and went over to where Hippomedon was speaking with the women. "Phyle! Daughters!" I called.

They turned and came to me. I hugged Deipyle and Argia, then kissed my little sister's cheek. Before I could ask them why they had come, Argia announced she was expecting again, and Deipyle said that she could not wait to see Tydeus.

"I've sent runners to the women's husbands," Hippomedon said.

"Is that why you came?" I asked my daughters and my sister. "To visit your husbands?"

"Antigone insisted," Phyle explained.

When we exchanged greetings, Antigone, it struck me that you appeared much the same as when you left Argos with your father years ago – except that you had exchanged the colorful skirts of a noblewoman for the plain gray gown of a priestess.

"King Adrastos, I've come to speak with my brothers," you announced, showing no sign of fear.

"Polynikes will be here by sunset. But Eteokles – we have no way to communicate with him."

"He may be dead," Hippomedon offered.

"I don't think so," you said. "Lady Athena told me they needed me here."

Amphiorax arrived next, and spoke privately with his wife; shortly afterwards, Polynikes and Tydeus pulled up in their chariots. Hippomedon had his men kill a goat for the evening meal, and by nightfall the men had scraped away some of the day's sweat and grime. We gathered by the campfire outside Hippomedon's tent to review the day's events. Polynikes reported that once again Eteokles failed to appear. "The Thebans are conserving their arrows and javelins," he added. "They held us back with slings, mostly."

"Perhaps they're running low on bronze for points," Tydeus speculated, wrapping an arm around Deipyle. "Those men up there look more scrawny every day, and I think there are fewer guarding the gates."

"There could be plague," said Kapaneus. "That often happens during a siege."

Hippomedon bared his crooked teeth in a grin. "That would mean Apollo's on our side!"

"There's no reason to suspect plague," said Amphiorax. "The day was very hot. Maybe they just wanted to stay out of the sun."

"That's the problem – we never know what is going on," said Polynikes, breaking a stick in two and tossing the pieces into the fire.

"Perhaps the goddess will help me change that," Antigone said. "She came to me in a dream: she said I was needed here to see that the laws of the gods were upheld by the king of Thebes – especially in his treatment of my brother."

"I'll treat Eteokles with honor," Polynikes said. "Little though he deserves it."

Antigone tilted her head to gaze at her brother. "It's possible she meant that *he* should obey the gods' laws in his treatment of *you.*"

"Hmph," grunted Polynikes. "Well, *he* is the oath-breaker. Not me."

The gods see things differently from mortals: so often we think they are saying one thing when they actually mean quite another. It didn't occur to me, at least not then, that Athena could mean a king of Thebes who was neither Eteokles nor Polynikes.

Amphiorax leaned forward. "What does the goddess want you to do, Antigone?"

She hesitated. "I'm not sure. She told me only that I was needed in Thebes." For a moment we were quiet; I thought I heard an owl, Athena's bird, hoot in the distance – or perhaps I imagined it. "I will go and speak with Eteokles," Antigone concluded.

Polynikes frowned; the more his sister said, the unhappier he became. "Why didn't you do that five years ago? That's when Eteokles broke his oath. He *was* the rightful king, until the day he should have passed power to me – so he *was* a king of Thebes who broke the gods' law in treatment of his brother."

Antigone shrugged. "The goddess sent me the vision only four days ago."

I stood and addressed my war-leaders. "We have a decision to make. Do we escort Antigone to a gate tomorrow so that she can speak with Eteokles, and perhaps arrange terms for peace?"

Amphiorax gave his opinion first. "We've lost a lot of men lately, to raids and desertions. And some Thebans, at least, may be ready to consider surrender. If it could end this war, it's worth trying."

"I don't want people to say I'm hiding behind my sister's skirts," said Polynikes.

"You've approached Thebes every day since we arrived," said Kapaneus, reaching over the boundary-stones of the campfire to poke the nearest log with a stick. Sparks shot up into the dark night air. "You've faced javelins, arrows, sling-stones and insults. No one doubts your courage."

Polynikes smiled a little at this, then turned to his sister. "Eteokles usually doesn't answer. What makes you think he'll listen to you?"

"He may not," she admitted, with painful honesty – no king could afford to show such self-doubt. "But I must do Lady Athena's bidding."

I clasped my hands behind my back. "Even if *he* doesn't listen to her, Polynikes, she may sway opinion inside the walls."

"Very well – but on one condition," said Polynikes.

"What condition?" Antigone asked sharply.

"That you leave when I tell you, if I judge it's too dangerous. Swear it."

You hesitated, Antigone, I remember. Unlike your brother Eteokles, you keep your word – so once given, you'd be bound by it. But Polynikes insisted. And after a few moments' consideration you agreed, sprinkling wine on the ground to seal the oath.

Haemon, what happened the next day outside the walls was this: your wife and I accompanied Polynikes to the Ogygia Gate. Our horn-players sounded the note, and Antigone stepped down from her brother's chariot and walked slowly forward, alone. In her gray priestess robes, carrying an olive branch, she was clearly seeking parley. But the bowmen on the walls trained their arrows on her nonetheless.

"I am the servant of Athena," she shouted up at the Thebans, louder than I would have thought a woman could manage. "Of Athena and the Kindly Ones! Harm me at your peril!" She maintained a steady pace.

The men did not release their arrows. "State your name and your mission!" their leader called down to her.

Finally she stopped, perilously close to the foot of the walls – no more than ten paces, about the same distance as the walls' height. "I am Antigone, daughter of Oedipus, sister to Eteokles and Polynikes! Eteokles, I would speak with you!"

The Theban archers and javelin-men stared at each other; then one of them cried, "It *is* her! I recognize her – Princess Antigone!" I was too far from the walls to hear what was said among the Thebans after that, but before long we saw the red crest of Eteokles' helmet appear above the battlements.

"So he *is* still alive," I said quietly, stroking Arion's neck.

From his chariot, Polynikes said sourly, "He's afraid to show his face to me. *Antigone* he'll talk to."

Though we could see their gestures, we could not hear all the words; Antigone told us the details later. It did not go the way I expected.

"Sister!" Eteokles shouted loudly. "I knew you lived in Argos before – but I didn't think you'd turn traitor!"

"I'm no traitor, Eteokles—"

"Yes, you are!" he interrupted. "You stay in the Argive camp – with Polynikes!" He held up a javelin; its bronze point flashed in the morning sun. "Ask our gods-cursed brother what happened to Ismene! His allies have shed the blood of many Theban women – why should I hold back from spilling the blood of a treacherous sister?"

Antigone turned to stare back at Polynikes, horror on her face.

In that instant Eteokles cast his javelin. It was an easy shot, and Antigone was not ready for it; he could have spitted her, if he'd wanted to. The javelin landed two full paces from where Antigone stood and buried its head in the earth, its shaft vibrating like a plucked lyre-string.

Antigone turned and shrieked: "You attack a priestess? Your own sister?"

"Go, traitor!" Eteokles shouted. One of his men handed him another javelin. "Leave, and take that pretender with you!"

She turned her back on Thebes with courage worthy of a warrior and walked back to Polynikes' chariot – slowly, with dignity. Before climbing into the car she dropped the olive branch and asked accusingly: "What happened to Ismene?"

"Come on, get in," Polynikes said.

"Not until you tell me!"

"She's dead," he told her. "She was hiding in a farmhouse north of the city – the men who found her didn't know who she was."

"They killed *Ismene?*"

"She didn't tell her name. And they say she resisted." He held out his hand. "Please, Antigone. It's done, and can't be undone."

Scowling, she accepted his hand and climbed into the car beside him. I nudged Arion with my knees and Polynikes' charioteer shook his reins; we led our forces back to the southern gate. I heard no more words pass between brother and sister along the way, but when we reached Hippomedon's camp – and my daughters and Phyle ran over to ask what had happened – Polynikes said, "You must go back to Athens as soon as possible. It's not safe for you here."

We explained the sequence of events. Looking dejected, Antigone said, "I've failed the goddess."

"Perhaps not," Phyle ventured. "You forced Eteokles to show himself. Maybe that's what Athena wanted."

Waving away a fly, Amphiorax said: "Possibly."

At any rate, I redeployed extra men from the two nearest gates to ensure the women's safety, in case the Thebans tried a raid overnight.

Thank the gods, no such attempt was made, and at dawn we sent them away without incident. Polynikes watched until all that could be seen was a cloud of dust in the distance; finally he said, "At least one of my siblings can keep an oath."

Then he turned to Kapaneus. "Let's try your battering ram." The rest of us agreed.

We led the extra men around to the Eudoxa, and called for reinforcements from other gates; over the course of the afternoon we sorted our soldiers into groups of similar height. Those of short to medium height were assigned to carry the ram; taller men would hold their shields high to protect our force from projectiles. Our best archers were positioned in the back. We talked through the plan, and rehearsed the maneuver in a field about an hour's march from our encampments. We held drills morning, afternoon, and night, so that the men would be used to the darkness; we wanted to attack before first light, so that Thebes' archers would have the sun in their eyes.

We damaged the gate; but as you know, it held. In the effort we lost twenty-three men, while our archers picked off only four or five Thebans. Polynikes' helmet was struck by a stone as big as my fist; a cheer of triumph came from above the wall when he staggered and fell to his knees. One of his Lions caught his arm and pulled him to his feet again, covering Polynikes with his shield.

Looking around the parapet, Eteokles shouted: "Away, traitor!"

Polynikes coughed, shook his head, then replied, "Oath-breaker!" He let his men hustle him back out of range of the defenders' missiles as we made our retreat.

When we reached our encampment, Polynikes removed his helmet and asked Hippomedon to see if it needed mending. I was surprised he even asked; several boars' teeth had been knocked off, but then I saw the ashen color of his face. As I slid down from Arion's broad back I said: "You should lie down, Polynikes. I'll call the healer."

He swayed when he stepped down from his chariot; Kapaneus helped him to the commander's tent and helped him shed his corselet and greaves. The healer arrived and probed his skull with cautious fingers. Polynikes coughed and belched, looking ill; the healer's assistant managed to thrust a bowl in front of his face before he vomited. The stinking mess was carried outside, and the healer prepared an infusion of willow bark, telling Polynikes to sip it slowly.

After finishing the medicine Polynikes set the cup aside and rubbed the bridge of his nose between two fingers. "I'm so tired of this," he said. "We're getting nowhere. Maybe he *does* have the gods' support as king."

"I'm not sure of that." This came from Amphiorax, who stepped into the tent and took a seat on a folding stool. "He showed his face again. He wanted to look brave. Ask yourself: why? We know it's not for our benefit, since he ignored us for so long. Eteokles needs to impress people *inside* the walls."

The sun was slanting low; I called the war-council to meet at Polynikes' bedside. After Amphiorax' words, he seemed to regain his resolve. Though still shaky, he declared his determination to make his challenge again the next day.

"We made progress today," Hippomedon said. "That gate is weakened."

"Let's set fire to it," urged my nephew Kapaneus. "If that doesn't completely bring it down, it'll do enough damage that we can smash in with the ram."

Kapaneus had suggested several times that we use fire as a weapon; Polynikes had always refused. He wanted to be king of a proud city and not a pile of ashes. But now he agreed.

We settled on a course of action: first, from behind shields, we would pelt the gate's wooden surface with thin-walled pottery containers of oil; these would shatter against the wooden surface and coat it. Then several daring men, including Kapaneus, would run forward with lit torches. We planned the assault to begin in the hour just before dawn; the Thebans might not be able to tell what we were doing until the whole gate was aflame, and the light of the sun rising behind us would make it difficult for the defenders to aim. Polynikes also hoped that Apollo, the patron god of Thebes, might favor our action at his holiest hour. To maximize confusion, strain their defenses, and eliminate the stores that sustained the enemy, we planned simultaneous attacks targeting storerooms just inside two other gates: there our men would scale the walls on ladders and lob jars of oil stoppered with cloth, trailing a long fabric tail to be lit just before throwing.

This all-out assault took several days' preparation and planning. Polynikes continued his challenges at the various gates – once, at the Ogygia Gate, Eteokles actually showed himself. Eteokles refused combat, though; Polynikes confided to me he was actually relieved, for he was still suffering after the blow to his head.

On the final day of our preparations, Polynikes went to the deserted Temple of Apollo. There he made an offering, asking that his dizziness be taken away and that the god of light bless our effort.

When we launched our massive, fiery assault, the screams from behind the walls were like Apollo's own music to us; the sight of flames and scent of smoke roused our spirits. Even though we lost more than two dozen men – including Kapaneus, who was felled by an arrow through the neck – and were forced back by Theban archers, we knew we had struck a damaging blow. By the end of the day the townsfolk seemed to have extinguished the flames, and though the Eudoxa Gate did not crumble – I think that would have comforted my nephew's shade – my men were proud of their efforts. I heard them speaking, when Polynikes was out of earshot, of how they'd kill the Theban archers, take their pleasure with the Theban women, and strip the best houses of their jewels and gold.

During our evening council I poured a libation for Kapaneus, and Amphiorax spoke solemn words of prayer for the others. I realized, soberly, that my war-council of seven now had only five of its original members.

Hippomedon said: "Those people won't put up with Eteokles much longer."

"They'd better not," said Amphiorax. "We used up almost all our oil."

"They could just open the gates tonight," Polynikes grumbled, rubbing the side of his head. "Do they hate me so much that they'd rather let the city burn than accept me as king?"

Silently I thanked the gods that my return to the Argive throne had been managed without fire or bloodshed. "These things take time," was all I could offer.

"We've only been here four months," Tydeus said.

Hippomedon stopped picking his teeth to ask: "Is that all?"

"Yes," Amphiorax confirmed, glancing up at the moon.

"Huh," grunted Hippomedon. "Still, they must have been short of supplies even before today. Now they'll be boiling their sandals for soup."

The whole of the next day was consumed with tending to our dead. The largest pyre was needed at the Eudoxa; but I rode Arion around to each gate and spoke with the men in the camps, reminding them that their friends and brothers had not died in vain. This was the largest war-force Hellas had ever seen; men would sing of our victory for a thousand years. The triumph would soon be ours. We only need hold firm a little longer!

From their high walls, the Thebans watched our funeral preparations. A few jeered; but their mood was different from when we built the pyre for Parthenopeus and his men. Now, I was certain, Thebans were suffering too – some must have died in the fires, and the rest were facing hunger and want.

Amphiorax led us in prayers for my nephew and his men; then, the pyre still burning behind me, I left command of the camp to Kapaneus' lieutenant and returned to my camp. Polynikes and Hippomedon rode south and west, for their camps outside the Ogygia and the Neaira; Amphiorax and Tydeus went to their posts. We planned no special action the next day.

The Thebans had other ideas.

They struck outside the Kleodoxa before dawn. The first I knew of it was the sound of the keras – three long blasts, signaling hostile attack; then the four staccato notes that indicated the Kleodoxa. I leapt from my breakfast table and grabbed my cuirass; my manservant quickly buckled me in and handed me my helmet. Arion was ready outside my tent. I gave a few quick orders to the camp commander, then summoned two more chariots to ride with me and three squads of infantrymen to quick-march along for support. Passing the Astykratia Gate, I confirmed that Amphiorax had already left with his own group of reinforcements, and the Blues remaining at the garrison were calm.

The skirmish at the Kleodoxa was over before I got there; Tydeus'

Boars, bolstered by the Blues, had done well, firmly repelling the Theban raid. "Killed at least half of them," Amphiorax reported. "Including that bastard Melanippus."

"Aha!" Delighted, I jumped down from Arion's back, wincing as I put weight on my bad leg. "That's marvelous news – he was their best! We'll make quick work of this now!"

"Don't be so sure of that," my brother-in-law said, wiping sweat off his brow. "He thrust his spear in Tydeus' belly before he died."

A wave of horror went through me. "Tydeus – he's dead?"

"Not yet. But soon. Come, I'll take you to him."

I led Arion over and tied his reins to a post near Tydeus' tent. My son-in-law was slumped against the trunk of a tree, surrounded by a spreading pool of his own blood. His loincloth was sodden with crimson; the shaft of a short spear still protruded from his belly. Two dozen Boars had gathered round in a half-circle, their faces bleak; they parted to let me through.

"Tydeus?" I said loudly, not sure if he was past hearing.

He turned his head slightly, and his mouth twisted in something between a grin and a grimace. "My lord king," he said, reaching out his hand. "My second father!"

"Send for the healer!" I said.

"No," grunted Tydeus. "Let him help another. One who might live."

I squatted beside him and took his hand; it was clammy and cold. He looked down at the spear in his abdomen. "Wouldn't let them pull it – not till you got here," he said with an effort. "My life will go with it."

I nodded. "Most likely."

A spasm of pain wracked him; he drew a hissing inward breath, and then spat blood. "They say I killed him, though. Melanippus."

"You did," Amphiorax confirmed.

"Bring me his body," Tydeus asked. "I want – want to *see* that he's dead, before I go."

My brother-in-law nodded. "I'll do it."

"Hurry," I urged, and Amphiorax left.

"My son," Tydeus gasped, blood dribbling from his lower lip. "You'll protect him, Adrastos?"

"Of course," I said, squeezing his hand, suddenly struck by how young he looked. "Of course. He's my grandson."

"Deipyle… tell her not to cry too much. Diomedes – that's the man she must think of, now. Teach him to – to remember his father."

"Yes." I looked up. Amphiorax was returning, with Polynikes and Hippomedon behind him – without, so far as I could tell, what Tydeus wanted. "Where's the body?"

Amphiorax grimaced and opened his mouth to explain, but Hippomedon answered first. "The Boars beheaded it already. No point bringing the whole thing." He came over with the dripping, slack-jawed head of Melanippus.

Tydeus smiled and held out his hands like a child reaching for a gift. I rose and took a step back, revolted and yet understanding the impulse. A man needed to know for sure that he'd sent his foe before him across the River Styx.

"It's messy," Hippomedon commented. Releasing his grip on the gray-streaked hair, he shook his wrist; blood and flecks of gore flew off. "You did a right job bashing in his skull, Tydeus."

Tydeus drew the gory relic to his chest like a man cradling a baby. "I can die content," he whispered. "Your blood – ambrosia to me, Melanippus." He stroked the side of the head that had been mashed to a pulp, mingling Melanippus' blood and brains with the filth and blood that already coated his hand. Then, to my horror, he brought his gore-smeared hand to his mouth.

"That's – that's sacrilege!" stammered Amphiorax. "An offense to the gods! To eat human flesh—"

"Tydeus," yelled Polynikes, "what in Hades are you doing?"

"Ambrosia," he repeated, not looking up from Melanippus' dead face. He sucked the gore from his hand, and stroked again the ruined skull of his enemy.

Revolted, I said, "His wits have gone." I reached down to take the gruesome object by the hair, but Tydeus pulled it back from me and put it to his lips as though to kiss it – or to lick the shards of the shattered skull.

Then the horns sounded, three long notes. "Attack! Boars, make ready!"

Tydeus' men grasped their spears and turned to face the walls. "Did you see that?" I heard one of them exclaim. "He *ate* the brains!"

Amphiorax stood over where Tydeus lay, still cradling Melanippus' severed head. "The gods will punish you for this sacrilege, Tydeus," he proclaimed, then turned and ran toward his chariot.

I glanced at Hippomedon and Polynikes. "We can't help him now. We've got to fight." They nodded, their faces grim, and hefted their weapons. I returned to Arion; sitting on his back I could see what was happening. It was another sally from the small port beside the Kleodoxa: I rode out to answer it, my spearmen sprinting alongside. For a time I knew nothing but the pounding of Arion's hooves, the sound of bronze singing against bronze, the scream of Theban arrows cutting through the air. We felled one, then two more; the enemy force began retreating towards the gate – and then, to my surprise, I saw a group emerge from a copse of trees, dragging something behind them.

What we had thought to be the main force of this second raid was only a feint; the main mission, it seemed, was being carried out by these other men. I suppose they wanted to recover Melanippus' body. They retrieved his head, at least – and they took my son-in-law Tydeus with it.

When the skirmish was over, the enemy forced back within their walls, I rejoined my war-leaders on a rise out of range of the Theban archers. I was still on horseback; Amphiorax and Polynikes stood on the ground to my right. Together we watched as the Thebans hung Tydeus' body above the Kleodoxa Gate for us to see.

"He's dead, isn't he?" I asked, feeling sick at the idea he might still be alive. How would I explain all this to my daughter? I swallowed hard. "I don't see him moving. He must be dead by now."

"Criminals," Polynikes growled, clenching his fists. He had been furious with Tydeus for having, as we believed, killed Ismene – but now that his brother-in-law was dead, he was enraged by the insult to the corpse. "To treat his body like that!"

"Tydeus ate human flesh," Amphiorax reminded him. "The gods could not let that crime go unpunished."

Amphiorax was always gloomy, but as he spoke, a cloud passed over the face of the sun, blocking Apollo's light. I remember that Polynikes shivered and swayed; my brother-in-law reached out a hand to steady him.

But my gaze returned to Tydeus. What agony his last moments must have been: the gaping belly wound and overwhelming thirst… the rope around his neck. "He *is* dead, isn't he?"

Again no one answered me. I pulled Arion's reins and turned away.

*

A knock at the door of the tomb interrupts Adrastos' story. Before anyone can say or do anything, the door opens. The bright light makes it impossible to distinguish the features, but the figure clearly belongs to a man carrying a spear.

"The king is on his way," he announces. "He's commanded that the area be cleared before he comes."

CHAPTER EIGHTEEN
ISMENE

Ismene looks up, relieved that the voice does not belong to Astakus. But the soldier is one of Melanippus' men; Astakus must still be outside. She glances at the four Argives, at her aunt and her cousin. What should they do?

Before Ismene can think of an answer, her aunt rises and steps forward, planting her hands on her hips. "Well, then, go clear it."

"Uh, my – my lady queen," stammers the soldier, "I didn't see you. But – um – I think the king wants *everyone* to leave."

Eurydike shakes her head. "*We* will wait for *my husband* here."

Ismene recognizes the tone her aunt uses with misbehaving boys. Eurydike never expected to be queen – and yet her firm demeanor, Ismene notes with admiration, is sufficiently commanding. Perhaps her years of motherhood have been good practice.

"My lady queen, I don't know…"

Moving to stand at his mother's side, Haemon says: "The queen and I will speak with the king when he arrives. If he wishes us to leave, he can send us away then. But I expect his orders refer to the people outside."

The man looks hesitantly from Haemon to Eurydike.

"Go on," says Eurydike, gesturing dismissal.

The soldier bows and shuts the door to the tomb; the lamp's flames dance in the draft.

His voice hushed but urgent, King Adrastos says: "*We* can't stay here until your father comes!"

"What, are you afraid?" Haemon challenges him.

The Argive laughs, but there is no humor in the sound. "Of course!"

Ismene looks at the foreign king, and reflects that others – warriors, kings even – are not always as brave as they seem to be.

It does not really *feel* like courage, within her now – more a readiness. But after listening to so many secrets, she knows it is time to share her own.

Perhaps she will appear braver than she feels.

"While we wait for Uncle Creon," she says, "I want to tell you what happened before Polynikes made his last challenge."

ISMENE

As Haemon told you, my maid was missing from the start. I hoped she had fled with her parents to Orchomenos – but as we learned later, that wasn't the case. In the meantime, another young woman took her place. Rhanis was a chubby, greedy girl, whose usual work was emptying the chamber pots and cleaning the hearths. But of course, an unskilled maid was my least concern.

Theban blood flowed the very first day, when Tydeus' javelin killed the youth who happened to be standing near the king. We all feared that death was only the first of many to come.

We prepared ourselves for a long siege. Lasthenes the Herd-Master said we should slaughter most of the male livestock brought within the walls. Bulls and steers, rams and wethers, he-goats and boars and even the ganders – nearly all were put to the knife. In order not to alarm the female animals and their young in the pens down by the walls, Lasthenes used the agora as the killing grounds. The flesh was dried so that it would keep – not smoked. Even then, Uncle Creon warned us to save our firewood. And our oil.

We soon felt want. Asparagus... that's my favorite, but we had none last spring. After the first few days the only fresh greens were what people could grow in their courtyards, or on the rooftops. I'd always liked the palace rooftop garden; now I took a greater interest in it, especially the quickly growing rows of radishes we planted around the rose bushes.

Thebes was hot, dirty and crowded. Uncle Creon's census showed we had three times the usual number of people within the walls. When he and the scribes compared this with the inventory of our storerooms and other caches of food – and reckoned all the usual bounty of spring and summer we would not collect – the leaders' faces fell. The trader Hyperbius gamely said that smaller rations would help him trim down his paunch, and Eurymedon, who commanded the javelin troops, tried to make a joke of it: "Since we'll be eating nothing but lentils and beans, we can fart the Argives to death!" But only Aktor the bronze-smith laughed.

We were assigned responsibilities and soon had a routine. King Eteokles chose war-leaders to supervise the forces at each gate, which kept most of the men busy; Uncle Creon was in charge of supplies; Haemon led morning prayers. My brother decided *I* should supervise the rationing of water. We had wells inside the city, but with so many more people we had to use that water sparingly.

So I watched the peasant women as they drew up the water from the dark depths and carried heavy jars to each quarter of the city, making sure that people got what they needed without taking too much. I rather enjoyed the work. I visited everyone: potters making clay sling-stones, herdsmen tending the penned animals, soldiers like my cousin Menoeceus patrolling the gates – I'd never known the people of Thebes so well. In idle moments I pretended I was a descendant of the River Ismenus that flows southeast of the city. The Ismenus brings water to many of Thebes' farmers and flocks; now I did the same.

The country people, so used to the open hills and plains, slept on the tiled and painted floors of houses throughout the city. My aunt spent her time settling disputes between city matrons and their unexpected peasant guests, while her daughters supervised tasks that were usually country chores: milking, cheese-making, and collecting eggs.

Delivering water occupied my mornings; in the afternoons I helped Udaeus and Rhodia care for the injured and infirm. Because old Rhodia's hands shook and her eyesight was poor, I prepared medicines and treated patients under her supervision. As the months wore on, more people fell ill; Rhodia said they needed fresh foods. In the palace, we still had mint and anise and chamomile, at least in small portions; but I thought longingly of the things the peasant women normally gathered in the hills and brought to the agora to trade: dandelion greens, celery, fennel and cress.

As spring drew to a close, the milk of the ewes and nanny-goats began to fail. We could keep a few goats fed on scraps and garbage, but Lasthenes decided to butcher all the ewes and lambs rather than feed them more of the city's grain. That gave us fresh meat for the summer solstice festival. But when our feast was done I found myself craving the mulberries, cherries, and little red strawberries we normally enjoyed as dessert.

I tried not to speak of such things, contenting myself with a few greens and radishes from the roof garden. The common people had only raisins and dried figs to supplement their bean stew. I frequently inspected the grape vines on the roof – the fruit was still inedible; I know, because I tried one – when I realized someone had been plucking the leaves. I suspected Rhanis: I once spied her at the bottom of the staircase to the roof, where she had no business, and she gave me a guilty look. But we were all hungry, so I said nothing.

Many things went unsaid as spring changed into summer, or were discussed only in private. I remember, Haemon, when I was helping Udaeus with a small sick boy, you stopped by to offer a prayer. Afterwards, while I sponged the child's forehead, you asked your colleague: "Was I wrong, to hope Apollo would send plague on the invaders?"

Udaeus scratched his large nose. "We're just lucky there's no plague inside the walls."

I cringed with dismay. Despite all the time I'd spent with Udaeus and Rhodia, neither had mentioned the risk of plague – which of course would be terrible in the overcrowded city. We'd suffered plague once before, while my mother and father still ruled; that stopped only when my mother's father gave his life to Apollo so that the city might be spared.

Another forbidden topic was the king's refusal to accept a duel with his brother. Polynikes' challenge became the most interesting event of each day. In the evenings there were wagers placed as to whether he would next be spotted with his olive branch at the Chloris or the Ogygia, whether it would be early in the day or when Apollo's chariot was directly overhead or in the afternoon.

At first no one dared ask the king why he did not take up arms against his brother; but later I overheard Lasthenes – whose herds now consisted of only a few scrawny sows and nanny goats – complaining to my cousin Menoeceus and the trader Hyperbius. "The king could end this cursed siege tomorrow," he grumbled. "All he has to do is go out and fight!"

Menoeceus nodded agreement, but Hyperbius shrugged. "I won't question the king's motives." Patting what had once been an ample belly, he added: "My wife says I'm far handsomer now!"

I thought I understood Eteokles' reluctance. Years before, a match between the twins would have been even. But Polynikes had trained with the Argive warriors for years – he had to have the advantage now. Waiting out the Argives seemed safer; everyone knows it's hard to take a walled city by force. Uncle Creon, who knew the history of Hellas better than any man, advised patience. We had stores to last months, even if we were all tired of lentil soup flavored with dried mutton. Thebes' gates were strong, our walls high and thick. Our archers – led by my cousin Menoeceus – were skilled; with Eurymedon's javelin-men and the slingers, they kept the Argives back from our city.

But many were restless. My aunt resolved more and more conflicts between the peasants and their reluctant hosts. Looking back, they seem so petty: a quarrel about a broken jug; a complaint about a farmer whose snores kept a tanner's family awake; a stolen mirror. Yet people came to blows over these matters.

Why, then, did no one betray Eteokles and open a gate to the Argives?

Captain Melanippus deserves much of the credit. He was the one who led his men – his son, Astacus, often among them – out through the sally ports at night. Their skin smeared with soot for concealment in the darkness, they spied on the Argives and listened to what the enemy soldiers were saying around their campfires. Melanippus reported that Polynikes was furious with the people of Thebes for their past betrayal, and planned to kill all our men and enslave the women.

Menoeceus narrowed his eyes at this. "But Thebans are his own people!"

Downing a swig of well-watered wine, Melanippus wiped his lips with a grimy hand. "Not anymore."

We were in the palace courtyard, just before dawn; the king always gathered his family and advisors to break our fast together. I was sitting near my cousin, and despite the weak light I could tell he was not convinced. "What use is an empty city?" he asked.

"Argos is crowded," Hyperbius said, his sandals crunching on the gravel path as he walked over to refill his cup. "King Adrastos has welcomed criminals from all across Hellas."

Menoeceus persisted. "Do you think Polynikes would give Thebes to such people?"

Hyperbius dipped his cup in the urn. "He could."

"Of course he would," Melanippus broke in. "Why not? His warriors think nothing of killing our peasants and raping their widows and daughters. I've seen those poor women in their camps – with bruises on their faces and blood on their thighs."

"Captain Melanippus!" objected Haemon. "Ladies are present!"

Melanippus looked at me first, before my aunt or any of my cousins. "I'm sorry, my lady Ismene. Sorry to relate such a thing. But it's the truth."

Feeling ill, I put aside my bowl of bread and milk.

"That's why we can't yield to the traitor," said Eteokles. "It's almost dawn. Time to get to your posts."

A few mornings after that, I was supervising water distribution near the Neaira Gate when a runner sprinted over, calling my name. When I turned to answer him, he cried, "Princess! Thank the gods you're safe!"

Puzzled, I pushed up my sun-hat. "Why shouldn't I be?"

The youth bowed. "My lady princess, the Argives say they've killed you. Please, come with me to the Kleodoxa Gate – Captain Melanippus and his men are very worried!"

My brother the king was on the scene by the time I got there; I remember the relief on his face when he saw me. My cousins Haemon and Menoeceus arrived soon after – Haemon squeezed my hand and Menoeceus gave me a hug. I felt guilty at exciting so much commotion. The report was just a mistake; I'd been in no particular danger. But we soon discovered that my maidservant was the one who'd died. Remembering Melanippus' description of how the Argives treated their captives, I felt sick to my stomach.

Then Polynikes joined the forces outside the Kleodoxa. He shouted that Eteokles was a coward for refusing to fight; for once, Eteokles climbed up to the battlements – but he yelled down that he'd *never* accept the challenge. When he and Captain Melanippus returned to street level, Eteokles explained he would let the Argives continue to think me dead. "If Polynikes has any natural feelings left, he'll be angry with Tydeus for killing you. If he doesn't, then it doesn't matter."

"Murdering innocent girls," Melanippus muttered. His gaze met mine; then he quickly glanced away. As if speaking to his dusty sandals, he said: "Tydeus' men call themselves the Boars – but even wild boars wouldn't do this."

Eteokles clapped the grizzled war-leader on the shoulder. "Let's make those Argives pay for their crimes."

A few nights later Melanippus, his son Astakus, and their men struck outside the Chloris Gate. They left through the sally port, allowing themselves to be sealed into a small chamber built into the wall; the inner door was closed and barred behind them before they opened the door to the outside world. Once they'd ventured out into the night, the two soldiers who remained behind closed and barred the outer door and waited for Melanippus' forces to return. Only when they heard the correct pass-phrase did they open the outer door; and only when the men inside our walls heard the second pass-phrase, and confirmed that the outer door had been sealed, were our raiders let back into the city.

Every day Eteokles and Uncle Creon and devised new phrases to be used as secret signals. "Kadmos and Harmonia turned into snakes," was one; "Serpent teeth make the best soldiers," another. My favorite was: "Thebes' strong walls were built with song." Each was designed to inspire our men by reminding them of our city's history, and to be specific enough that not even Polynikes could guess them.

The first raid saw one of the seven Argive warlords – Parthenopeus, I now know – cut down. Of course we rejoiced. Menoeceus led me up the narrow stone stairs, so that I could see the flames of the Argives' funeral pyre. In the dark of evening, there was no risk of my being recognized by the attackers.

I stared at the bonfire, smelled the smoke, and I wondered how many bodies were burning. "Will they go away now?"

As more Thebans joined us to watch, Menoeceus took my hand and helped me walk along the walls. "Well... I hope so."

"But you don't think so."

"Not yet," he said, squeezing my hand before he released it.

We stayed a long time up on the battlements, watching the funeral-fires burn and gazing up at the constellations overhead. My fellow Thebans jeered and shouted insults, but I was content to watch the flames. If only these Argive deaths would end this awful siege! Then all of us – including Menoeceus and me – could go back to the business of living.

The following afternoon, Rhodia and I were tending the herb garden on the roof of the palace when we were joined by my brother the king. Eteokles undid the buckle that fastened the chin-strap and took off his helmet, then scratched his sweat-damp hair. "Ismene, I have something to discuss with you."

"Of course." I set aside my trowel, got to my feet and followed him to the balustrade. Together we looked down over the crowded streets. It was hot and dry; even the children, who seemed scrawnier each day, rested in the shade instead of chasing each other through the streets.

"Captain Melanippus is doing Thebes a great service," he said.

"Yes, he's very brave."

"Ismene… he's asked to marry you."

I blinked. "He – what?"

Years before, when my parents' crimes were made known, I'd given up any thought of marriage. What man would want a wife with such a mother: a woman whose son killed his father and then married his own mother? The shame was greater for my sister and me than for our brothers. Haemon, until yesterday I thought *that* was why you and Antigone stayed apart.

"I've agreed," Eteokles continued. "He deserves to be rewarded."

I looked down at my unkempt gown, the dirt beneath my fingernails. "I'm the daughter of Jocasta by her son Oedipus! What kind of reward is that?"

My brother grinned. "The kind Melanippus wants. He already has a grown son, and he's sure Astakus will protect him if your children show any, uh, patricidal tendencies. Besides, he's not from the best family. Becoming the king's brother-in-law would be a huge step upwards."

As my astonishment faded, alarm took its place: Eteokles was serious. "Brother, no!"

"Why not? Melanippus may not be a king, but he's our best warrior!"

"But—" I stammered, unable to articulate my reason.

"Listen, Ismene. Nothing inspires a man to greater bravery than fighting to protect the woman he loves. You'll be helping Thebes."

I pulled away, looking past the balustrade down at the hungry children. Eteokles was right; my duty was to Thebes – not to what *I* might want. Still...

"I see you need time to get used to the idea," my brother said. "Let's talk again tomorrow. In the meanwhile – would it hurt you just to *smile* at him? You're pretty when you smile, you know – just like Mother."

It was little enough to ask; I nodded and said I'd try. Eteokles patted my shoulder and departed.

Watching him walk away and start down the stairs into the palace, I thought about what he'd said. Of all our mother's children, I most resembled her, although I lacked her sparkle. Somehow she had survived twenty years of marriage to a man – my grandfather Laius – she did not love, all the while ruling Thebes with grace and charm.

But my dismay must have been obvious: when I returned to the herb garden, Rhodia asked me what was wrong. So I told her that my brother wanted me to marry Captain Melanippus.

"A woman may have many reasons for not wanting to marry a particular man," mused the old midwife. "The two most common are that she dislikes him – or that she loves another."

I felt my cheeks flush and looked down; for once I was glad Rhodia's eyesight was poor. "I don't think either of those objections would satisfy my brother."

"Here's one that might." With her unsteady hands she picked a slow-moving insect off the chamomile leaf it was eating, and pinched it between her fingers. "A pregnant woman suffers more during times of hunger, as does the child in her belly. Three women gave birth during the last ten days, and two of them have no milk – their infants will likely die. Many babes birthed under these conditions are born dead; those that live are often idiots. Marrying and starting a child while we're under siege is folly."

I didn't know if this excuse would work either, but it was the best I had. I presented it to my brother the next day.

Frowning, Eteokles set down an inventory-tablet. "I'll always make sure you have enough to eat. And your child, if you have one."

"Please, Brother – I know you're doing all you can. But no one can be sure how long this siege will last."

He tapped his bronze stylus against the table. "I *could* just announce your betrothal," he said slowly. "There's no reason for you to marry till the war is won."

"Thank you," I said, nearly weeping with relief – I hadn't expected Eteokles to yield. I did not want a betrothal to Melanippus either; but that would be better, at least, than marriage.

He shrugged. "Given the times, it's best to keep all options open."

I realized my brother had additional motives. "What do you mean?"

Eteokles grinned like a small boy caught sneaking a fistful of raisins. "A betrothal rewards Captain Melanippus – but *wanting* something is even better motivation than *having* it. He'll do everything he can to prove his bravery to you. And if another man proves more useful later… well, I'll still have an unmarried sister."

The betrothal meant I sat with Melanippus and his son, rather than my cousins, during our pre-dawn council and the late-day meal; so I heard all the details of his exploits. He and his son were so proud of the blood they'd shed: the man surprised at the latrine near his camp outside the Astykratia Gate; the one with the severed hamstring who tried to crawl away; the one outside the Phthia Gate, too young to shave, weeping for his mother. Aktor and Lasthenes enjoyed these stories, and Eteokles often raised his cup and asked Melanippus to tell another. But they made me lose my appetite. Melanippus called me dainty, and when I left a crust of bread or a piece of boiled beef on my plate, he finished it himself.

My cousin Menoeceus' tales bothered me much less. He and his men repelled the Argives who tried to scale the walls one night with ladders, and every day they kept the enemy back from our gates with their arrows and javelins and stones.

Of course Captain Melanippus gave me his opinion of that. "Archers have their uses, but shooting men from a distance isn't *real* bravery. A *real* warrior meets his enemy face to face."

I was tempted to ask about the Argives whose throats Melanippus cut while they slept – but the king wanted me to be pleasant to my betrothed, for the sake of the city. So I only said, "The archers risk their lives too," and named several that had died.

His son Astakus laughed. "Half of those only died because they fell off the wall. One of them wasn't even shot; he just leaned out too far!"

"He's still dead," I snapped. Melanippus looked surprised by my irritability, so I quickly added: "But I'm no soldier. I just hope you'll be safe tonight."

I didn't ask about their plans. Once I made that mistake; Melanippus refused to tell me anything, saying: "You might go and warn Polynikes!" Of course that was absurd – I had no such intention. But I never asked again.

"Your beauty gives me reason to return," Captain Melanippus said, rather gallantly. He kissed my hand, and then said, "Come, Astakus – the sun'll set soon. We'd best make ready."

Life continued. The days were long and hot; the water level in the city wells dropped lower; faces were thinner, grimmer, grimier. I wondered if I'd ever dip my feet in the Chrysorrhoas again. Then you came, Antigone. By the time I learned of it, Eteokles had already sent you away. I expressed my disappointment to Menoeceus as I brought water the next day to the Phthia Gate. He joined me as I headed back to the palace, and reminded me that my brother wanted the enemy to continue believing me dead.

"What does that matter?" I objected, glad to have the chance to speak with him. Menoeceus listened to me in a way no other person did; to him I could express my doubts and fears. "It's been so long – if Polynikes and Tydeus were going to have a falling out they'd have done so by now."

Menoeceus shifted the shoulder-strap that secured his quiver of arrows. "He thinks Antigone might make Polynikes feel ashamed."

I squinted against the sun. "But he also says she's a traitor, allied with Polynikes – if that's true, wouldn't she just support Polynikes?"

We went several more steps before he said anything further. I remembered that a few months ago there had been sacks of barley stacked along the wall of the house we were passing; those had long ago been consumed. The city was less crowded now: not so much because of the people who had died, but because the livestock was gone and the supplies were dwindling.

"I don't know," Menoeceus said finally. "Maybe he doesn't want you to speak with your sister. He definitely didn't want other Thebans to hear her."

A few days later, the Argives tried the battering-ram against the Eudoxa Gate. We were taken by surprise: they'd kept the ram out of sight of our watchmen until that very morning. But our soldiers fought well; Menoeceus and Eurymedon were heroes, their archers and javelin-men felling many of the enemy. When I heard that Polynikes had been struck with a sling-stone, at first I hoped he was dead, because that would end the war – but later I was relieved to hear he'd survived. He made his challenge to Eteokles again the next day, so we knew the war would continue.

Soon after that came the attack with fire.

Many died. Eurymedon, Lasthenes and others were suffocated by the smoke as they tried to put out the flames in the storerooms; others, especially children and the aged, perished before they could escape their burning homes. Amazingly, the Eudoxa Gate held. Menoeceus' arrows brought down many attackers, and finally drove them back; but despite the best efforts of Aktor and Hyperbius – and all my water-carriers – several of our storerooms were destroyed. Other than the palace stores, only the storerooms at the Neaira, the Ogygia, and the Astykratia Gates remained.

Uncle Creon advised Eteokles to halve the ration. The last few donkeys kept for hauling burdens were brought to the palace kitchen for butchering. Servants set up racks on the palace rooftop, instead of the agora, to dry the stringy flesh – the king feared that such a temptation for the peasants would bring on a riot. Eteokles decided we could get by with two chariots per gate; he culled the horses, keeping only the twenty-eight best from the palace stables. The rest joined the donkeys as strips of meat drying in the sun, and their bones were boiled for soup, noble steeds and beasts of burden mingled together. Wealthy families who had kept their dogs finally sacrificed them to the stew-pot; all but two of Eteokles' hunting dogs found their way to the table. The offal from this slaughter fed the remaining sows and nanny goats for a while, and then they too were put to the knife. King Eteokles issued an edict forbidding the use of oil lamps. The ribs of Eteokles' two remaining dogs, which he fed from his own plate, stood out like the warp strings on an empty loom – and yet, scrawny as they were, I noticed people eyeing them at dinner.

The old and the young began to die.

Rhodia told me that many of the deaths among the elderly were suicides. Old men opened their veins rather than watch their grandchildren starve. Grandmothers took to their beds, refusing food and even water; usually they died within four days. Some begged Rhodia for poison, that the end might come quicker. Often she obliged. I know, because I helped to prepare the doses – but we were running out of belladonna. Soon she kept the last of the poison for those who wanted to put their children out of misery.

At the morning prayers, people began shouting at the king from the rear of the crowd: "End this, King Eteokles! Fight Polynikes!" The first time this happened, Eteokles pretended not to hear, though I saw how his back tensed. The next day, he reminded everyone that Polynikes and his Argives planned to slay Thebes' men and enslave the women – and someone called out: "At least that would be quick!" There was grim laughter at this, and a few other voices urged Eteokles to face his brother. Red-faced, the king turned to Melanippus, who was standing beside me, and hissed that he had better do more damage in his next raid.

He did – and in the effort he died. Melanippus and his men set out before dawn, attacking the enemy camp outside the Kleodoxa. They slaughtered as many Argives as they could manage, until Tydeus gave Melanippus a fatal blow. The soldiers said that even as he fell, he managed to thrust his spear-point into Tydeus' gut. Melanippus' men were forced to retreat; but when they returned without him, his son Astakus urged them back out with tears of rage, saying he would not leave his father's body unburied. They crept up quietly, hidden by the brush, and found Tydeus still alive – and in the act of eating the brains from Captain Melanippus' severed head.

As a diversion, Aktor and Menoeceus led a fierce attack nearer the gate; this gave Astakus the chance to snatch his father's head from the hands of the cannibal, while others dragged Tydeus into Thebes. As soon as they were safely inside, they told the crowd what they had seen.

The mob surged towards Tydeus' body, threatening to tear it limb from limb, but Astakus said that was too good a fate for him. "Let's hang this piece of garbage over the gate!" he screamed. "Let those barbarians watch the crows eat it!"

What followed was like a festival, but with each part turned inside out. I was supervising the distribution of water near the Kleodoxa, so I saw it all: instead of celebrating a god or a king, people cheered a corpse. Rather than fresh-faced maidens, blood-streaked warriors brought the offering – which was hideous instead of beautiful. They dropped Tydeus' body, dangling from a rope, over the wall; people climbed up to curse the corpse and our enemies. But when the celebration finally ended, there was no feast and no wine to enjoy. I heard one man say, "Maybe he was just hungry. If we hadn't hung him up out there, we could be chewing on roast Argive!"

The grisly joke spread quickly; that day I heard it at least three times.

Using some of our precious firewood, we burned Captain Melanippus' head in the agora in the late afternoon. People were especially kind to me, as his betrothed. I was sorry that he was dead – he was a brave man, who died for Thebes – but I did not miss him. When the ceremony was over, I expressed my condolences to his son Astakus, who was truly grief-stricken, and went into the palace. I joined my young cousins for a scanty supper, then went to spin wool in a dim corner of the megaron. I spent many evenings that way, losing myself in the rhythmic throwing of the spindle.

"I'm so sorry." Someone was standing above me, blocking my light.

I looked up; seeing Menoeceus, my heart skipped a beat. "What?"

He pulled over a stool and sat down next to me. "About Melanippus."

"Oh – oh, of course." I felt suddenly flushed, because he was staring at me intently. "He was a good man, and did his best for Thebes."

"I don't know about that, Ismene. I think he might have been prolonging this war."

I considered his words as I carefully wound the spun thread around the shaft of my spindle. "What do you mean?"

He lowered his voice. "You're Polynikes' sister – you know him better than anyone. Do you really think he plans to kill all the men of Thebes, and enslave all the women?"

"I couldn't believe it at first," I admitted. "But, he *is* here, attacking the city. And Melanippus reported that's what the Argives are saying—"

"But what if it's not true? What if it was *never* true?"

Menoeceus had always seen things that other people missed. Yet I struggled with his ideas. "Why would Melanippus invent such thing?" I asked, drawing out more wool from the tuft on my distaff.

"I didn't say he invented it."

I threw the spindle and let it fall, whirling. "You mean – Eteokles told him to say it?" I finally whispered. "Why would he do that?"

"Because it gave the Thebans a reason to fight, from the very beginning. To support Eteokles."

"But… killing and raping… that's what war *is.*"

"Yes." He shifted closer. "But every day since the very first, Polynikes has offered an alternative. What if it's genuine? Wouldn't it be better for Eteokles to accept the duel? It doesn't seem right for Eteokles to ask so many Thebans to die for *his* sake… the king should be willing to die for Thebes, instead."

I could hardly hear my own voice when I asked: "Are you joining Polynikes?"

He shook his head. "No. My loyalty is to Thebes. And unless this war ends soon, more Thebans will suffer."

"But if they fight each other in single combat, one of them will die," I said.

"One of them is going to die anyway."

His blunt statement brought sudden moisture to my eyes; I caught up my spindle and passed it to my left hand, then wiped my face. Menoeceus reached out and touched my arm. "I'm sorry, Ismene."

I glanced up at Eteokles on the throne, talking to Uncle Creon and Haemon and Aktor the bronze-smith. Astakus sat slumped nearby on a stool. His young face was still smudged with the soot the raiders used for night camouflage; his leather corselet was scratched and stained with the blood of slain enemies. He and his father had been fighting my brother's battle – Melanippus had given his life, and even his corpse had been abused.

Which Theban would suffer next? How many more would die? All so that one of my brothers could stay on the throne of Kadmos, and deny it to the other.

"You're right," I said. "I wish there was something I could do."

"There is. Ask him to meet Polynikes."

"*Me?*"

"Yes, *you*, Ismene." His hazel eyes glowed golden in the torchlight. "*Your* voice may make the difference."

After a moment I nodded. Everyone else had been brave; why not me? Menoeceus offered a smile of encouragement as I set aside my spindle and distaff. Then, though my knees trembled, I rose and approached the throne.

"Eteokles," I said. Then I cleared my throat and spoke more loudly: "Brother?"

Eteokles turned his head in my direction. "Ismene – how are you? We all share your grief."

"Captain Melanippus died for Thebes."

"Yes," he said, solemnly. "He did."

I pressed my lips together, willing myself to continue. "So – so why won't *you* fight for us, Brother? Why won't you face Polynikes?"

My words startled everyone, from my youngest cousin Pyrrha to old Uncle Creon. Rhanis, on her knees sweeping ashes out of the hearth, looked over in amazement; the soldiers drinking in the far corner turned to stare. The room fell silent, and everyone gaped at me – then, one by one, they turned their attention to my brother the king.

Eteokles' face darkened, but even he seemed taken aback. "Where's this talk coming from, Ismene? You saw what the Argives did to Melanippus. Do you want them to do that to the people of Thebes?"

"Of course not," I said, unsettled by all the attention. I had not thought this through; I should have been prepared to continue the conversation. "But—"

"You ask others to risk their lives for the city," interrupted Menoeceus. He strode over to stand beside me. "Why won't you risk your own, Cousin?"

The king slapped the arm of his throne. "I knew it!" he thundered. "Turning my own sister against me – perhaps I should fight *you*, Menoeceus!"

I sensed Menoeceus preparing an angry answer, but Uncle Creon pounded his staff on the tiled floor and spoke first. "My lord king!" he said loudly. "My son risks his life every day to protect Thebes. Can you say the same of *your* son?"

Confused by this remark, I looked at my uncle – as did my brother and everyone else in the megaron. For several heartbeats, silence reigned. Finally Eteokles said: "Has age addled your wits, Uncle? I have no son."

"I know," said Creon. "Why not? Polynikes, I understand, has *two!*"

Eteokles clenched both fists in anger at this unfavorable comparison to his twin; I saw the muscles knot like ropes all along his arms. Then, sudden as lightning, Eteokles' shoulders relaxed and a broad grin lit his face. "Uncle Creon – you're right! It's past time I sired a son."

I thought of Rhodia's advice against pregnancy during a siege – especially now that food was in such desperately short supply. But I had already said too much.

Besides, Uncle Creon had a different objection. "With what woman? You're not married."

It was true; unlike Polynikes, Eteokles was not married and had never made a serious effort to become so. Over the years I thought he was waiting to make a great alliance. Occasionally he entered into negotiations for the daughter of a foreign king – but these never bore fruit. Knowing what I know today, I think he feared that a marriage would reveal that the necklace of Harmonia was missing.

Eteokles was up to Creon's challenge; he shrugged, and scanned the megaron. His gaze stopped on my maidservant Rhanis, squatting by the hearth. "You there!" he said, pointing. "What's your name?"

Her eyes went round. "Rh-Rhanis, my – my lord king," she stammered.

My brother beckoned her forward. "Come here, Rhanis."

Rising from the tiles, she approached the throne; her face was plain, but the siege had slimmed her figure from plump to shapely. She pushed a lock of hair out of her face, leaving a smudge on her temple.

"You can't marry *her!*" Aunt Eurydike exclaimed, scandalized. "That's the chamber-pot girl!"

Eteokles chuckled. "I didn't say I would. But, Aunt, your husband is my wisest counselor – he's right, I should have an heir. And this girl seems sturdy. Look at those breasts, those hips!"

Though she was being discussed like a heifer, Rhanis' lips parted in wonder. To bear the son of a king – surely she never hoped for so much in her life. Sometimes the Fates offer even the least of mortals a golden opportunity.

"I'm healthy, my lord king," she breathed.

"Good." Eteokles glanced over at a steward. "See that she's scrubbed clean, and have her brought to my bed. Aunt Eurydike, you will supervise."

Our aunt looked horrified. Uncle Creon's lips twitched – whether from amusement or disgust I could not tell – and he bent down and said something to his wife. Reluctantly she rose, inclined her head to my brother the king, and followed Rhanis and the steward out of the room.

"There!" said the king, looking pleased with himself. "Never let it be said that I'm unwilling to do my duty! And you, Menoeceus: if you incite my sister – or anyone else – to traitorous talk again, I'll have you thrown from the walls. Do I make myself clear?"

Menoeceus bowed deeply. "Perfectly, my lord king."

Eteokles frowned, but then spoke to a few more people before departing himself, to jokes and ribald well-wishes. Most others also left, but I stayed, returning to the corner where I had left my distaff leaning against the wall. Menoeceus joined me once more.

"Well, I asked him," I said.

"Yes, you did," he said. "I'm proud of you, Ismene."

His warm praise made all the embarrassment and awkwardness of the evening disappear, the way a puddle shrinks in bright sunlight. I smiled a little and shook my head. "Not that it did any good!"

He smiled, and then said: "Your brother definitely knows how to distract people. Tonight everyone will be talking about the king and the chamber-pot girl, instead of the duel he should be fighting with Polynikes." Leaning closer, he continued: "But Father was right – it's the duty of men and women to produce children to follow us."

I remember thinking how handsome he looked. That was all I could think of, the sparkle of his eyes and the curve of his lower lip. Heat rose to my cheeks as the silence lengthened.

"Ismene…"

"Yes?" The word came out so softly, I wasn't sure he would be able to hear.

"I'm saying it wrong." He looked up towards the shadowed ceiling, and for a moment I feared he would end the subject altogether. Then he met my gaze and said: "You've always been my favorite cousin. But during these last few months, I've come to truly admire you. How well you work with the water-carriers: helping everybody from the wealthiest of the Spartoi to the tanners and the refugees from the hills. The way you assist Udaeus and Rhodia with those near death, and give them comfort in their last days. I've watched you coax new life from the soil, upstairs in the garden – and save lives after that terrible fire. And no matter how awful things get, you never complain." He bit his lip. "When – when Eteokles betrothed you to Melanippus... I was crippled with jealousy."

"Really?" My heart soared as though I had learned that the siege was over and the gates unlocked. I could not help but smile – and for the first time in my life, I felt that my smile might match the radiance of my mother's.

Menoeceus glanced around the megaron; except for us, it was empty. Then he bent his head to mine.

I'll remember that moment as long as I live. He wore a tunic of pale yellow wool with a pattern of leaves worked in brown thread along the border just the shade of his leather belt, a touch darker than his suntanned skin. The days of deprivation had left his face more angular, the muscles of his arms and legs starkly defined. I thought, as his lips found mine, *Apollo, handsomest of the gods, is also an archer.*

He kissed me – and the power of my own response shocked me. After months of short rations, you almost forget how to be hungry – but when at last there's something savory to eat, your hunger reappears, overpowering. The force of my desire for Menoeceus was like that – and, I think, his for me.

After a time we stopped to catch our breath, but he put his arm around me and pulled me close.

Leaning against Menoeceus' hard-muscled shoulder, I reveled in his warmth. I did not know what might happen the next day. I did not know whether Thebes would survive. All I knew was at that moment, for the first time in years, I was truly happy.

"May I come with you to your room?" he asked.

Without hesitation, I answered him by lifting my face for another kiss. Then I took Menoeceus' hand and led him through the dark corridors to my chambers. Sometimes the Fates *do* offer mortals a chance at happiness – the thought returned to me but without the cynicism I felt watching Rhanis and Eteokles. Instead I felt pure joy.

Menoeceus and I had known each other all our lives, but we had never before helped each other undress, had never lain down naked together. It was a mixture of familiar and unfamiliar, ecstasy and a little pain, the mundane and the marvelous.

After we spent ourselves, we lay together on my bed in the moonlight; the rays of Artemis' chariot poured through my window, outlining the strong curves of his shoulders and chest in soft silver. We did not speak of marriage; we did not speak of the future at all. We dozed for a while, and the moon slipped across the sky. When we roused ourselves to try again, we put to use what we had learned of one another's bodies, and the second time was better than the first. Eventually the sky outside my window grew lighter; Menoeceus stroked my hair and kissed me, and said that he must go.

With so little sleep, I should have been tired – but I wasn't; I felt as light as a butterfly's wing. I rose, dressed myself, and went to the palace courtyard. Rhanis was there, although not seated beside Eteokles. She looked almost pretty in an ochre-dyed tunic, against which the sun-lightened streaks in her freshly washed hair seemed like gold instead of straw. Her round face glowed at all the attention from the king's family and advisors. But while others stared curiously at the king's new concubine, I kept glancing at my cousin Menoeceus.

Uncle Creon was the first to speak. "My lord king," he said, "there's bad news. Rot discovered overnight in the barley at the Neaira storehouse – found when the bakers went to fetch the ration for this morning's bread."

My brother asked for details; as we ate our meager breakfast we listened to my uncle's report, which was sobering. Many pithoi were spoiled, the grain not even worth serving to horses. Eteokles turned to Haemon. "We must ask Apollo for guidance."

Solemnly we followed the king through the shadowed corridors of the palace and down the main staircase. Udaeus awaited us there, holding a small jug of wine; these days, Haemon's offering to the god consisted of only a few drops scattered on the ground. The crowd that had gathered was not as thick as in earlier days; many of Thebes' citizens were too exhausted, hungry or discouraged to attend the dawn ceremony. Those that had come mostly seemed interested in catching a glimpse of Rhanis – rumors about her had already spread – but when Haemon stepped forward in his rather dirty white robes the lewd comments died down.

As the sun's chariot burst over the horizon, Haemon began the prayer; when he had completed the first verse, the crowd chanted the response. Haemon poured the libation, then returned the jar to Udaeus and lifted his arms towards the rising son. "Apollo, guide us! How may your city be saved?"

We received no answer from the skies – but something stirred at the southwestern corner of the agora.

"What is it?" I whispered to Menoeceus.

He peered out over the crowd. "Someone being carried on a litter…"

"The Tiresias!" cried my cousin Pyrrha. "The Tiresias is coming!"

As the crowd parted, I could see the ailing old prophet, lying on a litter borne by two servants. His elder daughter Daphne walked on his right side, Manto on his left. I knew Haemon visited the seer every day, asking for guidance, but the Tiresias had not communicated anything useful since the start of the siege. The old man looked as dry and brittle as a locust shell. Even though it was warm, a blanket covered most of his body.

Menoeceus turned to his father, who stood just behind us. "Did you ask him to come, Father?"

Uncle Creon shook his head. "I just hope whatever he says will be more helpful than his last prophecy."

"His last prophecy was true," Menoeceus pointed out.

My uncle shrugged. "Yes, Thebes was in danger – but it was the messenger's report that helped us prepare. The Tiresias' warning made no difference."

"But it was *true*," Menoeceus persisted. "Maybe we just need to know how to listen."

Creon's shaggy white eyebrows lowered; it looked as if he and his son were about to argue, when my brother's voice rang out loud enough to be heard across the agora.

"Tiresias! We are honored by your presence." He looked down at the invalid on the litter. "As king of Thebes, I ask you: what must I do to win this war?"

The old man opened his mouth and licked his lips as if struggling to speak. People edged forward, trying to get a view.

"Be still!" Eteokles thundered. The crowd settled down; a squalling infant was somehow shushed by his mother. "Tiresias, we are listening."

The aged prophet's voice was surprisingly clear. "One man…"

We waited; I was almost afraid to draw breath, lest the sound disturb the prophet. I glanced at Menoeceus, but he didn't notice: he was staring intently at the Tiresias.

Finally Eteokles asked: "One man, what?"

The blind seer turned his head towards my brother. "One man must die… for Thebes." Then his mouth closed.

"One man," my brother repeated. Then, more urgently, "*Which* man?"

The Tiresias said no more. His daughters whispered to him, touched his hands and face, but he did not respond.

"Has he died?" Eteokles asked, a hint of hope in his voice. I could almost hear him thinking that if one man had to die to save Thebes, *he* would choose the Tiresias – so as to be rid of his frustrating, incomplete, inconvenient prophecies.

"He lives, my lord king," Daphne reported. "But he has returned to the deep sleep. In this condition we cannot wake him."

My brother muttered something under his breath that I could not distinguish. Then, raising his voice, he said: "Haemon, as chief priest of Apollo, you will meditate on the words of the Tiresias."

Haemon bowed. "Yes, my lord king."

"Now, Thebans: to your places!" Eteokles commanded. "Relieve the night shift!"

People streamed away in different directions; Menoeceus squeezed my hand before starting for the Phthia Gate. The Tiresias' daughters had the bearers carry the old prophet back towards his house. Haemon looked as though he meant to follow, but Eteokles caught his arm.

"You will tell *me* what the prophecy means before you inform anyone else."

He nodded. "I understand, my lord king."

I had my own duties to attend, supervising the women bringing water to those stationed along the walls. It was shortly after noon when I reached the Phthia Gate. The enemy garrison outside remained quiet; Polynikes had made his challenge at the Kleodoxa that morning. Menoeceus consulted with his lieutenant and came down to speak to me. A sheen of sweat lent a glow to his strong, tanned arms and legs; he was as handsome as an archer in a wall-painting. My heart skipped with excitement as he drew near.

Pouring him water, I asked: "What do you think the Tiresias meant?"

"It's clear enough." He drank down the cup of water and held it out to be refilled. "One man must die to save Thebes."

My hands shook as I poured again; precious water spilled on the ground. "Eteokles?" I whispered.

"He's the king. He's the one that Polynikes is challenging." His boar's tooth helmet gave his face a stern aspect. "Thebes is starving, but that doesn't matter to him. Someone will have to convince him, somehow."

"When Haemon explains it," I ventured, "maybe that will do it."

"Maybe." He raised his hand to stroke my cheek. "Shall I come to you tonight?"

I nodded.

We said little at first, that night; our lovemaking was urgent and intense, as though we sought the power of Eros to drive away all other thoughts. At last we pulled apart and lay on our backs, heartbeats gradually slowing from the gallop they had reached. There was a slight, warm breeze; it cooled the sweat on my skin.

I turned my head to look at him. "I love you," I whispered.

"And I love you, Ismene."

Moving closer, I rested my head on his shoulder. "I wish we could stay like this forever."

"So do I." He stroked my hair. "But only the gods have forever."

I contemplated this. Of course all mortals die. It is only a question of when, and how.

"There are only a few days' food left," he said. "The peasants have started boiling leather and wool to fill their stomachs – did you know that?"

I nodded. "But there's still some grain – and three nanny goats, I think. And two sows in that pen by the Ogygia Gate."

He kissed my forehead. "We have thousands of people to feed, Ismene."

I knew as well as he did that our meager stores would soon be gone. "Do you think Eteokles will sacrifice the chariot horses?"

"He'll have no choice, if things don't change. But they *must* change."

Later, I realized that Menoeceus was already contemplating the course of action that he took. But, mercifully, he said nothing of it to me – and I did not suspect.

"What shall we do?" I asked.

In answer he just kissed me. Then he slipped out of my bed saying I should sleep, and he had some things to take care of before the morning council.

In fact, Eteokles called no council; he led us directly out into the agora for prayers to Apollo. I saw, in the gray pre-dawn light, that the ceremony was better attended than it had been for months: everyone in Thebes had heard about the Tiresias' words. But that morning the blind prophet did not appear.

At dawn's first light Haemon made the libation and led the people in prayer; then the king asked him: "Priest of Apollo, you said you would meditate on the words that the Tiresias gave us yesterday. Do you understand their meaning?"

Haemon glanced at his father, then told the king: "Thebes' suffering will be short; the matter will be settled soon."

Relief spread through the agora like a ripple in a pond. "You have heard Apollo's priest!" declared Eteokles, raising his hands as if to bless the people. "Our suffering will soon be over!"

Menoeceus said loudly: "*How* will our suffering end, my lord king?"

The king turned, anger in his blue eyes. "I cannot say – we must wait for the gods to show us."

Pulling back his shoulders, Menoeceus continued: "I believe the answer lies at the Astykratia Gate, my lord king. Will you come with me there?"

Eteokles scowled at him. "Why? What treachery are you planning – to let in Polynikes?"

Behind me, Aunt Eurydike hissed; the crowd shifted uneasily, murmuring and pointing. I saw Uncle Creon lift his staff, preparing to vent his anger – but Menoeceus held up one hand. "Father, I thank you, but I can speak for myself." Facing Eteokles, he said: "No, my lord king. No such thing. But I do have a plan to help our city; and it can only be accomplished at the Astykratia Gate."

While Eteokles pondered this, it occurred to me that Menoeceus might intend to answer Polynikes' challenge himself. My throat tightened in alarm – but Menoeceus wore no sword, and a bow was no weapon for a duel.

"Very well," my brother finally said. He glanced at Hyperbius and Aktor and young Astakus. "Have your lieutenants take command from the night watch," he told them. "You will come with your king."

Half of Thebes, it seemed, followed; when our procession reached the Astykratia Gate, the king received the salute of the night guard's commander. "Has Polynikes been sighted here?"

The man shook his head. "No, my lord king."

"Very good." Turning to Menoeceus, he said: "So – why have you led me here?"

"I must climb to the top of the wall."

Eteokles smirked. "And I must go with you, I suppose, so you can show me something – or push me off?"

Menoeceus shook his head. "No, my lord king, that's not necessary. Stay below if you prefer." He handed his bow to his father; then he unbuckled the chin-strap and handed his helmet to his mother. He ran his hands through his hair, and then slipped the leather belt of his quiver over his head. I noticed there were only two arrow-shafts to be seen, and thought this strange – and then Menoeceus drew out a ribbon decorated with roses from the palace garden. Handing the quiver to me, he kissed my cheek.

"What's this?" asked Eteokles. "Are you going to signal the enemy with a garland?"

"It's not the enemy who should pay attention to this," he answered. Then he headed up the stairs.

I gripped the quiver, feeling its leather slightly damp with my lover's perspiration. I did not know what was about to happen, but I felt suddenly sick with fear.

When Menoeceus reached the battlements, he tied the ribbon around his head.

"No!" cried Uncle Creon, the first to comprehend. "Son, don't do it!" He moved toward the stairs, but his aged legs carried him slowly.

Menoeceus turned to look back at Thebes; his eyes met mine for the space of two heartbeats. Then, his voice loud and clear, he addressed the king. "King Eteokles: the Tiresias said one man must die to save Thebes. I am not vain enough to think myself that man. But my death will prove I am no traitor – and, I hope, give you the courage at last to accept your brother's challenge."

Then I realized that his garland was like those placed on animals about to be sacrificed on the altar. I screamed, "No – Menoeceus, *no!*"

But it was too late. He had already jumped.

*

Overcome, Ismene squeezes her eyes tightly shut and leans back against the wall of the tomb. But, though words have failed her, closing her eyes does not stop the memory.

Two hands – soft and warm – enclose hers. "Oh, Ismene," says Aunt Eurydike, "oh, dear girl."

Ismene yields to the older woman's embrace, resting her head on the comforting shoulder.

"My dear," Eurydike whispers, "you may be carrying his child."

Ismene pulls back to look at her aunt's tear-streaked face. "Really?" she asks, and then feels foolish. "I mean, isn't it too soon to tell?"

"It is soon." Eurydike smiles slightly, wiping her eyes. "But I was noticing that your breasts are larger."

Sensing everyone staring at her breasts, Ismene folds her arms across her chest. "We've been getting more food. That might be all."

"It might," Eurydike says. "But I hope – I hope it's more than that. It would be a blessing from the gods."

"A sign, perhaps," says Eriphyle, raising her voice as if to ensure that Antigone, in the darkness of the other tomb, will take note.

"And what about *my* pregnancy?" asks Argia.

"That could also be a sign from the gods," Haemon says, glancing at Eriphyle as if to verify, priest to priestess. "A sign that it is time for life, not death."

"If we're going to live," Adrastos mutters, "we need to get out of here before Creon arrives."

"Maybe Astakus has left," Ismene says. "I'll check." She gets to her feet, then steps around the people and her brother's grave-goods as she makes her way to the tomb's entrance.

Am I being brave now? she wonders, putting her hand against the door. But when she opens the door she does not see the soldiers – only her uncle the king.

CHAPTER NINETEEN
CREON

Arriving at the twin tombs, Creon surveys the area from his sedan chair. The guards are at their posts, but no crowds loiter nearby: the place has been cleared, as ordered.

But – though a quick glance at the position of the sun, halfway toward the western horizon, confirms the hour – there is *no one* present other than the guards. The person who asked to meet him here has not yet come.

Had he misunderstood? No, the messenger was reliable. There must simply be some delay.

"Down," he tells the bearers, and they lower the sedan chair to the ground. A slight breeze ruffles his thin hair; the weather is cooling, which makes him think of autumn and harvest time. Though the war is past, the rest of the year will still be difficult: the normal rhythm of agriculture has been totally disrupted. This only increases the importance of the meeting for which Creon waits.

A servant hands him his staff; he rises from the royal chair and makes his way to the tombs. Gritting his teeth, he realizes that the heap of flowers before Antigone's tomb is larger than the one before his nephew's. He moves past Astakus and the other guard, pushing away the offending blooms with the butt end of his staff – and hears what sound like muffled voices. He looks up in annoyance – the guards should know better than to whisper behind his back! – and realizes that the soldiers have not spoken: the sounds are coming from within Eteokles' tomb.

He gestures with his thumb, pointing to the bronze-bound door. "Who?" he says softly.

"Your family, my lord king," answers Astakus, echoing Creon's hushed tone.

Interesting. Creon has not expected this.

"Take your men over there to the knoll," he says softly. "Have my servants go with you, and keep anyone else well away – with the exception I mentioned earlier."

Nodding, the soldier complies. Creon edges closer, standing so that his ear almost touches the door. After a moment he recognizes the voice of his niece Ismene; and, as her narration continues, he realizes that she is addressing her sister Antigone, sealed into the adjoining tomb. He is aware of many events Ismene relates, but others surprise him – and light a spark of hope in a corner of his spirit he had thought would remain forever dark. His beloved son, Menoeceus, who sacrificed his young life for Thebes –

some part of him might yet live on!

The door opens suddenly, startling him; but his appearance is more surprising to those inside. "What a group we have here!" he says, his eyes adjusting to the darkness of the tomb. "Not only my family, but the Argive priestess and her retinue!" He moves further inside. "Sheltering the sister of our enemy Adrastos – a woman I ordered gone from Theban lands – and whispering stories to the niece condemned for her disobedience! Now you three defy me as well!" He studies Ismene, Haemon, and Eurydike in turn; for several breaths they remain guiltily silent, and Creon wonders how they will react to this show of anger.

Even though his heart is thawed by the thought that Menoeceus might have sired a child before his death, Creon knows a king dare not begin with leniency. Power is built on strength; a fortress cannot last on a foundation of yielding sand.

"Husband..." Eurydike begins.

"A wife should obey her husband's orders," he says sternly. "And I ordered Antigone shut away."

"Creon, I haven't disobeyed you. Antigone remains shut away on the other side of the wall. What harm is there in talking to her, comforting her? Must she die all alone?"

To this he has no answer. He turns to the next traitor.

"And you, Haemon – you defy me for a woman who deserted you?"

"Antigone didn't desert me. She left Thebes to care for her father – as a father, you should appreciate that!" Haemon meets his gaze directly. "And now: as Antigone's husband, Apollo's chief priest, and your eldest son – I ask you to break down that wall and release her before you anger the gods further."

Creon resists the urge to nod in approval. It is high time that his son begins standing up for what he wants – but he will not acknowledge this before foreigners. Instead he turns to his niece: "Ismene, I see you share your siblings' rebellious nature."

"I wish I could match their courage, my lord king," says Ismene. "Compared with them, I am nothing. But the bravest of all was your son Menoeceus."

Creon's throat tightens; he swallows hard, willing his eyes to stay dry. The memory of his son's death is more painful than a broken bone laid bare.

Haemon breaks in, sparing Creon the need to respond. "Ismene was just telling us – and Antigone – about him."

"I know," Creon admits. "I was outside the tomb, listening."

"Then, my lord king, you've heard that we were only sharing stories of the war," says the Argive priestess. "You know that we have not been plotting against you."

He tilts his head. "I'm not sure of that yet. I don't know why you're still here, Eriphyle, when I ordered you to leave. But..." he continues, moving into their midst, "I know it is my place to tell the end of the story. What happened after Menoeceus died. Antigone, listen well. And I call upon the ghost of Eteokles to bear witness." While the others exchange looks of confusion and then acceptance, he removes the stopper from a jar of wine among the grave-goods, then pours a libation for the shade of his nephew and predecessor. "Shall any word I speak be false, Eteokles, I bid you call out from the Underworld."

He hands the jar back to Haemon, who puts it away. Ismene brings over a folding wooden camp-stool from among the grave offerings: Creon takes a seat, and the others move so they are sitting near his knee. Creon looks at the foreign priestess, Eriphyle, with her three servants clustered in the shadows behind her.

"I welcome your words, king of Thebes," she says solemnly.

Creon nods. "Antigone, can you hear me?" he says loudly.

The answer from beyond the wall is muffled, but Creon can still hear the note of defiance so characteristic of his niece. "Yes, Uncle."

"Good. Then I shall begin."

CREON

My son Menoeceus leapt to his death from the same spot where my father, for whom he was named, sacrificed himself for Thebes. It is the highest spot on our walls, the one surest to bring a quick death. I imagine that my son saw the gods' will in the convergence of events, his own name, and the prophecy of the Tiresias.

I knew in advance of my father's actions what he planned to do. I did not try to stop him. But he was an old man: older than I am now, his life-thread already worn through. My son was a young man in his prime.

Even had I been able to climb the stairs in time, I could never have stopped my son from jumping. I would only have robbed his final moments of their dignity. But when I saw him step away, disappearing from view, it was as though my heart vanished too. I staggered; a soldier caught my elbow, so I did not fall, but I lost my grip on my walking stick and it thumped to the ground. I heard my wife's anguished wail, my other children's cries of horror, my niece Ismene's heartsick moan – and the clamor of the Theban crowd.

Then Haemon was at my side. "Father?" he was saying. "Father, are you all right?"

I clutched the arm of my eldest son. I still had living children, I told myself – and Thebes still needed me. "Yes," I told him, accepting my fallen staff from one of the soldiers. I pulled myself straight. "Thank you, Haemon."

My nephew the king approached, his face ashen. "Creon, your son – it's as the Tiresias said. One man's death, to save Thebes."

"Do you think that the Argives will just leave now?" I spat at him. "Menoeceus killed himself to remind *you* of *your* duty!"

Eteokles said nothing.

"He sacrificed himself for the city," I continued, "as your grandfather did! Your mother hung herself to prevent riots and chaos when her deeds were discovered; your father accepted blindness and exile." I looked past him, seeing that my wife had fallen to her knees, weeping; Ismene had her fist stuck in her mouth, as if to prevent herself from screaming, and my younger children – despite their tear-streaked faces – were trying to comfort them both. Moving so close that my lips almost touched my nephew's ear, I whispered: "There's only one way to end this war. If you won't go out to face Polynikes, I'll tell the city of the trick you and Megara used with the drawing of the tiles – and of the herbs you gave your brother to keep him from assuming the throne a year later."

"How – how do you—"

"Megara told her mother. Eurydike told me." I saw fear in his blue eyes. "I haven't forgotten who gave my daughter permission to wed Alkides against my will."

I turned my back on him and began climbing the stairs. No soldier attempted to stop me; a moment later both Eteokles and Haemon followed, with Aktor and Hyperbius close behind. When we reached the battlements, I saw my son lying on the rocks below but could not make out the details. "Aktor, what do you see?" I asked the bronze-smith, knowing his eyesight was keen.

Aktor peered downwards. "I think he's dead, my lord."

"Better if it was quick," said Hyperbius, touching my shoulder.

I nodded and rubbed my eyes. "I want to retrieve his body."

"Uncle, it's dangerous," Eteokles warned.

Shading his eyes, Aktor scanned the Argive encampment beyond the range of our arrows. He reported several pointing towards us – obviously they had seen Menoeceus jump – and a runner heading away.

"They're probably fetching Polynikes," Hyperbius speculated. "Or another of their commanders."

"We can ask for a truce to retrieve my brother's body," said Haemon.

"I don't think...." Eteokles began, and then stopped.

Hyperbius' interpretation proved correct. The Argives were curious enough to send for their commanders; in a short time several chariots arrived, as well as King Adrastos on his horse.

I drew a deep breath and yelled, as loud as I could: "Polynikes!" The sound echoed across the empty space beyond the walls, but I did not think he could hear me.

My son Haemon, so many years a priest, bellowed and waved. "Polynikes!"

We observed some movement, and then two of the men got out of their chariots and came forward, surrounded by their infantry holding up shields in a protective formation. As they approached I recognized one as Polynikes and the other as Amphiorax. When they were close enough for conversation, Polynikes shouted: "Is that you, Uncle?"

Eteokles grabbed my arm, but I ignored him. "Yes! Polynikes, will you allow our men to retrieve—" I paused, swallowing, then continued: "to retrieve the body of my son Menoeceus?"

The king's hand dropped from my arm; for a time there was silence – in the city down behind me; among all the archers, javelin-men, and slingers along the walls; and from the enemy. Then the enemy war-leaders spoke among themselves. They came to some agreement, and Polynikes turned back towards us. "We will honor your truce!" he shouted; meanwhile Amphiorax and a group of soldiers with blue-painted shields retreated, presumably to deliver the message to the others.

I looked at Eteokles, and at first I thought he would object. But then he nodded, and pointed to Aktor. "Take five men. Through the sally-port, not the gate." Turning to the ranking archer, he said, "Have your men keep their weapons trained on the enemy. The traitor out there could be lying. If they venture close, let fly."

It took longer than I expected: long enough to feel a drop of sweat trickle the length of my back, long enough to remember the first words and first steps of the son I had named for my father. Eventually I saw Aktor and his men down below. Both armies watched warily. A chariot-horse in the distance whinnied; the bow of an archer off to my left jerked, but he held his fire. Four of Aktor's men lifted my son's broken body and set him into the belly of a shield; then they hoisted their burden and shuffled back toward the walls. All the while Aktor and the fifth man kept their spears leveled outward. At last the outer door of the sally port swung shut behind them.

Then Polynikes brought his chariot closer. "I honored your truce, Creon! Now, will my brother Eteokles honor my challenge?"

Leaning against the stone battlement, I turned to my nephew the king. The details of his armor differed slightly from his brother's, but otherwise they might have been the same man – even to the red plumes of their helmet-crests.

Eteokles was trapped, and he knew it. He would never hold the soldiers' loyalty if I told them the truth of how he'd cheated to win the throne, especially after the misery of the siege. I suppose he could have pushed me off the wall; he was young and quick. But Haemon and Hyperbius were too close for him to manage it undetected.

"Tomorrow!" he shouted down to his twin. "Outside the Ogygia Gate!"

In the streets below a great cheer arose, quickly matched by one from the Argives outside the gate. Eteokles looked at me through narrowed eyes, then nodded as one nods to an opponent who has just won a game of senet. Then he turned and descended the stairs. Haemon, Hyperbius and I followed.

Leaning on my staff for support, I looked down at my son's body. His mother knelt, weeping, at his side; the shield in which he lay was like a cradle. *We are all born in blood,* I thought. And this ending – this sacrifice – would give birth to something else. *This is what you wanted,* I told him silently. *The war will end, now, one way or another.*

I bent down to straighten the garland of roses on Menoeceus' head. Then I took my wife's hand and, with the help of my youngest daughter, drew her to her feet.

Eteokles spoke with Haemon about preparations for Menoeceus' funeral. When he had finished, he embraced his aunt, cousins and sister, then told Hyperbius to gather the people of Thebes in the agora. Pyrrha and I helped Eurydike stumble back to the palace. Eteokles moved more quickly, of course; by the time we arrived he was standing on the terrace at the top of the grand staircase, looking out over the crowd. He waited for the rest of the royal family to ascend the stairs before he moved forward to address the people.

"Thebans, we have lost one of our best today," Eteokles began. "Menoeceus was my cousin, my friend since boyhood. He was the best of our archers, a true leader. We must mourn him; we must grieve."

As the king continued his eulogy, even I – though I had just lost a beloved son, though I had been filled with rage at Eteokles for the circumstances that led to my son's sacrifice – even I was moved and comforted. Eteokles spoke of his cousin's bravery and piety; he reminded us that in contrast to Menoeceus' steadfast loyalty, the traitor Polynikes was willing to destroy Thebes to satisfy his own ambition. He recalled other Thebans who had given their lives for the city: Lasthenes, Eurymedon, Melanippus. "Their valor will not be forgotten. We must honor their memory. Tonight at sunset we will bury my cousin Menoeceus at the Astykratia Gate – and tomorrow, to honor his shade, I will meet the traitor in single combat."

The people did not cheer this assertion as they had before; instead there was a respectful, somber silence. Thebans were considering the import of the moment, the fact that their fate would soon depend on the strength of their king's sword-arm.

Lifting a hand, Eteokles made a sweeping gesture that encompassed the city below. "For all those who have fallen, and all those we must protect – our wives and children, our aged parents – we must remain strong. We must defend our mother city against the enemy, against the traitor who brought them here. The walls and the gates must be well guarded." There were shouts of assent; then he concluded: "Go to your posts! And I, your king, will prepare for tomorrow."

He beckoned to me; as we stepped through the palace doors, he said, "We need to talk, Uncle."

I nodded, and followed Eteokles through the corridors to his study. He removed his war-helmet and set it on his work table; dismissing all his servants, he bade me take a seat. After the door was closed, he went to the side table where a jar of wine stood in a bronze stand. He poured two cups, without mixing in any water, and offered one to me.

"It's the last of the Chian," he said.

I accepted it, sprinkling a few drops on the floor to Menoeceus before drinking. It was rich and powerful and slightly bitter.

Eteokles sat on the couch next to mine, rather than at his work table. He spoke low, his voice full of regret: "I did not know what he meant to do."

I looked down, studying the blood-dark liquid inside the gleaming gold cup. "Nor did I."

"Well... it's as the Fates would have it." He sipped his wine, then set his goblet on the low table before us. "So now, Uncle, I need your help to ensure that I win – that *Thebes* wins, tomorrow."

Even with all that had happened that day, I understood his meaning immediately: he meant to cheat, if he could. Not that I condemned him for this – only men with large armies and thick muscles think that might makes right, and dismiss anything but force in battle as somehow impure. Strength is a gift of the gods – but so are clever ideas! After all, we worship Hermes as well as Ares. And Thebes was in grave danger.

"How?" I asked.

"You tell me." Apparently Eteokles had considered this matter for some time. "Your encounter with the Sphinx – it was not like her to kill herself. How'd you manage it?"

"That was before your time," I parried.

"True – just after my father married my mother." He smiled slightly, and took another sip of the Chian. "But the story of the Sphinx is one of the city's favorites: her contest of riddles, her sudden and extremely convenient death just afterward."

"The Sphinx killed herself," I said reflexively. "With her own blade."

"Did she?" A questioning spark lit his blue eyes. "I've heard the story many times. Old people love listeners, and sometimes their words reveal more than they realize."

Eteokles was always perceptive. The aged do appreciate an audience for their stories: just look at me now! Sometimes the young think we talk too much; but when one nears life's end, the past is something to be savored rather than hidden. One seeks admiration for past deeds – even ones once shrouded in secrecy, when those who might have objected are gone. Besides, my nephew was a man to appreciate cunning.

"I've heard, Uncle, that you have made a study of herbs and poisons."

"Yes," I acknowledged. "I have."

"Was that how you persuaded the Sphinx to end her own life – with herbs in her wine that made her do your bidding? Or with poison?"

"I was alone with the Sphinx when she died. Your duel with Polynikes will have many witnesses. I don't think he'll agree to share a wineskin with you first."

Eteokles leaned forward, forearms on his knees. "What about something on the edge of a blade? Something so that even a scratch would... would..."

I supplied the words he seemed hesitant to utter: "Would be fatal?"

He looked away then; the knot in his throat bobbed as he swallowed. This surprised me. He had asked me here to talk of trickery, of a sure way to slay his twin. And yet contemplating it clearly disturbed him. I had always thought Eteokles' reluctance was a matter of simple self-preservation: Polynikes had been living in Argos for years, training at arms with the fiercest warriors of all Hellas – he had to be the better warrior. Logically, waiting out the siege offered Eteokles a better chance of survival. And until that moment, I would have said that had matters been reversed – if Eteokles had been sure of his ability to prevail – he would have accepted the duel long before. But I realized that something more was at work.

Eteokles had shown little love or respect for his twin since the boar hunt so many years ago, so brotherly affection could not be the issue. Did Eteokles fear that fratricide would earn him the wrath of the gods – and curse him as Oedipus was cursed for slaying his father Laius?

"Polynikes has brought suffering and destruction to our city," I reminded him. "His war has meant the death of many Thebans. Including my son."

Eteokles nodded, still not meeting my gaze; he stood, and walked over to the window. "Yes. He's a traitor to Thebes, and must be stopped." He turned back to me; the summer sun behind him lit his coppery hair but cast his face into shadow, so that I could not read his expression. "That's why I need your advice, Uncle."

"You want poison for your blade. So that you need not be the better swordsman to win the duel."

He nodded.

"I doubt wolfsbane or hemlock could be made strong enough. I'm not sure about belladonna, and anyway the city's supplies are almost gone."

"What about snake venom?" he asked, walking back toward me. "A viper's bite is just a scratch, and yet it kills."

"Even so, venom takes time to work. Sometimes hours."

"Anything to improve my chances. *Thebes'* chances."

I studied my fingers. My son had given his life to force Eteokles to act; Menoeceus understood that protecting Thebes against the invaders was worth more than a single life – even when that life was his own. Now one of my sister's sons must die to preserve the city.

384

"I will see what can be done." With the aid of my walking-stick I rose to my feet. My nephew thanked me, and walked me solicitously to the door, where he told the servant waiting outside to summon Aktor and Hyperbius.

When I reached my rooms I dismissed the servants, telling them I wished to mourn alone. After they were gone, I dragged a painted chest out from beneath the bench in the far corner. I did not lift its dusty lid; the old cloaks and tunics in the chest's main compartment were of no interest to me. Instead, I grasped a section of the chest's carved decoration and twisted until I felt the secret latch slide free. Then I was able to pull out the hidden drawer that rested beneath the chest's false bottom.

Moving so that the afternoon sunlight illuminated the contents of this drawer, I examined the various vials of carved stone to make sure their beeswax-coated wooden stoppers still held. I checked the knots that closed the half-dozen small drawstring bags; each was as I had last tied it and none had been disturbed. Then I inspected the small boxes of terracotta and ivory, each sealed with a lump of dried clay into which I had pressed the side of my signet-ring so that only the shape of the setting's edge – not the carved seal – left its unique mark. All were intact.

Each container was different enough from the others for me to tell them apart, but none was a work of art. There were no gold clasps or precious stones, no painted Kretan decorations, no Aegyptian faience inlays. But the herbs and potions within were more precious than rubies or amethysts. Some could bring on visions; others would trigger nightmares. A few had the power to summon sleep. Others would ferry any mortal to the far side of the Styx. I chose a vial that I thought would serve my nephew's purpose, and slipped it into my tunic. Then I replaced the concealed drawer and pushed the chest back beneath the bench.

I walked over to the window to look out over the city. I must have stood there a long while, lost in memory. Old men do such things – especially old men who have lost a beloved son. I remembered the cheerful sound of Menoeceus' laughter when he was a toddling child. The toy wooden chariot he had played with, a gift from his uncle Oedipus the king. I recalled how proud he was the first time he shot bronze-tipped arrows from his small bow, then when he bested the other youngsters in a contest that spring. How impressive he looked in his war-corselet and greaves: so unlike his unathletic father... except that Eurydike always said he had my voice, and my way of tilting the head when listening.

Menoeceus had given his life for his city – I would ensure that his sacrifice was not in vain.

Eventually the servants knocked at the door, saying it would soon be time for my son's funeral.

I remember little of the ceremony; as my womenfolk wept, and my younger sons wiped their eyes, I found myself watching the king, wishing that he and his generation had chosen different – and better – paths. My daughter Megara could have obeyed me, and married a good husband instead of the drunken braggart who murdered her and her children. My son Haemon could have taken a new wife to replace the one who abandoned him. Eteokles and Polynikes could have remained the friends they were in childhood – they could have trusted and relied upon each other, like King Amphion and his twin brother Zethos. Then Menoeceus would not have jumped from Thebes' high walls.

But I could not change the past. I could only do my best to guarantee the future of the city.

When the ritual was complete, the crowd of mourners went back to their homes. Only a single torch led the procession back to the palace; we had none to waste. I told Eurydike to stay with Ismene that night; the poor girl was taking her cousin's death very hard – and I preferred to go about my business without observation.

I went to Eteokles' chamber before dawn. The king was already awake, dressed only in a loincloth; despite his royal edict, an oil-lamp burned on the bedside table, a silver hand-mirror beside it. I remember thinking that fussing over his appearance hardly seemed warrior-like, but then conceded to myself that a king needed to present an impressive countenance – especially on a day such as this.

"Uncle," he said simply. Then, to his manservant, he said: "Leave us."

I waited until we were alone, then withdrew the sealed stone vial from my tunic, along with a makeup brush I had taken from my wife's things. "This is for your sword, and your dagger."

He turned and walked over to his wooden arms-stand. Eteokles took the sheathed sword in one hand and his dagger in the other. I waved towards a low table; he carried the weapons to it and slipped each blade from its scabbard.

"The lamp, Nephew," I said. "We must take care."

Eteokles fetched the lamp and brought it over to the table. I took a seat on the nearby couch and cautiously worked loose the wax-coated wooden stopper from the stone vial, then placed the stopper on the table.

"First, the dagger," I said.

He grasped the weapon and held it up; I dipped the brush into the soapstone vial and then painted the mixture down the blade's sharp edges.

"Sheathe it carefully."

Eteokles did so, then picked up the sword in both hands. This took longer. I started with the tip of the blade – working an alternating path down each side, coating a handspan's length along one edge and then switching to the other. My vial did not contain enough to paint the entire length of the sword.

"If that's all you have," he said, "it'll have to do."

Getting to my feet, I held the bristles of the brush in the lamp-flame till they caught; then I dropped the miniature torch into an empty brazier in the corner. Cautiously I replaced the stopper and set the vial aside. "As you slide the blade back into the scabbard, the leather will spread the poison back from the tip towards the hilt. It should be enough." I picked up the sheath and held it as steady as I could using both hands; Eteokles slipped the blade slowly into place. We both exhaled with relief when that was done.

"Take heed how you draw either weapon," I said. "Don't nick yourself. And these blades may never be safe again. It would be best, once you've won the duel, to melt them down and burn the scabbards."

He nodded, and replaced the weapons on the wall. His boar's-tooth helmet looked as if it had just been polished; the bronze greaves glimmered in the lamplight and I realized that Eteokles wanted to impress more than just the people of Thebes.

"I suppose it will be odd," I said, "to face Polynikes after all this time."

Gesturing at the silver mirror that lay on his bedside table, my nephew made a sound that was not quite a laugh. "I see him every time I look in the mirror."

Some say that twins start as a single child in the womb; I think Eteokles felt this to be true in a way his brother Polynikes did not. He could have had Polynikes assassinated after his banishment – even before reaching Argos. It would have been much cleaner, much simpler, and I'd always wondered why he did not. Now I finally understood Eteokles' reluctance, both to fight Polynikes and to kill him. It would be too much like killing himself.

"I thank you, Uncle, for the sake of our city," he said, his tone suddenly brisk.

I left him and returned to my own empty rooms; Eurydike arrived, looking weary, as I was washing my face. We went through our morning preparations without speaking. My wife was still dazed with grief for our lost son – and while I mourned Menoeceus, I feared for Thebes. What if Eteokles lost – what mercy would Polynikes and his Argives show? Would he kill me? Probably. I hoped he would show mercy to Eurydike and our children.

After we dressed, Eurydike and I made our way toward the front of the palace. Ismene and my younger children joined us in the antechamber, where Eteokles – attended by his bedmate Rhanis – stood garbed for battle. The guards swung open the tall wooden doors, and we followed the king out onto the terrace. Dawn stretched glowing fingers across the eastern horizon, the morning star shining brightly between rosy streaks; the crescent moon shimmered through a few clouds in the west.

I surveyed the crowd filling the agora below. "Where's Aktor?" I asked my nephew. "And Astakus?"

Eteokles crossed his arms. "Outside, with their men; by now they should have flanked the enemy. My sentries report that the Argives have gathered almost all their forces at the Ogygia Gate to watch the duel."

Acknowledging my nephew's cleverness with a nod, I said: "You'll have most of Thebes watching too. Except, perhaps, the Tiresias." I did not see a litter.

"But one of his daughters is here." Eteokles gestured towards a small, slim woman with long straight hair; in the dim light it was impossible to tell whether she was Daphne or Manto. "Let's hope that she has favorable omens to report to her father."

Wearing his whitest robes, Haemon emerged from the palace behind us; he raised his hands and chanted a paean to Apollo. Then he handed King Eteokles a golden wine-cup. Eteokles declared: "May Apollo be with us!" and walked slowly down the marble stairs. When he reached the final tread, he poured out the libation. As dark droplets of wine splashed onto the cobblestones, I was reminded of the poison on the king's blades.

While the Thebans in the agora cheered, the king beckoned the rest of the royal family to join him and the people. We descended the stairway – Rhanis following behind – and Haemon led us all in a final prayer. Then Eteokles ordered the soldiers to relieve the night guard. A garrison would remain at each gate, but it seemed that everyone else remaining planned to follow us to the Ogygia Gate.

As the king stepped over to return the goblet to Haemon, his sandal struck a loose cobblestone; he staggered, and I reached out to catch his elbow. Those who were watching caught their breath with a collective gasp. Had the king fallen, that would have been the worst possible omen. Haemon said nothing, but looked grave as he took the goblet from his cousin.

But King Eteokles, quick as ever, turned to the crowd with a reassuring smile. "You see, Thebans, even if I stumble, I will not fall! And Thebes, too, will stay upright!"

The tension shattered as suddenly as it had formed. People cheered, whistled, jumped in the air for a better look at their king. A chant started: "Eteokles! Eteokles! Eteokles!"

The king's shoulders straightened; he lifted his hand, and the royal seal-ring of Thebes caught the sun, now risen above the eastern wall. "To Ogygia!"

He led us southwest through the city, towards the Ogygia Gate and the most sacred place in Theban history: where our founder Kadmos first arrived and slew the serpent that guarded Ares' sacred spring; where Kadmos sowed the serpent's teeth that grew into the earthbound warriors, the Spartoi, ancestors of our ruling elite; where the would-be queen, Dirke, met the fate decreed by King Amphion and his twin brother Zethos.

The stable master and his charioteers had made ready all fourteen chariots; as we drew closer I saw Hyperbius walking along the line, inspecting the horse-teams and vehicles. The sight put heart into the people of Thebes: twenty-eight beautiful steeds, their manes bound with colorful ribbons into rows of tufts; fourteen valiant charioteers, each ready to drive a warrior out to the battlefield.

Eurydike and Ismene led a crowd of women and boys too young to fight up the stone stairways on either side of the gate; as they fanned out along the battlements, all seeking good vantage points among the archers and javelin-men, Eteokles gestured to the herald stationed at the lookout-post nearest the gate. "King Eteokles of Thebes will answer the challenge of the traitor Polynikes!" the man bellowed.

In answer we heard the blare of a keras horn, and then Polynikes' voice came through the gate. "Eteokles, you coward, come out and fight!"

Eteokles did not deign to answer this directly. He went to his chariot, and motioned Hyperbius and the other warriors to theirs; spearmen formed up behind, and my son Haemon and I took our place as witnesses behind their shields. "Remember," Eteokles said to those nearest, "and pass the word down the line: respect the duel. Do not engage in battle without my order."

Hyperbius nodded, with a crooked grin like a merchant who knows he is about to get the better of a deal. "Yes, my lord king. Your men know the plan."

King Eteokles gave the order to open the gate. The guards drew back the massive oaken cross-bar with a heavy scraping sound; then the tall gates swung outward, opening for the first time since spring.

The Ogygia Gate is wide enough for eight men marching abreast; Eteokles and his captains had picked the tallest and most imposing spearmen they could find. They marched smartly, shields held level, the cadence of their sandals steady and uniform. Next came Hyperbius' chariot, and then the other chariots two by two – until Eteokles' chariot, which the rest of the spearmen, and Haemon and I, followed. From the walls, Thebes' women cheered their husbands, sons, and brothers.

Hyperbius and his charioteer had gone a few lengths beyond the gate, and stopped to form a center point; the other chariots formed up to their side in an arc that mirrored the curving line of the Argive forces. Polynikes, with his red-crested helmet and his shield painted with a lion, was easy to spot. Beside him was King Adrastos on his white mount. There was the warrior-priest Amphiorax, stocky and muscular, his shield painted solid blue. Behind them, the bristling spears of the Argive army were like a field of grain on a windless day.

Eteokles' charioteer brought the vehicle up to the central position, just beyond Hyperbius. Haemon and I followed, accompanied by four spearmen, and took places beside Hyperbius' chariot. Polynikes' charioteer brought his team closer, so that now the brothers faced each other at the center of a broad double arc of warriors.

Polynikes jumped down from his chariot; the driver handed him a spear. Walking out onto the packed earth between the armies, he shouted: "It took you five months, coward!"

Shield on his left arm, spear in his right hand, Eteokles stepped out of his chariot-car. "There's a special place in the Underworld for traitors!"

Taking two long strides, he hurled his spear. Polynikes dodged the missile easily, and answered by casting his own spear; its bronze point flashed in the sun before Eteokles deflected it with his shield.

"He should have waited," Hyperbius muttered. "Get close enough for a thrust."

But I understood Eteokles' strategy. He wanted the battle to be fought with sword, not spear. I saw how carefully he drew his gleaming sword from its scabbard before beginning to close the distance. Polynikes whipped out his with an easy, practiced motion.

The two combatants drew closer, circling one another just out of reach. Polynikes' dented greaves and battle-scarred shield offered a marked contrast to the bright polish of King Eteokles' armor; but in their height, their lithely muscled build, the lines of face and beard glimpsed beneath tiled helmets, the sons of Oedipus were virtually indistinguishable. They seemed, indeed, reflections of the same man.

At first, the two opposed armies watched in breathless silence: I could hear the sound of water flowing in Dirke's spring nearby, the scuffling of the twins' sandaled feet in the dust, the grunt as one brother parried a sword-blow with his shield. They feinted, clashed, retreated a few steps, lunged again. Polynikes bellowed, charging forward; Eteokles swung his shield around to block the thrust, but his brother's blade skidded along the curved surface and nicked his thigh, blood welling up in a crimson line. Twisting back from the blade, Eteokles arced his sword around to the side; Polynikes jumped back.

"First blood!" yelled someone in the Argive ranks.

Behind me, from above, came a woman's high-pitched voice: "Death to the traitor!"

The hush was broken: now the Argives beat their spears against their shields, and the Thebans answered in kind. Jeers and shouts of encouragement swelled all around; as if borne upon storm-tossed waves, the brothers' duel grew more furious. They charged, dodged, slashed with gleaming bronze as the sun rose higher. Their helmets' tall war-crests, both as red as the blood running down Eteokles' leg, whipped and bobbed with the movements of combat. I saw sweat-sheen on their arms and necks, fear and apprehension in both pairs of blue eyes.

Which twin would prevail – which would be king of Thebes hereafter?

They were perfectly matched in height and reach, but Polynikes seemed the stronger. He forced Eteokles backward, step by step – but Eteokles managed to keep changing the angle of attack, so that the combatants never came too close to the invading army or the defenders.

All Eteokles needed was a scratch – it would not kill immediately, but I was sure the poison would burn worse than salt in an open wound, and that moment of shock might give Eteokles an opportunity for a fatal blow. If not, he only needed to bide his time and wait for Polynikes to weaken. There would be pain, then numbness. Best to strike a leg, so that Polynikes would stumble – or his sword-arm, so that the weapon would drop from tingling fingers.

But Polynikes was battle-hardened. Eteokles could not manage even a scratch.

"They can't keep it up much longer, in this heat," I muttered.

Hyperbius must have heard me; from his chariot, he said: "I don't know, my lord Creon. They don't seem to be tiring. They may feel the rage of Ares."

"Thebes is at stake," Haemon said. "Apollo is watching."

Indeed the sun's blazing heat seemed to loan power to the brothers' fury, as though Apollo in his glowing chariot gave them strength. The ring of blade on blade, the low-pitched thump of a swing parried by a shield – each strike seemed more forceful than the last. Then Polynikes landed the most prodigious blow of all; Eteokles caught it on the bronze-bound edge of his shield – and Polynikes' blade snapped off at the hilt.

Thebans gasped in unison with the Argives; then their surprise gave way to cheering. I saw Polynikes' mouth drop open and his eyes go round as Eteokles darted forward and kicked away the fallen blade. Polynikes tossed aside the useless hilt and edged backwards, holding his shield high as he drew his dagger; Eteokles advanced, his sword slicing down towards his brother's unprotected neck.

Polynikes brought up his shield just in time to turn the blade aside, but the force of his brother's swing knocked his shield back into his helmet with an audible crack. Staggering from this blow to the head, he let his shield swing wide – and Eteokles pounced, thrusting his sword up beneath his brother's cuirass and deep into his belly.

"No!" howled the Argives, their cry of dismay masking Polynikes' roar of pain.

Eteokles looked as surprised as his twin; he lost his grip on the sword as Polynikes fell. The wound was a fatal one – but Polynikes was not yet dead.

The victor stepped closer to the injured man. Behind us, Thebans cheered wildly: the women with the archers and youths on the walls, the charioteers and spearmen to my left and my right.

Eteokles lifted a hand; gradually the tide of cheering ebbed. "Yield now, Brother," he commanded, "and die in peace!"

The wounded man managed to push himself up on his shield-arm; dropping his dagger, he grasped the hilt of Eteokles' sword and, with a grunt, pulled the blade from his own vitals. A torrent of blood rushed forth. Polynikes looked at the blade – but Eteokles seemed transfixed by the spreading pool of crimson. I wondered, in that instant, if he saw himself lying there.

So he was not watching his brother's right hand, did not notice the blade's wavering course towards his calf, unprotected by the bronze armor that shielded his shin, until the sword sliced his flesh.

Eteokles jumped back as if bitten by a snake; horror plain on his face, he stared at the fresh wound on his calf.

Polynikes laughed, choking, blood spilling from between his lips, and Eteokles' sword-hilt fell from his hand. "Join me in Hades, Brother," he sputtered. "In the place… for oath-breakers…"

I knew what Eteokles was thinking: in that scratch, he feared his own death. But Thebes still hung in the balance. "Eteokles!" I cried.

He glanced back at me, as dazed as a man roused from a nightmare. Then, like a wakened sleeper, he seemed to remember where he was and what must be done. He picked up his own sword, dripping with his twin's blood, and lifted it high.

"Now!" he bellowed.

A horn sounded from the wall behind me; then the air overhead filled with arrows, raining down upon the Argive troops. Amphiorax and his soldiers charged towards us, their blue shields like an ocean wave, while other Argives turned and fled.

The four men assigned to Haemon and me closed before us, their ox hide shields forming a barrier; they walked us backward step by step towards the gate while Hyperbius and the other chariot-borne warriors swept towards the invaders. When Haemon and I were inside, the gates swung closed behind us, and our guards helped their comrades wrestle the cross-bar into place.

Haemon assisted me up the stairs as quickly as my aged legs would carry me. I had witnessed my nephews' fight at close hand; I saw the rage and fear in their eyes, smelled the blood and sweat. Looking down from the battlements was a different experience – so must the gods look down upon mortals' wars.

I saw, before most of the enemy did, Theban forces under the commands of Aktor and Astakus closing in from the left and the right; I watched the Argive army crumble in disarray when Eteokles and Astakus fought together to kill Hippomedon. Then, when King Adrastos fled on his swift horse, the enemy's fighting spirit departed with him. The Argives under the command of Amphiorax fought on for some time, but our forces, urged by Eteokles, seemed to burn with Apollo's own flame.

From above, it was difficult to distinguish the sound of a single sword or spear striking against shield, or biting into flesh; the noise of battle was more like storm-driven surf pounding against a rocky shore. Soon I lost sight even of King Eteokles, although every now and again I glimpsed the red plumes of his war-crest. The scene below merged into an ebb and flow of dust clouds thrown up by horses' hooves and chariot wheels, a volley of arrows or javelins, a headlong rush of spearmen, the blare of battle-horns. But I could see the overall shape of the battle: the tide was moving out.

By mid-afternoon it was done.

It had gone from duel to battle to rout. Corpses and the groaning forms of the injured dotted the open space before the Ogygia Gate; all but two of our chariots were gone, making the circuit of the walls to slay or drive off any remaining enemy forces. Argive soldiers had dropped their shields to run; our men pursued them into the fields and forests. I heard later that Astakus' men slit the throats of two Argives found crouching in an abandoned pig-sty; another tried to hide in a grain storage jar, and was speared like a fish from above. No doubt many escaped, but the Argive army was no more.

When Hyperbius judged it safe, he called for assistance bringing in the wounded. I ventured out with my sons and the healers and the strong peasant women who offered to help.

I'd only seen so much blood once before, when Lasthenes put the herds to the knife. But a battlefield is a different thing. When we slaughtered the herds, it was orderly; nothing was wasted. This was the work of Ares and Chaos. Men lay sprawled, lifeless eyes staring vacantly up at the sky, their intestines spilling out in a sticky heap to make a feast for flies and crows. Some still alive moaned in pain, calling for water. Those in Argive armor we dispatched quickly, mercifully – along with Thebans that the healer Udaeus decreed too far gone for Apollo's art. Others we bandaged and then loaded onto their shields to be carried back through the gates.

I saw two peasant wives pointing down at the body of the man who had been Amphiorax; I recognized him only by his armor and the blue-painted shield that lay by his side – he'd taken a spear-thrust through the jaw that tore off most of his face. But the women knew he was an Argive captain, from his armor and his signet ring. "The Blues," one of them said, pointing at his shield. "They was always camped outside the Astykratia. That's where we should hang their captain!" Her companion agreed; taking his arms and legs, they scooped Amphiorax into his shield and began dragging it back toward the city.

But no one – healer or scavenger – came near Polynikes' corpse; it was as though it lay in a cursed zone. This zone I breached. I spat on the lifeless form, showing my disgust for the son of Oedipus who had brought such suffering on the city of his birth. Then, leaning on my walking-stick, I kept walking through the dead and the wounded, until I came to a man on his hands and knees, retching. It was Eteokles. I shouted for Udaeus, then squatted beside him.

Eteokles heaved again, then paused to look at me. "Uncle Creon."

Udaeus came running up behind me. "My lord king – how are you hurt?"

My nephew shook his head. "You tell me."

The healer eased Eteokles into a sitting position and examined him quickly. "I don't understand it – there are no serious wounds." He rested his palm on the king's forehead. "You haven't lost much blood, and it's a hot day – but your flesh is *cold*, my lord king." Looking puzzled, he bent down to examine Eteokles' feet and ankles. "It's as though you were bitten by a viper – but I see no bite-marks."

Eteokles glanced at me; in his gaze I saw pleading. "Argive treachery?" he suggested.

"Venom on an enemy's blade," I said firmly. Eteokles had been his own enemy – as much as, or perhaps even more than, Polynikes. "Is there anything you can do for him, Udaeus?"

The healer hesitated, as if reluctant to admit defeat. "No," he said at last. "Some men recover, but most do not."

"If you can't save me," Eteokles gasped, "see to my men. Go!"

"Yes, my lord king." Udaeus straightened from his crouch, but I stopped him before he could depart.

"Pass the word that Argive blades are not safe," I cautioned. "Any that are taken off the dead should be melted down and recast."

"A sensible precaution – but we may not be able to catch them all."

"Perhaps it will be enough. I expect that venom is hard to come by; not everything will be tainted." I let him go, and returned to my nephew.

"My sword," he gasped, and gestured at it, a few paces away from his pool of vomit.

I fetched it, holding it cautiously by the hilt, then with some difficulty I crouched down and eased it carefully into the scabbard he wore. "I'll make sure it's buried with you, my lord king." Then I added: "Thebes is safe. You have performed the duties of a king."

He smiled, briefly. "Your approval. At last."

"Do you wish to be taken to the palace – or to the agora? I can summon bearers."

He sat there, considering. "No," he said. "It's a king's duty to supervise the aftermath of battle, isn't it?" He made a sound indeterminate between laugh and cough. "Besides, I'd like to see the sacred spring one last time."

I called for assistance, and with the help of one of my younger sons and a sturdy peasant woman we carried Eteokles over to Dirke's spring and dipped out a cup of water for him to drink. Hyperbius came by; though my nephew was only able to manage a few words, I knew what he wanted. I told the trader to assemble swift parties for Orchomenos and Gla to bring food, wine, oil, and other supplies.

As the sun sank lower in the sky, others came to speak with the king: Astakus, to report that the northern frontier was secure, and that he had brought supplies from the deserted Argive camps; Aktor, who had pressed the enemy to the western edge of Theban lands. Haemon informed us that Apollo's temple in the east had not been desecrated, and he remained with me by the side of the dying king. As it became clear that the city was truly safe, the well-born women started venturing out as well. My wife and my niece and my daughters, learning that I was with Eteokles, came to share his final hours. His skin was growing clammy to the touch; Udaeus warned us it would not be long.

Many Thebans came to pay their respects, to thank the king for saving their city.   But one visitor was a complete surprise.   When first I saw the donkey-cart approaching from the south, I expected a peasant bringing supplies.   In the long shadows of late afternoon, I did not recognize Antigone until she reined in her donkey and stepped down from the driver's bench.   My son's jaw tightened as he recognized his wife, garbed in the gray robes of a priestess of Athena, but they did not speak.   Antigone went directly to her brother, who lay with his head cradled in Ismene's lap, but first addressed her sister. "Ismene, you're alive!" she observed accusingly.

"Yes, but Polynikes is dead," Ismene said. "And Eteokles…"

Eteokles' blue eyes opened wide. "Antigone? But… how?"

"Athena told me I was needed again."   She shook her head.   "I tried to prevent this when the goddess sent me the first time, but you refused to listen."

"Only one way… this could end," he groaned. "Polynikes…"

"*Polynikes*? What about *Eteokles*?" she answered, anger in her voice. "Aren't *you* to blame for this as well?"

I pride myself on reading people and events, but her expression and her words cast my mind into sudden doubt.   How much did she know?   What she said might mean only that Eteokles had denied his brother the agreed turn on Thebes' throne.   But her finger seemed to point at the sheathed sword.   Did my niece know – had the goddess told her – that Eteokles had fallen victim to his own poisoned blade?

Would she indict *me*, too?

I stepped between her and Eteokles. "If Athena sent you – and not the Kindly Ones – then the goddess of wisdom must have told you that King Eteokles acted to protect his city!"

"He broke the laws of the gods!" she snapped, insolence filling her voice. "Eteokles swore to share the throne with his brother!"

"Polynikes swore allegiance to Thebes, but led a foreign army against it!" I retorted angrily. "How many Theban lives have been lost?"

"Peace," Eteokles groaned.

Suspending our argument, my niece and I turned to look at the dying king. "Thebes… safe," he said.   His hands shaking, he pulled the royal signet-ring from his finger and held it up towards me. "Uncle… keep Thebes safe."

With Haemon's assistance, I knelt beside my nephew and accepted the signet ring from his hands. "That is my goal above all," I assured him.

Haemon touched the back of his hand to Eteokles' forehead, and then to his own. "May Hermes grant you safe journey to the Underworld."

"Oh, Eteokles," said soft-hearted Ismene, her face wet with tears. "If you see our parents, give them my love.   And… and Menoeceus…"

I tightened my hand on the royal signet. "Tell my son he was right," I whispered. "And your mother… tell your mother I miss her."

Eteokles did not respond to me – or to any of us.   Haemon put a finger behind the king's ear to check his pulse, then shook his head.   Without really thinking about it, I slipped the golden ring with its carved sphinx seal onto my finger.

Haemon helped me to rise. "King Eteokles is dead," he said. "Long live King Creon!"

I gave my first order as king of Thebes. "Take King Eteokles' body to the agora, along with the others who died for Thebes. Tomorrow we will hold funeral rites."

Antigone looked up at me. "What about Polynikes?"

I glanced towards his corpse. In the red light of sunset, the blood drenching the ground beneath him looked black as a crow's wing. "Let him lie where he fell, attacking his own city."

"He must have a proper funeral!" Antigone argued.

"He deserves no better than Tydeus," I shouted, enraged by her defiance. "Be glad I don't hang his corpse over the gate!"

"Uncle—"

"Silence!" I thundered, furious that my first orders should be questioned. "I am now your king – you owe me the loyalty that you owed Thebes. Anyone who defies me in this will not see the light of day again. Is that understood?"

I scanned the faces of my subjects. All bowed their heads respectfully except for Antigone. She stared at me with eyes as blue as Oedipus' had been, before he destroyed them – the same color as Jocasta's eyes, who had been both her mother and grandmother.

"Is that understood?" I repeated.

"Understood," said Antigone, lifting her chin. But she did not say that she would obey.

*

"I could not, Uncle," says his niece. Creon notices that the edge of anger and defiance in her voice has softened; instead, her tone is sorrowful. "The gods' law is higher even than a king's."

Creon looks down to meet the soft eyes of his wife Eurydike. She says nothing, but he knows she wants him to reverse his decision and free Antigone. Ismene, seated on the floor at his other foot, touches his knee – the gesture of a suppliant. She does not speak her request; she does not have to.

It is the Argive priestess, Eriphyle, who speaks. Her low and gentle voice is as lovely as her face. "King Creon, she is right. The law of the gods supersedes the law of mortal men."

Creon wipes damp palms against his thighs. He has convinced himself that for the good of Thebes he cannot relent: that he must stand firm as the city walls. Weakness leads to chaos, to defeat. Yet here, at the grave of his nephew, it is harder to remain adamant. Did Eteokles' stubbornness benefit the city? Did Polynikes'?

Before he can formulate his thoughts, there is a knock at the door. His listeners appear startled, but Creon knows who he has instructed his soldiers to allow through.

He calls out: "Enter."

CHAPTER TWENTY
CREON

Pulling himself up with his wooden staff, Creon rises to his feet. How stiff his knees are!

Against the blinding daylight, he cannot make out the face of the person standing in the doorway, but the silhouette belongs to a short and slender woman with long straight hair: a daughter of the Tiresias. A soldier stands behind her.

"You have brought your father?" Creon asks.

"Yes, my lord king," she replies. "Carried on a litter."

Creon turns back to the dim interior and explains: "I received a message from the Tiresias to meet him here. You are all welcome to join me. Even you and your people, Eriphyle."

He follows the Tiresias' daughter – Daphne, he decides, seeing a few strands of silver in her brown hair – towards where her sister stands beside the prophet's litter. The two men holding the front and back poles stand in an easy posture, as though the shrunken old man they carry weighs no more than a child. For a moment Creon tries to recall a time decades past, when the man now known only as the Tiresias was a merchant named Pelorus, a well-traveled seaman with a dark suntan and wiry strength. That identity seems long gone: Creon can hardly remember what Pelorus looked like. Only the prophet Tiresias remains: pale from months in his sickbed, hands gnarled and spotted with age, his wispy beard white as the thin clouds overhead. A black blindfold is draped loosely over his sightless eyes.

As Creon approaches the litter, he senses Haemon, Eurydike and Ismene just behind him. The Argives linger a few paces back.

"Well, Tiresias?" Creon asks.

"Creon," whispers the ancient prophet. His voice is weak, but evidences no confusion.

"Yes. You wish to tell me something?"

"Let her out," the old man says. "Let Antigone out."

For once, no riddles! But the instruction is difficult to follow. "Tiresias, I can't. She broke the law."

"Bad law." The old man wheezes, then coughs, the spasm wracking his thin ribcage. Manto bends over him, wiping spittle from his lips with a cloth, but he feebly pushes her away. "Not the gods' law. If you don't let her out – the gods will punish Thebes."

Creon hesitates. Always, he has put Thebes first. Even before assuming the throne. But a king who reverses his orders is no king. And Thebes needs leadership. "I decreed that Antigone would never see the light of day again," he says, bending close to the ancient prophet. "I am *king* now, Tiresias. How can I break my word without plunging Thebes into chaos?"

The Tiresias smiles crookedly – and suddenly Creon is able to see what eluded him before: the visage of the wily merchant Pelorus. "Don't break your word."

"What?" Creon feels the others edging closer, eager for a solution – as, in truth, is he. "How can I release her, then?"

The old man lifts a single finger. "I will show you the way."

Creon waits for more – but the old man says nothing. Slowly the finger falls, and the Tiresias lets out a rattling, raspy breath.

"What is it?" Creon prods. "Tiresias – what is this way?"

The prophet remains silent.

From behind Creon, the Argive priestess speaks. "I believe his spirit has left his body."

Manto, the prophet's younger daughter, begins to wail; Haemon comes forward and gently moves her aside. He sets his ear to the old man's thin chest, touches the brittle-looking wrist. Then he moves the blindfold from the unseeing eyes and closes the blue-veined eyelids. "He is dead, Father."

"No!" cries Eurydike, adding her wails to Manto's keening.

"He wanted to die," Daphne says, wiping tears from her face. "He's suffered so much these last few months. But he told us Apollo needed him to remain for a final task."

Creon thumps his staff against the ground in frustration. "Then why didn't Apollo let him finish it? He was about to tell us a way past this impasse!"

The Argive priestess takes a step closer. "Perhaps, King Creon, another god opposes Apollo."

"Maybe not," says Ismene. "Uncle, the Tiresias may have shown you the answer. His death may *be* the message from Apollo."

"What?" Creon is in no mood for riddles. "Speak sense, child!"

Ismene touches his arm. "Your words, Uncle, were not that Antigone should die. You said instead that she should never again see the light of day."

"You're a good listener, Ismene," he concedes, "but I don't see your point."

His son Haemon is quicker. "Father, the old Tiresias is dead; a new one must be chosen. And Apollo has selected Antigone!"

Manto and Eurydike's moans of grief ebb away; in the sudden silence Creon considers his son's words. The new Tiresias, if not blind already, must relinquish his or her eyesight in order to facilitate the second sight of prophecy. After becoming the Voice of Apollo, the new Tiresias never sees the light of day again.

If Antigone were to assume this role, Creon could release her without breaking his word – and keep Thebes safe from the gods' wrath.

"You are high priest of Apollo," he says to his son, both relieved and reluctant. "You have authority to determine the god's choice. But Antigone must consent."

"She will!" With an eagerness Creon has rarely seen in his eldest son, Haemon rushes back into Eteokles' tomb.

"How long will it take to break down the wall?" Ismene asks. "She's suffering – we should let her out *now*."

Creon looks up at the sun, now approaching the western hills. "There's still daylight."

"It will take some time, my lord king," says Eriphyle's dark-haired manservant. "The best thing would be to use a battering ram."

"Very well." Creon studies the fellow closely. "I assume you were among those who tried to break through Thebes' gates?"

The Argive coughs slightly, avoiding Creon's gaze. "Yes, my lord king – although obviously without success."

"Well, this should be easier," Creon says. "It's only mud brick."

"And no rain of arrows or sling-stones to hamper us." The dark-haired man scratches his nose and then glances at the priestess.

Just then Haemon emerges from Eteokles' tomb, a huge grin on his face. "Father, she's agreed!"

Creon feels his own heart lift with his son's smile, but he is careful to keep his own expression serious. There is work to do before the sun sets. He orders Astakus and one of his men to accompany the Tiresias' daughters and their father's body back to the city, then sets the rest of the soldiers to fashioning a battering-ram. The Argive manservant offers advice, helping select a straight pine tree; Haemon somehow supplies an axe.

Weary, Creon takes a seat on his sedan chair. Eurydike stands beside him, while Ismene exchanges a few quiet words with the Argive priestess. Eriphyle clutches her cloak close to her throat, though the breeze is not that cold; on the other hand, she may have caught a chill in the damp tomb.

Creon turns to watch the Argive manservant, advising Theban soldiers how best to lop off the pine branches. For a manservant, the fellow seems unusually at ease giving commands to soldiers. In fact, something about him is oddly familiar. Could it be that this middle-aged fellow was one of the Argive officers? Squinting, Creon examines him more closely. The way he holds himself, the stiffness in one of his legs: could he be King Adrastos?

The hair color is wrong – but no hairline is visible, and the man is clean-shaven. Creon realizes that the black curls are a wig.

The corners of Creon's mouth twist upwards in wry admiration. Adrastos is known to have escaped the final battle; the woman Eriphyle is his sister. Who could the other Argives be? Two young women – one with child. Adrastos' daughters Deipyle and Argia, most likely.

As Haemon and the limping Argive drag away a large branch, Creon taps his wife's arm. "Do you know who that man is?"

Unruffled, Eurydike asks: "Which man, my dear?"

Yes, he can tell: she knows. While he does not entirely like the idea of his wife keeping secrets from him, his respect for her increases. It is better that this truth remain hidden. No one should learn that King Creon spoke to King Adrastos and did not order him killed on the spot.

"Never mind," he says.

Eurydike bends to kiss his cheek. "I'm glad you're letting her out, my love," Eurydike says. "It means so much to Haemon – and to me."

With only a harrumph in response, Creon glances down towards the walled-in cave, darkening in the twilight. Releasing Antigone this way is a sly solution – but is that not characteristic of his service to Thebes? From behind the throne as well as on it: clever solutions save lives. Like how he used the Sphinx to keep his sister Jocasta from having to marry the wrong man, without starting a war. Of course Oedipus was arguably the wrong man as well – but the sequence of events proved that the gods and the Fates could not be foiled. And Antigone's release seems to be the gods' will.

By the time Apollo's chariot has reached the horizon, the men are ready with their battering ram. In twilight's fading glow, Creon watches the instrument deployed. Haemon lends his hand to the effort, as do Creon's sedan-chair bearers and the Argive in the dark wig. It takes less time than Creon expected to burst through. Eurydike and Ismene rush inside with food and drink; soon after, Haemon leads his wife out through the jagged hole, the black blindfold of the Tiresias already tied around her head. She stumbles a little, perhaps from weakness, but as they come closer Creon can see that she trusts her husband to guide her.

"So, niece, you will be the new Tiresias," Creon says.

She inclines her blindfolded head. "It seems the gods have chosen me."

"For years, the gods have been preparing her for this role!" Haemon's words gush forth like water from a spring. "As her father's guide, she learned the life of a blind person. And the Tiresias is servant to Athena as well as Apollo. Where has Antigone been these last few years? In service to Athena!"

"But not to Apollo," Creon says.

"*I* have served Apollo," Haemon answers. "I'll go with her, as her guide."

Eurydike grips Creon's hand. "Haemon..."

"Would you have your mother lose another son?" asks Creon.

"My place is with my wife," Haemon answers. "Mother, we'll be in Thebes sometimes."

"But, Haemon – will you be strong enough for this?" Eurydike asks, ever maternal.

"Traveling can be arduous," Creon adds.

Antigone juts out her chin. "I'm sure Haemon will do well," she says, resuming her usual defiance.

"Father, Mother – I'll manage. In this war I've gained strength. I haven't felt faint since the Argives came, and I've learned to defend myself. Besides, I've always wanted to travel. Now I can."

On his son's face Creon sees a newfound, manly confidence. Besides, the logic is irrefutable. "Very well."

Haemon declares that the ceremony should take place at the Temple of Apollo. Anxious to finish this before a crowd can gather, Creon offers his sedan chair to Antigone. A few soldiers remain to guard Eteokles' tomb, but the rest – including the Argives – come with them. As the small party climbs the hill towards the temple, Eriphyle and Haemon discuss the details of the ceremony. Eriphyle agrees to fulfill the role of the foreign priestess; Haemon reminds Antigone that once the rites are complete, she must not speak until the two of them reach Delphi.

When they reach the temple forecourt, Creon realizes that the dark-wigged Argive has disappeared; under cover of dusk, he must have slipped into the forest. Perhaps, Creon thinks, Adrastos has enough piety not to pollute the ceremony with his presence. At any rate, Creon does not mind; it is easier to have him gone. Though without his sedan chair the steep climb is arduous, when they reach the temple Creon feels better than he has in months.

Haemon leads Antigone and Eriphyle into the temple, while Creon eases himself into his sedan chair, just vacated and now resting on the ground. Temple servants bring folding chairs for the women, and cups of wine mixed with water. As he drinks, Creon ponders the implications of the ceremony soon to begin. The Tiresias is frequently a gadfly to Thebes' king: how irritating will it be for the Tiresias and his defiant niece to be one and the same person? Yet perhaps it will be easier to deal with only one instead of two separate individuals.

"I hope they'll come to Thebes often," his wife says to Ismene.

"Haemon did say he wants to travel, Aunt," his niece responds. "And the old Tiresias was in such poor health that he couldn't travel much. I expect Antigone will want to resume the earlier tradition."

Creon presses his fingertips together and nods. The Tiresias is supposed to be an itinerant prophet, spreading ambiguous messages of hope and doom across all Hellas. The king of Thebes need not expect more than his fair share of divine omens.

"Look," whispers one of the Argive women to the other. "Here they come."

She points up towards the temple, and Creon sees his son leading Antigone, still blindfolded, down the stairs. Eriphyle and the priest Udaeus follow. When they reach the center of the forecourt, Haemon's voice rings out in the notes of paean to Apollo. Creon and the others rise in respect for the god and move forward, forming a semicircle around the celebrants.

Haemon finishes the hymn, then turns to Creon. "My father and my king: your decree remains in force – but the sun has set."

Creon nods. "She may remove the blindfold."

Antigone lifts her hands to the back of her head and unties the strip of dark linen. She blinks in the torchlight, then gazes at each family member in turn. "I want to remember your faces."

"Oh, Antigone!" Eurydike sighs, her eyes shining with tears. Antigone steps forward and the older woman hugs her niece tight. "I wish there were another way."

Antigone pulls back gently. "It has to be done, Aunt. The gods are calling me." She moves next to Ismene. "I'm sorry I have not been a better sister to you."

"You have been who you needed to be, Antigone," the younger sister responds solemnly. "And now you will give up that identity, and be the Tiresias. You're so brave!"

"Am I?" Antigone responds. "You are the one who gave me the courage to live. Was it more courageous for me to leave with Father, or for you to stay and help Thebes heal?"

As the sisters embrace, Creon hopes that the new Tiresias will content herself with this sort of philosophical speculation and leave him and his kingdom in peace. But the glint in her eye when she turns to him holds an element of challenge. "Uncle," she says, not using his royal title.

"Yes?" They face one another like opposing warriors – like Eteokles and Polynikes, except that they have decided to work together. He hopes he has made the right choice.

"I know you love Thebes," she says.

He raises an eyebrow, waiting for her to continue.

"The gods will know it too."

He crosses his arms over his chest. "They already do."

"Of course." She purses her lips slightly, then inclines her head.

She turns at last to Haemon. With gentle fingers he brushes her hair out of her face and looks down into her eyes. "You are beautiful," he says. "My wife."

For once she does not argue; she reaches up to trace the lines of his forehead, his jaw. "And you are handsome, Husband. I will remember your face, just like this."

"Our path will be difficult."

"But we'll be together."

He kisses her, then holds her face in his hands for a moment, their eyes locked on each other – studying, memorizing, as if committing each other to heart. Creon realizes that his son has been struck by Eros' arrow at last.

Creon clears his throat. "Let's take care of this."

The ceremony is held infrequently, only upon the death of a Tiresias; and the man once known as Pelorus served as Voice of Apollo for more than a decade. The Tiresias before that, Creon's father, held the role for thirty-seven years; and his predecessor, a woman, served as Tiresias for decades, going back to a time before Creon's birth. So Creon, old as he is, has seen the rites only twice before.

Eriphyle walks to the center of the forecourt to tell the story. "The hunter Tiresias followed his dogs into the forest in search of game. He came across a small lake, fed by a waterfall: and bathing in that lake was the most beautiful woman he had ever seen. Unable to help himself, he jumps into the lake to seize her."

This version is not exactly as Creon remembers, but he supposes the story's details differ from one city to the next.

"Yet this is no mortal woman that he can overpower – it is the goddess Athena! Furious that a man has looked upon her nakedness, she drags him onto the shore."

In the light of the surrounding torches, the Argive priestess is beautiful: her blonde curls cascade over her cloak, and her milk-white arms are graceful as she enacts the gestures of the goddess.

"The hunter Tiresias falls at her feet. 'Forgive me, Goddess – I could not resist your beauty!' he says."

Beauty, Creon thinks, is a thing of danger and power, and for mortals so easily lost. He remembers his lovely daughter Megara, dead far too young. And then he remembers Jocasta – who stood beside him the last time this ceremony was performed – her beauty lasted longer, but now she, too, is gone.

"Athena looked down upon the man in fury. 'Then my beauty is the last thing you shall ever see!' And with that she struck him blind."

Eriphyle stops her narrative. Antigone kneels on the white marble tiles; Haemon stands behind her, holding her head between his hands. The priest Udaeus draws a blade; it flashes in the torchlight as he moves, quick as a striking snake, to pierce each of her eyes. Antigone gasps and cries out; blood runs down her face, and Creon cannot help but think of Antigone's father, blinded by his own hand when he learned the truth of his marriage to Jocasta. Creon feels his wife's fingers dig into his arm; grateful for the excuse to look away, he strokes Eurydike's hair with his free hand.

Udaeus, Thebes' most skilled healer, quickly cleans and bandages Antigone's wounds; Haemon helps her to her feet.

"Tiresias is forever blind," Eriphyle continues, "but far-seeing Apollo grants the gift of second sight. Tiresias is the Voice of Apollo, devoted servant to Athena! All Hellas hails the Tiresias!"

By custom, the new Tiresias leaves for Delphi at once to begin training at the site most sacred to Apollo, keeping silence until the gift of prophecy is sealed at the navel of the world. Darkness, of course, makes no difference to the Tiresias – but her companion needs the sun's light to guide the journey. So Haemon leads the new Tiresias up the temple steps, and the rest follow. Knowing his wife is not ready to depart from her son, nor Ismene from her sister, Creon decides to stay the night, sending a runner to the palace with the information.

The temple is accustomed to visitors. A young acolyte leads them to rooms normally used by those who need the priests' healing arts. Servants bring in a light meal; Haemon helps his wife take a seat on a three-legged stool. She rocks slowly back and forth, as if trying to banish the pain. "Udaeus says we can't give you more poppy juice until morning," Haemon tells her. "Would you like something to eat?"

The new prophet nods her blindfolded head. Haemon beckons a servant over and guides his wife's fingers to the food. "There's bread, and soft cheese with green onions. Here's some roast mutton." With his help, she quickly consumes the simple fare.

Creon shares a low table with Eurydike, Ismene, and the Argive women. Little is said, and he finds himself absorbed in the flavors of the meal – he has tasted nothing so delicious in years. Is it the knowledge that he is safe, despite being outside the walls? Perhaps the explanation is only that the servants of Apollo, skilled with healing herbs, also use their knowledge in selecting oils and spices.

Udaeus checks on the new Tiresias; she moans slightly as he adjusts the bandage over her right eye socket. "It will hurt less in the morning," he assures her.

She twists her lips wryly, as if she has something to say – but of course she cannot.

"I know," Udaeus says. "It *has* to hurt less than this."

She shrugs, then shakes her head slightly. Haemon says: "That's not what you were thinking, was it? You were thinking that you won't see the morning."

Her lips curve into a slight smile, and she nods.

"But you'll hear the birdsong," he says, taking her hand. "And you'll feel better after you sleep."

With Haemon's tender assistance she goes to a cot. He removes her sandals and helps her stretch out her legs, placing a pillow under her head and a woolen blanket over her body. She gropes and grabs his arm, then his hand, holding it fast.

"Don't worry – I won't leave you. I'll never leave you."

"They love each other," whispers the priestess Eriphyle, her observation tinged with surprise. Creon realizes suddenly that this is a woman who does not understand love, who does not know *how* to love. He had been thinking that Eriphyle reminded him of Jocasta, but in this the two women could not be more different.

"Of course they do," says Eurydike, managing somehow to look happy and sad at the same time.

Eriphyle looks from Eurydike to Creon. "Well, my lord king, you have released your niece. What about the rest?"

His brows draw together. "What do you mean?"

"The bodies of our husbands. Let us perform the funeral rites."

"The Tiresias said nothing about that."

"That was the old Tiresias," Eriphyle argues. "The new Tiresias will surely tell you to bury them."

Eurydike rests a hand on his arm. "Antigone was ready to die rather than let Polynikes remain unburied. She *will* tell you they must have the rites."

"She can't say anything yet," Ismene reminds them. "She's forbidden to speak until reaching Delphi."

"True," Creon says, pressing his fingers together.

"But," Ismene continues, "taking down the bodies will help people understand that the war is over. Our gates will be inviting, not gruesome."

"No," Creon snaps. "I won't reverse another of my decisions just because people ask me." While Antigone is away at Delphi, he will find a way to dispose of the bodies. Not that he wants to do them any honor, but Ismene has a point: the rotting corpses are disgusting, and may keep away traders, farmers, and herdsmen. But it must be *his* decision, with a sound reason. "It is time for us to sleep."

But the Argive women are not finished with their petition. "My lord king," Eriphyle says, "what if I offer you something in exchange?"

Creon rubs his jaw. If Argos were to ransom the bodies – that *could* allow him to relent without weakness. Trying to repress the hope that he feels, he asks gruffly: "What could Argos offer?"

"I remind you that we are in Apollo's sanctuary," she says warily. "You may not harm me."

"I do not harm my guests! What is your offer – tribute?"

Eriphyle presses her full lips together and draws a deep breath. She shakes her head slightly, and her blue-green eyes fix his gaze. "The necklace of Harmonia."

Creon is so startled by this answer that he almost fails to detect the reaction of the two younger Argive women. But his instinct, honed by decades in the Theban megaron, notes their expressions even without fully understanding them. "*You* have the necklace?"

Eriphyle's golden curls tremble as she nods. "Yes, Polynikes gave it to me – just before the armies set out."

He assumes an air of indignation. "That is the rightful property of Thebes' queen!" The accusation is successful: Creon notices the flash of anger in the eyes of the pregnant woman seated to Eriphyle's left. "Argia, I see you agree with me!" He turns his gaze on her. "Don't try to deny it. You are the widow of Polynikes; and this is your sister Deipyle, who was married to Tydeus."

Argia glares at him. "He gave Aunt Phyle the necklace so she would take his side." The young woman's anger and resentment – Creon cannot tell: is it towards Eriphyle, Polynikes or both? "He bribed her to choose war."

"It's *her* fault our husbands are dead," adds Deipyle.

The Argive priestess sits up straight. "Tydeus and Polynikes wanted this war more than anyone! You can't blame their deaths on me. *My* husband was the only one who opposed it."

"The *only* one?" Creon folds his arms across his chest. "What about the entire population of Thebes?"

Eriphyle inclines her head. "You're right, my lord king."

Her show of contrition affects Creon more than he wants to admit. Why, he wonders, does female beauty have such power over men – even graybeards like himself? *The gods have made us this way*, he tells himself. Because they have the same weakness. Even Zeus would struggle to stay enraged after seeing Eriphyle's feathery eyelashes sweep down to touch her rounded cheeks, watching her full red lips quiver uncertainly. By Aphrodite, the woman is as beautiful in her way as his daughter Megara once was – as was his sister Jocasta! And, it would seem, for the same reason.

But the advantage of Creon's years is that such loveliness no longer completely scrambles his wits. "How many deaths might have been prevented – your husband, my son, so many others – but for your vanity in taking the necklace?"

Moisture shines in her large eyes, the color of a sunlit sea. "I cannot say, my lord king. But I offer it to you now, in exchange for the bodies."

Creon is swayed by the woman's beauty; he is grateful for an excuse to rid Thebes' gates of the rotting Argive meat; and yet his anger and indignation remain. "You offer stolen property – Harmonia's necklace belongs to Thebes!"

"In exchange for something you should do anyway," she retorts, "obeying the laws of the gods!"

She is right, of course. Still, he vents his disgust. "What women do for the sake of beauty!"

"No worse than men, for the sake of glory," she replies. "I remind you, my lord king, that you promised not to harm me."

"And I will not. But the gods, if they show any justice, will punish you." The anger on Argia's face suggests to Creon that the gods may have already chosen their instrument.

"That is up to them." Eriphyle lifts her hands to her throat and works free the agate-headed silver cloak-pin that holds the garment shut. She sets the cloak aside, and then unwraps the finely woven linen veil from around her neck, revealing the gleam of polished gold: a necklace in the form of two serpents twined together, their heads resting in the valley between her creamy breasts. She reaches back behind her neck and unhooks the clasp; then she holds the precious item out to him. "Will you accept this ransom, King Creon?"

The tiny grains of gold forming the serpents' scales glitter in the firelight. The four small but perfectly formed sapphires of the serpents' eyes shine with a dark, mysterious glow – perhaps the glow of the power with which the god Hephaestus imbued the sacred object, the power to keep its wearer forever young and beautiful.

For so many years these sinuous golden curves adorned his sister's slender throat – until at last she hanged herself in shame, the truth of her incestuous marriage revealed.

"My eyes are not what they were," he says gruffly, not wanting to admit that they are full of tears. "Ismene, the necklace was once in your safekeeping, and your sight is still sharp. Is this truly the treasure of Harmonia?"

Ismene accepts the necklace from the Argive woman holds it to catch the light of the nearest torch. She traces the twisting lines of the serpents' embrace with a finger, peers down at the polished sapphire eyes. "Yes, Uncle, it is."

"Then we have an agreement, my lord king?" asks Eriphyle.

"We do," says Creon. "Tomorrow we will take care of the bodies."

Phyle nods her blonde head and reaches for her cloak. "Then, if you will excuse me, my nieces and I will retire to our camp."

Creon watches the three women leave, wondering briefly how they – and Adrastos – will be received in Argos after the defeat, especially when it becomes known that Phyle sacrificed the lives of so many men for the sake of vanity.

He grunts and shakes his head. Enough with Argos! He has his own city to rule. Tomorrow there will be funerals to arrange; lumber from some of the ruined houses and storerooms can feed the funeral pyres. Then the cleanup and rebuilding can continue. There will, no doubt, be opportunities to make things more efficient; he already has ideas about how to reconfigure the storeroom near the Eudoxa gate.

"Here, Aunt Eurydike," Ismene says, interrupting Creon's thoughts. "You're the queen of Thebes now. So Harmonia's necklace belongs to you." She places it into Eurydike's hands.

Creon watches his wife turn the precious heirloom in her hands, an expression of respect and awe on her face. "I don't know, Ismene. I was a pretty maiden once, but now I'm a plain old woman. Do you think this could really make me beautiful again?" Her voice is full of doubt, but he detects a faint note of hope as well.

There is movement on the far side of the room; the new Tiresias pushes herself up, despite her husband's protests. "You must rest, now, Antigone – ah, Tiresias. We have a long journey to begin tomorrow!"

The blindfolded woman shakes her head vigorously, then points across the room.

"What do you mean?" Haemon asks. "We can't stay here – we have to go to Delphi for your training."

Antigone nods assent, but then swings her feet over the site of the cot and points once more, her finger indicating the general area where Creon, Eurydike, and Ismene sit. She clasps both hands to her throat, then shakes her head from side to side.

Looking worried, Haemon shouts, "Udaeus – something's wrong! I think my wife's having a seizure!"

As the healer hurries over, the new prophet clenches her fists, frustration evident on her face. She opens her mouth as if to speak, then clamps it shut and gropes for her husband's arm. "I don't think it's a seizure," Udaeus says.

The blind woman pulls herself up to stand; then, with one finger, she traces an arc across her neck and then points again. Her aim is vague, but when Ismene says, "Is it something to do with the necklace?" the blindfolded head nods vigorously. She takes a step towards her younger sister.

"Would you like to hold it, my dear?" Eurydike asks. "I don't mind."

She makes a strangled, wordless sound, her agitation obvious.

"It must be frustrating that you can't see it," Ismene says.

The Tiresias shakes her head again, then stamps her foot against the floor. With her husband's help she walks over; Ismene vacates a chair for her, and once the blind woman is safely seated Eurydike places the necklace into her hands. She clenches it tight in one hand, shaking it as though in anger.

"This caused your brothers' death," Creon ventures.

She nods, then holds the necklace up and sweeps it in a circle that encompasses everyone present and shakes her head in negation once more. Despite several more guesses, Creon and the others cannot determine what she is trying to convey. Finally she rests it on her knees; pointing to the treasure with her right hand, she makes an obscene gesture with her left, extending the forefinger and little finger but curling closed all the rest.

Haemon touches her shoulder. "Are you trying to say the necklace is obscene?"

The Tiresias nods. She holds two fingers close together, then gestures with both hands far apart as if to say her husband has guessed only a fraction of a larger whole.

"Did Phyle cheat on her husband with Polynikes?" Ismene asks. "Is that what you want to tell us?"

Hearing this suggestion, Creon lifts an eyebrow; Ismene *is* a good listener. That relationship could well have happened.

But the new Tiresias shakes her head. Either that affair did not happen, or that is not the message she is trying to convey. "I must speak," she whispers.

Eurydike gasps in horror; the priest Udaeus' jaw drops. "You can't!" cries Haemon. "Not before reaching Delphi!"

"She has already spoken," Creon points out, "so she might as well continue. What do you have to say?"

The blindfolded face turns his direction. "This necklace is cursed."

"Do you mean it's a forgery?" Ismene asks, her cheeks coloring. "It can't be. I'm sure it's what Mother used to wear."

"It *is* the necklace Mother wore," confirms the Tiresias. "But it is cursed. It has always been cursed."

Udaeus bends closer. "I don't understand, Tiresias. How can that be? You agree this is the necklace given to Harmonia, the daughter of Ares and Aphrodite, when she wed our city's founder Kadmos."

The blind woman smiles slightly. "Harmonia was born to Aphrodite and her lover Ares. But who made the necklace? Hephaestus – Aphrodite's husband."

Creon strokes his chin, comprehending. "He cursed the necklace out of jealousy."

"Hephaestus could not punish Aphrodite and Ares. He shamed them, by catching them together in his net of bronze and displaying them naked for the rest of the Deathless Ones to laugh at – but his wife still bore the child of another. He wanted to make the descendants of that affair suffer; it was the only way he could get revenge."

"The Tiresias," Ismene says, "I mean, the last Tiresias – he warned me never to wear it."

"And my daughter Megara *did* wear it," adds Eurydike. "Look what happened to her."

"And to Jocasta," Creon says. If he had perceived the heirloom's evil nature earlier, could he have saved his sister from her fate? Shaking off the thought, he says: "Eriphyle was the last to wear it – and for its sake she let her husband and Argos march to defeat."

Eurydike looks at the shining golden serpents. "What should we do with it?" she asks worriedly. "*I* don't want it!"

"Let me take it to Delphi," says the new Tiresias, "and offer it to the god's treasury."

"That makes sense," Haemon agrees. "It can't harm Apollo – and the Oracle can keep it safe from anyone who might seek to use its power."

"Very well." Creon reaches up to straighten his crown. "Niece, I hope the gods will not punish you for breaking your silence prematurely."

"Some things are worth risking punishment for." Her smile is wry.

Creon's throat tightens. "Yes. They are."

This matter decided, those remaining in the temple are finally able to rest. When Haemon and the new Tiresias – her silence resumed – depart at first light the next morning, Eurydike holds Creon's hand tight, watching until the pair disappears in the distance. "Do you think they'll be all right?" she asks worriedly.

Creon takes a deep breath before answering. The roads are full of thieves and his son Haemon, despite being toughened by the last few months, is not the strongest of men. Transporting the cursed necklace could add further danger – as might the breaking of the new prophet's silence.

But none of these thoughts would comfort his wife. Instead he chooses to say: "No one dares attack the Voice of Apollo."

Then it is time to see to the day's business: returning to the city, Creon orders the enemy war-leaders cremated, and Polynikes interred in the tomb originally meant for him. One of Creon's men, a fellow with sharp eyesight, reports seeing a man on a white horse watching the ceremonies from a distance; but Creon knows Adrastos is no longer a threat. Still, it is a relief the following day when his men confirm that Eriphyle and her nieces – and their Athenian escort – have left Theban lands.

With the funerals, trade negotiations, and the work of organizing the rebuilding, several days pass before Creon can manage a quiet word with Ismene. It is late afternoon when she arrives at his private study; he offers her a cup of wine and pours one for himself, savoring the vintage and the knowledge that – with the siege over and their supplies restocked– there is no need for austerity.

"You listen to everyone," he says to Ismene. "Tell me, what are people saying?"

"People are excited about Rhanis' pregnancy," she says. "They like the idea of Eteokles leaving behind a child."

"And Menoeceus."

"I hope so," she says, blushing.

He smiles. "What else have you heard?"

Ismene hesitates, then tucks a dark curl behind her ear. "Some people don't believe that Antigone and Haemon left for Delphi. I've heard rumors that they're dead."

"But they saw the broken wall and the empty tomb – then they saw Polynikes buried there. Besides, it was too soon for Antigone to have died of hunger and thirst."

His niece shrugs. "I know. People are saying she hanged herself, like Mother."

"By Apollo!" Creon looks up at the painted ceiling-beams. "How could she hang herself in a cave? The ceiling isn't high enough, and there's nothing to tie a rope to – even if she had had a rope, which she didn't!"

Ismene smiles faintly. "People don't always think things through."

"And what's supposed to have happened to Haemon?"

"Well – one version is that he broke down the wall and found her. And when he discovered she was already dead, he hanged himself too." Ismene takes a small sip from her goblet. "They say that's why you allowed Polynikes to be buried, and the Argive bodies cremated – as an apology to Haemon's ghost."

He rubs his face with both hands. "Once he returns to Thebes with the new Tiresias, I suppose those rumors will stop."

"Honestly, Uncle…" she pauses, then blurts: "Most people are just happy that the war is over, and there's food on the table again. Many think you were right to condemn Antigone – Polynikes did so much damage to the city."

Creon pulls himself up with his staff; taking his cup, he walks over to the window. The city of Thebes is bathed in golden light slanting over the western hills – a place of beauty once more – but with the equinox past, the nights are coming earlier. "Well, my dear: you and I know the truth. Over the last fifty years, I've caused the deaths of three women in order to protect this city, and I was never blamed. If the people want to judge me guilty of this one, even though I'm innocent – perhaps that is a kind of justice. As long as Thebes is secure, I am content."

Having started rumors in the past when they were needed, Creon knows how difficult they are to extinguish. And in this case it is not necessary.

He is still not sure whether freeing Antigone was the best choice – but it was the only choice. That is the duty of a ruler: making the required decision, and dealing with the repercussions. He has other decisions to make: appointing a regent for Eteokles' child, should Rhanis bear a boy; finding another heir, if the babe proves to be a girl. And in the meantime, so long as breath remains in his body, he will take care of his city.

Creon scatters a few drops of wine out the window, then turns back to Ismene and raises his cup. "May the gods bless Thebes."

AUTHORS' NOTE

Beware! The following contains *serious spoilers*. If you haven't finished the book, there are a number of twists and surprises that we hope you'll enjoy before you read this authors' note. We urge you: return to the narrative and come back to this page later!

Having read through to the end, if you'd like to understand the reasoning behind some of the choices we made in telling this story, please continue.

WAS SOPHOCLES WRONG?

The most familiar version of this myth for modern audiences is probably Sophocles' version of the Antigone story; it is the basis of several operas and numerous theatrical adaptations such as Jean Anouilh's play *Antigone*. Readers who know this version of the story might wonder why Antigone is still breathing at the end of *Antigone & Creon: Guardians of Thebes*.

But in other versions of the myth it is clear that Antigone did survive. According to some, she and Haemon have a son – which conflicts with Sophocles' play, in which both Haemon and Antigone die while only engaged. There is a third myth fragment in which Antigone and Ismene are murdered by Laodamas, the son of Eteokles; some accounts instead have Ismene murdered by Tydeus. The mythical tradition features many inconsistencies.

We love Sophocles. We respect him greatly, or we wouldn't have borrowed so heavily from *Antigone* and *Oedipus at Colonus* to create *Guardians of Thebes* and from *Oedipus Rex* for our novel *Jocasta: The Mother-Wife of Oedipus*. However, Sophocles has a Shakespearean tendency to pile on deaths (or rather, Shakespeare has a Sophoclean tendency, since Sophocles' plays predate the Bard's by two thousand years). And the classical Athenian playwrights often bent the myths to make contemporary political statements. So although Sophocles' Antigone hangs herself, that is not the only possible outcome.

In fact, it seems an unlikely one. We realized – as Creon does – that it would be extremely difficult to hang yourself in a cave. Sophocles may have chosen that type of death as homage to the death of Jocasta (although he wrote *Antigone* before he wrote *Oedipus Rex*).

As Sophocles may have done, we grappled with the contradictory versions of the myth to find a resolution that made sense to us, while still enabling our characters to interpret events to suit themselves. Antigone and Haemon both depart from Thebes, shedding their old identities and in Antigone's case even her name; in a sense, their former selves have died.

ISMENE

The myths surrounding Ismene, like those involving her older sister, are also contradictory. In Sophocles' *Oedipus at Colonus*, Ismene performs an unseen, off-stage ritual to purify her father. In *Antigone* she tries to assist her sister in performing the funeral rites for Polynikes – suggesting that Ismene was not, after all, killed by Tydeus during the war – but Antigone spurns her help.

Of the four children of Jocasta and Oedipus, Ismene is certainly the softest, the least well-defined; she is often a dramatic foil for her more hot-headed siblings. Traditionally a supporting character rather than a protagonist, Ismene leaves fewer traces in the myth. Some accounts have her betrothed to a man named Atys, who was killed by Tydeus in the war but who seems to play no major role. Instead, we decided to link Ismene to Melanippus and to her cousin Menoeceus, allowing the reader to hear their stories from her perspective.

THE CAVES

A technical challenge in creating this book was how to seal Antigone in her cave and yet allow her to interact with others. It seems unlikely that King Creon would permit people to gather outside the sealed entrance in plain view, and shouting through a brick wall would not have lent itself to the sort of revelations we planned for the narrative.

But the archaeological record suggested a solution. Just outside modern Thebes is a pair of caves that once served as royal tombs. (You can see a photo of them on our website, www.tapestryofbronze.com.) The director of the Theban archaeological museum took Victoria to the site and told her that they are supposed to be the tombs of Polynikes and Eteokles. These twin caves served the needs of our story so perfectly that we felt almost as if we were discovering the past instead of writing fiction.

ARGOS

The Argive myths contemporary with this fundamentally Theban story are fascinating, but extremely complicated. To maintain our focus on Thebes, we have simplified and abridged. Rather than three rival kings, our story features three powerful Argive houses. We've also skimmed over some of the interactions between Argos and other city-states such as Sikyon.

ALKIDES / HERAKLES

There are so many stories about Herakles (Hercules in the Roman tradition), spanning so long a time frame, that even discounting the many fantastic episodes they could not belong to a single man. Like many students of the myth, we suspect that because Herakles was so popular, storytellers freely inserted him in many other tales.

But the many legends of Herakles agree that this was not his given name; originally called Alkides, he took the name Herakles – meaning "glory of Hera" – in an attempt to mollify the anger of the queen of the gods. And tradition holds that Alkides *was* married to Creon's daughter Megara; in a fit of madness, he murdered his wife and children, and his punishment was to perform a sequence of labors for King Eurystheus of Tiryns.

So far as we can tell the myths do not mention Argive involvement in Alkides' punishment; this is our invention. Traditionally, Alkides flees to Delphi, where the Oracle – uncharacteristically, manipulated by the goddess Hera – sentences him to servitude in Tiryns. But the archaeological record strongly suggests that Tiryns may have been a vassal state of Argos, and Hera was certainly the patron deity of Argos. Furthermore, as the goddess of marriage it seems logical that Hera should be the deity from whom a man who has murdered his wife and children should seek forgiveness.

Herakles is also known for having supplied the horse Arion to Adrastos – and yet he does not play a role in the war of the Seven against Thebes. To us, the pieces seem to fit together: the murderer Alkides seeks Hera's forgiveness at Argos, gives the steed Arion to the Argive king Adrastos, and then is sentenced to perform tasks for King Eurystheus of Tiryns which are only just beginning when Polynikes and the Argives move on Thebes.

WARFARE

During the Bronze Age, attacking a walled city was an extraordinarily difficult military challenge. The two best-known examples from the approximate time period of our story are the Trojan War, which the myths would place about a generation later, and the taking of Jericho in the Old Testament (getting the dates of Greek myths to line up with the chronology of the Bible is challenging, but the fall of Jericho seems to have been somewhat earlier). In both cases the aggressors won, but Troy was only defeated through Odysseus' famous ruse; Jericho was conquered because of the treachery of Rahab the prostitute, and the collapse of the walls which some attribute to sonic warfare, others to an earthquake, and still others to God.

It was not until the Assyrians started building siege machines several centuries later that the walls of cities became truly vulnerable; the later Hellenes such as Alexander the Great, and then of course the Romans, advanced the art of siege warfare through still more sophisticated devices. We have included a crude battering ram in the story; though it is not explicitly mentioned in the myth, the device our characters use is so simple that it did not feel anachronistic. The efforts to scale the walls with ladders, Kapaneus' attempt to burn down a gate (and getting killed while doing it) and Tydeus' cannibalism are supported by the various myths.

Estimating the size of the army is difficult. Legend has it that Helen's lovely face launched a thousand Hellene ships to attack Troy; before that, those attacking Thebes claimed to have the largest army ever seen. Of course, many armies probably claimed to be the largest force in history. We have based the size of the attacking force in our narrative on our best understanding of the populations at the time, assuming that unlike the Trojan expedition – a force drawn from more than two dozen cities all across Hellas – the army led by Polynikes and Adrastos was primarily Argive.

ETEOKLES' WIFE

As far as we can tell, Eteokles' wife is not mentioned in the myths. There is evidence that two of Creon's younger daughters, Henioche and Pyrrha, served as regents to his son Laodamas: the historian and fabulist Pausanias mentions a tripod with these names from his visit to the Temple of Apollo at Thebes many centuries later. So possibly one of these women was Eteokles' wife and the mother of Laodamas; but if so, why is the widowed queen never mentioned?

To us this suggests that Eteokles might have chosen a less prominent woman to bear his child. The missing necklace of Harmonia might have been an embarrassment that motivated him to postpone marriage. This idea led to our creation of Rhanis.

THE TREASURES OF HARMONIA

The legends make it clear that there were two treasures of Harmonia: a dress, made from material woven by the goddess Athena and a necklace created by the god Hephaestus. Harmonia was the daughter of Ares and Aphrodite; the cuckolded Hephaestus put a curse on his gift. While it may have bestowed beauty on its wearers, it did not bring them good fortune.

We showed both treasures throughout our prior novel *Jocasta*, but decided to dispense with the dress by burying Jocasta in it. There were several reasons for this decision. First, we used the belt from *Jocasta* for her death at the end of that novel, so the characters could now feel that the dress was cursed. And besides it would be easier – and psychologically more likely – for Polynikes to run off with just his mother's golden necklace than for him to smuggle out his mother's dress as well.

Traditional versions of this story make Eriphyle (often given the epithet "hateful") far less sympathetic, and characterize her decision to side with her brother against her husband as bribe-induced treachery, for which she is later murdered by the sons she bore to Amphiorax. The writer Apollodorus suggests that Harmonia's necklace did not reach Delphi for a few more generations, but we have shortened its path to achieve a more complete closure in *Guardians*.

OEDIPUS AND ARGOS

The myths do not state that Oedipus and Antigone spent time in Argos. On the other hand, there is no evidence that they did not. Forming a relationship between Adrastos and Oedipus enabled us to introduce the Argives earlier in the story. Besides, the myth makes clear that Adrastos welcomed those spurned by others; having him play host to Oedipus lets us explore the development of that character trait.

THE TIRESIAS

The prophet Tiresias appears in myths associated with several generations and is supposed to have lived for seven lifetimes; in addition Tiresias is said to have been transformed from a man into a woman, and later back to a man. In this volume as well as in the other books in our series we have made "Tiresias" a title rather than a proper name, with a new person assuming the role when a Tiresias dies.

ARION

The horse Arion appears in several myths. In one, he is the child of Poseidon and Demeter, and can speak like a human. In others, he is the means by which Adrastos escapes death after the rout at Thebes. He is also the gift of Herakles to Adrastos.

In the Mediterranean of the Late Bronze Age, riding on horseback was still relatively rare. Artistic representations and physical remains show that horses were generally smaller than they are today, more like large ponies and better able to pull chariots than carry grown men in armor. However, there seems to be evidence that horse riding was happening in other geographic locations – and the myth of half-man, half-horse centaurs suggests an observer spotting a man on horseback without fully understanding the context.

THE PEACHES OF IMMORTALITY

One of the questions we always ask ourselves when figuring out a novel is why something did *not* happen. Why were Antigone and Haemon not together from the start?

The myths paint a confusing and contradictory picture of their relationship. By some accounts, they had a child together. In others, they are merely betrothed. Antigone is known for having accompanied her father Oedipus during her exile; to be of any use to him, she must have been more than a child. Yet women married young during that period, usually between fourteen and eighteen. If Haemon and Antigone loved each other – in Sophocles' *Antigone* Haemon kills himself out of grief at losing her – then why didn't he go with her and her father, or else insist that she remain in Thebes with him? We searched for a plausible reason to keep Haemon and Antigone apart.

We decided on sexual dysfunction caused by low blood pressure. This would contribute to Antigone's sense of inferiority with respect to her mother's beauty. It would explain why Haemon, feeling inadequate and ashamed, did not go with her or insist that she stay in Thebes.

It also gave us a way out of the problem. Leaves from the ginkgo tree (the silver fruit tree) were rumored to have been of assistance in this situation (the actual efficacy of gingko leaves is questioned). It also gave us the chance to show a traveler from the east, who was on his own search for the peaches of immortality – a genuine legend from China. The similarity of this story to those found in other traditions – the apple in Genesis, and the golden apples of the Hesperides – show that some stories seem to be universal.

WRITING

Each novel we've tackled so far has had different artistic challenges. While writing *Jocasta*, we were learning how to write (and how to write together). The Niobe trilogy presented other difficulties – different characters, different places and a long period of time.

The writing of *Guardians* was extremely challenging. We had many new characters to develop. We spent a lot of time researching and imagining siege warfare – from both sides of the walls. We wanted to tell two parallel stories – Antigone sealed away in the cave and all the events leading up to it. Furthermore, everything was made more difficult by the events in our personal lives. Alice has been excruciatingly busy in her day job and with family obligations. Victoria suffered a serious ski accident, which meant that months were co-opted by pain and physical therapy. So creating this novel took longer than our previous endeavors.

Nevertheless, we feel that *Guardians* offers something special. Every generation must learn to stand up for what is right. It can be risky, but often it's the only way to make a difference. And each person should examine his or her motives when making important decisions. It turns out that few things are as clear-cut as we first believe, especially when we pause and step into another person's sandals. The stories of Antigone and Creon and their friends and relatives, despite the passing millennia, remain relevant today.

DO YOU WANT TO KNOW MORE?

If you liked *Antigone & Creon: Guardians of Thebes*, you may want to try other novels in the Tapestry of Bronze series. They include the Niobe trilogy:

Children of Tantalus: Niobe & Pelops
The Road to Thebes: Niobe & Amphion
Arrows of Artemis: Niobe & Chloris

And of course, *Jocasta: The Mother-Wife of Oedipus* – which ends just where *Antigone & Creon: Guardians of Thebes* begins.

You can also visit our website: www.tapestryofbronze.com. There you will find reviews, maps, a pronunciation guide, a bibliography and information on how to contact us, in case you have questions beyond those we have addressed here.

Thanks for joining us in our tapestry of the Bronze Age!

Victoria Grossack & Alice Underwood

CAST OF CHARACTERS

MORTALS

Adrastos (1). Argos. King of Argos. Son of Talaus; brother to Eriphyle, Pronax, and Astynome; husband to daughter of Iphis. Children: Argia, Deipyle, Aegialeus. One of the seven against Thebes, stationed outside the Phthia Gate.

Adrastos (2). Argos. Son of Polynikes and Argia; grandson to Adrastos (1).

Aegialeus. Argos. Son of Adrastos (1); brother to Argia and Deipyle.

Aktor. Thebes. A bronze smith; one of the seven defenders of Thebes; he guards the Chloris Gate.

Alexida. Argos. Daughter of Amphiorax and Eriphyle; sister to Alkmaeon, Amphilochus, Eurydike (2) and Demonassa.

Alkides. Thebes, Tiryns. Son of Amphitryon and Alkmene. Marries Megara. Children with Megara: Creontiades, Deicoon, Ophites. Incredibly strong man.

Alkmaeon. Argos. Son of Amphiorax and Eriphyle; brother to Amphilochus, Alexida, Eurydike (2) and Demonassa.

Alkmene. Thebes. Widow of Amphitryon. Son: Alkides.

Amphilochus. Argos. Son of Amphiorax and Eriphyle; brother to Alkmaeon, Alexida, Eurydike (2) and Demonassa.

Amphion (deceased). Thebes. Former king; fraternal twin brother to Zethos; husband to Niobe. Children: Children: Alphenor, Chloris, Phaedimus, Damasichthon, Ilioneus, Sipylus, Tantalus, Kleodoxa, Eudoxa, Ogygia, Astykratia, Neaira, Ismenus, Phthia. Known for building the walls of Thebes.

Amphiorax. Argos. Marries Eriphyle. Children: Alkmaeon, Amphilochus, Alexida, Eurydike (2), Demonassa. One of the seven against Thebes, stationed outside the Astykratia Gate.

Amphitryon (deceased). Tiryns, Thebes. Married to Alkmene. Son: Alkides.

Antigone. Thebes, Argos, Colonus. Daughter of Jocasta and Oedipus; wife to Haemon; sister to Ismene, Polynikes and Eteokles; half-sister to Oedipus.

Argia. Argos. Daughter of Adrastos; sister to Deipyle, Aegialeus; marries Polynikes. Children: Thersander, Adrastos (2), Timeas.

Astykratia (deceased). Thebes. Daughter of Amphion and Niobe, one of the gates is named for her.

Astynome (deceased). Argos. Daughter of Talaus, sister to Adrastos (1), Pronax and Eriphyle.

Chloris. Formerly Thebes, now queen of Pylos, married to Neleus. Daughter of Amphion and Niobe, one of the gates is named for her.

Creon. Thebes. Son of Menoeceus; brother of Jocasta; husband of

Eurydike (1). Children: Haemon, Megara, Menoeceus, Henioche, Lykomedes, Megareus and Pyrrha. Some of the children are only mentioned as part of a group.

Deipyle. Argos. Daughter of Adrastos; marries Tydeus. Son: Diomedes.

Demochares. Thebes.

Demonassa. Argos. Daughter of Amphiorax and Eriphyle; sister to Alkmaeon, Amphilochus, Eurydike (2) and Alexida.

Diomedes. Argos. Son of Tydeus and Deipyle; grandson of Adrastos.

Dirke (deceased). Thebes. Wife of former regent, the spring outside the Ogygia Gate is named for her as it is where she died.

Eteokles. Thebes. Son of Jocasta and Oedipus; brother to Antigone, Ismene; identical twin brother to Polynikes; half-brother to Oedipus. One of the seven defenders of Thebes; he guards the Ogygia Gate.

Eriphyle (Phyle). Argos. Daughter to Talaus; sister to Adrastos and Pronax; marries Amphiorax. Children: Alkmaeon, Amphilochus, Alexida, Eurydike (2), Demonassa.

Eudoxa (deceased). Thebes. Daughter of Amphion and Niobe, one of the gates is named for her.

Eurydike (1). Thebes. Wife to Creon. Children: Haemon, Megara, Menoeceus, Henioche, Lykomedes, Megareus and Pyrrha. Some of the children are only mentioned as part of a group.

Eurydike (2). Argos. Daughter to Amphiorax and Eriphyle; sister to Alkmaeon, Amphilochus, Alexida and Demonassa.

Eurymedon. Thebes. A javelin thrower; one of the seven defenders; he guards the Eudoxa Gate.

Eurystheus. Tiryns. King of Tiryns; cousin to Alkides.

Haemon. Thebes. Son of Creon and Eurydike, brother to Megara, Menoeceus, Henioche, Lykomedes, Megareus, Pyrrha; married to his cousin Antigone

Harmonia (deceased). Daughter of Ares and Aphrodite, married to Kadmos, first owner of the necklace of Harmonia

Hippomedon. Argos. One of the seven war commanders against Thebes; he attacks the Neaira Gate.

Hyperbius. Thebes. A trader who has traveled widely. One of the seven defenders; he guards the Neaira Gate.

Iphis. Argos. Father-in-law of Adrastos; grandfather to Argia, Deipyle, Aegialeus. Head of one of Argos' three houses.

Ismene. Thebes. Daughter of Jocasta and Oedipus; sister to Antigone, Polynikes, Eteokles; half-sister to Oedipus.

Jocasta (deceased). Thebes. Daughter to Menoeceus (1); sister to Creon; wife to Laius; wife to Oedipus. Children: Oedipus, Antigone, Ismene, Polynikes, Eteokles.

Kadmos (deceased). Thebes. Legendary founder of Thebes.

Kapaneus. Argos. Nephew to Adrastos through Astynome; father of Sthenelus. One of the seven against Thebes; he attacks the Eudoxa

Gate.

Kleodoxa (deceased). Thebes. Daughter of Amphion and Niobe, one of the gates is named for her.

Labdakus (deceased). Thebes. Former king of Thebes; father of Laius.

Laius (deceased). Thebes. Former king of Thebes; married to Jocasta; natural father of Oedipus.

Lasthenes. Thebes. Master of the herds. One of the seven defenders; he guards the Astykratia Gate.

Megara. Thebes. Daughter of Creon and Eurydike, sister to Haemon, Menoeceus, Henioche, Lykomedes, Megareus, Pyrrha; marries Alkides. Children: Creontiades, Deicoon, Ophites.

Melanippus. Thebes. Father to Astakus and captain of the guard. One of the seven defenders; he guards the Kleodoxa Gate.

Melanthe (deceased). Thebes. Also known as the Sphinx.

Menoeceus (1) (deceased). Thebes. Father of Creon and Jocasta; a nobleman of Thebes – one of the Spartoi. Known for having sacrificed himself to lift a curse off of Thebes.

Menoeceus (2). Thebes. Son of Creon and Eurydike. Brother to Haemon, Megara, Henioche, Lykomedes, Megareus, Pyrrha. One of the seven defenders; he guards the Phthia Gate.

Mnesikles. Korinth. Messenger between Korinth and Thebes.

Neaira (deceased). Thebes. Daughter of Amphion and Niobe, one of the gates is named for her.

Neleus. Pylos. King of Pylos, husband of Chloris, father of Nestor and others.

Nestor. Pylos. Son of Neleus and Chloris.

Niobe (deceased). Thebes, Lydia. Queen of Thebes, wife to Amphion. Children: Alphenor, Chloris, Phaedimus, Damasichthon, Ilioneus, Sipylus, Tantalus, Kleodoxa, Eudoxa, Ogygia, Astykratia, Neaira, Ismenus, Phthia.

Oedipus. Thebes, Korinth, Argos, Colonus. Son of Laius and Jocasta; adopted son of King Polybus and Queen Periboea of Korinth. Husband to Jocasta. Father and half-brother to Antigone, Ismene, Polynikes and Eteokles.

Ogygia (deceased). Thebes. Daughter of Amphion and Niobe, one of the gates is named for her.

Parthenopeus. Argos. One of the seven against Thebes; attacker of the Chloris Gate.

Pelorus. Thebes, Delphi, Colonus. The original name of the Tiresias in *Guardians of Thebes*.

Periboea. Korinth. Queen of Korinth; Oedipus' adoptive mother.

Phthia (deceased). Thebes. Daughter of Amphion and Niobe, one of the gates is named for her.

Phyle. See Eriphyle.

Polybus (deceased). Korinth. King of Korinth; married to Queen Periboa;

adoptive father of Oedipus.

Polynikes. Thebes and Argos. Son of Jocasta and Oedipus; brother to Antigone and Ismene; identical twin brother to Eteokles; half-brother to Oedipus. Marries Argia. Children: Thersander, Adrastos, Timeas.

Pronax. Argos. Younger son of Talaus; brother to Adrastos and Eriphyle.

Pyrrha. Thebes. Daughter of Creon and Antigone; sister to Haemon, Megara, Menoeceus, Henioche, Lykomedes, Megareus.

Rabbit. Thebes. Hare-lipped nursemaid serving Alkides, Megara and their children.

Rhanis. Thebes. Serving woman in the palace.

Rhodia. Thebes. Old mid-wife.

Sthenelus. Argos . Son of Kapaneus; great-nephew to Eriphyle, Adrastos, and Pronax.

Talaus (deceased). Argos. King of Argos. Children: Astynome, Adrastos, Pronax, Eriphyle.

Thersander. Argos. Son of Polynikes and Argia; grandson to Adrastos (1).

Theseus. Athens. King of Athens, this is not the original Theseus who battled the Minotaur, but a different man using the same name to improve his claim to the throne. Our research shows that the stories associated with the Minotaur-Theseus probably occurred several centuries earlier, in the Minoan period. *Guardians of Thebes* is set in the period known as the Mycenaean.

Thoas. Korinth. Regent of Korinth.

Tiresias. Thebes, Delphi, Athens and all Hellas. A seer considered the Voice of Apollo and a servant of Athena.

Tydeus. Kalydon, Argos. Marries Deipyle. Son: Diomedes. One of the seven Argives against Thebes; attacks the Kleodoxa Gate.

Udaeus. Thebes. Healer and a priest of Apollo.

Zethos (deceased). Thebes. Fraternal twin brother to Amphion; husband to Thebe. Master of the herds in his time. Son: Idmon.

DEITIES

Aphrodite. Olympian, goddess of love. Married to Hephaestus; lover to Ares. Daughter Harmonia by Ares. Patron of Korinth.

Apollo. Olympian, god of light (the sun), prophecy, music, healing and plague. Twin brother of Artemis.

Ares. Olympian, god of war. Lover of Aphrodite. Daughter: Harmonia.

Artemis. Olympian, goddess of the hunt and childbirth and associated with the moon. Twin sister of Apollo.

Athena. Olympian, goddess of wisdom, war and weaving. Patron of Athens.

Demeter. Olympian, goddess of the harvest. Mother of Persephone.

Dionysus. Olympian, god of wine. Son of Zeus and Semele, a daughter of

Kadmos and Harmonia.

Hades. God of the Underworld.

Hephaestus. Olympian, god of crafts and the forge. Married to Aphrodite.

Hera. Olympian, goddess of marriage. Patron of Argos.

Hermes. Olympian, god of lies, thieves, messengers; guides the newly dead to Hades.

Hestia. Goddess of the hearth, she gave up her throne in Olympus to tend the central fire.

Persephone. Daughter to Demeter and Zeus; wife to Hades after he abducted her.

Poseidon. Olympian, god of the sea, horses and earthquakes.

Zeus. Olympian; king of the gods. God of oaths and hospitality (xenia).

CPSIA information can be obtained at www.ICGtesting.com
Printed in the USA
BVOW031431190513

321116BV00012B/354/P